P9-DFK-366

Acknowledgements

Far more people help in the creation of a novel than just the authors. The story that would become DEAD SIX began as an online serial at www.thehighroad.org titled *Welcome Back, Mr. Nightcrawler*. Thank you to the good folks of THR for letting us play in their yard. We would like to thank Chris Byrne and the Gun Counter for fixing the "computer situation." Their generosity is much appreciated. Special thanks go to Marcus Custer for his technical/tactical advice, he's like having your own personal Jack Bauer, only without all the yelling and whispering. John Shirley helped out big time on knives as did Ogre Rettinger on information security and Jeff More on the border. Once again, Reader Force Alpha rode to the rescue with their proofing, critiques, and vast stores of useful knowledge. Thank you all.

DEAD SIX

"And by thy sword shalt thou live . . ."

Genesis 27:40

Prologue: Cold Open

VALENTINE
Sierra Vista Resort Hotel
Cancun, Quintana Roo
Southern Mexico
February 17

There was an angel standing over me when I opened my eyes. She was speaking but I could barely hear her. Every sound was muffled, as if I were underwater, except for the rapid pounding of my heart. *Am I dreaming? Am I dead?*

"On your feet, damn it!" the angel said as she grabbed my load-bearing vest and hauled me from my seat. My head was swimming, and every bone in my body ached. I wasn't sure where I was at first, but reality quickly came screaming back to me. We were still in the chopper. We'd crashed. The angel was pulling me toward the door. "Can you walk? Come on."

"Wait," I protested, steadying myself against the hull. "The others." I turned to where my teammates were sitting. Several of them were still strapped into their seats, but they weren't moving. Dim light poured through a

3

gaping hole in the hull. Smoke and dust moved in the light, but behind that there was blood *everywhere*. My heart dropped into my stomach. I'd worked with these men for years.

"They're dead, bro," Tailor said, suddenly appearing in the door frame. At least one of my friends had made it. "She's right. We've got to get out of here before they start dropping mortars on us. This isn't a good place to be."

Still terribly disoriented, I shook my head, trying to clear it.

"You're in shock," the angel said, pushing me through the door of our wrecked NH-90 helicopter. "What's your name?" she asked as we stepped onto a large, tiled surface.

"V . . . Valentine," I stammered, squinting in the early morning sun. "Where are we?"

"In a pool," Tailor said, moving up a steep embankment ahead of me. "Ramirez is dead. Half the team's gone." He dropped the magazine out of his stubby, short-barreled OSW FAL and rocked in a fresh one. "Hostiles will be on us quick. You locked and loaded?"

My head was clearing. I looked down at the DSA FAL carbine in my hands and retracted the bolt slightly. A .308 round was in the chamber. My good-luck charm, a custom Smith & Wesson .44 Magnum, was still in its holster on my left thigh. I was still alive, so it hadn't let me down. "I'm ready," I said, following Tailor up the incline.

Our chopper had crashed in the deep end of a huge, pear-shaped swimming pool that had been mostly drained of water. It sat at an odd angle, still smoking, the camouflage hull absolutely riddled with bullet holes. The walls of the pool's deep end prevented the chopper from flipping over, but it was leaning to the side. There were deep gashes in the tile where the rotor had struck. The rotor had blown to pieces, and fragments were scattered everywhere.

"What happened?" I asked. The angel didn't answer at first. I remembered then; her name was Ling, the one who hired us. She followed me up the embankment, clutching a suppressed Sig 551 assault rifle.

"We crashed," she said after a moment, as if I didn't know that. We cleared the top of the incline. A handful of armed people waited for us in the shallow end of the empty pool. Aside from Tailor and me, only three were dressed in the green fatigues of my company, Vanguard Strategic Solutions. I closed my eyes and tried to catch my breath. Ten of us had left on this mission. Half hadn't made it. *Goddamn it . . .*

"You alright, Val?" Tailor asked. "I really need you with me, okay?"

"I'm fine," I said, kneeling down to check my gear. "Just a little rattled." We'd crash-landed in the middle of a deserted resort complex. The city had once been covered in places like this, but now they were all abandoned. In front of us stood a cluster of white towers that must have been a luxury hotel once. About a hundred yards behind us was the beach and ocean as far as the eye could see. The place had probably been evacuated back when the fighting started. It was dirty from disuse and littered with garbage and debris. Several plumes of smoke rose in the distance. Cancun had seen better days.

Ling brushed the dust from her black body armor. "Mr. Tailor. You're in charge now, correct? We must keep moving." I believed she was from China, but there was no accent to her speech.

With Ramirez gone, Tailor had just been promoted to team leader. He quickly looked around, taking in our surroundings. "And where in the hell do you want to go? This part of town is covered in hostiles." His East Tennessee twang were more pronounced with his anger.

"Somewhere that is not *here*. I have multiple wounded," Ling said, nodding toward the rest of her teammates, all members of the same mysterious *Exodus* organization. Like her, they were heavily armed and dressed in black. They were clustered in a tight circle near the edge of the pool, waiting for instructions. In the middle of them was a teenaged girl being tended to by their medic. "We have to get her out."

"Look, damn it," Tailor exclaimed. "We'll save your precious package. That was the deal." He jerked a thumb at the young girl as he spoke. "Let me try to get help again." Tailor squeezed the radio microphone on his vest and spoke into it. "Ocean-Four-One, this is Switchblade-Four-Alpha."

While Tailor tried to raise the base, our team sharp-shooter, Skunky, ran over to see if I was okay. He was a skinny Asian guy and was in his mid-twenties, same age as me. "Dude, you're alive."

"I'm fine," I said, standing up. "What happened?"

"They hit us with some kind of big gun right after we took off. It punched that hole in the chopper. The pilots were hit with frag. We made it a few miles, but it was too much damage. They were trying to set us down when the pilot died. That's how we ended up in the pool."

Tailor looked over at us, flustered. "I can't raise the base. This is bad, really bad."

"Switchblade-Four-Alpha, this is Stingray-Two-Zero," a new voice said, crackling over our radios.

That was the call-sign for our air support. One of Vanguard's Super Tucano turboprop attack planes roared overhead and began to circle our position. Vanguard was one of the best-funded private military companies in the business. We could provide our own air support if we needed to.

"Stingray-Two-Zero, this is Switchblade-Four-Alpha," Tailor said. "What's your status?"

"We were going to ask you the same thing, Four-Alpha," the pilot replied. *"We've lost communication with the airfield. It looks bad down there."*

"We've got multiple wounded and multiple KIA. We need an immediate medevac. Five of us, six Exodus personnel, and the package. Eight confirmed KIA, including the crew of the chopper." Switchblade-Four was down to just me, Tailor, Skunky, Tower, and Harper.

As Tailor talked to the pilot, trying to figure out what was going on, I looked over at Ling and her people and at the young girl that we'd gone through so much trouble to acquire. I didn't know who the girl was or why Exodus wanted her so badly. She had to be important, though, since Ling had offered us an ungodly sum of money to go into Cancun, guns blazing, to rescue her. The fact that we'd be violating the UN cease-fire hadn't seemed to bother her.

Tailor let go of his radio microphone. "Pilot says there's an armed convoy headed our way up Kukulkan Boulevard.

Looks like Mendoza's militia. They saw us go down, I guess. Couple trucks full of guys and some technicals. He'll provide cover, but he's low on ammo."

"Just like us," Skunky interjected.

Ling put her gloved hand on Tailor's shoulder. "I need you to get your men moving," she said. "I'll contact my people to see if I can find out what's going on."

As Ling trotted off, Tailor turned back to us with a worried look on his face. "Val, Skunky, c'mon, we gotta go." Nodding, I followed him as he waved to the others. Standing away from the Exodus people, we huddled up. "Listen up, Switchblade-Four," Tailor said, addressing us as a team. "We're in some serious shit here. I don't know what's going on back at the base. I got a bad feeling." Tailor looked over his shoulder as an explosion detonated to the southeast. The Tucano had begun its attack run.

"This is the third time we've broken the cease-fire this month," Skunky said, anxiously grasping his scoped, accurized M14. "You don't think . . ."

"I know what *I* think," Tower, our machine gunner, said. Sweat beaded on his dark face. "I think they *left* us here."

That got everyone's attention. Being abandoned in-country was every mercenary's worst nightmare.

"It doesn't matter," Tailor said. "Everybody shut up and listen. I don't trust these Exodus assholes. When we start moving, y'all look out for each other. If we have to, we'll ditch these guys and head out on our own."

I flinched. "Tailor, they've got wounded and a kid. And where in the hell do you think we're gonna go?"

"Don't argue with me!" Tailor snapped. The pressure was getting to him. "We'll figure it out. Now get ready.

We're moving out. Keep your spacing, use cover, and watch for snipers."

"*Get some!*" the rest of us shouted in response.

"Mr. Tailor, I've got some bad news," Ling said, approaching our group. She had a satellite phone in her hand. "I don't think anyone's coming for us."

"What?" Tailor asked, his face going a little pale.

"Something happened. According to my people, the UN shut down all of Vanguard's operations about an hour ago."

"The UN?" Tailor asked, exasperated. "But the Mexican government—"

"The Mexican Nationalist government dissolved last night, Mr. Tailor. I don't have all the details. I'm afraid we're on our own."

"All we have to do is get to the safe areas in the city, right?" Harper asked. Since the cease-fire, half of Cancun was controlled by UN peacekeepers.

Ling took off her tinted shooting glasses and wiped her brow on her sleeve. "I don't think that's wise," she said, putting the glasses back on. "All employees of Vanguard have been declared unlawful combatants by the UN. I'm sorry, but we need to go, *now*." We all looked at each other, and several obscenities were uttered. We were now on our own in a country where we'd made a *lot* of enemies.

"They sold us out," Tower said. "I told you!"

Tailor spoke up. "It don't matter. Let's move." He took off after Ling. The rest of us followed, spacing ourselves out in a small column. Ling rallied the Exodus personnel, and they followed her as she climbed over the edge of the pool. Two of them were always within arm's reach of the strange young girl. We quickly moved across the courtyard of the resort complex, heading for the buildings. The grass was overgrown, and the palm trees were untended.

Tailor tried to contact the pilots for an update but got no response. It was obvious something was wrong. The small attack plane zoomed back over the resort in a steep right turn, ejecting flares as it went. An instant later, a missile shrieked across the sky, trailing smoke behind it. The Super Tucano exploded in mid-air, raining burning debris into the ocean below. A Rafale fighter jet with UN markings roared overhead, turning to the east.

Our entire group froze in disbelief. This day just kept getting better and better. Beyond the noise of the fighter's engines, the distinctive sound of a large helicopter approaching could be heard.

Tailor grabbed my shoulder and pulled me along. "Move, move, move!" he shouted, breaking into a run.

"Into the hotel, quickly!" Ling ordered. Behind us, a huge Super Cougar transport helicopter descended past our crash site and set down in the courtyard. Like the fighter jet, it bore UN markings. More than twenty soldiers, clad in urban camouflage and blue berets, spilled out of the chopper. They fanned out and immediately started shooting at us. Rounds snapped past my head as I ran across the hotel lobby. I jumped, slid across the reception desk, and crashed to the floor below. I landed on top of Tailor. Harper landed next to me.

"What do we do?" I asked, climbing off of Tailor. The water-damaged lobby was illuminated by hazy daylight streaming through the huge, shattered skylight. The wall in front of us was pockmarked with puffs of plaster dust as bullets struck. The reception desk was heavily constructed out of marble and concrete, so it provided decent cover. The hotel interior was ruined from disuse and stunk of rot.

"Why are they shooting at us?" Tailor screamed.

Ling was crouched down next to Tailor. She shouted in his ear. "I *told* you, they declared you unlawful combatants. We broke the cease-fire. They're just following orders!" She then reached up, leveled her assault rifle across the counter, and ripped off a long burst. "Protect the child!" The Exodus operatives under her command obeyed her order without hesitation. The two men guarding the young girl hustled her, crouched over, to the very back of the room. The rest started shooting, causing the UN troops outside to break their advance and dive for cover.

I glanced over at Tailor. "What do we do?"

Tailor looked around for a moment, the gears turning in his head. He swore to himself, then raised his voice so he could be heard over the noise. "Switchblade-Four! Open fire!"

My team was aggressive to the last. Tower opened up with his M60E4. The machine gun's rattling roar filled the lobby, making it difficult to hear anything. I saw a UN trooper drop to the ground as Skunky took the top of his head off with a single, well-placed shot from his M14. Harper's FAL carbine barked as he let off shot after shot.

I took a deep breath. My heart rate slowed down, and everything seemed to slow with it. I was *calm*. I found a target, a cluster of enemy soldiers advancing toward the lobby, and squeezed the trigger. The shortened alloy buttstock bucked into my left shoulder as I fired. One of the UN troops, much closer, tried to bolt across the foyer.

Two quick shots and he went down. Another soldier crouched down to reload his G36 carbine. The palm tree he was hiding behind didn't conceal him well. The blue beret flew off in a spray of blood as I put two bullets through the tree.

I flinched. Something wet struck the right side of my face. Red droplets splashed my shooting glasses. Ducking back down, I reflexively wiped my glasses, smearing dark blood across them. Harper was lying on the floor, a gaping exit wound in the back of his head. Bits of gore and brain matter was splattered on the wall behind him.

I tugged on Tailor's pant leg. He dropped behind the counter. I pointed at Harper. My mouth opened, but I couldn't find anything to say. "He's dead?" Tailor asked, yelling to make himself heard as he rocked a fresh magazine into his weapon.

I nodded in affirmation. "We have to move! We're gonna get pinned down!"

"Got any grenades left?" Tailor asked. I nodded. He got Ling's attention. "Hey! We'll toss frags, then I'll pop smoke. They'll find a way to flank us if we stay here."

Ling shouted orders to the rest of her men. Tailor and I pulled fragmentation grenades from our vests and readied them.

"Frag out!" We lobbed them over the counter. The lobby was rocked by a double concussion as the explosives detonated nearly simultaneously. Dust filled the room, and the remaining glass in the skylight broke free and rained down on top of us. Tailor then threw his smoke grenade. It fired a few seconds later, and the lobby quickly filled with dense white smoke.

"That way!" Ling shouted, pointing to my right. At the far wall was a large doorway that led into the main part of the hotel. Her men filed past us at a run, stepping over Harper's body as they went.

One of Ling's men stopped. He was a hulking African man, probably six-foot-four and muscular, so broad that the rifle he carried seemed like a toy in his hands. "Commander, come on!" Behind him, a Chinese man fired short bursts through the smoke, keeping the UN troops busy as we fell back into the building. Then came the young girl, flanked by her two bodyguards.

The girl looked down at me as they hustled her by, and everything else dropped away. Her eyes were intensely blue, almost luminescent. Her hair was such a light shade of platinum blond that it looked white. It was like she was looking right through me. "I'm sorry about your friends," she whispered. At least, I could've sworn she did. I don't remember *seeing* her say anything, but I definitely *heard* her.

Tailor grabbed me by the arm. "Val, *go*, goddamn it!" It snapped me back to reality. He shoved me forward and we followed Ling's people into the building.

LORENZO
Disputed Zone
Thailand/Myanmar Border
September 6

Men with AK-47s waited for us at the gate, illuminated by the headlights of our stolen UN 6x6 truck. The guards approached the windows. One of them was wearing a necklace strung with dried human fingers.

"Decorative bunch," Carl stated.

The voice in my radio earpiece was not reassuring. "Lorenzo, I've got three at the gate. Two in the tower. FLIR shows *lots* of movement in the camp." Reaper was a quarter mile up the hill, one eye on the glowing blobs on his laptop screen and the other on the road to make sure the actual United Nations troops didn't show up.

I was signaled to roll down the window. Complying let in the humid night air and the scents of cook fires and diesel fuel. The lead guard shouted to be heard over the rumble of our engine. My Burmese was rusty, but he was gesturing with the muzzle of his rifle toward the only building with electricity, indicating our destination. I saluted. The guard returned it with a vague wave.

The heavy metal barricade was lifted and shuffled aside. Carl put the truck into gear and rolled us forward. "They bought it." The gate was shut behind us, effectively trapping us in a compound with a thousand Marxist assholes. My driver smiled as he steered us toward the command center. "That was the hard part."

"For you," I responded as I took my earpiece out and shoved it back inside my uniform shirt. Scanning across the compound showed that our aerial reconnaissance had been spot-on for once. The main generator was right where we thought it would be, ten meters from the loading dock. The machine was a thirty-year-old monstrosity of Soviet engineering, and our source had reported that it went out constantly. *Perfect.*

More soldiers, if you could use the term for a group this

disorganized, were watching our big white truck with mild curiosity. Many of the local peacekeepers moonlighted smuggling munitions, so our presence was not out of the ordinary. I opened the door and hopped down. "Wait for my signal," I said before slamming the door.

Carl put the truck into reverse and backed toward the loading dock as a pair of soldiers shouted helpful but conflicting directions at him. The truck's bumper thumped into the concrete. The tarp covering the rear opened, and a giant of a man stepped from the truck and onto the dock. My associate, Train, spoke in rough tones to the thugs on the dock, pointing to the waiting crates of mortar rounds. They began to load the truck. The rebels paid him and Carl no mind. The various UN peacekeepers they had on the take changed constantly. Only the officers, like I was pretending to be, actually mattered.

The guard at the entrance held the door open for me as I walked up the steps. The building had once been part of a rubber plantation, and this had been a reception area for colonial-era visitors. It had been rather nice once but had slid into the typical third world shabbiness of faded paint, peeling wallpaper, and spreading stains. The air conditioner had died sometime during the Vietnam War, and giant malarial mosquitoes frolicked in the river of sweat running down my back. There was a man waiting for me, dressed nicer than the others, with something that casually resembled a uniform. The guard from the door followed me inside, carelessly cradling his AK as he stood behind me.

"Good evening," the warlord's lieutenant said in

heavily accented English. "We were not expecting you so soon, Captain."

"I need to speak with your commander," I said curtly.

He looked me over suspiciously. I had practiced this disguise for weeks. The fake beard was perfection, my coloring changed slightly with makeup, my extra inches of height hidden with thin-soled boots and a slight slouch, and my gut augmented with padding to fill out the stolen camouflage uniform. I had watched the Pakistani captain, studying his mannerisms, his movements. I looked exactly like the fat, middle-aged, washed-up bureaucrat hack from an ineffective and corrupt organization.

Since the receptionist didn't pick the AK off his desk and empty a magazine into my chest, I could safely assume my disguise worked. I watched the guard over the tops of the Pakistani's spectacles. I had replaced the prescription lenses with plain glass after murdering the real captain this afternoon. Finally the lieutenant spoke. "Do you need more money?"

"Those border checkpoints won't bribe themselves open," I responded, my accent, tone, and inflection an almost perfect impersonation. I made a big show of looking at my watch. Carl and Train had better be loading that truck fast. "I must be back soon or my superiors will suspect something."

"General is busy man," he said, the sigh in his voice indicating what a bother I was being. He gestured toward his subordinate. "Search him."

I raised my arms as the soldier gave me a cursory pat down. I was, of course, unarmed. I couldn't risk the possibility that one of these amateurs might take their job seriously. Bringing a weapon into the same room as a rebel leader was a good way to get skinned alive. The search I received was so negligent that I could have smuggled in an RPG, but no use crying over spilt milk. I lowered my arms.

"Let's go." The lieutenant motioned for me to follow. The three of us went down a hallway that stank of cigarette smoke. The light was provided by naked bulbs that hummed and flickered with a weak yellow light. We passed other rooms flanked by soldiers. Quick glances through the windows showed village laborers, mostly old women and children, preparing narcotics for shipment. Revolutions need funding too. Finally we reached a set of double doors with a well-fed guard on each side. These boys were bigger, smartly dressed, wearing vests bristling with useful equipment, and kept their rifles casually pointed at me as we approached.

The general's personal bodyguards and the lieutenant exchanged some indecipherable dialog. I was patted down again, only this time it was brutally and invasively thorough, making me glad that my weapons were in the truck. The guard pulled my radio from my belt, yanking the cord out from under my shirt. He started to jabber at me.

"Regulations require me to have it at all times," I replied. The guard held it close to his chest, suspicious. "Fine, but I need it back when we're done here." The two led me into the inner sanctum while the lieutenant and the first guard returned to their post. That just left me with two heavily armed and trained thugs to deal with. The odds were now in my favor.

Now this room was more like it. Most warlords learned to like the finer things in life. While their army slept in mud huts and ate bugs, they lived plush and fat. Being the boss does have its perks. The furnishings were opulent, but random and mismatched, a shopping trip of looting across the country. It was twenty degrees cooler as a portable AC unit pumped air down on us.

The warlord was waiting for me, reclining in an overstuffed leather chair, smoking a giant cigar, with his feet resting on a golden Buddha. This man had spread terror over this region for a generation and grown obscenely rich in the process. He'd also become soft and complacent, which worked to my benefit. He was grizzled, scarred, and watching a 56 inch TV on the wall, tuned to some situation comedy that I couldn't understand. The volume was cranked way too high. "You want see me, Captain?" he grunted, puffing around the cigar. "What you want?"

He was ten feet away. I had a guard standing at attention on either side of me. "If I am to continue smuggling ordnance for you, I will need more money." I put on an air of meekness, of subservience, while in reality I was taking in every detail, calculating every angle. My pulse was quickening, but I gave no outward indication. I coughed politely against the cloud of Cuban smoke.

"Eh? I already pay you. Pay you good. Maybe too good . . ."

"They set up another checkpoint just north of the river. I'll need cash to pay off the garrison commander there."

The warlord sighed as he stood. "UN troops so greedy." He limped over to the wall and pulled back a tapestry, revealing a vault door, just where the informant had said it would be. "Old days, we just kill each other.

Peacekeepers make it so complicated now. Peacekeepers . . ." He snorted. "No better than my men, but with pretty blue hats." No disagreement from me on that one. The UN was less than useless, though their ineptitude created plenty of business opportunities for men like me. "Maybe someday my country not have war. Then my men get pretty blue hats, and we can go to other countries and rape *their* women and take *their* money. Hah!"

I waited patiently for him to spin the dial. That vault was state of the art, rated TXTL-60, and would have required quite some time and a lot of noise for me to defeat on my own. Better to just have the man open it for you. I glanced over at one of the waiting guards. He had a Russian bayonet sheathed on the front of his armor. He smirked, taking my look to be one of nervousness. After all, what did he have to worry about from a middle-aged Pakistani who was just padding his paycheck? The guard turned his attention back to the TV.

"How much you need?" the warlord asked. The lock clicked. The vault hissed open.

The man at my right snickered along with the laugh track as my hand flew to his sheathed bayonet. "I'll be taking all of it." Steel flashed red, back and forth, and before either guard could even begin to react, they were dead. I jerked the knife out from under the second guard's ear and let the body flop.

"Huh?" The warlord turned and saw only me standing. His bleary eyes flicked down to see his men twitching on the ground, then back up at me, dripping bayonet in hand. Then he said something incomprehensible but obviously profane as understanding came. The general's pistol started out of his holster. I covered the distance in an instant and ran the knife up the inside of his arm before driving it between his ribs. I removed the gun from his nerveless fingers and left the old man tottering as I went back for my radio. The warlord went to his knees as I hit the transmit button.

"I'm in."

Carl came back before I even had the earpiece back in place. "Truck's loaded. Status?"

Stepping over the dying warlord, I glanced inside the vault. It was about the size of a walk-in closet. Rebellions ran on cold, hard cash. There were stacks of money inside. A quick check revealed that much of it was in euros and pounds, which was good, because many of the regional denominations weren't worth the effort to carry out.

"Status? Filthy rich. The intel was right on. Train, bring three of the big packs. You've got two guards in the entrance, three more in the hallway. Carl, you got a shot at that generator?"

"No problem."

"Execute," I ordered before noticing that the warlord was still breathing, gasping for air around a perforated lung, one useable hand clamped to his side, the spreading puddle of blood ruining the nice Persian rug beneath. I squatted next to him. "I must've hit you a little lower than expected. You should already be dead. Sorry about that."

"Who . . . who . . ." the old man gasped.

"You don't know me. It's nothing personal, just business." The lights flickered and died as Carl killed the generator. It was pitch black inside the old plantation. I rested next to the dying man and waited. The warlord finally breathed his last and embarked on his short journey to Hell. A moment later the door opened and a hulking shadow entered. Train pressed a tubular object into my hands and I quickly strapped the night-vision device over my head. The world was a sudden brilliant green. "You get them all?"

"Smoked 'em," he answered as he handed me my suppressed pistol. The can was warm to the touch. "Where's the cash?"

The two of us stuffed as many bills as would fit into the three big backpacks. I threw on one, and Train, being half pack animal, took the other two. I took point and led us out. One more guard blundered into the hallway from one of processing rooms. We didn't even slow as I put a pair of nearly silent 9mm rounds through his skull. Bodies were scattered around the entrance. It had started to rain. Carl started the truck as Train climbed into the back. I handed up my pack of cash.

I crawled into the cab and pulled off the NVGs. "Let's go." Carl nodded and put the 6x6 into gear. I kept my pistol in my lap, and I knew that Train was ready to fire a belt-fed machine gun through the fabric back of the truck, just in case the alarm was raised before we made it out.

The rain comes hard in Burma. The gate guards barely even paid us mind as the truck approached. I watched them through the windshield wipers as they sullenly left the security of their overhang to move the barricade. The man with the finger-necklace glanced back toward the command post and shrugged as he noticed that the lights were out again. We rolled through the gate uncontested, the muddy jungle road stretched out before us. We were home free. I activated my radio. "Reaper, we're out. Meet us at the bridge."

"On the way," was the distorted reply.

"We did it," I sighed. The spirit gum pulled at my cheeks as I yanked the fake beard off and tossed it on the floorboards. The glasses and idiotic blue beret followed. "There had to be close to a mil in the vault."

"That was too easy," Carl said, always the pessimist.

"No. We're just that *good*."

There was a sudden clang of metal from the back, then a burst of automatic weapons fire. I glanced at Carl, and he was already giving the truck more gas. Somebody had raised the alarm. "Told you so."

"Lorenzo, taking fire," Train shouted into the radio. Then there was a terrible racket as he opened up with the SAW. Bullets quit hitting our truck, which was a relief, since it just happened to be filled to the brim with high explosives.

I checked the rear-view mirror. Through the raindrops I could see headlights igniting. They were coming after us, and they were going to be really pissed off. Train had just popped the men who would normally be moving the barricade, so that would buy us a minute, but our stolen truck would never outrun all of those jeeps on this kind of road.

It could never be simple. "Go to Plan B," I said into the radio.

We reached the bridge over the Salawin River nearly a minute ahead of our pursuers. A hundred yards long, it was the only crossing for miles and had been built by captives of the Japanese army in the waning of World War Two. The wood creaked ominously as our heavy truck rumbled over it. We stopped halfway across and bailed out. Headlights winked through the rain three times from the other end of the bridge, confirming that Reaper was waiting for us. Train tossed a bag of money to Carl and the detonator to me. He shouldered the other two bags with one hand and carried the SAW like a suitcase.

The three of us walked to the waiting Land Rover. I could hear the approaching rebel vehicles. "Bummer about the ordnance," Train said. "That would've been worth some serious dough back in Thailand."

"Beats having our fingers end up on a necklace," Carl muttered.

We reached the waiting vehicle and piled in. Reaper scooted over as Carl got behind the driver's seat. Carl always drove. He spun us around through the mud so we could head toward the border. I glanced back at the bridge, noting the swarm of flashlights swinging around the UN truck. I waited until we were several hundred yards down the road before pressing the button.

The C4 that Train had stuck to the crates of munitions detonated. The truck was destroyed in a spreading concussion that blew the pursuing rebels into clouds of meat and turned the Say-Loo River bridge into splinters.

My crew gasped at the intensity of the display. "Impressive," I agreed before turning my attention to counting the money.

LORENZO
Bangkok, Thailand
September 7

My group had the private back room of the restaurant to
ourselves. The food had arrived, the mood was happy, and
the piped-in music was loud and had lots of cymbals in it.
The crew was in high spirits. The job was a success. Some
Burmese scumbags were a lot poorer, and we were a
whole lot richer.

Reaper, our techie, was proceeding to get drunk. He
was young, skinny, and it didn't take a whole lot of alcohol.
Carl, our wheelman and my second-in-command, was
slightly less sullen than usual, beady rat eyes darting
back and forth while he chain-smoked cheap unfiltered
cigarettes. Train, the muscle, was his usual good-natured
self, laughing at every stupid comment. I was enjoying
some nuclear-hot curry death mushroom dish and basking
in the glow of another excellent score.

The beads leading into the private room parted, allowing
a giant whale of a man in a three-piece suit to enter the
room. He was taller than Train and probably weighed
more than my entire team put together. He was freakishly
large. My crew was instantly quiet. There was a slight
motion to my right as Carl drew his CZ-75 and held it
under the table.

"Lorenzo, I presume." The fat man pulled up a chair
and sat. The chair creaked ominously under his mass. "Is
that supposed to be your first name or your last?"

I finished chewing, savoring the eye-watering pain. "Neither. Who the hell are you?"

"My name is not important. I am the man that provided the information for your latest job. I take it that the warlord's vault was full, as promised."

I had never met the informant in person. The job had been arranged through intermediaries. That was normal in my line of work. The fewer people who knew me, the better, yet the fat man had found me, and I did not like being found. "We had an agreement. Your share will be left at the drop tomorrow."

Bald and sweaty, the giant shrugged. He was obese, but there was something about the way that he moved that suggested there was a lot of dense muscle under all that blubber. "Do not be alarmed. This is not a trap. Keep the money. Consider it a tip. You see, I work for Big Eddie." He trailed off as he spoke, smiling with that strange quality of the slightly schizophrenic. He must have noticed my unconscious flinch at the name. "Big Eddie has an assignment for you."

My crew exchanged nervous glances. *Oh hell no.* Everyone here knew what working for Eddie entailed. They all looked to me for confirmation. I slowly put my chopsticks down. "I retired from his organization. Me and your boss are square."

"I am afraid you are mistaken," the fat man stated. "Our employer does not believe in retirement, merely extended leaves of absence, and then only at his convenience. You have been away from the fold so long. He merely arranged this last assignment as a test to see if you had maintained your previous skill sets."

I had always known that some sort of reckoning would come. Standing to leave, I pulled some Thai baht from my wallet and threw them on the table. I had no interest in anything related to Big Eddie, one of the most brutal crime lords in history and an all-around bad dude. Prior jobs performed for the man had left me independently wealthy, but with a lot of scars and a trail of bodies from here to Moscow. "Come on, guys; let's go."

"Our employer insists that you are the only person who can complete this assignment. Your knowledge of languages, of disguises, your ability to blend in with any culture, to infiltrate any group, and your gift for violence are legendary. He spoke *very* highly of you, that there is no place safe from you, no item you cannot steal, no target you cannot eliminate. You, sir, are the best of the best, and he is prepared to compensate you generously for your valuable services."

It didn't matter how much money he was talking about, because it just wasn't worth it. "Tell him to find somebody else."

The fat man laughed, but it never reached his eyes. "Our employer said you would say that." He placed a manila folder on the table and shoved it toward me. He passed other folders to Carl, Train, and Reaper. "He said you should look at this before you make any rash decisions, Mr—" And then he called me by my real last name.

I froze. There was no way he could have known that. He opened the folder.

Pictures. Lots of pictures.

My crew began to flip through the pages of their files, eyes widening in shock, mouths falling open. Carl began swearing in Portuguese. Reaper, dumbfounded, stood and pulled his Glock from his waistband, letting it dangle, folder still open in his other hand. Finally, he raised the gun and pointed it at the fat man's head and snarled, "You're threatening my mom?"

"Of course." The fat man wiped his brow with a silk handkerchief as he began to read from my folder. "Mr. Lorenzo, your adoptive family consisted of six siblings, oh my, I do love large families. Robert, Jenny, Tom, George, Pat." He shoved a list of addresses toward me, paper clipped to a series of photos. "Big Eddie knows where each of them lives, where they work, what they do, and how to reach them at any time. Should you attempt to contact them, Big Eddie will find out, and he will be most displeased."

"They know about my daughter?" Train asked in disbelief, his big hands crunching the edges of the folder.

"You bastard." I knew he was not bluffing. Eddie was capable of *anything*. They must have been gathering this information on me for years.

"All five of your siblings are married. You have nine nieces and nephews, with one bundle of joy on the way," he told me as he passed me another stack of photos. School photos. I was across the table before he knew what was happening, my knife open and pressed hard between his second and third chin.

He didn't even flinch. "Your mother lives with your sister Jenny now, still in your hometown. On Tuesday evenings she goes to her book club. During the week she babysits while Jenny goes to work as the night manager of an International House of Pancakes."

I twisted the knife, and a small trickle of blood splattered on his white collar. His little pig eyes were hard and cold as he stared me down. "Your oldest brother, Robert, is, surprisingly enough, a federal agent. I take it he has no idea what you do for a living. He has a lovely home in the suburbs, a beautiful wife, a son, and two lovely daughters. You will take on this assignment or Big Eddie will take care of them first. You know how he feels about police officers."

"And if I just cut your throat and disappear?" I hissed, leashed anger bubbling to the surface.

"You won't. We've studied you. You will do what it takes to protect your family. Plans are in place so that if I do not return, or if you are not observed attempting to complete this assignment, then your family will pay the price. You may try to warn them, you may try to protect them, you may even attempt to locate our organization. If anyone is capable enough to try, it is you. But you cannot save all of them. You know how great our employer's reach is, and there is no place in this world where you can hide them all. At the first sign of a failure to fully cooperate, a terrible bloodbath will be on your head."

He wasn't bluffing. Eddie was more powerful than most governments, a shadowy figure involved in every criminal enterprise on the planet. I had never met him, and like many who had done his bidding, I suspected he wasn't a lone individual at all, rather a very ruthless organization. Either way, if Eddie wanted somebody dead, it was only a matter of time. I withdrew the Benchmade, wiped the blood on the fat man's shirt, folded the blade, and put it back in my pocket.

I lived under an assumed name. We all did. In this world, anything that was precious to you became a liability, potential leverage against you. How had Eddie found them? Where had I screwed up? I knew that if I tried to warn them, even if they believed me, there was no way I could protect them all. I slowly sat back down. My crew followed my example.

"That's better. Here is your mission packet. There are three phases. As you can see from the deadline, time is of the essence."

I opened the proffered folder, read a few lines, then laughed out loud. "You've got to be kidding. This is impossible."

"The clock is ticking, Mr. Lorenzo. Complete this mission or we will kill everyone you have ever loved." He gestured at the mushroom dish. "Are you going to finish that?"

"Shoulda just shot him," Carl muttered before downing the last of his beer. He crushed the can in his fist and tossed it out the fourth-floor window of our seedy Bangkok hotel room. Odds were that the can hit a tourist or a prostitute. "Suicide, this job, I tell you that. Better to run."

Train rubbed one callused hand across his face. Haggard, he looked like he'd aged ten years in the last hour. "And then what? Hide? Where are we gonna go?"

"*We* aren't the problem," I stated. Each of us was fully capable of going to ground and totally disappearing. The four of us exchanged knowing glances. If we thwarted Big Eddie, we were going to be knee-deep in dead babies. I hadn't even spoken to my family in years. They thought I was some sort of international businessman. I sent them a Christmas card once in a while, that kind of thing, but it wasn't like we were close. I'd checked out of the normal world. But I couldn't let my brothers and sisters pay for my sins. They weren't like me. They were *good* people. They were the only people who had ever shown me any kindness in my miserable youth.

We were quiet for a long time as my crew mulled over our predicament. Finally, I broke the silence. "Eddie's men will be randomly watching these people. As soon as any one of them is contacted, they'll kill all the others. We could maybe save some, but I don't want to take that chance. I'm in. If any of you want out, I understand. Take your share and go. If Eddie sees that I'm on my way to the Mideast, he'll know I'm working the job. It might buy you some time to get to your people."

Reaper immediately raised one bony hand. "I'm with you, boss." He was the youngest member of my crew. I had hired him in Singapore, where he'd been avoiding extradition to the US for a host of felony charges, and put him to work as our technical geek. I was the closest thing he had to a father figure, and that was just sad.

"This is going to be the toughest thing we've ever done," I warned. "There's no shame in backing out. We're probably going to get killed if we're lucky or thrown into the worst kind of prison you can imagine if we're not."

"I'm in," Reaper repeated with a lot more force than you would expect from looking at him. I had known that whatever I had voted for, Reaper would have my back.

I nodded. "Carl?"

My oldest friend grunted as he leaned forward in his chair. We had worked together for a very long time. When we had first met, Carl had been a Portuguese mercenary helping to overthrow an African government. Between the two of us we'd killed piles of people in dire need of killing, and a quite a few who had just been in the wrong place at the wrong time. We'd robbed, conned, stolen, and murdered our way across four continents. The contents of Carl's folder were a mystery. He was like my brother, but I didn't know what he had left behind in the Azores all those years ago. He wasn't exactly the conversational sort.

Carl shrugged. "Whatever . . . I'm in."

The last member of my crew hesitated. I knew that Train's folder contained pictures of his estranged wife and little girl. Omaha, Nebraska wasn't out of Eddie's reach. Train's ex had divorced him while he had been serving time. She didn't like being married to a criminal, but she apparently had no moral problems cashing the checks he mailed to her after every single one of our jobs, either. Train loved his young daughter more than life itself, and I could see that fact roiling around behind his eyes as he made up his mind.

"I can't," he said simply. "Sorry, Lorenzo."

I nodded.

"Ah, Train, come on," Reaper whined. "We need you, big guy."

"I don't trust Eddie," Train spat. "And you'd be an idiot to trust him. He knows about my kid, man. I've got to go get her."

I extended my hand. He hesitated only briefly before crushing it in his big mitt. He was one of only a handful of people in this world that I actually trusted. I had worked with Train for nearly a decade and his decision didn't surprise me at all. For a man who could snap a neck with one hand, he had a remarkably soft heart. "Watch your back," I ordered.

He gave me a sad smile. We both knew that this was the end of a long run. "No problem, chief."

Train took his share of the money and slipped out that night. At the time, none of us had realized that our hotel room had been bugged even though we had swept the room.

The next morning I had awoken to a knock on our door. When I answered, gun in hand, the messenger was gone, but there had been a cardboard box left there addressed to me. The size and weight told me what it was even before I opened it. Train's severed head had been neatly wrapped in newspaper. The only other contents were a note.

I AM WATCHING YOU.

Chapter 1:
Job Security

VALENTINE
ATC Research & Development Facility
North Las Vegas, Nevada, USA
January 18
0330

I made my way around Building 21, rattling door handles as I went. It was the second time I'd checked this building during my shift, and I didn't expect to find it unsecured. Still, the night-shift maintenance guys had a habit of leaving doors unlocked as they did their rounds, so I often had to relock them during *my* rounds.

Finding nothing out of place, I returned to the front of the building. Mounted on the wall next to the front door was a small metal button, resembling a watch battery. I retrieved from my pocket an electronic wand, and touched the tip of it to the metal button on the wall.

Nothing happened. "Goddamn it," I grumbled, wiping both the button and the end of the wand with my finger.

The wand was my electronic leash. As I hit the buttons across the facility, the wand recorded the time that I was there, thus proving to my employers that I was actually doing my job. However, if there was any moisture at all on either the button or the wand, it wouldn't register.

I tried the button again. Still, nothing happened. Swearing some more, I pulled a small cloth out of my pocket and wiped down the button and the tip of the wand. Yet again, nothing happened. A pulse of anger shot through me, and I threw the wand against the steel door of Building 21. It bounced off, leaving not so much as a dent, and clattered to the concrete sidewalk below.

I took a deep breath and looked around. The sprawling ATC facility was dark, lit only by the amber lights around the buildings and along the roads. To the south, the omnipresent glow of the Strip lit up the sky. The night air was cool but had the familiar dusty stink of Las Vegas.

I looked down at the wand and frowned. Everywhere I'd been, everything I'd done, and *this* was what I was reduced to. I had seen combat on four continents and had survived it all, only to be utterly defeated by badly designed electronics. I sighed loudly, though there was no one around to hear.

I picked up my wand and made one last attempt. Touching it to the button, the wand beeped loudly and registered the hit. Muttering to myself, I stuffed the wand back into my pocket and returned to my patrol truck. Building 21 was last on my scheduled rounds; I had nothing else to do but drive around for the remaining three and a half hours of my shift.

As I drove, I listened to a late-night radio program

called *From Sea to Shining Sea*. It was basically four hours of people talking about conspiracy theories, aliens, ghosts, and stuff like that. Most of it was a bunch of hooey, in my opinion, but it was often entertaining. Listening to the conspiracy theories regarding Mexico, the United Nations, and Vanguard Strategic Services always gave me a chuckle. They had *no idea*. The host, Roger Geonoy, was talking about secret government black helicopters or something with a guest. The guest was a frequent visitor to the show and only called himself "Prometheus." He never gave his real name. Because, you know, *they* are listening. I barely paid attention as they went on about the supposed shadow government and its stealth helicopters. I did get another chuckle when Prometheus insisted that these choppers are sound-suppressed and can fly in what he called "whisper mode." I'd ridden in enough helicopters to know just how freaking loud they are.

As Roger Geonoy listened to Prometheus blather on about black helicopters and cattle mutilations, I remembered my last helicopter ride in detail. The noise of the engines, the roar of gunfire. The sickening sound of bullets hitting the hull. The shrieking of the alarm as we dropped into a drained swimming pool. The ragged, bloody hole in Ramirez' head. Doc's guts spilled out onto the floor of the chopper.

"Sierra-Eleven, Dispatch," my radio squawked, startling me. I realized that I'd been sitting at a stop sign for minutes on end. *From Sea to Shining Sea* had gone to commercial break. My heart was pounding.

Shaking it off, I answered my radio. "This is Sierra-Eleven."

"Electrical Maintenance needs you to let them into Building Fourteen," the Dispatcher said.

"Uh, ten-four," I replied. "Ten-seventeen." I took a deep breath and returned my attention to doing my stupid job.

Hours later, I pulled my patrol truck into a parking space behind the Security Office. Putting the truck in park, I finished the paperwork on my clipboard, recorded the mileage, and cut the engine. My breath steamed in the cool January air as I stepped out of the truck and made my way into the office.

"Mornin', Val," my supervisor, Mr. Norton, said as I passed his office en route to the ready room. "Anything happen last night?"

Pausing, I leaned into the doorway for a moment. "It was quiet, Boss." Leaning in farther, I handed him my paperwork. "Is McDonald here yet?"

"Yeah, he's on time today," Mr. Norton said. "Have a good weekend, Val."

"You, too, boss," I said, leaving the doorway and making my way down the hall. I pushed open the door to the ready room. My relief, McDonald, was standing by the gun lockers, seemingly half awake. He was *always* seemingly half awake and had a perpetual five o'clock shadow on top of it. I found him tiresome.

He had the muzzle of his pistol in the clearing barrel as he chambered a round. Stepping past him, I opened my own gun locker, drew the .357 Magnum revolver from the holster on my left hip, and placed it inside.

"Why do you still carry that thing? We've got the new nine-mils, you know," he said, holstering the pistol he'd just loaded.

"I shoot revolvers better," I answered, not looking at him. "Not much to pass on. It was quiet last night. Some contractors are working by the old warehouse on the south side, so make sure Gate Ten is closed and locked after they leave." I slung my gun belt over my shoulder and made my way out of the office and into the parking lot.

I found my Mustang and cranked it up. My radio was playing the morning news as I drove home, but I found it hard to pay attention. I'd lived outside of the United States for years; domestic news was something I was used to just ignoring. Frowning, I changed radio stations and listened to music for the rest of my commute home.

My apartment building was halfway across town. It didn't look like much, but it was cheap for Vegas and wasn't in a really bad neighborhood. It was an old motel that had been converted to apartments. The rooms were small, but there weren't a lot of gangbangers and hookers hanging around all the time, and the cops weren't there every night.

I made my way upstairs to the second floor. As I approached my door, I saw my next-door neighbor leaning against the railing. She smiled. "Hey," she said, sounding tired. She removed a pack of cigarettes from her jacket pocket.

"Mornin', Liz," I said, leaning against the railing next to her. She was wearing a blue uniform, like me, but she wasn't a security guard. Liz was a paramedic, and like me she also worked the night shift. She usually got home about the same time I did. Her curly red hair was pulled into a bun under her cap.

"Long night last night?" I asked as she dug for her lighter.

"Jesus Christ," she said. "Goddamn tweakers." Liz had been a medic for ten years and had seen just about everything.

"Here," I said, handing her my Zippo lighter. "You okay?"

"Thank you. I'm fine—my partner just had to fight with this one asshole." I'd never met Liz's partner, but apparently he was a big dude. That was probably for the best, as Liz herself stood barely five foot three. She paused while she lit her cigarette. She then snapped the lighter closed but didn't hand it back to me.

"That's an interesting logo on there," she said, holding my lighter up. It was matte black and engraved with a skull with a switchblade knife clutched in its teeth. I'd had the lighter a long time, and it was pretty scratched up. "Were you in the military?"

I didn't say anything. Looking over at Liz, I saw that she was studying me intently. "I was," I said at last. "Air Force. A long time ago."

"You're too young to have done anything a long time ago."

I chuckled. "I enlisted when I turned eighteen."

"I figured," she said, handing me the lighter. "You seem like the type. Was that your unit logo or something?

"This? No. I was in the Security Forces. I did one stint in Afghanistan before I got out."

"What'd you do after that?" she asked.

"I went to work," I said awkwardly. I didn't know Liz all that well, and I wasn't used to talking about myself with people. "I was a security consultant for a few years."

"Consultant? What kind of work did you do?" she asked.

"Uh, the usual stuff," I said awkwardly. "Can't really tell you."

"Oh, whatever," she snorted, exhaling smoke.

"No, really," I said. "I signed a nondisclosure agreement." Leaving out the fact that my company no longer existed, I made a big show of yawning. "Hey, I think I need to hit the rack."

"You sure you don't want some breakfast? It's my weekend to have the kids. I'm making bacon and eggs in a little bit."

"Thanks, but I'm really tired," I said with a sheepish smile. I turned and unlocked my door.

"Hey, Val," Liz called after me just as I stepped inside. "I do PTSD counseling on the side. If you ever need to talk . . ."

I smiled at her again. "Thank you. I'm okay, really," I said, before closing the door. I locked it, dropped my backpack on the floor, and plopped down in front of my computer. I had one e-mail waiting for me.

Michael Valentine:

> *Have you considered my offer? You're an excellent soldier and you risked your life to save someone precious to us. Our organization could use people like you. I hope to hear back from you soon.*

> > > > > *Song Ling*

The e-mail was from a randomized address, so I had no idea where it was sent from. It included a footnote with a long phone number for me to call if I was interested, and it said that I could call that number from anywhere in the world.

Leaning back in my chair, I took a deep breath, and rubbed my eyes. I closed my e-mail browser and stood up. I wanted to take a shower and go to bed. I hoped that I wouldn't have nightmares this time, but I knew that I would. I always did.

VALENTINE
Las Vegas, Nevada, USA
January 18
1245

I awoke to the sound of my phone ringing. Noticing my clock, I realized I'd only been asleep for a few hours. I reached over to my nightstand, grabbed my phone, and looked at the display. I didn't recognize the number.

"Hello?" I asked, my voice sounding groggy.

"What're you doing, fucker?"

"Who *is* this?"

The voice laughed. "Has it been that long, bro?"

"Tailor?" I asked.

"What are you doing?"

"I'm sleeping. How did you get this number?"

"Well, get up! I'll be there in about half an hour."

"Be *where*?"

"At your apartment."

"What? How the hell do you know where I live? How did you get this number?" Tailor didn't answer. "Never mind. What do you want?"

"I'll tell you when I get there. Get dressed, I'm taking you to lunch. Don't dress like a slob, we're going someplace nice."

"But—"

"*Val*. Trust me."

I was quiet for a few seconds. "Fine. This better be good." I hung up on him, ran my fingers through my hair, and got up.

Twenty-five minutes later, there was a knock on my door. Now fully dressed and mostly awake, I crossed my small apartment and looked through the peephole. I saw Tailor's misshapen head, distorted through the tiny optic, his eyes hidden behind Oakley sunglasses. I opened the door.

"Tailor." His head was slightly less misshapen in person. Tailor grinned. He hadn't changed a bit. His dirty blond hair was buzzed down to almost nothing, as always. He was dressed casually but still looked uptight. He was wearing a nice leather jacket.

"Val." He stuck out his hand. I took it, and we shook firmly. "Long time no see, bro."

"C'mon in," I said, stepping aside.

Tailor looked around my apartment. "This is where you live? What'd you do, spend all your money?"

"I've got plenty of money in savings," I said testily. "I just wanted to keep a low profile. This place isn't bad." Tailor then noticed my blue uniforms hanging against the wall.

"You're a security guard?" he asked incredulously. "You've been in how many wars? And now you're a security guard?"

"Ain't much demand for my skill set, you know," I said, looking for my jacket. "Where are we going?"

"I found a steakhouse."

"You're buying me a steak? What? Okay, what the hell is going on?"

"Don't worry about it. I'll tell you about it over lunch." I looked at him hard for a moment. I was about to tell him to get the hell out of my apartment and go back to bed. Something told me to hear him out, though. I felt that I owed him that much; he'd saved my life more than once. I nodded, put on my sunglasses, and followed him out the door.

"It's good to see you again," I said from the passenger's seat of Tailor's Ford Expedition, looking out the window. Neither one of us had said anything since we'd left my apartment.

"You, too, bro," Tailor replied, his voice sounding unusually upbeat.

"So, where are we going?" I asked as he drove me across town. We were headed downtown, toward the Strip.

"Ruth's Chris," he said. "It's over on Paradise."

"Dude, that place is expensive."

"When did you become so *cheap*, Val?" Tailor asked. "Besides, I'm buying. Don't worry about it! You think I'd drag you out of bed and not buy lunch?"

"*Yes*," I said, folding my arms across my chest.

"Fair enough." A lopsided grin appeared on his face. "But I didn't this time."

A short while later, I found myself sitting at a booth in the steakhouse, waiting for my food. Tailor sat across from me. We both sipped glasses of Dr. Pepper and talked about nothing.

"Okay, Tailor, what's this all about? I haven't heard from you since Mexico. Now you show up on my doorstep and buy me an expensive steak. What's going on?"

Tailor set down his Dr. Pepper. "Have you thought about going back to work?"

"I *have* a job," I said, sounding a little huffy.

"What do you make, ten bucks an hour?" Tailor asked, sarcasm in his voice.

"I make *eighteen* bucks an hour," I said, sounding more than a little huffy this time. "And no one shoots at me. Also? I haven't been to a single funeral since I started."

"Okay, how's that working out for you? Are you happy?"

"What?"

"Are you happy doing this? Going to work every day like a regular guy? Is that what you want?

"Well, I . . ." I fell silent, and remained quiet for a long moment. I took a deep breath. "I *hate* this," I said quietly. "It's like . . . I try so hard to fit in, to understand people, to make this work. But I *can't*. I just . . ."

"You know what the problem is, Val?" Tailor asked, interrupting me. I raised my eyebrows at him. "You're a *killer*."

"That's not it," I protested.

"The *fuck* it's not," he said. "How long have I known you? Four years, right?"

"Since Africa," I said, remembering my first deployment with Vanguard. It seemed like a lifetime had passed since then.

"Right. And you know what I've learned in all that time? You're a badass. You don't think you are, and you've got that baby face and stupid smile, and you act all quiet and shy. But when you strip all that away, you're a killer."

"So?" I asked. His analysis of my personality was making me uncomfortable. I looked around the restaurant, studying the other customers, watching the doors as people came in and out.

"See what you're doing right now? You're checking the exits, aren't you?" Tailor said.

"Fine. So I'm the problem. I'm some kind of badass that can't understand how to fit in the real world, just like in that old Kurt Russell movie. Is that it?"

"No. The problem isn't that *you* don't understand. It's that *they* don't understand," he said, moving his arm to indicate the other people in the restaurant. "*They* don't live in the real world. They haven't seen the things that you've seen or done the things that you've done. Most of these people have never killed a man or buried a friend. Hell, most probably have never even *fired a gun*. And there you sit, concealing a 44 Magnum, watching the exits, surrounded by people who just don't *get it*. You're a *killer*, Val, and no matter how long you work a bullshit nine-to-five job, you're not gonna change that."

I didn't respond for a few moments. "You're more perceptive than you look," I said at last, rubbing my eyes.

"The question is," Tailor went on, "what changed? It didn't used to bother you. I know you have nightmares,

Val. Everybody has nightmares. Everybody has regrets. Well, except me. *I* don't. But most people do. It didn't used to eat you up. It's eating you up now. I can see it on your face. What happened?"

"*Mexico* happened, Tailor," I said flatly, looking him in the eye again.

Tailor took a deep breath and leaned back in his seat. "That was ugly, wasn't it?"

"Ugly? We got stranded in hostile territory, abandoned, left to *die*. We barely got out alive. So yeah, I guess you could say it was *ugly*."

"We got out, didn't we?"

"Only because of Ling and her people."

"It doesn't matter," Tailor said, taking another sip of his soda. "We lived."

"Tell that to Ramirez's family."

"Ramirez didn't *have* any family, Val," Tailor snapped, setting his glass down hard. "None of us did. It's why we were good at our jobs. It's why we got the good jobs, the good pay, and the good equipment. It's why we were on the Switchblade teams in the first place. We had nothing to come home to anyway. Ramirez is dead. Harper is dead. Tower is dead. *Everybody dies*, Val. You don't get to pick how or when. I worked with Ramirez longer than you. Don't you *dare* use his death as an excuse to mope around like a teenaged drama queen!"

I didn't say anything, and I didn't look at Tailor. We were briefly interrupted as the waitress brought us our food.

"Is that what's eating you, Val?" Tailor asked at last, chewing expensive steak with his mouth open. "Survivor's guilt?"

"You don't understand," I said quietly, cutting my steak.

"How the hell do *you* know what I understand?" Tailor said to me. "I've been doing this longer than you, Val. You think you've seen some shit? I've seen some shit, too. The difference is, I *deal with it* instead of letting it screw me up. Until you do that, nothing's going to change for you. Living in this dump, punishing yourself with a stupid job and a stupid life isn't going to make you feel any better."

I ate my steak in silence, not sure what to say. We were quiet for an awkwardly long time before either one of us spoke. I set my fork down and looked at my former partner. "What's this all about, Tailor? I know you didn't drive all the way to Vegas and buy me an expensive steak just to yell at me about my angst."

Tailor took a moment to finish chewing before he spoke. "I've got a job offer for you."

I raised my eyebrows. "I'm listening."

"You'd have to leave soon. Like in the next week or so."

"I'd have to break my lease."

"Will that be a problem?"

"No, I just won't get my deposit back. Who's it with?"

"I don't know," Tailor said, flatly.

"What do you mean, *you don't know*?"

Tailor leaned in, his voice hushed. "I think it's a front for the government. They're real hush-hush about everything. They just call it *The Project*. They're offering twenty-five K a month, plus expenses."

I almost choked on my Dr. Pepper. "Christ, that's like three hundred thousand dollars a year!" My annual salary with Vanguard had been about a hundred thousand dollars a year, plus operational bonuses. I only got paid that much because I was on one of the Switchblade teams.

"Tax-exempt," Tailor added.

"What? From a US company? No Medicare or Social Security?" By US law, if you were out of the United States for three hundred and thirty days of a year, you didn't have to pay income taxes. This capped out at eighty thousand dollars. Everything above that was taxable income.

"You get paid what you get paid. They told me they'd take care of the IRS aspects of it."

"And you're just trusting these people?"

"Val, they've already deposited a twenty thousand dollar signing bonus into my bank account. I trust *that*."

"Money talks, huh?"

"Money talks."

"Have you told anyone else about this?"

"I called Skunky," Tailor replied, sipping his soda.

"Really? How's he doing, anyway? Haven't heard from him."

"He lives in California now."

"Eew," I said, making a face.

"I know, right?"

"You know, you're not the first one to offer me a job," I said.

"Really? Have you been looking?"

"No. Every couple of months I get an e-mail from Ling. She wants me to sign up with her group."

"Val, that crazy Chinese bitch ain't gonna sleep with you."

"What? That's not—"

"Oh, the hell it's not," he interrupted, grinning. "Come

on, Val, I know you. You've got a thing for Asians, and I watched you drool all over her from the moment she showed up. The puppy love was cute, Val, it really was."

"Hey, that *crazy bitch* saved our lives."

"Well, we wouldn't have been there if Exodus hadn't hired us in the first place. We were expendable. And we *paid* for it."

I sighed. "I know. It's why I haven't answered. Her group considers me some kind of hero, I think, because I saved that kid we rescued."

"Val, her group . . . how much do you know about them?"

"I've done some research. It's hard to find much. They're like global vigilantes. They kill slavers, drug runners . . ."

"That's just the beginning," Tailor said. "They're a very secretive, very well-funded transnational paramilitary organization. They're like a cult. They go around the world, shooting people and blowing shit up in the name of the greater good or something. The UN considers them a terrorist group."

"They didn't think too highly of Vanguard, either, Tailor."

"Look," Tailor continued, "I'm saying you might want to think twice before getting involved with some crazy terrorist group because you're bored and you're trying to get laid. I mean come on, this is *Nevada*. If you want to screw an Asian chick so bad, just go to a whorehouse."

My mouth fell open. "You . . ." I cracked a smile and began to laugh. "You're a *dick*, you know that?"

"Yeah, I know," he said matter-of-factly. "Even still, you

shouldn't rush into something like that when you don't know anything about it."

"Says the guy who shows up on my doorstep and tries to get me to take a mysterious job with a mysterious company he doesn't know anything about," I said, a wry grin appearing on my face.

"Okay," Tailor admitted, "but we'll be there together. If there are any problems, well, we'll deal with it. We've been in bad situations before."

"The money's too good, Tailor. Something stinks."

"I know," he said again. "I think it's something to do with the Middle East."

"As in Afghanistan? I really don't want to go back to Afghanistan, Tailor."

"No, I think they're going to send us someplace that the US ain't supposed to be. I think that's why the pay is so good, and that's why there's so much secrecy."

"Huh," I said. "How'd you find out about this?"

"Friend of a friend got me in touch with this guy named Gordon Willis."

"Who's he?"

"I don't know. He's pretty cryptic about everything, but he's obviously got a lot of money behind him. All he'll say is that he represents the best interests of the United States."

"That sounds, um, *ominous*."

"Right?" Tailor asked. "I know, Val, I know. Like I said, the money's real good. Everything I've seen from these people is on the ball. They pay in advance. And their cars have government plates."

"You're really going along with this?" I asked.

"I'm already signed up and everything. I ship next

week. That's why I'm here, Val. I want you to go with me. Whaddaya say?"

I was quiet for a long moment, as our waitress brought us our check. "You know, last night at work I got bitched out by an employee at the facility. She showed up at the south gate at about zero-two-hundred and wanted a temporary badge. The south gate doesn't open until zero-six. So instead of going to the front gate, she sat there and bitched out the dispatcher on the phone until he sent me down there. Then she bitched *me* out until I issued her the temporary badge."

"That's bullshit," Tailor said. "You should've told her to go to the main gate or sit there all night."

"I can't. We're always getting nasty-grams in the e-mail from the Branch Office, reminding us that serving the client is the number one priority, that we're there to make things better for them, blah blah blah," I said, waving my arm theatrically. "Basically, if I enforce the rules I'm supposed to enforce, people complain and I get in trouble. If I *don't* enforce them, people complain and I get in trouble."

"Why don't you look for a new job?"

"Like I said, it's hard to get jobs with my skill-set. Normal jobs, anyway. I mean, what am I going to do, sell cars? Flip burgers? And I don't have anything else going on. I don't really have any friends here. I don't have a girlfriend. I mean, I guess I could go out to bars or whatever and try to pick women up, but what am I going to say? *Hey, baby, I know I'm emotionally damaged and unstable, and I spent the last five years shooting people for money, and now I'm a security guard and everything, but why don't you overlook all that and come have sex with me in my crappy little apartment?"*

Tailor let out a raucous laugh. "Then come back to work, Val. To hell with it."

"Yeah . . . yeah. I mean, why not? I can't possibly hate my life any more than I do now. Screw it, let's do this. It'll be good to work with you again."

"You sure, Val?"

"I'm sure. Hey, what did Skunky say when you called him?"

"He wasn't interested." Tailor shrugged. "Says he's got his own thing going on or something."

"I'm glad he's doing better than me. Come on, take me home. I've got some arrangements I need to make." Tailor grinned and stuck his fist across the table. I made a fist with my left hand and bumped it against his.

VALENTINE
Las Vegas, Nevada
January 19
1059

"Mr. Valentine! It's good to see you," the man said earnestly, giving me a firm handshake. "My name is Gordon Willis. This is my associate, Mr. Anders," he said, indicating a tall, muscular man with tan skin and cropped blond hair. Anders looked like an old Waffen SS recruiting poster. The *Übermensch* grunted. "Please, sit down," Gordon said then, indicating a chair on the opposite side of a cluttered desk.

Sitting down, I studied Gordon for a moment. He was in his late thirties or early forties, with a slick haircut and an expensive suit. He smiled with perfectly straight, perfectly white teeth, and observed me with piercing blue eyes. I immediately distrusted this man. He was slick, but my gut told me he was a snake. I tried to ignore it and listened to what he had to say.

"I trust Mr. Tailor has filled you in on the job opportunity I can offer you?" he asked, folding his hands on the desk in front of him.

"Uh, yes," I said, trying to quell my unease. "He didn't have a lot of details himself, but he told me about the pay. Twenty-five thousand dollars a month?"

"Yes!" he said, beaming. "Tax exempt, of course."

"How . . . how is that possible?" I asked. "The tax law says that—"

Gordon interrupted me with an obnoxious little chuckle. "Mr. Valentine, I'm sure you have a lot of questions. I'm afraid that there are a lot of things I simply can't tell you unless you sign. All I'm at liberty to say is that you won't have to worry about paying any taxes. We'll take care of the IRS documentation and filing for you. You'll keep every cent of what you earn."

"Who are you people?" I asked flatly, my eyes narrowing. "What's this all about? I can tell that this isn't your office," I said, moving my arm to indicate the small storefront we were sitting in. "You probably rented this place out a week ago."

Gordon sat back in his chair and studied me with a knowing grin on his face. "Mr. Tailor was right about you," he said. "You're very sharp." He then pulled a large manila envelope out of his desk drawer. He opened it and began to read to me. "Your real name is Constantine Michael Valentine, yet you somehow managed to get *Constantine* left off of your military ID." My mouth fell open, but I didn't say anything. I hadn't heard anyone say my real first name in years. "You served a four-year term of enlistment in the United States Air Force, including a six-month combat deployment to Afghanistan. You were involved in an incident there, and while you were discharged honorably you have a reenlistment code of RE-3. They asked you not to come back."

"Okay, so you were able to pull my DD214," I said. "Are you with the government?"

Gordon set the papers down before speaking. "Something like that. I'm afraid I really can't say much more at this time. Ever since Mr. Tailor indicated that you might be interested in the job I'm offering, we've been doing a very thorough background check on you. I know that you went from being a career contractor with Vanguard Strategic Solutions International to working as a night-shift security guard for a local defense contractor. Your annual income is about one quarter of what it was last year, and that doesn't include the generous operational bonuses or hazard pay that Vanguard was famous for."

"So?"

"So, Mr. Valentine, your friend Mr. Tailor told me that you're *better* than this. And you know what? I agree. I've studied your entire dossier, going back to when you were in high school. I know what happened to your mother, and I can only imagine the effect that had on you."

"Mr. Willis," I said coldly, "You have no *idea* the effect that had on me."

"Ah, I see," he said, his voice softening. "I apologize, Mr. Valentine. I didn't mean to bring up bad blood. All I was trying to say is that I think what I'm offering is perfect for you."

I sighed, pinching the bridge of my nose between two fingers as I did so. "Mr. Willis, what exactly *are* you offering me?"

"Straight to the point." He beamed. "I like that. You wouldn't believe how many guys we get through here that get intimidated when we pull out their file. I'm not going to lie to you," he said, leaning in closer. "This job is going to be dangerous. You'll have to be able to deploy right away."

"I see. That shouldn't be a problem. How dangerous are we talking here?"

"As I'm sure you've guessed," Gordon said, "absolute discretion is required. Look at the world situation right now, Mr. Valentine; war in Mexico, war in the Middle East, war in Southeast Asia and Africa, more in-fighting in Russia, and an uneasy cease-fire in China with a thousand-mile-long DMZ along the Yangtze River. The world is spiraling into chaos and our country's conventional military and intelligence assets just aren't enough to deal with it all."

"I've been shot at in half the places you just listed, Mr. Willis," I said. "I'm *well* aware of the geopolitical situation."

"I'm sure you are, Mr. Valentine. Since joining Vanguard you've been on—" he trailed off as he checked my file— "*five* major deployments overseas. Nearly five years of your life fighting other peoples' wars. I'm offering you a chance to serve *your* country again. There's a critical situation developing, and we need the best people available to manage it before it gets out of hand."

"Don't you have the CIA and Special Forces for that?" I asked. Something about this whole thing stank. The money was too good, and the facts were too few.

"As you can imagine, they're stretched thin as is," Gordon replied.

"I can't imagine you're having trouble recruiting people with the money you're offering."

"You wouldn't think so, but many of our candidates have the same professional paranoia as you, Mr. Valentine. Due to the nature of the situation, I'm simply unable to disclose much more than I've told you before you sign. Many otherwise promising candidates have balked at the lack of information."

I chewed on that for a moment. It was disquieting, to be sure, but I had a feeling there was more to it than that. "I see. Am I to assume that this will be a combat operation?"

"If all goes well," Gordon said, "the combat will be minimal. We're trying something new in our area of operations. You'll be trained in mission-specific skills above and beyond door-kicking and trigger-pulling. As I said, the utmost discretion is required. I'm also required to inform you that while you're away, you'll only have minimal contact with loved ones back home. We regret this, but security is necessary until the operation is completed."

"What kind of time frame are we looking at here?" I asked.

"Hopefully, we'll have everyone home by Christmas. Now, I'm sure you've heard that before, so I'm not going to mince words. The contract is for an undetermined period of time not to exceed three years. You're ours until the mission is over, basically. Obviously, at the pay rate we're offering, it's in our best interest to accomplish the mission as soon as possible." Gordon let out a convincing chuckle at his own joke.

"Tailor told me he got a signing bonus."

"Ah, yes!" Gordon said, retrieving another manila envelope from his desk. He opened it and placed a piece of paper in front of me. It was a standard government direct-deposit form. "If you'll fill this out," he said, "we should have that in your bank account in three to five business days."

"And . . . you're sure there won't be any problems with the IRS? This is all going to my regular checking account with the Las Vegas Federal Credit Union and I'm not going to have the tax man breathing down my neck?"

"Don't worry, Mr. Valentine," Gordon said, grinning. "We're bigger than the tax man." That sounded more ominous than promising. I realized then that the big guy, Anders, was still standing in the corner behind Gordon and hadn't said a word the entire time. He observed me with a bored look on his face, but I didn't doubt that he'd made a plan to kill me the moment I walked in the door. These guys undoubtedly knew that I had a concealed-firearm permit, but they hadn't said anything about it.

"Who, exactly, is *we*?" I asked, looking over the contract Gordon had pushed in front of me. It was full of vague legalese and only referred to Gordon's organization as *the party of the first part.*

Gordon grinned. "I'm afraid you'll have to sign to get filled in on all of that, Mr. Valentine," he said and set an ornate pen down in front of me. "All I can say until then is that you'll be serving the best interests of the United States and will be protecting your country from enemies foreign and domestic."

I picked up the silver pen. It had XII, the Roman numeral for the number twelve, engraved on it. I wondered what it meant. I took a deep breath and signed the document. Gordon smiled.

"I guess I'll have to call my boss and tell him I'm not coming in Monday," I said.

"Don't worry about that," Gordon answered. "We'll take care of everything. You can take the direct-deposit form with you if you don't have your bank routing number available right now. Within forty-eight hours, you should receive a packet with everything you need to know. You'll be deploying within two weeks."

"Deploying where?" I asked, handing him back his pen.

"Everything will be in the packet," he said. "Until then, take some time to get your affairs in order. You'll likely be out of the United States for an extended period of time." Gordon stuck his hand out. I hesitated, then took it. He had an excessively firm handshake. "Welcome aboard," he said and stood up. I gathered my papers and stood up as well. "You did the right thing."

"I hope so," I said, taking my papers and turning to leave.

"Mr. Valentine?" Anders, the big guy, said as I opened the door. I turned and looked back at him. "If you fail to arrive at the deployment location at the appropriate time, we *will* come get you. It'll be best if you're punctual."

"I get it," I said and closed the door behind me. *What the hell did I just do?*

LORENZO
Confederated Gulf Emirate of Zubara
January 20

The marketplace was busy, the large Sunday crowds nervous. Change was coming, and the people could feel it. I made my way through the bustling place, gray and incognito as usual, dressed like the locals in a traditional white thobe and checkered headdress. In my line of work, you never stick out. It keeps you alive longer.

There were three sections of Zubara City (Ash Shamal, Umm Shamal, and Al Khor). Each was a narrow sliver of land extending into the Persian Gulf for a couple of miles. Half a million people were packed on those three little peninsulas, mostly Sunni, some Shiite, a mess of imported workers, and I was spending my day in the poor, dangerous one, Ash Shamal.

Nobody used the country's official name, or the abbreviation CGEZ. The Americans or Europeans who ended up here usually called it the Zoob. The rest of the world just referred to the tiny country as Zubara.

I got to the entrance of the club fifteen minutes early so I could survey the area. This neighborhood was one of the oldest in Ash Shamal, but there was much new construction underway. It was also one of the more traditional. It was interesting to note the fundamentalist graffiti that was popping up in many of the alleys, and even more interesting was that the local authorities hadn't bothered to cover it up. Either there was too much of it to keep up with, the official government types didn't bother to come into this neighborhood, or the cops actually agreed with the message. Either way, it was a grim omen.

Zubara was a relatively modern state, dragged kicking and screaming into the twenty-first century by the current monarch. Bordered by Qatar and Saudi Arabia, the tiny nation wasn't nearly as rich as its neighbors but was relatively clean, organized, and, by Arab standards, efficient. Zubara was one of the jewels of the Persian Gulf, but that appeared to be changing with the current power struggle, and my specialty was to capitalize on the inevitable chaos that would result.

I had spent my entire adult life in various third-world countries. I'd seen revolutions, famines, wars, and the utter collapse of societies. I made my living on the fringe of mankind. I didn't know what was going to happen here yet, but I knew *something* was coming.

Zubara would be just another job, just a little more difficult than normal, or so I tried to convince myself. It had been six months since I had been drafted for this job. Six months since Eddie had brutally murdered one of my crew just to let me know how serious he was. Half a year of preparation and groundwork to pull off an impossible mission. There was a bitter taste in my mouth as I prepared for this meeting.

I walked around the block to scope out the back entrance, just in case. There was some construction going on across the street, but the workers all looked like the normal Indonesians and Filipinos that did all the grunt labor in this country. I saw no indications of a trap. Making my way back to the front, I leaned against the corner of a building and watched the club. The man I was supposed to be meeting would probably be running late, like pretty much everything in this part of the world. I couldn't spot anyone else surveying the place, so it was either safe or they were really good.

Waiting gave me time to think, which was unfortunate, because right now thinking about what I was doing just made me angrier. This job sucked. It was suicide, and I had been forced into it against my will. It was going to take months to accomplish, but once this gig was completed, I was going to devote my life to finding the man who put me in this situation. I vowed that I was going to go on a killing spree that would become the stuff of legend.

My thoughts of murder were interrupted when a black Bentley parked in front of the club. The luxury car didn't seem out of place on the same street as a vendor selling live chickens, but that was the nature of the Middle East. The driver exited and held open the back door for his charge. The man that stepped out was in his forties, wearing a brown suit, white shirt, and no tie. This was pretty fashionable apparel in the region and was what all the cool terrorists were wearing.

He was early. *Amazing.* The driver stayed with the vehicle. I waited a few extra minutes, watching for anything out of the ordinary before I followed him into the club. The interior was dark and cooled by rows of ceiling fans. Inside, the social club was far nicer than its drab outside appearance suggested. It was relatively crowded by middle-aged men smoking hookahs, playing chess, and bitching about local politics.

The server acknowledged me as I entered, but I waved him off as I spotted the man I was looking for sitting at a table in the back. The server retreated deferentially.

The man saw me approaching and nodded once. I pulled up a chair and sat. "Lorenzo," he said before taking a sip of his pungent tea. "I didn't recognize you."

"That's the general idea," I responded. Say what you will about the man-dresses, they were actually pretty comfy and enabled me to conceal a few weapons. Even still, they do make you look like a big stupid marshmallow, and you can hardly run in one. I'd taken a few days to brush up my Arabic and perfect the local accent. I'd grown my beard out, and my natural features enabled me to pass for a native Zubaran rather easily. After all, I had a knack for blending in wherever I went. "Good to see you again, Jalal."

Jalal Hosani smiled. "No, it is not good, I am afraid. You are a wanted man in this country, if I recall correctly." His English was perfect. It should be, since he'd attended Oxford, paid for by his friends in the Qatari royal family.

"Actually, no. You're thinking of Syria, and the UAE . . . oh, and I think the Saudi courts want one of my hands. This is my first time in lovely Zubara. It's kind of nice, except that whole pending revolution thing. So, what brought you here?"

"Business grew difficult in Baghdad," he said with a

casual wave of his hand, as if a couple hundred thousand American troops interrupting his illicit arms dealing was a minor inconvenience. Jalal pulled a silver cigarette case from his suit. He offered me one. I shook my head. "Still the health nut, I see."

I only smoked when the cover required it. "Cardiovascular fitness comes in handy in my line of work."

"About that." Jalal lit his cigarette and took a long drag. "What is your work this time?" He waited for me to respond, and when I didn't, he continued. "I see . . . Usually your work involves the involuntary transfer of wealth and countless murders. I can safely assume this will be the same?"

"But of course," I replied as I pulled a fat envelope from my man-dress and passed it over. "As usual, you don't want the details. I was never here."

Jalal raised his eyebrows as he flipped through the stack of money. He looked around the room as he shoved the money into his coat. "That is a considerable sum," he said. "A considerable sum indeed. You do realize, however, that there are men hiding in this country who are with organizations you have stolen from. In fact, I know that one *very* dangerous man happens to frequent this very club on occasion. I could just keep the money, say who you are, and—"

I cut him off. "I know who hangs out here." Everyone knew Zubara was a safe haven for various terrorist organizations. Diplomatically, the government was friendly to the US, and tolerated the Israelis, but the official government was growing weaker by the day. "Maybe you talk, and I end up on an Al Jazeera video getting my head sawed off?" I had robbed, conned, or defrauded every major criminal organization on earth at some point. It had made me both a lot of money and a lot of enemies. "We both know that won't happen, because you know I'd find a way to take you with me, and besides, I pay way better than those cheap bastards." I gestured toward the envelope. "That's the first installment. I'll pay you double what I paid you in Dubai."

"It was only a hypothetical."

"And just so you know, I'm doing this job for Big Eddie. So if you *hypothetically* cross me, you *hypothetically* cross him, which means that he'll track you down to the ends of the earth and *hypothetically* feed your entire family into a wood chipper."

His eyes grew wide as he processed that information. Regardless of who you were in the criminal underworld, you were afraid of Eddie. He was evil incarnate. It was my ultimate trump card, because no one on Eddie's naughty list lived for long. Jalal's demeanor changed and he gave me a big smile, always the businessman. "Of course, my friend. How can I be of service?"

Jalal Hosani was a facilitator, not a man who got his hands dirty. He knew people. When you are operating in a new area, you had to have intelligence, and that meant knowing the right people. Jalal knew the right people. Of course, he would also sell me out as soon as it benefited him. So I had to make sure that the math stayed in my favor, because I actually kind of liked Jalal, snake that he was, and killing him would make me . . . sad. Sort of.

"Later on I'm going to need a source for equipment,

weapons, vehicles. Usual stuff, but right now I need information. I need to know what's really going down in Zubara."

"The emir is having a battle against one of his generals for control of the government," Jalal said as if this were common knowledge. "The pro-Western factions are siding with the emir, the fundamentalists and Iranian puppets are siding with the general. It hasn't become violent yet, but it is only a matter of time."

I nodded. "I know that much. What I need to know is who all the players are, and then I'm going to have you do a few introductions for me. Which side are you on?"

"General Al Sabah is a very dangerous man, but the emir should not be underestimated." My old acquaintance appeared to give it some thought. "I suppose I will wait and see which side wins. That is always the side to be on."

"I killed a guy named Al Sabah once."

"It is a common name." Jalal shrugged. "Either way, most of the army is loyal to the general and his personal guard is growing with many foreign"—he paused, looking for the right word— "volunteers."

"You mean fundamentalist nut-jobs who got tired of getting their asses kicked up north decided to get a different job where they could still sock it to the Great Satan?"

"Something like that. Now let us get down to business." We spoke for another half an hour, during which he provided me with the low down on the various players in this unfolding drama. I was careful to give him no information about what I was actually doing here. I asked random questions about unrelated things, to cloud the issue just in case he was planning on betraying me. The meeting was beneficial, and I learned quite a bit more about the inner workings of Zubaran politics. Finally we were done, and Jalal, late for his next appointment, excused himself. We would be in touch.

I leaned back in my chair and watched him leave. The power struggle complicated things. Politics in this part of the world was like a high-speed chess game where the losers got put in front of a firing squad. Heightened tensions led to heightened security, which could prove to be a pain. If the situation deteriorated too quickly, it might spook our mark, and ruin Phase One. We would have to adjust accordingly.

A moment later the server approached me with a menu. The young man greeted me with a great deal of respect. "We did not know you were going to be visiting us today, Khalid." He addressed me by the fake identity I had been cultivating here over the last few months. "How can I be of service?"

Zubaran food was relatively bland for this part of the world, but it was tolerable, and scheming always made me hungry. "Kusbasi kebab, and make sure to spice it up this time. And fetch a chess board. I'll be meeting Al Falah for a match shortly."

He snapped his heels together and retreated toward the kitchen. The service here was excellent, as it should be, since I was their new landlord. I had bought the club outright as soon as I had arrived in Zubara. I checked my watch. My next appointment should be on the way.

At least for now, Phase One was proceeding according to plan.

Chapter 2:
If You Die, They Don't
Have to Pay You

VALENTINE
Quagmire, Nevada, USA
January 30
1420

It was quiet in my Mustang, save for the noise of tires on gravel, as I made my way down the long, winding road to Hawk's home. I hadn't been down this road in months, not since I'd first settled in Las Vegas.

Hawk's real name was John Hawkins. I'd met him in Afghanistan years prior. He'd been the team leader of Switchblade 4, my team, before moving into the training section, then retiring. It had been Hawk who'd taught me how to shoot a revolver and instilled in me a love of Smith & Wesson .44 Magnums. Glancing in the rearview mirror, I saw that Tailor's Expedition was right behind me, shrouded in the cloud of dust my car was kicking up. Our two vehicles were laden with nearly all of my worldly possessions. It was surprisingly little, all things considered.

The dirt road passed through a barbed-wire fence, but the gate had been left open. Up ahead, I could see Hawk's ranch house and the barn beyond it. Several trees shaded the house from the afternoon sun. I could see a couple of horses absentmindedly chewing their feed, paying us no mind.

I came to a stop near Hawk's Dodge turbo-diesel pickup truck, and Tailor parked next to me. I stepped into the cool desert air, glad that I'd worn a jacket. Tailor joined me a second later.

"Place hasn't changed much," Tailor said, looking around.

"Look, he's got solar panels on the roof now."

"Hawk likes to live off the grid," Tailor said. "He's got his own water supply, his own food supply, and his own electricity. You could ride out the end of the world here."

I chuckled. "That's probably his plan." As we approached the house's large front porch, the door opened. Hawk stepped out into the afternoon air, squinting slightly in the light. He looked the same as ever, tall and fit, with rough features and hard eyes. His hair and goatee had more gray in them than they used to, but overall he was doing pretty well for a guy in his fifties. Hawk was wearing a tan button-down shirt, faded blue jeans, and cowboy boots. As usual, his Smith & Wesson Model 29 revolver was in its custom-made holster on his right hip.

Tailor and I both began to grin as we climbed the short steps. Hawk greeted us with a smile and roughly shook both of our hands. As always, his handshake nearly crushed mine.

"Goddamn, boys, it's good to see you," he said, his voice raspy and harsh. "How the hell are ya?"

"Doing just fine, sir," Tailor said.

"How 'bout you, kid?" Hawk asked me.

"Things are looking up."

"C'mon in, boys. Let's sit down before we start unloading your truck." Hawk opened the door and led us into his house. We followed him into the kitchen, where he had us sit down before opening the fridge. He still walked with a slight limp.

"You boys want a beer?"

"Uh, no thanks." I hate beer.

"We're driving," Tailor said. "Got any Dr. Pepper?"

Hawk turned around, closing the refrigerator door. He had in his left hand one large can of beer, and in his right hand two cans of Dr. Pepper. "I bought a case after Val called me," he answered, sitting down. "So, boys, why don't you tell me what's going on? Tailor, I haven't heard from you in a year. Val here hasn't e-mailed me in a couple of months. Then all of a sudden I get a call, asking me if I can store his stuff. So what's going on?"

"We're not supposed to talk about it," Tailor said. "It's a job. We're going to be gone for a long time, probably over a year."

"A job with who?" Hawk asked, sipping his beer.

"We're . . . not really sure," I said. Hawk set his beer down and raised his eyebrows. "I mean, I think it's the government. It's all very hush-hush."

"How's the pay?" Hawk asked.

"Insane," Tailor responded.

"We're not supposed to talk about it," I said, echoing Tailor's words.

"Don't give me that bullshit, boy," Hawk said. "You know I ain't gonna go calling the newspaper or anything."

"Does Quagmire even have a newspaper?" Tailor asked.

"Sure as hell does. The *Quagmire Sentinel*. Yesterday's front-page headline was about the truckload of chickens that overturned on the highway outside of town. There were chickens everywhere. Now, do you have any idea where they're sending you?"

"All they'd tell us was that it was someplace where the US doesn't have any ongoing operations," Tailor said. "So I'm guessing somewhere in the Middle East, probably."

"Or somewhere in Africa," I suggested.

"Christ, I hope not," Tailor said. "I don't want to go back to Africa."

"Me, either," I said. "But that's the thing, Hawk. They won't tell us anything. They just had us sign a three-year contract."

"Kid, are you telling me you signed a contract when you had no idea who you're working for or where you're going? Why would you do that?"

"Twenty-five *large* every month," I said. "They've already dropped a twenty-K signing bonus into my checking account."

"Damn," Hawk said. "That's good money. Hell, I haven't made that kind of money since Decker and I retook that diamond mine from the rebels. We got paid in cut stones. I still have some of 'em in the safe downstairs. Anyway . . . boys, are you sure about this?"

"No, I'm not," I said honestly. "But . . . Hawk, I tried living the regular life. I had a normal job and everything."

"You hated it, didn't you?" Hawk asked, studying me.

I hesitated briefly. "Yeah. I hated it. I don't know what's wrong with me. After Mexico . . . Christ, Hawk, most of my friends are dead now. How could I want to go back to that life? What's wrong with me?"

"Goddamn it, Val, we've been over this," Tailor said angrily.

Hawk interrupted him. "Hold on, Tailor. Val, we all go through this eventually. You get over it, and you go on to the next job. You miss that life because it's all you've done. You miss the money, the excitement, the shooting. It's normal. Anyway, you're good at it. I've never seen anyone run a six-gun like you. The first time I handed you a .357 you shot like you'd been born with it in your hand. Why do you think I talked Decker into hiring you? I saw what you did in Afghanistan. You cleaned out that Hajji nest like a pro, and practically by yourself."

"I got kicked out of the Air Force for that," I said.

"Forget 'em," Hawk responded. "The bureaucrats that run the military these days don't know talent when they see it."

"I know. Honestly? I don't feel bad about wanting to go back. I feel bad that I *don't* feel bad about wanting to go back."

"No point in trying to be something you're not, Val," Tailor said. "That's why I called you for this. I figured you wanted to go back as much as I did."

"Tailor's right," Hawk stated, a hard gleam in his eye. "You're a natural-born *killer*, boy, and you always will be.

You're guaranteed to be miserable until you accept that."

"It's a good thing Tailor called," I said. "I was about to accept Ling's offer and join Exodus."

"I knew it!" Tailor exclaimed. "Hawk, will you talk some sense into him?"

"Kid, Exodus is bad news. Now, I know they helped you get out of there after things went to shit in Mexico, but that's probably only because you saved that Oriental girl's life. They're dangerous."

"So were *we*," I said.

"But we were professionals," Hawk replied. "They're true believers. That's a different kind of dangerous. Better to stay away from it."

"I don't have the best feeling about this gig, either," I said.

"You don't have to go."

"I already signed the contract."

"So? If you need to disappear, we can make that happen. It'll be a huge pain in my ass, but it's doable. I've done it before for other folks."

"No. I don't want to go on the run."

"The money's too good to walk away from," Tailor said.

"No kidding," I concurred, cracking a smile. "I'll be living large when I get back."

"Well, let's get to unloading your stuff, then," Hawk said, setting his empty beer can on the table.

As darkness fell, Tailor, Hawk, and I sat on the front porch, watching one of the most beautiful desert sunsets I'd ever seen. Hawk leaned back in his chair, sipping a beer. Tailor and I sat next to him, studying the shades of red and purple that filled the sky as the sun slowly sank beneath the mountains. Real moments of peace are hard to come by in life, and no one wanted to ruin it by talking.

The sun slowly disappeared, and the stars were increasingly visible overhead. It was cold out, and our breath smoldered in the chilly air. Hawk looked over at Tailor and me. "Now you listen, boys," he said, taking another sip of his beer. "A long time ago, I was on a job that paid too good to be true, too. More than twenty years ago now, I think. It was before we went legit and founded Vanguard. It was just Switchblade back then."

"What happened?" I asked.

"We were straight-up mercenaries. We worked for just about anyone that had the cash to pay us, and we didn't ask questions. We always got the job done, too. We spent most of our time in Africa. Business was good. Until this time we got in over our heads. We . . ." Hawk hesitated. "We basically overthrew the democratically elected government of Zembala."

"Where's that?" I asked.

"It doesn't exist anymore," Hawk replied. "It's called the Central African People's Republic now. The government of Zembala was corrupt, teetering on collapse. They had tribal conflict, religious conflict, and the Cubans screwing around there, too."

"Fucking Cubans," Tailor and I said simultaneously.

"We had been paid to protect the president of Zembala. He was a real piece of work, let me tell ya. He was a lying, whoring drunk, and the validity of the election results were questionable. Anyway, he was hoarding the cash from the state-run diamond mines, trying to fund his army to keep the Commies from overthrowing him. We protected him. He didn't trust anyone from his own country. Too much tribal bullshit. We didn't have a dog in that race, so he trusted us. But we got a better offer." Hawk paused for a moment. "The Montalban Exchange, some big international firm, offered us a lot of money to kill the president."

"That didn't work out, did it?" Tailor asked.

"Christ Almighty, it was bad," Hawk said, finishing his beer and crushing the can in his hand. "Decker went for it. We killed the president. That was easy. It got complicated after that. We left the capital for Sweothi City, getting our asses kicked the whole way. There were only a few of us left. The Montalbans were supposed to have a plane there to extract us."

"There wasn't a plane, was there?" Tailor asked.

Hawk laughed bitterly. "Hell, no."

"How did you get out?" I asked. "Did the Montalban Exchange help you?"

"No, they didn't. They just left us to die. We hooked up with some Portuguese mercs and made a run for it. Decker sacrificed one of our guys, young fella named Ozzie, to distract the Cubans. He pulled it off, though. The rest of us managed to get on a plane to South Africa. Lost a lot of good men in that mess . . ." Hawk trailed off, looking toward the darkened mountains.

"Holy shit," Tailor said. "Ramirez never talked about that."

"And yet the story sounds strangely familiar," I said, giving Tailor a hard look.

Hawk opened another beer. "None of us talked about

it. We made a mistake, and it got a lot of people killed. Well . . . even if we hadn't been there, the same thing probably would've happened. And Africa's *Africa.* Every time some politician sneezes over there a hundred thousand people get slaughtered."

"Africa sucks," I said, looking up at the stars. The time I'd spent there hadn't been so pleasant, either.

"It is what it is," Hawk said quietly. "You boys be careful over there, now. Always have a way out. Don't trust the people you work for. Remember, if you die, they don't have to pay you."

"Okay, Hawk," I said.

"I *mean it*, boy," he said harshly. "I've been to too many goddamned funerals already."

VALENTINE
Kelly Field Annex
Lackland Air Force Base, Texas
February 4
0545

Southern Texas was warm, even in February. It wasn't unpleasant, but it was a far cry from the harsh winters and lake-effect snow of Northern Michigan, where I'd grown up.

The last few days had been a whirlwind. Tailor and I had been flown from Las Vegas to San Antonio. From there we were hurried to a military installation that they tried to keep secret, but I knew it was Lackland Air Force Base. I'd gone to Air Force basic military training and

Security Forces School here. They kept us cooped up in an old barracks for several days. Each day, more and more people would arrive. All told, there were forty-two of us living in the barracks, that we knew of.

Food, in the form of military MREs, was brought to us, and we weren't allowed to go outside. All cell phones had been confiscated, and those that had kept theirs hidden had found that they had no signal anyway, meaning our hosts were probably jamming them somehow. They also took all of our personal identification documents, like passports and driver's licenses. This caused all manner of outrage, but our employers insisted that these effects would be returned when the mission was complete.

People came and went from the barracks, but they weren't part of our group. No one knew who they were, so we all guessed that they were associates of Gordon Willis. I had to hand it to Gordon: he'd certainly managed to recruit an interesting bunch. As Tailor and I talked to, and got to know, the people that were presumably our new teammates, we learned quite a bit about them and how much we all had in common.

For starters, almost all of us had combat experience. Most were ex-military, like me, and of those, a few had been kicked out or had spent time in the Fort Leavenworth military prison. Others had an intelligence background, and most of us spoke foreign languages. Tailor and I spoke Spanish fluently. Very few of us had any close family. None of us were married.

There were a few women in the building, too, but they were confined to a different part of the barracks and weren't allowed near us. We didn't know how many there were. I guessed that they were afraid someone would end up pregnant or something. It seemed silly to me.

So there I was, standing on the ramp, looking at a plain white Boeing 767 jetliner that was waiting for us. The sun wouldn't be up for another hour. We stood there in a big cluster, smoking and joking, waiting for them to tell us to board the plane. A few of us, including Tailor and me, had formed into a little circle.

"Where are we going?" someone asked. "Anyone heard?" I turned around. The guy that had asked the question was named Carlos Hudson. He was a black guy from the south side of Detroit, originally. He was the only other Red Wings fan in the whole bunch, so he and I had hit it off.

"They haven't told us anything," I said. "They issued us a bunch of hot-weather gear, though. We're going to the Middle East."

"Oh, yeah, definitely," Tailor said, standing next to me.

"Why would they send us to there?" someone else asked. "What are forty-two guys going to do that half the US military can't?"

"Maybe we're going to Iran or somewhere, then," Hudson suggested. "You know, someplace the US ain't supposed to be?"

"Could be the Sudan," another guy chimed in.

"I do *not* want to go back to Africa," Tailor said for the umpteenth time, puffing a cigarette.

"Don't worry, boys, we're not going to Africa," a woman's dusky voice said. That's when I saw her. She was tall, probably fve ten or so, and had auburn hair pulled back into a ponytail. She had curvy features hidden beneath khaki cargo pants and a sage green fleece jacket. A green duffel bag was hoisted over her shoulder, and it looked like it weighed as much as she did. She was flanked by three other women, but there was something about her . . .

"Who are you?" Tailor asked.

"McAllister," she said, sticking her hand out.

Tailor glanced at me, then shook her hand. "My name's Tailor," he said. "William Tailor. So, where *are* we going?"

"Zubara," she said.

"Where?" someone asked.

"The Confederated Gulf Emirate of Zubara," one of the other females, a tall black woman, said.

"It borders Qatar and Saudi Arabia," McAllister added. "The US has no real presence there."

"How . . . how do you know this?" I asked, stumbling on my words for some reason.

McAllister smiled at me. She had a mischievous . . . no, a *devious* smile, and beautiful green eyes. "I'm going to be in charge of our communications network when we get there. I've spent the last three weeks learning how their telecommunications setup works. Can't drop me in blind with equipment I've never seen and expect me to make it work." She maintained eye contact with me for what felt like a long time but in reality wasn't. "Anyway, that's all I know," she said then. "Well, we're getting some really good equipment, too."

Before I could think of anything else to say, the door of the plane opened, and the stairs were lowered down to the tarmac. A moment later, a black Suburban pulled up next to where we were all standing. Three men got out.

Two looked like standard-issue contractor types, with their tactical cargo pants and tactical vests and whatnot. The third looked like something out of an old movie. He was probably sixty or so, with white hair and a black eye patch over his left eye. His face had hard lines in it. His remaining eye could bore a hole in you. He wore a bomber jacket that was undoubtedly older than I was.

"Alright, listen up!" he said. His voice was harsh and raspy. "I need you all to fall in and board that plane in an orderly fashion. This is your first assignment, and it's an easy one, so try not to *fuck it up*! I know you have a lot of questions. We have a long flight ahead of us. You'll be briefed in the air."

"But, um, sir, Gordon Willis told us that we'd have briefings and training before we deployed," some brave soul said.

"You were *lied to*, son. Now get on that plane so we can get going."

"Um, sir, who *are* you?" the same person, a red headed guy, asked. Some people just didn't know when to quit.

The old man, for his part, cracked an evil smile. "My name is Hunter, son. Colonel Curtis Hunter. I'm the *boss*. Now move out!"

We'd been in the air for a few hours, just wandering around the plane, killing time. The Boeing 767 jetliner was meant to hold hundreds of passengers in its standard form, but there were only about sixty seats in the front of the plane we were on. The rear was all for cargo. Tailor and I sat next to each other, talking, when Hunter's harsh voice came on over the intercom. "Listen up. Everyone wake up. I'm coming back to give you the first part of the briefing. McAllister, King, you two come up front."

I watched as McAllister and the tall black lady from the tarmac got out of their seats and made their way forward. After a few minutes, they returned, each carrying a bunch of manila envelopes. They walked down the aisle, handing them out to everyone.

"Thank you, stewardess," a smartass named Walker said. Walker was one of the guys that had been to Leavenworth. He'd been an Army Intelligence interrogator. Apparently he'd gotten in trouble for killing an insurgent prisoner in Iraq. He was short and suffered from obvious Little Man Syndrome. I had no idea how a dipshit like him scored high enough on the ASVAB to make it into Intelligence in the first place. "Could you bring me a Coke and some peanuts?"

"Shut your face, pencil-dick," McAllister said, dropping Walker's packet in his lap. Several guys started to laugh. Walker's face turned red, and he stood up. He grabbed McAllister by the arm, causing her to drop the rest of her packets. She was four inches taller than him.

"Listen, bitch," he started, looking up at her. She turned and punched him square in the face, just like that. He recoiled and let go of her. Blood came trickling from his nose. He came at her again, grabbing her with both hands. The next thing I knew, I was out of my seat, standing in the aisle.

"Val, what are you . . . ?" Tailor asked. I ignored him and moved toward Walker and McAllister. "Oh, goddamn it, Val," Tailor said, getting out of his seat and following me.

"What do *you* want, Valentine?" Walker didn't let go of McAllister. A couple more guys stood up. Walker was about to get his *ass beat*.

"What the hell is going on back here?" Colonel Hunter yelled, his rough voice clear over the drone of the engines. He had appeared from up front, flanked by two of the ambiguous security men. Both had their hands under their vests, probably ready to draw pistols.

"I'm fine, sir," McAllister said, pushing Walker off. She seemed embarrassed that people had come to her defense.

"I'm sure you are, Sarah," Hunter said, working his way through the crowd. "Mr. Walker, what is your problem?"

"Sir," Walker said, defiantly staring Hunter in the eye, "I just made a joke and this bitch—"

"That's *enough*, Mr. Walker." Hunter cut him off. He moved in closer. "Now you listen to *me*, boy. We aren't even in-country yet. If you're going to give me problems before we even get there, so help me God I will drop your ass into the ocean. I'm not joking. That's not some empty threat. You belong to me now. If you don't make it to Zubara alive, no one in my chain of command will give a shit. So I suggest you sit down and shut your mouth before you piss me off."

Walker looked around nervously. The rest of us had backed away, leaving him virtually alone with the scary senior citizen. After a long moment, he deflated. "Yes, sir." He sat back down.

"Better," Hunter said. "Sarah, Anita, please hand out the rest of the packets. Let's get this briefing started." McAllister and King both resumed handing out the materials. Tailor and I returned to our seats at the rear of the abbreviated passenger compartment and were the last to get the handouts. McAllister handed me mine without so much as making eye contact.

"Did I piss her off somehow?" I asked Tailor. He just shrugged and opened his packet. Inside was a bunch of documents, maps, and photographs.

"Gentlemen," Hunter said, using the aircraft's intercom so we could hear him, "as you're all probably aware, our destination is the Confederated Gulf Emirate of Zubara." There were screens all along the passenger section that displayed the briefing. The cabin lights darkened, and a large map of Zubara appeared. There wasn't much to it. It was a patch of desert with three little peninsulas sticking out into the Persian Gulf on the eastern side. Its borders touched Qatar in the north, Saudi Arabia in the west, and the United Arab Emirates in the southeast. The map then changed, from one of the entire country to one focusing on the three urbanized peninsulas.

"The capital city, and really the only city in Zubara, is Zubara City. It's made of three sections, Ash Shamal, Umm Shamal, and Al Khor. Over a million people are packed into these three pieces of land, including large numbers of immigrant workers from Pakistan and South Asia. For years, Zubara was a reclusive Middle Eastern emirate, founded on the supposed site of some ancient port city. It's rich in oil and natural gas but was very isolated. Without foreign investment, Zubara was unable to fully tap its natural resources, leaving the country much poorer than its neighbors.

"This made it a breeding ground for radical Islam.

Over the years, Hezbollah, Hamas, and especially Al
Qaeda were able to do a lot of recruiting here. Things
started to change ten years ago. The old emir went on a
vacation to Switzerland. His son, the current emir, had
built a loyal following in the country's military and told
his old man not to come back. Things have more or less
been improving ever since." The map disappeared, and
the picture of a middle-aged, mustachioed man, in an
expensive-looking suit and traditional Middle Eastern
keffiyeh headdress, appeared.

"This is the current emir," Hunter explained, "Salim
ibn Meheid. He's tried very hard to force Zubara into the
twenty-first century. He's attempted to crack down on
terrorist recruiting and financing, has formally recognized
Israel, though relations with the Israelis are strained, and
has opened his nation's economy to foreign investment
and development. As a result, billions of dollars are pouring into his country now, and oil and natural-gas output
has doubled.

"There are problems, though. The biggest problem is
this guy, General Mubarak Hassan Al Sabah." The picture
changed again, this time to a man with a goatee in a gaudy
tan military uniform, decorated with ribbons and medals.

"General Al Sabah has gained the loyalty of the army.
Most of the army is made up of conscripts from poor
families and volunteers from places like Iran, Iraq,
Pakistan, and Yemen. General Al Sabah has created a cult
of personality and has done everything short of openly
defying the emir. The emir's economic policies have
brought a lot of change to Zubara, and many Westerners.
And while he's tried to crack down on the financing of

terrorism, the general has proved an obstacle to that. General Al Sabah wants to be the Saddam Hussein of Zubara. He's built a network of contacts and allies, from the Iranians to Al Qaeda. All of his allies don't necessarily like each other now, but he apparently is able to keep them from killing each other long enough to focus on the Americans. Despite the emir's efforts, Zubara remains a safe haven for terrorists. This is where they do their banking. This is where their families live. This is where they recruit. This is where they go on vacation."

Hunter paused for a long time. "Gentlemen, I think you're beginning to understand why such tight security has been necessary in this operation. What we're doing here is radically unconventional. We're running a major operation with a skeleton crew. You make up the bulk of our forces. We have the support of the emir and a few people loyal to him, but we'll largely be on our own."

"What exactly is our mission, sir?" that same redhead asked.

"We're going to bring the war to their doorstep, son," Hunter replied. "We can't invade Zubara. It's not diplomatically or militarily viable. In any case, any attempt to bring in Americans would probably result in a coup attempt against the emir, which would surely bring the country into civil war. The mission would be over before it began. So we're doing things differently. It's called Project Heartbreaker. After you get off this plane, you're never to mention that name to anyone, *ever*. Anyway, through heavy use of human intelligence and years of planning, we've been able to track down a large number of bad people in Zubara. We know where these people live, where they work, and who they're dealing with. We're going to find them and kill them."

"Is that it, sir? Go to Zubara and kill a few terrorists?"

"You, ginger," Hunter said, pointing at the talkative redhead, "no more from you today. It's a lot bigger than that." "We're bringing the war to their home front. The enemy will discover that there are no safe places, anywhere, for them to hide. Our small operational group is going to try something that's never been tried. Gentlemen, welcome to *Dead Six.*"

Tailor and I looked at each other, grinning. Despite my trepidation about my new employers, I liked where this was going. I returned my attention to Colonel Hunter and his briefing.

I had been in a deep sleep when someone pushed me on the shoulder. I sat up quickly, having been startled awake. I was in the window seat and had been leaning against the fuselage of the plane, using my jacket for a pillow. I looked to my right. Tailor was nowhere to be seen. The cabin was darkened, most of the window shades were pulled down, and it seemed that almost everyone was asleep. Sitting next to me was Sarah McAllister.

"What is it?" I said, rubbing my eyes.

"Hey." She sounded almost awkward. "I, uh, wanted to thank you, for, you know, standing up."

"It's okay," I said. "I mean—"

She cut me off. "But I can take care of myself. I don't need you to come galloping to the rescue."

"I saw that. You clocked him pretty good."

"I used to play hockey," she said. "When I was in high school."

"Seriously? Me, too."

"That's great," Sarah said flatly. "Listen. I know you and the others were trying to help, but you have to let me handle things or I won't get any respect around here. Does that make sense?"

It made a lot of sense, actually. "I wasn't trying to embarrass you. I just . . . it just happened, you know? I didn't really think about it."

"I know. I'm not trying to be a bitch or sound ungrateful, but there are four women here in the middle of all of you guys."

"You probably had wieners thrown at you from day one."

"Oh my God," Sarah said, rolling her eyes. "You have no idea."

"I didn't do that to get in your pants, if that's what you're thinking." I was being honest with her about that, too. Of course, I had no *objections* to getting in her pants, either.

Sarah smiled. "The funny thing is, I actually believe you. You know . . ." Sarah's voice trailed off and she leaned in close to me, squinting quizzically. I pulled back a little bit, not sure what she was doing. "Holy crap," she said, still too close to my face. "Your eyes are different colors."

This always makes me self-conscious. My left eye is blue. My right eye is brown. People usually react like that when they first notice. "Yes, they are."

"Are you wearing contacts or something?"

"No, I'm not." I gently pushed her back a little bit, out

of my personal space. "I was born like that. It's called heterochromia."

"That's *so* weird," she said absentmindedly. "I'm sorry." Then she grinned. "I'll get out of your face now. I'll see you later, Valentine." Sarah touched me on the shoulder as she stood up and left the seat. I shook my head slightly and smiled.

LORENZO
February 5

Terrorist mastermind Ali bin Ahmed Al Falah sat across from me in the smoke-filled room. His guards watched me suspiciously. "Goat-fucker," he spat as my rook took his knight.

"Indeed," I replied as I pretended to study the board. For somebody who was supposed to be so damn nefarious, Falah sucked at chess. It was more challenging to put up a good match and then let him win than it was to actually play somebody good. And I didn't even like chess. "Your turn."

"Your mother was a whore, Khalid." Falah twirled the end of his bushy white beard. He looked vaguely like a Wahhabi Santa Claus as he contemplated his next move. I had left myself dangerously exposed and he could have checkmate in two, but apparently Falah was only strategic when it came to financing suicide bombings.

I had gotten to know Falah rather well over the last few months. As the new landlord of his social club, it had of course been necessary for me to meet my most prestigious customer. It had turned out that Khalid and Falah had a whole bunch in common and had become friends. Falah had taken a liking to my character and had taken Khalid under his jihadi wing.

Falah, wanted by both the Americans and the Mossad, was staying in Zubara, effectively out of their reach. Neither nation was willing to take official action in the tiny country right now, as perceived foreign involvement would only weaken the besieged pro-Western emir in the eyes of the populace. The old man talked a big game about sacrificing for the cause but had no desire to become a martyr himself.

There was a loud noise from downstairs in the social club, and one of the guards, an angry young man by the name of Yousef, went to check it. Falah always traveled with an entourage. Terrorists are kind of like rappers that way. Hell, his personal vehicle was a ridiculous yellow Hummer H2. It sounds ostentatious, but it wasn't really that odd in a country where this much oil money was flowing.

"Have you thought about what I suggested yesterday?" I asked.

He looked up, playing coy. "About the missiles?"

I nodded. "Yes. Remember, I am new to this, but I want to do anything in my power to help the cause. I do not mean to pry, but I believe our warriors could use the weapons."

"Ah, my young friend, I appreciate such enthusiasm," Falah laughed. "Of course, surface-to-air missiles would be incredibly valuable in the jihad against the American barbarians murdering our brothers."

I smiled. It was incredibly difficult to not ram my thumbs through the old man's eye sockets and wrench his miserable skull from his shoulders. It was even more difficult to pretend to be his buddy. The man I was playing a friendly game with was responsible for blowing up churches, businesses, and schools. I had no problem with killing, but I tried to keep my killing limited to scum like Al Falah. "Yes, of course."

Falah made his move. We had been playing chess together several times a week for months now. Occasionally he got one right. He leaned back and gestured proudly at what he had done. I barely noticed. "Ha. Get out of that."

"Hmm . . ." I made a big show of puzzling over his latest strategy. Inside I was praying that he was going to go for my offer of a meeting with the fictional arms dealers. The entire thing was totally fabricated. If he was stupid and greedy enough that he went for the deal, then it enabled me to end his pathetic life early and utilize his resources for Phase Two. I moved a pawn to enable him to beat me more easily. "Your turn."

"They will return soon, correct? I've thought about what you've told me about these businessmen you met, Khalid," he said, pausing for dramatic effect. "Tell them that I am willing to meet to discuss their offer. If it is as reasonable as you say, I will arrange the purchase."

"Most excellent, sir," I replied. *You'll be dead in a couple weeks, asshole.* "I will contact them immediately."

Falah gave me a devilish grin as he moved his queen. "Checkmate!"

"Indeed."

Chapter 3:
The Zoob

VALENTINE
Fort Saradia National Historical Site
Confederated Gulf Emirate of Zubara
February 5

I didn't know what time it was locally when we arrived at our destination. I knew it was the middle of a moonless night. Our plane had landed at Zubara's only international airport but had taxied away from where the commercial airliners would offload passengers. Instead, our plane stopped at the far end of the airport, where the private and charter jets landed.

From there we were herded into a large, unmarked white bus. The bus's windows were so darkly tinted that you couldn't see out. The cargo from the plane was off-loaded onto the bus and a pair of trucks. The entire caravan was leaving the airport through a back gate within a half hour of the plane touching down. Compared to the seemingly endless flight from the United States, everything happened remarkably fast once we hit the ground.

I wasn't able to see anything of the city as we passed through it. The brief glimpse I got between the stairs of the jet and the door of the bus had told me little. It was cooler out than I thought it'd be, probably in the sixties. The air smelled of dust, burning natural gas, car exhaust, and an inadequate sewer system. It reminded me of Mexico.

The drive from the airport was long, but as near as I could tell, it was because we were winding our way around a cluttered city. I assumed the driver, who was one more of Colonel Hunter's security men, was taking a roundabout route to wherever it was we were going. It was the better part of an hour before the bus came to a stop. We all stood up in the aisle, clutching our backpacks, waiting for the line to begin moving, as Hunter's security guys tried to hustle us along. Tailor and I were two of the last ones off.

Stepping out into the cool night air, I took in my surroundings. We were in some kind of large compound surrounded by twenty-foot walls. The walls were made of stone, and looked old. Inside the walls were five large buildings, all of which looked new, plus a few old buildings off to one side.

"This some kind of fort?" Tailor asked.

"Looks like it," I replied. "Those buildings are new, though. So are those lights," I said, noting the new amber streetlights in the compound. "Looks like it's been improved over the years."

"This is Fort Saradia," Sarah said from behind me. I turned around quickly when she spoke, a little bit startled.

Tailor looked at me funny and cracked a smile but didn't say anything.

"You know about this place, don't you?" Tailor asked.

"We got briefed before you guys. This place was a fort for the British in the nineteenth century. It was expanded over the years. The Zubarans used it as a small army depot for a long time. That's why half the wall looks new. They closed it down about twenty years ago. I guess they were going to turn it into a university or something, but that didn't pan out, either. Now it's a protected site."

"And that's why we're here, isn't it?" Tailor asked. "Because no one will come poking around, and those walls mean people can't see in."

"Pretty much," Sarah said.

"We can't spend all of our time here," I mused. "If we keep going in and out of the same place all the time we'll get spotted eventually."

"Nah, I bet this is just a staging area," Tailor suggested. "We probably won't spend much time here."

"You guys won't, but I will," Sarah said, grabbing her duffel bag as one of the security men tossed it onto the pavement. "All of my equipment is set up here."

"See? Like I said, it's a staging area," Tailor repeated. "A command center."

"There's my bag," I said. My large GI duffel bag had been dropped onto the pavement. I stepped forward and slung it. "So . . . where do we go now?" I asked. Tailor and Sarah just shrugged. Looking around, I could see that everyone else was just as puzzled as we were. A couple of the buildings looked like dormitories or barracks, but none of us knew what to do now.

The small cluster of security types standing around was no help. They'd hardly acknowledge us, much less tell us anything. Four of them were carrying carbines, too, so none of us got too pushy. All they would tell us was that Colonel Hunter would be along to brief us again. I wondered why they felt it necessary to have the briefing outside in the parking lot instead of in a building or something. I was tired, and so was everyone else. After a few minutes, I set my duffel bag down and sat next to it. Others did the same. A few minutes after that, the bus backed out of the large gate it had come in and departed, leaving us to sit on the ground.

Probably twenty minutes later, a white Toyota Land Cruiser came rolling up from the interior of the compound. It stopped a short distance from where we were all sitting. The doors opened. From the passenger's side, Colonel Hunter climbed out and strode toward us, flanked by yet another security guy. Most of us stood up as he approached.

"Gentlemen, welcome to the Zoob," he said, raising his voice so all of us could hear. If you don't know already, we're currently at Fort Saradia, a few miles outside of the city. This will be our base of operations for the time being. Over there," he said, pointing to our right, "is the dormitory. Each of you has been assigned a room there. Your name is on the door of your room. The doors aren't locked. Grab your gear, find your room, and get some rack time. We'll be getting you up for more briefings in a few hours. Any questions?"

One guy spoke up. "Sir, what—"

Hunter cut him off. "Tough, I'm not answering any

now. Move out!" Without so much as another word, Colonel Hunter and his entourage of security men piled into Land Cruisers and drove off, leaving us to carry our bags all the way to the dormitory. Tailor and I looked at each other, shrugged, and picked up our bags.

The dormitory had three levels. The stairs were on the outside of the building, with a set on either end. They led to an enclosed walkway that was flanked by rooms on either side. Tailor and I made our way down the first level, checking the doors on each side for our names. Each person's name was written on the door in magic marker.

I found my room eventually. It was on the north end of the third floor. "Valentine" had been written on the door. Someone had also drawn a rough picture of a heart with an arrow through it. Grumbling something unpleasant, I opened the door and stepped into the dark room.

A dusty smell filled my nose, and it took me a moment to find the light switch. As the old fluorescent light above my head flickered to life, it revealed a Spartan little room. It couldn't have been more than twelve foot by twelve. It looked like a college dorm room that had been abandoned years before. The walls were bare white cinder block, with no decorations. A simple bed with a thin mattress was shoved into one corner. A military-surplus wool blanket and a small pillow had been tossed onto it. Against one wall was a set of metal shelving. A small closet was situated on the other wall.

I set my bag down and began to explore my new room. On the far wall was a window and a door. The window was darkly tinted, and didn't open. The door opened outward to reveal a small balcony. From my balcony, in the cool, dry night air, I could see over the wall of the compound. The amber glow of Zubara City could be seen to the east. The wind was gusty and cold, so I went back into my room.

The other door in the room led to the bathroom. I crossed my room and pulled that door open. "Hey!" someone yelled, startling me enough that I stumbled back into my room. It had been a woman's voice. A second later, Sarah McAllister appeared in the doorway.

"Hey!" I said as she stepped around me, walking into my room like she owned the place. "What the hell?"

"Are you stalking me or something?" she asked.

I felt my face flush. "You're in *my* room!"

"I guess we share a bathroom," she said.

"I guess," I said. "Weird that they didn't separate males and females."

"This isn't summer camp," Sarah said, grinning.

"Do we have a shower, then?" I asked, poking my head back into the bathroom.

"Sort of," Sarah replied. To my right, at the very end of the room, was a square section that looked like the base of a shower. At about knee high, there was a spigot and two knobs. The spigot led to a hose, which in turn led to a shower head, clipped to the wall just above the spigot.

"Huh? So . . . what are you supposed to do, sit down in this thing?"

"I don't know," Sarah said. "You could use the spray-hose to wash yourself, I guess. There's nowhere on the wall above to clamp it, so we can't use it like a regular shower. Also, there's no curtain."

"And what the hell is that?" I asked, indicating another spray-hose. This one came out of the wall next to the toilet.

"It's for washing your feet," Sarah explained. "Most toilets over here have them. Local custom is you wash your feet after using the bathroom."

"What about your hands?" I asked.

"That's optional," she said, smiling.

"So this is it, huh? A shower, um, *thing* with no curtain, a toilet with a spray-hose on it, and a bare tile floor with a drain. Zubaran bathroom technology is a bit wanting."

"I'm going to take a shower," Sarah said. "Or I'm going to try. So get out of here. The door doesn't lock, so don't open it until I'm gone. *Stalker*."

"I'm not stalking you!" I protested as Sarah shoved me out of the bathroom and slammed the door in my face. "Psycho," I muttered to myself as she turned the water on.

Exhausted, I kicked my boots off and climbed into bed. Pulling the rough wool blanket over me, I rolled over and was asleep in minutes.

I was abruptly woken a short while later. I sat up in bed, startled, not entirely sure where I was at first. Sarah stood over me, wearing nothing but a *short* pair of gym shorts and a T-shirt. Her hair was wet. She smelled nice; she *looked good.*

"Hey, Valentine," she said. "Do you have any toilet paper?"

"Huh? What're you doing in my room again?" I mumbled.

"*Toilet paper.* There isn't any. Did you bring some?"

"Actually, I did." I sat up. "I always bring toilet paper."

I reached over and dug into my duffel bag. I handed her a roll that was wrapped in a plastic bag. "Anything else?"

"No, that's everything," she said, stepping back into the bathroom. "Nice try, though." She flashed me a smile before closing the door again.

"You're welcome!" I yelled at the door before laying back down. I had a smile on my face as I rolled over to go back to sleep.

VALENTINE
February 28

For the rest of the month of February, we remained cooped up in Fort Saradia. We had classes every day on topics ranging from fieldcraft to local history. Gordon Willis made several appearances to tell us what a great job we were doing and remind us of the importance of operational security. He seemed pretty useless, actually.

There was a lot of physical fitness training, too. It had been less than a year since I'd left Vanguard, but I'd gotten pretty out of shape. The first morning they had us running laps around the inside of the compound I thought my heart was going to explode. Tailor was even worse off than I was, since he was a smoker.

What we *weren't* getting was any firearms training, which bothered me, but I understood why. Fort Saradia didn't have a range of any kind, and was only a few miles outside of the city. There was no way to do a lot of shooting without drawing attention.

At least we did have weapons. I'd been inside the main

building a few times and had caught a glimpse of the arms room. It was stocked with some of the most modern equipment I'd ever seen, and it was all brand new. Our armorer was a jovial guy named Frank Mann. He sported curly black hair and a bushy black mustache, and was eminently proud of his arms room. He'd been around the block a few times himself, so he, Tailor, and I became friends. In any case it's always a good idea to make friends with the armorer.

Tailor and I didn't tell him about the handguns we'd smuggled. Even though they'd prohibited cellular phones and some other items, they'd never bothered to search our belongings. I suspected Frank wouldn't care. He was as big a gun nut as Tailor and I, and I'd seen him packing what I assumed was a personally owned Glock .45 several times.

Toward the end of the month, things began to pick up. Every day it seemed that there were fewer and fewer of us. The word was that we were being divided up into small groups and sent off to safe houses to begin conducting operations. Sarah hinted that they'd been watching us to see whom we got along with, and who we'd work well with. Frank told me that he'd been issuing weapons to the people that were leaving. It seemed like things were finally going to begin. I was excited; sitting around in the compound had grown tiresome.

On the very last day of the month, I was told to report to the small briefing room in the admin building. It was mid-afternoon as I made my way across Fort Saradia. The sun was high in the sky; it was warm but not hot. A strong wind blew from the north. Every time it would gust, it'd kick up another huge cloud of dust. Other than the howling wind, the compound was quiet.

I was apparently the last one to arrive in the small briefing room. Colonel Hunter and Sarah were standing at the front of the room, talking quietly. A laptop was set up on a table, hooked up to a projector. A portable screen stood at the head of the darkened room.

"About time," Tailor said, sitting at one of the desks with a notebook.

"Are we taking a test or something?" I asked, sitting next to him. I briefly wondered if this was one of those crazy dreams where you're back in school and have to take an exam you haven't studied for.

"They're shipping us off," Hudson said from across the room. Sitting next to him was Wheeler, the guy who kept asking questions on the plane. He and Hudson had both been in the Rangers together. Wheeler was a slim, freckled redhead. Despite being from New York, he was a country boy. Wheeler had grown up hunting in the woods of upstate New York, or as he always pointed out, the "unpaved" part of the state.

"To where?" I asked.

"Downtown," Colonel Hunter explained, facing us at last. "You boys are ready. I'm shipping the four of you off to one of our safe houses in the city."

"Al Khor," Sarah said. "It's the upper class of the three peninsulas of Zubara City. It's where most of the government ministries are and where most of the Westerners live. It'll be easier for you to blend in there, but you will operate throughout the city."

"So, we're the last ones to leave, and we're getting an

easy assignment," Tailor said. "Did we screw up somehow, sir?"

"You're the last team to leave, Mr. Tailor, but you'll probably get the first mission. I've actually been impressed with you boys, so I'm assigning you all to the same chalk."

"Just the four of us, sir?" Wheeler asked.

"You'll be fine," Hunter replied. "Mr. Tailor, you're in charge of this chalk."

"Yes, sir!" Tailor answered crisply. I groaned. Tailor kicked me in the shin under the desk.

"From your records, I know that Mr. Tailor has the most combat experience of you four," Hunter said. "Mr. Valentine, you're second-in-command."

"But, sir," Wheeler protested, "I mean, no offense to Valentine, but Hudson and I have been through a lot. We did two tours in Afghanistan together."

"I know that, Mr. Wheeler. However, Mr. Valentine has seen combat in Afghanistan, Africa, Bosnia, China, Central America, and Mexico. I didn't make the chain-of-command decision lightly. Do not question me, ginger."

Tailor snickered.

"Holy shit, Val," Wheeler said, looking over at me. I just shrugged.

"Moving along," Hunter said, "your first target is this man." Sarah pressed a few keys on the laptop. An image of a young Gulf Arab man, probably no older than me, appeared on the screen. He was wearing the traditional thobe and headdress. He had a baby face, with a thin mustache and a neatly trimmed beard on his chin. "His name is Abdul bin Muhammad Al Falah. He's a young up-and-comer in the Zubaran terrorist network. He's used his family's money and political connections to try to make a name for himself."

"He looks like a kid, Colonel," Tailor said.

"He's twenty-six," Hunter replied. "He's also, by all accounts, just a spoiled rich man's son. Our intelligence assets believe this is all a game for young Mr. Al Falah. And he's not been directly involved in any terrorist operations so far."

"So why is he important?" Hudson asked.

"He has connections. They're grooming him to be a player when he gets older. Your first assignment, gentlemen, is to locate and capture Mr. Al Falah."

"*Capture*, sir?" I asked.

"The junior Al Falah knows people," Sarah said, still sitting in front of her computer. "He'll be a very useful intelligence asset. He's relatively young and inexperienced, too, so it should be easier to extract information from him." Her voice was colder than usual as she spoke.

"Miss McAllister is right," Hunter said. "We need him alive, for the time being. You will interrogate him."

"Are we supposed to make him talk?" Wheeler sounded nervous with the idea. "Aren't there, like, *rules* about that now?"

Hunter scowled. "Rules? Does extracting information from this young man make you uncomfortable, Mr. Wheeler?" He didn't wait for a response. "You're not in the army anymore. This young man has been helping recruit the assholes who've been blowing up your old compatriots. I don't want rules, gentlemen, I want results."

"So, how are we supposed to find him?" Tailor asked.

"Our intelligence assets are working on that, Mr. Tailor," Hunter replied. "You'll be assigned to observe him yourself, and you'll be given a list of places he frequents. He's not a difficult man to track, and he has no reason to suspect he's in any danger here. Zubara has been a safe haven for terrorists for years. This should be an easy one."

"I'll be assisting during operations," Sarah said, taking over from Hunter, "as a sort of dispatcher. I'll be in radio contact with the other operational teams. I can update you on intelligence, give you instructions, and assist in translating if you need it. You've all been assigned radio call signs. Wheeler, yours is *Ginger.*"

"Hey!" Wheeler protested. Tailor broke out in a laugh.

Sarah ignored our adolescent humor. "Hudson, you're *Shafter.*"

"So the *black man* gets to be Shafter, huh?" Hudson growled. "Hell, why not *Dolemite*? Or how 'bout *Black Dynamite*?" The room immediately fell silent. Sarah looked at Colonel Hunter, not knowing what to say. Hudson could only maintain his indignant expression for so long before he started laughing. "Lord, girl, where did you come up with these?"

"They're randomly chosen by computer," Sarah insisted.

"Bullshit!" Wheeler snorted. Hudson slapped the desk and let out a raucous laugh.

"Gentlemen," Hunter warned, frowning. *Kill joy.*

Sarah continued. "Tailor, your call sign is *Xbox.*"

"Xbox?" Tailor asked, sounding laughably butt-hurt. "Seriously?" Wheeler folded his arms across his chest and gave Tailor a look of smug satisfaction. I chuckled.

"And Valentine, your call sign is *Nightcrawler*."

"Nightcrawler?" I repeated. "How did you come up with *that*?"

Hunter finally cracked a smile. "You should've heard some of the ones she came up with for the other boys. Mr. Walker's call sign is *Lilac*."

"I thought you said they were randomly chosen by computer?"

Sarah tried as hard as she could to look innocent. "They are! Why would you think otherwise?" She flashed me a little smile and winked. Tailor, noticing, kicked me under the desk again.

VALENTINE
Ash Shamal District
March 11
1900

"This is Ginger. I've got eyes on the target," Wheeler said over the radio.

"Roger that," Tailor responded, his voice very hushed in my earpiece. *"I see him, too. He just passed my position."*

"Ginger, Control," Sarah said over the radio, her voice very professional. *"Do you have a positive ID on the target?"* It was very important that we had the right guy, after all.

"Uh . . . stand by." Wheeler and Hudson were both in our van, which was parked farther down the darkened alley to the south. To the north was the target building. It was a small building, only one story, constructed out of

stucco and brick like most of the older buildings in the city. It looked out of place, though, surrounded by several huge, new, corrugated-steel warehouses. On the south side of the target building was a bright amber light. The rest of the alley was dark. Previously, our intelligence assets had made sure the other nearby street lights were out of commission, vandalized with a pellet gun.

"Control, Shafter," Hudson said. *"I've got a positive ID on our target. He's got three others with him."* The van had an impressive assortment of gadgets and equipment, including state-of-the-art night vision and thermal optics.

"Copy that, Shafter," Sarah said, ice in her voice. *"You are cleared to engage. Capture the target. Kill the others. Control out."*

It was *on*. Shrouded in darkness, I peeked around the corner, looking north, up the narrow alley. Abdul bin Muhammad Al Falah and three compatriots slowly made their way toward me, talking loudly in the darkness. Al Falah and one skinny man were dressed in traditional Arab thobes, dark ones because it was cool out, and checkered headdresses. They were flanked by two serious-looking men in brown suits, probably bodyguards. Our target had what appeared to be a laptop bag slung over his shoulder. *Good.* It was likely we'd get at least some intelligence from his computer. Al Falah and his friend were having an animated conversation, their voices echoing loudly down the narrow alley. They acted like they didn't have a care in the world as they approached me.

The building at the end of the alley was some kind of terrorist hangout, used mainly for recruiting and propaganda. Al Falah frequented the place. Almost every night he would take a walk down the alley with another potential recruit. He'd go on and on about the jihad and other bullshit, wowing the recruits with his family connections and promising their families large monetary rewards if they would sign up to kill Americans. At first, I couldn't believe how brazen they were, walking down a public street discussing this stuff. After a few days, I realized that this was the reason we'd been sent to Zubara in the first place. *They'd never see it coming.*

"*This is Xbox*," Tailor whispered, his voice hushed in my earpiece. "*They just passed my position. Four of 'em. The target, another individual, and two big fuckers, probably guards.*"

"Roger," I said, still peeking around the corner. Tailor was hiding behind a wall that separated the target building from a warehouse to its south. In the darkness, Al Falah and his escorts had walked right past Tailor's position without noticing him. His bodyguards were complacent, it seemed. *Good. Complacency kills.*

I looked down at my watch. The final call to prayer of the day would begin at any moment. There was a mosque only a block away. Once the call to prayer began, the traditional music would start blaring over a set of loud-speakers. This would last for a couple of minutes, and would give us a little cover if we had to make some noise.

I was wearing tan cargo pants, a black shirt, a black jacket, and a tan baseball cap. I looked unmistakably American, but I was dressed similarly to most of the Westerners running around Zubara, except for the holster on my left hip and the body-armor vest under my shirt. I reached under my jacket and drew the Sig 220 pistol I'd been issued. With my other hand, I reached into my jacket's inside pocket and pulled out a suppressor. I quickly screwed the two together, while taking one last look around. The sky was glowing from the lights of the city, so much so that I couldn't see any stars, even though it was clear out. All around us were typical city noises; we were only one block away from a busy main thoroughfare. The alley itself was peaceful, save for the prattling of Al Falah and his friend.

Suddenly, from the north, a recording of a man singing in Arabic began. It was 1907. The call to prayer had begun. I took a deep breath. "This is Nightcrawler," I said, whispering into my radio. "I'm moving." With that, I stepped around the corner, suppressed pistol held behind my back, and began walking purposefully toward my target. I kept my head down, so the brim of my ball cap hid my eyes. I hunched over, trying to hide how tall I was. My heart was pounding, but I wasn't really scared. I doubted Al Falah's half-assed bodyguards were much of a threat.

"*Xbox moving*," Tailor whispered. To my north, past Al Falah and his compatriots, something moved in the shadows, another figure coming up behind them on the sidewalk. Tailor's shape was silhouetted against the amber light of the building at the end of the alley. The body-guards hadn't once looked behind them yet.

I was getting close now. Looking up, I saw that the two bodyguards had noticed me. One stepped in front of the rest and began to approach. The other hung behind. Still, neither had looked behind them. Tailor continued his approach unnoticed.

The lead guard said something to me in Arabic, his voice raised to make himself heard over the blaring music. Al Falah and the other man stopped. I didn't understand the language, but I definitely got the gist from the tone of his voice. The thug was a tall man, with a bushy mustache. His right hand was beneath his brown jacket, resting on the butt of a gun. I made eye contact with him for the first time. He held his left hand up, signaling me to stop, still talking. He grew angry when he realized that I was a foreigner and took another step closer. He was only a few feet in front of me now. Young Mr. Al Falah had an obnoxious grin on his face; his friend seemed nervous.

My eyes darted to the left. Tailor was right behind the other bodyguard. His hands came up, extending his own pistol. He fired a shot; the muffled pop of the suppressed .45 round discharging was barely audible over the singing that echoed through the alley. Tailor's target dropped to the sidewalk.

The bodyguard in front of me turned around quickly, having heard the discharge. Before he knew what was happening, I had my own pistol up and put a .45 slug into his left ear. My gun was on Al Falah before the body hit the sidewalk. He and his friend both turned to face me, eyes wide, staring at my pistol. Tailor's .45 popped twice more, and Al Falah's friend fell to the ground, two gunshot wounds to his back.

Al Falah looked down at his companion, then turned around to see the muzzle of Tailor's suppressed pistol. He turned back to me, skin pale, eyes fixed on my pistol, and raised his hands slowly. A puddle formed on the sidewalk beneath him as his bladder let go.

An instant later, Tailor snapped open a collapsible baton and struck Al Falah on the neck. He cried out in pain and dropped to the sidewalk, falling into his own piss. I watched the street while Tailor zip tied our prisoner's hands. Al Falah looked up at me one last time before Tailor pulled a black bag over his head.

"Ginger, Nightcrawler," I said over the radio, "We got him. Get up here." I unscrewed the suppressor from my pistol and reholstered it. I then snapped open my automatic knife, cut the shoulder strap on Al Falah's bag, and pulled it off of him.

Without turning on its headlights, the van sped up the alley, coming to a stop right next to us. The sliding side door opened. Hudson jumped out, grabbed Al Falah, and effortlessly threw him into the van. He climbed back in, and I followed, laptop bag in hand.

Just as the call to prayer died away, Tailor noticed Al Falah's friend, lying facedown in his own blood with two bullets in his back. He was still alive. He groaned slightly and tried to move. Without blinking, Tailor stepped forward, shot him in the back of the head, then jumped into the van, pulling the door closed behind him.

We backed down the alley until we came to the cross street, turned on the headlights, and sped away into the night. Tailor called Control over the radio to inform them of our success. I slumped against the wall of the van and looked down at my watch again. *1909. Not bad.* Hunter had been right. It'd been remarkably easy.

Stepping forward, Tailor roughly pulled the black bag from Al Falah's head, knocking off his checkered headdress in the process. The young terrorist looked around, still groggy from the sedative and from being clocked by Tailor. His eyes grew wide as he became aware of the surroundings and his situation. He was handcuffed to a chair in the basement of our safe house. We had him shoved off into a corner. The only illumination was from a bright lamp we'd set up. I had to shake my head at the whole scene; it was like something from a bad spy movie.

Al Falah looked at Tailor, fear in his eyes. His mouth was slightly open, but he didn't, or maybe couldn't, speak. He then looked over to me; his eyes darted down to the pistol on my left hip. We'd removed our jackets in order to openly display our weapons.

To my left was Hudson. Al Falah seemed especially intimidated by him. Hudson, for his part, just folded his muscular arms across his chest and stared the skinny terrorist down, not saying a word.

"Do you speak English?" I asked. Our prisoner's eyes darted back to me. He didn't say anything.

"I know you can understand me," Tailor said, leaning in a little closer. He was probably right; almost all educated Gulf Arabs spoke English. "So we can do this the easy way, or we can do this the pushing-your-shit-in way. What's it gonna be, ace?"

Al Falah, for his part, seemed to have found a little bit of spine. He closed his mouth and sat up a little straighter in his chair, staring defiantly at the wall behind us. Tailor straightened up, then looked over at Hudson and me, grinning. It seemed that Al Falah didn't want to do this the easy way.

"Wheeler, go get Sarah," Tailor said then, talking over his shoulder. Wheeler, who was behind us, near the stairs, nodded and headed up to the main floor of the safe house. A few moments later, he clomped back down the stairs. Behind him, Sarah gracefully made her way down, clipboard in hand. She followed him across the darkened room.

The prisoner's eyes grew wide again when Sarah stepped into the light. He stared up at her shapely figure, and his mouth fell open again. She was taller than he was. She looked back down at him, not saying anything. Wheeler pulled up a second chair, and slid it next to her. She sat in it, crossing her legs and laying the clipboard in her lap. She clicked open a pen, leaned forward, and spoke to Al Falah in Arabic.

He looked back at us, then back at her, then back at us again, seemingly confused. Sarah repeated whatever it was that she'd said, her voice a little bit harsher. Al Falah seemingly balked at this and said something back.

"What'd he say?" Hudson asked.

"He just called me a cunt," Sarah said. "Said he doesn't have to answer to a woman."

"Really?" Tailor said. Without another word, he stepped forward and punched Al Falah across the face. The terrorist's head snapped to the side, and he cried out in pain. "Ask him now."

Sarah repeated whatever it is she said to Al Falah. His voice wavered, but the young terrorist apparently didn't tell Sarah whatever it was she wanted to hear. She looked up at us and just shook her head.

Tailor shrugged. "Okay, asshole," he said and punched

Al Falah again. Hudson stepped around Sarah and violently struck our prisoner himself. Al Falah's head snapped back, and the young Arab cried out. Tailor and Hudson took turns hitting him a few more times. Hudson was strong as an ox and had to take it easy. A real shot from that man would have cracked Al Falah's skull.

"What are you asking him?" I said, looking down at Sarah.

"This kid is just a small fry. His uncle, Ali bin Ahmed Al Falah, is the real target. I'm asking about him."

I looked back up at our prisoner. Tailor and Hudson had stopped pummeling him for a moment. One eye was puffy and swelling shut, and blood was running from both his nose and lip. It was unpleasant, but this was war. If any of us were captured, we could expect worse. Sarah remained cool but seemed uncomfortable with what was happening. Nonetheless, she repeated her question, her voice sounding cold and harsh.

The young Al Falah spent a few moments staring at his lap, breathing heavily, blood dripping onto his clothes. He lifted his head back, still panting, and looked over at Sarah. He took a deep breath. Sarah lifted her clipboard just in time to block a blob of spit and blood. I had to give the kid credit; he'd certainly found his backbone. Not that it was going to do him any good.

"Oh, that's *it*," I said, speaking to Al Falah for the first time. I lifted my right foot and booted our prisoner in the chest. He gasped in pain, rocked back on his chair, and fell over backward, smashing his hands between the chair and the concrete floor. I moved forward, planting my right foot into his chest again, and drew my pistol. Holding the

Sig .45 in both hands, I looked down at Al Falah, the sights aligned with the bridge of his nose.

"Valentine, no!" Sarah exclaimed, coming up out of her chair and putting her hand on my shoulder. "We need information from him."

"Tell him if he doesn't start talking I'm going to blow his head off," I said coldly. *The Calm* had overtaken me, as it often did right before I had to shoot someone. Sarah had sensed the change. She hesitated. *"Tell him,"* I repeated, more firmly. Sarah stepped around me. Al Falah's eyes were focused on the muzzle of my pistol and nothing else. Sarah leaned down and spoke to him. Al Falah sputtered something back.

"What'd he say?" Hudson asked.

Sarah stood up and sighed. "He says he's prepared to die. I think he wants to. He's scared shitless. He thinks it'll make him a martyr."

"Fuck that," Tailor said, squatting down next to our prisoner. He reached into his pocket and drew his knife. With the push of a button, the blade snapped forward out of the handle. Tailor reached down and grabbed Al Falah's face with his left hand. "Tell him that if he doesn't start *talking,* I'm going to start *cutting parts* off him. Tell him we're *not* going to kill him. I'll just cut off his ears, his nose, his tongue, and put out his eyes, and knock out his teeth, and dump him on the side of the road somewhere. He can live the rest of his shitty life as a beggar, or he can kill himself and not get his virgins. I'm not gonna do him no favors."

"I . . ." Sarah said, hesitating.

"Tell him!" Tailor shouted, poking the very tip of his

blade into Al Falah's face. There was no doubt that Tailor would do it.

Sarah steeled herself, leaned back down to our prisoner, and spoke to him again for a few moments. His eyes grew wider as he processed her words. He looked over to me, with the muzzle of my pistol still pointed between his eyes, then over to Tailor and the knife poking into his face. Apparently the short, scary Southerner with the disfiguring razor was the more frightening prospect of the two of us. Falah hesitated for what seemed like an eternity.

"I . . . I . . . okay," Al Falah then sputtered, speaking English for the first time. "I will tell you. I will tell you! Please . . ."

"That's more like it," Tailor said. He pushed the switch on his knife, and the blade disappeared back into the handle. I took my foot off of Al Falah's chest and holstered my pistol. Tailor and I then grabbed the back of his chair, hoisted him up, and set our prisoner upright again.

"Your uncle," Sarah said, sitting back down in her chair. "Ali bin Ahmed Al Falah. Tell me everything you know about him." The young Arab took one last look around the room, lowered his head slightly, and began to talk. He had a *lot* to say.

Stepping onto the roof, I saw Sarah silhouetted against the lights of the city. She was standing by the wall that ran around the roof of the house, smoking a cigarette. Hearing me open the door, she turned around briefly and nodded. I returned the nod, and stood beside her.

Below us was the small villa that we used for a safe house. The house itself was big, with no less than six bedrooms, two and a half bathrooms, and a big common area downstairs. In addition to that, it had a huge basement. Basements were rare in homes in the Middle East. The safe house also had a tall wall around it. Next to the house was a large carport that held four vehicles. In front of the house was a sort of garden with a grove of tall palm trees and a mess of ferns at their bases.

"Are you okay?" I asked, looking out over the city. "I didn't know you smoked."

"I don't," she said, exhaling a puff of smoke. "I mean, I quit years ago. I bummed one off Tailor. I just . . . sometimes when I get stressed I have one. That's all."

"Oh, I see. What's wrong?"

"I thought you were going to kill that guy."

"Sarah." I paused for a moment while I struggled to find the right words. "I *did* kill a man tonight. One of Al Falah's bodyguards."

"I know! I ordered you to. It's just . . . I don't know. I'm being stupid. I've never been part of an interrogation like that before."

"I was a little surprised to see you here," I said.

"I was surprised when they called me out. I guess the other Arabic speakers were busy. Walker was probably busy pulling somebody's fingernails out. I was told that normally I wouldn't leave the compound much. I'm not even supposed to know where all of the safe houses are!"

"You've never done an interrogation like that before, have you?" I asked.

"No. I suppose you've done a lot of them, right?"

"Not really," I said truthfully. "I was mostly a trigger-puller. We had intel specialists do that kind of thing."

"Tailor seemed like he was enjoying himself," she said hesitantly.

"Well . . . Tailor is *crazy*. He's always been like that."

"How long have you known him?"

"Years now. Since we were in Africa together."

"Do you really trust him?" Sarah asked, putting out her cigarette on the top of the wall and looking over at me.

"With my life," I replied. "I don't know if I'd trust him with anybody else's, though."

Sarah looked at me sideways, eyebrows raised. She then let out a sardonic chuckle. "You're funny, Mike," she said, calling me by my given name for the first time. We stood together, looking out over the lights of the city, for what seemed like a long time. Neither one of us said anything.

"You did fine, by the way," I said at last.

"What?"

"In the interrogation," I continued. "You really kept your cool in there. You really seemed like you knew your stuff."

"I've been trained," Sarah said, "by, um, our employers for Project Heartbreaker. I just didn't know how intense it was going to be."

"It gets easier. I mean, it sounds horrible, but you get used to it."

"I hope so," Sarah said. "We're just getting started."

"You hear something?" I asked.

"Oh, yeah." She looked back over at me. "We've got a list of targets a mile long. Terrorists, financiers, support people, recruiting people, you name it."

"You know all of the targets?" I asked incredulously.

"What? Oh, no. I just got a peek at it. It's not just names, either. It's places. Gatherings. *Events*. This is going to get *ugly*, Mike."

"That's what I figured," I said. "So, what happens to our boy downstairs?"

"Hunter's sending someone to come get him. I don't know what they're going to do with him now."

"They'll either make a deal with him in exchange for being a continuing source of information, or they'll put a bullet in his brainpan and dump him in the ocean. Either way, sucks to be him."

Sarah nodded. "His computer wasn't even password protected, either. There's a *lot* of information on there. Hunter was happy."

"Heh . . . I'm glad. So, do you know what's next?"

"His uncle. He's the next target for you guys."

"I figured. When?"

"Soon. Hunter said your chalk did so well that he's giving you that mission next. We've got some more intel to gather, but that's your next job. They'll be sending me information to brief you soon."

"Good."

"Mike . . . I saw something else. You know, when I was digging around. They're expecting heavy casualties for Dead Six. The operations they're planning are high risk and are planned with minimum possible manpower."

I sighed aloud, looking back out over the city. "Great."

"You just be careful out there, okay?" she said quietly. She was staring at me intently. We held eye contact for a long time.

"I will," I managed.

"What's *up*?" Tailor said, strolling through the door onto the roof, lighting a cigarette as he went. He was unusually upbeat and had a stupid grin on his face. He paused when he realized Sarah and I were alone together. "Am I, uh, interrupting something?" he asked, cigarette in mouth.

"No, no," Sarah said, stepping away from me. "I was just giving Valentine some info on what's happening next."

"We're going after his uncle, right?" Tailor asked, referring to the captive in our basement.

"Sure are," I answered.

The expression on Tailor's face changed almost imperceptibly. My friend might not have been *certifiably* nuts, but he sure did enjoy this kind of thing a little too much. "*Good.*" He grinned.

Chapter 4:
Secondary Target

LORENZO
March 13

Falah had sounded nervous on the phone as he apologized for postponing our appointment due to family trouble. I played the concerned friend, even went so far as to offer my assistance, but he wouldn't elaborate about what was wrong. It wasn't until afterward that I got the word on the street that Falah's favorite nephew had disappeared. The bodyguards provided by his uncle had been found shot to death, along with one of their new recruits. I'd only met the kid once. He'd struck me as another obnoxious rich kid, wannabe-terrorist asshole.

Nobody had any idea who'd taken him. It wouldn't have surprised me if the senior Falah wasn't waiting by the phone for the ransom call right now. There was a subset of the criminal underworld that specialized in kidnapping the kinds of targets whose parents wouldn't involve the authorities. It was dangerous, but drug lords' kids were especially lucrative. But I knew of most of the crews who did that kind of thing professionally, and I didn't think any of them were operating around here.

Even the lowest of the low had families, easy targets that could be exploited for money, revenge, or leverage. Hell, I was a perfect example. Eddie had learned my real name, tracked down my family, and just like that, he owned me.

My family wouldn't even recognize me now. My older brother, Bob, the federal agent, always the righteous, morally grounded, overachieving tough guy would certainly slap the cuffs on me myself if he had even the slightest clue about the things I'd done, and he'd probably sleep well at night afterward. But he, and all the rest, were family, and I *owed* them. They wouldn't understand, but I was doing this for them.

In a way, I could understand Falah's worry. Even scumbags had loved ones. I just hoped he got that shit cleared up fast so I could hurry up and kill him.

VALENTINE
Al Khor District, Safe house 4
March 20
0745

Tailor and I made our way into the basement of the safe house, having been rousted out of bed by Sarah. We were surprised to find Colonel Hunter waiting for us, flanked as always by a pair of his nondescript security men. Several chairs had been set up. A laptop sat on a small table, hooked up to a portable screen. Wheeler and Hudson had been called away a few days prior and hadn't yet returned.

"Good morning, gentlemen," Hunter said. "I apologize for dragging you boys out of bed so early, but we've got work to do. We're ready to move."

"Are Hudson and Wheeler coming back, sir?" I asked as we sat down.

"I'm afraid not. I have them on another assignment right now. You two will be on your own. I have confidence in you."

Tailor and I just looked at each other. Sarah's face was a mask, but there was concern in her eyes.

Hunter turned on the big screen and began his briefing. "This is Ali bin Ahmed Al Falah. He's a Saudi national by birth but has lived in Zubara for over ten years. He's a wealthy, influential landowner and has connections to the Saudi royal family. He's also a *player*." The man pictured was short and overweight. He was wearing a traditional checkered headdress and had a thick white beard.

The picture changed. It was now a much younger Al Falah, dressed in camouflage and holding an RPD machine gun.

"This is Al Falah in 1984," Hunter continued. "At the age of twenty-six, he dropped out of a Saudi religious university to join the jihad against the Soviets in Afghanistan. He fought with the mujahedin for two years before being wounded and returning to Saudi Arabia."

The picture changed again. This time Al Falah was shaking hands with an all-too-familiar man, and smiling.

"We believe this picture was taken in 1997 or so. Yes, that is Osama bin Laden. As I said, Al Falah is a player.

He's very wealthy, both from his father and from his dealings in the oil and natural gas industry. He's respected, considered pious, and has an enormous family. Though polygamy is rare in Zubara, he's got three wives and probably nine children. He lives in a large walled compound outside of the city. Nice place—fountain, palm trees, you name it. He's got many servants and quite a few Indonesian slave girls as well."

Tailor and I were taking notes. Hunter told us it wasn't necessary. Sarah handed each of us a fat manila envelope.

"Everything you need is in here," Hunter said. "Al Falah never does anything himself. He's always the behind-the-scenes man, the one pulling the strings and providing the funding. We believe getting shot in the ass in the 'Stan probably led to this attitude. He raises enormous amounts of cash for various terrorist groups. He has several influential charities in Zubara, Kuwait, and the UAE that are all fronts for donating money to organizations like Hezbollah, Hamas, and Al Qaeda in the Arabian Peninsula."

"I'd do this one for free," Tailor muttered under his breath.

Hunter didn't seem to hear him. "Fortunately for us, this is one of the rare occasions where removing the man will remove the means. Al Falah does what he does through force of personality. He's well liked and respected. He goes to Friday services at mosque . . . well, *religiously*. He always fasts during Ramadan. People are happy to do business with him. Your mission, gentlemen, is to kill Ali bin Ahmed Al Falah. You can use any means you see fit. You are to keep collateral damage to an absolute minimum to keep the

Zubarans from getting antsy. You can request any equipment you wish, but no other personnel are available at this time. Failure is not an option. Any questions?"

"This is . . . wow," I said, looking through the stack of documents.

"Welcome to Big Boy Town," Hunter said, cracking an evil grin. "You boys were picked for this assignment because I believe you can handle it. I didn't say it'd be easy. I'm giving you two a lot of leeway. Just get the job done. The best place to hit Al Falah is here," Hunter said, pointing to a picture that had appeared on the screen. "This is a social club that Al Falah frequents. It's a coffee house, or a tea house or something like that. Men go there to smoke hookahs, play chess, and shoot the shit. It's also one of very few public places he's regularly seen."

"How often does he go there, sir?" Tailor asked.

"Several nights a week, usually," Sarah said. "He likes to play chess with his friends."

"Where does this information come from, sir?" Tailor asked, looking at Colonel Hunter. "Is it reliable?" He seemed uncharacteristically concerned.

"Our intelligence assets are dependable enough, son," Hunter replied crossly. "We have our own people as well as contacts in the Zubaran intelligence services. This is an important job. This will be our first major hit."

"Anything else we need to know, sir?" I asked.

"As a matter of fact . . ." Another picture appeared on the screen. This one was of a pretty nondescript Gulf Arab man, in traditional dress, and was taken from far away. "Your secondary target is this man. He's the new proprietor of the social club. He appeared on the scene a few months ago. We don't know anything about him other than his name, *Khalid*."

"Why's he important, sir?" I asked.

"He's hosting Al Falah," Sarah said. "He's a facilitator. We've picked up some unusual electronic chatter coming from the club. A lot of encrypted phone traffic, stuff like that. We have reason to suspect Khalid is part of the enemy's support network."

"Even if that's not the case," Hunter said, "everyone in Zubara knows who our target is and what he does. Part of our objective is to make the man on the street afraid to deal with the bad guys. So Khalid is your secondary target. Your tertiary targets are Al Falah's bodyguards and assistants. Eliminate as many of them as possible."

Tailor and I exchanged a knowing look. I felt a predatory grin split my face as I returned my attention to the briefing. This was the kind of job I'd signed up for.

VALENTINE
Ash Shamal District
March 25
1757

"Our boy's here," I said, looking through a pair of compact binoculars. Tailor was lying next to me, doing the same thing. One floor down and across the street from us, a bright yellow Hummer H2, followed by a white Toyota Land Cruiser, pulled to a stop in front of the social club. "Would you look at that?" I asked. "That's a pretty pimp ride he's got." Tailor chuckled.

The Land Cruiser's doors opened, and four men, presumably bodyguards, piled out. They were all dressed in cheap-looking suits without ties. As I watched, the driver got out of the Hummer, hurried to the other side of the vehicle, and opened the passenger's side door.

"There he is," Tailor said as a short, heavyset man in traditional Gulf Arab garb climbed out of the large yellow SUV. Tailor and I laid eyes on Ali Bin Ahmed Al Falah for the first time. We'd been coming to the same spot for days, watching the social club, waiting for him to make an appearance. Today we finally got lucky.

We were on the second floor of a half-completed building that stood directly across a divided street from the social club. It was going to be an office building of some kind, but construction had been halted. The second floor had large floor-to-ceiling windows on the sides. The glass wasn't installed yet. We lay on the floor, side by side, shrouded in the darkness the unfinished building provided, watching our target. The sun was low in the western sky behind us. People passing by on the narrow street had no idea we were there. Our vehicle was parked in the narrow alley behind the building, concealed from view.

Tailor reached into his backpack and pulled out a hand-held device that looked like a satellite dish. He put on a set of headphones. "Let's see if we can hear what they have to say." Neither of us spoke Arabic, but we could connect the parabolic microphone to our radios and transmit the intelligence back to Control.

Al Falah made his way toward the glass front doors of the establishment, with his driver walking just behind. The other bodyguards fanned out and did a half-assed job of observing the area. As Al Falah approached, another man in similar Arab attire appeared from inside. The two men greeted each other warmly, grasping each other's right hands while putting their left hands on the other man's right shoulder. They then exchanged kisses on each cheek.

"That must be Khalid." I squeezed the transmit button on my tiny microphone. "Control, Nightcrawler. We have eyes on the primary, secondary, and tertiary targets. Intel was correct. This is the place."

"*Copy that, Nightcrawler,*" Control replied, all business. Anita King was on the radio instead of Sarah.

"Control, Xbox," Tailor said, "I'm transmitting now."

"*Copy that . . . receiving,*" Anita said. I could hear Al Falah and Khalid speaking in Arabic in the background. We observed Al Falah and Khalid for several minutes, until they disappeared into the club, followed by Al Falah's entourage.

"Did you get all that, Control?" Tailor asked.

"*Uh . . . roger that,*" Anita said. "*They were just greeting each other. Said something about a chess game, and that they were going to discuss a proposal.*"

"What kind of proposal?" Tailor asked.

"*They didn't say. Observe the area for as long as you can, then withdraw without being detected.*"

"Roger that, Control," I said. "Out."

Tailor looked over at me, then back through his binoculars. "I'm hungry."

"So, what do you think?" I asked. "How you wanna do this?"

"I say we get a scoped rifle and just pop him from here."

DEAD SIX 125

"Sounds easy enough. Do we have a scoped rifle?"

"There's an SR-25 in the safe house we can use. It's got a suppressor, too. From right here, we can lay down some fire, drop a bunch of these guys, and then bug out through the back."

"Did you get a good look at the bodyguards?" I asked. "I think they've got sub-guns."

"Probably little MP5s or something under their suit coats," Tailor agreed. "Probably can't shoot for shit. We should be okay." It was about sixty yards from our position to the front door of the club.

"Cripes, we should've brought the rifle with us. We could've popped him just now and had it over with," I said. We'd been ordered to observe the club and try to get a feel for Al Falah's routine. We knew where Al Falah lived, of course, but it had been deemed too risky to attempt to hit him there.

"Yeah," Tailor said, not really listening to me. "Can't see much in the windows. They're tinted. Al Falah won't sit by the windows out front anyway. He's a big shot, right? He'll have a private room in the back or something."

"Worse comes to worst we could enter the club," I suggested, even though I knew that wasn't a good idea. "Hell, no. Not with just the two of us. No, we'll have to hit him here. We'll only get one shot. If we fuck this up he'll go underground and we might lose him."

"You're right." I set my binoculars down. "You wanna take the shot, or you want me to?"

"You take the SR-25," Tailor said. "I'll grab a carbine and provide cover fire." Tailor wouldn't come out and admit it, but I was a more accurate shooter than he was.

He was correct in his assertion that we'd only have one shot, too. There wouldn't be much room for error.

"I don't like it," I said. "Just the two of us versus five bodyguards—"

"That we *know* of," Tailor interjected.

"Right. Next time he could have more. One shot, maybe two, since the rifle's an autoloader, before his bodyguards can get him behind cover. A rifle I've never shot before, and who the hell knows who zeroed the scope or when." We didn't have access to any kind of a shooting range, and I doubted they'd let us risk taking the rifle out into the desert someplace to test-fire it.

"You're right," Tailor agreed, setting down his binoculars as well. "If they get Al Falah into that club, we'll have to go in after him. So you better drop him on the first shot. That's the best chance we got."

"Why are there only two of us? We could really use Hudson and Wheeler for this."

"I don't know," Tailor said. "I don't like it, either." I could only wonder what kind of operations the others were involved in if they could only spare two of us for a job they insisted was so important. As I continued to watch the social club, I couldn't help but worry that things were going to get ugly, fast.

LORENZO
March 26

The disassembled pieces of my pistol were strewn on the kitchen table of our rented apartment. I wiped the slide down with a rag while my crew slept. I found that I always woke up early on game day. Nervous excitement, I suppose.

It never hurts to recheck your equipment. I put a few drops of Slipstream lube on the frame rails of my STI 4.15 Tactical 9mm before fitting everything back together. The gun was a stubby work of lethal art. Phenomenally accurate and reliable, it was the pistol I used when performance was more important than deniability. I had a few Bulgarian Makarovs and old Browning P35s for that. I worked the slide back and forth quickly, feeling the familiar slickness of oiled metal on metal. I checked the chamber before aiming at Al Falah's picture that had been taped to the wall. The tritium sights lined up perfectly on the bridge of his nose as I pulled the trigger. The hammer fell with a snap.

Ali bin Ahmed Al Falah dies today.

The old terrorist bastard had dropped by the club yesterday. He was still distraught, but he wasn't going to let that get in the way of business. Our meeting was on.

An eighteen-round, flush-fit magazine went into the STI. I pulled back the slide and let it fly, feeding a Hornady hollow point into the chamber. If everything went according to plan, that same bullet would end up in one of Al Falah's bodyguards by the end of the night. He'd beefed up the number on his security detail since his nephew's murder. Sure, Al Falah was still calling it a kidnapping, but at this point I knew that was wishful thinking.

The call for prayer could be heard coming from the corner mosque as the sun rose. It was a mournful sound but I had spent so many years in places like this that I found it kind of comforting.

I showered, put on the obnoxious perfume that all of the men in this region wore, and dressed in my Zubaran thobe, vest, and head scarf. I'd tailored this one a bit with a few extra pockets, and I could hike up the idiotic skirt and run if I needed to. The reflection in the bathroom mirror was that of an Arab landlord who had become friends with a terrorist. Today would be the last day that this identity would ever exist.

If I were just here to assassinate this man, life would be simple. Murder is easy, no matter who the target. I needed him for so much more, hence the effort of fabricating Khalid. Al Falah needed to quietly disappear. A business meeting meant that he would probably have greater than normal security, but he would also need his computer to arrange the transfer of funds. I needed that computer for Phase Two and I needed Al Falah himself for Phase Three.

I splashed some water on my face and stared into the mirror. This was too damn complicated. If anything went wrong, there was going to be hell to pay. Shutting the faucet off, I dried my hands and prepared myself for what I had to do. My crew had woken up by the time I came out. The three of us ate breakfast in silence. There was a lot riding on today, and we all knew our jobs.

I holstered the pistol under my thobe, along with two more magazines and the Silencerco suppressor that would be attached to the end of the STI's threaded barrel. My radio went into another pocket.

"You ready?" Carl asked rhetorically, still chewing his Captain Crunch.

"I'm going down to the club," I answered in Arabic. "I'm expecting a busy day today."

VALENTINE
Al Khor District, Safe House 4
March 26
1955

I had the jitters. I always did before an operation. My nerves would smooth out as I got into the swing of things. Tailor and I were in the basement of the safe house, preparing our gear, getting ready for what was coming. Neither of us spoke. We'd go over the plan again later.

I'd gone through this routine many times before, and the jitters always passed, but it was different this time. It was just Tailor and me. No backup, no fire support, and our entire egress plan was to get in our car and drive away.

We'd gotten the word earlier in the day. Al Falah would be returning to the club tonight to broker some kind of arms deal with Khalid. Intelligence had given us the time of the meeting, but few other details. It was *on*.

But still my mind wandered. I had a lot of questions, many that I didn't dare to ask. I wondered about this intelligence. Where did it come from? Do they have someone inside Al Falah's network somewhere? Why not have *that guy* kill him? I wondered what happened to Wheeler and Hudson, too. Though they were supposedly assigned to our chalk, we hadn't heard from them in days.

I chided myself. So many questions, but now was not the time to worry about them. I returned my attention to my gear. Standing up, I slid on my body armor and adjusted the straps until it snugly conformed to my torso. It was a low-profile vest, black in color, with pockets front and back for hard protective plates. The plates, designed to stop rifle fire, were made of ceramic and were thinner and lighter than any I'd ever seen.

On my left hip was a high-ride concealment holster for my revolver. Tailor flashed me a smirk when I pulled the big wheelgun out of my bag, but I paid him no mind. It was my good-luck charm, and I had a feeling I was going to need some luck tonight.

I put on my jacket. It was loose-fitting, and like my body armor and T-shirt was black in color. In Zubara, it was still fairly cool out in March once the sun went down. I wouldn't look too out-of-place with a jacket on. The dark color of the jacket made it hard to tell I was wearing the armor vest underneath it.

Reaching down, I picked up my primary weapon and shouldered it. I pulled back the charging handle, observed that the rifle's chamber was empty, and let the bolt close. I then looked through the scope. The Knight's Armament SR-25 sniper rifle felt heavy in my hands. Its twenty-inch barrel was capped with a sound suppressor. A folding bipod was attached to its railed hand guards. I began to partially disassemble it so it'd fit in a discreet padded case.

While I did this, Tailor got his own equipment ready. His weapon was a 5.56mm FN Mk.16 carbine, also with a suppressor. The carbine had the short, ten-inch barrel installed, making it very compact. Tailor removed the suppressor, then folded his carbine's stock. He was then able to fit it into his backpack.

As Tailor and I finished packing our gear, I realized Sarah had come down the stairs. Hunter had left her with us, as he'd been called away for something else. I wasn't sure why they left her at the safe house instead of bringing her back to the base where she belonged, but I was happy to have her around.

"Be careful," she said simply. The look on her face told me she wanted to say more.

"We'll be fine," I said, hefting my bag. I didn't mean to be dismissive of Sarah. It was just that I had my game face on and it was hard to be sociable. I looked her in the eye and touched her on the arm as I walked past. She didn't follow Tailor and me as we made our way up the stairs.

"Where *is* he?" Tailor whispered in frustration.

"Punctuality is not considered a virtue over here," I said absentmindedly, scanning the front of the club through the SR-25's scope. It was a lot more crowded than I would've preferred. By my count there were more than a dozen patrons, all of them Arab men, most of them in traditional garb, in the club now. I could see a few of them sitting by the windows, smoking, playing chess, and having animated conversations with a lot of hand gestures and laughter.

I looked up from the scope of my rifle and over at Tailor. His carbine was on the floor in front of him. He was propped up on his elbows, watching the front of the club through binoculars. I could tell he wanted a cigarette, but we couldn't risk the light signature. In order to have a clear shot, we had to get a lot closer to the window than I liked.

Another ten minutes slowly ticked by as the jitters got worse. Finally, a yellow Hummer H2 pulled up to the curb and parked, trailed by the same white Toyota Land Cruiser as last time. I quickly hunkered down behind the rifle as Tailor picked up his carbine and looked through the ACOG scope mounted on it. The jitters melted away. My heart rate slowed down. I felt my body relax as *The Calm* washed over me again.

A rough-looking man with a brown suit jacket and a bushy mustache got out. It was the same driver from the previous day. Through the rifle scope I could tell that he had a compact submachine gun hidden under his suit jacket. He hurried around to the passenger's side and opened the door.

Ali bin Ahmed Al Falah stepped out of his truck. He was on the opposite side of the Hummer, and I didn't have a clear shot, but there was no mistaking his squat stature and white beard.

"That's our boy," I whispered. "You confirm?"

"I confirm," Tailor said.

"Control, Nightcrawler," I whispered into my microphone. "We have eyes on target."

"*Roger that, Nightcrawler,*" Anita said, her voice distant and professional. "*You are cleared to engage.*"

"Copy," I said, flipping the SR-25's selector switch from *safe* to *fire*. Al Falah, trailed by his driver, made his way toward the door of the social club. This time he had a large black briefcase in his hand. His four other bodyguards had piled out of the Land Cruiser and fanned out. To my dismay, they seemed more alert than they had the previous day.

"I'll hit his driver first, then switch to the other bodyguards," Tailor said. "You take out the primary target first, then the secondary target." The mission priorities were Al Falah, then Khalid, then the bodyguards. However, our *practical* priorities were to take care of the people who could shoot back as quickly as possible.

The front doors of the club opened. I recognized Khalid through the scope. As soon as the club's doors closed behind him, I swiveled the rifle on its bipod, placing the illuminated crosshairs between Al Falah's shoulder blades. I wasn't going to attempt a head shot, even at this close range, with a rifle I'd never fired before, not when it was this important. My finger moved to the trigger, and I exhaled.

Crack! The suppressed rifle's report sounded like a .22. The bullet smacked into my target in a puff of blood, a little higher than where I'd aimed, and tore right through him. Al Falah dropped to the ground like he'd been hit with a bat.

"He's down," I said calmly. Tailor fired off a double tap. Al Falah's driver went down as I swiveled the rifle toward Khalid. The other men standing around began to scurry like cockroaches. The patrons of the club seated next to the windows reacted in horror. Several got up. In a moment, the entire place would empty into the street. "I've lost Khalid!" I was getting tunnel vision through my scope. Somebody was shooting back at us.

"He's behind the Hummer!" Tailor said, firing off another double tap. There was someone crouched down behind the Hummer's engine block, concealed from my view. I didn't even see Khalid bolt for cover after I'd shot.

He's fast, I thought. I then cussed at myself. *Damn it. I should've waited for them to shake hands. Probably could've gotten both of them with the same bullet.*

The two remaining bodyguards were hunkered down behind the Land Cruiser as Tailor began shooting at it. One of them was foolhardy enough to bolt for Al Falah; I caught him in my crosshairs and put a round through him as he ran. He stumbled as the bullet hit and face-planted onto the sidewalk.

I still didn't have a shot on Khalid. Swinging the SR-25 around on its bipod, I put two more rounds into Al Falah's body, just to make sure. The terrorist convulsed as the bullets hit him. Al Falah was *quite* dead.

Switching back, I rapidly fired into the boxy yellow truck, hoping a bullet would punch through and hit Khalid. Shot after shot, holes appeared in the hood and fender. Then my rifle *stopped.* I looked at the action; a fired case was sticking sideways out of the ejection port, mashed between the bolt and the breech face.

That same instant, Al Falah's surviving bodyguard raised his submachine gun over the ventilated hood of the Land Cruiser and ripped off an entire magazine at us. The bullets impacted all around us, kicking up clouds of plaster and dust as they hit. The noise panicked the patrons of the club, and they began to stream out onto the sidewalk, running in different directions. It was time to go.

Tailor roughly slapped me on the shoulder as he got up, changing magazines as he did so. I stood up, slung the SR-25's carrying case over my shoulder, and followed Tailor, trying to clear the jam as I moved.

We headed back into the building. A Range Rover

came speeding around the corner and screeched to a halt next to the Hummer. Four more guys, armed with submachine guns and short-barreled Kalashnikovs, jumped out of the vehicle and fanned out. The bodyguard hiding behind the Land Cruiser leaned around the vehicle, pointed in our direction, and began shouting. As Tailor and I hit the stairs, our hiding place on the second floor of the half-completed building was hosed with automatic weapons fire.

LORENZO

Half a year of my life . . . wasted.

That was the first coherent thought that ran through my mind as Ali bin Ahmed Al Falah's chest puckered into a grapefruit sized exit hole right in front of me. Scarlet and white bits rose like a cloud as he went to his knees, heart torn in half and still pumping.

I had been on the receiving end of gunfire so many times that I instinctively bolted for cover behind the nearest vehicle. Flinching involuntarily as I wiped the fine mist of Al Falah off my face, I honed in on the shooter's position across the street. I wasn't the only one. "Achmed, up there!" the first bodyguard shouted as he lifted his MP5. Two rapid shots came from the building, and the guard went down hard, disappearing from view on the other side of the yellow Hummer. One of the other bodyguards returned fire.

My ear piece crackled. *"Who's shooting? What the hell's going on?"*

"I don't know! I didn't fire!" The sniper hammered two more rifle rounds into the fallen man's back, and now the closest bystanders realized what was happening and ran away screaming.

"*Who did, then?*"

"A sniper wasted Falah." I pushed myself tight against the wheel as the sniper fired a couple of rounds into the Hummer. The window shattered, and the nearest guard fell, missing half his face. A Range Rover screeched to a halt and the rest of Falah's men piled out.

"*Witnesses?*"

"Bunches," I replied.

Carl said, "*Roger that.*" Then there was a stream of profanity so vile that it made me cringe more than the incoming sniper fire. "*A public killing! This ruins everything!*"

The voice on the radio changed. It was Reaper. "*Lorenzo! We still need his computer.*"

"*Get it! Get the case!*" Carl bellowed across the channel. "*I'm on the way.*"

I risked a peek. The other guards were blasting the crap out of the building. Bystanders were running for their lives. Bodily fluids were draining all over the street, and there it was, a plain leather briefcase, still clutched in Falah's twitching hand. I had to move now, because some asshole had just blown my carefully laid plans. Starting toward it, I stuck one hand under my thobe and grabbed the butt of my STI. I had spent three months wearing a dress, and I was not leaving without that damned case.

The shooting had stopped. The new guards were shouting and pointing at the sniper's building. One young man jumped from the vehicle and sprinted toward me. He knelt next to his former boss, barely even registering that I was there, recognizing me from previous visits. The Range Rover tore away, probably in pursuit of the shooter. *Good.*

"Khalid! Call for doctors!" he shouted. It took a split second for me to realize that was supposed to be my name. Look one way, look the other. People moving, pointing, talking on cell phones, no other guards in sight, this could still work.

"At once!" I answered as I reached down and grabbed the case. Al Falah's hand wouldn't let go when I pulled. He had it clutched in a literal death grip. I tugged harder, hoping that the guard would keep trying to hold the contents of Al Falah's chest in rather than pay any attention to me.

The guard looked up in confusion. "What are you doing? Why—" I kicked him in the teeth, sending him reeling into the gutter. Jerking the case into my arms, I ran back into the club. I pushed past the startled onlookers, their attention mostly on the bodies in the street. Some of them were just realizing that I had booted a man with a submachine gun in the face and robbed the dead. I jerked up the thobe and ran like hell back into the club, through the kitchen, past the startled employees, out the back door, and into the alley. I heard the door slam closed behind me.

I rounded the corner. The stinking alley was empty except for overflowing dumpsters and graffiti-sprayed walls. Carl wasn't here yet. "Where are you?" I hissed. "I've got it. I'm at the back of the club."

His voice was slightly distorted in my ear. "Coming. I almost got hit by some crazies having a car chase or something."

I glanced back to the club. Nobody had followed yet, but it wouldn't be long. I jerked my head around at the noise of an engine. A vehicle pulled into the alley, only it wasn't Carl's van, but another car full of angry Muslims, and I immediately recognized the driver screaming into his cell phone as Yousef, one of Al Falah's men.

No cover, no place to hide. No time to run. Yousef's eyes widened when he saw me there, splattered in his boss' blood, stolen briefcase in hand. He was probably on the phone with the guard I had just booted. Ten yards to that vehicle, Yousef behind the wheel, one passenger, no other options, and the 9mm was in my hand before I even thought about it. Car doors flew open as my STI cleared leather.

Time slowed to a crawl. The passenger was quicker, coming up out of the vehicle, stupidly leaving cover, stubby black MP5 rising. Dropping the case, my hands came together, arms punching outward, the gun an extension of my will. The front sight entered my vision, focused so clearly that the bad guy was only a blur behind it. I stroked the perfect trigger to the rear.

The sound should have been deafening, but it seemed more of a muted thump in the narrow alley. The heavy 9mm had virtually no recoil, and I fired as fast as the sights came back into place. The man with the submachine gun fell, his weapon tumbling from his hands. My muzzle moved, seemingly on its own, over the driver's windshield where Yousef, face betraying his shock, was slower to react, cell phone falling from his open hand as he wrestled with his seat belt. The glass spiderwebbed as I opened fire, obscuring my target. Uncertain as to his fate, I continued firing, pumping round after round through the car. The slide locked back empty. The spent magazine struck the ground as I automatically speed-reloaded.

I had done this kind of thing a few times.

Carl's white van careened wildly into the alley, locked up the brakes and narrowly stopped inches from the car's bumper. "Down! Down!" he screamed out the window, creating a weird off-time effect as my radio earpiece repeated it a millisecond later. Without hesitation I flung myself into the garbage. The muzzle of a Galil SAR extended from the van's window as Carl fired over my head. The cracks of the .223 were ear-splitting compared to my 9mm.

Rolling over, I could see dust and debris spraying from the club's rear exit. The guard I had kicked a moment ago was sliding limply down the door frame, already on the way to his seventy-two-virgin welcoming committee.

"Let's get out of here!" Carl shouted. I scrambled to my feet, grabbed the case, and ran past the shot-up car, keeping my gun up, scanning for threats, and pulled myself into the already moving van. We sped off into the streets, Carl's beady eyes flickering rapidly back and forth, looking for cops. I reholstered my gun and watched as my hands began to shake.

"Did you get the computer?"

"Yeah, I'm fine. Didn't get hit. Thanks for asking," I replied.

He rolled his eyes. I opened the case, and inside was

the unharmed laptop. So at least we hadn't screwed *everything*. Months of planning and preparation, Phase One almost done, Phase Two ready to go, and all screwed because some mystery person whacks *my* target in public. *Damn it. Damn it*. Could we still pull this off? We had to. We sure couldn't afford to fail.

I closed my hand into a fist as the trembling continued. I was going to figure out who screwed us, and I was going to make them pay.

Chapter 5:
Grand Theft Auto

VALENTINE

"Nightcrawler, Xbox, this is Control, report! Give us a status update!" Anita sounded anxious over the radio.

"We're fucking busy right now!" Tailor snapped. We quickly moved down the two flights of stairs and out the back door of the building. We stopped at the fence. Tailor went through the hole we'd cut first, his carbine pointing to our left, up the alley. I followed, pointing the heavy SR-25 to our right. I was startled when four muffled shots rang out; one of the bodyguards had come around the corner, and Tailor had cut him down. The man crumpled to the ground, his MP5K clattering on the pavement.

Moving quickly, I opened the door of our truck, an extended-cab Toyota pickup, and tossed my gear onto the backseat. I then climbed into the driver's seat. Tailor jumped into the passenger's seat. I put the pickup into gear and stepped on the gas.

"Look out!" Tailor yelled. The bodyguards' Range

Rover had pulled into the alley ahead, blocking our exit. They got out and started shooting. Worse, the alley wasn't wide enough to turn around in. Swearing aloud, I threw it into reverse and stomped on the gas.

We backed down the alley entirely too fast. Tailor fired through the windshield, his suppressed rifle hissing and snapping loudly in the passenger cabin. The enemy took cover behind their truck and returned fire. Several stray rounds peppered the front of our vehicle.

Scrunching down, hoping the engine block would provide me with protection, I tried to navigate the Toyota down the alley in reverse by using my side mirror. Rounds came whizzing through the windshield. I hit the walls five or six times, smashing through garbage cans and terrifying stray cats. Seconds later, Al Falah's bodyguards piled back into their truck and started down the alley after us.

We exploded onto the main road, still in reverse, and were nearly broadsided by a minibus. I cut the wheel to the right and stomped on the brakes. Cars swerved around us, horns screaming as they went. I put the pickup back into drive and hit the gas. We got moving just as Al Falah's men made it onto the street.

I sped along, having turned the wrong way to use our preplanned egress route. They were in close pursuit. At that time of the night, the roundabouts in Zubara were clogged with traffic. I didn't want to get in a gunfight in the middle of a traffic jam, too many bystanders, too many witnesses. I hung a quick right, turning down a narrow side street. Such streets in the city had one lane going each way, with a small roundabout at each intersection. In the middle was a raised concrete divider, almost like a sidewalk, making left turns difficult.

The street was mercifully free of traffic, but within seconds, Al Falah's men began firing at us again. Rounds entered through the back window and hit the tops of our seats. Tailor and I were hunkered down about as far as we could go.

"Will you please shoot *back*?" I screamed. He turned around, twisting to his left, and returned fire through what was left of the back window. Hot brass peppered me in the side of the head. I flinched and almost went off the road. "Be careful!"

As Tailor swore at me, we came to the first roundabout. My heart fell into my stomach as I realized a large truck full of sheep had broken down in the middle of it, blocking the road. Several cars were stopped around it. There was no way past. At the last instant, I cut the wheel to the right. The Toyota bucked as we jumped onto the sidewalk. I had to swerve again to avoid hitting a planted palm tree. It was hard to see clearly; the windshield was full of bullet holes and was covered in a spider's web of cracks.

I laid on the horn as terrified pedestrians jumped out of our way. Clear of the traffic jam, I swerved back to the left, ripping off the truck's passenger-side mirror on another palm tree as we landed back on the street. The pursuing Range Rover was right behind us now. Two men were leaning out of the windows, firing at us with pistols. I snarled in pain as a round clipped my right shoulder, causing me to almost lose control of the truck. The sudden swerving of the vehicle made Tailor drop his spare magazine as he was trying to reload.

To hell with this, I thought. "You buckled?"

"What? Why?" Tailor shouted back. I floored the brake pedal.

The Range Rover smashed into the back of our truck, crumpling the bed and tailgate. Our perforated rear window shattered completely. The big SUV considerably outweighed our little pickup. We fishtailed to the left; the Range Rover went on and crashed into a parked car.

Our ride was trashed, but we were stopped, and we were alive.

Dazed, I unbuckled myself, opened the door, and literally fell to the pavement. I somehow managed to get to my feet and looked over at our pursuers. The driver and the front passenger hadn't been wearing seat belts. They appeared injured or dead. The airbags had deployed.

I looked around. Cars drove by, slowing down to gawk at the wreck. We didn't have much time. With my left hand, I swept my jacket to the side and drew my revolver. I brought the gun up, pointing it at the Range Rover, but pain shot through my right shoulder as I attempted a two-handed hold. I remembered then that I was bleeding, and was suddenly aware of the pain. Holy *crap* did it hurt. I winced, but continued on, holding my .44 Magnum one-handed.

Approaching the SUV carefully, I looked for signs of movement. I stumbled as I walked, and couldn't hear very well. The driver begin to stir behind his airbag. He tried to open his door, but it crunched up against the smashed tailgate of our pickup.

He didn't see me. I fired. A fat .44 slug tore through

his head, splashing the airbag with blood. I fired again, putting a bullet into the passenger. He looked dead, but I wanted to be sure.

There was a third man in the backseat. He sat up, obviously dazed. There was a cut on his forehead; blood was pouring down his face. He placed his hand on his head as he came to, not noticing me at first, but he froze when he saw the big .44 leveled at him. His eyes went wide. My hand was shaking. I could hear sirens in the distance. We had to go. We weren't supposed to leave witnesses. I pulled the trigger again. The terrorist disappeared behind the door in a small puff of blood.

My ears were ringing. My heart was pounding. I was injured. *The Calm* had worn off, and I was half in shock. I took a deep breath, reloaded, then holstered my revolver. I moved to the passenger's side door of our pickup. Tailor was starting to come around, but he was in a daze.

"C'mon, bro, we gotta split," I said. "Cops are coming."

"Yeah . . . yeah . . . okay . . . You get 'em?"

"I think so. C'mon, let's go!" I grabbed the SR-25 and its carrying case from the backseat. My shoulder screamed in protest as I hefted the rifle, but I didn't have time to worry about it. Tailor stumbled and nearly fell down but was able to retrieve his backpack, his carbine, and the spare magazine he'd dropped onto the floor of the truck. We then hurried away from the scene of the crash, heading up the street a short way before turning into a narrow alley.

Rounding the corner, we were immediately illuminated

by headlights. *Oh, hell.* The vehicle, a small French Renault, came to a stop just under a streetlight. I could see the driver. He appeared to be a Westerner.

Not sure what to do, I leveled the SR-25 at the Renault. "Get out of the car!" The man hesitated, then raised his hands, seemingly in shock. I squeezed the trigger. The suppressed rifle cracked thinly in the night air, and the Renault's left-side mirror exploded as a 175-grain match bullet tore through it. "Now!" I ordered. The driver stepped out of the vehicle. I lowered my rifle and moved toward him. "I'm sorry," I said without looking at him. "We need your car."

"Bloody hell! Just take it! Don't shoot!" He was British.

Tailor stepped up to him. "Drop your cell phone," he said levelly, even though he still looked a little wobbly.

"Are you mad? You're taking my car, do you have to take my bloody mobile, too?"

I'm not going to repeat the swath of obscenities that Tailor let out at that point, but an instant later the unlucky British man dropped his phone onto the ground. Tailor stomped on it, smashing it.

"Get out of here!" he yelled. The terrified man ran off down the street.

"You drive," I said.

"Why?"

"I'm *bleeding*, that's why!" I said as I tossed my weapon into the little French car's backseat.

"Fine," he said. We got in, Tailor put the car in gear, did a three-point turn in a narrow driveway, and we took off down the alley, away from the crash scene, just as the police arrived.

LORENZO

We drove south toward our apartment. After a few minutes I was positive that nobody was after us. Our vehicle was as bland and common as could be had in this city, even though Carl had worked it over so that we had some speed on tap if necessary.

Carl's Portuguese accent was a lot more pronounced when he was enraged. "Everybody knows Falah's dead. We're screwed!" he bellowed as he slammed his fist into the steering wheel. His eyes flickered back to the mirror as the sound of a siren went behind us, but it was heading for the scene of the crime and not our way. He continued, slightly calmer. "What now?"

"Pull over." My mind was racing. The mission depended on making Al Falah disappear. "Nobody has to know he's dead."

"And how're we supposed to do that, genius?" Carl pulled us into the lot of the Happy Chicken on Bakhun Street and parked the van behind a brand new Audi A8.

I got on the radio. "Reaper. Come in."

"Gotcha, boss."

"You've got the police band. Figure out where they're taking Falah."

Carl's eyes studied me in the rear-view mirror. "You've got to be shittin' me . . . No. You're not," he sighed. "We're gonna die."

"Eventually."

Reaper was back in a matter of seconds. "Security

forces are freaking out. How many people did you guys kill down there?" I looked at Carl and held up two fingers. He gave me one back, but he used his middle finger. "Never mind. Ambulance is en route to the hospital in Ash Shamal under police escort."

I glanced back the way we had come. The hospital was just off Bakhun, which was the major four-lane through this peninsula. The ambulance would have to pass us. We could still intercept them. "Reaper, I want you to flood their emergency system with calls. Give them a bunch of shooters randomly killing people at the *north* end of Ash Shamal," I ordered. Carl looked at me in confusion. "Let's see what we can do about that police escort." Zubara was a relatively quiet city by this part of the world's standards. If they just had a bunch of people get popped in the district, they would be quick to jump at another call.

"Too late." Carl glanced back. "I hear sirens. Here comes the ambulance."

Through the window, I saw a pudgy, well-dressed Zubaran approaching the Audi with a sack of fast food in hand. He raised his key fob, and the car's alarm beeped. "I've got an idea."

There was no time for subtlety. I slid open the van door and hopped out. I could hear the sirens now, too. They would be passing by any second. The driver of the Audi was just sitting down as I caught the closing door with my body. He looked up in surprise and started to say something. I grabbed the keys from his hand, slugged him hard in the mouth, and jerked him onto the pavement.

The Audi started right up with a purr. I slammed it into gear and roared out of the parking lot. A dozen cows had given their lives for this interior. "Nice car," I muttered as I shifted into second. Oncoming traffic had to stomp the brakes to avoid hitting me, then I was out on the road, northbound, the GPS told me in Arabic.

On the other side of the divider a police car zipped by, blue lights flashing, heading south. Right behind it was the ambulance. Zubaran emergency vehicles used that obnoxious European-style siren. I grabbed the radio. "Carl, I'll take the cop car. Run the ambulance off the road!" I shouted as I cranked the wheel and gunned it over the mound of dirt that served as the divider. German cars have great suspension but I still managed to almost bite my tongue off as I crashed onto the southbound lane. I hastily put my seat belt on. The GPS told me I had just done something very bad.

Drivers in this part of the world didn't pull off to the side for emergency vehicles. If you're dying in the Middle East, don't do it during rush hour. Traffic here was a constant battle of wits and honking horns. The ambulance was weaving between cars ahead of me. A Toyota tore off my passenger-side mirror, and the driver honked. Revving the powerful engine, I was doing sixty by the time I passed the ambulance. The police car, some little Euro sedan, was right ahead of me. The Audi pulled alongside effortlessly.

The cops glanced over in confusion. The look here for security forces was Saddam Hussein-style mustaches and big mirrored shades. I drifted right into them, slamming into their side, shoving them hard to the right. The cops started yelling, and the passenger was going for his gun. I drifted left a bit, then swerved back with more energy, smashing the hell out of their little car.

The driver overcorrected, turning too far to the side, and the car spun out of control in a haze of rubber smoke before crashing violently into the rear end of a parked SUV. I applied the brakes and came to a smooth stop.

The cop car was at an angle, sideways, half on top of the other vehicle. Those guys wouldn't be causing me any trouble for a bit. I could see the flashing lights of the ambulance as it slowed to a crawl behind me. Stepping on the clutch, I shifted into reverse. "Carl, where are you?"

"Right behind the ambulance," he replied.

"Hit the brakes," I said as I stomped on the gas. Even in reverse this car was pretty damn quick. I braced myself as the Audi's trunk collided with the front of the still-moving ambulance. My world came to a violent lurching halt. The rear window shattered and glass ricocheted around the cab as the air bag knocked the shit out of me.

It took me a blurry second to get the seat belt unbuckled and to collapse out the door into the street. Got to hand it to those Germans, they crash test their stuff really well. I staggered to my feet and pulled my gun. It wasn't necessary though. The ambulance crew were groggily moving, knocked silly by the impact. The siren was still wailing.

Carl was at the back of the ambulance, dragging Al Falah's corpse out. The cars around us had stopped, and there had to be at least a dozen eyes on us. I limped around the back to help. "Hurry up," Carl grunted as he pulled the limp body toward our van. I grabbed his legs and lifted. He weighed a ton. We got to the van and tossed him inside, I was in right behind.

The van's tires squealed as Carl got us out of there.

VALENTINE
Al Khor District, Safe House 4
March 26
2355

Tailor and I were surprised to find Gordon Willis waiting
for us back at the safe house. As before, the big guy
named Anders was with him, giving us a hard stare but not
saying a word. Suffice to say, Gordon wasn't happy. The
two of us sat on folding chairs in the middle of the big
house's living room while Hal, one of our medics, worked
to patch us up. I was sitting there, shirtless, as Hal worked
on the wound on my shoulder. All while Gordon royally
bitched us out.

It turned out Gordon's cool demeanor came unraveled
when he was mad. It was a little amusing to see the
smooth-talking slickster sputtering and raising his voice.
Yelling didn't really suit him. He wasn't unhappy about Al
Falah; we'd done quite well in that regard. As we
described what happened, I could see the anger in his
eyes. We failed to kill the secondary target Khalid. We lost
our vehicle and had to exigently acquire a new one. Worst
of all, we were *seen*.

I honestly don't know what the hell he expected. We
were ordered to do the hit in public in the middle of the
city; of *course* it was going to make noise. I thought that
was the *point*.

Looking over at Tailor, I could tell he was kind of
tuning Gordon out too. As Gordon blathered on about

operational security and his expectations of us, Hunter stood quietly in the corner. Sarah leaned against the wall behind him, looking at me with an expression on her face that I couldn't read. I wondered what she was thinking. One of Hunter's security men stood by the door, giving Anders the stink eye.

After a few minutes of ass-chewing, Gordon visibly shifted gears, and the slickness returned. He plopped down on the couch across from Tailor and me and began to speak once more as I put my T-shirt back on.

"Well, what's done is done," Gordon said, straightening his tie. I wondered why in the hell he was wearing a suit. "Now we need to focus on the next mission. I need you two to be ready to move on this in a few days."

Tailor and I looked at each other. I *was* able to read the expression on his face. I had a bad feeling too. "What's the next mission, sir?" I asked.

"Ms. . . . uh . . . McAllister, right? Ms. McAllister, would you hand them the mission packets, please?" Sarah rolled her eyes and stepped forward, handing out manila envelopes to each of us.

"Your next mission will be pretty simple, boys. You're going to return to the social club you snatched the younger Al Falah from and clean it out. The other two men in your chalk . . . um . . ."

"Wheeler and Hudson," I interjected, my voice flat.

"Yes, Weiner and Hudson," Gordon replied, "will be rejoining you for this one. It'll be a straight-up enter-and-clear. Are you up to it?"

I sighed and looked over at Tailor. He nodded at me, ever so slightly. "What's the plan, sir?" I asked after a moment. Tailor and I listened as Gordon went over the plan. He droned on for a long time. The man sure liked listening to himself talk. He asked us if we had any questions.

"When do we roll on this?" I asked.

"In the next few days," Gordon said. "Word will be sent down soon, so be ready to go on short notice. Anyway, gentlemen, I need to get going." Gordon stood up. Tailor and I followed suit. Gordon shook my hand vigorously, squeezing tightly, then did the same to Tailor. He then nodded at Anders, and the two of them strode out of the room.

"You heard the man, boys," Hunter said after Gordon was out of earshot. "Be ready. The order to move will come down without much warning. You're going to be operating at a high tempo for the time being. I need you boys to stay sharp. No alcohol, no sneaking off, nothing that will slow you down, until further notice. Tailor, I need you and Valentine to plan your routes to and from the target building, including contingency plans. I trust things will go smoother this time?"

"It would've went smoother if we'd had some backup," Tailor said.

Hunter shook his head. "Gordon had the rest of your chalk on a wild goose chase. We sent a dozen men to hit a building, and no one was even home. Complete waste of time, unlike your next job, where I can promise you'll have a target-rich environment."

"Roger that, Colonel," Tailor said.

"Outstanding." Hunter turned to the medic. "Hal, you're coming with me. Singer's chalk is coming back from a mission tonight, and they've got some injuries. The doctor could use your help."

Hal nodded and began to pack up his jump bag. "Valentine, make sure you change that bandage in the morning," he told me. "I'll check you out when you get back to the fort."

"Sarah, do you want to come back to the compound tonight, or do you want to come back tomorrow?" Hunter asked.

"I, uh, need to pack my stuff, Colonel," Sarah said, seemingly surprised by the question.

"That's fine," Hunter said. "You can ride back to the fort in the car that brings Hudson and Wheeler here. Let's go, Conrad," he said, addressing his security escort. It was the first time I'd heard him name one of his bodyguards.

After a few moments, Hal finished packing up his bag and shouldered it. With that, Hunter, his security, and the medic left, leaving the three of us alone in the big house. Sarah flopped down on the couch where Gordon had been sitting.

"This isn't looking as good now," I said after a long moment.

"At least we'll have full chalk this time," Tailor said. "What happened today was *bullshit*."

"What are you going to do?" Sarah asked.

"What can we do?" I said. "We're going to do the mission and hope we don't get killed."

"I don't know about y'all, but I'm going to *bed*," Tailor said, standing up. Without another word, he disappeared up the stairs, leaving Sarah and me alone in the dimly lit living room. I stood up and sat down next to her on the couch. The metal folding chair was making my butt hurt, and I was still sore from the crash.

"Where'd you get the tattoo?" she asked, breaking the awkward silence after a few moments. She'd seen it while I'd had my shirt off. "Were you in the military?"

"Air Force."

"Really? Me, too. What did you do?"

"Security Forces. You?"

"Radio Communications Systems. I cross-trained as a Cryptologic Linguist after four years. Did three years of that after a year at the DLA," Sarah said, referring to the Defense Language Academy in California.

"So that's how you speak Arabic," I said. Sarah nodded. "Hell, I was all proud of myself for learning *Spanish*. And I only did that after all the time I spent in Central America."

"In the Air Force?"

"Uh, no. I was in Afghanistan for six months, but I got out after that. I was hired by, um, a contractor, after that."

"You did construction?"

"No, not that kind of contractor. I worked for Vanguard."

Everyone had heard of Vanguard. We'd been in the news a lot last year. "You were a *mercenary?*" she asked incredulously.

"Basically," I said. "Tailor hooked me up here. How 'bout you?"

"I . . . This is embarrassing, but I ran into some financial problems. I had this boyfriend that . . . well, he was an asshole. Basically, he spent all of my money, ran up my credit cards, stuff like that. He got into drugs. I tried to help him. Before it was over, my credit was ruined. The cops arrested him, found his cocaine in my apartment. I lost my security clearance. My career was over. I got out last year. There's plenty of work out there for people with my background. Almost none for people who can't get a clearance, though."

"So how'd you end up here?"

"I was living in a crappy apartment, working a crappy job, when I was contacted with this offer. How could I refuse? A chance to go do something again, to use the skills I learned."

"And make a pile of money while you're at it," I suggested.

"Obviously," she said, smiling again. "I don't know why I'm telling you all this. You're easy to talk to. So, where'd you get the tattoo?"

"What? Oh. I got it in Nevada." I turned toward her and rolled up my left sleeve, showing her the tattoo on my shoulder. It was a skull clutching a switchblade knife in its teeth. It had the words "Abandon All Hope" written around it. "It was after we got back from Bosnia. This is the Switchblade logo."

"Switchblade?" Sarah asked. "Didn't you just say you worked for Vanguard?"

"Vanguard Strategic Solutions International," I said. "But the Switchblade teams were the best the company had. We were the lifers. Most guys worked short-term contracts, six months to two years. A few of us stayed full-time. We got better training, better benefits, better equipment, and much better pay."

"Sounds good," Sarah said, sounding unconvinced.

"It was dangerous as hell," I said honestly. "But my team was lucky. We did really well. Then Mexico happened."

"You were there?" Sarah asked. "During the fighting, I mean?"

"You could say that. Our last mission was an absolute clusterfuck. We lost . . ." I trailed off for a second. "Well, we lost damn near everybody. Our chopper was shot down in Cancun, and the UN came after us."

"Wait, what? Why?"

I paused for a moment. "It's . . . complicated."

It must have been obvious I didn't want to talk about it. "I'm sorry," Sarah said. "How are you feeling? You had a pretty rough night tonight." She lightly placed her hand on my leg.

"I'm . . . fine," I said, my heart rate suddenly increasing.

"I was worried about you." She didn't break eye contact.

"This isn't the first time I've been shot. I got lucky. This will heal up okay. It'll just be another scar," I answered, obviously full of shit.

"Whatever you say, Mr. Tough Guy," she said, that devilish grin appearing on her face again. A moment later, the smile faded. She stared into my eyes for what seemed like a long time, her mouth open slightly. "Hi," she said, leaning in a little bit closer. The tone in her voice was ever-so-slightly different now. Then she leaned forward and kissed me, *hard*.

"Sarah, I—"

"Just relax," she whispered, her mouth inches from mine. "It'll be fun. I promise." This had all come out of nowhere. I was so dense about stuff like this and was never much of a ladies' man. I wasn't sure what to do. But as Sarah pushed me back onto the couch and climbed on top of me, it became pretty clear what *she* wanted to do. I wasn't about to argue.

LORENZO
March 26

Reaper was clicking away madly, his Rob Zombie T-shirt stained with energy drink, head bobbing back and forth rhythmically to whatever was on his iPod as he glared at the gibberish on Falah's laptop screen.

"He looks kinda like a *galinha* when he does that," Carl said from the kitchen table. Then he moved his head back and forth, except Carl had no rhythm to speak of, and no neck, either, so it was more like he moved his face back and forth in a very poor imitation of the scarecrow-like Reaper.

"He does have that chicken vibe going on," I replied as I moved the ice pack to a different spot on my face. That airbag had really clocked me. As soon as the swelling went down enough, I was going to go shave. The police were already looking to question Khalid about today's events. Too bad he no longer existed.

"I can still hear you guys," Reaper said without looking up from his multiple screens. He had been engrossed in those since we had gotten back.

"How?" I asked incredulously. I could hear the metal coming out of his earpieces from across the room. That mystery was going to go unanswered as Reaper suddenly pumped his fist in the air.

"Cracked it!"

Thank goodness. This was big, but I had faith that Reaper could do it. "Well, that's a little anticlimactic," I said. Carl grunted in agreement and popped open another beer. It wasn't that you couldn't get alcohol in Muslim countries; you just had to know where to look. "Me crashing a hundred-thousand Euro car was way cooler."

Reaper yanked out the earpieces. "I'm in. I've got everything. His password protection was pathetic. I own you, punk-ass bitch! Ha!" he shouted like he had just won a multiplayer death match rather than broken into a terrorist financier's personal files.

I approached and stood over Reaper's shoulder. "Look for anything on Adar. We need his contact info. If it isn't under Adar, look for the Butcher. It's time for Al Falah to call his pet psycho home."

I called the Fat Man at the number provided in the folder from Thailand. I'd already had Reaper take a shot at figuring out where it originated, but it was even more secure than my personal communications, bounced off of who knew how many satellites and scrambled in every way imaginable.

The Fat Man knew who it was before I even spoke. "Hello, Mr. Lorenzo. How goes it?"

"Phase One is complete. We've implemented Phase Two," I said.

"I shall pass that on to our employer. We had heard that there had been a few complications." His voice was without inflection. He wouldn't even give me a clue if he had just woken up or if it was late at night. Nobody even knew what time zone Big Eddie was in. "Nothing you couldn't handle, I assume."

"Of course not."

"By the way, some of our men attended your niece's dance recital. Rachel, I believe her name was. Let's see, she belongs to your brother, Robert. They recorded the recital for Big Eddie. He commented that she is very graceful and talented for such a young girl."

"I told you. I'll *do* the job," I stated.

"Of course you will. Eddie just likes to keep track of his employees. It is what makes him such an effective leader. Keep up the good work." Then he hung up. I carefully put my phone away before smashing my fist into the wall.

Chapter 6:
From Sea to Shining Sea

VALENTINE
Ash Shamal District
April 1
2005

"*Xbox, this is Shafter,*" Hudson said over the radio, breathing hard. "*We're in position.*"

Tailor looked over at me. I nodded, and he spoke into his radio. "Copy that. Stand by. Control, Xbox, we're standing by."

"*Xbox, Control,*" Sarah said, sounding as calm and distant as ever. "*Execute. Be careful,*" she added, her voice softening just a bit.

I smiled to myself. "This is going to be a turkey shoot," I said, observing our target building through binoculars one last time. "You think they'd have beefed up security after we snatched the Al Falah kid out here."

"They did," Tailor corrected. "Look. That guy right there, he's got a rifle."

"What is that, a G3?" I asked absentmindedly. "Look, another guy in the doorway. Looks like he's got a sub-gun."

"I think they're wearing vests," Tailor said. He patted the driver on the shoulder. "Let's go. Shafter, Ginger, stand by to execute. When you hear shooting, enter and clear. Watch for friendlies—we'll be coming in from the other side."

Hudson acknowledged. Our driver, a guy from another chalk that everyone called Animal, flipped on the headlights and stomped on the gas. Our up-armored van roared down the narrow street toward the social club.

The little side street had several cars parked on either side. Tonight was the most popular night, and it seemed that the disappearance of Al Falah hadn't deterred the enemy from using the place. The two armed clowns outside wouldn't pose a problem. Our plan was laughably simple: take out the two armed guards outside, then enter and kill every son of a bitch in the place. Tailor and I would enter from the front, while Hudson and Wheeler would enter from the rear. The rear door led down into a basement, where we believed there might be a weapons cache. Animal was going to stay with the van. He was from Singer's chalk; he'd been hurt and couldn't run, but he could still drive.

The terrorist with the G3 rifle was meandering up the street, checking the parked cars when he was illuminated by our headlights. I saw him clearly; he was wearing black fatigues, a ski mask, a blue body-armor vest, and a chest rig for spare magazines. He looked pretty squared away, and our van's windshield probably wouldn't stop direct hits from a 7.62x51mm weapon.

That didn't deter Animal. He swerved the van right at the terrorist. I braced myself. The man in the black fatigues dodged to the left. He wasn't fast enough. Our heavy, armored van came to a stop with a crunch of twisting metal and shattering glass. The little Toyota sedan we hit crumpled and was pushed up onto the curb. The man in black was pinned between our van and the Toyota, his legs and hips crushed.

"Move, move!" Tailor shouted, pulling the van's right-side door open. I shouldered the paratrooper SAW I was carrying and headed for the door. I heard two quick shots as Animal leaned out the window and blasted the pinned terrorist with his .45. I ignored it as I ripped off a short burst at the man guarding the door, my machine gun roaring loudly in the narrow alley. The 5.56 mm bullets punched through him, splattering blood on the wall behind. He was so surprised he hadn't even gotten his weapon ready.

I came up to the door. Tailor was right behind me. Stepping over the body, I reached forward and yanked the door open just as a long rattle of automatic fire could be heard from behind the building. I held the door open, and Tailor tossed in a pyrotechnic distraction device. We would've used grenades, but we didn't know where Hudson and Wheeler were. A couple seconds later the device detonated, blasting the room with a head-splitting concussion.

Tailor and I stormed inside, weapons at the ready. The doorway dog-legged around into a main room. We rounded the corner. The social club was in chaos. Men were running in every direction, shouting and screaming in Arabic.

Billiards tables lined one wall, and couches lined the other. The air stank of smoke from cigarettes, hookahs, and our flash-bang. Terrorist propaganda and Islamic flags were plastered all over the walls.

Men ran toward us, trying to get out of the building. They were either too confused and didn't realize we were there, or thought we were their own armed guys. It didn't really matter. I leveled my machine gun and squeezed the trigger.

It was a massacre. Tailor and I moved laterally across the main room, firing at anything that moved. A door burst open and a pair of men came running in, armed with assault rifles, but we cut them down before they even realized what was happening. The crowd of terrorist recruits turned, trying to escape down the stairs, tripping over overturned chairs, bodies, and each other as they fled. It didn't do them any good.

"We're in the basement," Wheeler said over the radio. The men trying to flee out the back entrance were gunned down as they came upon Wheeler and Hudson.

The whole thing was over in a matter of minutes. I stood amongst the carnage in the social club, pulling a fresh belt of ammunition onto my weapon's feed tray. The machine gun in my hands was hot to the touch; I'd gone through a hundred-round belt in less than two minutes. Probably two dozen bodies lay on the floor, ripped apart by gunfire. The air stank of powder, smoke, and death.

Tailor lit a cigarette, his carbine dangling from its sling. "April fool, motherfuckers," he said, snapping his Zippo lighter shut. My hands started to shake. *The Calm* was wearing off, and soon I'd be hit with a flood of emotions as adrenaline dump shocked my system.

The only people we'd let out of the building alive were three Indonesian girls Hudson and Wheeler found in the basement. They were drugged up and had been used as playthings by the terrorist recruits. We found a weapons cache also. AK-103 assault rifles and GP-30 grenade launchers from Russia. G3 rifles from Iran and Pakistan. Rocket-propelled grenades and launchers from China. Thousands and thousands of rounds of ammunition. So we dumped some gas, popped a thermite grenade, and burned it all.

As we hurried outside, we noticed that the air reeked of gasoline. In the few minutes we were inside, Animal had kept himself busy by dousing all of the cars parked on the street with gas. As we backed down the street, Hudson tossed a road flare out of the van, igniting the gas and setting the whole row of cars ablaze, just like the building.

The fire quickly spread to the neighboring warehouses. Before long, the entire block was engulfed in flames. It took the city firefighters all night to put the inferno out. In the morning, they found an Ace of Spades playing card stuck to a light pole at the end of the street. Our little calling card been Colonel Hunter's idea. I liked it.

LORENZO
April 10

I stood on the balcony of our apartment. It was part of a complex at the south end of the city, near the intersection of old world and new money, oil-rich and third world poor. The compound itself was relatively modern, but more importantly, it was landscaped in such a way that we had quite a bit of privacy. We had some university students sharing one wall, and an old couple below us, but they all kept to themselves. We entered only through the attached garage, and that was in a van with tinted windows. The ID I had used to set up the lease was a top-of-the-line forgery of a Zubaran Oil Ministry employee who worked weird hours, and our only paleface, Reaper, never went outside anyway. We might as well have been invisible.

The balcony was where I came to contemplate. Every wall inside our hideout had something mission related tacked up, as I had to memorize a lot of facts and faces, but that could get obnoxious after a while. I had brought the manila folder from Thailand with me and had been absently flipping through the photos. It had been a long time since I had seen most of those people, and I had never met any of the kids, and now they were all going to die if I didn't play my cards right.

Over the last few weeks there had been shootings, bombings, and all manner of craziness. Normally Zubara was a quiet place, but now there were blue uniformed SF troops on every corner, and random checkpoints set up by the secret police. There was a war going on, and it was making life difficult for us honest criminals.

I suppose I could call myself an honest criminal. I had tried being a regular criminal, but I found that I didn't have the stomach to lie to and steal from normal folks. Terrorists on the other hand had lots of money, were fun to lie to, and nobody seemed to mind when I occasionally

killed them. And it was easier to sleep at night since I was
able to convince myself that I used my sociopathic
tendencies for good. *Mostly*.

The local news was full of stories about random
murders and disappearances. Somebody was going down
a checklist of the Zoob's terrorist underworld like a bad
issue of *The Punisher*, and the worst part was that we had
no idea who it was. The word on the street was that it was
the emir's secret police killing men loyal to General Sabah,
but from what I had seen, this was too professional for
those thugs. My money was on the Israelis, but even that
didn't make any sense. The hits were stirring up the
fundies and talk of revolution was becoming more and
more common. If the emir lost power, then the Izzies
would have yet another oil-rich country hating them and
funding Hezbollah and that struck me as a bad thing, but
then again, I had never been the diplomat type.

So if it wasn't the emir, and it wasn't Mossad, who was
raising so much hell in the area? It couldn't be the CIA, as
they were way too obvious. I had no evidence, but I was
sure that whoever had blown Falah's heart out was one of
them. Having some sort of hit squad mowing down the
people that I was supposed to be infiltrating was definitely
screwing with my work. It didn't really matter, though. I
just had to keep a low profile until I could get to Adar.
Piece of cake.

The sliding door opened and Reaper appeared, gangly
and squinting at the sudden brightness. The boy really
needed to get more sun, but that would take him away
from his precious computers and high-speed Internet.

Reaper was an interesting case. He'd been one of those

super-genius kids, awkward and goofy as hell I was sure, and he'd been attending MIT when he was fourteen. When I'd met him six years ago he'd been on the run from the law. Ironically enough, he had the most serious criminal record of my crew. My rap sheet only showed a handful of juvenile offenses whereas Reaper, the child prodigy, had been an overachiever and been indicted for several hundred counts of felony fraud, hacking, and embezzlement before he was old enough to drive.

Time magazine had written a cover story about him. Reaper had used that as his resume when he'd asked to join my crew.

He shuddered. "Man, it's hot."

I chuckled. "Wait until summer. It's barely ninety. How's your machine thingy coming?"

He shrugged. He'd been working on the device for Phase Three for weeks now. His room was covered in bits and pieces of the complicated gizmo. "I thought about going with a low-inductance capacitor bank discharge, but I said hell with it, the explosive pumped flux compression generator will be so much *cooler*."

"You know, I dropped out of high school specifically so I wouldn't have to know what any of those words meant."

"I thought you dropped out to commit a triple homicide."

"Quadruple," I corrected him. "All I need to know is will it work and will it be ready in time?"

I knew it would be. Reaper had an IQ that was off the charts. He could process data like I could languages. "Starfish will be good to go, but we'll need a couple of test runs out in the desert, just to make sure."

"You named it Starfish?" It didn't resemble a starfish,

it looked like a big tube in an aluminum housing. "That's cheesy."

"Cheesy *awesome*," he answered with pride. I'm sure the name had some sort of geeky historical reference. Reaper changed the subject and pointed at the folder in my hand. "You been thinking about your family?"

I shrugged. "A little, you know . . ." In actuality, I was terrified a bunch of my nieces and nephews were going to get shot in the head for something that they didn't even know about, but I couldn't let that show to the kid. He needed me to be sure, indomitable, fearless, all that leadership crap.

Reaper looked slightly embarrassed. "You worried about them?"

"Only if we fail." The rest went unsaid. We both knew what would happen then: Eddie would kill everyone that had ever mattered to us just out of principle. But he hadn't come out here to talk about that. "What've you got?"

"Adar bought the spoofed e-mails. He just wrote back. He's leaving Iraq today. He'll be back in a couple of days."

I nodded. As long as he had the box, everything would be fine, but from everything I had learned, he *always* had the box. It was his prized possession and life-insurance policy. "Good. We'll intercept him at his safe house outside of town."

"You think he's as scary as the rumors make him out to be?" Reaper asked. The word on Adar made him sound like some sort of jihadi Jack the Ripper. If Adar had been born into some other society, he probably would have been a serial killer. But luckily for the young murderer from Riyadh, Falah had recruited him and put his natural talents for cruelty to good use for their cause. "I mean, come on, we've dealt with some crazies, but this guy takes the cake. Dude, he like *eats* people and stuff."

"No big deal." I clapped my young associate on the back. "So he's bug-nuts crazy and I get to kill him. I told you this job has some perks."

"There's more," Reaper said. "I just heard on the news, they're evacuating the American embassy. There's a big mob protesting in front of it. The State Department said that all Americans need to leave Zubara right away." His grin exposed a bank of grossly crooked teeth. "I'm guessing that doesn't apply to us."

I hadn't been back in my home country in forever—too many laws, too much order. Life out on the fringe was much more to my liking. "It looks like the Zoob's heating up. Don't worry, we'll be out of here before the place totally melts down."

"I don't know, chief," Reaper said slowly, like he was the one with all the experience. "This shitty little country is important to a lot of powerful folks, shadowy, scary, secret government crazy shit. I wouldn't be surprised if there was a bunch of stuff going down."

Oh, not again. I rolled my eyes. "You've been listening to that conspiracy theory talk-radio show again, haven't you?"

"From Sea to Shining Sea?" Reaper shrugged. "You know, it isn't always just space aliens and Reptoids of the Hollow Earth. Their political analysis is awesome. Way better than the propaganda you get from the regular news. You really should listen. I've got it streaming right now if you want."

I snorted. "If I'm ever commissioned to rob Atlantis, I'll tune in. In the meantime, you worry too much."

"I'm just saying, I got a bad feeling about this is all."

VALENTINE
Fort Saradia National Historical Site
April 11
1230

"Cover me, goddamn it!" Tailor snarled as fire poured onto his position.

"Hang on, hang on," I said. I had a situation of my own to deal with. There were at least four bad guys coming up on my left.

"I need help now or I'm gonna die! Shit. I'm hit!"

I could see where Tailor went down. I started for him, but the distraction cost me. I didn't see the guy with the chainsaw until it was too late.

"Come and save me, damn it."

There was blood everywhere as I was cut in half. "Too late. I'm dead." I tossed the vibrating controller on the couch. Tailor swore at me first and then the Xbox.

The biggest open room on the first floor of the dorms had been turned into the rec room. We'd scrounged up a couple of games, a bunch of free weights, and a dart board. Our chalk was enjoying the break. Wheeler was spotting Hudson, as our big man bench-pressed enormous amounts of weight. Wheeler saw that we were toast and got excited. "About time. Our turn. Wrap it up, Hud."

Hudson grunted as he shoved up three hundred pounds for the ninth time. He was actually scary. "One. More."

"You suck, Val," Tailor whined as his character was curb-stomped to death. "You completely and utterly suck. You sucked so hard you choked on your suck. You suck at horde mode."

I raised an eyebrow. "It's this stupid controller. I hate playing shooters on a console. A keyboard and mouse is superior in every way."

Before Tailor could rebut and begin another nerd argument, Hudson racked the weights and stood up. "Get outta my chair, Tailor." He grinned. "Let me show you how it's done."

"How about me and you play, Hud?" Tailor asked him. "Let these uncoordinated monkeys go play Candy Land or something. Leave the horde to the real men."

"It's my turn," Wheeler insisted. "Just because it's your call sign doesn't mean you can hog it all day. Here, I'll pull all the weights off for you, and we'll see if you can do just the bar. Val, you better be ready to spot so he doesn't drop it on his concave chest and hurt himself."

Tailor flipped them both the bird as he passed over his controller. "Screw you, Wheeler, you soulless ginger. It ain't my fault I want to enjoy the finest recreation that Club Sara-Dia has to offer."

"Saradia," Hudson corrected as he flopped onto the couch. "Say it with me. Saw-radia."

"Sara-*Dia!*" Tailor exclaimed, needlessly accentuating his twang.

"Now you're just messing with me," Hudson muttered.

"What?" Tailor asked. "Sara-Dia."

"Hell, I can't tell if you're Southern or handicapped," Wheeler said. "But I repeat myself."

We were becoming a tight crew. One of the things I'd missed after leaving Vanguard was the camaraderie. It was good to have the R&R time together. Too bad it was temporary.

One of the colonel's security men appeared in the doorway. "Tailor, Valentine, Mr. Willis needs to speak to you right away." He didn't even wait for the response.

Tailor groaned. "Oh, what now?"

"Come on, man." I headed for the door. "This is why we're paid the medium bucks."

"I'm management. I should be getting bigger bucks." Tailor reluctantly followed. He stopped at the doorway to shout at Hudson and Wheeler. "Sara-*Dia*!" Then he ducked around the corner as Wheeler chucked an orange Fanta can at him.

The two of us headed across the courtyard. Tailor seemed to be in a better than normal mood, but shooting people in third-world nations was his element. "How's Sarah doing?"

"She's good," I replied, suspicious. "Why?"

"I bet," he said, smirking. I raised an eyebrow at him. "Val, I know you two are getting it on. She jumped your bones in the safe house, didn't she?"

I chuckled. "As a matter of fact—"

Tailor laughed. "I hope you at least turned the couch cushions over." I felt my face flush, and Tailor laughed at me again. "It's about time, anyway. That girl's been after you since the day you met."

"This whole thing is insane," I said. "I mean, it's

174 *Larry Correia & Mike Kupari*

intense. I feel like a teenager. I don't know how it's going to work out, but—"

"Goddamn it Val, there you go again!" Tailor said, interrupting me. "Quit overthinking it! You always spaz out and scare the girl off."

"When did I ever," I began.

Tailor interrupted me again. "Remember Teresa?"

"Oh . . . right," I said.

"I'm always right," Tailor insisted. I was dubious about that claim, but in this instance he was. Teresa had been a medical assistant with Vanguard, and she was the last woman I'd almost had a relationship with. I more or less pushed her away. I had to give myself credit, though. I was trying *really hard* to avoid doing the same thing to Sarah. "I'm serious. Stop being such a big spaz-girl. I can't have you worrying about some bullshit angst when we're out in the field."

"I'll be fine," I said. Tailor doused his cigarette as we entered the building. Gordon Willis and Colonel Hunter were waiting for us in the classroom.

Gordon greeted us enthusiastically. As always, he was wearing a suit. Anders was there also, leaning against the back wall, looking bored. "Mr. Tailor! Mr. Valentine!" Gordon said, vigorously shaking our hands. "Great to see you boys again. Damn fine work you're doing out there. Your hit on the terrorist recruitment house went off without a hitch. Now, our Zubaran counterparts were pissed that you caused so much collateral damage." Gordon leaned in closer and theatrically lowered his voice. "Off the record, boys, I don't give a shit about that. I'm glad to see you mopping the floor with hajji."

"Wait a minute," Tailor said. "You sure as hell gave a shit *last* time."

"I see where you're coming from, Mr. Tailor. Last time there was some concern that making too big of a splash too soon would cause some of our known targets to go to ground. We were able to keep things under control, and that didn't happen. The plan now is to kick it in high gear, keep hammering the enemy, so they don't have any safe places to hide."

Tailor and I looked at each other. I could tell Tailor wanted to get in Gordon's face, but I shook my head ever so slightly. He just frowned and sat down.

"Have you had a chance to look over your mission packets?" Gordon asked as I took my seat. We hadn't. "Well, I guess that's why we're having this briefing, isn't it?" Gordon said, laughing at his own joke. Tailor and I ignored him and opened our packets. "As you can see, gentlemen," Gordon continued, "we don't have a lot of information on the next target. His name is Adar. We believe that he is originally from Saudi Arabia. We don't know if Adar is his real name. We also suspect that he has ties to the Saudi government, but we're not sure what those ties are."

I looked through my packet as Gordon talked. This guy had spent years running all over Southwest Asia killing American and British soldiers. There was only one photograph, and it was taken from far away. He was a pretty nondescript looking guy, with short hair and a trimmed mustache. He was braced against the cinder block wall, looking out a window, carrying a Russian SVU bullpup sniper rifle affixed with a sound suppressor.

"I've heard of this guy," Tailor said. "Read about him on the Net. They say he's killed over a hundred Americans. The army thinks he's a myth, nothing but terrorist propaganda."

"If only that were the case," Gordon said, doing a very good job of feigning sincerity. "Adar is quite real, and that number is probably accurate. We don't know who he really is, who he works for, or who trained him, but he's a definite threat. Eliminating him will help me prove to my superiors that Project Heartbreaker is a worthwhile cause."

"So we've been able to track him down, then?" I asked.

"Exactly!" Gordon said, sounding upbeat. "He keeps a home in Zubara, in the village of Umm Bab, near the Saudi border."

"So, the US has been trying to find this guy for years, but all of a sudden we find out where he lives? How do we know this information is good?" I asked.

Gordon didn't bat an eye. "Twenty-four hours ago, we intercepted an e-mail from Adar. He's returning to Zubara and will be staying at his house here. However, if it turns out Adar isn't there, we'll just cancel the operation and go back to square one. If the information proves to be accurate, you two are going to go in and kill Adar."

"What? Just the two of us again? What about Hudson and Wheeler? They were assigned to *me*." Tailor was visibly agitated now.

"The operational plan calls for two shooters, Mr. Tailor," Gordon said dismissively. "I wasn't able to get clearance for any more than that."

"Shouldn't this get the priority?" I asked. "I mean, we need to get this guy, right?"

"I'm going to level with you boys," Gordon said, leaning in closer. "My superiors don't consider Adar a priority target. Eliminating him is a way of garnering more support for Project Heartbreaker, especially from people in the Pentagon. I was able to get approval for this operation, but you two are the only ones I was able to commandeer, if you will, to do the job. People in my chain of command have security concerns. It's not that I don't trust you, but . . . well, let's just say that this operation will be a little unorthodox."

I wasn't sure what to think. Gordon sounded sincere, but he *always* sounded sincere. Adar certainly was a worthy enough target; I'd heard of him too. I sure as hell didn't like the sound of *unorthodox* though. "It's not that killing Adar isn't worthwhile, sir," I said cautiously. "It's just . . . look, we almost got killed on our first mission because we were outnumbered. If we'd had Hudson and Wheeler with us, the complications would've been avoided entirely. Because there were just the two of us, we had to improvise."

"And you lost one of my trucks," Hunter growled, speaking for the first time.

"Exactly," I said. "With more eyes on the target, more shooters, we could've wiped out all of Al Falah's bodyguards in a less than a minute. As it was . . . well, things went to shit."

"I understand where you're coming from, Mr. Valentine," Gordon said, looking me in the eye. "I don't like having to take risks like this. But it needs to be done.

This Adar has killed over a hundred American soldiers. Let's *get* this guy. Can I count on you boys?"

Tailor and I looked at each other again. "We'll get the job done, sir," Tailor said.

"Great!" Gordon said, slapping me on the shoulder. I winced as pain shot through my arm; he managed to hit me right where the bandage was. "You boys go ahead and look over those mission packets. There's a lot of information in there. I'll be contacting you as soon as we have confirmation that our target is on the ground." Gordon's cell phone began to ring. "Excuse me," he said, answering it. He left the room with his phone in his ear and Anders in tow.

We waited until we heard the outside door close. "Colonel, you didn't buy any of that horseshit, did you?" Tailor asked. "Isn't there some way we can get more guys for this?"

Hunter's face was a mask. "I'm afraid not, son," he said, turning to leave. "It's not my decision. Wheeler and Hudson will be staying here. You boys relax now, but stay sharp. And don't discuss this with anyone, not even your teammates. You won't get much notice for this one. Don't leave the compound." With that, Hunter left the room, leaving Tailor and me alone.

Chapter 7:
Black Helicopters

VALENTINE
Fort Saradia National Historical Site
April 15
1700

Colonel Hunter and Sarah were waiting for us in the classroom. One of Hunter's security men had come looking for us in the chow hall and ordered us to go in for a briefing.

"Gentlemen, I'm glad you made it," Hunter said, sounding slightly agitated. "I know this is short notice, but you two are rolling out tonight. We believe our target has returned to his compound." Sarah handed each of us a fat new mission packet, full of maps and photographs.

Tailor and I sat down in the classroom, opening our packets as we did so. "Has this Adar guy come back, then, Colonel?" I asked.

"We believe so," Hunter said. He clicked his laptop and a video appeared on the big screen at the front of the room. It was footage from a thermal camera, taken from an aircraft. A pair of SUVs could be seen rolling into a compound. Eight people got out after they stopped.

"This is Adar's place in the village of Umm Bab. It's about fifty kilometers southwest of here. This video was taken fourteen hours ago."

"Wait, what's that?" Tailor said, pointing at the screen. Hunter replayed the segment of the video. It appeared that one of the people was being dragged into the house, struggling.

"We don't know," Hunter said bluntly. "Our boy has an ugly reputation. That individual could likely be his next victim. That's not our problem."

"Where did we get this video?" I asked. "Do we have a drone out there?"

"Yes," Sarah said from the back of the room. "Our, um, support network was able to acquire several UAVs for us."

"We've had UAVs watching Adar's compound since Gordon came and talked to you boys," Hunter said. "Nothing's come up until today. No one has left the compound since this was filmed. You'll be rolling out shortly. Gordon wanted to move sooner, but I told him I wasn't going to try this in broad daylight. You'll have the cover of darkness at least."

"Wait, how do we know that Adar's there, then?" I asked. "Did someone on the ground ID him? Are we just going by this footage?"

Hunter and Sarah exchanged a glance. Hunter then came around the table and leaned against it. He looked tired. "Yes," he said flatly. "Look, boys, I'm not any happier about this than you are. Frankly, I think this whole mission is bullshit. I told Gordon I don't want my men risking their lives on his pet projects when we're running with a skeleton crew to begin with. I was overruled on this one."

"Is there any way we can get more guys, Colonel?" Tailor asked.

"No, Mr. Tailor, there isn't," Hunter replied.

"So how are we going to get there?"

"A truck will be waiting for you by the gate," Hunter said. "First you'll need to go to supply. Get your gear and draw your weapons before you get on that truck."

"Wait, we're going to just *drive* there?" Tailor asked incredulously.

"Don't worry about it, Mr. Tailor," Hunter said dismissively. "Your transportation needs will be taken care of. The organization that has oversight of our little mission has a few assets. Everything else you need to know is in your packets, including aerial photos of the target compound. You'll need to plan your operation while en route."

"What? Colonel," I began.

Hunter cut me off. "This is *not* a democracy, Mr. Valentine!" he barked. "Now get your ass to supply and get kitted up! Move out!" Tailor and I looked at each other, and stood up. Sarah gave me a worried glance as we left the classroom.

VALENTINE
Confederated Gulf Emirate of Zubara
April 15
2045

"Control, Nightcrawler, radio check," I said, squeezing the transmit button on my headset.

"*Read you loud and clear, Nightcrawler,*" Sarah replied, all business.

"Alright, let's go over this one more time," Tailor said, concentrating on one of the aerial pictures of Adar's compound. We were in the back of a large, windowless van driven by Hunter's man, Conrad. He ignored us as we talked. The interior of the van was lit by a red light. "We'll use the assault ladder to hop the wall here," he said, pointing a gloved finger at a spot on the picture.

"Right," I said. "We'll come down behind the shed, here, and stash the ladder there."

"We then move across the compound to the back door, here," Tailor continued.

"Then we enter and clear. As if it's going to be that simple."

"It is that simple. Doing that without getting killed is the hard part."

I leaned in close to Tailor so that Conrad couldn't hear me. "This whole thing is screwed up, dude. We're going to clear a house that we *know* has eight people in it, with just the two of us. We don't know the interior layout. We don't know their security measures. All we know is that one or two guys patrol the yard every half hour or so."

"What I want to know is how we're supposed to get close to the place by just driving up to it," Tailor said. He had a point. The compound was in the middle of the village of Umm Bab. "Too much risk of being seen. Small town like that won't have much traffic at night."

"Well, why don't we ask him, then?" I suggested, nodding my head toward our driver.

"What the hell, why not?" Tailor agreed. "Hey, buddy?"

he said, moving to the front of the van and tapping the driver on the shoulder.

"What is it?" Conrad said, seemingly irritated that we were talking to him.

"How the fuck do you intend to get us to that compound without getting our asses shot off?"

"Yeah," I said, chiming in, "what are we going to do, just drive up to the front gate and hop over it with this gay little ladder they gave us?"

Conrad was visibly annoyed now. "I'm not driving you to the target," he answered curtly. "I don't even know where it is. I don't know what your objective is. I had no idea it was a 'compound' until you two idiots told me. I'm just dropping you off at a predetermined location. Someone else is taking it from there."

"Wait, what?" I asked. "Where are we going from there?"

Conrad sighed. "Again, guys, I *don't know*. I don't *need to know*. I'm just the driver, okay?" He spoke to us like an elementary school teacher lecturing his class. "Maybe you two should just concentrate on whatever it is you're doing back there and let me drive."

"Listen, asshole," Tailor said, his eyes narrowing. Before he could say anything else I put my hand on his shoulder and shook my head. He plopped back down to his seat, flipping Conrad the bird as he did so. "Pissed me off," Tailor muttered as he picked up his packet again.

I leaned back against the wall, rubbing my eyes. We'd been driving for over an hour, and I had no idea where we were. They hadn't issued us much in the way of equipment, either. We were each given a set of fatigues, in the blotchy A-TACS pattern, and body-armor vests.

We wore night-vision goggles up on our heads. The goggles themselves were state of the art and were lighter than any kind I'd used before.

Another piece of equipment I'd never used before was the strange weapon in my hands. "What the hell *is* this thing?" Tailor asked, as if he'd read my mind. We'd each been issued a weird, boxy little .45-caliber submachine gun with a folding stock and a fat suppressor on the end.

"It's a KRISS Vector," I said after a moment. "I read about these in a gun rag. They came out a few years ago." Each of our weapons was painted to match our fatigues and was topped with a holographic sight.

We carried the rest of our gear in pouches on our vests. Tailor had been issued some kind of tactical PDA with a GPS locator built into it. It had the coordinates preprogrammed, as well as a bunch of mission-specific information. I wondered why in the hell they didn't just give us that in the first place instead of bothering to print out the mission packets. My .44 was on my left thigh. I had a feeling I was going to need some luck tonight.

After a seemingly endless drive, the van rolled to a stop. "We're here," Conrad said, looking at us in his rearview mirror. "This is where you two get off. Leave your mission packets in the van." Tailor opened the back doors and climbed out.

"Where are we?" I asked, stepping out after him, slinging the folded assault ladder over my shoulder. The van had pulled off to the side of a long dirt road that cut through the desert. Far off in the distance, I could see the amber glow of Zubara City. The moon wasn't out yet, and the stars were bright overhead.

Conrad shut the van's engine off and killed the headlights. Suddenly it was dead quiet; nothing could be heard except the faint sound of the wind and the rustling of our equipment.

"We're in the middle of nowhere," Tailor said, his face illuminated by the small screen on his GPS. "What the hell? We're even farther from the target than we were at the fort!"

"Hey man, are we in the right place?" I asked, approaching the driver's side door of the van. Conrad had gotten out and was leaning against the van. He reached underneath his 5.11 vest and retrieved a pack of cigarettes.

"We're in the right spot," he said nonchalantly, lighting up. "Your ride will be here shortly. Smoke 'em if you got 'em." Tailor just shrugged, leaned against the van himself, and lit up a cigarette.

Minutes ticked by. None of us spoke. I gazed up into the night sky; it was the first time I'd been able to see the stars since I'd arrived in Zubara. I don't think any of us wanted to ruin the rare quiet moment we were having.

The quiet was suddenly interrupted by a low beeping sound. Conrad pulled out a device that looked like a pager and read the little display. "Your ride is here," he said, putting the gadget back into his pocket. Tailor and I looked around. No lights could be seen on the road. Not a single car had driven by in the few minutes we'd been standing there.

"Where?" I asked. Conrad just shook his head like I was stupid. A moment later, I heard a dull *thwup-thwup-thwup* noise. It sounded like a helicopter off in the distance.

"Is that a chopper?" Tailor asked.

"Something like that," Conrad said. I wondered what in the hell he was being so coy about. I quickly found out. The *thwupping* noise grew louder, but the helicopter still sounded far off in the distance, and it was difficult to tell which direction it was coming from. Then I saw a black shape slowly moving across the sky; the helicopter was a lot closer than it sounded.

"Now, what the hell is *that*?" Tailor asked as the helicopter approached.

"I have no idea," I said. Seeing new and strange things had become the theme of the evening, it seemed. I'm something of an aviation buff. As a matter of fact, I have a private pilot's license. But I'd never seen anything like the machine that was setting down in the desert in front of us.

It wasn't very big, maybe the size of an old Huey. Its hull was painted black and was made up of oddly curved and faceted surfaces. The chopper looked like a bastard love-child of a Huey and the RAH-66 Comanche. It kicked up a cloud of white dust as it touched down onto the bleached, rocky Zubaran desert, but it still was ridiculously quiet. The muted whine of turbine engines could be heard over the dull *thwupping* of the rotor. The rotor blades themselves appeared to be very wide and were oddly shaped.

"It's a stealth helicopter," I said, somewhat in disbelief. There I was, working for a secret government organization, engaged in an honest-to-goodness black operation, and I was about to climb onto a genuine *black helicopter*. I shook my head. Tailor laughed to himself.

The chopper settled onto the desert floor, and an

off-kilter-looking door slid open on the side of the fuselage. The interior cabin was lit with a red light.

"Let's go!" Tailor said, slapping me on the shoulder. He took off toward the chopper at a jog, and I followed. We both crouched down as we approached the aircraft. The unbelievably quiet rotor was still turning. We climbed into the small cabin. A bench was in the middle, with five seats facing outward on each side. As we sat down and strapped ourselves in, the sliding door closed itself.

"Here," the copilot said, reaching back toward me. He was wearing a black flight suit and a helmet with night-vision goggles mounted on it. He handed me a bulky little flash drive. "Updated mission information." I took it from him and handed it to Tailor. Tailor pulled the PDA out of its pouch on his vest and plugged the drive into it. We both studied the screen as the helicopter lifted off, carrying us into the night sky.

I closed my eyes briefly, trying not to think about my *last* ride in a helicopter.

"Thirty seconds!" the copilot said. "We won't touch down." Tailor and I nodded. The stealth helicopter was running dark, flying low over the desert floor toward the village of Umm Bab. We were slowing down now. I unbuckled my seat belt and readied myself.

"We're at the LZ!" the pilot said. The door on the chopper slid open. Cool, dusty desert air rushed in. "Now!" Without replying, Tailor stood up, made his way to the door, and jumped out into the darkness. Following suit, I stepped up to the door, bent down, and jumped out.

We were a little higher up than I thought. I landed

hard, swearing aloud as I flopped onto the rocky desert floor, rolling onto my side. We were so obscured by fine dust that I could hardly see anything. Tailor grabbed me and pulled me upright as the muted sounds of the stealth helicopter faded away. The dust cloud began to settle, leaving us alone in the desert.

"Where are we?" I asked as I quietly chambered a round on my weapon.

"That's Umm Bab over there." He pointed toward the amber lights in the distance. "Control, Xbox," Tailor whispered into his headset. "We're on the ground."

"*Copy that, Xbox,*" Sarah replied. "*Proceed to the target.*" There was some static interference as she spoke. We were a long way from the fort.

"Roger," Tailor replied. "Let's move, Val." Flipping down his night-vision goggles, he took off toward Umm Bab at a fast walk, submachine gun held at the low-ready. I pulled my own NVGs down over my eyes and turned them on. The dark desert was now bright green. The stars overhead were incredibly bright, and the lights of Umm Bab were almost blinding.

I stood up and followed Tailor. I unfolded the stock on my weapon and turned on the holographic sight, setting it for night-vision mode. Carrying the assault ladder on my back, I moved through the darkness in silence. It took us a long time to reach the outskirts of the village. The moon was set to rise at 0122, and we wanted to be out of the open desert before that happened.

Tailor broke into a run and took cover behind a high wall that surrounded a large house. Once he was in place, he signaled for me to follow while he kept a lookout. I quickly ran to him, crouching down next to him against the wall. "Over there," he said. "The target house is just down this street. Follow me to the alley. Watch out for dogs." In Zubara, like many Middle Eastern countries, one could occasionally find packs of feral dogs roaming the streets.

Tailor nodded, stood up, and quietly moved toward the alley. I followed, constantly watching our backs while Tailor led the way. We came to the end of the wall. Tailor leaned around it. He used hand signals to tell me it was clear, then disappeared.

Checking our six one last time, I peeked around the corner. Tailor was a few meters up the alley, crouched behind a large trash bin, waiting for me. I could see no other movement in the alley, and mercifully no lights. The alley itself was narrow, barely wide enough for a truck to drive down. The back walls of compounds lined either side. There was no movement, except for single a black cat trotting along the wall. I signaled for Tailor to advance again. He moved forward, another twenty meters or so, before crouching down in front of a parked pickup truck. The cat took off running and disappeared. Tailor leaned around the vehicle and signaled for me to move forward. In this fashion we leapfrogged toward our target as quietly as possible.

Just after midnight, we arrived behind Adar's compound, in the exact spot we'd picked out from the aerial photos. I began to unfold the ladder, locking it into its extended position. I leaned it up against the ten-foot wall. Tailor and I froze when we heard someone loudly talking in Arabic on the other side of the wall. Tailor mouthed the word *shit.* I whispered that I'd go check it out and began to climb the ladder as quietly as I could.

Reaching the top of the wall, I laid eyes on Adar's compound for the first time. The house was large, square, and made of white stone. A lush garden of palm trees and ferns sat in the middle. There was also a fountain, loudly splashing water into an artificial pond. I was grateful for this as the noise of the water could cover our footsteps.

Below me was the shed, and *directly* below me, leaning against the wall I'd just climbed, was an Arab man wearing a suit. He was smoking a cigarette and talking to somebody on his cell phone. *Shit.*

I turned around and looked down at Tailor. I held up one finger, telling him that there was one guy. I pointed down, indicating his location. I held my hand to my head, mimicking a phone, to tell Tailor what he was doing. Tailor nodded and dragged his finger across his throat. I nodded back.

Turning around again, I shuffled forward onto the top of the wall, as slowly as I could, so as not to make noise. The man was oblivious to my presence. His lit cigarette was as bright as a flashlight through my goggles, and it illuminated him clearly.

I brought my weapon around, being very careful not to let it touch the top of the concrete wall. I waited. I didn't want to interrupt the call, just in case he was talking to somebody who might tip these guys off.

After a moment, he snapped the phone closed. I was ready. Leaning a little bit farther forward, I aimed for the top-rear portion of my target's head, just as he began to walk back to the house. The suppressed submachine gun clicked and hissed as I fired a two-round burst, and the man collapsed to the ground, blood pouring out of the back of his perforated skull. The strange submachine gun had surprisingly little recoil.

I gave Tailor the thumbs-up and took one last look around the compound. There were bright lights on the front of the house but none on the rear. Seeing no movement, I climbed over the wall and dropped ten feet to the ground below. I landed hard in the dirt between the shed and the wall, and my ankle stung a little. I ignored it, ran forward, and grabbed the dead man's feet. As Tailor cleared the top of the wall, I dragged my victim into the darkness behind the shed.

Above me, Tailor carefully maintained his balance while he pulled the ladder up over the wall. He handed it down to me. I held it as he quickly climbed down. Once he was on the ground, he covered the courtyard with his weapon as I laid the ladder down in the dirt behind the shed.

"Control, Nightcrawler, we're inside the compound. Proceeding to the house."

"*Roger that, Nightcrawler,*" Sarah replied, her voice still shrouded in static. "*Is that you behind the shed?*"

"Uh, affirmative," I said.

"*Understood. I see three heat signatures.*"

"One of the tangos," Tailor said. "He's down."

"*Copy that,*" Sarah replied. "*We just got the UAV in place. We'll be providing overwatch.*"

"Roger that. Out." I was happy for the cover of the aerial drone, of course, but I wondered why in the hell they didn't have it there from the get-go.

"Nice work," Tailor said, indicating the dead man. "You see the back door?"

"Yes," I said, peering around the shed. The house was only about fifty feet from our position, but we'd have to bolt across the courtyard and hope we weren't seen.

"I'll cover you."

"Roger," I said, as Tailor positioned himself to cover the courtyard with his weapon. He gave me the high sign when he was ready. "Moving!" I said, and ran toward the house as quickly and as quietly as I could. I was across the courtyard a moment later. I took a knee, and leaned around the corner of the building, covering the courtyard for Tailor. He then ran from the shed to my position, and crouched down next to me.

Together we moved to the back door of Adar's safe house. It was locked.

"Can you pick it?" I asked.

"Probably," Tailor replied, lifting his night-vision goggles up onto his head. I covered him as he pulled out some bump keys and began to work on the door. It wasn't the best lock ever designed, and thankfully the door wasn't dead-bolted. It was open in a few seconds.

I turned off my NVGs and lifted them off my face. Giving my eyes a moment to adjust to the darkness, I nodded to Tailor. We readied our weapons, and Tailor quietly opened the door. It led into a large kitchen, but no one could be seen, and the lights were off. Tailor and I crept inside, silently closing the door behind us.

Music could be heard from the next room. It sounded like a radio or a television, and we could hear men talking in Arabic. We moved through the kitchen, and I risked a peek around the corner into the other room.

It was a living room. Against the far wall was a huge television. Four more men sat around it watching a porno flick. Cheesy music, grunting, and moaning resonated though the house. I looked back at Tailor and told him what was happening through hand signals. Three men were sitting on a couch, facing the television. Their backs were toward us. The fourth sat in a chair off to the side. He'd be able to see us if he looked away from the TV.

Through hand signals, Tailor told me what he wanted to do. Tailor crawled up right next to me, very slowly so as not to make noise, and stood up. We simultaneously leaned around the corner, bringing our weapons to bear. A short burst from Tailor's Vector tore into the head of the man sitting in the chair. Tailor's target slumped forward, his blood pouring down his neck.

At the same time, I put the reticule of my holographic sight on the back of the couch and held down the trigger. The .45 rounds ripped through the couch in puffs of fabric and stuffing. I swept from right to left, stitching bullets across them. The men gasped as bullets tore into them, but they were quickly silenced. Tailor switched targets and emptied the rest of his magazine into the three men as well.

It was over in seconds. They never knew what hit them. We both quickly changed magazines and moved into the living room, doing our best to cover all angles. The men on the couch had been thoroughly ventilated. A few stray rounds had gone into the far wall, but the television was still blaring pornography at an unpleasantly high volume.

A cloud of smoke hung in the room, and the air smelled like burnt powder.

This is too easy, I thought, but I wasn't about to get complacent. Complacency is what had gotten these assholes killed. We still hadn't found Adar, and we knew from the surveillance that three more individuals were in the house.

"Control, Xbox," Tailor whispered. "Main floor clear. Four more tangos down. Sweeping the building now." I could barely hear Sarah's voice. She was drowned in static. Tailor tried again, but he got the same result. Something in the area was interfering with our transmissions.

Tailor pointed up. He proceeded to an ornate staircase, weapon shouldered and at the ready. I followed, constantly swiveling my head around to make sure no one was coming up behind. The top of the stairs revealed a wide hallway, with a few doors on either side. Strange music resonated through the upper level, and it included people chanting in some language that wasn't Arabic. At the end of the hall was a closed door that probably led to the master bedroom.

Tailor started down the hallway, and I followed. Most of the doors on either side were open, and we carefully checked each one before proceeding past. One was locked, so we kept going.

A toilet flushed. Tailor and I froze and swung our weapons toward the bathroom door just as it opened. The man inside was buttoning his shirt back up when he saw us. He had a pistol in a shoulder holster. His eyes grew wide, and he reached for it, but he wasn't nearly fast enough. His white shirt splashed red as we both hit him with a two-round burst. He fell over backward, hitting the hardwood floor with a thud.

Tailor immediately swung his weapon toward the door at the end of the hall. I swung mine back toward the stairs. Back to back, we waited for a long moment. Nothing happened. The strange music was the only sound that could be heard. The upstairs of the house must have been sound-dampened or something. Sweat trickled down Tailor's blackened face. He nodded at the door at the end of the hall and started toward it. All of the rooms in the upstairs hallway were now empty. If Adar was in the house, he was through that door.

The bizarre chanting music grew louder as we drew closer, but it was muffled enough that I still couldn't tell what language it was. As we approached the end of the hall, I felt strange. Apprehension grew in me. My heart rate sped up. *The Calm* was wavering. Something was wrong.

I put a hand on Tailor's shoulder. He stopped and looked a question back at me. My mouth opened, but I couldn't think of anything to say. Looking irritated, Tailor just jerked his head at the door and reached for the handle. He signaled me to go right while he'd go straight. It's hard to properly cover the angles in a room when there're only two of you. We'd have to be quick. He hesitated for a long second, hand hovering over the handle, then grabbed it and slammed the door open. Together, we rushed into the room.

The bedroom was huge. Directly opposite the door was a large four-poster bed, with some kind of big painting hung above it. Against the far wall was a mirrored dresser, a desk, and what looked like a vanity.

Adar stood in the middle of the room. He was taller than I thought he'd be. He was also completely naked and splattered with blood. He clutched some kind of curved dagger in his hand.

In front of him, hanging from the ceiling, was a woman. Her hands were bound over her head. Her hair, matted and wet, hung down in her face. Blood dripped from her ravaged body onto plastic sheets spread across the floor. She'd been utterly mutilated. Adar had split her open like he was cleaning a game animal. Bloody lumps that appeared to be internal organs had been neatly arranged on the dresser. Behind them was an iPod and a set of speakers, the source of the strange music.

My stomach lurched. My mouth fell open. It felt like my balls were trying to crawl up into my stomach. It took me a moment to process what I was actually seeing. I could hear a strange buzzing in my ears over the bizarre rhythms of Adar's music.

"Jesus Christ," Tailor said, turning toward Adar. I don't know why neither of us fired. The whole thing was surreal.

Adar, as if noticing our presence for the first time, turned toward us. His face was a mask. If he was surprised or afraid, he didn't show it. My heart was racing now. My knees were weak, and I thought I was going to fall. I wanted to turn and run out of the room. Adar spoke to us then. He said something in Arabic that I didn't understand. Blood trickled from the corner of his mouth as he talked. I looked over at the dead girl again, then back at Adar. I felt numb. Adar smiled. I closed my eyes . . .

"*Val!*" Tailor yelled, startling me.

I blinked, realizing then that my revolver was in my hands. Confused, I slowly reholstered it.

"*Nightcrawler, Nightcrawler, Control, what's your status?*" Sarah asked, the concern in her voice obvious. I tried to speak but couldn't.

That's when I saw Adar. He was lying on the floor, on his stomach, in a huge pool of blood. Some of it was his, some of it was the girl's. A gory wound protruded from the center of his lower back. There was another exit wound on the back of his neck; he'd been nearly decapitated.

"Get it together, goddamn it!" Tailor yelled, grabbing my body armor and shaking me.

"I'm . . . what happened?" I asked. "I think I blacked out."

"You fucked him *up* is what happened!" Tailor said, letting me go. He walked across the room, stepping over Adar's corpse, and smashed the iPod. The horrid music silenced, Tailor keyed his microphone. "Control, Xbox, radio check."

"*Loud and clear, Xbox,*" Sarah replied, relief obvious in her voice. "*What's your status?*"

"The target's dead," Tailor said. "We're fine. Stand by." He looked up at me. "Why didn't you just shoot him with your submachine gun?"

"I don't know." I didn't remember shooting Adar. "Why didn't *you* just shoot him?"

Tailor hesitated. "I don't know, either," he said. "Fuck it, it's *done*. Let's check for intel and get the hell out of here. This place is freaking me out."

Nodding, I looked around Adar's room. The mirror behind him had shattered, presumably from my bullets passing through him. The painting above the bed depicted a horrific monster, a mass of tentacles and teeth, devouring a girl. I looked back over at Adar's victim. I felt dizzy, turned, and threw up on the floor.

"You alright, Val?" Tailor asked, calmer now.

"No," I replied. "We can't leave her like that!"

"What? Val, we gotta go, man, we don't have time to —"

"We can't leave her like that!" I shouted, standing back up.

"Listen, goddamn it!" Tailor said. "She's dead! You can't—"

"Tailor, *please*," I said, much more quietly this time.

He mouthed another curse word. "Fine. Let's hurry this up. We have to get out of here." I closed my eyes as I held the girl's feet. Tailor stood up on a chair and snapped out his automatic knife. He used it to cut the ropes that she'd been hung with and grabbed her shoulders. He helped me gently lower her body.

"Oh, *God*," Tailor said, making himself look up at the ceiling. The girl's head had flopped back as we carried her; her eyes were gone. Empty red sockets stared up at my partner. "This is fucked up. This is *fucked up*," he said. Doing our best to ignore it, we carried her to Adar's bed and wrapped her in the sheets. Tailor quickly looked away, sweat trickling down his face.

"Hey look," I said, noticing for the first time a small safe. It was mounted in the wall next to the bed, and was open.

"Let's . . . let's check it out," Tailor said, regaining his composure.

Inside was a stack of American hundred-dollar bills. "Wow."

"There has to be fifty thousand dollars here," Tailor said. He began stuffing the money into his assault pack.

"I don't suppose you're going to report that," I said as I rummaged through the safe, stuffing documents into my pockets. At the very back of the safe, my hand touched something solid.

"What's that?" Tailor asked as I pulled it out.

"I don't know," I said. It was a small wooden box wrapped in a plastic bag.

"Take it. Grab everything else you can find. We've gotta bounce, man. We been here too long." We took one last look around the room but didn't find anything else. As we turned to leave, I pulled an Ace of Spades out of my pocket and dropped it onto Adar's back.

He hadn't stopped smiling, even in death.

Chapter 8:
The Intern

LORENZO
April 16

The house was too quiet.

I should have known something was wrong as soon as I saw the compound's front gate left open. After doing a quick pass by, we had modified the plan. Carl had parked a klick down the road, and I had snuck up on the isolated compound, consisting of a single large house surrounded by a ten-foot brick wall, on foot. It had been purchased by Al Falah as a safe house for his associates.

Approaching as quietly as possible, I had paused and scanned the gate repeatedly. The plan had been for both of us to sneak in, kill Adar and anybody else there as quickly as possible, grab the box, and get the hell out, but now that situation looked fishy. So I'd snuck in to take a quick peek. I was wearing body armor, covered with ammo and explosives, and had a short AR-15 carbine, and even weighed down that much I was far stealthier than most. Not trying to brag, but I would have made a damn good ninja.

The compound had appeared utterly dead, so I had sprinted right up to the door. Lights were on but nobody was home. Sweeping inside, I paused as I saw the first perforated corpse. "Somebody beat us to it," I said into the radio as I surveyed the destruction in the living room. Brass casings rolled underfoot and the room stank of the recently dead.

"What do you mean?" Carl's voice said in my ear.

"I mean that the guards are dead and the place is shot to hell. Somebody's been here already."

"Did they get the box? If those no-good thieves got the box, I swear I'm gonna—"

"Dude, we are no-good thieves. Chill." I moved quickly through the room, careful not to step in any of the spreading puddles. Empty extended Glock magazines were on the carpet. Could this be the work of the same hitters that had screwed up Phase One?

I kept my rifle up as I moved through the house. It was dead silent, but there could still be somebody here.

"I bet it was those guys that almost botched the Falah job." There was a single body half in the bathroom with a cloverleaf of bullet holes in his chest. I approached the bedroom door quietly, my suppressed 5.56 carbine at the ready, the red dot of the Aimpoint sight floating just under my vision, though I had a sneaky feeling that Adar wasn't going to be a problem. The bedroom door slowly swung open. Adar was obviously dead. There was a second form under a blood-drenched sheet. I lifted it slowly.

I must have made some sort of strange noise into the radio.

"Lorenzo? What is it? Are you okay?"

"Better than the residents. It's a bloodbath in here." I hadn't seen anything like this since Chechnya. That girl had been mutilated, dissected. Somebody had shot the hell out of Adar, too. I did a quick once over of the room, discovering that the stories about the Butcher of Zubara hadn't been exaggerated. "Carl, Adar cut this girl . . . like . . . I don't know what."

"No time for that. Find that box. Hurry before some-body else shows up."

Blood was *everywhere.* Adar hadn't just been dropped, he'd been methodically taken apart. There was a blood-stained Ace of Spades playing card left on the perforated corpse. *What the hell?* Then I noticed a discarded revolver speed loader, five spent cases, and a single live .44 magnum cartridge. I picked up the round and examined it.

"Clint Eastwood was here."

"Huh?" Carl responded. *"Quit screwing around."*

Shoving the cartridge into my pocket, I kept searching. The safe had been cleaned out, Adar's belongings had been rifled through, and I felt a sinking feeling in my gut that what we had come for was already gone.

The shooters had missed something.

"One second." Having years of experience looking for bugs and planting them, I knew that most people would have missed Adar's hidden camera. Apparently he liked to record his torture sessions. I followed the wire back behind the bed and found the recorder. It was still running. Maybe this would tell me who our mystery shooters were. I took the DVD out of the machine and hurried back down the stairs.

"I can't find the damn box."

Carl swore over the radio again. *"Someone took it already, you think?"*

"I think so. I'm leaving the duplicate anyway. Odds are whoever took it doesn't know what it's for, but the prince's people have to think it's been destroyed." I took a small box from a pouch in my armor. It had been carved to very exacting specifications from some very specific pieces of wood. Pressure on some hidden indentations caused the intricate box to slide open, revealing the delicate key inside. I pulled the duplicate out and held it up to the light. This part had been trickier, since there were no recorded measurements for the actual device, but I was about to melt it into slag anyway, so it didn't really matter. I twisted the base of the key, and dozens of tiny pins moved freely down the sides of the shaft. I placed it in the safe and started setting the bomb.

The incendiary device would immolate the entire room, burning a hole through the floor in seconds. This whole house would be nothing but ash and bones in a matter of minutes, and it was all so Adar's extended family would think his box was toast. I set the timer for five minutes. Plenty of time to be down the road.

"Hurry up," Carl said. *"I'm getting nervous."*

"I know," I answered, already heading for the exit, knowing with dread certainty that the box had probably been taken from the upstairs safe by the shooters. I made sure the DVD was still in place. Those shooters had my box, and I had to get it back, no matter what.

"Lorenzo, you better hurry."

"What?"

"*Two cars full of bad guys pulling into the compound. Run!*"

I ran downstairs and crouched near the rear exit. The door was open, and the arriving headlights illuminated the back wall of the compound. The cars pulled to a stop and doors opened. Someone began to sing, drunken and off key. Adar must have been planning a homecoming party, and more guests had just arrived.

Not wanting to find out what kind of people a terrorist invited to a torture party, I tried to think of a way out, *something, anything*. If I made it to the back wall, I would surely be spotted before I could scale it. I could try to Rambo my way out, but from the noises coming from the yard, there were several bad guys.

"Carl, how many we got?"

"*Couldn't tell. It was too dark when they pulled in. Want me to come in shooting?*"

"Hold on that. I've got an idea." I moved quickly back into the home. The doorbell rang, long and raspy, and someone on the other side laughed. I had seen the fuse box in my search. The bell continued, the user obviously becoming frustrated. I pulled my pack off, removed my night-vision monocular, and strapped it onto my head. In another pouch was a small Semtex charge, and I squished it against the circuit breakers.

The ringing quit, and loud knocking started. The laughter was gone, and now voices called out with some concern. The radio initiator blinked green in my hand, we had contact. The charge would only kill the lights in the house, but hopefully this would be enough of an edge. I moved back toward the side entrance.

Now they were pounding on the front door. I pulled a frag from one of the MOLLE pouches on my armor and, staying low so as to not blot out the light coming through the peep hole, slid up to the door. I pulled the pin but carefully kept the spoon down until it was wedged tightly against the door's base plate. The grenade had a five-second fuse, and it would be one heck of a surprise for our party guests. It's those little touches that show you care.

Back toward the side door now. The pounding turned to kicking. I kept moving, wanting to get some space between me and that frag. The side door was in view, the rear wall of the compound visible through the portal, still illuminated in the headlights. A shadow moved on the back porch: a man with a gun. They were coming. I flipped down the monocular, and the view for one eye turned a pixilated green.

"Adar!" one of the men on the back porch shouted. The front door cracked and splintered on its hinges.

"Hide-and-seek time." I took a deep breath and mashed the initiator.

There was a *bang* as the house plunged into darkness. My world was now a super illuminated green. I raised the AR to my shoulder, realized that I had not turned down the Aimpoint for night vision use as the dot appeared blindingly fuzzy, cursed under my breath, turned the knob to dial it down, and moved my hand back to the grip. Behind me the front door crashed open.

Five.

A man in a suit and headdress moved through the rear entrance into my sight, blinking stupidly, pistol held before him like a talisman to ward off evil.

Four.

I flipped the selector to semi and pulled the trigger twice, the dot of the Aimpoint barely moving as it bounced across his torso. The suppressor was deadly silent, but each bullet still made a very audible *chuff* noise as it violated the speed of sound.

Three.

I moved forward, sidestepping, gun still at the ready, slicing the pie, more of the back porch swinging into view. The first man was falling, a second man was behind him, looking surprised in my pixilated world, lifting his Tokarev sideways, gangster style. The dot sight covered his face. *Chuff.*

Two.

There was movement behind me, the rest of Adar's guests piling into the entryway, surprised by the darkness. A few random gunshots rang out as they attacked the shadows.

One.

The concussion of the grenade was sharp inside the structure. Even with a few walls between us I could feel the impact in my eyeballs. Gliding over the bodies of the men that I had just shot, I took the corner slowly, watching for movement. Somebody started screaming.

There were two figures standing in front of the fancy fountain, easy targets. The carbine met my shoulder, but I stopped. Only one of the targets was a man, the other was female. The man had a subgun in one hand, and a rope leading to the bound wrists of the young woman. Her head was hung down, hair covering her face. He was staring, slack jawed, at the smoking front door of Adar's home and his dying and injured companions.

Having seen that poor girl upstairs, I just reacted. I flipped the selector to full auto. The man never knew what hit him as I stitched him from groin to neck in one burst. The bullets were tiny, but they were *fast*, and at this range they fragmented violently, ripping through flesh and leaving softball-sized exit wounds. He stumbled back, falling into the fountain with a crimson splash, jerking the rope and sending the girl sprawling. I dropped the mag and reloaded as I scanned for threats, trying to break the tunnel vision. *Clear.*

Instead of heading for the back wall, I sprinted toward the captive. She appeared to be in a state of shock, probably a young Filipina worker. I'm a killer, and a thief, and a con man, and a hired gun, but I was not a monster, and in Zubara, girls like this were treated like slaves or worse.

"Come with me," I said in Arabic, helping the girl to her feet, then quickly switching to Tagalog. "Come with me now or these men will kill you." She looked at me, stunned or bewildered, probably drugged and incoherent.

"Lorenzo, what's happening?" Carl's voice was tense.

"Pick me up at the front gate," I replied tersely. "We need to go, lady." I gestured with my gun in the direction to move. "Now!"

"You're an American!" she shouted in English. "Oh, thank God!"

"Uh . . ." *That was unexpected.* "Yes! I'm here to rescue you . . . or something. Let's go."

The van barely slowed as I shoved the still-bound girl into the back and climbed in after her. The incendiary bomb detonated with a brilliant flash that crackled from every window. I slammed the door as Adar's burning compound shrank in the distance.

VALENTINE
Fort Saradia National Historical Site
April 16
0400

Alone in my room, I sat on the floor, my back to the wall. I was still wearing my cammies. My body armor was lying on the floor next to me. The door to the balcony was open; a cool breeze drifted into the room.

On the floor next to me was Adar's strange little box. I'd given it a half-hearted examination; it was some kind of puzzle box, made of wood, ornately carved. It looked very old. I tried for a minute to open it but quickly gave up.

I don't know how long I'd been sitting there when I heard someone knocking on my door. I didn't answer it. I didn't want to talk to anyone. After a few moments, the knocking stopped, leaving me alone with my thoughts. Our trip back from Adar's compound had been long, but I barely remembered it. We'd been debriefed by Gordon as soon as we'd returned to the compound. He, of course, had been overjoyed, especially at the intelligence we'd gathered. Tailor neglected to mention the fifty thousand dollars he'd stuffed into his backpack. I'd forgotten to turn over the puzzle box.

I couldn't sleep. Every time I closed my eyes, I could see that dead girl hanging from Adar's ceiling. I wondered what her name had been; where she'd come from, how she'd ended up there. It reminded me so much of what happened to my mom, it *hurt*. My stomach was still twisted into knots, hours later.

I took another swig from the large plastic bottle in my hand. I'd managed to bum some booze from one of the other guys. I didn't know what in the hell it was. It tasted terrible, but it was alcohol, and it was potent. It'd *do*. As I took another drink, my bathroom door suddenly opened. Sarah walked into my room.

"Hey," I said, not looking up at her.

"Mike? Are you okay?" she asked, standing over me.

I raised my eyes up to hers. "Not really," I said. I took another sip.

"What happened?" she asked, sitting on the floor next to me. She saw the bottle in my hand. "Are you drinking?"

"Yes, I am!" I said, loudly slurring my speech and saluting her with the bottle. Sarah grabbed it out of my hand. "Hey!" I protested, but she ignored me. She lifted it to her nose and made a face when she sniffed it.

"What is this stuff?"

"I was drinking that," I said testily.

"I think you've had enough, Mike," she said firmly.

"Just leave me alone, okay?" I snatched the bottle back from her.

"Mike, please, just tell me what happened. I'm here for you. *Talk* to me."

"No, goddamn it, I don't want to *talk* about it!" I snapped. "I just want some peace and quiet! You think all because you screwed me it gives you the right to march in here whenever the hell you want?"

Sarah huffed loudly and quickly stood up. "Look, I read the report, okay? I know what you found in there."

I let out an obnoxious drunken snort. "Oh, do you? So you know that he cut her open, cut out her organs, and put them on his shelf like bowling trophies?"

"Oh my God," Sarah said. We'd kind of left that part out of our report.

"So don't barge in here and tell me I can't have a goddamned drink!"

"I'm just trying to *help* you."

"I don't need your help!" I shouted, slamming the plastic bottle down on the concrete floor. "You're not my damned mother! She's been dead since I was a kid. You know what? I get by just fine."

Sarah's expression softened a little. "How did she die?"

"She was murdered. I came home one day and found her cut to pieces, just like that girl. My dad's dead too. So are half my friends. You know what? I don't *care*. I *kill people* for money. Shooting people is my *job*. I can handle it. I always handle it. I don't need your help. I don't need your pity. And I don't need *you*. So just march your little ass the hell out of here and leave me alone!"

Sarah's eyes flashed with anger. "I don't need this. Go ahead, drink it all! Drink yourself to death if you want. I hope you choke on it!" She turned on a heel and stormed out of my room, slamming the bathroom door behind her.

A pulse of anger surged through me. I picked up the ancient puzzle box and threw it against the door as hard as I could. It crunched loudly as it hit, and fell to the floor, broken. I stared at the bathroom door, breathing heavily. I just wanted to be left alone. I just wanted Sarah to come back. I wanted another drink. I didn't want to drink anymore.

A sickening pit formed in my stomach as I realized what I'd done. *Good job, Ace*, I thought. *You managed to drive her away, too.*

"Shut up," I said aloud. *It's not my fault. I had a bad night.* There was comfort in self-pity. I lifted the plastic bottle to my lips and began to gulp down the rest of the pungent mystery alcohol. It burned on the way down, and I thought I was going to throw up. I let the empty bottle clatter to the floor.

I slumped back against the wall and closed my eyes. The room was spinning, and it wouldn't stop. My thoughts became even more sluggish than they were before, and it was difficult to concentrate on anything. I had a hard time remembering what I was so upset about. I drifted off to sleep.

LORENZO

The van slalomed around the corner as we headed back toward town. I bounced painfully against the wall. The girl I had rescued was sitting next to me, head flopped back on the seat, totally out. Apparently she'd been drugged by the bad guys.

"Easy, Carl, don't get us killed."

"Don't you tell me easy! Plan, Lorenzo, we had a plan. Who the hell is this broad?" He swung us around a truck full of sheep, and when I say full of sheep, I mean that literally, like it was piled full with legs sticking out the top.

"She was not part of the plan. I would have remembered that."

"They were going to torture her. I couldn't just leave her. She sounded like an American before she passed out. We can just drop her at the embassy gates and take off."

"Is that what you think now?" He gestured out the window at the Zubaran police vehicles streaking in the direction we had come from. "Cops crawling everywhere. And you forgot, because of the mobs of angry assholes, they evacuated the embassy."

To accentuate his point, I saw a man on the sidewalk getting the hell kicked out of him by some of the Zubaran secret police. "Okay, our place is closer. Get us off the streets." The whole city had gone nuts.

"I'm not taking her to our place. With what we're working on, nobody can see that."

"Do it, Carl." I ordered. My crew was loyal, and I seldom had to pull rank, but this was *my* crew, and it wasn't a democracy. The driver swore, his beady eyes glaring at me in the rearview mirror. We reached the compound in minutes. We entered through the attached garage so no one would see us carry the girl in.

Reaper met us at the door. He had a Glock shoved in the front of his pants. "What happened out there? Police bands are screaming about some massacre. Did you get the box? Hey . . . who's the babe?"

"Lorenzo decided he's Batman, sneaking around at night and rescuing people," Carl spat. I ignored him and carried the girl up the stairs and into the apartment. I laid her gently on the couch. She was still out.

"Where's the box?" Reaper asked.

"Somebody beat us to it and whacked Adar." I put the DVD in his hand. "The shooters are hopefully on this, and we need to figure out who they are. We need that damn box."

"On it, chief." He ran for his computer.

I flopped onto the couch next to the girl. My hands were starting to do the post-action shake. No matter how many times I did something like this, that part never changed. Carl sighed, folded the stock of his stubby Galil, and set it on the coffee table.

"Pretty bad in there, I guess?" he asked slowly, sitting down. We had been working together for over fifteen years now. We'd met in Africa, where he had been working as a mercenary, and we had both gotten screwed over by our respective employers. Working with me had proven more lucrative, and we'd been together ever since, through all sorts of craziness, and it still took me a moment to realize that Carl was *trying* to be comforting. He just wasn't very good at it.

"I shot three of them. Took out some more with a grenade." I shrugged. "The guys before me made a real mess."

Carl regarded me suspiciously, wheels turning, probably wondering if I was going soft on him. "Couldn't happen to a nicer bunch." He gestured at the girl. "And what do we do with her now?"

I studied her for the first time. She was young. Probably in her twenties. I had thought that she was from the Philippines when I had first seen her, as most of the servant girls in Zubara were imported from there or Indonesia. They were literally a slave class. Now I wasn't so sure. She would have been unusually tall for a Filipina and didn't look quite like most of the servant girls I had seen here. She was snoring peacefully in a drug-addled haze. One eye was badly bruised, and it made me glad that I had shot those men.

"I couldn't leave her. You should have seen the girl upstairs," I said. Carl didn't respond. Acts of mercy were few and far between in his life. I patted her down: no documents, no passport. Something caught my eye. "Check this out." I held up her wrist. She had a gold ring on one finger.

"What's that say?" he asked, squinting his beady eyes.

"California Polytechnic University, San Luis Obispo."

"Think she stole it off a tourist, I hope?"

"I'm thinking that we're going to need to come up with a pretty good cover story for when she wakes up." I gestured around the room. Hundreds of pictures were tacked on the walls. Posters of Al Falah, Adar, building schematics, road maps, and miscellaneous paper littered every corner of the room. A scale model of the Phase Three target was on the coffee table, and there were at least ten visible guns, and that wasn't counting the RPG in the corner.

Carl took his time responding. He would have just left her there. Hell, I don't know why I hadn't just left her behind. We were thieves, not heroes. "You're the one with the imagination. I just drive good and shoot people."

"Guys, come check this out," Reaper called excitedly from the other room. "I've got your shooters."

We entered the makeshift computer room and hovered over Reaper's shoulder. He was playing some Finnish goth-metal over the speakers. "I'm skipping past the torture porn. This Adar guy was one screwed up son of a bitch . . . and *here* is where your shooters come in."

"Why isn't there any sound?"

"Audio's all screwed up, chief. It's all static. The DVR probably didn't burn the disk properly."

"Slow it down." There were two men, dressed in camo, faces smeared with black greasepaint. They were armed with blocky submachine guns. One was just over six feet, kind of stocky, and left handed. The other was thin, a lot shorter, probably about my size. Both were Caucasians. "They're Americans."

"How can you tell already?" Reaper asked.

"That's Remington A-TACS camo. Not that common. They're either Americans or Canadian airsofters. Look how they move, too. Pretty typical Western CQB doctrine."

The two had entered the room at the same time, weapons shouldered. The shorter one covered the room to his front, while the taller one peeled off to the right. *They've done this before.*

Their professionalism seemed to fall apart a second later as the bigger one froze when he saw the girl hanging from the ceiling. Adar turned toward the shooter with a strange look, almost a smile, on his face.

The shorter of the two shooters kept his weapon pointed at Adar. The other one just flipped out. First he said something to Adar, but the Butcher didn't seem to respond. He just stood there, smiling. It was creepy. The shooter then dropped his subgun, leaving it to hang on a single-point sling, reached down to his left thigh, and drew his handgun.

"What the hell is *that*?" Reaper asked.

"That's a .44 magnum," I said as the shooter put a round into Adar's left knee. The kneecap exploded into blood and pulp, and the Butcher of Zubara dropped to the floor. The other infiltrator flinched and covered his ears as the powerful weapon discharged.

From there, the shooter proceeded to take Adar apart piece by piece, systematically. Adar tried to say something, holding up his right hand, only to get it blown off. The next round went into Adar's left bicep, mangling his arm in a spray of blood.

The shooter's accuracy was impressive. The fourth slug went into Adar's gut. The fifth went into his neck, nearly taking his head off. The shooter then reloaded automatically, mechanically, without thought. *Damn, he's fast.* He had the gun reloaded and the cylinder closed before the emptied speed loader hit the floor. I absent-mindedly pulled the .44 shell out of my pocket. I flipped it end over end between my fingers as I watched.

After the execution, the two shooters seemed to argue for a moment, then cut the mutilated girl down.

The pair then quickly ransacked the bedroom. Before they left, the tall one dropped the Ace of Spades onto Adar's bleeding corpse. A grotesque grin remained on the Butcher of Zubara's face.

"Who are these *fodas*?" Carl asked.

"Who the hell carries a *revolver* anymore?" Reaper asked.

Somebody who's really good with one and knows it, I thought. "Like I said, Dirty Harry."

"Look at these guys!" Carl was pissed. "What's with the camouflage? Kids these days all want to wear camouflage and gear and play dress up! How are they going to explain that if they got picked up by the cops?"

"They'd just shoot the cops." A professional should never be this brazen when there were more subtle ways available to pop somebody. "Play back when they're arguing." The taller shooter was young. He didn't have a killer's face, but there was no hesitation when he'd stitched those massive slugs through Adar. "He's definitely American. Looks pretty corn-fed. He's a pasty northern Midwesterner, probably has a cheese-wedge hat at home."

"How can you tell when you can't hear what he's saying?" Carl asked suspiciously.

"It's in the way he moves. I do this for a living, remember? His mannerisms, his gear, his clothing, all point to the USA. He might as well be wearing an Uncle Sam hat."

"I guess. Well, when you play an Arab, I don't recognize you, down to the dress and the perfume. You say he's American, I believe you," Reaper said.

"Go back a bit." Carl frowned. "These guys have to stick out. How many Americans are in Zubara?"

"Officially? A couple thousand," Reaper replied automatically. "And thousands more assorted Europeans. Mostly in Al Khor. If these guys have been operating in the poor side of town, they'd totally stick out."

"Reaper, grab my notepad from the living room. We've got contacts in every district. I'm going to give a few of them a call."

Reaper nodded, adjusted his Glock, and left the room.

"Kid's gonna shoot his balls off, carrying his gun like that." Carl said. Reaper flipped him the bird on his way out.

"We don't have very good health insurance in this

business, either," I muttered, studying the faces of my new adversaries. These men were standing in the way of me completing Phase Three. Until I had that box, all of our work was worthless. Without that box, our families belonged to Big Eddie. I did not know who these mystery shooters were, but my new mission in life was to find them and kill them if I had to. I blew up the picture until it became grainy, zooming in on the tall one. These men knew their business. This was going to be a challenge.

There was a sudden crash and a surprised yelp from the living room. Carl and I both drew our guns and moved apart. I disengaged the safety on my STI and pointed it at the doorway. Carl took up position behind the desk, CZ extended in front of him.

"Reaper?" I shouted. "You okay?"

Our guest had awoken. Reaper stumbled into the doorway, his arms raised in a surrender position. The girl stood behind him with his Glock 19 pressed into the base of his neck. I didn't have a shot.

"Sorry, chief," he said slowly.

The girl glared over Reaper's shoulder. The drugs must have worn off enough for her to come to, and she was obviously angry and confused. Her eyes darted about between us. "Nobody move! I'll shoot this guy right in the head," she ordered. I had been right. She was an American, and she apparently knew how to use that Glock. "Who are you people? What am I doing here?"

"That's kind of complicated."

She tightened her grip on the Glock. I could imagine a 9mm exploding through Reaper's head. "Give me the short version, asshole!"

"Okay. So there I was, minding my own business . . . and I ran into some very bad men who had you tied up and were taking you into a house where you were going to be tortured to death on video. I, uh, rescued you." The girl looked kind of out of it, disoriented and scared. She was still under the influence of whatever drug they had given her. And her finger was resting on the trigger that decided whether one of my crew lived or died. "We're friends."

"You expect me to believe that?" she shouted, blinking rapidly. Reaper cringed as she banged the Glock into the base of his skull.

"Look, we're not your enemies. See?" I slowly placed my 9mm on the table and stepped away. "Carl, put your gun down."

"But—"

"Do it!" I ordered. Even worse than her killing Reaper would be the noise. Our complex was crowded with rental villas, and I had no doubt that Zubaran fuzz would be crawling all over a gunshot call within minutes. Carl grudgingly responded and placed his CZ on the floor. "My name is Lorenzo. I saw that you were in danger, and I helped. I brought you back here, because the streets are covered in cops, and all hell has broken loose out there. Let me help you." Why had I brought her to our hideout? Damn needless complications.

"Okay, I don't think you're with those men that grabbed me, but who are you, really?" She was scared, but she was hard, and her grip on the gun didn't loosen. "You're an American, at least."

"You first," I suggested soothingly. Plus it gave me a

moment to try to think of some sort of plausible cover story.

"I'm with the US government," she snapped.

You have got to be fucking kidding me. "Good," I said as calmly as possible. If I had brought a fed or a spy back to our hideout, it was either screw the mission or kill her. Neither one sounded like a good option. I caught Carl casting me a look, letting me know how stupid he thought I was. "We're on the same side. We're on a top-secret mission. And if you blow Special Agent Wheaton's brains all over the walls, you're going to have some explaining to do to your superiors, and I probably won't be able to get the security deposit back on this apartment."

When you have to lie, you might as well reach for the stars.

"Are you Dead Six?" she asked unsteadily. Her eyes had narrowed to dangerous slits, and her teeth were a hard white line on her darkly tanned face. I paused, not sure how to answer. "Are *you* with Dead Six?" she repeated.

Fifty-fifty chance on this one. "Yes."

"I knew it!" she shouted as she stepped back from Reaper. The muzzle of the Glock was swinging toward me. The 9mm hole looked unnaturally large as the contents of my stomach turned to ice. I threw myself to the side, but I already knew it wouldn't be fast enough.

Click.

Reaper disdained holsters, and since he tended to just shove the gun in his pants, he usually carried chamber-empty. Carl and I called him a sissy for doing that, but as I hit the floor, I was mighty glad Reaper was a sissy.

The girl apparently knew guns, and she instinctively

reached up with her left hand and began to rack the slide. The world seemed to dial down into slow motion as Reaper spun and charged her, his stringy black hair rising like a halo. He hit her hard, and they both disappeared into the living room.

I was up in a flash, moving toward the scuffle. In the corner of my vision, I saw Carl scooping up his gun. Reaper and the girl were wrestling for the Glock, the muzzle pointed upward between their faces. He was much taller, but she was stronger than she looked.

Beginning to lose the struggle, she let go of the gun and threw her elbow into Reaper's temple. His head snapped back like his neck was a spring. Our techie went to the ground in a heap, but at least he took the Glock with him.

Carl had drawn down on her. "Don't shoot!" I shouted as I leapt over Reaper. "Too loud!" The girl had gone into a crouch, hands open in front of her face. Carl turned and disappeared from the room. *Thanks for the help there, buddy.* The girl circled, waiting for me. Apparently this chick knew how to fight, and I didn't like hitting girls.

"Just calm dow—" She cut me off with a snap kick at my groin. I swept one hand down to block, but it had just been a feint. She hit me with a back fist on my cheek hard enough to rattle my teeth. That hurt. I stepped back, eyes watering, and cracked my knuckles one-handed. "Oh, it's gonna be like that, huh?"

"I'm not going to let you kill me, too," she spat. She charged with a scream, throwing wild punches. She was desperate, but I was a professional. I dodged and swept them aside, waiting for a clean shot. She fought surprisingly well for a girl, and if it wasn't for the fact that I was going to have to knock her the hell out, I could almost admire the ferocity.

Suddenly Reaper's terrible music began to blare, painfully loud. The speakers on the computer probably near overload. *What the hell?* Carl came storming back into the room. He had my pistol and was screwing my sound suppressor onto the end of the threaded muzzle. It was difficult to hear him over the noise. "I'm too old for this hand-to-hand crap." He raised the 9mm and fired. The Zubara phone book sitting on the couch exploded into confetti. The *thump* of the silenced gun was barely discernible over the wailing guitars. He turned the gun on the girl. "Cool down, missy, or your head gets the next one."

Eyes wide, she slowly raised her hands in surrender. I slugged her hard in the stomach, knocking the wind out her and sending her to the floor. Violence against women doesn't count when they start it, and I wasn't going to trust her as far as I could throw her. Somebody banged on the other side of the living-room wall. Our neighbors were probably cursing us.

"You got her, chief?" Carl asked with a grin. "I'm gonna turn this garbage down. Kids today, Reaper, how can you listen to such noise?" Our techie moaned on the floor in response.

"Reaper, you okay?" I asked. The girl had gotten to her hands and knees, gasping. Flicking open my Benchmade, I placed the knife against her neck. She felt the steel there and froze, knowing that this fight was over. Reaper grunted, indicating that he would live. "Good. Grab some rope."

♠ ♠ ♠

The three of us and our captive were in the living room. The music was turned off, and everyone was a whole lot calmer. The girl was sitting on the loveseat, hands tied behind her back and, just to be safe, ankles tied together, too. I had my suppressed pistol in my hand, Carl had a beer, and Reaper was holding an ice pack against his head. "No wonder they drugged her," he muttered.

"Okay, let's try this again, without all the hitting and shooting and stuff. Who are you, and why were you being held by Adar's men?"

"What's an Adar?" she asked.

"Evil, crazy guy, planned on doing really bad things to you and then selling the video to demented freaks to masturbate to, but sadly he's on an express train to hell right now. That's an Adar," I said patiently. "And your name?"

She answered sullenly, realizing that she might as well cooperate. "My name's Jill . . . Jill Del Toro. I used to work at the American embassy."

"Used to? Who were you with? State Department? CIA? NSA?"

"Um . . . the Department of Agriculture."

I raised one eyebrow. "Okay, then. Please tell me that was some sort of cover, and you're some sort of super spy or something?" I didn't want to think that somebody from the Department of Cows and Plows had almost been the death of my team of professional killers.

"No, that's Rob Clancy stuff. I was temporarily on loan to the State Department, but I was basically a receptionist . . . well . . . I was an intern."

"Tom Clancy," Reaper corrected. "Wait . . . intern? What the hell?"

"You got beat up by an intern," Carl laughed. "Oh, man. That's good."

"I'm working on my master's degree, political science, and was doing a tour of US aid programs around the Middle East. Did you know they actually have dairy farms in Saudi Arabia?"

"Fascinating. Stick to the subject," I ordered, gesturing with my 9mm for emphasis.

"I found out about something that I wasn't supposed to. I saw them kill the assistant-ambassador. The Dead Six guys tried to shoot me, but I ran. I got lost in town, and that's when those crazy guys grabbed me and stuck a needle in my arm. I woke up here." She sighed. "I swear, I don't know much about Dead Six, but I know you plan to kill me, so let's get this over with. I'm not going to beg."

"Tell me what you do know about Dead Six first."

"I know you're some sort of secret death squad. The ambassador was told not to talk about it by your boss, that Gordon guy. You guys killed Jim Fiore for asking too many questions, and I was just in the wrong place. I don't know anything!" The girl looked like she could cry, but was too mad. "Screw it. So let's do this, you *pinche pendejo* cowards."

"Did she just call us what I think she called us?" Reaper asked.

"I think so." Carl chuckled approvingly.

The girl was tough, and pretty, too. Even tired, dirty, with one blackened eye, and being generally disheveled, I could tell that she was probably normally very attractive in an athletic kind of way. Her hair was long and extremely dark. On the other hand, I was probably old enough to be her dad, or at least her dad's younger brother. "Calm down. We're not Black Flag, or Dead Six, or Ninja Force Alpha, or whatever, and we're not going to kill you," I said.

"Really? Who are you then?" There was a sudden hope in her voice. She studied the pictures and maps on the walls, the piles of weapons and equipment, and the model building on the table. "Wait a second . . . What the hell are you?"

"Well, we aren't the good guys," Carl grunted, "if that's what you're hoping for."

"We're criminals," I stated. "You got a problem with that?"

"But . . . you're not going to kill me?"

"Only if you give me a pressing reason," I responded, deep in thought. This Dead Six, whatever the hell that meant, was who had Adar's box, and, if this Jill was telling the truth, which my gut told me she was, then I now held something that *they* wanted.

I had a witness to their black op. I wasn't adverse to the idea of arranging a trade. Worst case scenario, I could use her as bait. Sucked for her, but that wasn't my problem. I jerked my head at Reaper. "Check her out." He looked at me in confusion. I sighed. He really didn't get to spend much time around women that weren't being paid to pole dance. "On the *computer*."

"Oh, gotcha," Reaper replied as he left the room, returning a moment later with his laptop. He started doing his thing while Jill glanced between us suspiciously.

It only took him a few seconds. "You're dead," he said without looking up. "Officially at least."

"That was quick." I said.

"It wasn't like I had to look hard." He flipped the screen around so I could see it.

It was on the *Drudge Report*. The headline said Four US Embassy Staff Killed in Zubara. It took me a second to scan the article. Apparently during the evacuation, an embassy car had been struck by gunfire then firebombed. It was a terrible tragedy, killing the assistant to the ambassador, two US Marines, and an intern. This was sure to cause even more strain in the already tense relations, blah blah blah. I turned the screen so Jill could see it. "That's a nice picture they got of you," I said.

"Oh my God." Jill turned almost as white as Reaper. "I can't believe this."

"I hate to break it to you, but some very powerful people have decided that you being alive is inconvenient," I replied, wheels turning. Dead Six had marked her for death. I could use her. *Which meant that she needed to trust me.* "Believe it. You've got nowhere to run." I pulled out my knife and flicked it open. "If you promise to quit hitting us and taking my people hostage, I'll let you loose. But if you try to run off, I'm going to have to shoot you, okay?"

"I promise."

"What are you doing?" Reaper asked, suddenly wary at the idea of turning this particular firecracker loose. "You sure this is . . . ?" He trailed off as I glared at him. "Never mind."

"Jill, is it?" She nodded. I proceeded to cut the rope

around her wrists. "The way I see it, you have a problem. You've been declared dead by some sort of black operations guys. Official channels will only hurt you, not help you. This country has gone crazy. There's a war going on, and you're now in the middle of it. If the government finds you, then you're dead. If the secret police find you, then you're dead. And if you get picked up by the kind of people I saved you from tonight, you're worse than dead. You will need the assistance of, shall we say, a criminal element to get out of this country alive. Preferably honest, and dare I say, charming criminals, versus the standard underachievers who gravitate toward that career field."

She rubbed her wrists. "And you know where I can find some people like this, I assume?"

"Perhaps. We have a very difficult job to do, and I think that you might be helpful. You don't have any moral qualms about helping us out, in exchange for us getting you out of the country, do you? Considering that the kind of people I rob are the kind of people who want you dead."

"Okay," Jill answered after a long pause. "This . . . this is a lot to process. Can you really help me?"

"I can, but you have to help us first."

"You can't be serious, chief," Reaper stated. The side of his head was turning a nasty shade of purple.

Jill nervously looked around the room, obviously unsure of what to do. "Well, you saved my life. What is it you need from me? How can I possibly help you guys?"

"We'll worry about that later," I said, sounding as reassuring as I could. I'm really good at sounding reassuring when I need to. "For now, welcome aboard."

Carl began to laugh, a deep, rumbling belly laugh. The mercenary did not laugh much.

"What's so funny?" I asked.

"We got us an intern. Haw!"

While Carl was busy changing the license plates on the van and Reaper was tending to his bruised face and ego, I showed the video of the two shooters to Jill. I made sure to back it up far enough for her to see what I had saved her from. She visibly cringed and had to look away when she saw the mutilated girl.

"That would have been you," I said patiently. "Now I need you to keep watching." If anything should make her thankful for me coming along, that had to be it. Watching Adar get blasted seemed to cheer her up. Unfortunately she didn't recognize either of the Dead Six operatives.

"The only ones I ever saw was a really normal-looking white guy, probably forty-five or so, named Gordon. The other two I didn't get as good a look at, well . . . because they were trying to kill me. One had real short hair, looked like a former soldier, the other I didn't see hardly at all, but he was this really big, muscled blond guy. All of them wore suits. Gordon did all the talking," she explained. "Sorry. I don't even know if Gordon was his first name or last."

"Won't be his real name anyway," I responded. "Start from the beginning."

She sighed as she pulled up a seat. I could tell that she was exhausted and emotionally fried. "Originally I was working out of the embassy in Doha, Qatar. It's a lot bigger. But they were short clerical staff here, so I got volunteered.

At the time everybody told me how *boring* Zubara was supposed to be. I had never even heard of the place before. It wasn't supposed to be anything big, just catching up on basic paperwork so the ambassador could go around shaking hands. This was supposed to have been my last week, then I was going home."

"Bummer," I said, shoving her a bottle of water and a couple of pills. She looked at the pills suspiciously. "Ibuprofen," I explained. "Sorry about punching you, but you brought it on yourself. Then what happened?"

"Well, there really aren't that many Americans here, and those that do live here are pretty self-contained, oil or natural-gas guys, with their own compounds, so it wasn't like they ever needed us. There really wasn't much for us to do. It isn't like this is an important assignment. The ambassador's this old guy, used to be the mayor of some town in Kentucky, got the job because he worked on the president's political campaign. He just drank and slept all day." She actually smiled at the thought. "That's your tax dollars at work."

I just nodded. I hadn't paid taxes in, well, *ever*.

"Then it started getting crazy."

"I was here for that part." I didn't add that I had probably contributed to that state of affairs.

"Some men had been killed while trying to murder some of the locals. They appeared to be Americans. The Zubaran security forces freaked out at us, but the ambassador assured them that it wasn't us. Then more and more bad things started happening, and we got the word to pack. It was the assistant to the ambassador, a guy named Jim Fiore, real nice guy, who took care of all the day-to-day stuff. He kept calling people in Washington, trying to figure out what was going on."

"Like who?" I asked. If I could narrow down what kind of operation Dead Six was, it might help me track them down.

She shrugged. "It wasn't like I got to hear the calls. That's way over my piddly clearance. I just know that he was in his office on the phone non-stop for two days. He used to talk to this old army buddy of his all the time, I think he's an FBI agent now, but other than that, I don't know. There were three of us left to help Jim at that point. We were mostly just shredding papers, and it wasn't like there was anything important in there, it was just standard procedure. There was a mob outside the gates, protesting, burning flags, and it was pretty scary, but they hadn't turned violent yet other than throwing some rocks at the gate."

"When did this Gordon show up?"

"It was the last day of the evacuation. Everybody else had left except for us and some of the Marines, but they were all manning the gate. I had been assigned to be Mr. Fiore's secretary. His regular one had been diagnosed with pancreatic cancer last month and had to fly home . . . uh, never mind, doesn't matter. So I was working for Jim, and he was still making phone calls. I was in back shredding papers when Gordon came barging in." Jill's voice grew quieter. "He started yelling, telling Jim that he needed to shut up, and quit asking questions, that none of this was his business. Jim got all angry and said that Dead Six was destroying the country. That was the first time I had heard the name."

"So they shot him?"

"Oh, no, not then. The Marines would have torn them apart, I don't care who they were. No, when Jim said Dead Six, Gordon got all quiet, like he was surprised at the name, and said that they were done here. Then he left. It wasn't until later . . ." Jill paused to wipe under her eyes. It almost made me feel bad for using her. "About twenty minutes later we left for the airport with an escort, two Marines, both really cool guys that I knew. We were almost there when the Marines got a call that that there was another riot on the route that we were on, and we were supposed to take a different way. We pulled off onto this quiet street and there was another government car there waiting to meet us."

I nodded. That's probably how I would have done it.

"Two guys, the Marines acted like they recognized them, they walked right up to the windows like they were friendly as could be and just started . . . started shooting . . ." Jill paused for a really long time. "I'm sorry . . ."

Brutal. "How'd you get out?"

"They shot the guards in the front seat first, probably because they were more scared of them. They just shot *forever*. Mr. Fiore was hit, blood was going everywhere, but he opened the door and managed to get out while they were reloading."

"Typical mistake. Bullets act weird when you're shooting through window glass. You get a lot of deflection with handguns," I explained. She looked at me with bloodshot eyes. She had been crying. It made me uncomfortable. "Sorry."

"Mr. Fiore, Jim, was a tough dude. He grabbed the big

blond one and I just ran. I ran while they shot him over and over and over. I didn't look back, but I could hear him screaming. I *felt* the bullets go by me. I just ran between the houses until I couldn't anymore."

Jill had started weeping. This wasn't exactly my cup of tea. What was I supposed to say? *Sorry your life is ruined and your government wants you dead, but shit happens.* I awkwardly reached over and patted her on the knee. It seemed like the human thing to do.

She continued. "I hid in an alley for hours. I didn't speak the language. I was scared to death. When I finally saw a police officer, I ran over to him. He talked to me long enough to find out I was an American. He called someone on his radio. Then he had me sit in the back of his car while we drove across town. I thought he was taking me to the police station, but instead he took me to those assholes who drugged me." She wiped her nose and sniffed, regaining her composure. "And after seeing that video, thanks for taking care of them."

I smiled. She was actually kind of cute. A little while ago she had been trying to kill me, and now she needed a *moment*. "It was no problem." I wasn't the best at comforting people, but I was pretty good at killing people.

"Look, I'm about to pass out. I've had a hell of a day. Do you have a place I can sleep?"

I nodded. "Yeah, we've got a spare bedroom. Just . . . you know."

"Don't try to escape or you'll shoot me," she replied. "Where would I go? Who would I call? I've got no family. I can't call my employers. I'm assuming that everybody I know has their phone tapped already. Don't worry. I won't do anything stupid."

I showed her to the spare room. There was no window, no phone, and the way I slept, she would have to be a ghost to sneak out, but I would rig the door with a motion detector after she fell asleep. The apartment had an alarm, and I'd arm the perimeter, too, just in case. "You've got a bed, pillow, and a minimal number of roaches. Sorry I don't have any spare girl clothes, but I can come up with something tomorrow. The bathroom's that door there, complete with actual toilet or squatty hole and spray hose. Personal preference, I guess."

Jill paused in the doorway. "I just realized. You saved my life, and I don't even know your name."

I gave her a weak smile. "I'm Lorenzo. The skinny one you beat up is Reaper. The hairy one is Carl. And if you're wondering, yes, those are all made up and won't do you a bit of good."

"Good night, Lorenzo. And thanks." She closed the door.

Carl was waiting for me around the corner. "You're an idiot," he whispered.

I nodded. "So what's new?"

The short Portagee folded his burly arms and glared at me. "You're jeopardizing the whole job to take in some broad. You forget the part where Big Eddie kills everybody if we screw up? How does this help us?"

"I take it you heard her story?"

"I listened in. She doesn't know squat about these Dead Six *fodas*. She's useless."

"Helping her was the right thing to do," I said.

Carl snorted. "And since when did you start caring about what's *right*? I've known you a long time, Lorenzo. You don't care about right and wrong. When you meet people, they go in one of two groups: Are they a threat, or can you use them somehow? I was surprised you cared so much about this family of yours, that I've never heard you talk about, to risk your neck."

That was because the people in that folder were the only people who had ever been decent to me, but that went unsaid. "I like a few people."

"I shouldn't count," Carl replied.

"Of course not. You're unlikable," I said. Carl nodded as if this was the wisest thing he'd heard. "Look, I've got other things in mind for the girl. Dead Six will be looking for her. She's an in against them. And if they want her bad enough, they'll trade us that damned box."

Carl rubbed his stubbly face as he thought about that. "That's cold, even for you. I don't know. I'm gonna have to sleep on that. Whatever you do, don't tell Reaper. The kid will never go for it." He turned and walked away, shaking his head.

Sometimes it's hard being the bad guy.

The Fat Man picked up on the first ring. "Hello, Mr. Lorenzo."

Did he ever sleep? "We've completed Phase Two, but there's been a complication."

"Our employer does not like *complications*."

"Adar is dead, but his box is missing."

"My goodness. That certainly is bad news. I do hope that this will not unduly hinder you."

"I need information. I need to know about an American operation being conducted in Zubara called Dead Six. At least, the operatives I saw were American. I believe they have the box. If any of Eddie's people hear anything, I need to know."

"But of course," the Fat Man said. "Is that all?"

"That's all. Is this the part where you randomly threaten children to keep me in line?"

"Good-bye, Mr. Lorenzo." And he was gone.

Chapter 9:
The To-Do List

VALENTINE
Fort Saradia National Historical Site
April 16
0900

I opened my eyes to the sound of someone pounding on my door. My head throbbed with each blow. Using the wall to prop myself up, I struggled to my feet and answered the knock.

It was Conrad, Hunter's security man. Next to him was another guy I'd seen before but whose name I didn't recall. They were dressed like twins in 5.11 vests and Oakley sunglasses. "Valentine, come with us," Conrad said bluntly.

I looked at my watch. "What's happening?"

"Just come with us." Conrad put a hand on my shoulder and pulled me out of the room.

"Hey!" I protested, groggily. My left hand reflexively reached for my S&W .44; it was still in its holster.

"Hold it right there!" Conrad's partner shouted, immediately producing a pistol from under his vest. He held the Sig 220 in a tight two-handed grip, pointed at my right ear.

"Whoa whoa whoa!" I said, raising my hands, head pounding with each word. "Everybody calm down! What the hell's going on here?"

"Put your hands behind your head!" Conrad's partner demanded.

"Do it," Conrad said. He yanked my .44 out of its holster and stuffed it into his waistband. I had little choice; I slowly laced my fingers behind my head. Conrad then shoved my face into the concrete wall. Pain shot through my skull at the impact. They kept me pinned as my hands were pulled behind my back and roughly zip-tied together. Conrad spun me around, and his partner punched me in the stomach, *hard*.

I doubled over, gasping for air. Conrad was holding my zip-tied hands and wouldn't let me fall. "Hunter is waiting for you," he said. The two men shoved me toward the stairs and marched me across the compound. Conrad had his hand on my shoulder while his partner stayed a few paces away, ready to shoot me if I ran.

It had been a long time since I'd been that hung over, and I wasn't handling it well. The morning heat was oppressive. Once we cleared the shade of the covered hallway, it felt like the sun would burn my hair off. I squinted in the light, and my head ached with each step.

Other Dead Six personnel watched quietly as I was paraded across Fort Saradia. I was furious. Beyond that, a small pit was forming in my stomach. As we grew nearer and nearer to the admin building, I began to wonder if Hunter was going to have me shot.

"Wait, wait, we gotta stop." I leaned forward and threw up.

"Heh, looks like our boy doesn't feel so good," one of the security men said. Conrad and his partner had a good laugh at my expense before dragging me along again.

As we approached the administrative building, Sarah stepped out into the morning sun, putting on sunglasses as she cleared the door. She froze when she saw me being pushed along by Hunter's men, blood trickling down the side of my head, hands tied behind my back. Her mouth opened, but she didn't say anything. I just looked at the ground.

A few minutes later, I was sitting outside of Hunter's office, being watched by one security guy while Conrad was inside talking to the colonel. After a short time I was marched in and pushed into a chair in front of Hunter's desk.

Looking around, I realized I'd never actually been in the office before. It had once belonged to Fort Saradia's commanding officer. It was under new management now. Several screens were mounted in various places, and bundles of wires were strung along the floor and ceiling. Maps of the city, of the CGEZ, and of the entire Middle East were hung on the walls. The air stank of cigar smoke. The two security men loomed over me as I sat there.

Hunter regarded me quietly. His gaze was hard and unsettling. He had only one eye, but it could look at you twice as hard.

"Colonel?" I began, choosing my words carefully.

"What did I do?" I struggled to think clearly; my head felt like it was full of peanut butter.

"Gentlemen, take a walk," Hunter said, dismissing his two men. As they left the room, he turned his attention to me. "Miss McAllister informed me that you were drunk off your ass last night and seemed unstable. And now Conrad tells me you went for your weapon when they woke you."

Hunter paused for effect. "Mr. Valentine, we're having this little chat to determine if you're still fit to go on missions. So tell me, son, what the hell is your problem?"

"It was . . . bad . . . last night, sir. I did things I regret. I was under a lot of stress. I took it out on Sarah, and I shouldn't have. But I don't understand why I got dragged in here at gunpoint."

Hunter studied me for a moment before speaking. "I know all about you and McAllister, by the way. I know you've been diddling each other like a couple of high-school kids. I don't give a damn about that. I'm only telling you so you're not under the impression that anything happens around here without my knowledge. What I do give a damn about is one of my best men trying to drink himself stupid after a mission, especially given the operational tempo we're dealing with. I seem to recall telling you no alcohol until further notice. As a matter of fact, you're supposed to go out again tonight."

"But sir!" I protested. "I'm—"

"Hung over?" Hunter interjected. "I can see that. You look like hell, Mr. Valentine. You reek of alcohol. What the hell were you drinking, Av-Gas?"

"I . . . don't really know, sir. I don't remember much."

"I bet," Hunter said. "I'm asking you again, now, what's your problem?"

"There were some things we left out of our report, sir," I said quietly. "About what we found in Umm Bab."

"Oh?" Hunter asked, raising the eyebrow above his eye patch. I spent the next few minutes recapping the grisly scene we discovered in Adar's bedroom. My voice broke a few times as I talked about the mutilated girl.

Hunter quietly let me finish. "Well, that makes sense now," he said at last. He thought about it for a long, uncomfortable moment. "I guess you're lucky."

"Sir?"

"You heard me. My first inclination was to throw you in the brig for a couple weeks. Unfortunately, we don't have time for that, and we're too short on personnel. You will not jeopardize this mission. Another episode and I'll send you home."

I couldn't believe what I'd just heard. "Send me *home*?"

"Well, I'll send you back to Gordon Willis. He'll probably make you disappear. I doubt you'll end up back wherever it is you came from. I've only sent one person back so far, and I don't know what happened to him. If you follow orders until the project is over, you won't have to find out. Am I making myself clear, Mr. Valentine?"

"Perfectly, sir," I replied.

"Outstanding," Hunter said.

"Sir, can you untie me now?"

"In a minute. Listen up. Your next mission is very important. So far, the project has been going well. Very well. We have the enemy running scared, and the rumors are flying. Many suspect Americans, but we're too aggressive. Most think it's the Israelis, or the emir's secret police. The nice thing about shaking the bushes like that is that once in a while something good comes running out."

"I'm not sure I follow you, sir."

"We've been approached by a contact that wants to make a deal. She's willing to exchange information for protection. We're working on setting up the meeting now. The name she gave us is Asra Elnadi. We believe she's a former partner of one of the local arms dealers, Jalal Hosani."

"I've heard that name before."

"Mr. Hosani is on our to-do list. He's been running guns to anyone in the region with the cash to buy them. As a matter of fact, we think he provided most of the weapons you torched in Ash Shamal. But he's not the issue right now. Our contact says she left Hosani to go work with one of his competitors, a Russian syndicate run by one Anatoly Federov. He's on the list, too, and he's higher up on it than Hosani. He's not only running guns but is providing explosives and advisers. The training he offers is a lot better than the Iranians."

"So what's the deal?"

"It's simple, really. She wants to meet with our people. She'll divulge everything she knows about both Federov and Hosani if we get her out of the country."

"Do you think she's worth the trouble?"

"I do. So here's what's going to happen." Colonel Hunter spent the next few minutes giving me a brief rundown of his mission plan. I listened intently, despite being in pain and having my hands tied behind my back.

It was simple enough. One of our people would meet Asra at a predetermined location. We'd screen her, make sure she checked out, and would then bring her to one of our safe houses. If she was legit, we'd get her out of the country. Hunter seemed reasonably confident that things would go smoothly, but operational experience had dulled my optimism somewhat.

Half an hour later, I left Hunter's office and headed down the hall to the security office, rubbing the raw spots on my wrists where the zip ties had been. My head still ached, and all I wanted to do was crawl back into bed.

Conrad was sitting at a desk, clicking away at a laptop when I walked in. I spotted my .44 sitting on a shelf behind his desk. "I'm here for my gun," I said simply. I really didn't feel like having another conversation with this asshole.

Conrad didn't look up from his screen. "Well, if it isn't Doc Holliday looking for his big shootin' iron."

My head still throbbed, and I felt a surge of anger shoot through me. "Just give me my gun so I can go," I said, stepping closer to Conrad's desk.

"The colonel thinks you're hot shit. That's the only reason you didn't end up in the Gulf," Conrad said, grabbing my revolver from his shelf. "You know what I think?"

"I don't really care," I stated. "Just give me my gun."

"I think you're just a dumb kid who's in way over his head," Conrad said, pretending to examine my revolver. He then set it down on his desk with a clunk.

The muzzle was facing toward me as I grabbed the .44.

As I stood up, I flipped the gun around in my hand and extended my arm. I aligned the sights on the bridge of Conrad's nose. I'd had enough of these people.

I pulled the trigger.

Click! Conrad raised an eyebrow as the revolver's hammer fell on an empty chamber. I pulled the gun in close to my chest and hit the cylinder release. The security man had unloaded it before giving it back to me. I could tell the moment I picked it up. Smart move on his part.

He put his hand on the butt of his gun. "You trying to scare me or something? I'm with the *organization*," he sputtered, like I knew what he was talking about. "You're a fucking *temp*. You're *nothing*."

"I'll see you later, asshole," I said. I holstered my gun, turned on a heel, and left the office.

I made my way downstairs and out the front door, almost crashing into Sarah as I stepped back into the heat. "Michael!" she said, seemingly unsure of what to say. "What happened to you?"

I almost laughed. "What *happened?* Hunter was ready to shoot me, that's what happened!"

"Michael, I didn't mean for—"

I cut her off. "No. Just stop. I learned a long time ago not to fish out of the company pond, and this is why. As soon as I piss you off, you run to the boss, and I get the *shit* kicked out of me. So just stay away from me, alright? I got a mission to plan." I stepped around her and walked away, not looking back.

It took me a few minutes to get back up to my room. Sweat was trickling down my face by the time I made it to the third floor of the dorms, and I thought I was going to pass out. I locked the door behind me, cranked the air conditioner up, and sat down on my bed.

I noticed something shiny on the floor by the bathroom door. It had fallen out of the old Arabian puzzle box. The object was silver in color and had a silver chain attached to one end. I grabbed the chain and picked the trinket up.

It was roughly cylindrical, a few inches long and maybe as big around as a ballpoint pen. Surprisingly heavy, the object was intricately carved and looked as it if had many moving parts. It also looked very old. The top of the object, where the chain was attached, appeared to be a knob. I gently tried to rotate it to see if anything would happen.

To my surprise, the thing audibly clicked and more than a dozen tiny metal pins of varying lengths popped out of the shaft. Rotating the knob the other way caused the pins to disappear again.

I sat back down on my bed, playing with the trinket, wondering what it was. It seemed like a key of some kind, but that was only a guess on my part. Whatever the object was, it was still in my hand when I fell asleep.

I told myself it was a coincidence, but I had the most macabre, horrifying nightmares of my entire life.

LORENZO
April 16

I was wandering the local market when my cell phone buzzed. It was secure, encrypted, and not very many people had my number. *Caller unknown.* Glancing around, there was nobody close enough to eavesdrop, and there was enough background hum from the various vendors and customers that listening in would be difficult. Half the Arab world was on a cell phone at any given time anyway.

"I heard you were looking for me," Jalal Hosani said, cutting right to the point. I had been trying to reach him all week. If anybody knew what was really going on, it would be the local neighborhood arms smuggler.

"I need some information."

"As do I." There was a long pause on the other end of the line. "Are you involved in what has been happening?"

"Not my style. You know that." I had the professional reputation of being a man of subtlety. "I was actually going to ask you the same question."

Jalal actually laughed. "Are you serious? I've been afraid to stick my head out in public for fear of losing it to these men leaving the playing cards."

I paused in front of one of the carts. They actually had good-looking chili peppers, and I was a bit of a connoisseur. Even the smell was *hot*. I gestured for them to fill a bag. "So, how's business treating you?" I asked as I passed over a few riyals to the eager vendor and put the peppers with the rest of the supplies I'd purchased.

"Well, half my customer base is dead or hiding, but the other half has been stocking up on guns in response, so overall it has been good. At this rate we'll be in full-fledged revolution in a matter of months." Jalal said that like it was a good thing, simply a business opportunity. "Why are you curious? I thought a *patriot* such as yourself would be glad to see such enemies of your homeland eliminated."

I wasn't going to lie. If it wasn't for Dead Six having my

box, they could burn the entire city down and I wouldn't give a damn. "They took something that belongs to me. I need to find them."

"Not that I know where they are, but if I were to find such a thing, that information would be incredibly valuable to many people. I'm sure General Al Sabah, for instance, would be willing to pay a fortune."

"So would Big Eddie," I responded as I stopped in front of another booth featuring camel, the other, other white meat. *Yum.* "He's got deeper pockets than the general, but you know how he feels about being exclusive," I bluffed. I didn't have access to Eddie's resources, but I would cross that bridge when I came to it. "Does the name Dead Six mean anything to you?"

"Perhaps," Jalal responded after a moment of thought. "I will be in touch." The call ended.

I shook my head. Hopefully Jalal would come up with something. That man had his finger on the pulse of the city's criminal heart. Now I was just going to have to work my sources until I found something about Dead Six that I could use. *Well, why the hell not?* I ordered a pound of camel. You only live once.

The short walk back to the apartment compound gave me a chance to think. I had one weapon I could use against Dead Six to get them in the open, young Jill Del Toro, but I was hesitant to utilize her. The idea made me uncomfortable. Carl had been right. I used people. That's what I did. It didn't mean I had to like it.

Carl had said that he was surprised that I was sticking my neck out for my family. They weren't even my blood relations, but they had taken me in. They were the only people who'd ever been good to me. I had grown up on the streets, son of a drug-addled whore and a homicidal beast of a man. I'd been put to work stealing as soon as I was old enough not to get caught, and I had been an overachiever in that respect. By the time I was ten, there wasn't a lock I couldn't pick, no pocket I couldn't get into undetected. I had been a tiny shrimp of a kid, and though that had been handy for fitting through various unsecured windows, it had made me look like an easy target for the other predators. I had solved that by developing a reputation for savage violence. Pipe, knife, chain, brick, it didn't matter. I never fought *fair*. Cross me and I kill you.

I had kept that attitude into adulthood, and it had served me well. There had only been one point in my life where I hadn't had to fight to survive. It had been brief, but I had appreciated it. The people in that manila folder were responsible for that, and I would be damned if I was going to let Big Eddie hurt them for it.

If that meant I had to hurt some other seemingly decent person . . . so be it. In the end it was all just an equation. Whatever I had to do to reach my goals was what was going to happen.

So why did I feel like such an asshole? I sighed as I ascended the steps to our apartment, bags in hand. This was why I stuck to robbing criminals, terrorists, and scumbags. The unfortunate downside of my time with a real family was that I had developed a finely tuned sense of guilt, damn Gideon and all his morals. I had managed to utterly squash my conscience for years, but it was bugging me now.

The apartment smelled . . . *really* good. "Okay, we're in a Muslim country, where did you guys find *bacon*?"

Carl poked his head around the corner from the kitchen. "Same place I find beer. Whenever you buy groceries, everything is too hot or weird with tentacles and eyeballs and shit."

"You do realize that the greatest thing your explorer ancestors ever accomplished was introducing the chili pepper to Thailand? That was awesome. That whole slave-trade thing . . . not so good." I tossed my headdress on the couch and followed the smell of pig. Carl was cooking and Reaper was sitting at the table, listening to his conspiracy-theory radio.

Carl looked at my bags as I started unpacking. "You bought camel? Fucking *camel*? See? What did I just say?"

I realized the shower was running. "Where's the girl?" I asked suspiciously.

"Jill's in the bathroom," Reaper replied dismissively.

I thought about it a second. "How long?" I snapped.

Reaper looked up, stringy hair in his face, disheveled as usual. He tended to keep weird nocturnal hours, fueled by sugar and energy drinks. "Uh . . . ten minutes?"

"There's a window in there." If she ran, it could ruin everything. I was across the apartment in an instant and jerked open the bathroom door. The room was fogged with steam. Jill was just stepping out of the shower, naked, absolutely gorgeous, and reaching for a towel. I froze.

"Hey!" she shouted as she quickly covered herself. "You mind?"

I backed out and closed the door.

Carl was waiting for me as I returned. "Thought of that. Window's too small, and it's a twenty-foot drop onto asphalt." He shoved me a plate. "Jackass."

Reaper was looking at me in awe. "So . . ."

I nodded. I was guessing that Jill worked out. *A lot.* "Smoking hot."

"I knew it," he sputtered, then grinned. "You know, we haven't had a girl on the team since Kat—"

"She's not on the *team*," I snapped. "Don't get too attached. Got it?"

Reaper looked down. "I just meant . . . never mind." He stuck his earpieces back in. Carl studied me for a moment. I gave him a look just daring him to respond. He went back to his bacon.

Jill joined us for breakfast a minute later. Apparently Reaper had decided to help out and had loaned her a Rammstein T-shirt. She accepted the offered plate and sat down across from me, looking a bit indignant. "Next time you should knock."

I took my time and finished chewing. "Next time you shouldn't get kidnapped by terrorists."

"Touché," she replied. "Fair enough. But just so you know, I'm not going to try and escape, I promise. Who am I going to run to? The cops? That worked *real* good last time. So . . . mind if I ask a few questions?" When I didn't respond, she must have taken that as a yes. "What kind of criminals are you?"

The other two looked to me and waited, as if saying, *this should be interesting.* "The strong silent type that doesn't talk about their work in polite company," I replied slowly. "As in, it's none of your business."

"Okay, fine. How about, what do we do now?"

Pausing, I wiped my mouth with a napkin. It wasn't like I could just tell her I was waiting for some sort of contact so I could trade her for the box. I took a moment to compose my response. "*You're* going to lay low. *We're* going to find Dead Six."

"Well, I know why I don't like them, but what's in it for you?" She was suspicious of my motives, which meant she wasn't stupid.

"Let's just say that they have something I want and leave it at that."

"When you find them, are you going to . . . *kill* them?" she asked.

"That's a definite possibility. Does that offend you?"

"No. I just wanted to see if you needed any help." Jill actually smiled. "It's still kind of sinking in, but these people ruined my life. As long as they're out there, I can't go home."

I don't think she realized yet that she could never go home. Once you've witnessed a rogue government operation murder US citizens and they'd already reported you as KIA, it was time to just walk away and get a new name. She was now on the official to-do-list. "This isn't amateur hour. We're highly trained professionals. What exactly are you bringing to the table?"

"I can take care of myself," Jill responded.

"No kidding," Reaper said. His face was still swollen. "Where'd you learn to fight like that? Not that I couldn't have, you know . . . taken you out, but you surprised me is all." Carl and I both openly scoffed at him. Reaper couldn't fight his way out of a cardboard box. "Whatever."

"My dad owned a martial-arts studio. He taught us how to defend ourselves. I grew up in kind of a rough neighborhood, so it came in handy a couple times. Dad was a good teacher, used to fight professionally even."

Carl scowled. His favorite thing in the world, other than chain-smoking and complaining, was to watch people beat each other bloody senseless on TV. There wasn't a lot of televised bullfighting, I suppose. "Del Toro . . . Tony 'the Demon' Del Toro?" he asked. Jill nodded in the affirmative. That must have been impressive or something from the approving look Carl gave her. "Like ten years ago, I watched him on pay-per-view almost tear this guy's arm off. I hate those Brazilian jujitsu guys. Guy needed his arm tore off, cocky *fodas*, so I remember the Demon."

"Being able to punch out Reaper is great and all, but we're talking about a team of assassins who've been ripping through fundamentalist murderers like it's nothing," I said coldly. "Do you even know how to shoot?"

"Dad taught me how to use a gun," Jill said defensively. That alone meant nothing. There were lots of people that *thought* they knew how to shoot. Usually if they could hit anything, they were too slow, or if they were fast, then they couldn't get reliable hits under stress. The kind of shooting I was good at was all about putting a bunch of bullets into my opponent before they could do it to me, and that was not how most recreational types did it.

"Uh-huh. Do you speak Arabic? Can you pass for a local?" In fairness, I already knew the answer to those. And with a little bit of coaching, I could easily get her to pass for one of the local imported Filipina workers: she had the features. Worst-case scenario, the women in the old part of town all wore hoods, and in the most traditional didn't even let their eyes show. "Can you *not* stick out like a tourist?"

"Well . . . no."

"Ever killed anybody?"

She shook her head.

"Thought so. You're going to stay here, keep your head down, and do exactly what I tell you to. When we come up against Dead Six, they won't hesitate. You run into that guy with the .44 magnum from the video and he'll *eat* you."

"Phrasing!" Reaper injected. Jill scowled at him.

"So to speak," I corrected.

"Your old man retired now?" Carl asked, trying to return the conversation to something more interesting to him. "Haven't seen him fight in forever."

"Passed away," she said. "I lost both my parents in a car accident. My brother was a Marine, just like dad had been, but he was killed in the war a couple years ago. I've got no close family left. So there won't be anybody demanding to see my supposedly dead body, either."

"They burned the embassy car anyway. If these guys are as professional as they seem, they probably found another girl to stick in the car before they lit it up. Nobody is going to recognize that body anyway," I said. "Hell, that's probably why they burned the car. They wouldn't have bothered if they'd nailed all of you." I didn't add that that was how I would have done it.

"And if I was missing, presumed taken by the terrorists, then that would have forced a big response from the government," Jill added. She caught on quick. Dead Six was running quiet. I'm guessing having the American populace watching the news and demanding a rescue mission was not on their itinerary.

Reaper chimed in. "There won't be an official investigation anyway. These black ops always squash that. There won't ever be an autopsy to show it isn't really you, either. Dental records won't matter. I bet you ten bucks they already cremated them all!"

Reaper was talking out of his ass. "When did *you* become such an expert on secret government operations?"

"I tell you, man, you really need to listen more. The truth is out *there*." He was getting defensive. "Roger Geonoy had an expert on *Sea to Shining Sea* last night. See, there's an Illuminati plot to control the world's oil supply, but that's just the beginning."

"Oh, not again," Carl muttered.

"Seriously," Reaper said, wide-eyed. "A cabal of powerful European bankers and stuff, it all makes *sense*. Did you know that the US government couldn't account for billions of dollars last year? Where do you think it all goes, man? It's for the secret war against the Illuminati."

"And they're going to release Loch Ness Monsters into the Gulf to disrupt the tankers," I added. "How nefarious."

"Only if the aliens from Roswell he's always talking about say so," Carl said. "Shut up already, Reaper."

"What is it that he does for you . . . exactly?" Jill asked.

"He's the brains of the operation."

But the kid wasn't going to be deterred. "Okay, so you don't believe in *my* conspiracy theories, but we're conspiring to break into a thousand-year-old secret vault for a mythical crime lord, so we're trying to track down a secret government death squad that kills witnesses, and there's apparently a conspiracy to overthrow the emir, but the second I say Illuminati, I'm the crazy one."

"Yes," I answered without hesitation.

Jill looked around the table. "Maybe I was better off with the terrorists."

Chapter 10:
Hurt

VALENTINE
Ash Shamal District
April 16
2345

Ash Shamal was the poorest of Zubara's three urban districts, and the most dangerous. Parts of this district were hotbeds of Islamic fundamentalism, and the streets weren't safe for Westerners, especially at night. Much of that was our fault. Since Project Heartbreaker had begun, it had stirred up a hornet's nest on the poor side of town. The locals were outraged over Dead Six's dirty work. Most of them seemed to think it was the Israelis. Certain people used this misconception to their own personal advantage.

By *certain people* I mean General Mubarak Al Sabah. The emir considered the popular general to be a threat, but for whatever reason couldn't just have him shot. Word on the street was General Al Sabah's faction of the army was making deals with local terrorist cells. Now, most of these so-called *cells* were just groups of angry, ignorant locals that claimed to stand against "Zionism" and "American Imperialism" and all that bullshit. In reality, they had no training, no equipment, no organization, and most of them weren't eager to go off and die for the jihad.

That was, of course, until General Al Sabah started using his connections to equip and train the locals. He was slowly building a small army in Ash Shamal. They were, at best, poorly trained rabble, little more than cannon fodder. But we believed Al Sabah was going to make a move on the emir soon, and he'd need all of the help he could get.

Facilitating these jihadi militias was one Anatoly Federov, the Russian arms dealer Hunter had briefed me about. He supplied them with brand-new hardware from Russia and advisers on how to use the equipment. Al Sabah, in turn, promised to be a very powerful friend to Federov when he managed to overthrow the emir.

Dead Six had no intention of letting that happen. From what I'd heard, we had plans to kill both Federov and General Al Sabah himself. One thing at a time, though. In order to kill someone, you have to find them, and find a way to get to them. Powerful people surrounded by many heavily armed friends are notoriously difficult to get to, for obvious reasons.

That is, unless the powerful person's disgruntled business partner decides to cut a deal with the people gunning for him in order to save her own ass.

Enter one Asra Elnadi. According to our information, Ms. Elnadi was an Egyptian-born businesswoman who had been educated in Paris. We didn't know a lot about her history beyond that. We did know that for a few years

she had been the business partner and lover of Jalal
Hosani. Yet something went wrong, and Asra left Hosani
in order to team up with Federov, taking a bunch of his
business contacts with her. Federov became a major
player in the Gulf; Hosani's business stagnated, and he
went from being a rising-star arms broker to a second-rate
gunrunner.

Hell hath no fury like a woman scorned, or so goes
the ancient cliché. Project Heartbreaker had brought a
different kind of hell to Zubara, and people like Asra were
scattering like cockroaches. Normally you step on the
roaches as they run, but occasionally you make a deal with
one to get to another, more powerful cockroach.

Okay, that analogy kind of fell apart, but you know what
I meant. Through some unknown—to me, at least—back
channel, Ms. Elnadi had managed to contact Dead Six
and offered to squeal. She was afraid of us, sure, but she
was more afraid of her current boyfriend. There was only
one problem: despite her expensive European education
and status as an international businesswoman of ill
repute, Ms. Elnadi didn't speak English. Furthermore,
she had an intense distrust of men and apparently insisted
on meeting face-to-face with a woman, one who spoke
either Arabic or French.

The result of all this skullduggery and intrigue was that
I found myself driving across town in a nondescript Toyota
Land Cruiser, sitting next to Sarah McAllister in awkward
silence.

We were taking two vehicles. Sarah and I were riding
in the Land Cruiser, and would be the ones to actually
make contact with Asra Elnadi. Tailor, Hudson, and

Wheeler were following us in a van. The plan was for them to hang back until we arrived at the meeting, then fan out and provide overwatch as best they could. Asra wouldn't be expecting Sarah to arrive alone, but we feared that too much of a show of force would spook her. If we lost her, we'd probably never find Hosani or Federov. If all went well, the only people she'd actually see would be Sarah and me.

"Shafter, Nightcrawler, radio check," I said, squeezing the transmit button as I talked.

"Loud and clear," Hudson replied.

"We're almost there," I said to Sarah, keeping my eyes on the road. I was tense, and not just because I was uncomfortable being around Sarah. Keeping a low profile for the mission meant that I'd be alone, at least for a short time, if things went south. It also meant that instead of wearing full battle rattle and carrying a rifle, I was in street clothes and a wearing a low-profile vest with thinner plates and less coverage. In a big backpack in the backseat was my FN Mk. 17 7.62x51mm carbine. With the short thirteen-inch barrel fitted and the stock folded, it could be concealed in a pack with a couple of spare magazines.

Sarah had barely said anything to me the entire trip. She wasn't enjoying the ride any more than I was, but we had a mission to complete. We were both trying really hard to be professional.

"Are you armed?" I asked as I maneuvered the Land Cruiser through a roundabout.

Sarah seemed surprised by the question. "They gave me a forty-five." Sarah, like me, was wearing an untucked, short-sleeved shirt over her T-shirt and body armor to conceal her weapon.

"Okay," I said. "If the shit hits the fan, fall back to the truck and let me cover you. If I get hit, get in the truck and leave without me."

She was quiet for a moment. "Mike, you don't have to."

"Yes, I *do*. You're a mission-essential asset. It's my job to get you in and out of there alive. If it gets bad, you grab our target and get her out. If you can't do that, leave her with me and get yourself out. This is how it works. Okay?" She briefly looked like she was going to argue with me, but simply nodded.

Asra Elnadi insisted that we meet in a freight yard near the Ash Shamal docks. She told us that she'd be coming alone. This simplified things for us a little, as we'd only have one person to exfiltrate. Nothing complicates a simple extraction mission more than the would-be extractee showing up with an entourage of friends and family.

Using a GPS unit in the truck, I navigated my way through a labyrinthine maze of old warehouses and stacked shipping containers. The Ash Shamal docks were one of the busiest ports in the Persian Gulf, and the surrounding facilities were huge. They were also uncontrolled. There were no fences, no cameras, no access control points, and as near as I could tell, no security. The harbor police occasionally did patrols through the docks at night, but those patrols had fallen off as violence had risen in the district. The police in the Zoob were probably either sympathetic to General Al Sabah's fermenting revolution or didn't want to get killed in it.

It was just after midnight when we finally arrived at the

predetermined meeting point. It was a large, open area surrounded by walls of shipping containers stacked four and five high. There were a couple of small buildings and a long, metal sunshade, under which dozens of forklifts and utility vehicles were parked. Along the rear of this concrete pad was a massive warehouse. The area was dark, save for lights on the front of each of the buildings.

I killed the headlights as we slowly rolled into the open, noticing an Audi sedan parked between two forklifts. "Xbox, Nightcrawler, I think I have eyes on the package. Where are you?"

"We're almost in position," Tailor replied. *"Okay,"* he said after a few moments. *"I can see you."*

"Where are you?"

"I'm on top of a stack of conex boxes to the south of you. Gotcha covered, nice and quiet." This meant that Tailor was providing overwatch with a suppressed rifle. It was too dark for me to see where he was, but from on top of any of the stacks of containers he'd have a commanding view of the area, especially using the thermal scope Frank had pulled out of the armory.

"Nightcrawler, Shafter," Hudson said. *"We're just around the corner. We can be on top of you in a couple seconds."*

"Roger that," I said as I got out of the truck.

I looked over at Sarah. "You ready?" She nodded again, not looking at me. I reached into my pocket and took out a flashlight. I flashed it at the Audi three times, paused for a few seconds, then flashed it a fourth time. The Audi's headlights flashed back at me five times. The dome light came on briefly as the driver's door opened. A slender female figure climbed out of the car and closed the door behind her.

Sarah and I approached slowly. I stayed a few paces behind Sarah and scanned the area. Even though I had Tailor watching me and some backup, something was bothering me. I felt vulnerable.

"Stay here," Sarah said. "I'm going to go talk to her." She then keyed her own radio microphone. "Xbox, I'm making contact with the package now."

I waited for him to acknowledge Sarah before speaking. "If this takes too long, I'm going to grab her and throw her in the truck. If she tries to get back in her car, draw down on her."

Sarah looked a question at me. "Hunter's orders," I said. "She's coming with us whether she likes it or not. I was told to shoot her if she tries to run. So you need to make sure she understands that the only way she's getting out of this alive is if she does what you tell her. If she gets cold feet, I'll put a slug through her. If I don't, Tailor will. Clear?"

"Yeah, clear," Sarah replied, walking away from me. I didn't know what the hell she was being so touchy about. The fact that Asra Elnadi was a woman didn't make her a good person. She was a black-market arms dealer who sold weapons to terrorists. If she hadn't come to us first, she'd have probably ended up dead when we went after Federov. Maybe it was a chick thing.

I was standing about fifty feet away from Sarah when she addressed the target in Arabic. I constantly scanned the surroundings. I was gripped by a sense of unease that I just couldn't shake. Was it because of the previous night, or was it something real?

"*I've got the package in tow*," Sarah said over the radio, sounding relieved. "*So far so good.*"

I activated my microphone again. "Xbox, Nightcrawler, you see anything?"

"*Negative,*" Tailor replied. "*It's quiet. Why? Something up?*"

"Just a bad feeling."

"*Hang on,*" Tailor said. "*I just had a door open. . . . There's a couple guys walking up some exterior stairs.*"

It might not be anything, I thought, just somebody working late, but it didn't make me feel any better. I couldn't see anything moving in the darkness. "Xbox, where?"

"*Two hundred meters due north of you. They're on a catwalk on that three-story warehouse. Shit, they just walked behind something. I lost them.*" I could see the building in question but couldn't make out any details from here. There was a long pause as Tailor searched through his scope. "*They were carrying boxes or something, but it's hard to see details through this thing.*"

Sarah seemed to have our contact under control and was gently leading her my way. I wished she'd hurry the hell up. Asra was babbling away, nervous. The arms dealer had a high-pitched voice. Something she said seemed to spook Sarah, and they started moving quicker. She sounded nervous over the radio. "*The package thinks she might have been followed.*"

My attention focused back to the warehouse. I'd just caught a tiny flicker of movement at the top.

"*Okay, I got visual on one of them again. He's setting down his box.*" Tailor sounded uncertain. "*Wait. Shit. It's a weapon, I say again, he's got a weapon. Get out of there, Nightcrawler! Engaging!"*

Sniper. "Understood, moving!" I said, breaking into a run. There was no cover where we were. We had to get out of there. "Sarah!" I yelled, digging the Land Cruiser's keys out of my pocket. "Get her in the truck!"

"I heard him!" Sarah said, grabbing the package by the arm and pulling her along. Asra balked at this and began chattering at Sarah. She seemed like she wanted to know what was going on. There wasn't time for that. I caught up with the two women, took Asra by the other arm, and hauled her roughly back to our Toyota.

She struggled and bitched at me. I looked over at Sarah as my left hand went to the butt of my gun. "Tell her that Federov is coming for her, and if she doesn't get into that truck right now I'm going to fucking *shoot* her." Sarah conveyed my warning to Asra. The arms dealer's eyes went wide, and she complied with my command. I hurried for the front seat. Muffled cracks echoed across the storage yard; Tailor had started shooting.

"Xbox, do you have—" But a deafening *bang* cut me off. Bits of metal flew from the hood of our truck. I lurched to the side and threw myself to the pavement behind the car. The next bullet exploded through the engine block, destroying it. Asra started screaming. "Out! Out!" I shouted, crawling toward the women. Windows shattered as huge bullets lanced through our ride.

Sarah reacted quickly, getting as low as possible. I reached up, got a handful of Asra's suit jacket, and yanked her to the ground. We were pinned. The sniper had something huge, and by the rate of fire, semiautomatic. Our Toyota wasn't cover, it was just concealment.

"Got one. Shit! Can't spot the other guy. Shot's blocked. Moving!" Tailor shouted.

A hole as big around as my fist punched through the Toyota's side panel. The bullet dug a divot into the ground, launching stinging asphalt bits. If we ran for the nearest conex, not all of us would make it, but if we sat here, we were as good as dead.

Asra stood, panicking, trying to flee. Sarah knocked her down before I could. A bullet whined through the space she had just filled. Sarah threw her body on top of our package to hold the struggling woman down.

This day just kept getting better and better. The sniper had disabled our vehicle first so we couldn't run. The only reason we hadn't been hit yet was luck.

"This is Shafter. We've got multiple vehicles inbound from the east at a high rate of speed. We got more company!"

"Copy!" I said. Another heavy slug plowed through our truck, showering me with shattered safety glass. "Hurry!"

"Got you, fucker," Tailor gasped as he opened fire. The gun was suppressed, but the supersonic bullets cracked by over our heads. *"He's down! I got him!"*

I rolled over. Sarah was still on top of the flailing woman. "Are you hit?" She shook her head. Asra was in shock, covering her ears with her hands and babbling like an idiot. "Shut her up!" Fluids were pouring from our perforated truck. More bad guys were inbound. It was time to go. "Shafter, we need extraction, *now!*"

♠ ♠ ♠

I scanned nervously out the window as we raced away from the scene of the shootout. This was exactly why we always tried to use multiple vehicles. The colonel was going to be pissed that we'd lost another one. Wheeler was driving, Hudson was riding shotgun. Tailor was in the back of the van, scanning out the rear window with his rifle in his lap. Sarah and I were in the back, too, as was our guest. Asra Elnadi was still prattling on about something.

"What's she saying?" Hudson snapped.

"She says she's very sorry. Federov must have had her tailed, and . . ." Sarah scowled. "Mike, she says you'll regret roughing her up, and that she'll complain to our superiors and have you punished."

I looked over at her incredulously. The arms dealer was an attractive woman of about forty. Her mascara was running badly. She glared back at me with an indignant look that said *don't you know who I am?*

I made a face at her and turned toward Tailor. "What took you so long back there?"

"There was a crane in the way. I couldn't get a shot. I had to run a ways."

"If you didn't smoke so damn much, you'd have gotten there faster."

He turned around and grinned at me. "You ain't worth that!"

Conex containers were flying past as we sped out of the port, pulling onto a main road. Wheeler had been trying to keep our speed reasonable, so as to not draw attention to us, but he floored it now that we were in the open.

"Damn it. A bunch of sedans just pulled out behind us," Tailor snapped. "They're on us."

"They weren't in visual range," Wheeler said tersely. "How're they following us now?"

"She's been bugged," Hudson said. Asra shrieked at me as I ripped her purse away, but sure enough, I found the little tracking device a second later. I passed it forward, and Hudson tossed it out his window. Too bad they had a visual on us now, which meant we either had to lose them the old-fashioned way, or shoot it out. "Pat her down, Sarah." Sarah didn't complain, but Asra Elnadi certainly did. "Tell her that she can either let you do it, or I will." Once that was translated, it finally shut her up.

We raced south, toward the main part of town. There was more traffic here, which we could use to our advantage. "I'm going to get on the parkway," Wheeler said as he took the turnoff. It made sense. It was way too easy to get lost on the backstreets. Hudson was on the radio with Control, trying to get us some help. Several sets of headlights were gaining rapidly on us. They'd followed us onto the parkway.

"Shit! Shit! Shit!" Wheeler suddenly applied the brakes. Traffic had slowed to a stop.

"Oh, God, what *now*?" I asked in frustration. Then I saw the flashing lights. Zubaran security forces had set up a checkpoint. Two police cars were parked there, along with an army APC, and the road had been funneled down to a single lane in the center. Camouflaged soldiers and blue-suited police officers were stopping each car, checking the occupants. One car had been pulled off to the side to be searched.

This was new. Our antics had been causing the Zubarans some serious problems, but this was the first time we'd run into a random checkpoint.

"It's the damned curfew!" Wheeler said, looking around anxiously. There was nowhere to turn off. They'd placed the roadblock such that anyone pulling onto the parkway would be committed, and flipping around would bring us right back to the pursuing mobsters.

"They've stopped," Tailor reported from the back. "They see the cops too." At least Federov's men weren't stupid enough to start a gunfight with the police right there, but we were trapped. "We've got to go through. Hide your guns."

They were still searching that one car, and it appeared they only left room enough to search one at a time. We might get through this. Other cars were being waved through with just cursory examinations. But then again, we were a carload of obvious Westerners. Dead Six had provided us all with forged documents for just this contingency, but if the car got searched and they found our weapons, we'd have a serious problem.

"Let me do the talking," Sarah suggested. She was the only one of us that spoke the language.

Hudson thought about it for a second and then struggled to maneuver his bulk between the seats so Sarah could get up front. It was rather difficult for him, but finally we got Sarah into the passenger's seat before we were close enough for the troops at the checkpoint to see us.

It took forever for the line of cars to move forward. The soldiers ahead seemed to be as unmotivated as third-world armies normally were on this kind of duty. We had a good chance of breezing right through this. As an added bonus, we'd be long gone before Federov's men could make it through. There were over a dozen soldiers and cops manning the checkpoint, but only a few of them seemed to be engaged in doing any actual work. The rest stood around shiftlessly, smoking or talking to each other.

Tailor stashed his rifle under a blanket. "Everybody stay calm, but if this goes south, lay down as much fire as you can. Wheeler, drive right between those cop cars and get us the hell out of here. Sarah, your job is to make sure we don't have to do that? Got it?"

Sarah just nodded. Hudson was sitting on the other side of Asra now, looking really uneasy. He and Wheeler had spent a lot of time manning checkpoints in Iraq, and I figured he'd much rather be on the other side of the roadblock right now. "Wheeler, be cool, man. Just be cool."

A few minutes later it was our turn. Wheeler rolled his window down as a soldier walked up to the van. The soldier was young, but he seemed like he was on the ball. He kept one hand on the pistol on his belt as he scowled at the carload of Westerners. The back of the van was dark, and had no windows. He didn't seem to have a flashlight.

The soldier said something. Wheeler just smiled and passed over his papers. Sarah responded in Arabic, but the soldier snapped back at her harshly. He either didn't like being addressed by someone he wasn't talking to, or he didn't like being addressed by a woman. He studied Wheeler's papers intently, looking for any discrepancies. It was just our luck that we'd found one of the only people in the Middle East who gave a shit about doing a good job. Even better, he spoke English.

"Americans?"

"Yes, sir," Wheeler responded, cheerful as he could be. "We're working on the natural-gas pipeline for Zubara National Energy."

The soldier nodded but seemed suspicious. "What is your business in Ash Shamal? This is a dangerous place for Americans at night."

Wheeler had already thought of the cover story. "We had to pick up some diagrams at the Ash Shamal branch office. It took longer than expected, and I got lost in the dark."

The other soldiers were all sitting on their asses, but many of them had rifles close at hand. The cupola on top of the armored car was manned and equipped with a machine gun. The car ahead of us pulled away, giving us a clear shot to freedom. Wheeler's eyes flicked nervously forward. The young soldier was nodding as he thought about Wheeler's story.

"Foreign criminals are murdering people in this part of the city. There was a shooting down at the harbor. Do you know anything about that?"

"No, sir," Wheeler replied cautiously.

"No?" The soldier asked sarcastically, and leaned farther in. Sarah tried to speak to him again, but he ignored her. *Damn it, why wouldn't he just let us go?* His gaze lingered on Asra and her smeared makeup. Then he studied me and Hudson for a moment. My carbine was in the backpack between my legs. I moved one hand to the sliding-door latch. The soldier removed his head from the window and addressed Wheeler loudly. "Step out of the car. All of you, step out of the car."

"Officer, can't we—" Wheeler began to speak but

stopped as the soldier suddenly yanked out his pistol and stuck it in our driver's face. "Whoa! Hey, man! Relax!"

"Out of the car!" the soldier shouted. The other soldiers and police officers looked up in confusion. The APC gunner swung the machine gun around so it was pointed at our van.

I didn't have my own window. I could only see the soldier's extended gun hand now. More troops appeared behind us, curious at the commotion. They tried to look in through the tinted back windows. Tailor reached under the blanket. Sarah was shouting something in Arabic. The soldier was shouting back at her. Somebody banged something hard against the opposite side of the van. Asra flinched so violently that it made me jump.

Then there was a gunshot. *The Calm* slowed everything down. I looked just in time to see the soldier's gun move down out of recoil. Wheeler said something unintelligible. A small amount of blood splattered against the interior of our windshield.

"Drive!" Tailor shouted. The rear glass shattered as he opened fire through it, killing a soldier. Another gunshot roared through the van. Sarah had pulled her .45 and fired out the driver's side window, right past Wheeler's face. I slid the side door open and brought my carbine up even though the stock was still folded. The soldier that had been questioning us was hitting the pavement, a hole between his eyes. I pointed the carbine up at the gunner in the cupola and fired five or six times. The first shots missed but at least one went home, dropping the gunner down into his hatch in a puff of blood. I shifted to the next target, a police officer who was clumsily trying to draw his pistol. Two rounds went through his chest. The soldier next to him was trying to bring his rifle to bear, which had been slung across his back. We began to move as I popped off three more shots. I watched the soldier collapse to the ground as we sped by.

Tailor kept firing at the checkpoint through the back window, forcing the troops to keep their heads down as we made our getaway. He flipped around as I slid my door closed, noticing the blood on the inside of the windshield. "Who's hit? Wheeler? Sarah?"

"I'm fine!" Sarah shouted.

"I'm okay," Wheeler hissed, concentrating on the road. "Asshole shot me in the arm."

Tailor turned back around. "Get us out of here." He went back to shooting.

Asra had been screaming. I hadn't heard her over the gunshots. "Shut up!" Hudson bellowed at her as he moved up between the front seats. "Let me drive," he said. "Let Val look at that, man."

"I'm okay!" Wheeler snapped. "I'm fine! Let me drive!"

Tailor dropped the empty magazine out of his carbine and looked over his shoulder. "Val, we—" He was cut off as the van swerved violently to the right. Tires squealed, and we were thrown around the cabin.

When I looked back to the front of the van, Sarah was reaching over, holding the steering wheel. Wheeler was slumped forward and wasn't moving. Just like that, he was gone.

It took us over an hour to get to the safe house, even though it wasn't all that far from the port. The Zoob had already been in a heightened state of alert because of our exploits and the subsequent spike in terrorist attacks. A shootout at the docks and another at a police checkpoint had put the city on lockdown. We had to go very far out of our way to avoid more checkpoints.

Two vehicles were waiting for us at the safe house. One of them was driven by two of Colonel Hunter's security men. They grabbed Asra Elnadi and drove off with her before we even got in the door. The other, a van, was driven by Hal and one of the other medics.

Other than some cuts and bruises, I was unscathed. The same went for Tailor, Hudson, and Sarah. Wheeler was dead. The bullet had struck him in the bicep, traveled through his arm, and entered his chest through the armpit opening of his armor vest. He hadn't even known that he was dying. There was nothing we could have done for him. My shirt was sticky with his drying blood.

After the four of us had been seen by the medics, we assembled outside by the garage. Hal backed his van up to the open garage door and gave us a body bag. Together, and in silence, Hudson, Tailor, and I stripped Wheeler of his equipment. When that was done, Tailor and I stood back while Hudson quietly said a few words to his old friend. We then carried Wheeler's body to the medics' van. It was the closest thing the affable former army paratrooper would ever get to a proper funeral.

"Tailor?" Hal said, approaching us after a while. "Hunter wants you to come back for debrief."

"What?" Tailor said, sounding agitated. "We had kind of a bad night."

"I know, but he wants you to come back. Valentine,

McAllister, he said there'd be a car for you two sometime tomorrow."

Sarah seemed suddenly uncomfortable. "Wait a minute. Don't they need me to debrief Asra?"

"You're not the only one that can speak Arabic, you know. Besides, you're exhausted. You're in no shape to do any work tonight. Tailor just has to give a report. Then he can go to bed."

"Why not just bring us all back?" Hudson asked. He hadn't spoken in a while. "They need someone to stay here and watch the house or something?"

"Well, there's only one extra seat in the front of the van," Hal said. "And . . ." he hesitated. "I didn't figure anyone would want to ride in the back with Wheeler."

"I will," Hudson said. "It's no problem."

"You sure, man?" Tailor asked.

"Yep," Hudson said. "Wheeler and me, we zipped six of our soldiers into body bags last time we were deployed. We carried them away. Stayed with them for as long as we could. I'll ride with him one last time. I owe him that much. He never would've come over here if it wasn't for me."

"Okay," Hal said quietly. "We need to get going now."

"There any food in this place?" I asked. Hal just shrugged. "Yeah, I'll be fine. I just need to get some sleep."

"Take it easy, bro," Tailor said as he climbed into the van. It disappeared through the gate, leaving Sarah and me standing alone under the stars. We had the big house all to ourselves. *Awkward . . .*

"Mike, I'm sorry about Wheeler," she said as we went inside. "Are you okay?"

"I just need to take a shower."

"Me, too," she said. Fortunately, the big house had two bathrooms, so it wasn't an issue. The medics had brought fresh clothes for us to the safe house, so we wouldn't have to run around in blood-stained khakis for the rest of the night.

After my shower, all I wanted was to get some sleep, but sleep just wouldn't come. The longer I lay there, the madder I got that I couldn't sleep. I rolled over, then rolled over again. I was too hot, so I cranked up the air conditioner. Then I was too cold. Then my foot itched. Then I had to go to the bathroom. Then . . .

"Fuck!" I snarled, throwing my pillow across the room. "Goddamn it!" I stood up and began to pace around in the darkness. The clock on the nightstand said 4:45 and I was still awake. I stormed across the room, picked up the clock, yanked the cord out of the socket, and threw it against the wall. It smashed into pieces of broken plastic.

I stood there, breathing heavily, ridiculously mad but unsure of what I was mad at. I just wanted to go to sleep and forget things for a while.

Wheeler was dead. Yesterday he was there, today he was gone, just like that. I had no one to talk to, nothing to distract me, and no alcohol to numb me. All I could do was sit there, awake when I should be sleeping, thinking about how I'd watched my friend die and what I could have done differently. It was *killing* me.

There was a quiet knock on my door. It was Sarah. "Mike, are you okay?" she asked. Her voice was slightly raspy, like she'd been crying.

"Yeah, I'm . . . yeah . . ." I said, even though I was

anything but okay. Sarah opened the door a little bit and peeked in at me.

"Can I come in?"

I sighed. "Sure," I said and sat down on the bed. I turned on the stupid-looking lamp that sat on the nightstand. Sarah was wearing the same short shorts and T-shirt she'd been wearing the first time she came into my room, our first night in-country. It was strange, but she looked a little older now.

"You broke your clock," she noted. "And you look like hell." I became suddenly self-conscious and looked around for my T-shirt.

"It's been a bad night."

"I know," Sarah said. She crossed the room and sat down next to me. "I've been in my room crying for an hour."

"Are *you* okay?" I asked, looking over at her.

"I don't know why I was crying," she said. "I don't feel anything. I didn't feel anything when Wheeler died. I didn't feel anything when I killed that solder. I didn't feel . . ." Tears welled up in Sarah's eyes, and her hands started to shake. "I didn't feel anything at all."

"That's normal," I said. "It's adrenaline. You're going through adrenaline dump right now. Makes you crazy."

"How do you *do* this?" she asked, wiping her eyes. "I saw you. You shot those three guys dead like it was nothing. It took like four seconds. I mean, oh my God, how do you do it?"

I shrugged. "It's what I do. It's all that I do, I guess. I try not to think about it."

"I just want to go home," Sarah said, sounding like she couldn't cry anymore. "I hate this country."

Me, too. "But, hey, we're alive. Right now that counts for a lot."

"Thank you," she said. Sarah then yawned widely.

"You should get some rest," I suggested. "You're exhausted. I am too."

"I know," she said, rubbing her eyes. "I just don't want to be alone right now. This big house is too quiet." Sarah looked down at her lap for a moment, then back up at me. "Is it alright if I sleep in here?"

"What?" I said, surprised. "I mean . . . sure. If you want."

"Don't get the wrong idea," she said more sternly. "I just don't want to be by myself. Okay?"

"It's fine."

"Are you sure?" she asked.

"I'm sure," I said, trying to sound reassuring. "Lay down." Sarah thanked me again, gave me a small kiss on the cheek, and slid under the covers on the right side of the bed. I turned the lamp back off and laid my head on the pillow. This time sleep quickly overtook me.

It was daylight out when I awoke. My clock was still smashed on the floor, so I wasn't sure what time it was. I took a deep breath and closed my eyes as the events of the night before came back to me. I relived, in my mind, watching Wheeler die, and I quietly swore to myself.

There are always doubts when a teammate dies. You question yourself, and your confidence is shattered. *Did I do everything I could? Was there any way it could have been avoided? Did something I do cause him to get killed?* The hardest thing to do after losing one of your own is to go back into combat again, burdened with the knowledge that your surviving teammates are all counting on you. I've known guys that could never get over that hurdle, and I've seen it end careers.

In my case, that wasn't really an option. There was nothing I'd have liked more than to simply quit and go home, but it seemed like the only way to go home early was in a body bag.

It was then that I noticed something warm and soft pressed against me. Sarah, still asleep, had wrapped her arm and one leg around me. She quietly slept, her face a few inches from my right ear, her auburn hair splashed across the pillow.

God, she's beautiful. Sarah opened her eyes then, as if my thinking about her woke her up.

"Hey," I said, looking into her eyes.

"Hey, you," she replied. "You make a good pillow."

"I'm glad you think so. I can't feel my right arm."

"I'm sorry," Sarah said with a little smile. "You want me to move?"

"Not really," I confessed. "This is . . . nice. A nice way to wake up."

Sarah agreed. "Yeah," she said, squeezing me a bit tighter. "So tell me. Why is it every time you almost get your ass shot off you end up in bed with me?"

I had no idea how to answer that. I just looked at her, mouth slightly open, and she giggled. "Um . . ."

"Yes?" she asked.

"Because you're the Queen of Crazy Town?" I suggested tentatively.

Sarah gently pushed my face away and laughed. "I can

see where I gave you that impression. What time is it, anyway?"

I shrugged. "My clock is still broken."

"Well . . . they'll call before they send a car," Sarah said. "We could be here all day. They're trying to limit traffic outside the compound during daylight hours or when the roads are busy. You know, because of the checkpoints." Sarah trailed off and exhaled heavily.

"Listen," I said. "You did good out there. You weren't trained for that kind of job, but you held it together. You did what you had to do. No hesitation, nothing. I'm impressed." I really was.

"You don't have to say that to make me feel better."

"I'm not," I said sternly. "Your quick thinking is probably the reason more of us didn't get killed. I'm proud of you."

"Thank you," she said softly. She kissed me sweetly.

Smiling, I turned toward her a little and gently brushed a stray strand of hair out of her face. She closed her eyes as I caressed her cheek. Her right hand slid up to my shoulder, pulling me closer to her. I scootched over a bit and kissed her, deeply. She made a very soft, pleasurable sigh and ran her fingers through my buzzed hair.

I rolled onto my back, pulling Sarah with me. Straddling me, she only stopped kissing me for a moment and pulled her shirt off over her head. She leaned forward again, kissing me passionately, her hair tickling my face and my neck.

Sarah and I made love for a long time, and, for a while, I was able to stop thinking about all the things that were bothering me. Like how horrible it was that we were fooling around like a couple of high-school kids on prom night just hours after we watched one of my guys bleed to death. Or how I treated her the night I got drunk. Or what was going to happen between us after this. However it played out, it was going to be *complicated*.

At that moment, though, with her in my arms, I didn't worry about any of that. I was *alive*, goddamn it, and so was she. For the time being, that was all that mattered.

VALENTINE
Fort Saradia National Historical Site
April 18
1230

I stepped into my room and closed the door behind me, looking down at the sheet of paper in my hand. Hunter had given it to me after Sarah and I returned from Safe House 5.

It was a BOLO, or "be on the lookout" alert, passed down from Gordon Willis. The photocopy was about a young woman named Jillian Del Toro. She had been an intern at the US Embassy in Zubara, on loan to the State Department from the Department of Agriculture. She was a low-level employee but apparently had access to one James Fiore, the assistant ambassador. Fiore had been killed by the enemy after the US Embassy was evacuated. According to the dossier I'd been given, Jill Del Toro was apparently selling embassy secrets to General Al Sabah's intelligence people and had gotten Fiore killed.

Del Toro was still at large. She wasn't considered

dangerous, but she was a traitor, and Gordon wanted her brought in, dead or alive.

I studied the picture of the young woman. Miss Del Toro was twenty-five years old, fresh out of college. She was beautiful, with dark hair, bright eyes, and a very pretty face. Maybe it was just me, but she didn't look like a traitor. I was probably being naïve, I thought, but something about this whole thing didn't sit right.

Of course, very little of what was passed down from Gordon Willis sat right with me. I tossed the BOLO on my bed and sat. As I did so, I noticed the strange key that I'd found in Adar's safe, still sitting where I'd left it.

I reached over and picked up the ancient-looking trinket and examined it again. Turning the knob on the base caused dozens of tiny pins to pop out of nearly invisible recesses in the object's shaft. I twisted the knob the other way, and the tiny pins smoothly disappeared.

Sarah and I hadn't really gotten any sleep, and I was tired. I was off for the rest of the day and decided then that I was going to take a nap. Before I could lie down, there was a soft knock on my door. The door opened and Sarah stepped into my room, quietly closing the door behind her.

"Hey, you," she said, smiling widely when she saw me. I felt a smile appear on my own face as I stood. She met me in the middle of my room, stepping into my arms and kissing me.

In some subtle way, Sarah was a different person to me now. At first, she was just some chick I thought was hot. Then we talked a bit, and then we slept together. But now we'd been in combat together, bled together, buried a friend together. We were more than friends and lovers now. We were *comrades*.

"Hey yourself," I said, not letting go of her. "What's going on?"

"What's that in your hand?" she asked, indicating the strange trinket I was holding.

I held it up. "I don't really know, but watch this." I twisted the knob again, causing the pins and teeth to reappear. Another twist of the knob retracted them.

"Wow," Sarah said, taking it from my hand to examine it. "Where'd you get this? It's pretty."

Suddenly, I felt uncomfortable. "I found it the other night," I said, sitting back down on my bed. "It was in a safe in Adar's house."

Sarah looked down at the trinket, apparently not bothered by where I'd gotten it. "Why didn't you report it?"

I shrugged. "Hunter didn't ask about it, so I figured they weren't looking for it anyway. It's just some doodad I found. I've collected a bunch of crap since I've been here, you know. Besides, I forgot about it. That was kind of a bad night."

The expression on Sarah's face changed subtly. "Yeah, it was," she said. All at once I felt butterflies in my stomach. Something was bothering her. "We need to talk about that," she said.

I sighed, lowering my eyes. "Okay." I patted the bed next to me so Sarah would sit down. "So let's talk."

"You hurt me," she said, crossing her legs as she sat down. "I came in here trying to help you. You screamed at me, swore at me, and told me to get out." Sarah's voice was perfectly calm as she spoke. I felt like curling up into a ball.

"I was drunk," I said after a moment. Sarah's eyes flashed. I raised my hands in surrender before she got too upset. "I'm not using that as an excuse," I said quickly. "I'm really not. It's just a fact. I had a bad night. Seeing that girl . . . it just . . . I was still in shock. I couldn't handle it. It doesn't matter, though. I shouldn't have taken it out on you. Like you said, you were trying to help me, and I pushed you away. I'm sorry. I'm not just saying I'm sorry, either, I really mean it. I . . . I didn't mean to hurt you."

"Well, you did," she said coldly, fidgeting with the key in her hands. I started to say something, but she interrupted me. "But you know what? It's okay. I mean, it's not okay, but it's okay."

I gave her a sidelong glance, not really sure what to say. Sarah laughed, lightening the mood in the room just a little bit. "Have I mentioned I'm crazy?" she asked.

"I gathered," I said, allowing myself a half smile.

"I'm also confused." Sarah exhaled heavily and continued fiddling with the key, trying to think of what to say. "After the other night, I think I got it," she said. "I mean . . . Jesus Christ, I killed a guy, and I cried my eyes out. You go out and do that every day, and they just expect you to keep on doing it and not break down. You broke down, didn't you?"

I looked down at the floor, lowering my head just a little. "When I saw that girl, I . . ."

"I know," Sarah said quietly. "I know. It really bothers you when men hurt women, doesn't it?"

I was surprised by the question. "I guess. I mean . . ."

"I can tell," she said. "Even when you were dragging Asra Elnadi along, you were very careful with her. You probably didn't even bruise her arm."

"I would've shot her if she ran," I said levelly. "Just like I was ordered to."

"I know," Sarah said. "It would've bothered you for a long time, though, wouldn't it?" I nodded my head slightly. "I read your file. I know about your mom. That had to have been awful."

I had just been a teenager when she'd been robbed and murdered by some random meth-heads. "It was, but it's been a really long time."

"I didn't get you at first, you know," she said. "I mean, you're cute and everything, but I didn't think you'd be good for much more than a roll in the hay."

"You think I'm cute?" I interjected, trying to deadpan.

"Shut up," Sarah said, grinning and giving me a little shove. "I'm serious. I didn't think we'd . . . you know . . ."

"Yeah," I said. "This is kind of intense, isn't it?"

Sarah nodded. "But I get it now. I know you guys are under a lot of pressure out there. I mean, oh my God, look at how many people we've lost already!"

"Sarah—"

"I'm not finished. That doesn't change what happened. I came here to help you. You yelled at me and made me feel like a piece of shit." Sarah's cool words hurt me like I was being stabbed. "And I need to know where we stand, right now. Because if this is how you are . . . I'm sorry, I mean, I know what you're going through now, but if this is how you are, I'm not going to be a part of it. I spent three years in a bad relationship, and I'm not going through it again."

I was quiet for a few moments as I tried to figure out what to say. The thought of driving her away terrified me. The thought of trying to build a relationship with her, in the middle of war, also terrified me. I wasn't sure which scared me more. Sarah gave me a hard look, swallowed, and spoke again. "Mike, if you want me in your life . . ."

"I want you in my life," I said awkwardly. "You're just . . . you're amazing. I can't even tell you. I—"

Sarah gently placed a finger over my lips, silencing me. "It's okay. I just needed to hear you say that. Thank you."

We sat together, quietly looking into each other's eyes for a long time. Butterflies danced around in my stomach, and I couldn't think of anything else to say. Right then I knew that I was falling in love with her. It was an amazing feeling, and it scared the hell out of me. I didn't even know if either of us was going to make it out of Zubara alive.

As I looked into her eyes, I asked myself, is it worth the risk? I realized that I'd already made my decision, even before I asked the question. This woman had seen me at my best and at my worst, and she still wanted to be with me. What kind of fool passes that up?

I took the silvery trinket from Sarah's hand, opened the chain, and gently hung it around her neck. She'd said it was pretty.

"Are you giving me this thing? Too cheap to buy me a real present?" She laughed.

"I found this thing that night," I said awkwardly. "So . . . I'm giving it to you, as a promise of a fresh start."

Sarah crinkled her brow at me. "That is so cheesy, but really sweet too. So yes, I accept your token of apology." She laughed again. "Oh, I almost forgot. You're off for the next three days at least."

"The next three days? Are you serious?"

"I talked to Hunter for you. I convinced him you and your chalk need a break. So you don't have anything to do for the next three days but lounge around the fort and relax."

"What about you?"

"I have a briefing I have to be at in . . ." Sarah glanced at her watch. She wore it upside down, so that the face was on the underside of her right wrist. "Four hours. I don't have anything to do until then."

"I can think of something," I said coyly, knowing I sounded more dorky than suave.

"Oh really?" Sarah said, sounding coy herself, as she moved in to kiss me again. "Sounds interesting . . ."

Some time later, Sarah and I lay together in my bed. She was asleep in my arms. Her hair smelled like strawberries. She was a quiet sleeper.

I don't know how long I lay there, holding her in my arms, thinking about things, before I feel asleep. What chance did Sarah and I have in this place? What else could I do? Could we get out somehow? Even if I could find a way to escape Zubara, would I be able to convince Sarah to go with me and leave everyone else behind?

Chapter 11:
For the Good of
the People

LORENZO
April 20

I punished the bag until my knuckles bled.

It was an eighty-pound leather punching bag that I'd found used in a local market. Some duct tape, and it was good as new. I'd hung it up in the corner of the garage and was using it for some stress release. I worked out religiously every morning, but this was different. I'd already been striking the bag furiously for half an hour, and stinging sweat was leaking into my eyes.

I imagined that the bag was Big Eddie. If I could get my hands on whoever he was, I was going to absolutely destroy him. The nerve, the *audacity*, to threaten me, to force me into this . . . I was going to make him pay. I'd worked for him for years, doing his bidding, stealing things, killing people, robbery, extortion, you name it. I had been his lapdog, and I didn't even know if he was real.

Disgusted with what I'd become, I had eventually walked away, naively thinking that I could be safe from his machinations. But somehow he'd figured out who I really was, and that had given him leverage. With a shout, I stepped back and side kicked the bag so hard that a jolt of electricity traveled up the bones of my leg.

I switched my mental picture, and now the bag was the Dead Six operatives. My life was growing complicated, and I didn't like that one bit. My elbows left skin on the bag as I nearly bent it in half with the impacts. Nobody knew a thing. Reaper's electronic digging couldn't find them. Hosani hadn't called me back. None of the urchins, scumbags, villains, and criminals I'd contacted had a clue who they were. They were ghosts.

They'd slip up eventually. Everyone did, and then I would take them. But what if I couldn't find them before Eddie's deadline? Or even worse, what if their operation finished, and they just went home? And the worst possible scenario: Adar's box had already been shipped back to the US and was sitting in some CIA warehouse where they had no clue what they even had.

If that was the case, then I would just have to proceed without it. And that meant my odds of success went from slim to near zero. If the pace of the killings tapered off, then I was going to have to assume the worst, and then I would have to do my worst. I'd have to stick Jill out in the open and see what happened.

Here I was, perfectly willing to take an innocent woman and basically sentence her to death. What kind of monster was I?

You're soft. Weak. I slammed the bag again and again,

breath coming in ragged gasps. Even a couple of years ago, I would have handed her off in a heartbeat. The problem was that she wasn't just a number in an equation now. She'd been living here for a couple of days. She was a decent, kind, trusting person. She was the sort of person that I had avoided all of these years, because they were exactly the type that I didn't want to hurt. I hung out with evil for a reason. She was just a scared girl who only wanted to go home.

With that bleak thought, the last of my energy evaporated, as even I have my limits, and I just hugged the bag close to stop the swaying. Every muscle in my body was on fire, and sweat drizzled down my face and onto the bag, but the leather was cool under my skin.

"Anybody ever tell you that you're kind of intense?"

I hadn't heard her enter over the rhythmic pounding in my ears. Jill was standing at the base of the stairs into the apartment, watching me. I pushed away from the bag. "Yeah, I get that once in a while. . . . What're you doing up so early?"

"Couldn't sleep," she said with a shrug. The bruised discoloration around her eye had subsided and she was looking better. "I've got a lot on my mind. You know."

I walked around the front of the van. "Understandable. But if you've come to talk about it, you've really got the wrong guy," I said as I picked up my shirt. My torso and limbs were crisscrossed with scars from bullets, knives, burns, and shrapnel, and most of them had not been stitched up by actual medical professionals, either. It always made me a little self-conscious.

"If I wanted somebody in touch with their emotional

side, I'd talk to Carl," she replied sarcastically. "Wow. You know, you're pretty ripped for an old guy. . . ."

"I'm not *that* old." Well, I had been in junior high the year Jill had been born.

"Easy there. I was just trying to make a joke. Seriously, though, you're going out looking for Dead Six again today, aren't you?"

"That's the plan," I answered as I pulled the shirt over my head. It was instantly drenched with sweat. My muscles ached. "I'm going to check out Al Khor today." It was the safest, and therefore most boring, part of town. It was also the most modernized section and was where the Americans and Europeans tended to live. There was a possibility that someone over there had seen our shooters.

She was regarding me strangely. "Take me with you."

I stopped. "Why?"

"I've been cooped up in here for days. I'm bored."

As a professional liar, I'm a master of knowing when I was being lied to. I just waited. She rolled her eyes. "Fine. It's just something I have to do. I have to feel like I'm doing *something*. This might just be business for you, but this is personal to me. These people killed my friends, and they tried to kill me. Then they burned them. They were good men, and they deserved better. I have to do this."

Sighing, I studied her. I could understand that feeling. I could even kind of respect it.

"Please?"

I didn't say anything as I pushed past her and climbed the stairs. My silence must have hit a nerve, as she immediately blew up. "Damn it, Lorenzo! I'm not some useless child. I don't care what your stupid secret mission is! I—" She was cut off as the bundle of clothing hit her in the face.

"Get dressed," I said from the top of the stairs.

"Is this a burka?"

"Sort of. If you're going to be here, you might as well learn how not to be totally useless. I said get dressed. You coming or what?"

It is surprising how foggy it can get along the Persian Gulf in the mornings. A fat gray cloud hung over the city, and only the lights at the tops of the buildings in the Khor district were visible as we crossed the bridge.

"Is this really necessary?" Jill asked through the bag that was covering her head. "Can I take this off yet?"

"Think she's lost enough?" I asked Carl. He shrugged. "It's for your own good, Jill. If you're captured, this way you can't be tortured into telling them where our hideout is."

"You mean if I run away, I can't sell you out," she snapped. "Well, duh. I was lost in the first couple of minutes, but that was a while ago, and now we're on the Gamal bridge going over the ocean. I can tell. The embassy is only a couple miles from here. It's the only big bridge in town, and it sounds like we're on a big bridge, so unless we drove all the way to Dubai while I wasn't paying attention, can I please take this stupid bag off now?"

Carl leaned over from the driver's seat. "She's got a point."

"Next time, it'll be a blindfold *and* a gag," I muttered. "Okay. Take it off."

Jill complied. "See? Told you."

"Goodie for you. Now listen carefully. I'll be talking to a lot of people. You're going to do exactly what I tell you, when I tell you, and you are not going to talk. At all. You sound like an American and walk like an American. Hell, you've been eating American food, and you even smell like an American. Keep your head down, shoulders slumped, because you're too damn tall, and stay behind me."

"I've been around this part of town before," Jill replied.

"Not like this you haven't. There's a lot of women around, and in Khor, most of them are dressed pretty normal. You're not one of them. You're invisible. You're going to play my obedient little wifey-poo, which means you carry the shopping bags and mostly just watch. I'm going to teach you how to blend in. We'll be in radio contact with Reaper back at base if we need him."

"What's Reaper do?"

"Besides play video games and watch porn?" Carl responded. "I'm not sure."

"Reaper's tapped into *everything*. Hacking, information piracy, anything complicated. In a way, he's as good at what he does as I am at what I do. Hell, he could screw with the traffic lights here from our apartment if we need him to." In truth, behind Reaper's pathetic tough-guy facade lurked the soul of an über-nerd who should have been working for NASA.

"What's your job, Lorenzo?"

I smiled. "I'm management." In actuality I wore a few hats, none of which Jill needed to know the specifics of. I was the master of disguise, the acrobatic second-story man, the con, the swindler, the lady's man, certified locksmith and safecracker, a ruthless fighter with hand or blade, and wasn't too shabby as a gunslinger. "These guys do all the work. I take the credit."

"What's Carl do?"

"Drive and shoot stuff," he explained. "People are stupid, so talking to them, that's Lorenzo's job."

"Carl's always my backup when we work. He's the getaway driver and heavy artillery."

"How many guns do you have in here?"

"A few . . ." And an RPG and a mess of Semtex, but she didn't need to know that.

"Can I have one?"

"No," Carl and I responded simultaneously.

This part of town was sleek, modern, damn-near swanky. Most of the buildings looked new, all glass and concrete. It had been less than a decade since the current emir had deposed his father. The old emir had been a pretty typical dictator, and he'd stuffed his Swiss bank accounts fat while most of his people lived in poverty. The current emir was a decent enough sort by all accounts. Sure, he was still ruthless and brutal, but he'd decided that the days of his country being a cultural backwater were done. He'd made friends with the West, told the Fundies to chill out, brought in big-time infrastructure investments, and even went so far as to say crazy, controversial stuff like Israel shouldn't be burned into nuclear oblivion. Like I said, pretty decent by this part of the world's standards.

And Al Khor was the shining example to the rest of the world that Zubara didn't suck anymore. I don't know if the emir was jealous of the nearby UAE or Qatar, but he was doing his best to keep up with the Joneses. Fueled by oil money, Zubara now had three hospitals, a university, luxury hotels, a big museum, a fancy new zoo, and, very impressively for a city of under a million residents, *two* Bentley dealerships.

Too bad the emir had stepped on so many toes in the process, because the line of people mean enough to take him down was getting longer and longer.

"*Sabah! Sabah! Sabah! Sabah!*" the crowd at the end of the street chanted, led by some professional agitator in a black hood with a bullhorn. They were a hundred yards away, and there were probably fifty of them, all relatively young and nicely dressed, probably students, and they were stacked in front of one of the tall municipal buildings. They were waving signs with pictures of a bearded man wearing a purple beret. Since there weren't any rocks or Molotov cocktails being thrown, it was relatively boring.

I stopped to watch. Jill halted obediently behind me. In true chauvinistic style, I had loaded her with a bunch of bags full of items purchased from the local shops. If you were going to be questioning merchants, it helped to spread a little love in the process. Jill had followed me for hours now, not understanding a word that passed between me and the various people I'd spoken with. I wondered if she was sick of it yet.

Glancing back, I saw that she was waiting patiently, burdened down by fifty pounds of miscellaneous crap that was probably just going to get thrown away after Reaper picked through it for souvenirs. Interviewing merchants looking for Dead Six had been an utter waste of time. Only Jill's dark eyes were visible under the blue silk scarf.

Those eyes drifted over to the protestors, then back to me, wondering what was up.

The sidewalks were relatively crowded with the late lunch crowd, and we were right in front of a café filled with government employees, who were trying to eat and watch the protestors at the same time. Nobody was close enough to hear me speak English, so I leaned in.

"General Sabah's supporters are getting braver. See, with all of the killings lately, his followers are getting fired up that the emir isn't doing enough to stop it. If the emir loses enough support from the right people, then I bet you money the general is ready to have a coup to restore order, for the good of the people, of course."

Jill looked around nervously. I signaled that she could speak. "They talked about the general at the embassy. That's one of the reasons we got the order to get out. He hates Americans."

There was a concrete bench nearby, and these sandals were hurting my feet. I gestured for her to take a seat. A bunch of pigeons immediately surrounded us. They were probably escapees from the rooftop cages that littered the city. Pigeons here were a delicacy, and these once-fat things were reduced to scavenging for crumbs. I shooed one away.

"Men like him hate whoever is convenient to put them into power, and then they'll hate whoever's convenient to keep them in power. Sabah's side is supported by the Iranians. The emir screwed up. The Zubaran army hardly has any natives in it. Once the people started getting rich, they farmed out all the low-paying jobs to imported labor, and they included the army in that." I gestured around the street. "Notice that all of the waiters, taxi drivers, janitors, they're all Indians, Filipinos, Malays, or Sri Lankans? Sabah did the same thing with the military, but he filled it with Iranians and Syrians."

"So why doesn't the emir just fire the general?"

I pointed at the mob. "Because of useful idiots like them. The emir wouldn't just fire Al Sabah, he'd execute him if he could get away with it. But then half the city would get burned down, and that's assuming the emir's got the manpower to take him anyway. I'm guessing probably a quarter of the security forces would go with the emir, if that. Either way, an overt move by either one to topple the other would blow this place right up. I've seen it before."

"Where?" Jill asked, obnoxiously curious.

"Sixteen years ago I helped overthrow the democratically elected government of an African country," I explained. "It wasn't pretty. When a country collapses, the scumbags run free, raping and murdering. It's like nothing you can imagine. Think slaughter on an industrial scale. You take any city, take away their electricity, food, and water for a week, and it'll turn into *Mad Max*, guaranteed. And there's always some asshole ready to take those things away for his own benefit. I've seen it up close in Africa twice, Mexico, Chechnya, Haiti, Burma, Afghanistan, you name it, anyplace that has fallen apart, I've been there, and I see it coming soon to Zubara. I can *smell* it."

Jill studied the mob. "You've seen a lot of suffering."

I snorted. "I've *caused* a lot of suffering. Naw, that's just what I do. I seek out chaos. I make my living off the men that cause chaos. Assholes like Sabah are my meal ticket. Regular thieves steal from normal people. I steal from assholes."

"So, you're trying to say you're Robin Hood?" Jill scoffed.

"No, of course not. Assholes just have more money, and it isn't like they can cry to the cops when they get taken. It's worked out well for me."

"So, you justify being bad by only victimizing bad people."

"It's like karma, or something . . ." I trailed off as I noticed a black limo roll past us. It parked before the protestors at the front of the building. Apparently the mob was blocking the garage. A group of blue-uniformed security forces came down the government building's steps and surrounded the limo, rifles shouldered. The mob pulled back instinctively in the face of the guns. A young man in a designer suit stepped from the back of the limo.

"I think that's the Interior Minister," Jill said. "He's like the emir's nephew or something. He came to an embassy function once."

I surveyed the crowd. The students were full of noise but weren't so tough facing half a dozen men with rifles. In fact, they were quieter now. The chanting had stopped. The black-hooded agitator with the bullhorn was suspiciously missing.

"Jill, get up. Let's go." I stood. She started collecting the bags. I grabbed her arm. "Leave them."

The emir's nephew was met by an older man in a suit. They greeted each other warmly, surrounded by their loyal security forces. The young man adjusted his tie and smiled. My eyes narrowed as I picked out one person moving against the tide of the mob. Jill sensed the urgency in my grasp and sped up. We walked quickly back the direction we'd come. "Don't run. Don't look suspicious. Don't look back. When I push you down, cover your ears and keep your head *down*."

I glanced back. We were too far away to understand whatever it was the suicide bomber screamed. Probably just a teenager, he opened his vest, exposing stacks of gray wrapping his torso, and raised his arms wide. There was a long moment in time as the security forces and the nephew froze and the crowd right around the bomber instinctively recoiled. The pigeons leapt skyward in a cloud. I threw my arm around Jill's shoulders and took us both to the pavement.

The blast rippled across the ground and through my lungs. The concussion was massive. A wave of sound and energy rolled over us. Windows half a block away shattered.

Lying there, eyes clenched shut, hands pressed flat over my ears, I kept my weight on Jill, but no secondary explosions came. I uncovered my ears. First I could only hear a high-pitched whine, and that eventually settled into car alarms. Then I could finally hear the screaming of the wounded. As I rolled over, a wall of smoke and dust hung around the front of the government building.

People were wandering, dazed, bloody. Mangled bodies were splayed everywhere. The limo was twisted back into itself, jagged metal protruding. Severed limbs and bits of tissue littered the street. The shattered steps that had held the Interior Minister were coated in a red slurry of ribs and organs. The mob was *gone*.

Children were crying. A dog was barking. Where the hell had a dog come from? Already people were pulling out their cell phones. Some idiot's first inclination was to use his camera phone to take a picture of the carnage.

I got shakily to my feet. The café we'd been standing next to was a mess. Tables overturned, awning broken and hanging at a bizarre angle. One of the waiters was down, a giant chunk of hurled glass embedded in his throat, gurgling and thrashing on the sidewalk. Jill grabbed my thobe and hauled herself to her feet. Her facial scarf was dangling down her chest as she looked about in bewilderment, a stream of blood trickling from her nose.

"Got to keep going," I ordered. I put my hand on her shoulder and propelled her in the correct direction.

"Okay. Okay." Snapping back to reality, Jill realized her face was exposed and pulled the scarf back into place. We walked briskly down the street, part of a herd of humanity trying to get away from the terror. I guided her into an alley. Already I could hear the first sirens.

The alley was dark and cool. I got us behind a loading dock. "Hold your arms out," I ordered. Jill was confused but did exactly as I ordered. I ran my hands down the insides of her arms, then through her voluminous robes, patting her down, looking for blood. I'd seen people bleed out from shrapnel wounds to arteries without even knowing they'd been hit. Torso clear, legs clear. *No blood except the superficial amount on her face.* "Are you all right?"

"I'm . . . I'm fine. All those people . . ."

"Dead," I responded as I took my radio earpiece out of my shirt. "Nothing you can do about it. Hang on! Carl, come in, Carl!"

"What was that?" he bellowed in my ear.

"Suicide bomber. We're moving back toward Ensun and the Gamal Parkway on foot. Once we're clear of the responders, I'll call for pickup."

"*Stay low and watch your back,*" Carl ordered.

"You, too." I pulled the earpiece out. "We've got to keep moving. This place is going to be swarming with security forces fast, and we don't want to get picked up for questioning." Jill nodded quickly. Her head was still in the game. *Good.* I took a handkerchief out of my vest and roughly wiped the blood from under her nose. "Keep your head down and keep up with me."

We went out the other side of the alley and started walking. The streets were full of workers now as people flooded out of their respective buildings to see what was going on. A pillar of black smoke rose into the air behind us.

The war had just arrived in Al Khor.

We were back in the apartment within an hour of the bombing.

My crew sat around our kitchen table. There was a white leaflet in the center. These things had been posted all over Ash Shamal within minutes of the explosion. I'd had Carl pull over and pick one up from one of the little kids that were passing them out on every single corner in the neighborhood.

The leaflet told all about how over twenty innocent students, most of them from this very district, were peacefully protesting in front of the interior ministry and had been massacred by the emir's personal guard. Apparently there had been another attack by the Zionist murderers, this one against the emir's own family, and he was still too emasculated to root them out; rather, he reacted in a heavy-handed and inept way against the innocent students of Ash Shamal's madrassa. Zubara needed the strong leadership of General Mubarak Al Sabah to get us through these tough times, not the Jew-loving emir . . . so on and so forth.

"That's such bullshit," Jill spat as Reaper finished translating it for her. "That's not what happened at all."

"Reality never matters," I muttered. "Just feelings. Get the masses riled up enough and you can do anything. Propaganda doesn't have to be true—it just has to *feel* true to enough stupid people. Make them feel picked on, then fill them full of hope about how you'll change stuff. Works every time."

"I so hate this place." Jill put her head down on the table. "Have you got any more of that ibuprofen? My head's killing me," she muttered through her arm. Shockwaves tend to have that effect on people. Reaper got her the bottle.

Carl glanced at me. "The bomb, how big?"

"At least twenty pounds. I was too far away to get a good look, but I'm guessing it was packed in nails or something from the mess it made."

"Good thing you weren't close enough to get a good look or we wouldn't be talking right now. These guys ain't fucking around," Carl responded. He'd been at the receiving end of a bombing during a job involving the Tamil Tigers several years back. That one had been wrapped in industrial staples. My friend still had one embedded in his back. It occasionally set off metal detectors. Carl didn't like bombs, unless he was the one setting them.

I sighed. This was it. If the country was moving into a full-blown revolution, then Dead Six was sure to bail. It was now or never. I glanced over at Jill. It was time to put her out there and see who tried to kill her. She still had her head down. She'd had a really tough day. *Shit.*

"How're you doing, Jill?" Reaper asked, a real note of concern in his voice.

"I'm fine," she lied. She slowly raised her head and moved her long hair out of her eyes, neatly tucking the stray strands behind her ear. She was remarkably composed, all things considered. "I've just never seen anything like that before. It was terrible, absolutely terrible."

"It's probably going to get worse," I added, "before we can get you out of here safely." *Lies.*

"So what do we do now, chief?" Reaper asked hesitantly.

I didn't know what to do. My one option sucked. Even the hardened killer, Carl, didn't like it, and Reaper would probably openly revolt. *I have to figure out how to play—* then my phone buzzed. It was from another unknown number. I flipped it open.

"Hello, my friend," Jalal Hosani greeted me. "I do not have much time."

I covered the speaker and mouthed *Hosani* to the others. Jill looked round, still confused. She was still in the dark about everything related to this job, and I intended to keep it that way. "What've you got?"

"I have some information about those friends you've been seeking to reunite with. I'm happy to say that they're still in town. I will need you to meet me the day after tomorrow. I will call you that morning with the location."

"Thank you, my friend." I said. "And how *appreciative* will I need to be for you doing this favor for me?"

"Do you remember how appreciative you were of the favor I did for you in Dubai? I believe that five times that should suffice."

I had paid him a hundred thousand American dollars for what he'd done for me that time, and that had been outrageous. So now Jalal was asking for *half a million*. "You've got to be kidding . . ." Reaper and Carl looked with mild curiosity. I took a pen and wrote *$500 K* on the bottom of the leaflet.

"Holy shit," Reaper said.

"Be cheaper just to beat it out of him," Carl suggested.

"Believe it or not, there are other people who would be even more appreciative of this information. But we are such old friends that I thought you should have the first opportunity. And also, I do believe that I will be going on a vacation shortly after, as the climate around here has gotten a little *warm* for my tastes, so I would like physical appreciation, rather than digital."

He wanted half a million in *cash*. "Physical?" I responded slowly, looking to Reaper, who thought about it for a second, then nodded in the affirmative. "Okay. But two days is short notice—are you cool if it is European appreciation?" Reaper hurried from the room.

"English, Euro, or other?"

"You picky bastard. Well, mostly British, God save the Queen, and some Continental, because I do love all those pretty colors, you know how it goes. And for this much love, it had better be damn worth it."

"Such a sense of humor! You are a good friend. I

will be in touch." He sounded happy, and he should
be.

I put the phone away. "Greedy, conniving son of a
bitch."

"What just happened?" Jill asked.

"For information on Dead Six, Lorenzo just agreed to
fork over half a million bucks," Carl explained. "Lorenzo
has always sucked at negotiation."

Jill seemed absolutely stunned. "Where in the world
are you going to come up with that kind of money? That's
insane!"

Reaper came back into the room with a backpack and
a big silly grin on his face. He dropped it in the middle
of the table with a theatrical grunt. Carl, temporarily
inconvenienced, was forced to move his beer out of the
way. "I'll have to pull some out and recount it," Reaper
said as he unzipped it. This particular bag was mostly U.K.
pounds, neatly stacked 100 pound notes, fifty per stack,
rubber-banded together. There were at least fifty stacks in
this particular bag that we had smuggled into the country.
Reaper pulled one out and flipped through it. "I'll have to
check today's exchange rate first."

Zubara had been a British protectorate, and they still
had a lot of influence here. So we'd smuggled in mostly
pounds. We also had a mess of euros, dollars, and a giant
pile of local riyals.

Jill made a whistling noise as she opened the bag wider.
"The movies always make it look so much bigger. . . .
How'd you get all this?"

I'd been stealing professionally for years from everybody from Al Qaeda to FARC, from the Yakuza to the

Russian Mob, and I was about the best in the world. My exploits were the stuff of legend. I was worth a lot more than Jill could easily comprehend. I wasn't even really sure how much I had stashed in various encrypted accounts around the world dating back to my days working for Big Eddie. Personally, I was easily worth millions. I could have given up this lifestyle years ago, but then again it had never been about the cash. It had been about the *challenge*.

"I told you assholes always have more money," I answered with a smirk.

Chapter 12:
Broken Arrow

VALENTINE
Location unknown
April 21
0700

Nine of us sat in the back of a V-22 Osprey, wondering where in the hell we were going. Well, eight of us were wondering. The ninth, Anders, seemed like he knew what was going on, but he wouldn't tell us anything. We'd been suddenly roused from bed and rushed to the desert, where we'd been picked up by the Osprey.

Anders wasn't really part of Dead Six. He answered only to Gordon and seemingly came and went as he pleased. I'd heard that he'd helped on a few missions, and he had a ruthless reputation. He never spoke to anyone else, and his background was a complete mystery. Holbrook was former Navy and said that he'd spotted a SEAL trident tattoo on Anders' forearm. Other than that, we knew nothing about the guy.

Tailor and Hudson were with me, as was Singer's entire chalk. Also with us was a new guy, a heavy-set dude with a buzzcut. His name was Byrne, and he was Wheeler's replacement. Like me, he was former Air Force. We'd heard that new guys were showing up here and there to augment our losses. Obviously, those rumors were true.

Singer *had* been around since day one, and he was a solid team leader. Tall, lanky, and possessed of a sick sense of humor, Singer had probably the best track record of any of the chalk leaders, a fact which drove Tailor insane. With him were Holbrook, Cromwell, and Mitchell, all good guys.

We were roused out of bed in the middle of the night and were driven out into the desert again. Instead of the stealth helicopter they'd flown us around in before, I was surprised to be picked up by the awkward-looking tiltrotor aircraft.

We'd been in the air for over an hour. No one talked; it was too loud in the back of the aircraft. We were all wearing earplugs, and most of my teammates had fallen asleep. The tiltrotor's cramped cabin was illuminated by red overhead lights. Anders sat toward the rear, away from the rest of us, and was carefully studying something on a PDA.

We were all fully kitted up in battle rattle, too. My Mk 17 rifle was slung across my chest, with the muzzle hanging between my knees. My vest was covered with magazines, grenades, and other ridiculously heavy crap. We'd even been given fancy new A-TACS camouflage fatigues to wear.

Pulling my hat down over my eyes, I tilted my head

back and tried to fall asleep. I figured the Osprey would either have to land or refuel sooner or later, and maybe then Anders would tell us what was going on. Until then, I was going to rack out for a while.

I don't know how long I'd been asleep when Anders kicked me, but it couldn't have been very long. Startled, I sat up, pulling my hat off my head. Anders had strolled, hunched over, down the cabin and roused all of us. He turned around at the front of the cabin, sat in one of the chairs, and addressed us as a group.

"Listen up!" he said, raising his voice over the dull roar of the engines. "This mission is the highest priority operation we've received. You men make up the best teams Dead Six has, and that's why you were selected for this operation. You need to understand that everything you're about to hear is need-to-know only. Do not discuss this operation with anyone. Not your friends, not the other chalks, not the admin pogues, no one! Am I making myself clear enough? If there's an OPSEC breach on this, I'm going to fuck your world up. Understood?"

We all nodded haltingly. None of us liked being threatened by this douche bag.

Anders continued unfazed, holding up the PDA so we could see the screen. We leaned in to try to make out the small picture he was showing us. "Your objective is this. This is the warhead to a Russian RT-2PM Topol ICBM. It has a yield of five-hundred and fifty kilotons."

Anders pushed a button on his PDA, then held it up again, showing us a new picture. "This is what the physics package of the warhead looks like if it is removed from the reentry vehicle. This part is where the nuclear reaction takes place and is all that is required to produce a yield. As you can see, this part is small enough to fit in the trunk of a small car." The eight of us looked at each other. "I think you can see where this is going," Anders said dispassionately. "This particular warhead, so far as we know, was removed from its missile and was to be destroyed in accordance with the START treaty. It disappeared years ago and has never been accounted for. At this moment, the warhead is on a truck, headed for a remote airfield in Yemen. From there, we expect it to be flown covertly to Zubara and delivered to General Al Sabah. For obvious reasons, we're not going to allow this to happen. We're flying nap-of-the-Earth right now. We'll arrive at the target site just before dawn and intercept the warhead before that plane takes off. Our mission is to secure the warhead and eliminate anyone involved in the delivery. We will take *no* prisoners. Any questions?"

We had none. "Good," Anders said. "Each chalk will operate as a fire-team. The plane will be waiting on the ground when we get there. Tailor, take your chalk and secure the aircraft. Singer, take your chalk and secure the truck. It's probably escorted, and there could be heavy resistance. Be aware that the situation can change at any time. If we get there and it's obvious the plane hasn't been loaded yet, I want both teams to hit the truck. No matter what, we have to secure that warhead."

"What will you be doing during all this?" Singer asked.

"Whatever I feel like. I have the RADIAC equipment," Anders said curtly. "I'm also a trained medic. I'll be on the ground with you and will direct you over the radio as the situation develops. Do your job."

I sat back against my seat and looked at the floor. The tension in the air was making me uncomfortable. Nobody liked being around Anders. Why would they only send eight guys, plus Anders, for such an important mission? You'd think they could at least spare a third chalk to stop General Al Sabah from obtaining a nuclear weapon! *What the hell is going on?*

VALENTINE
Somewhere in Yemen

Tailor had his arm over my shoulder as I helped him along. Blood trickled from a wound on his right calf, and he was limping pretty badly. The wound didn't look that bad, but even "minor" gunshot wounds hurt.

We hobbled down the ramp of a damaged An-74 transport plane, back out into the early morning sun. The notional airstrip we were at didn't look like it had been used in decades. There was nothing left but a short, cracked runway, a ramp half covered in desert sand, and one road leading off into the hills. The terrain around us was rugged and mountainous. A cold wind blew steadily across the flat spot the airfield had been built on.

We'd arrived right in the middle of the transfer of the nuclear warhead. It had already been loaded on the plane, but the convoy that transported it hadn't yet left when we came upon the airfield. We took them by surprise, landing right in the middle of their deal.

It was a bloodbath. More than twenty-five bodies littered the area around the transport plane. A convoy of trucks sat shot-up and burning behind the damaged aircraft. Once we had confirmed that the weapon was on the plane and not in the trucks, the modified Osprey had done a strafing run with a chin-mounted gun turret. Both chalks had struck with the element of surprise and liberal use of 40mm grenades. The Yemenis had been quickly overwhelmed.

Which isn't to say that things went well for us. Singer was on the ground in front of us, gurgling and gasping for air. Blood poured from a sucking chest wound near his armpit. The bullet that hit him had missed his ceramic plate and plunged deep into his chest, probably tearing through his lungs.

Cromwell had ripped off Singer's vest and was hastily applying a pressure dressing. It just wasn't enough. "Christ, I can't stop the bleeding!" he cried. "Hang in there, boss! Where's Anders? Anders! I need a medic!"

Anders strode up from behind the wreckage of a 6x6 truck, satellite phone in hand. "What's the matter?" he asked casually, stuffing the phone into a pouch on his vest.

"I can't stop the bleeding!" Cromwell repeated. "I need your help!"

Anders, not moving with any particular urgency while Singer suffered, squatted down, smacked Cromwell's hand aside, and began to inspect the wound. He stuck his face in close.

"There's nothing I can do," Anders said emotionlessly. "Tension pneumothorax. He sucked in too much air from the entrance wound. His lungs have collapsed." He stood up and wiped the blood off on his pant legs. Singer had stopped moving. "He's dead." The tall operative then turned on his heel and headed for the ramp of the An-74.

"Hey!" I said, unable to hide the anger in my voice. "Tailor's hurt, too!" Tailor winced as he put weight on his hurt leg and babbled a short stream of obscenities.

"He'll be fine. You've got combat lifesaver training, right?" Anders said, not looking at me as he walked up the ramp into the aircraft.

"Fuck you, Anders!" Tailor said. Anders ignored him and disappeared into the plane. "Shit . . . Val, I gotta sit down. Help me out here." I supported Tailor's weight as he lowered himself onto the edge of the plane's cargo ramp. He extended his wounded leg. "Take a look at that, will you?"

Slinging my rifle behind my back, I snapped out my automatic knife and cut his pant leg away. He had a nasty gash in his left calf. I pulled out a bandage and applied pressure to the wound. Tailor grunted and swore as I did so.

"Cromwell," Tailor said, forcing himself to talk through the pain. "You okay, buddy?"

Cromwell and Holbrook were kneeling next to Singer. Holbrook gently pushed Singer's eyelids down.

"He's gone," Cromwell said. Furious, he stood up and stomped away. Holbrook fell onto his butt and sat there, staring at his dead friend.

"Holbrook?" I asked.

"Singer's dead, man. Singer's fucking dead." He put his bloody hands over his face.

Their chalk's fourth man, Mitchell, had caught a round in the throat on the way out of the Osprey and was dead on the spot. Hudson and our new guy, Byrne, stood back cautiously, scanning the horizon for reinforcements. The

Osprey we'd arrived on had landed and was waiting for us.

Anders came out of the plane, stowing the radiation detector. He was talking on the radio. "Tarantula, this is Drago. Package is secure . . . Roger that." He strode down the ramp and started giving orders. "Valentine, Holbrook, bring that nuke out here. I've got a strike team coming to secure it."

"Strike team?" Tailor snarled. "Where were they while we were getting shot at?"

Anders glared at him, nostrils flaring. "We needed to get here before this thing moved." Anders saw Holbrook sitting there, with his head in his hands, and came over and kicked him in the side. "Get off your ass. I gave you an order."

Suddenly, Holbrook stood, bloody hands clenched into fists. "You let Singer die!"

Anders shrugged. "Shit happens."

Holbrook lost it. He swung for Anders's face, but the big man moved shockingly fast. He easily ducked aside, but followed up with an elbow that got Holbrook square in the face. Then Anders hurled him headfirst into the ramp. Tailor and I barely got out of the way. Anders's heavy boot slammed down on Holbrook's back. Holbrook cried out in pain.

Singer's chalk was tight, and Cromwell saw his buddy go down. He came running. Anders saw him coming and calmly readied himself. Cromwell threw a punch that Anders easily blocked. Anders then slugged Cromwell in the teeth. Cromwell swung wildly, but Anders let it sail past before surging forward and grabbing Cromwell by the armor and then wrapping his big left arm around his throat. Somehow Anders had pulled his combat knife and it was pressed against Cromwell's jugular.

Instinctively, I jumped up, pulling my rifle around from where it had been slung behind my back, but Anders was too quick. A pistol appeared in his other hand, and, faster than I could blink, I was staring down the barrel of a .45. I froze. Anders's pistol was a big H&K Mk23. He spoke very slowly. "Got a problem, Valentine?"

I was *Calm*. I didn't say anything, but Tailor did. "Fuck you, Anders!" Of course, *he* wasn't the one with a gun stuck in his face. Now Tailor had his .45 out and leveled at Anders. "Let Cromwell go!"

"Safety that sidearm and place it on the deck, Tailor, or I shoot your girlfriend in the face."

"Easy, Tailor," I suggested. Holbrook was moaning, trying to rise. Cromwell was turning red; his eyes were focused on the blade pressed against his neck. Hudson had come running and was now covering Anders with his SAW.

The hulking operative took it all in calmly. He showed no fear at all. "Shoot me and you walk home." There was nothing but barren rocky desert as far as the eye could see. We'd have better odds of surviving a walk across Mars. Anders glanced around. "I hear Yemen is nice this time of year."

Tailor slowly lowered his weapon. "Stand down, Hudson," he ordered. Anders waited, keeping his gun on me for longer than he needed to, just because he was a douche. Finally he put his arm to his side, but he didn't holster. Anders let go of Cromwell, and he fell, gasping, to the ground.

"That's better. Now quit your crying and secure that package before I get angry." Anders turned and walked away. He casually stepped over Cromwell. "Get this piece of shit onto the bird."

We watched as the second Osprey dusted off. Anders's mysterious strike force had arrived a few minutes before and secured the package, all while keeping a suspicious eye on us. Thankfully, Anders went with them. Holbrook and Cromwell were both still dazed. Hudson and Byrne were helping them onto the aircraft ahead of us. I was supporting the still-limping Tailor. In the distance we could see dust from approaching Yemeni reinforcements. They were still a ways off.

"Hey, Val. Remember back in Vegas when I said you were a killer?"

"What about it?" I grunted as I helped him along.

"Well, you ain't in the same league as Anders. That fucker *scares* me."

"Tailor, can you see where this thing is going?"

"Yeah, I can," he replied. He pulled out a cigarette and lit it. Tailor's hands were shaking.

"The money isn't looking so good anymore."

He had talked me into this, and he knew it, but it wasn't in Tailor's nature to admit making a mistake. "Not really."

"We need to make a Plan B, bro."

"You think so?"

"I think so. I think we might need to disappear in a hurry. They obviously think we're expendable. Have you checked your bank account?"

"No, why?"

"I can't access mine from the computers at the fort."

"You think they're not paying us?"

"I've heard the others talking. Nobody can check their accounts. Hunter said he'd ask Gordon about it. Remember what Hawk said?"

"If we're dead they don't have to pay us. Son of a bitch," Tailor said tiredly. "I think you're right. I think we might need to ditch these guys. This is Mexico all over again."

"Got any ideas?" I asked as I helped him up the ramp.

"Not really."

"I might."

VALENTINE
Al Khor District
April 22
2100

It was a typically warm and dry night as Tailor and I made our way down the sidewalk, trying not to draw attention to ourselves. Al Khor had the most Westerners of any of the Zoob's three urban districts. A few weeks prior, it wouldn't have been unusual to see quite a few Brits and Europeans out and about.

Things had gone downhill since then, and now Westerners were abandoning the city. A string of car bombings and other attacks kept most Westerners indoors at night. The streets of the city were still jam-packed with traffic, and the sidewalks were only a little less crowded, but you could feel the tension in the air as the tiny little nation held its breath.

Project Heartbreaker was at the same time wildly successful and a miserable failure. We did indeed have the terrorists on the run here. Several of our chalks were sitting at safe houses, idle, because there wasn't much to do. We were literally running out of targets. To that end we'd begun casting the net wider, expanding operations into neighboring Qatar and the United Arab Emirates.

According to our intelligence contacts, including those ostensibly working for the Emir, the terrorists were scared shitless. Horror stories about the men who leave the Ace of Spades had spread as far as Afghanistan and Indonesia. The local press had picked up on it here and there, too, but the Zubaran government had, for the most part, quashed that before it became an issue. Dead Six had become the Bogeyman that terrorists looked under their filthy beds for.

At the same time, the Confederated Gulf Emirate of Zubara was slowly tearing itself apart. The fear and chaos we'd caused was intended to be inflicted only upon the terrorists, but it had quickly spread to the wider community. General Al Sabah was now positioning himself to be the new Iron Man of the Arabian Gulf, and had half the Zubaran Army on his side. The emir was on shakier ground than ever. It seemed very likely that the emir's regime would fall, not to Islamic Fundamentalist fanatics as originally feared but to a militant opportunist who wanted to become a world power broker overnight.

The entire situation was a confusing mess that threatened to send the region spiraling into chaos. On top of it, we'd paid a steep price for our questionable success. Almost one-third of our personnel had been killed in action at this point.

I was terrified of what would happen to Sarah if we stayed in the Zoob. So Tailor and I had talked it over for a long time. I then talked to Sarah, while Tailor talked to Hudson, and that was as far as the talking went. There were others I liked, others I'd have liked to bring in, but I couldn't trust anyone else. We were getting out.

That was easier said than done, of course. I could, I suppose, have just gone to the airport, whipped out my passport, and tried to buy a plane ticket, but that would've created questions. In any case, I was sure Gordon's people had mechanisms in place to catch us if we tried to run. So we'd have to be clever.

I'm not really that clever. I'm not the guy that comes up with cool tricks or brilliant plans. Neither is Tailor, regardless of what he might tell you. But you don't have to be clever if you have clever friends.

Tailor stood watch while I entered a phone booth outside an Internet café. Zubara still had pay phones aplenty, unlike the United States. Foreign workers fresh from South Asia didn't have cell phones that worked in the country, so they often made use of the pay phones until they got situated. I had a cell phone myself, of course, but it was issued by Dead Six, and I wasn't about to use it for this.

I pulled from my pocket a wrinkled piece of paper. Scrawled on the paper, in my own handwriting, was a long telephone number. Using a prepaid international calling card that I'd bought with cash, I dialed and waited. It took several seconds to connect, then began to ring.

Ling answered the phone on the second ring, sounding a little sleepy. I had no idea what time it was where she was. For that matter, I had no idea where she was.

"Um, hello?" I said awkwardly, hoping like hell she wasn't pissed that I'd ignored her e-mails.

"Who is this?" Ling asked firmly.

"It's Valentine. Remember Mexico?"

Ling was quiet for a second. "Michael Valentine? This is a surprise."

"I'm sorry," I said. "I hope I didn't wake you."

"It's three o' clock in the bloody morning here," Ling said, not actually sounding irritated. "Of course you woke me. Are you calling to take me up on my offer?"

"Actually . . . I need your help."

"Is that so? What sort of help?"

"I'm in kind of a bad spot here, and I need to get out of it."

"Where are you?"

"The Middle East."

"It would help if you were more specific, Mr. Valentine."

"I'm in the Confederated Gulf Emirate of Zubara."

Ling paused for a moment. "Oh. Oh, I see. Yes, I can see where you might be in some trouble then. How did you come to be there?"

"That's a long story."

"Can I safely assume that you've been getting into trouble there, or perhaps causing trouble yourself?"

"That'd be a safe assumption," I said, nervously looking around. Tailor gave me a thumbs up through the glass.

"Very well," Ling said. "What sort of help do you need, then?"

"I need to get out of here," I said flatly. "As soon as possible. Normal methods of transportation aren't workable. I need to just disappear."

"Just you?" Ling asked.

"No, me plus three others. People I trust. I don't care how we go, and right now I don't even care where we go, we just need to go."

"What's going on?"

"Look, I can't stay on the line too long. If we're gone too long they'll notice, and then there'll be questions, and that will cause problems."

Ling chewed on that for a moment. "I see. I see. So tell me, honestly. Why should I help you? How can I even trust that you're not now working for someone trying to set a trap for my organization?"

"Because a bunch of my friends died trying to help get that girl off that boat before she disappeared. Because I, personally, risked my life to keep her safe, even though you never even told me why she was important. I have money. I'll pay if I have to. I just need your help."

"As luck would have it," Ling said after another long pause, "I'll be in that part of the world shortly. Do you have a way for me to contact you?"

"Not securely, no," I admitted. "I have a phone, but it's probably monitored. I'm on a pay phone right now."

"I see. Okay, I'll need you to call me on May fourth. We'll set up the meeting then.

"Meeting?"

"Yes. I want to meet with you face-to-face. If all goes

well, we'll have no problem getting you and your friends out quickly after that."

"Can't we all just go the first time? Things are circling the drain here."

"We can do it my way, or I can go back to bed, Mr. Valentine," Ling said, ice in her voice. "It's up to you."

I exhaled. "Okay, okay, we'll make it work. I'll call you on May fourth and we'll go from there."

"Good," Ling said. Her voice softened just a bit. "Please be careful."

"Thank—" Ling hung up on me before I could finish thanking her.

Chapter 13:
Hasa Market

LORENZO
May 3

I was in the kitchen when my phone buzzed, indicating a new text message.

> *Hasa Market. 4:00 at the fountain.*
> *Wait for further instructions. Come alone.*

I scowled. *Come alone?* Why did he need to specify that? Did he somehow think that this was all some sort of scheme to get him into the open? Was he afraid Dead Six was coming for him, too? Or maybe he thought that I just wanted to get the info out of him and then cheat him out of the money. . . .

Or it was a trap for me. There were plenty of people in this country who would pay Hosani good money for my head. "Carl, check this out," I called.

My partner joined me a second later. He only glanced at the phone for a second. "Trap, it sounds like, maybe."

"Could be. But we need the info. It's worth the risk."

"You going alone?" Carl asked suspiciously.

"Of course not. Hasa is a busy place. It's that fish *souk* right off the docks at the end of Umm Shamal. Plenty of places for you guys to stay incognito."

Carl shook his head. "No vehicles in there. I can blend in. Reaper, not so much." That was true. Our techie was about the palest white boy we were going to find in five hundred miles. I had given Jill crap about walking like an American, but she was a master of disguise compared to Reaper. "I miss Train."

I missed Train, too. The big guy had been a virtual killing machine and had been great backup for situations like this. "We'll stick Reaper in the van back a ways. He's our ride out if we need him. We'll stay in radio contact." I tried to keep Reaper away from the hands-on part of the work. It wasn't exactly his area of expertise. But he was street-smart enough to keep his eyes open for anything suspicious.

"One problem," Carl said slowly. "What about the girl?"

"Aw, hell." He had a point. We couldn't just leave Jill here alone. I suppose we could have tied her up, but that didn't really go along with trying to get her to trust us. If this meeting didn't go well, she was still my ace in the hole. The other times I had gone out since she'd been here, there had always been at least one member of my crew here to make sure she didn't try anything stupid. She had behaved, so far. *Drugs were an option.*

Then Carl surprised me. "We take her." He caught my look of confusion. "Extra eyes we could use. I saw her after that bomb went off. She was tough. Most folks don't do that good first time they see a bunch of guts blown all over the street. We used to have a girl on the team."

He knew how much I hated when he brought up that bit of our past. "Her and Kat don't have very much in common," I said.

Carl shrugged. "Personality? No. But both pretty girls, skinny but still with big tits and a nice ass. The good parts are in common." As usual, Carl was a subtle poet of a man. "Pretty girls come in handy in this business, go places we can't, talk to people we can't. But that's not what I meant. This girl, she's a good girl."

"Carl, oh man, I can't believe this," I laughed. "You're getting soft in your old age. She's grown on you, hasn't she?" I didn't think Carl was capable of actually *liking* anyone.

That got him. He raised a meaty hand threateningly and waved one stubby finger in my face. "We'll stick her in the van. Make her feel helpful. This don't change nothing. It sure don't change the plan. So don't you give me no shit about getting soft. I've burned fucking *villages*. Got it?"

"Got it."

"Good." He folded his arms. "That said, I don't like your backup plan no more."

"Me either," I said slowly, but it wasn't like he had a better idea. For us, it was either find Dead Six or die. Nothing else would stop Big Eddie's rampage. "Hosani had better come through."

The four of us were gathered around the kitchen table. I had just outlined what was going down this afternoon.

Reaper pulled up a Google Earth view of the Hasa neighborhood on one of his laptops.

"That's a pretty open area, Chief," Reaper said. "I can't see them trying to take you out in the middle of all that." The market was right off the docks. There were warehouses to the north, and a school and a mosque to the southwest. There were three roads in. At any given time of day, the place was packed with witnesses.

"If it is a trap, they'll send another text, telling me to walk somewhere else quieter. That gives them a chance to see if I've got anybody tailing me." I nodded at Carl. "You'll need to be discreet."

"What do you want me to do?" Jill asked quickly. It was almost like she was eager to prove that she was worth something.

I glanced at Carl. He shrugged. I already knew his opinion.

More than likely, nothing was going to happen. Hosani would give me an address or something, and I would slide him the backpack of cash. That was it. Odds were that this was going to be relatively boring. But then again, I had thought the same thing about Al Khor, and that had ended up with blood raining from the sky.

I placed the Bulgarian Makarov in the center of the table with a metallic clunk. "You said you know how to use this?"

She looked at me suspiciously for a second, then back to the gun, then back at me. "Who am I supposed to shoot?"

"Nobody in particular. You're going to be a lookout if Hosani tries to bring in help or if Dead Six shows up. Early warning, that's it. This is just for self-defense."

"Got anything bigger?"

"No. You get the *chick* gun." I rolled my eyes. "That's one of the most common guns in this part of the world for a reason. It works. It's concealable. And that's really important because like most shitty countries, Zubara's got strict gun-control laws. So unless you want to go to prison forever, don't get spotted with this. If you need to ditch it, I'm not worried about it, just drop it in a garbage can and keep walking."

Without further hesitation, she picked up the gun. I noted that she was careful to keep it in a safe direction and her finger was indexed outside the trigger guard. Maybe she had been taught well. "It's . . . double action. The safety works backwards from Dad's Beretta . . ." It took her a second to find the magazine-release. The Makarov had its magazine release button in the heel of the grip, unlike most American guns. She dropped the magazine on the table, then pulled the slide back, looking inside the empty chamber. She grinned maliciously. "Do I get bullets, too?"

I had to admit that she had a pretty smile. "We'll work up to that."

VALENTINE
Fort Saradia National Historical Site
May 3
1030

Tailor, Hudson, Byrne, and I were already sitting in the classroom when Hunter came striding in, Sarah in tow. "I'll be brief, gentlemen," he said, opening his laptop and hooking it up to the display screen. "You're moving out shortly."

"We were told that we've got a lock on our next target, sir," Tailor said.

"That's right," Hunter replied, bringing up a picture on the screen. "This is your target, Jalal Hosani." Hosani was an average-looking Middle Eastern man, with styled hair and a scruffy, stubbly goatee. He was dressed in a brown suit and a white shirt with no tie, as was the fashion. "He's going to attempt to flee Zubara today. He's not going to get out of the country alive."

"How do we know this, Colonel?" I asked.

"Asra Elnadi," Hunter replied. "During her interrogation, she told us that one of Hosani's bodyguards was an ex-lover of hers, and they kept it on the sly. She was able to contact him and get him to sell out his boss."

"No employee loyalty," Byrne suggested.

"Not in this business, son," Hunter said. "With his boss skipping town, this guy's probably out of a job anyway. So he tipped off our contact without knowing who she's working for."

"How do we know this information is credible?" I asked.

"I made it clear to Ms. Elnadi that there would be severe consequences if the information she gave us proved to be false," Sarah said coolly. "She's afraid of us. I don't think she'd try anything stupid, especially since we've kept her alive so far."

Hunter switched the screen to a map of the city. "The target will be attempting his escape from a small warehouse that he owns in the Hasa Market, in Umm Shamal.

This warehouse is right on the pier. According to the information Ms. Elnadi gave us, Hosani owns a boat. His escape plan is to load up his boat, hoist anchor, and sail away. Asra's ex-boyfriend told her that he's meeting some-one in the warehouse around sixteen hundred hours, and that he'll be leaving immediately after.

"There are several places he could go, so if we lose him he's probably gone for good. Your mission is to intercept Jalal Hosani at the docks and kill him. There are no secondary targets. Tertiary targets are any of his employees and bodyguards that you encounter."

"We're going to kill him in the middle of Hasa Market in broad daylight?" I asked. "Sir, that's one of the busiest markets in the city. It'll be packed by mid-afternoon."

"I'm aware of that, Mr. Valentine, but it is this or nothing. Any questions?"

We had plenty of questions. We spent the next two hours in the classroom, formulating the plan.

LORENZO
May 3

I had been dropped off several blocks from the Hasa Market and had walked in. Umm Shamal was the middle peninsula and was relatively middle-class, so I wore jeans, a soccer jersey, and a good pair of running shoes instead of sandals. I carried the money in a small backpack.

I liked baggy jerseys. They were handy for hiding stuff, including the relatively soft Level IIIA armor vest. My STI 4.15 Tactical was on my hip, concealed beneath my shirt. Between it and the two spare longer twenty-two-round magazines on my off-side, I had sixty-three rounds ready to go. Also concealed on me was my Greco Whisper CT knife. It had a five-and-a-quarter-inch blade and was perfectly balanced. If Hosani tried anything, I was going to stick to my promise to take him with me.

There was one benefit if I bought it today. Once Big Eddie found out, that would probably get Carl and Reaper off the hook, temporarily. But he had leverage on them too, so even though they couldn't do this job, he would find some way to use them again. Believe me, I'd thought about faking my own death rather than finishing this job. But if Eddie ever got any inkling that I'd cheated him, he'd kill every single person in that folder.

The market was bustling with humanity. It was a miniature city, with buildings made from portable stands and wandering streets of weathered stones. This was where all the small-time fishermen sold their catch, so it was the best place in the city to get fresh fish. The violence in poor Ash Shamal and rich Al Khor hadn't really hit here yet. This was the part of town where the actual work got done. This was the home of the regular people, and they just wanted to live their lives in peace, earn their money, and raise their kids. Too bad for them they were stuck between a bunch of fanatics.

There was a line of speakers placed over the central row of booths. They were playing traditional music, which was actually kind of pretty in a haunting way. Every now and then the music would cut out and a fast-talking announcer would tell the customers about some special at one of the booths.

The fountain dated back to the British and was styled to be vaguely ancient Greek. It was out of place between all the tan brick buildings. I took a seat on the edge of the fountain, waited, and watched bus drivers and school teachers buy sea bass. My Bluetooth earpiece wasn't very out of place in this group.

"I don't see anything yet," Carl said. I knew he had stationed himself at the opposite end of the market near the corner of the school. He had dressed in full-on man pajamas and baggy vest. Carl was too stocky and muscular to pass for a Zubaran, but there were a lot of foreigners in this country, actually more foreigners than natives since the boom began, and he had grown a bushy beard that would make any mullah jealous. "I'm at the bootleg DVD table."

"Anything interesting?"

"They've got a Robert DeNiro five-pack. I'm watching the windows on the mosque. If I was gonna snipe you, that's where I'd be."

That was comforting.

"Lots of traffic, but nothing suspicious," Reaper said. He and Jill were parked about a block away to the south.

I noted a man standing near one of the fish stands. Skinny guy, wearing Ray-Bans, he was making good use of the crowd to cover himself but was obviously watching the people clustered around the fountain, waiting for something. He had the look of a local, so that was probably one of Hosani's men.

My phone buzzed. The text was short.

Walk north. Go to the first warehouse.

So the exchange wasn't going to be in public. The thin man saw me looking at my phone, right on schedule, so now he knew who I was. I bent down, as if to tie my shoe, but primarily so he couldn't see me speak. "Got the message. Moving north to the first warehouse. I've got at least one guy watching me. Stay low." I adjusted the backpack and started pushing through the crowd in the direction of the docks.

VALENTINE
Umm Shamal District
May 3
1555

Hasa Market was a sprawling, confusing maze of tiny shops, stands, and carts that emanated out from an old fountain in the square. To the north were a trio of warehouses on the pier. Tailor parked our Land Cruiser between a mosque and a small schoolhouse on the west side of the square.

Hudson and Byrne were supposed to park their vehicle on the opposite side of the square. As much as we could, we always took two vehicles on a mission. It gave us a backup option should we not be able to make it to our own vehicle. Also, we figured that with all of the chaos we were about to cause in Hasa Market, we'd have less chance of getting snagged by the cops if we split up.

The situation still sucked. Four of us were going into an unknown building against an unknown number of opponents. Because we had to go through a crowded marketplace in the middle of the afternoon to get to that building, we could only bring weapons that we could conceal, i.e., handguns. Going into a gunfight with nothing but a handgun is stupid and should be avoided if at all possible.

Unfortunately, it wasn't possible. Hunter had suggested that we use compact assault rifles, concealed in backpacks, that we could drop if we needed to disappear into the crowd. Gordon Willis had overruled him on that one, apparently. He said it caused an unacceptable risk of getting made.

It seemed the risk of us getting our asses shot off trying to go into a gunfight with nothing but pistols didn't bother him. By that point I'd had more than my fill of Gordon Willis. But there was nothing we could do except carry on with the mission and try not to get killed.

Tailor and I made our way through the cluttered mess of Hasa Market, doing our best not to be noticed. We were both wearing khaki cargo pants, dark T-shirts to conceal body armor underneath, sunglasses, and untucked shirts to hide our sidearms. We looked undeniably American, but even with the recent chaos, no one seemed to pay us any mind.

The market stunk of fresh fish, and squawking seagulls filled the air. The rows of booths, carts, and shacks weren't laid out in any discernible order. They were gaudily decorated with what looked like Christmas lights, loud-speakers playing music, and signs in six languages. Most of the shoppers at Hasa Market weren't Zubaran citizens, or even Arabs. Most were imported labor from India, South Asia, and the Philippines.

The market sold more than just fish. Goods of every variety could be bought, from bootleg DVDs to clothes to medicine of dubious medical value imported from Asia. As Tailor and I made our way past various stands, the vendors would blurt sales offers out at us in broken English, telling us they had a great deal that was perfect for our needs.

"Lo siento, no hablo Inglés," is all we'd say in return. Tailor and I both spoke Spanish fairly well and had decided that with this many witnesses around, we'd avoid speaking to each other in English if at all possible. Half the world spoke English, including people in the Middle East. You'd be a lot harder pressed to find a Middle Easterner that spoke Spanish.

I did have to speak English into my radio, so I squeezed the transmit button and spoke softly. "Control, Nightcrawler, target building in sight." Tailor and I studied the warehouse though the crowd, trying to discern the best way in.

"*Control copies*," Sarah replied. Hearing her voice in my ear comforted me in a strange way. "*You are cleared to engage. Be careful.*"

LORENZO

The noise of the market was muted here by the thick walls of the surrounding buildings. The skinny guy was still following discreetly. I had to cross a narrow street, and, glancing both ways, I saw no vehicles other than parked delivery trucks. It was late enough in the afternoon that all the day's deliveries had been made. It smelled like fish.

There was a man, wearing a nice suit, waiting for me at the side door of the first warehouse. "Mr. Lorenzo," he said in rough English. "I need search you before come in."

"Tell Hosani to kiss my ass. If he's got a problem, me and my big bag of money will just go home."

The guard nodded. "He said you say something like that. I just want make sure you right man." He opened the door into darkness.

The interior of the warehouse was dark and cool. Crates were stacked up in neat rows. The roll-up door at the rear of the building was open, and a few small fishing boats were tied there, as well as one nice fifty-footer.

I spotted Hosani in the shadows under the catwalk by the glowing ash of his cigarette. There were a couple other men standing toward the back of the warehouse, and, from the sound, at least one pacing the metal catwalk above. If he wanted to take me out, I was well and truly screwed.

"Hey, Jalal. You didn't need to bring your whole gang," I said with forced joviality, mostly so Carl would hear and know that there were a lot of men with guns here.

"Don't flatter yourself," Jalal said. "This is how everyone in my line of work has to travel now, in groups, and in secret. I'm only doing this as a favor, and then I'm getting on that boat"—he waved his cigarette toward the back of the warehouse—"and going someplace safe."

"I thought this was good for business."

He adjusted his coat as he put his lighter away, exposing the butt of a compact pistol. Hosani sold guns, but I'd never seen him actually use one. He really was nervous. Earlier I had thought Dead Six was unprofessional because of their lack of subtlety, but now I could see the logic behind it. Their targets were *terrified* of them.

"These Americans who leave the playing cards, they're only part of the reason I'm leaving. This Dead Six, as you called it, is part of something bigger. I do not think they even realize who they are really working for." He trailed off with a wry smile. "But as they say, why buy the cow when you can get the milk for free? My appreciation?"

"Of course." I tossed him the backpack. He unzipped it and glanced inside, rifling quickly through the stacks of British currency. "You can count it. I won't be offended."

"I don't feel like sticking around any longer than I have to," he responded as he zipped the bag back up and put it over his shoulder. "I've got to warn you, Lorenzo. I don't know what Big Eddie's commissioned you to do, but it isn't worth going after these people."

"That's not an option."

VALENTINE

We paused for a moment, allowing our eyes to adjust to the darkness. We were in the warehouse. I slid my sunglasses up onto my head and pressed onward. The small side door we'd come through led into the main room of the warehouse, but it was stacked from floor to ceiling with racks and shelves full of boxes. Voices could be heard echoing through the building, but we couldn't see anyone. We crouched down and quietly weaved our way through the maze of racks and crates. The roll-up door at the north end of the warehouse was open to the docks, flooding the center of the floor in brilliant daylight. Above that door was a metal catwalk. There was someone up there. We'd have to take him out before Hudson and Byrne came in, otherwise he'd be above and behind them as they entered from the other side of the building.

I came to a spot where I could see the main floor through a narrow gap between two crates on the shelf in front of me. Tailor had his 1911 Operator drawn and watched my back as I tried to ID my target.

There were at least four more men in the building aside from the man on the catwalk. Two of them were standing off to the side, in the shadows, probably more bodyguards. The other two men were more interesting.

One of them was a fit-looking man wearing a soccer jersey and jeans. He had on sunglasses and had a scruffy, unshaven face, so I couldn't get a good look at him. A backpack was slung over his shoulder.

The other man was facing away from me. He wore a dark suit and had a lit cigarette in his hand. I couldn't quite make out what he was saying over the noises of the city and the harbor, but he was discussing something with the man in the soccer jersey. He paced as he talked, and turned around so I could see his face. There was no doubt about it. It was Jalal Hosani. I looked over at Tailor and nodded. Through hand signals, I told Tailor I was going to shoot Hosani from our current position. Hosani was only about fifty feet away, I could make the shot easily. Tailor told me he'd cover the catwalk.

I aimed my revolver through the gap in the crates,

placing the tritium front sight on Jalal Hosani's chest. I wasn't going to attempt a head shot at this range. If he was wearing a vest, the impact of a fat .44 hollow point would still probably break some ribs. Hudson and Byrne would be in the building before he could get away.

Hosani turned away to face the man in the soccer jersey. I adjusted my sight picture and aimed in between his shoulder blades as Jersey Guy tossed him a backpack. Hosani opened the bag and rifled through it. My finger moved to the trigger. I exhaled.

LORENZO

Jalal took a long drag off of his cigarette and shook his head as he exhaled. "Very well, my friend. It's your funeral, as they say. For my part, I—" Jalal's white shirt exploded in a spray of red, and a sledgehammer weight collided with my chest.

Jalal's blood was on my face, in my eyes, and I could taste it in my mouth. He collapsed into me, clawing at my shirt, but he was already dead and didn't even know it yet. I stumbled and fell, taking us both to the concrete. The bullet that had torn through his torso was stuck in my vest, and waves of pain radiated out from the bruised tissue underneath.

There was more shooting. Muzzle flashes back and forth across the warehouse as Hosani's guards went down, one after the other. There was a scream from above, and the man on the catwalk flipped over the edge and landed a few yards away, bones audibly cracking on impact.

It was the shooter from Adar's video, the tall one with the .44. He was moving smoothly down the aisle of crates. He had this calm look on his face, just kind of concentrating, like he was reading an interesting book or something. I shoved the twitching corpse off and jerked my pistol out. I didn't have a shot. He caught the movement and ducked down as I started cranking off rounds. My bullets flung splinters from the surrounding boxes as I scrambled to my feet. I kept firing, forcing him to keep his head down as I moved.

I flinched as a bullet impacted a support beam right next to me. There were multiple shooters. Jerking my head in the direction of the shot, I saw the shorter man from the Adar video vaulting over a railing. He disappeared between the crates. Now I had at least two of them hunting me.

I slid to my knees behind a crate. "Carl! Dead Six is here!" I instantly dropped the mag, stuffed the partially expended one in my pocket, and slammed a new one home. Pain radiated through my chest with every breath, and that was even after the bullet had zipped through Hosani. That wasn't a pistol, that was a cannon.

There was movement in the sunlight at the open dock door as someone else swept inside. *I have to get out of here.* There was a door to the side, offices or something. I leapt to my feet and sprinted through the doorway. It was a hallway, several doors branching off in each direction. *Shit.* Speeding right to the last door, I discovered it was locked. I took a step back and kicked it open, flinging it open with a bang. It was just a janitor's closet. No windows. No exit. The shooters were moving up behind me. I was trapped.

VALENTINE

Wooden crates splintered and fragmented above me as I ducked behind a crate and hoped that its contents were substantial enough to stop handgun fire. The man in the soccer jersey had spotted me.

I reloaded, punching my revolver's ejector rod and twisting a new speed loader into the cylinder. I then squeezed my radio's transmit button. "Xbox, I'm pinned down! Get this guy off me!"

"I'm on it!" Tailor replied. Seconds later more gunshots echoed through the warehouse as Tailor opened up with his .45. *"You can move!"*

"Roger! Moving!" I replied, coming to my feet again. I snaked through the maze of crates and shelves, revolver held out in front of me in both hands as I moved.

"Xbox, Shafter, we're entering now!" Hudson said over the radio. Tailor acknowledged him, and I wondered what in the hell had taken Hudson so long. I realized then that it had only been a minute since I'd fired the first shot.

"I've lost that shooter!" Tailor snarled, frustration obvious in his voice. In less than a minute we'd wiped out all of Hosani's guards except one. It kind of pissed me off, too.

I cleared the maze of crates and found myself in the open area in the middle of the warehouse. Jalal Hosani's corpse lay splayed out on the floor in a large pool of blood, a ragged hole between his shoulder blades.

"Careful," Tailor warned as Hudson and Byrne approached. "We still got one shooter out there, the guy in the jersey."

"Which way did he go?" I asked, kicking Hosani's corpse to make sure he was dead. He was. I dropped an Ace of Spades onto his back.

"You two," Tailor said, pointing at Hudson, "cover us. Val, follow me, I think he went through this door." The four of us split into pairs again. Hudson and Byrne exited the way they'd come in, through the open dock door. Tailor extended his 1911 and led me behind another shelf of crates, through a door that was hidden behind it.

It led to a short hallway. Our two teammates stayed behind, covering the doorway while Tailor and I made our way down, weapons at the ready. There were two doors on one side and one door on the other, but all three were closed. At the end of the hallway, there was a partially open door. A small sign above the door read Custodian in English and Arabic. It was a janitor's closet. A backpack with a broken strap lay on the floor, a few feet from the door.

My eyes caught a flash of movement in the darkened closet. Tailor and I spread out to either side of the hallway and continued to inch forward. We were wide open, and doorways were fatal funnels.

Shit, I thought bitterly. *I wish we had grenades.*

"Hey! Why don't you come out and die like man?" I shouted. I looked over at Tailor and shrugged. When all else fails, *negotiate*.

LORENZO

Please, don't let them have any grenades.

"Hey! Why don't you come out and die like a man?"

one of them yelled. Despite his raised voice, he sounded very calm, almost conversational.

"Why don't you come down here and get me then?" I shouted around the corner. The closet was decent cover, the walls were solid, and if they wanted me, they had to come down that fatal funnel of a hallway. The first one to stick his head down here was going to die, and they knew it.

"Who the fuck are you?" one of them yelled, clearly agitated. Apparently they weren't used to somebody speaking English. He was obviously a Southerner.

"Nobody worth dying over," I responded. "You better hurry. Somebody had to hear all that shooting. You don't have much time."

"We'll make time," stated the calm one.

Carl came over the earpiece. He was out of breath. *"Some skinny guy saw me coming in the market and tried to stab me, so I broke his head."* So Jalal's man had tried to stop my friend. That was a fatal mistake.

"There are at least three shooters. They've got me pinned down."

"I'll circle around," he said. I could hear the Dead Six men talking back and forth in hushed tones down the hallway. The nearest two were speaking in Spanish, but they shouted at someone else in English that they would take care of me.

"We're on the way," Reaper said. *"But I'm stuck behind some trucks."*

"I'm coming to help." The female voice over the radio took me a second to process. I could hear the van door open.

Idiot. "Jill, stay put!"

BOOM BOOM BOOM BOOM

I jerked away from the doorway as the walls shattered. The giant .44 Magnum slugs tore through the building materials with unbelievable fury. The smell of solvents filled the air from leaking containers. I stuck my gun around the corner and fired several wild rounds in response.

"Val! Holy shit, look at all this money!" They'd found the backpack.

"That's mine!" I shouted. "Assholes!"

"Not anymore, motherfucker!" shouted the obnoxious one. *"Ha!"*

VALENTINE

"This is taking too long," I said, dumping a fresh speed loader into my .44. "C'mon, man, we gotta go!" Tailor nodded, slung the backpack full of money, and led the way. I backed down the hallway, keeping my gun trained on the closet at the end of the hall. We'd already told Hudson and Byrne to head back to their vehicle, and the cops would be all over Hasa Market before too long.

"Control, Xbox," Tailor said, speaking into his radio. "Target neutralized. Egressing now. Will update as I can." Sarah acknowledged him on the radio as we reached the door at the other end of the hallway.

"It's your lucky day, asshole," I said to the man in the closet, even though I doubted he could hear me. Tailor and I then turned and bolted back through the warehouse.

LORENZO

It was quiet. I risked a peek. I couldn't see anything, but that didn't mean they weren't just waiting quietly to blow my head off.

"Lorenzo, there are four of them. Two came in the back. They're heading west toward the street." Carl said. *"Those two fodas from the video just walked out the front. They're heading south through the market, trying to play it cool."*

The ones with the box were the ones that mattered. "Tail them. I'm on my way," I responded, already heading for the exit. I shoved the STI back in its holster as I hopped over the bodies of Jalal and his men. There was no way I was going to let them get away.

The market was continuing as normal. The walls of the old warehouse and the music must have muffled the gunshots enough not to spook the crowd. I walked quickly, as running would have drawn too much attention. A woman gasped and pointed at me. Glancing down, I realized that I was still splattered with Jalal's blood. "Shit," I muttered.

"They're moving south," Carl reported. *"I'm on them."*

"Where?" I hissed. The woman was pointing at me and pulling on her husband's sleeve. I ducked my head and turned, moving deeper into the throng.

"By the fountain."

"Reaper, move up on the entrance. Be ready to roll. Carl, we need one of them alive."

Carl came back. *"I've been made."*

Then there was a gunshot.

VALENTINE

Guns holstered, Tailor and I pushed our way back through Hasa Market, south, where our vehicle was waiting for us. We nervously eyed the crowd as we walked, checking over our shoulders for the guy in the soccer jersey. I didn't know who he was, but I knew he wasn't just another militant asshole.

There wasn't time to worry about it. We'd been lucky, so far, in that no one had heard the shots or called the police, but I didn't want to find out how long that luck would hold. All we had to do was make it back to our truck and we were home free.

Not necessarily, I thought bitterly, remembering the night Wheeler died. We cleared the tangled mess of the marketplace and came upon the open area that surrounded the old fountain at the center. Like the rest of the market, it was choked with people, but it wasn't nearly as claustrophobic as the maze of shops and carts.

Gun. I noticed it so instinctively that I almost didn't realize it. Everything slowed down as *The Calm* kicked in again. On the other side of the fountain there was a man with a gun. He was short and squat, with a dark face and a scraggly beard. He was staring at me intently, and through the bustle of the crowd I could see him trying to bring a pistol to bear. He was dressed in local garb, but, like the man in the soccer jersey, I didn't believe he was some random Zubaran citizen.

Before I'd finished processing that, I realized my gun was clear of its holster and that the front sight was aligned on the man with the gun as he brought his own pistol up. His eyes grew wide as a gap appeared in the crowd; I had a shot. I fired.

I *missed.* My bullet struck the edge of the fountain, blowing off a small chunk and ricocheting off into the distance. My revolver's roar echoed through Hasa Market, and all at once everyone froze, heads turning to see what was happening. People around us stared at us wide-eyed, mouths agape.

"Oh, shit," Tailor said, his .45 already drawn. More shots rang out as the man with the gun fired at us, using the edge of the heavily constructed fountain as cover. Tailor and I shot back, moving laterally as we fired, trying to hit the gunman without killing anyone in the crowd.

All at once the marketplace was in chaos. People screamed and began to stampede in every direction. Tailor and I were nearly crushed by a throng of people trying to get away from the shooting. We couldn't even see the shooter through the morass of panicked shoppers, much less get a bead on him.

"We're compromised!" Tailor shouted, straining to be heard even though I was only a few feet from him. "Let's get the hell out of here!" He struggled to reload his .45 while he talked.

Following his lead, I lowered my now-empty revolver and began to push my way through the crowd. We headed west, toward the mosque. Our Land Cruiser was parked in an alley between the mosque and a school next door. After a few seconds, the crowd thinned a little, and I had room to breathe. I emptied my gun's cylinder and reached for my belt again.

Someone crashed into me as I drew the speed loader from my belt, causing me to drop it. My speed loader bounced off the concrete and rolled away. Swearing, I shoved the hapless person aside and crouched down, grabbing my loader.

I stood up, pausing to twist the cartridges into the cylinder, when someone shouted at me to stop in heavily accented English. I froze and looked up. About ten feet to my left was a Zubaran police officer. His pistol was pointed between my eyes. He held a radio in his other hand.

Two puffs of blood and uniform material erupted from the Zubaran police officer's side as Tailor double-tapped him. The cop staggered, and Tailor put a third round into his head. He dropped to the concrete like a sack of potatoes, his pistol clattering as it hit. I made eye contact with Tailor, nodded at him, and we took off at a run toward the mosque.

Looking back through the crowd, I couldn't see the stocky man who had shot as us by the fountain. But as we crossed in front of the school, I noticed a woman in a black burka running determinedly in our direction across the lawn of the mosque. She produced a small pistol from somewhere just as I rounded the corner into the alley.

LORENZO

I spotted the two Dead Six operatives fifty yards ahead, moving fast, straight for the mosque. That had to be where they'd left their car. I raised my gun, but there were too many terrified people stampeding between us, then they were around the corner of some booths and out of sight. "Damn it! Carl, flank around the mosque and hit them from the other side. Reaper, get your ass up here now."

I took off after them, darting between people. Some lady saw my gun and bloodsoaked countenance and screamed. That caused a bunch of other people to shriek and point, and a lot of them were already on their cell phones. This was so not good. *"Reaper!* We need immediate evac!"

"Almost there!" he responded.

There was a winding alley between the one-story school and the much taller mosque. The east end dumped into the market, and the west onto a quiet street. That's where I would have parked. I caught a glimpse of a khaki-clad figure duck into the alley. *Got you.* I moved up along the school wall, gun at my side. I was going to drop whichever one I saw first, then try to shoot the legs out from under the other.

Most of the people from the market were moving away from the two Caucasians and the men chasing them, and maybe that's why the woman with the veil stuck out so quickly. Jill Del Toro was coming across the lawn of the mosque, directly toward me, only she was going to reach the alley a few seconds before I was. She reached into her clothing and out came the little Makarov.

I ran faster, forcing myself forward. Jill brought the gun up in both hands, but she made the classic mistake of letting her gun lead around the corner, telegraphing her presence. And *he* had been waiting for it. One hand clamped around her wrist, jerking her forward. Jill disappeared.

Chapter 14:
Anger Management

VALENTINE

I grabbed the woman's arm with my right hand, crushing her thin wrist as roughly as I could. I used her momentum, vaulting her around the corner. She cried out in surprise as I wheeled her around a full two-hundred and seventy degrees, and gasped for air when I smashed her against the wall of the mosque, my forearm on her neck. In the same instant I brought my own gun up, leveling it between her eyes, and I froze.

The veiled woman was now staring down the barrel of my .44 Magnum, dark eyes wide with fear. Her right hand went slack, and the little Makarov pistol clattered to the pavement. She stopped struggling, and I asked myself why I hadn't already fired. I couldn't find an answer. Tailor asked what was going on. I didn't answer him either.

I reached forward with my gun hand and ripped the woman's veil off of her head. The black veil covered a very pretty face. She was young, with tanned olive skin and

night-black hair. She was Hispanic, or maybe of
Philippine ancestry, and she looked . . . *damned familiar.*

Holy shit, I thought, suddenly remembering where I'd
seen that face. "Jillian Del Toro?" I asked cautiously. Her
eyes suddenly went even wider, and the color flushed out
of her face. I couldn't believe it. It was the woman Gordon
had put out the BOLO on.

I noticed something out of the corner of my eye:
movement. Everything moved in slow motion as I
watched, my consciousness still enveloped by *The Calm.*
The man with the soccer jersey was approaching from
my right, weapon drawn. He was running straight at me,
hoping I wouldn't notice him in the mass of panicked,
fleeing shoppers.

I yanked Jill Del Toro's arm forward as hard as I could,
twisting to the right as I did so. She gasped in pain again.
I let go of her hand and clamped my right arm around her
neck. I pulled her against me and tightened my arm as I
brought my revolver over her left shoulder and leveled it
at the son of a bitch in the soccer jersey.

"Lorenzo, look out!" Jill Del Toro screamed. I
tracked him with my gun and fired. Jill winced as the
gun discharged a foot from her face. He dove aside. The
.44 slug smacked the corner of the school, smashing a
small piece of brick into a cloud of dust.

I tightened my grip on Jill and hunched down behind
her. The man in the jersey, Lorenzo, hovered just around
the corner, where I couldn't get a shot at him. He didn't
seem willing to risk a shot at me under the circumstances,
either. Tailor was coming up behind me, pistol drawn.

"Just let the girl go," he said from around the corner.

He spoke flawless, generic, unaccented English. "We can all just walk away."

"Listen, asshole," I growled, slowly backing down the alley. "I've had just about enough of you today. Why don't you come out so we can finish this?"

"Yeah," Tailor said, "we got your girl and your money bag. Having a bad day?"

We could hear police sirens in the distance. "What's it gonna be, ace?" I asked calmly, continuing to back down the alley, pulling the young woman with me as I went. "Cops are coming."

"Lorenzo!" the woman cried out, fear now obvious in her voice. I caught a flash of movement at the edge of the school. My revolver barked as I popped off another shot, taking another chunk off the corner of the building. Jill cried out again.

A couple of long seconds ticked by, and there was no response. Tailor and I made eye contact. I dropped the muzzle of my gun as he crossed in front of me, weapon held at the ready. He checked around the perforated corner of the school as I covered the opposite corner.

"He's gone," Tailor said, stepping back around the corner. He looked at Jill. "Guess your boyfriend got cold feet, bitch."

I couldn't help but smile at the absurdity of the situation. I yanked Jill Del Toro around and began to force her back toward our car.

LORENZO

I left her.

"Fall back, Carl. Fall back!" I ordered. The sirens were wailing. The security forces would be here any second. Everything was ruined. Jill had gotten herself captured. Dead Six had won. She was as good as dead. The mission was screwed. The only option left was self-preservation. I would have to figure out what to do about Eddie later. "Hurry."

"*I'm almost there!*" Carl responded.

"Leave them!"

The van tore around the edge of the school. I waved both hands overhead so he'd see me. Reaper stomped on the brakes, and the van screeched to a halt. I yanked open the side door. "Back up, grab Carl, and let's go."

"Where's Jill?" Reaper shouted.

"*Go!*" I bellowed.

But he hesitated. "She's one of *us*."

I froze, half in, half out of the van. My first inclination was to reach forward and smack Reaper on the side of his stupid head. In a minute we'd be fighting half the cops in Zubara. I was a thief. You run. That's what thieves do.

But he was right.

Something *snapped* just then.

I couldn't leave her.

Things had changed. She wasn't just bait. Jill wasn't just somebody I could use and throw away anymore. Reaper was right. She was one of us. "Son of a bitch!" I grimaced. Reaper must have seen it. Instead of putting the van into reverse like I had ordered, he stomped on the gas, narrowly avoiding running down a bunch of innocent bystanders, and headed straight for the alley.

"Carl, turn around and take them out!"

He was out of breath from running. *"Make up your mind!"*

The alley was probably forty yards long, five yards wide, and their car had to be parked either in it or on the exiting street. Trying to walk down that alley would get me killed, and shooting it out down the alley would only get Jill killed, and either way the cops were going to kill all of us in a second anyway. I needed to get on top of them, *fast*. The school wasn't very tall at all. I had an idea. "Reaper, pull right up to the front door of the school."

"What?"

"Just do it! Then back up and block that alley."

He did as I said, actually crashing our bumper into the front steps. But I didn't feel it as I was already out the side of the moving vehicle before impact. I stepped onto the bumper, the hood, the windshield, and finally onto the van's roof. I ran, jumped, and caught the edge of the roof with my hands. Pulling myself up, I scrambled onto the roof of the school.

I ran up the angled tile of the roof, parallel with the alley. This was idiotic. Half of Zubara was probably watching this moronic stunt, and I was sure that I'd be nicely silhouetted for the police snipers. The STI materialized in my hand as I approached the edge. Glancing downward, there were the assassins. The tall one was struggling against Jill, trying to force her into the backseat of a car, while she was fighting like crazy, but he outweighed her by eighty pounds. The Southerner was watching back down the alley, wearing *my* backpack, 1911 extended, waiting for me to appear at the end.

"What are you doing?" he shouted. "Cops are coming. Just shoot her already!"

The tall one grunted a response that I couldn't understand. He was hugging Jill's arms tight, but she just kept swinging her legs and jerking her head back into his face. I had no idea why he hadn't already shot her. Dead Six must have decided they wanted Jill alive for some reason. There was no time to think. The second Reaper appeared at the end of that alley, that psychopath was going to light him up. I punched my gun out, sights lining up on the Southerner's head.

There was a door into the alley from the mosque. It swung open directly behind the man, and he instantly spun toward it. There was a kid, probably all of six years old, standing there, and the kid was right behind my target. I was putting two and a half pounds of pressure on a three-pound trigger when I froze, thinking of the bullet that had passed through Jalal that was still throbbing, stuck in my vest.

I couldn't kill a kid. I'd never killed a kid.

The child looked at the Southerner, at his gun, and then over his shoulder, right at me. The Dead Six operative instinctively turned, following the kid's gaze. He saw me, eyes narrowed, and his gun flew up. Chunks of tile erupted skyward as I moved back from the ledge. Bullets just kept tearing through the mosque, searching for me, as he ran for the car.

At the end of the alley, our white van appeared, blocking their exit. They would cut Reaper to ribbons. I had to take them out *now*.

I took a few steps back, trying to remember the exact

position of their car, hoped I was right, then ran forward
and jumped off the edge.

VALENTINE

Jill Del Toro struggled mightily as Tailor snapped off
several rounds at the man she'd called Lorenzo. I turned
back to our Land Cruiser and, despite the girl's thrashing,
pulled the passenger's door open. We had zip-ties in the
glove box, and I was going to restrain the girl in my
arms before I gave in to the temptation to *shoot her*.
The terrified young child had disappeared back inside.
We were out of time and had to get the hell out of there.

"Just shoot her and let's go, Val!"

CRUNCH! I looked up in surprise as Lorenzo fell off
the roof of the school. He put a dent in the roof of our
Land Cruiser as he landed. He tried to do a shoulder
roll to dissipate his impact but ended up rolling down
the windshield and falling off the hood of the truck. He
disappeared over the truck as he hit the pavement on the
other side.

He reappeared a split-second later, pistol leveled at me
across the hood of the truck. He was listing slightly to one
side, and blood started to trickle down his face, but he had
a killing look in his eyes.

"Lorenzo!" Jill screamed again. Before Lorenzo could
turn around, Tailor was behind him, pushing his pistol
into the back of his skull.

"Drop it, motherfucker!" Tailor growled. Lorenzo let
his gun fall. Then there was more movement as someone

ran up the alley from my left. I'd been so fixated on
Lorenzo that I hadn't noticed. Neither had Tailor, who,
with a metallic CLANG, crumpled to the pavement as he
was smacked in the head with a goddamned shovel.

LORENZO

CLANG!

Carl hit the Southerner unbelievably hard, collapsing
the man in a heap.

I told him to take one of them alive.

The tall one shoved Jill down as his hand flew to his
gun. Carl was already diving behind the trunk as the
Magnum spit flame. I hit the ground as he reflexively
turned on me next. Brick dust rained down on me when
he fired, pulverizing the wall where I had just been. The
shooter with the hand cannon was circling the back of the
car, wearing that look on his face again, like everything
else in the world had just stopped, and that all that
mattered was taking out the garbage.

Carl was going for his pistol but was struggling to get it
out, snagged on the unfamiliar clothing. The left-handed
shooter came smoothly around the back of the car, doing
the math, deciding to take me out first, like he had all the
time in the world, mammoth handgun leveled right at my
face. Time dilated until I could see the cylinder rotate
another giant hollow-point into position behind the barrel.
Guns are scarier when you can actually see the bullets.

He twitched at the last possible instant, .44 slug digging
a divot into the pavement next to my face, fragments

raking bloody chunks from my upraised hands. The shooter jerked as another round struck him in the chest. I looked through the open door to see Jill shooting him with my pistol, then back in time to see him go down.

The police sirens were right on top of us. Reaper was honking the horn.

"Come on!" Carl shouted. He had leapt to his feet, tossed the shovel, and was trying to pick up the man he'd knocked out, pulling him by one limp arm. I moved to help but saw the man crawling around the back of the car, his buddy's 1911 in hand. Carl grimaced as the bullet struck him in the back. "Aaarg! I'm hit!"

"Run!" I shouted. The shooter ducked back down as Jill started punching holes in the trunk. I grabbed Carl by the vest and tugged him along. "Back to the van!" Jill kept shooting. "Jill, move!" She finally complied and ran after us. We reached the van a second later, and I shoved Carl in first. Jill leapt in after him. A new .45 caliber hole magically appeared in the sheet metal next to my hand. My opponent stood up and reflexively dropped the empty magazine from the .45 in his hands. He cursed as he realized he didn't have a reload. I made eye contact with my nemesis.

This isn't over.

There were flashing police lights coming up behind him. He tossed the empty gun into the car and went back for his friend, who was still wearing my backpack. I dove into the van and jerked the door closed. "Drive, Reaper, drive!"

Reaper did his best to get us out of there and managed to scrape all the paint off our passenger side on an approaching police car. The screech of metal on metal filled the compartment. Carl grimaced.

"How bad?" I asked.

"You know how hard it is to get a clean, untraceable vehicle? How much work I put into this engine? I'm gonna have to burn it now. I didn't want to have to use the spare yet. It ain't as nice—"

"I meant the bullet."

"Vest stopped it, bet I piss blood tonight, but I better drive before *galinha*-boy kills us all." Carl crawled forward and started yelling at Reaper to get into the passenger seat. There was a brief lull as Reaper got out of the way; then the van really started to roar. Even kidney-punched with a .45, Carl was the best getaway driver in the business. We still had a chance.

I was lying on the floor of the open cargo area, breathing hard and sliding about as Carl took us around corners on two wheels, sirens screaming right outside our back window, when I saw Jill looking at me strangely. "You okay? Are you injured?"

She didn't answer for a long enough time that I started to worry she'd taken a blow to the head. Then she finally spoke. "You came back for me. You weren't going to. You were going to save yourself, you could have, but then you came back."

"Yeah." That made me uncomfortable. Of course I had been ready to ditch her. I don't know why I'd changed my mind, but she had ended up saving my life, not the other way around. "Can I have my gun back?" She realized that it was still in her hands, then passed it over. "Go take a seat and buckle in."

"Thank you," she said softly as she moved forward.

Every cop in Zubara was going to be looking for our van. "Reaper, get on your computer and get rid of this pursuit. I want zero security forces communication. Screw with them however you want."

"All of them?" he asked, opening his machine. He sounded eager. I didn't normally just turn him loose like that. It was kind of scary.

"Use your imagination." There were two police cars directly behind us on the narrow street. "Carl, you want a hand losing these guys?" I shouted.

"If you don't mind me doing *all* the work!"

That sounded like a yes. I pulled up the rug in the back and opened a secret compartment, took out the stashed carbine, turned on the Aimpoint, and pulled back the charging handle. One thing I liked about this particular type of Toyota van was that you could open the back window. The muzzle cleared the window as I took a sight picture. It was difficult with the swaying of the shocks, but this wasn't rocket science.

Unlike Western police agencies that relied on communication, tire spikes, and road blocks, Zubaran cops hung their guns out the windows and randomly started shooting, which was a whole lot more dangerous to the neighborhood than it was to the people they were pursuing. I was doing the populace a favor. I pumped half a dozen rounds through the radiator of the first car before the cop panicked and jerked the wheel to the side, spinning out of control. The second car T-boned them.

I rolled the window up and sank to the floor. Reaper was clicking away like mad, destroying thousands of man-hours' worth of Zubara's communications programming, Carl was driving like a Formula One champion, and Jill was just watching me with this indecipherable look on her face, probably thinking about how, for the first time in her life, she'd just shot somebody, and it had saved a life. My life.

It had been a long afternoon. And it had all been for nothing.

"*Control, this is Nightcrawler, we've got a situation.*" I recognized that voice, even distorted over an unfamiliar radio. He sounded like he was in pain.

"*Go ahead, Nightcrawler,*" said an unfamiliar woman's voice. "*Are you alright?*" I could sense a note of *personal* concern slipping through the professionalism.

"Where's that coming from?" I asked quickly.

Carl took one hand off the wheel long enough to hold up a small radio. "It fell off the one I knocked out." He risked a look back at me. "Told you I do all the work around here."

"*I'm okay. Xbox is hurt. I've lost the cops and I'm heading to the safe house.*"

"*Nightcrawler, what's Xbox's status?*" the girl asked.

"*I don't know.*" He sounded worried. They weren't just teammates. They were friends. *Nightcrawler* . . . so that was the name of the guy I had to kill. *What a stupid call sign.* "*Xbox took a bad hit to the head. Some asshole hit him with a shovel!*"

"Where'd you find a shovel anyway?" I shouted.

Carl shrugged. "I passed some construction guys digging up pipes. You know, knock one cold, to interrogate. Seemed like a smart idea at the time." Good thing that the shovel was the official martial arts weapon of the Portuguese. It came from all of that dairy farming and hitting cows they had in their genes or something.

We were now listening in to Dead Six's encrypted communications. This was huge. "Carl, have I told you yet today that I love you?"

The next voice that came on was older, gruff. He had the air of command. *"This is Big Boss. Nightcrawler, was the target neutralized?"*

"Yes, sir."

"Are you sure, son?"

"He was dead before he hit the floor, sir. The guy he was meeting with got away. I don't know who the hell he was. He looked like a local, but he didn't fight like a local. He was good. Really good, sir. That girl that Bureaucrat put the BOLO on was there, too. I almost had her, but she escaped. She's working with the shooter. Called him Lorenzo."

There was a pause. *"Understood, Nightcrawler. Did you notice anything else about this man? Any way to identify him?"*

"He was average looking, could've been Arab, could've been Mexican. I couldn't really tell. He did carry some kind of high-cap 1911. Xbox tried to take him prisoner, but that kind of backfired on him. Are the others okay?"

"Shafter and Anarchangel are on their way to the safe house. Zubaran communications are going wild. People saw you. You screwed up out there, son. I want a full briefing as soon as you get back. Bureaucrat will be mad as hell."

"Reaper, can you track this?" I asked hopefully.

"I can try. Give me a second, though," he responded.
He was right. Eluding pursuit was more important. "I'm
routing every cop in the city back to the Hasa Market
where we're holed up in a hostage standoff." The boy was
creative when you gave him some leeway. "We've got a
room full of school kids and a sack of anthrax!"

"Don't overdo it," I warned.

The radio crackled one last time. *"Nightcrawler out."*

You just wait.

The stolen radio sat in the middle of the computer
table, volume cranked all the way up. Reaper had
removed the back plate and attached a few mysterious
wires to various things and was tapping away on his
computer, looking at waves, graphs full of quickly scrolling
numbers, and other things far beyond my meager comprehension. He'd already made sure that the radio didn't
have any sort of tracking device that could lead back to us.
He was in the zone. I had pulled up a chair and was sitting
there, pad of paper and pen in hand, scribbling furious
notes each time someone from Dead Six spoke.

It had taken forever to get home. After being routed in
the wrong direction, the police had actually caught on that
they were being screwed with. Then Reaper had introduced
a ferocious virus into their system, crashing the entire
Zubaran security forces' communication network. We had
parked the van in a ditch a few miles away and then
walked home.

Jill, apparently not sure what else to do, was sitting
across from me, nervously fiddling. The one called
Nightcrawler—or Val, as Jill had said the Southerner had

called him—had roughed her up pretty good, but she seemed okay to me. I'd been too engrossed with the radio on the walk home to talk to her. Carl had checked Jill's minor injures, then had grabbed a beer, flopped onto the couch, and was watching TV. The selections in this part of the world were out of date and he was watching the end of a poorly dubbed episode of *Three's Company*. He ripped the Velcro on his vest and tossed it on the floor, absently rubbing the bruise on his back.

Dead Six's communications were thoroughly connected. Within ten minutes of Reaper's virus attack, they had informed all of their operators that the security force's comms were disrupted and to take advantage of that if they needed to. It pissed me off that some of our work might somehow benefit these jerk-offs.

"Any luck?" I asked.

"I can't get a fix on the transmissions. This encryption is intense," Reaper muttered. "Whoever set this network up is good, really good."

"You're better," I stated. "Find them."

"It doesn't work like that," he said. "It's all about the math. If we hadn't found this unit already open, I wouldn't ever have cracked it. Even then, I can't access any of the other channels. I can't triangulate location because they're bouncing these things off everything. Their crypto guy's got mad skills."

I scowled. Reaper was usually unbearably cocky about this kind of stuff. I didn't like him sounding humble. That couldn't be good. Shaking my head, I went back to the chatter. This was the operational channel of the day, and Dead Six was apparently a busy bunch. I had noted every call sign used or referred to, and they had mentioned eight different individuals so far. I had no idea if that was all of them or just a fraction.

I got the impression that this channel was for the operators in Zubara, but from the dialog I could tell that this was bigger, and there were other active channels, and probably command channels beyond that. Big Boss was the operational commander. He answered to somebody called Bureaucrat, who apparently had a sidekick called Drago, but neither one of those had spoken yet.

There were two other operations being conducted today in the Zoob. Unfortunately they all spoke in vague generalities about their locations, like "we're on the street," or "by the mosque," or "we're waiting in the parking garage." No names, just random call signs. Nothing I could use to track them. The people they were either murdering or spying on were simply referred to as the targets, never by name.

"Nightcrawler, this is Control." It was the girl from earlier. Her voice was young, American. Her tone told me that she was close to this Nightcrawler. *"Big Boss wants an update on Xbox's status."*

The voice that came back sounded tired. *"He's got a concussion. I think he'll be okay. He's pretty screwed up, though, kind of . . . like punch-drunk stupid or something."* His accent was from the northern Midwest, Michigan, or maybe Wisconsin. It wasn't thick, though. He'd probably traveled. There was another voice in the background. I recognized the accent. *"Yes, I am talking about you, asshole. . . . No sign of traumatic brain injury. Um, I think. It's hard to tell with him. He's awake, anyway."*

It sounded like the Southerner laughed and then said *"Tell Sarah Ah said hi,"* or something like that. He sounded like he was from East Tennessee, and not from the rich side of town. I quickly scribbled "Sarah?" after the note for Control.

"How are you doing?" she asked. That was real concern. I was right. There was some emotion there.

"I'm fine. Had a close one today, but I'm fine," Nightcrawler answered slowly. The kid didn't just sound physically tired, but weary, burned out. *Good.* From what I'd heard in the last little while, their operational tempo was brutal. They were being driven hard, and hopefully that meant they would slip up soon.

"What happened?" Control asked.

"It was that girl. The one Bureaucrat wanted so bad. I don't know. I just . . . she caught me off guard." I glanced over at Jill and gave her a big thumbs-up. It would have been better if she had shot him in the face, but she was new at this and wouldn't have thought of a vest. Jill shrugged. Nightcrawler continued. *"Then there was that other guy, the one with the tricked-out 1911. The girl called him Lorenzo. He's good. He, I don't know, fell off the roof of this mosque, landed on our truck, and started shooting."*

"He fell off the roof? He kept shooting after that?"

"It wasn't that high. I mean, I fell off the roof of the barn once when I was a kid. I ended up in the emergency room, though."

"I didn't *fall*," I said to the others. "I meant to do that."

"Don't worry," Control said. *"We'll find him. I need you to be careful out there."*

"*Don't worry. I'll be fine.*"

Damn right you're fine. You didn't report my sack of money, either, you piece of shit. "They're sloppy on the radio," I said.

"You're just annoyed," Jill said.

Control came back. "*They want to debrief you right away. Big Boss is sending a car to pick you up. I'll . . . I'll see you soon.*" She was trying to be professional, but was . . . she was in *love* with him. *Holy crap, this gets better and better.*

Nightcrawler came right back. "*I'll—wait a second. What?*" There was some commotion in the background. "*I don't have your radio. . . . What do you . . . Son of a bitch! Control, Xbox's radio is missing. Repeat, his radio is gone.*"

"Are you sure?"

Brief pause. "*Yes. It's missing.*"

"No!" I shouted as I leapt from my chair. "Damn it, no!"

"*Hang on.*" Sarah, or whatever her name was, went right into full-blown damage control. "*Attention on the net. ComSec breach. I say again, ComSec breach. Emergency protocol in force, Zulu One. I repeat, Zulu One.*"

Then the radio went to static.

They'd changed to a different encrypted channel. "Reaper!"

"They're gone," he replied.

"Not good enough! Find them," I bellowed.

"I'm trying, but this stuff is hard."

Gone!

A bubble of rage uncorked from my soul, rumbled to

the top, and erupted like a festering boil. All this work, all the killing, all the effort, all for nothing.

I just lost it.

With an incoherent roar, I picked up my chair and hurled it into the kitchen, shattering it against the far wall. "This Nightcrawler asshole has screwed me *three* times now! *Three times*!" I slammed my fist through the nearby Sheetrock, scattering tacked-up photos of the Zubaran underworld like confetti. "Falah, Adar, and now Hosani! And I even kind of liked Hosani! Worthless asshole cock-sucking son of a bitch!"

Jill and Reaper recoiled as I stomped past. "Every step of the way, every part of this suicide mission, complicated because of that piece of shit. *Damn it*! Not only does he have *my* box—he's got *my* money! And I've got—" I kicked a hole through the kitchen door. "*Nothing*! It isn't enough for him to ruin my life, but *no*, I get to make him rich, too. I swear I'm going to gut him like a fish. I'm going to pull his eyes out and skull-fuck him to death! I'll tear his throat out with my *teeth*!"

Carl, having seen a few of my outbursts over the years, calmly turned up the TV volume and sipped his beer.

The neighbors started banging on the wall, demanding quiet. My first inclination was to pull my gun and shoot them through the wall. If they wanted loud, I'd show them loud. But I just stood there, breathing hard, chest heaving, veins popping out in my neck, left eye spasmodically twitching, fists clenched so hard that I was shaking. Big Eddie was going to murder *everyone*, and all because I couldn't catch Dead Six.

So what the hell do I do now?

"Are you done throwing your sissy tantrum?" Carl asked over the sounds of *Walker, Texas Ranger* speaking in Arabic. "Or should I go get more furniture for you to break?"

Deflated, back to the wall, I sank slowly to the floor. "I'm out of ideas."

Reaper had instinctively moved his body to protect his precious computer equipment from my fury. He'd rather me toss him across the room than one of those hard drives. "I can keep trying," he assured me. The kid wasn't used to me not having all the answers. "There's got to be a way. You always figure out something."

I shook my head. "We need to start thinking about how we can protect our families. How can we get all of them out of Big Eddie's reach?" But I knew that was futile before the words even left my mouth. He had us by the short hairs, and there was nothing we could do. "Jill, you did your part. I'll get you out of the country. I've got resources, friends. You—"

"Lorenzo!" Jill snapped. "You're not out of options yet."

I laughed, and it wasn't a happy noise. If only she knew. Up until a few hours ago, *she* had been my final option. But somehow things had changed. I stood up. "You don't have a *clue* what you're talking about," I said.

Jill's eyes narrowed dangerously. "Yes, I do." Her voice was barely a whisper, but somehow that got everyone's attention more than my ranting. "We all heard what they said. This Bureaucrat wants me dead, and I'll bet you money that's Gordon. You can still use *me* to get to *them*. I know you've already thought of that."

That perked Carl's interest, and he turned down the TV to listen to my response.

"I wouldn't do that."

"Yes, you would. I'm not stupid, Lorenzo. That's why you've kept me around. I figured that out in the last few days. I could see it in your eyes. You didn't like it, but I was insurance."

"I wouldn't do that *now*." That time I said it with more force.

And she knew I was telling the truth. "What changed?"

I didn't have an answer. "Nothing."

But she wasn't going to be deterred. "There's no such thing as *nothing*."

Reaper shook his head. "No way, man. Bullshit. Lorenzo wouldn't sell you out. That's . . ." He turned to me, scowling. "No way."

I looked Reaper square in the eyes. "I was going to do what I had to do. This isn't about me. This is about your mom, and Carl's family, and a bunch of little kids I've never even met, and for Train. I know what Eddie can do. I've seen it. What would you do if you were in my place?"

He looked around hesitantly. "I don't know."

I turned back to Jill. "But I'm not selling anybody to Dead Six."

Jill smiled. "So, you *do* have a heart."

It was really *tense* in that apartment right then. "Look, sorry about . . ." I waved my throbbing hand at the new holes in the wall. "Whatever. Just leave me alone. I'll . . . we'll think of something in the morning." I went to my room and closed the door, utterly defeated.

She didn't bother to knock.

I was sitting on the edge of the bed, staring at the

folder of family photos in the dim light, absently spinning that blood-stained .44 Magnum cartridge between my fingers, and I looked up to see Jill's silhouette in the doorway, hands on her hips. "Carl wanted me to tell you that he and Reaper went to pick up the spare car." Closing the folder, I set it aside. "What's that?" she asked.

Sighing, I responded. "This? This is a forty-four Magnum round. It came from the man that shot me today. And these," I said, gesturing at the photos, "are a bunch of innocent people who are going to be hurt because of what I am."

She waited. "Well . . . what are you?"

I shrugged. "I don't know anymore."

"I do," Jill said. She came inside and softly closed the door behind her. There was a sudden energy in the room. "I know *exactly* what you are."

I recognized the look that she was giving me. I'd seduced more women than I could count, but it wasn't like they *knew* me. I couldn't do this. Not with her. This wasn't right. I stood. "Listen, I—"

"You're a thief, and a liar, and an all-around jerk," she said with this mischievous little smile. "You're this just *horrendous* asshole that takes advantage of everybody around him, and uses people whenever it's convenient. And you're so *short*. I don't know what the hell I'm thinking."

That was unexpected. "Me, either."

"But . . ." Jill was closer now. She stopped, so close that I could just barely feel the soft curves of her body against me. It was electric. It had been a *long* time. "You're also the man that saved my life."

Her fingers were soft on my cheek. Then I was pulling her tight. Against all reason, I kissed her. She responded, quickly, aggressively. She felt so very good. "You don't have to do this," I said, and I meant it.

She whispered in my ear. "I know."

Wide awake, I stared at the dark ceiling, listening to the night sounds of Zubara coming from the open window and Jill's rhythmic breathing next to me. Her head was resting on my shoulder, and she had fallen asleep with one hand caressing the mottled scars on my chest.

Man, I needed that.

I moved the hair from her face, and she shifted slightly tighter against me in response.

What the hell was I doing? Men like me weren't allowed to have relationships. It wasn't that I wasn't attracted to her. . . . *Are you kidding?* She was beautiful and had an unbelievable body. No problem there. I'm only human. There was nothing I'd rather do, but I actually . . . hell. *I don't know.* It wasn't like I was used to *feelings.*

Jill was different than the others.

But I couldn't afford affection. Affection was weakness. I'd only ever had one serious relationship, and that had ended really badly. In the terrible world I inhabited, sex was business and love was for suckers. Loyalty was just something that could be used against you by anybody more ambitious than you were, my current predicament being a perfect example.

On the one hand, I felt like the biggest jerk in the world, like I was somehow taking advantage of this poor scared girl who had looked to me for protection, though it wasn't exactly like I had initiated this. On the other hand, I was thinking about how stupid I was. The cold, calculating part of my brain was warning me that Jill was probably just doing this to cement her chances of me not selling her out, that somehow she was better at emotional manipulation than I was. Maybe the con was getting conned.

Then again, I was at least a decade older than her, probably more. Since I spent my days murdering scumbags, it seemed odd that I would have some sort of moral hang up about that, but I did feel like a dirty old man. On a strictly practical note, it made me really glad that at forty I had the physical conditioning of an Olympic athlete. *Holy crap, the girl is energetic. Or maybe I'm just getting old.*

So I lay there, beating myself up, yet somehow feeling strangely happy. It was kind of weird.

Jill stirred. "You awake?" she asked softly.

"Just thinking is all."

I could see the whiteness of her smile in the dark. "Don't worry. We *will* find them." That hadn't been what I was thinking about at all. In fact, this was the first time in weeks that every one of my thoughts hadn't been driven by revenge. And for some reason, I liked how she said *we* would find them.

"You know, Jill, you're really pretty when you're homicidal."

She giggled. "You think too much. Wanna go again?"

Maybe life doesn't have to totally suck.

Chapter 15:
Pancakes

LORENZO
May 4

For some reason, despite massive setbacks, Dead Six boning me at every turn, being half a million dollars poorer, getting shot the day before, and still unable to get Adar's box, I felt better today than I had in quite a while. I had gone out onto the balcony and was staring at the sun just beginning to light the morning fog. Carl joined me a few minutes later, leaned on the balcony, and regarded me suspiciously. As usual, we were the first up. "You kids get that out of the way finally? Been sniffing around each other like horny teenagers since she got here."

The call to prayer began to resonate across the city. "Why, Carl, my good man. I have no idea what you're talking about."

He grunted. "Sure. So, what now, genius?"

I had been thinking about that. "You've seen the e-mails to Al Falah. The big meeting is on for June eighteenth. So we've got just over a month to get ready for the Phase Three."

"So we go in, but without Adar's box, we just die? Good plan."

"I might be able to pick it."

Carl nodded. "It's like a thousand years old and has something like *two hundred* tumblers, and if Reaper's numbers are right, you've got ten minutes maybe to get through before a couple hundred pissed off Saudis start shooting at you."

We had been through all this before, but it never hurt to go over the options again. "Explosives."

Carl knew his bombs better than I did. "That much reinforced material." He held up a stubby finger. "First, too loud. Pissed Saudis, remember?" Then another. "Second, you won't be able to smuggle enough in to make a shaped charge that can punch through."

"What if I were to find explosives inside the palace?"

"Ten minutes," Carl said. "Good luck. It's true what they say." He took a swig of his beer, breakfast of champions. "Getting laid makes you dumb."

"There are four other keys in existence. Adar only had one. We've got a month. We could steal one of the others," I suggested. Carl started to count on his fingers again. "I know, I know. One's been missing since the Third Crusade. The others are well guarded, and any attempt to take them would cause the vault's security to triple and probably get the meeting canceled." Adar, the exiled heir, had been our only hope.

"Maybe we try something different," Carl said.

"Find Big Eddie and kill him before he kills us? I'd

love to. Since nobody knows who he really is, if he's really even one man at all, and he works through layer after of layer of anonymous intermediaries, how do you suggest we do that?" I had been Big Eddie's single most effective thief for years, and I had never met the man. The intermediaries I had worked for had never met the man, either, and the second I started looking, he'd somehow know. "It'd be like catching the devil."

"I was just sayin'. I suppose I could just lay around in my underwear, get drunk, and watch TV until we run out of time."

"That's always an option. I'll keep working the streets. Dead Six will screw up. They're only human," I said. My phone buzzed. "Unknown number," I said suspiciously as I opened it. "Yeah?"

"Hello, Mr. Lorenzo." It was the Fat Man, sounding as ominously vacant as usual. "Our employer was wondering if you had made any progress in retrieving his box."

Oh, now it was *his* box. "Not yet. Dead Six is slippery."

"I understand. Disappointing, but I do understand. Big Eddie believes in fully supporting his employees with all of our organization's resources. His eyes are everywhere. Be ready on the eleventh. I will be in contact at exactly seven-fifteen in the morning, Zubaran time. I will give you the exact location of Dead Six. You will need to act quickly. There will be no second chance."

I was so shocked that I almost said thank-you.

"And as your immediate supervisor, I need to warn you. Big Eddie is concerned that you are not showing proper motivation. Motivation is very important, Mr. Lorenzo." His voice was urgent. "Fear and pain, these are good motivators, but loss . . . loss is the finest of them all. Please don't make me have to motivate you further. If I do not get a favorable report from you on the eleventh, I will be forced to use extreme motivation. Do you understand me, Mr. Lorenzo?"

"I hear you." *Psycho.* "Just get me the location and I'll handle the rest."

"I like pancakes." Then he hung up.

What the hell? Carl was looking at me strangely. My face must have betrayed my confusion. "The Fat Man's going to give us Dead Six next week."

My burly companion was actually shocked. "That's like a miracle."

"And he said he likes *pancakes.*"

"Huh?"

My phone buzzed again a moment later. I had received a video message. There was no sound. It was the Fat Man, the bloated monstrosity, wearing a giant white suit, almost filling my phone's screen. His bulk was squeezed impossibly into a restaurant booth, plate after empty plate stacked before him. He was shoveling pancakes into his mouth like some sort of industrial harvesting machine, barely pausing to breathe. He made a show of seeing the camera, stopped mid-mouthful, and made a big fake smile. His dark, empty eyes didn't smile with his mouth. His face was stained with whipped cream and syrup. The lettering on the window behind him was backward, but read IHOP.

The camera angle changed, moving over his shoulder, and sitting at the table directly behind him were my mother and my younger sister, Jenny, still in her uniform, probably taking a break from work, having an animated conversation, oblivious to the sociopath stuffing himself a few feet away. The camera panned back to the Fat Man, and he waved at me.

The son of a bitch was in Texas, personally keeping tabs on my mom.

Is it still considered a miracle if it comes from the devil?

VALENTINE
Fort Saradia National Historical Site
May 4
1205

Sarah was anxiously waiting for me in her room when I returned. My trip outside the compound had taken longer than I'd expected. The real trick had been convincing the guys at the motor pool to not log that Tailor and I took one of the vehicles for two hours. That hadn't been a problem, either. Things were getting bad enough that few of us that were still alive gave a crap about the rules anymore.

Sarah opened the door quickly when I knocked, and kissed me as I stepped inside. "I was worried," she said. The situation in the Zoob had been steadily deteriorating, and our shootout with that Lorenzo guy at the Hasa Market hadn't helped. It was getting difficult for us to move around the city quickly, as we had to spend a lot of time going around checkpoints.

"Sorry it took so long," I said. "Traffic. We had to go way the hell out of our way to avoid being stopped."

"I know," Sarah replied. "I'm just glad you're back. How did it go?"

"We're on," I said. I retrieved a piece of paper from my pocket. "She'll be here soon. She wants us to meet her in person. If she's satisfied that we're legit, she'll arrange to pick us up shortly after that."

"Wow," Sarah said. "Wait, she wants to meet all four of us? In person?"

"I'm afraid so. We're going to have to find a way to get you, me, Hudson, and Tailor out in town, together, without raising any suspicions."

"Shit," Sarah said. "I could talk to the other controllers. They could cover for us."

"Can you trust them?"

Sarah's expression sank. "I don't know. I can't believe we're just going to leave them. I mean, Anita is my friend."

I put my arms on Sarah's shoulders and looked down into her eyes. "Listen to me. I know this is hard. I don't like the idea of leaving Byrne, Frank, Cromwell, or Holbrook behind, either. I've been through a lot of shit with those guys. But it took a lot of doing just to get the four of us out. The more people I try to bring in, the greater the risk of compromise."

"I know, I know," Sarah said, sounding exasperated. "I get it. We need to be secretive about this, otherwise your friends will get pissed and leave us."

"I'm not worried about that," I said. "Sarah, if Ling thinks I'm screwing with her she'll have us all *killed*. These are dangerous people."

"I don't like it."

"I don't like it, either," I said honestly. "But it's the best I could do. Look . . . if you're having second thoughts, we don't have to go. Tailor and Hudson can go by themselves."

"Mike, you don't have—"

I interrupted her. "Yes I *do*, damn it. If you stay I'm staying. I'm not leaving without you."

Sarah's eyes widened slightly as what I'd just said sunk in. She shook her head slightly and gently put a hand on my cheek. "You're so stupid," she said. She then leaned in and kissed me, deeply and for a long time.

"What do you mean, 'stupid'?" I asked. We leaned in close together, so that my forehead was touching hers. I looked down into her eyes.

Sarah smiled. "I mean you say ridiculously sweet things like that and you're not being ironic. You're completely sincere, and you have no clue how rare that is. You're like a character in a bad romance novel."

"Well, it's your own fault, you know. You jumped me, remember?"

"I know," Sarah said. "Crazytown, remember? I warned you."

"You did. But listen," I said, seriousness edging back into my voice, "I'm asking you. Please, leave with me. This whole thing is going to hell in a ham sandwich. We have to get out while the getting's good. So let's go! Run away together."

"Go where?" Sarah asked. "I mean, really, Mike, where can we go?"

"Anywhere we want," I said, trying to sound more confident than I really was. "We can travel the world for a while until this whole thing blows over. I don't think Project Heartbreaker is going to be around much longer.

This country is falling apart. After things calm down, we can go home."

"Can I at least leave a note for my friends, warning them to get out?"

"Why not? They'll assume we bugged out on them anyway. It's not like I was planning to fake our deaths or anything. Tailor will be pissed, though."

"Fuck him," Sarah said dismissively. "He's the one that got you into this mess, isn't he? If he gives you any shit, I'll break his stupid face." She smiled again, and a surge of triumphant relief washed over me. I knew she was hesitant to just disappear and leave the others behind. I'd been terrified that she'd want to stay behind.

"I have something for you," Sarah said. She handed me a brown envelope. It contained all of my personal identification documents, including my passport, that had been taken from me before we left the States.

"How did you get these?" I asked.

"I have access to the safe," she said, eyes twinkling mischievously. "It's not like anyone goes in and checks to make sure your papers are still there."

I shook my head slightly. "You're amazing, you know that?"

"So tell me," Sarah said after a moment. "Who is this Ling woman? You haven't exactly been forthcoming about your history with her. Is she like an ex-girlfriend or something? You need to tell me the whole story."

Sarah was right. I owed her that much. I had avoided talking about Mexico the entire time I'd been in Zubara. As time went on, the parallels between our doomed mission in Mexico and Project Heartbreaker had made me increasingly uncomfortable.

"No, nothing like that," I said honestly. "I met Ling in Mexico last year when the situation had already gone to shit for Vanguard. We'd been contracted by the Mexican Nationalist Government to help secure some trouble areas in the southern part of the country. Some drug lords turned warlords had cut out little empires, so the government hired Vanguard to do a lot of high-risk operations."

"High-risk operations?" Sarah asked suspiciously.

"VIP protection, search-and-destroy missions, things like that. It was our biggest contract ever. Decker, my old boss, hired a ton of extra guys and brought in every team in the company."

"Including yours," Sarah said.

"Switchblade Four. We got the most critical assignments, raids on the bad guys, ambushing militia convoys, stuff like that. We were making progress until the UN moved in. Thirty thousand peacekeepers came in and unilaterally cut a cease-fire with the warlord in Cancun."

"Where does Ling come in?"

"We'd been sitting on our asses for days when she approached Decker with a business proposal. She said that there was a Cuban-flagged freighter docked in Cancun that was full of weapons going to the warlords, but she doesn't give a crap about the weapons. She says there's something else on the freighter, something her group, real secretive bunch, really wants. A girl."

"A girl?"

"Fourteen years old. A prisoner. Ling told Decker,

that her organization was willing to pay a crazy sum of money if we'd provide airlift and help get this girl back."

"Why did they bring you guys in?"

"I'm not sure. I never really asked her, and she didn't volunteer a lot of information. Anyway, Decker asks for volunteers, says there'll be a huge operational bonus to the team that goes. We volunteered."

"What happened?"

"Well, we got the girl," I said, my voice softening just a bit. "Stirred up a hornet's nest. Our chopper got hit on the way out. We went down at this abandoned resort hotel, landed right in an empty pool. Then the UN showed up and started shooting at us. Once the government collapsed, Vanguard was declared war criminals."

Sarah was suspicious. "This group that Ling works for, who are they?"

"Exodus." The look on Sarah's face told me she'd heard of them.

"Are you sure?" Sarah asked.

"That's what she told me."

"I thought they were a myth. Wow."

"I know, right? The whole thing was crazy. But it was *so* much money."

"Mike, tell me what happened," Sarah said, looking into my eyes.

I took a deep breath, glanced away for a second, then met Sarah's gaze again. I hadn't told anyone aside from Hawk the full story of what happened in Mexico. "Exodus thinks I'm some kind of hero."

VALENTINE
Umm Shamal District
May 5
0200

It took us over two hours to get to Ling's designated meeting spot. As was the usual case now, we had to go way out of our way to avoid downtown areas, major intersections, and other places where there were likely to be military or police checkpoints. The tiny Emirate of Zubara was holding its breath, waiting for the civil war to start.

It had taken some doing, but Tailor had managed to talk the motorpool into letting him sign out a Land Cruiser without it going in the books. I don't know who he begged, threatened, or bribed, but whatever he did, it worked. He, Sarah, Hudson, and I rolled out of the gate at Fort Zubara without so much as a second look from the guys standing watch.

The location Ling had given me was a construction site. The project, a shopping complex funded by a European firm, had been suspended indefinitely due to "security concerns," so we'd probably have the place to ourselves.

Hudson was driving as we pulled off of the street and into the site. The whole project was just a big hole in the ground surrounded by stacks of supplies and materials, much of which appeared to have been vandalized and looted. The gate at the front truck entrance had been left open, just as Ling said it would be.

No one said anything as we followed the road deep into the hole that was to be the foundation of the shopping center's underground parking lot. I was nervous. The last time I'd worked with Exodus it had cost several of my teammates their lives. They were a bunch of trigger-happy fanatics. If anything went wrong, the four of us would probably end up dead.

We stopped about fifty feet from an abandoned crane in the very center of the site. At least we wouldn't be visible from the road. It was about as secluded as you could get in the middle of a city. As per Ling's instructions, Hudson blinked the headlights three times, then turned them off.

Several floodlights snapped on. Startled, I squinted into the blinding light. I looked over at Hudson, nodded, and opened my door.

"Be careful," Sarah said from the backseat.

I tried to give her a reassuring smile. "I'll be fine."

Stepping onto the ground, I closed the door behind me and moved slowly to the front of the Land Cruiser. I took off my overshirt, revealing both my holstered revolver and my body armor. Holding my right hand up in the air, I slowly drew my gun with my left hand and laid it on the hood of the truck. I then stepped forward, both hands in the air over my head.

For a few tense moments, I walked toward the crane, almost holding my breath. I was following Ling's very specific instructions to the letter, and they hadn't shot me yet, but I couldn't shake the sense of unease. I was vulnerable, helpless, and hated it. A bead of sweat trickled down my head, and it wasn't just from the warm night air.

Ling appeared from behind the crane, alone. She

confidently strode toward me, closing the distance in a matter of seconds.

"You can put your hands down now, Mr. Valentine. It's fine," she said, not quite smiling.

Feeling silly, I slowly lowered my hands. "You're alone?" I asked, looking around.

"Of course not," she said. "My men are observing you and your friends. Just a precaution. Please do not take offense."

"None taken," I said, looking down into her dark eyes. "Thank you for coming. I need your help."

"So you insist." She looked past me at the Land Cruiser. "You can tell your friends to come out. I won't have them shot." The corner of her mouth turned up in half a wry smile.

I nodded and squeezed my throat mic. "It's clear. C'mon up." I looked back at Ling. "You want them to leave their weapons?"

"No, it's fine," she said dismissively. "I'm not worried."

"You don't have to drop your weapons," I said into my microphone. "Bring my gun up." I heard doors slamming behind me as my friends climbed out of the truck.

"So, Mr. Valentine, to business," Ling said, not wasting any time. "I apologize for dragging you out here like this, but I always prefer to deal face to face."

"I remember," I said flatly.

She didn't bat an eye. "And frankly, I'm curious to just who it is you wish me to help smuggle out of this country." Tailor tapped me on the shoulder and handed me my gun. I quickly holstered it. "Ah, Mr. Tailor," Ling said, "it's good to see you again."

Tailor nodded but didn't say anything. I then introduced Ling to Hudson and Sarah. Sarah seemed to pique Ling's interest a bit.

"I think I understand now, Mr. Valentine," Ling said, excessively polite as always. "Is this your girlfriend?"

"Uh . . ." I mumbled, surprised by the question.

"Yes," Sarah said levelly. "I'm his girlfriend." She gave Ling the evil eye, but the Exodus operative either didn't notice or didn't care.

"This makes more sense now," Ling said thoughtfully, looking at Sarah. She smiled. "Yes. Well, this is very unorthodox, but I see no reason I can't help you while I'm here. Like you said, Mr. Valentine, my organization owes you a great deal, and we've never had a proper chance to repay you."

"You'll help us get out of Zubara?" I asked.

"Yes," Ling replied. "Unfortunately, it won't be right away. We have business in the region and aren't ready to leave yet."

"How long will it be?" I asked. "I'm not trying to look a gift horse in the mouth, but time is a factor. Things are rapidly going south here."

"I'm aware," Ling said. "However, I still have a job to do myself. Your transportation out of Zubara is a freighter that my organization owns and operates, and it's still at sea."

"You flew here, right?" Tailor asked. "Can't we fly out on that plane?"

"No, you can't," Ling replied, almond eyes narrowing slightly. "I, too, have orders I must follow. The freighter is the only method of transport I'm to make available to you four. It will arrive when it arrives and leave when we've finished here. You can choose to be on it or not. It was the best I could do."

"It'll be fine," I said.

"Mike, I don't know about this," Sarah said quietly.

"Yeah, man," Hudson said. "Are you sure about this?"

"Guys, please," I said. "This is our only shot. Remember what happened to Singer? I trust *these* guys more than I trust Gordon Willis and his cronies."

"You're right." Hudson nodded.

"I trust *you*," Sarah said, looking up into my eyes. I smiled at her, then looked over at Tailor.

His brow was furled unhappily. He didn't say anything for a moment, then nodded. "Fuck it, we don't have a choice."

"Okay," I said, looking back at Ling. "We're in. How do you want to do this?"

Ling smiled as if oblivious to the near-argument we'd just had right in front of her. "Here," she said, handing me something from her pocket. It was a cell phone. "This is secure. A number I can be reached at is programmed into it. Use it sparingly and keep it with you. I'll contact you when we're ready to leave. I'm afraid it might be short notice."

"It's fine," I said. "We'll make it work. Do you have an approximate time frame?"

"Possibly a week. I know that's a long time, given your circumstances, but as I said, it was the best I can do." She looked down at her watch. "I need to be going now. We've been here too long, and I have a lot of work to do myself. It was good to see you again, Mr. Valentine." Ling smiled at me. "Please be careful. I'll be in touch."

VALENTINE
Fort Saradia National Historical Site
May 8
0800

It had been several days since our meeting with Ling, and there'd been no word from her since. This wasn't unexpected, but it was nerve-wracking. The goal now was to stay alive long enough for Ling to get us out of the country. It would suck to get killed so close to being home free.

There was another problem, too. The longer we waited, the greater the chance one of us would get second thoughts. I knew Tailor wouldn't change his mind. Once he made a decision, he always went through with it, even if it wasn't really a good idea. I wasn't so sure about the rest of us.

Especially Sarah. The idea of just leaving her friends and running away from Project Heartbreaker bothered her, a lot. Hell, it bothered me. Aside from Tailor and Hudson, there were a quite a few guys that I was friends with, and I hated to think what would happen to them after we disappeared. But I didn't know them that well. I wasn't sure if I could trust them. If I told them we had a way out, what would they do? Would they report it to Hunter or Gordon Willis? Would they want to come along? If so, would Ling and her people agree to that, or would they call the whole thing off since we tried to change the deal?

My greatest fear was that Sarah would decide she didn't want to go. There was no way I was leaving without her, either, so that meant I had to stay as well. That thought terrified me. Not because I was worried about myself; I was worried about what would happen to Sarah. I didn't think I could bear it if anything happened to her.

Project Heartbreaker was falling apart around us. I didn't know how Gordon and his people would handle doing damage control and cleanup. There was the possibility that it might involve Mr. Anders just murdering us. One way or the other, I really didn't want to wait around to find out.

Despite all this, the missions didn't stop coming, and they seemed to get more and more ridiculous as time went on. Our casualties had been severe. We were losing guys left and right, and yet they kept asking more and more of us.

We had just gotten briefed by Gordon on our next operation. Our chalk, plus Cromwell, Holbrook, Animal, and another new replacement named Fillmore, were all present. Our assignment was, to be blunt, *fucking ridiculous.*

Seems there was this Spanish billionaire-aristocrat-industrialist named Rafael Miguel Felipe Montalban who was the head of the Montalban Exchange, one of the largest and wealthiest corporations in the world. According to Gordon, this guy was using his money to fund General Al Sabah in Zubara and had his hands in other things as well. Conveniently, he was sailing up the Persian Gulf on his insanely luxurious yacht, the *Santa Maria.*

No problem, right? We'll just blow up the yacht, take

this guy out, and be home before beer-thirty. But no, Gordon says, that won't work. Instead we were to be inserted onto the yacht via helicopter, storm the ship, and capture Rafael Montalban alive. We were then to retrieve him and his personal laptop computer and bring them back to base.

Basically, Gordon was asking us to risk our lives to capture a guy when it was completely unnecessary. They were tracking Montalban's yacht by satellite. They had an armed UAV ready to drop a pair of guided bombs onto it at a moment's notice. If they wanted this guy out of the picture, all they had to do was say the word and he'd be on the bottom of the Gulf.

Except Gordon wanted him *alive*. He wouldn't even explain why. Eight of us were going to board two of Gordon's stealth helicopters, fly out over the ocean, and board Montalban's yacht in force. Just like last time, he was only sending in eight guys when dozens would be preferable. He assured us that Montalban's security detail, though highly trained, would be caught completely off guard and that we'd have the initiative the entire time.

I thought Tailor was going to blow a gasket. Holbrook and Cromwell didn't really get vocal until Gordon explained that Anders was coming along to provide support. Gordon probably very nearly avoided getting *decked*.

I explained that I'd never been trained on rappelling from a helicopter, much less onto the back of a moving ship at night. Gordon said rappelling wouldn't be necessary. The yacht was big enough that it had not one but two helipads, one on top and one on the stern.

We'd been given a lot of information on the *Santa*

Maria. Photos taken from the UAV stalking it. Plans from the builder, reports on Montalban's security people. The plan was simple enough. Chalk 1 would touch down on the helipad at the top of the ship's superstructure. They would then proceed in and take control of the bridge. Chalk 2 would land at the stern, enter the ship, disable the engines, then begin hunting for Rafael Montalban. Once we captured him, the choppers would pick us up. We'd fly off, and the UAV would prang the *Santa Maria*, sending it to the bottom and killing everyone still alive on board.

The two helicopters would orbit the area for as long as fuel permitted. One would have a machine gun to provide fire support. Anders would be riding in the other, armed with a sniper rifle, to pick off targets of opportunity on the deck. Anders was going to be riding in Holbrook and Cromwell's chopper. I imagined what a fun ride *that* was going to be.

Chapter 16:
Surface Tension

VALENTINE
Somewhere over the Persian Gulf
May 9
0155

Dark water flashed below us as the strange black helicopter skimmed the deck at speed. Inside, we were bathed in red light as we made final checks on our equipment and communications.

Tailor, Byrne, Hudson, and I huddled together, going over the plan one last time. Just inside the starboard-side door sat a crewman manning a machine gun. The stealth helicopter flew with its doors closed to maintain its small radar cross-section. When the door opened, the entire gun mount swung out, allowing the chopper to lay down suppressive fire.

"We have the target on FLIR," the copilot said. "Stand by. Touchdown in three minutes."

"Going dark," the pilot said, and the internal red lights

switched off. My active hearing protection minimized the noise of the chopper, but I could hear the pounding of my heart. It was that last-minute adrenaline spike that you get right before showtime. With the onset of that adrenaline, my pulse slowed and my thoughts coalesced as *the Calm* washed over me. Tailor reached over and slapped me on the shoulder.

"Thirty seconds!" My grip on the cut-down Benelli M4 shotgun tightened. The side doors quietly slid open, and the chopper was filled with the roar of rushing air. The door gunner slid his weapon mount into position. Below us, I could clearly see the *Santa Maria,* well-lit and steadily cruising though calm seas.

My stomach felt the sudden drop as our helicopter rapidly descended upon the *Santa Maria's* aft helipad. The yacht rushed up toward us, and with a heavy *thud* we were on the deck.

Tailor was out the door first, his carbine up and ready. I was right behind him. Following me was Hudson with the SAW, and then Byrne with another carbine. As soon as we were clear, the chopper dusted off. The door gunner opened up as the chopper ascended, raking the foredeck with a stream of tracer fire. We moved together in a tight line, rushing for the superstructure, trying to cover as many angles as possible. Shouting could be heard. An alarm sounded.

The aft superstructure served as a hangar for a small helicopter. We kicked in a personnel door and entered as our second chopper landed above us. The ship's interior lights were on. A door at the opposite end of the hangar opened as we passed by the *Santa Maria's* helicopter. Two

men in suits, armed with MP7 submachine guns, burst
into the room. They hesitated for a brief moment when
they saw us. We'd caught them completely off guard.
Tailor cut down one while I put a magnum buckshot load
through the other. Both men were dead before they hit
the floor.

"Clear!" Tailor said.

"Clear! Reloading!" I repeated, thumbing another shell
into my shotgun.

"Clear!" Hudson and Byrne repeated.

"Alpha Team, this is Bravo Team," Tailor said. "We're
in the hangar. What's your status?"

"Bravo Team, Alpha," Holbrook replied. *"We're crossing
the sundeck, heading for the bridge. We—shit!"* A long
burst of automatic weapons fire rattled over the radio.
"Encountering stiff resistance."

"Roger that." Tailor looked back at us. "Engine room.
Let's go!" We followed Tailor into the bowels of the *Santa
Maria*, encountering terrified crewmembers as we went.
The engine room was on the lowest deck, in the aft of the
yacht.

We cleared a tight, spiraling staircase and immediately
came under fire from down the passageway. Tailor
jumped back in the stairwell, stumbling backwards and
crashing into me.

"Shit," he snarled. "That was close."

"What?" I asked.

"I think they've got guys at both ends of the passageway. The hatch to the engine room is sealed."

"Frag?" I asked, mind racing.

"Frag," Tailor concurred. We each pulled a hand

grenade from our vests. Squeezing side by side, we moved as close to the doorway at the bottom of the stairwell as we could and pulled the pins. At the same time, we reached around the doorway and threw our grenades. Mine went aft, Tailor's went forward. They went bouncing down the passageway. We withdrew into the stairwell and crouched down. Men were shouting in the corridor. The *Santa Maria* was rocked by two deafening blasts a second later as the grenades detonated.

"Move, move, move!" Tailor shouted. We spilled into the passageway as rapidly as we could, weapons leading us around the corners. Tailor angled to the left, while I angled to the right. The two men that had been guarding the hatch to the engine room were dead.

I dove to the deck as a burst of automatic weapons fire roared behind me. Bullets zipped over my head and pocked the hatch to the engine room. Tailor fired off several short bursts in response. I rolled over onto my back, leveling my shotgun down the passageway just in time to see Hudson crouch in front of me, SAW shouldered. He ripped off a long burst while Tailor reloaded.

"Byrne!" Tailor shouted. "We'll hold 'em off. Get that fucking hatch open!"

"Moving!" Byrne replied. He was carrying on his back a compact Broco cutting torch. The three of us provided him with covering fire as he set his equipment up. Without hesitating, he pulled welder's goggles down over his eyes and ignited the torch.

Byrne first cut a small hole in the hatch and punched out the circular piece of hot metal in the center. I warned my teammates and tossed in another grenade. The blast slammed the narrow corridor. Byrne fired the torch up again and resumed cutting.

Minutes ticked by at an agonizingly slow pace as our teammate cut his way through the watertight hatch. We were vulnerable in the narrow passageway, and the ship's security complement knew right where we were.

"I'm through!" Byrne shouted as he extinguished the torch. Tailor and Hudson covered forward while Byrne and I went aft to clear the engine room. A couple of full-force kicks and the cut-through hatch slammed to the deck in a deafening clatter. The engine room was dark and filled with smoke from my grenade. We switched on our weapon lights, sending bright columns of light piercing into the hazy darkness.

A crewmember was lying on the floor by the hatch with blood leaking out of his ears. He wasn't moving. I couldn't tell if he was unconscious or dead.

"Damn," Byrne said, looking down. "Do you—" *BRRRRRRRP!* One of Rafael Montalban's security men appeared from behind a fixture. His MP7 was extended in one hand, like a pistol, while he covered his bleeding ear with the other.

Snapping the shotgun up, I fired. Two loads of buck-shot tore into the bodyguard in a splash of blood. As he hit the deck, I caught movement out of the corner of my eye. I swung my weapon around, firing twice again, dropping another crewmember that was running toward me. I quickly scanned the engine room for any more threats. Then I noticed Byrne lying on the floor, staring up at the ceiling, his right eye wide open. What was left of his left eye was hidden under a puddle of blood. A bullet had punched right through his safety glasses and into his head.

Enveloped in *the Calm,* I didn't feel anything as I looked down at his lifeless body. No, that would come later.

"Clear!" I shouted. "Man down!" Tailor and Hudson came in a second later. I was crouched by Byrne's body, thumbing more shells into my shotgun.

"Goddamn it!" Hudson cursed, punching the wall so hard I thought he'd break his hand. He looked down at me. "What are you doing?"

"I'm taking the torch," I said. "We might need it again."

Tailor quietly swore to himself. He then squeezed his throat mic. "Alpha Team, this is Bravo, engine room secured, what's your status?"

"This is Alpha!" Holbrook replied, sounding shaken up. *"We've got the bridge secured. Commo equipment is trashed. They're trying to retake it, but we'll hold 'em off. Animal is down, KIA."*

"Roger that," Tailor said flatly. "We're down one, too. Disabling the engine now. We're then going after the target."

"Good luck," Holbrook said, and the radio went silent.

Our first objective was complete. The *Santa Maria* was dead in the water. The engine was disabled, the radio was smashed, and the bridge was controlled by Holbrook's chalk. It was now up to the three of us to find Rafael Montalban and capture him.

The two choppers circling were watching for lifeboats or swimmers. No one had left the yacht. Rafael Montalban was on board somewhere. Tailor figured that he'd be holed up in the security office. It was at the end of a passageway on one of the lower decks, and was defensible. If we didn't find him there, we were going to head to his stateroom next. If he wasn't there either it was going to be a room-by-room, deck-by-deck search until we found the son of a bitch.

We encountered almost no resistance as we crossed the yacht. Sporadic gunfire could be heard coming from above us. Holbrook reported that Montalban's security force made their attempt to retake the bridge, and failed. We expected the remainder of the security contingent to be protecting the man himself.

We were right. We came under fire as soon as we set foot in the passageway that led to the security office. Instead of a few disorganized guys in suits with machine pistols, we were now encountering guards in body armor, armed with G36C carbines and Benelli shotguns. To make matters worse, we were outnumbered.

But *they* were out*gunned*. The *Santa Maria* shuddered with another concussion after Tailor sent a grenade rolling down the passageway. As soon as it detonated, Hudson leaned around the corner and laid down suppressive fire. Tailor and I quickly advanced up the corridor. There were several compartments on either side of the passageway, with a few of Montalban's remaining bodyguards using the doorways as cover. We were sitting ducks as we moved down the hall. We had to use overwhelming firepower to keep their heads down.

My shotgun wouldn't penetrate their vests, but a shotgun with a holographic sight on top of it makes for comparatively easy head shots. We brutally cut down the rest of Montalban's security force in that passageway. When the shooting stopped, six men lay dead on the deck in a mix of spent brass and spilled blood. The air stunk of smoke and burnt powder. Only the three of us remained standing.

I used the brief lull to pull more shells from the bandolier across my chest and thumb them into my shotgun. The weapon was hot to the touch. My cheek was sore from the pounding the stock gave it. Even an autoloader could be rough with three-inch Magnum buckshot.

As expected, the hatch to the security office was sealed from the inside like the engine room had been. According to the ship's schematics, these were security features in the event the *Santa Maria* was overrun by pirates. The security office was designed as a sort of panic room where Rafael Montalban and his personal guards could hold out until assistance arrived.

No assistance was coming. Our choppers had impressive electronic warfare suites and were effectively jamming all transmissions that weren't on select frequencies, like our radios. And your typical pirate didn't have access to a Broco torch.

My teammates covered me as I fired up the torch and began to cut through the hatch. This one was less substantial than the engine room hatch had been, and the cutting went faster.

It was done. Tailor was ready, Mk 16 carbine shouldered. I dropped the torch, doffed the welder's goggles, and clicked off the safety on my shotgun. Hudson had just finished loading a fresh hundred-round nutsack into his saw and nodded at us.

Tailor kicked in the hatch. The last three bodyguards were waiting inside, sporting compact assault rifles and body armor. My team swept into the security office all at once. We didn't use grenades this time. We needed Montalban alive.

The first guard was ducked behind an overturned metal desk. He fired off a burst as we came into the room. Hudson replied with the SAW, tearing through the desk and ventilating the man trying to hide behind it. At the same time, another guard leaned around a corner, G36C shouldered. Tailor and I hit him at the same time. The guard was ripped apart by the barrage of buckshot and 5.56mm rounds and collapsed to the deck.

We didn't stop. Moving through the office, we turned a corner. A hammer weight slammed into my chest as a loud handgun discharged in front of me. I yelled that I'd been hit and stumbled backward, falling to my butt. The shot was answered with a hail of gunfire that was over in a second.

"Val! You alright?" Tailor asked, crouching beside me.

"I'm fine! I'm fine!" I gasped, looking down at my chest. The bullet had blown open two of the shotgun shells on my bandolier and lodged in my front armor plate. I was okay.

Tailor extended a hand and helped me to my feet. I shook my head and stepped around the corner. Two men had been holed up at the back of the office. One was a big guy in a dark suit, with an ear bud. He was dead on the floor with about a dozen exit wounds in his back. His pistol lay on the deck in a pool of his blood.

The other man was still alive. He was an older gentleman, with graying hair and a neatly trimmed goatee. He had an aristocratic air to him and was wearing what looked to be a very expensive suit. He stood against the wall, eyes wide, with his hands on top of his head. Hudson had the barrel of his SAW practically shoved up the man's nose.

My eyes narrowed. "Rafael Montalban?"

"Yes," the man replied. "What is the meaning of this?" I had to give the guy credit. He hadn't pissed himself or anything. He had some semblance of backbone at least.

"Don't worry about it," Tailor said harshly. "You have a computer?"

"I have many," Montalban replied with an aloof sniff.

"We're only concerned with the one," Tailor said. "You know the one I'm talking about." Tailor was bullshitting the guy. All we'd been told was to get his laptop. We had no idea which laptop or what they were looking for.

Rafael Montalban frowned. "You've been well informed. It seems I have a leak in my organization. I'd speak to my head of security about it, but I'm afraid you just killed him." He nodded to the dead man on the floor.

"Just show us where the laptop is, playboy," Hudson growled. "I ain't in the mood for any bullshit."

"It would seem not," Montalban said, his English only had a hint of a Spanish accent. "Very well. It's in a safe in this office. This way." Hudson led Rafael Montalban around the corner. Tailor and I looked at each other and shrugged. *I can't believe that worked.*

Tailor bent over and picked something up. "Here," he said, handing it to me. "He shot you with this."

I looked down at the gun in my hand. It was a Korth .357 Magnum revolver, beautifully engraved, with a brightly polished blue finish. The grips were genuine ivory and had what I guessed was the Montalban family crest inlaid in them in gold and silver. I'd just been shot with a ten thousand dollar gun.

After Rafael Montalban opened the safe and retrieved the laptop, Tailor made him boot it up and enter the password. He then shoved the laptop into his backpack and keyed his microphone. "Control, this is Xbox. Bravo Team has secured the package and the target, repeat, we have the package and the target, both intact. Requesting immediate extraction."

Gordon Willis himself came on over the radio. *"Excellent work, boys!"* he said enthusiastically. *"Your ride will be there shortly. Over and out!"* Tailor rolled his eyes.

"Xbox, this is Control," Sarah said then. *"What's your status?"*

"One KIA on our team," Tailor said. "It was Anarchangel."

"Control, this is Joker," Holbrook said, sounding very tired. *"We've got two KIA, Animal and Linus. I'm wounded but still mobile. Copy?"* Sarah acknowledged while the three of us swore aloud. Linus was Cromwell's call sign.

I didn't really listen to the rest of the radio chatter. We were ordered to gather up and stand by for extraction at the aft heliport. We still had to use caution. Most of the *Santa Maria*'s crew was still alive. Even though we'd wiped out Rafael Montalban's security detail, there was no telling who'd be waiting around the corner, ready to be a hero.

"Gentlemen," Rafael Montalban said, sounding detached and aloof. "Surely we can come to some sort of understanding? I assure you I can triple whatever it is you're being paid. People died tonight, yes. Your people and my people. But we can all walk away from this." Montalban then winced as Hudson roughly pulled his arms behind his back and secured them with a zip-tie.

"There's no going back for us," Tailor said, lighting a cigarette.

"I see," Montalban said, discomfort apparent in his voice. "I'm going to ask you again. Let's talk about this like civilized people. Believe me, gentlemen, I'm a man of means. And I'm *not* a man to be trifled with. I have powerful friends."

"I think you better shut your mouth, playboy," Hudson said roughly. "Your friends ain't here."

Tailor gestured at our prisoner. "Bag this motherfucker." Rafael Montalban was forced to his knees. Hudson pulled a heavy black sack over his head and slapped him upside the head to shut him up. Tailor led the way down the corridor as we marched the Spanish billionaire topside.

I looked at the ornate revolver in my hand again. Feeling a slight twinge beneath layers of *Calm*, I ejected the one spent case and five unfired rounds and stuffed the gun into a pouch on my vest. Rafael Montalban wasn't going to need it anymore.

The extraction from the *Santa Maria* went smoothly enough. The other chopper landed first, depositing Anders onto the deck. He collected the laptop from us as soon as we made it topside. Holbrook and Fillmore boarded that chopper with Anders. It lifted off and hovered nearby while the other one set down.

As Hudson, Tailor, and I shoved Rafael Montalban

onto our stealthy helicopter, we noticed the survivors of the Santa Maria's crew quietly watching us from a distance. Some looked angry, others looked terrified, but most appeared in shock. None had offered any further resistance after we'd wiped out the security detail.

I looked at them one last time as we lifted off. They were all dead, and they didn't even know it. It felt wrong. A lot of people had died, and I found myself wondering why. The helicopter's door slid shut as we ascended into the night sky. I quickly grew tired as the chopper droned on. *The Calm* was wearing off, and I began to get the shakes. I was experiencing adrenaline dump. Closing my eyes, I tried to concentrate on something else.

I couldn't wait to see Sarah when I got back. I'd probably go straight to bed and fall right to sleep. Holding her in my arms helped me forget things for a little while. In the morning, we'd probably hold a memorial service for the three men we'd lost. I'd been to several such services already. There were no bodies this time. Our friends' remains had been unceremoniously dumped into the ocean.

The events of that night strengthened my resolve to escape Project Heartbreaker. We'd gone from meticulously hunting terrorists to recklessly killing the employees of a European billionaire, with no regard whatsoever for our safety. I'd had *enough*. I was done doing Gordon Willis's dirty work. He could find another damned errand boy.

My thoughts were interrupted when the chopper's copilot called my name. I left my seat and went forward.

"You have a call," the copilot said, handing me a headset.

"Who is it?" I asked, my voice raised so I could be heard over the noise of the chopper's engines.

"Gordon Willis," the copilot replied. I pinched the bridge of my nose, took a deep breath, and put on the headset.

"This is Nightcrawler."

"Nightcrawler," Gordon said. "Listen up. Damn fine job you did tonight. I'm proud of you. But something's come up. We have a slight change in our game plan. Can you handle that?"

"What kind of change?" I asked, my voice flat.

"I just got confirmation from Drago," Gordon said, referring to Anders by his call sign. *"Everything we need is on that laptop. Excellent work securing it with the password already entered."*

"So, what's the change?" I repeated.

"We no longer need Rafael Montalban alive. Liquidate him immediately."

"What?" I snarled, furious. "Three guys *died* trying to get that asshole, and now you tell us you don't need him? What the fuck are you doing, Gordon? Who in the hell is making these decisions?"

"Nightcrawler, I know you've had a bad night, but—"

"I haven't had a bad night, goddamn it!" I snapped, shouting into the microphone. "A bad night is when you get a flat tire or you break your cell phone. Tonight I killed a bunch of people and three of my teammates died, and now you're telling me it was for *nothing*?"

"Mr. Valentine!" Gordon barked, ignoring radio protocols. *"We'll discuss this when you return. Believe me when I say that tonight's operation was* not *for nothing.*

Larry Correia & Mike Kupari

You have your orders. Carry them out." The radio fell silent. I ripped the headset off and threw it to the deck. I closed my eyes tightly for a moment, swearing to myself. Taking another deep breath, I regained my composure and warned the pilots about what was going to happen.

"What was that all about?" Tailor asked. I didn't say anything in response. I just pointed at Rafael Montalban and dragged a finger across my throat. Tailor's eyes flashed with anger.

"Jesus Christ, you gotta be shittin' me," Hudson said, shaking his head.

I steeled myself; I had my orders. I turned to face Rafael Montalban and pulled the bag off of his head. He squinted in the red light, obviously confused.

"What's happening now?" he asked, still sounding defiant. "Have you come to your senses, young man?"

"This is where you get off," I said levelly.

"I . . . don't understand," Montalban replied hesitantly.

"You will." I pushed a button on the hull. The chopper was filled with a windy roar as the door behind our prisoner slid open. His eyes grew wide at the sudden realization of what was happening. He looked out at the blackness behind him, then back at me.

My .44 was already in my hand. I fired from the hip, putting the bullet through his chest. He didn't even scream. Before he could crumple to the floor, I kicked the dying man in the chest. Rafael Montalban, aristocrat, billionaire, industrialist, and head of an international conglomerate, tumbled out the door and disappeared into the darkness. Holstering my revolver, I closed the door and sat back down. I held my head in my hands.

♠ ♠ ♠

The subsequent trip back to Fort Saradia was long and uneventful. I slept through most of it. The choppers had landed somewhere in the desert again. The five of us piled into a large van for the long drive back to the city. I didn't wake up again until we crossed into the fort.

Upon arrival we were immediately herded into the briefing room. Colonel Hunter and Sarah were both waiting for us. We shuffled into the room, still in our body armor, weapons slung, and tried to sit at the desks with all of our gear on.

When I stepped into the room, I made eye contact with Sarah, who was standing back by Hunter. I knew I looked like hell. I wanted nothing more than to stride across the room and take her in my arms. I didn't think the colonel would approve. I managed a smile for her to let her know I was okay, even though I wasn't really. I just didn't want her to worry, even though she undoubtedly would anyway.

The debriefing went by quickly. Hunter just wanted to get through it while the mission was fresh in our minds and let us get some sleep. It had been a tough run. Holbrook had a bandage on his arm. I had a .357 slug stuck in my vest. Three of our teammates were on the bottom of the Persian Gulf. Bad op.

We all chimed in during the debriefing. Sarah recorded and Hunter listened intently as we retold the events of the mission, from beginning to end. Fighting fatigue, I explained the entry into the engine room and how Byrne died. The image of him lying on the floor, left eye socket filled with blood, flashed in my mind and I stumbled on my words. Tailor interjected and continued the narrative.

Hunter leaned against a desk, arms folded across his chest, and listened quietly as I explained the events of the return flight. His one eye studied me as I recalled Gordon's order to kill Rafael Montalban. Sarah put a hand over her mouth when I described dropping him into the ocean.

"So tell me," Colonel Hunter said, "where is this laptop? You retrieved the target's laptop computer, correct?"

"Yes, sir," Tailor replied.

"So where is it?" Hunter repeated.

"We gave it to Anders," Tailor said, sounding confused.

"What?" Hunter said, anger rising in his voice.

"Anders was waiting for us on the deck of the ship," Hudson said. "He took the laptop from us. Did we do something wrong, Colonel?"

Hunter didn't say anything for a moment. "No, boys, you did fine. Where is Mr. Anders now?"

"He stayed on the chopper after it dropped us off, sir," Holbrook said. "He's wherever those stealth birds go, I guess."

"I see," Hunter said, rubbing his chin. It was obvious that something was very wrong, but he didn't want to discuss it with us. At that point I was so tired I didn't really care. I just wanted to go to bed and forget this day had happened. "That's all I have for you, gentlemen. Go get some rack time. You won't have anything else scheduled for as long as I can manage it. You've all been busting ass for a long time. You deserve a break. Tonight, after sundown, we'll have a memorial service for Cromwell, Byrne, and Blutarsky. Dismissed."

We all got up to leave. Sarah crossed the room and threw her arms around me. She squeezed me tightly, then stepped away.

"I was worried," she said simply.

"I'm okay," I said, smiling a little. "It was a bad night. But I'm okay."

"Ms. McAllister, you can smother Mr. Valentine with affection later," Colonel Hunter said. "I need to speak with him. You, too, Tailor." Sarah's face turned red, and I felt myself flush a little.

"Oh, for God's sake, Val, everyone knows," Tailor said. "It's not a secret."

"Did you guys think you were keeping it a secret?" Holbrook asked, standing by the door. "Wow, that's funny," he said humorlessly, then stepped out of the classroom. Hudson and Fillmore followed.

"I'll see you later," Sarah said, squeezing my hand. She left the room, leaving Tailor and me alone with Colonel Hunter.

"Is something wrong, Colonel?" Tailor asked.

"You're goddamned right something's wrong," Hunter growled. "I'm not yelling at you, son, don't worry. You boys took a bad situation and made it work, like you always do. Matter of fact, I'm damned proud of you all."

"With all due respect, sir," I said, "this is *bullshit*. You told us we'd be fighting terrorists. You told us we were taking the war to their backyard. You said we were accomplishing something here. So what did we accomplish by kidnapping some rich guy off of his yacht? What did we accomplish when I murdered him and dropped him in the ocean? What the fuck are we *doing* here, sir?" I realized then that I'd almost been yelling at Colonel Hunter. He didn't seem fazed.

"I don't know," Hunter said.

"Um . . . what?" Tailor asked.

"I don't know what you accomplished, boys. I'm going to level with you here. I saw Gordon's intelligence on Rafael Montalban. His organization definitely was funneling money to General Al Sabah and other radical elements throughout the region. We've known about that for years."

"Then why haven't we done anything until now, sir?" I asked, more than a little confused.

"It's . . . *complicated*, son," Hunter said. "This stuff is way above my pay grade. We're talking about national foreign policy stuff here. International business, transnational interests, and supranational organizations. Rafael Montalban was connected. He had ties to the leadership of the European Union. He had ties to the UN Security Council. He had . . ." Hunter paused. "Well, let's just say the man had a lot of powerful friends."

"And we took this guy out," Tailor said. "Is that good?"

"I don't know," Hunter said. "He was a power player, but he was just one man. There are many others to take his place. Rafael Montalban has a younger brother, Eduard, who will probably take over for him. Killing one man won't break the Montalban Exchange. It won't stop the flow of money to the enemy. Christ, if that was all it took, we'd have killed all those sons of bitches years ago."

"What sons of bitches?" I asked.

"Never mind. Doesn't matter. Anyway, boys, I want to thank you for the work you've done. You two, in particular, have been the sharp end of the stick for Dead Six since your first operation. And it hasn't gone unnoticed."

Tailor and I looked at each other. "What do you mean?"

"For my part," Hunter said, "I'm going to tell Gordon that I'm taking you two off the mission roster. Hudson also. Hell, Holbrook, too. Fillmore, he spent the last two months sitting in a safe house. He's raring to go, still. But you boys need a break."

"I appreciate that," Tailor said.

"Gordon Willis wants to see you both," Hunter said. "He'll be here in a few minutes."

"What the hell does he want now?" I asked ruefully.

"I think he wants to offer you two a job," Hunter replied.

"What?"

"Project Heartbreaker is a temporary assignment, as you two are aware. I'm sure you've guessed that we have a much larger organization that's supporting our mission here. Well, we also have an active paramilitary branch that's always recruiting. I think Gordon wants to offer you a position there."

"Wait," Tailor said. "Who the hell does Gordon work for, exactly? The CIA?"

Hunter didn't blink. "Just like when you signed up for Project Heartbreaker, there are a lot of things you don't get to know until you sign the paper. Even then, there are a lot of things you don't get to know. I know you're angry. Just . . . think real hard before you make any rash decisions, boys. We could use you. It would probably be . . . better if you signed on. It's not always like this. I've been doing this for a long time. There are a lot of things going on right now that I don't like. Back in the old days a cocksucker like Gordon never would've . . ." He trailed off. "Never mind. Excuse me, gentlemen. I'm tired, too. Stand by. Gordon will be here in a few minutes. Remember what I told you." Colonel Hunter left the room without another word.

"He didn't *tell* us anything," Tailor grumbled. "I'm sick of all this innuendo and double-talk. People need to quit dropping hints and shit. They either just need to tell us straight up or shut their mouths."

"Skullduggery gives me a headache," I said, rubbing my temple. My shoulders sagged from the weight of my body armor and gear. I still had a shotgun slung across my back. I just wanted to take a shower and go to bed. I was in no mood for any of Gordon's bullshit.

But even when Gordon wasn't around, he could still piss you off. Another twenty minutes ticked by before Gordon strolled into the classroom. He had his suit jacket hanging over the crook of his arm. He tie was loosened and his shirt collar was unbuttoned. It was as casual as I'd ever seen him. He was wearing a leather shoulder holster with a Glock tucked under his left arm. He looked like a TV cop.

"Mr. Valentine!" he said jovially, vigorously shaking my hand. Gordon was one of those people who seemed like he was trying to crush your fingers during a handshake. "Mr. Tailor! Good to see you both. How was your flight?"

"I shot a man and kicked him out of the helicopter, Gordon," I said.

"I know. Nicely done, Mr. Valentine. Excellent work rolling with a changing situation. I know things were tense, and I know you gentlemen have been under a lot of pressure. Please believe me when I say your efforts are paying off."

"Is that so?" Tailor asked.

"It certainly is!" Gordon said. "We've been watching you two very closely. I'm prepared to offer you, both of you, full-time positions with my organization."

"What organization is that, exactly?" I asked.

Gordon smiled. "You know the drill, Mr. Valentine. Need-to-know. And unless I can count on you to make a commitment, you don't need to know."

Tailor lit a cigarette, not bothering to ask if it was okay to smoke in the classroom. "What exactly are you offering us?"

"A full-time job," Gordon replied. "You two would start right away. We'd have you on the next flight out of Zubara. You'll head back to our training center stateside for indoc and processing. After a couple weeks of R&R, of course. Paid R&R. You two have more than earned it."

I was speechless. Tailor kept asking questions. "So we'd just leave?"

"I'm going to level with you," Gordon said, leaning in conspiratorially. "And this goes no further than you two. Project Heartbreaker is winding down. Your mission tonight was probably the last major operation we're going to take on."

"What? What happened?"

"I had to fight to make Project Heartbreaker happen," Gordon said. "My superiors never really believed in it. It was a constant struggle to get funding and resources. That's why you were always so short on manpower and equipment. That's also why we ran you so hard. We had no choice. I never wanted to send you two out on missions, alone, with no back up. A lot of decisions made over my head forced my hand, I'm afraid."

"Like risking our lives to capture some guy then changing your mind later and ordering me to kill him?" I asked bitterly.

"Yes, like that," Gordon said. "I hated to do that, Mr. Valentine. I still think Rafael Montalban would've been an excellent asset. But the situation changed, and so did my orders. I asked you to carry them out, and you did. That sort of dedication and ability to adapt to a dynamic situation is why we're having this conversation right now. It's no accident your chalk was sent after Rafael Montalban. My organization needs people of your caliber."

"Okay, okay," Tailor said, interjecting before I could say anything else. "What would this position involve?" I couldn't believe it. *Is he seriously interested in Gordon's offer?*

"You'll work for me. Things are changing quickly. I need people I can count on so we can stay on top of things. I need people who can carry out tough jobs despite limited resources and information. The pay is *far* better than you're making now. You won't have to deal with any bureaucratic bullshit. You two will answer only to me."

I found it darkly humorous that Gordon didn't consider himself a bureaucrat. "You mean like Anders?"

"Yes!" Gordon beamed. "As a matter of fact, Anders is my right-hand man. You'll be working with him a lot. He's spoken highly of you both."

"I'll bet," I said. "Did he tell you he let Singer bleed to death without even trying to help him?"

"I was fully briefed on that operation, Mr. Valentine. I know that was tough, but the import—"

I cut him off. "Tough? *Tough?* Is that what you'd call that? We've had thirty percent casualties, and you call that tough?"

"You need to control your temper," Gordon snapped. "I'm trying to offer you a job!"

"Don't fuck with me, Gordon. I've seen full well what your jobs involve! And I'm sick of this shit!"

Tailor stepped between me and Gordon, trying to calm me down. I don't know if it was fatigue, stress, or a combination of the two, but I was on the verge of blowing up completely. My heart was pounding in my chest. I was so mad I was almost shaking.

"Fine!" Gordon said, gesturing sharply with his hands. "I'm trying to do you a favor. If this is how you want it, forget it. Mr. Anders warned me about this. He told me that when things start to get tough and you lose a couple guys, you fall apart. I didn't believe it. I've seen your record. But you know what? He's right. You can't handle it, Valentine. You're not cut out for this. This was a mistake. I need solid, dependable men. I don't need guys that turn to mush when we take a few casualties. Shit happens. People die. That's the way it is."

Something clicked just then. I stepped back and straightened myself out. My eyes narrowed. My face went blank. Tailor saw the expression on my face. His eyes went wide, and he turned to Gordon.

"Listen, you wanna leave now," he said. "Val had a bad night. Bad timing, you know?"

"It doesn't matter," Gordon said. "Forget the whole

thing. You two want to go down with this ship, you're more than welcome. We can always get more. You know how many people there are like you out there? Half burned-out shooters, desperate for their glory days and the old run-and-gun, who jump at any offer we give them? They're all so eager, and they don't ask a lot of questions. You, for example."

"Gordon, I'm warning you," Tailor said.

"I'm not afraid of you, Valentine," Gordon said, looking at me over Tailor's shoulder. He gestured to the pistol under his arm. "I'm not some paper-pushing desk jockey, you know."

"Gordon, there's no way you're going to get that gun out before Val blows a hole in your chest. Everybody just calm down now!"

"I'm perfectly *calm*," I stated. "I'm not angry at you because my friends died. We knew the risks when we signed up. I'm angry because my friends died as a direct result of your incompetence and blatant disregard for our lives. So I'm going to have to decline your offer." I turned around and walked away, but paused at the door. "Gordon, if I ever see you again, I'll kill you." I turned and left the room.

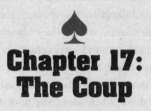

Chapter 17:
The Coup

LORENZO
May 10

The news was grim. There had been an explosion at the palace. The emir was dead. Until further notice, a curfew was in effect at eight o'clock every evening. The radio's volume had been turned up, and the crowd of foreign workers, mostly Pakistani and Sri Lankan, gathered at the café were all listening carefully, many of them surely wondering just how bad it was going to get, but too poor to leave their relatively good-paying jobs to fly home. The news report ended on the high note that the heroic General Sabah had personally assured the destruction of the Zionist backed criminals, and all the workers went back to their cheap food.

"Tomorrow's the big day. Are you nervous?" Jill asked.

"Of course not," I lied. "I eat commando death squads for breakfast."

The two of us were not that far from our apartment.

415

Tired of waiting for the Fat Man, and feeling the need to keep busy, we had continued our search for Dead Six. It had been just as fruitless as before. Zubara was a big city, and nobody we talked to recognized the Americans of Dead Six. I don't know where they bought their food, or who did their laundry, and apparently none of them had ever taken a taxi, and it was really pissing me off.

Jill Del Toro's education was coming along. She'd been my shadow for the last few days. She no longer walked like an American in public, and I was pretty sure I'd gotten her to the point that she was street-smart enough to not just get randomly murdered on her own. Today she was playing a relatively convincing imported Filipina. I'd helped her with her makeup so she'd look more forgettable. She looked like a cleaning lady and I looked like I should be unclogging drains.

It turned out that both of us were fluent in Spanish. Jill's paternal grandparents had been Mexican immigrants, and her dad had met and married her mom while stationed in Subic Bay. So we could converse freely here, as hardly anybody except for the occasional Filipino or European spoke Spanish in the Zoob and it didn't stick out in public like English did.

She'd come along pretty well. If she had the inclination, I thought she could actually have a future as a criminal. She was certainly a good liar. "I'm not worried, either," Jill said with confidence.

The last few days had been kind of awkward. Neither one of us talked about what had happened between us, which was good, *I think*, because that would have just needlessly complicated things. I had to keep my mind on business. "There's something important I need to talk to you about."

"Yes?" Jill responded quickly.

"It's about tomorrow's job," I said.

"Oh." She went back to her food, stabbing an olive with her fork.

"I don't know what's going to happen. This could be something simple and I can just walk right in and grab the box, or it could be crazy. I just don't know. We're going to have to come up with a plan on the fly. So I might need your help, I might not."

"I'm ready. Dead Six ruined my life, Lorenzo. I'll do whatever I have to do. I already showed you I'm willing to shoot them. What more do you need me to prove?"

I smiled. *She was aggressive.* "That's not what I meant. Tomorrow, we either succeed or fail. After that, it's on to Phase Three, and that's my problem, not yours."

"When will you tell me what that even is?"

"You really don't want to know. Let's just say that it's stupid and dangerous. But that's not what I'm talking about. What I'm trying to say is that after tomorrow, you're done."

She looked up from her lunch. "What do you mean?"

"I told you that if you helped me, I'd help you. I've had Reaper working on fake papers for you. I've got contacts I can refer you through. Basically, after tomorrow, you can go back to the US if you want." I would need to walk her through all the details of setting up a new life, but she didn't belong here, in this disintegrating shit hole, not anymore.

"Home?" Jill seemed shocked. Not upset, just surprised. "I . . . I don't know what to say."

"We'll worry about tomorrow first." I noticed some blue uniforms coming down the street. The security forces were randomly rousting people off the streets for questioning. It would be best to avoid that. I pulled out my wallet and threw down some riyals. "We'll talk about it later."

VALENTINE
Fort Saradia National Historical Site
May 10
1400

Following Sarah, I stepped out into the harsh desert heat. We made our way down the stairs of the dorm, followed by everyone else who'd been inside. Sarah and Anita had gone around banging on doors, telling everyone to follow them to the chow hall. She'd come to my room last.

Everyone kept asking her what was going on. She would only tell them she didn't know why, but Colonel Hunter had ordered an all-hands meeting. Something big had gone down. We hadn't had a meeting like this since our first night in-country.

For my part, I could guess what was happening. Gordon had told me that Project Heartbreaker was winding down. I wondered if, hell, *hoped* that the Project had been canceled and that we'd all be going home.

We all filed into the chow hall, and people began to sit down. Several of Hunter's security people were standing around, looking just as confused as the rest of us. My old buddy Conrad was there, too, looking as dickish as usual.

Aside from the support staff, only fifteen members of Dead Six were present. I knew another ten or so were still out at safe houses throughout the city. Even still, a lot of faces were missing, and almost a third of the guys present had been wounded.

Even our support staff hadn't been untouched. Sarah, Anita King, and another controller whose name I couldn't recall were there. But the fourth controller, a woman named Evelyn Majors, had been killed in action. She'd been sent in to a captured enemy safe house to help gather intelligence. The whole place had been wired. It blew up, killing her and all of Hansen's chalk. A couple of the logistics guys had been killed by a suicide bomber downtown.

We sat around talking for a few minutes. The dull roar of conversation quickly dropped away when Colonel Hunter came purposefully striding into the room. He stopped at the front of the chow hall, near the carts where the food was served.

"Listen up, everyone," he said, his raspy voice echoing through the now-quiet cafeteria. "Two hours ago there was an explosion at the Royal Palace. The emir is dead. It's been confirmed. General Al Sabah has declared martial law and has effected a nationwide curfew. He's deploying half the Zubaran Army throughout the city in order to lock everything down.

"Not all of the Army is on his side. According to our information, one of the emir's sons is still alive and is trying to rally support. General Al Sabah claims that the emir's son assassinated his father in a coup attempt. We have every reason to believe that General Al Sabah was the one behind the bombing. Either way, a civil war is about to break out in this country, and our support network is gone."

"What does this mean, sir?" someone asked.

Hunter looked thoughtful for a second. "Without Zubaran support, we can't function. We can't get supplies in and out of the country, and half of our best intelligence came from the emir's secret police. This is a crippling blow to our operations. Project Heartbreaker has failed." Hunter let that sink in for a moment before continuing. "I've been in contact with higher authority. I spoke with Gordon Willis half an hour ago. Project Heartbreaker has been terminated. Dead Six is being disbanded. We're all going home."

The chow hall erupted in clapping and cheers before Hunter could even finish saying it. Sarah leaned over and hugged me tightly in my seat. I could scarcely believe it, even though I'd sort of known this was going to happen. I was going to have to call Ling and tell her we wouldn't be needing her assistance after all. A big smile formed across my face.

"Okay, okay, listen up!" Hunter shouted. "Getting home is going to be a long and painful process, folks. There's going to be out-processing, nondisclosure agreements, and more paperwork than you can imagine. We're still working on getting all your pay problems straightened out, too. Worse, you're not leaving Zubara on a plane."

"How are we leaving then, Colonel?"

"The situation in the Zoob has deteriorated enough that they're not willing to risk our jet. Tomorrow night, around midnight, a boat will be coming for us. It'll moor at the dock on the north side of the fort. You're all going to board that vessel, and you'll be on your way. Before ten people ask, I have no idea where that boat is going. I won't be on it."

I barely listened to the rest of Hunter's briefing. He went on about how we needed to pack our stuff and start breaking down everything in the fort as quickly as possible. Instead my attention was focused on Sarah. She was beaming at me, a bright smile on her face. We were going to have to have a long talk about the future, about *us*. I knew it wasn't going to be easy, either. But after everything we'd been through already, I knew we could make it.

As it would turn out, I didn't know *anything*.

LORENZO
May 11

My phone sat in the middle of kitchen table, and I just watched it . . . waiting. The others had joined me, and the four of us were in a circle, kind of quietly looking at that phone like it was a magic oracle that was going to spit out the answers in a rhyming riddle or something. We had spent the last week preparing for today. Our equipment had been checked and rechecked. My crew was ready for anything. I didn't know what the Fat Man's message would bring, but I knew with dead certainty that he would call. Big Eddie's people were extremely reliable.

And punctual. The phone buzzed. I pushed the button for speaker phone.

The Fat Man spoke. "Dead Six is supposed to leave

Zubara tonight. They will be told to gather in the old Fort
Saradia compound to await evacuation. A boat is supposed
to pick them up at midnight."

Reaper was already pulling up a map of the area and
getting details on the old British fort. "How many men?"
I asked.

"Approximately twenty-five remaining combat personnel
and a dozen or more support staff. They will have all their
equipment, and they will be alert. The last of them have
been recalled already. Fort Saradia was their base of
operations. All of their personnel will be on-site before
sundown. They will need to be inside before the curfew to
avoid suspicion."

Reaper turned his laptop so I could see the fort. It was
a big square of tall mud-brick walls on the coast just
west of the Ash Shamal peninsula. A single road led to
it, weaving through encroaching housing and terminating
right at the front gate. The fort itself was big enough to fit
a football field inside and had several interior buildings.
That was a lot of area to cover. "Do you know where the
box is being kept?"

"I do not have that information."

Of course. "Anything else you can give me?"

"I would strongly suggest that you accomplish your
mission before midnight. You do not want to be there
after midnight."

"What happens then?"

"I cannot tell you, but Dead Six will be dead by dawn.
Do you understand me, Mr. Lorenzo?"

I hope you choke on a pancake and die. "Tell your boss
I'll get the box." I hung up. The group was quiet as I

studied the satellite photo of the fort. Something was going down, something huge.

Tonight I would bring the fight to Dead Six.

VALENTINE
Fort Saradia National Historical Site
May 11
1500

I found myself alone in my room, packing my belongings. Almost all of my clothes were stuffed into my duffel bag. In the short time I'd been in the Zoob, I'd somehow managed to acquire a second duffel bag's worth of crap, and I was busy sorting through it all.

All of the gear I'd been issued was on my bed, laid out for sorting. We were told to just throw away the various fatigues and other clothing we'd used. Colonel Hunter told us to keep our body armor and weapons with us until we were on the boat and out of Zubaran waters. The situation downtown had rapidly deteriorated, and there'd been sporadic fighting throughout the tiny country. Rumors were flying about the emir's son planning a last-ditch attempt to retake the Royal Palace. We all figured Zubara would be a war zone before the night was out, and we wanted to be ready in case anything spilled over onto our doorstep.

So the Mk 17 SCAR-H carbine I'd claimed back in February was lying on my bed, complete with grenade launcher, weapon light, and ACOG scope. I hadn't yet reassembled it after giving it a thorough cleaning. That rifle and I had been through a lot together, and it hadn't let me down. I wished I could keep it.

My body armor and load-bearing vest were on the bed as well. The armor still had Rafael Montalban's .357 slug buried in it. My vest was stocked with ammunition and even a couple of grenades. The colonel had been adamant about us being ready to fight in case something bad happened, and none of us argued with him. There was no sense getting killed on your last night in-country.

I'd lined my various souvenirs up on the metal shelf that sat against the wall of my room until I figured out where I was going to pack them. The strange wooden puzzle box that I'd found in Adar's safe was there, and I'd managed to sort of put it back together. Next to it was Rafael Montalban's elaborate Korth revolver. I'd found my harmonica, too, which I was happy about. I hadn't played it once since I'd been in the Zoob and had actually forgotten I'd brought it.

On the floor next to the shelf was a backpack full of money. It was my share of the loot we'd stolen from the man named Lorenzo. We'd split it four ways between Tailor, Hudson, Wheeler, and myself. Hudson was taking Wheeler's share. He said he'd make sure Wheeler's parents got the money. I had no doubt in my mind that he'd honor that promise.

I'd planned to use that money to pay Exodus for safe passage out of Zubara. Happily, I wasn't going to need their services now, which meant I could keep the money. My share amounted to about a hundred and twenty-five thousand dollars' worth of British pounds. I also had, stashed somewhere else, a smaller pouch with my half of the money from Adar's safe. *The spoils of war . . .*

I called Ling on the phone she'd given me and told her

the good news. She congratulated me but said that if the situation changed I could still call her. We'd made a deal and she'd honor it, she said. She told me that her people would be in Zubara for a few more days, though they were still leaving earlier than planned because of the looming civil war.

There were two quick knocks on my bathroom door, and Sarah came into my room. I smiled as soon as I saw her, and her eyes lit up. We embraced and kissed.

"Hey, you," she said, looking up into my eyes. "Getting all packed up?"

"You know it," I said. "I can't believe how much crap I've accumulated since I've been here. I hope they don't charge us for luggage." I laughed.

"I wonder how long it'll take us to get home?" Sarah said. "I mean, this boat could be going anywhere."

"It could be weeks," I suggested. "Or longer. Who knows? Hell, who *cares?* The important thing is we're getting out of here."

"I can't believe it," Sarah said, looking down. "After everything we've been through, all the people we've lost, we're just leaving. It was all for nothing."

I sighed. She was right. A lot of people had died, and we had nothing to show for it. "I know," I said. "The important thing is we're still alive. We have each other. We're going home. All things considered, I'll settle for that."

Sarah gave me a sad smile. "Me, too. So, uh, where are you going when you get home?"

"I don't really have a home," I said. "The closest thing I have to family is a cranky old bastard named Hawk. He

lives in a little town called Quagmire, Nevada. I'll probably go there, since I don't have anywhere else to stay.
What about you?"

"I managed to get an e-mail off to my mom, telling her
I'm coming home," Sarah said excitedly. "She doesn't even
know where I've been. Not really, anyway. I gave her a
story, told her I was working as a translator for an oil
company. I'll probably go back to Modesto, where she
lives. I don't have anyplace else to stay either."

I chewed in my lip for a moment. "Modesto is a long
way from Quagmire," I said.

"You know, I hate living in California anyway," Sarah
said, smiling again. "I could, I suppose, be talked into
leaving. You know, with the right incentive package."

I raised an eyebrow theatrically. "Baby, I've got an
incentive package right here," I said, gesturing to myself
while grinning stupidly.

Sarah laughed out loud. "You're cute when you're
being a retard, you know that? Are you asking me to move
in with you?"

"Eh, you might want to let me find a place to live first,"
I said.

"Oh no, it's not going to be that easy," Sarah said, eyes
twinkling. "You're going to have to meet my mother first."

"Oh boy," I said without enthusiasm.

"Stop it, my mom is a sweet lady."

"Wow," I said after a moment. "This is all surreal. We're
really doing this, aren't we? Holy shit. We're going home!"

"I know, right?" Sarah said, squeezing me again.
"Thank God."

I closed my eyes, holding Sarah tightly. "Thank God."

LORENZO

Carl and I sat in the van. It had turned out to be the hottest day so far this year, so of course, the air conditioner in our secondary van had died. We had one other vehicle stashed in a storage unit but it would stick out way too much in this neighborhood. The heat was like a stifling blanket, burning the air in my lungs. Sweat dripped down my back and pooled in my armpits. I finished the bottle of water and tossed it. Tonight was the night.

"You ready?" Carl asked from behind the wheel.

"Yep." I cracked the vertebrae of my neck after securing the transmitter around my throat. This was it. "Radio check."

"I can hear you fine. I've got a clear view of the gate, and the guards don't seem to be checking anything," Jill said. *"I think it's too hot for them to care."*

She was out of sight, a couple hundred yards up the road, closer to the fort. Alone, unarmed, and ready to step out into traffic on a moment's notice. She sounded excited.

"I've got you, chief," Reaper's voice echoed in my ear. I knew that he would be sitting in the darkened apartment, half a dozen screens open in front of him, joystick in hand, four radio channels going at once, processing absurd amounts of information, and totally in his element. Even though he was ten miles away, Reaper was going to be my eyes. "Little Bird can see the van just perfect, nice and bright on thermal, too."

Circling high overhead was Reaper's favorite toy and the single most expensive thing that I had ever purchased, and that included sports cars, yachts, and houses. Little Bird was basically the world's fanciest remote-controlled plane. Well, at least that a regular person could actually purchase. No matter how bad Reaper wanted one, we couldn't afford a Predator drone.

L.B. had a wingspan of only ten feet. When you took it apart, the whole thing fit into two big suitcases. It wasn't fast, it didn't have any guns, but what it did have was the ability to stay in the air for damn-near forever running off what was basically a glorified leaf-blower engine, all while snooping with every type of camera you could think of. It was like having my own portable spy satellite.

Old Fort Saradia was visible at the end of the road. Those twenty-foot walls had been built over a hundred years ago by the British Empire. There were only two entrances, one off the road, and a smaller one on the opposite side overlooking the rudimentary dock, and thermal showed that both of them were being guarded.

Inside the walls were several other buildings. Some old battered historical things, then a couple of large steel buildings that dated back to the forties, and finally a dorm that had been built more recently when Fort Saradia had been used briefly as the oceanographic institute for the emir's new university. The whole thing was supposed to be unoccupied now except for a couple of caretakers.

"You gonna stick with the plan this time, Lorenzo?" Carl asked.

"Sneak into a den of professional killers, find the box, walk back out. Right?" I was nervous, but I tried not to let it show. The shakes would come later, now I needed to be cold and professional.

"Walk in the park," Carl muttered. I knew he didn't like this at all. He wanted to go with me, but Carl was a warrior, he wasn't built for stealth. And no matter how satisfying it would be, kicking in the door, guns blazing, was just going to get us all killed.

Rather, I was going to do what I did best. And that meant being one sneaky son of a bitch. I needed to be fully in touch with my inner ninja. I checked my gear again. I was moving light. Speed and silence mattered more than firepower. Forty of them, one of me, it didn't matter what I was armed with. If I got caught, I was going to die. I had my STI, several extra mags of 9mm ammo, the excellent Silencerco suppressor, a pair of knives, one fixed blade and one folder, radio, lock picks, night-vision monocular, and finally a length of piano wire tied between two small wooden dowels. I'm an old-fashioned kind of guy.

My clothing was neutral, all gray and tan, cargo pants, plain long-sleeve T-shirt, soft desert boots, one of those cargo vests with ten million pockets, and even a khaki ball cap. The Dead Six types that we had seen tended to be dressed in that contractor-chic style, so I hoped that if somebody spotted me, their first inclination would be that I was just one of them, and by the time they recognized that I wasn't, they'd be quietly dispatched.

After some internal debate, I had worn my lightweight, concealable armor vest, because even though it made me a little less mobile, this was a very trigger-happy bunch that we were dealing with. It would stop pistol rounds, but rifle bullets would still zip through like it was made of butter.

Now we were waiting. From the Fat Man, we knew that all of Dead Six was coming here, and with the curfew in effect, they couldn't risk being randomly pulled over anymore than we could. Once Carl dropped me off and picked up Jill, he was going to park out of sight.

We were hoping for a vehicle that I could either carjack or ride unnoticed. Preferably the latter, as the former introduced some real bad complications into the mix. It was too early in the evening to start popping people. Reaper had already notified us of a couple of potentials, but they had been traveling too closely together. Luckily, the fort was the only thing at the end of this road other than shabby ramshackle housing, so if it was any sort of decent vehicle, it was obvious where it was going.

I didn't like this plan. There were way too many things to go wrong. But if this didn't work, then I was going to be reduced to trying to climb over walls that were probably under video surveillance. "I hate winging it," I muttered. Carl grunted in affirmation.

"I've got a truck on camera. He's at the base of the road, ETA, one minute," Reaper said. *"No thermal hits from the back."* Carl started the engine. The plan was to come up behind potential vehicles and tail them to the last roundabout. If it was a good one, we'd go for it. If it wasn't, then we'd take the turn and come back here to wait for the next target.

It was a Mitsubishi truck, with a ragged tarp covering the back. It passed us slowly. The driver was a blond Caucasian and the passenger was a black guy, so they probably didn't live here. It didn't have a tailgate, so that was one less thing to worry about. "This one looks good," I whispered. Carl nodded and rolled out behind him. "Jill, the white truck. Get ready to intercept." I pulled the hat low onto my head and placed my hand on the door handle. The metal was scorching hot to the touch.

"Have visual. Truck's coming toward the roundabout. Distraction time," Jill reported matter-of-factly.

"Good luck, everybody," I said. The van rolled up behind the Mitsubishi. "Now, Jill. Go! Go!"

I opened the passenger-side door. We had disabled the interior lights. The truck was slowing on the roundabout. We had one shot. Jill was dressed as a local, weighed down with bags of groceries. She blundered right into the path of the truck, playing oblivious to the hilt. The driver of the Mitsubishi hit the brakes. Red lights illuminated my world. I was out of the van in a heartbeat, Carl pulling the door closed behind me. I could see the passenger's profile in his mirror, his attention on Jill.

The tarp was dusty with talcum-powder sand. Trying not to make a sudden impact against the shocks, I slid under and right onto the burning heat of the truck's diamond-plate bed. The horn sounded, making me flinch involuntarily. I heard Jill shout back at the driver and could imagine her shaking her fist.

"I'm in," I whispered.

Jill heard and continued on her way across the road. Carl pulled through the roundabout and headed in a different direction. I lay on the metal that was hot enough to fry bacon and tried not to cry. The truck rolled forward. I slowly shifted myself around on the greasy, hot surface until I was squished in the shadow of the cab as much as possible. After another minute we left the paved road and the tires began to make a different noise on the gravel. We were getting close. The brakes whined as we stopped.

"*You're coming through the gate,*" Reaper informed me.

I could barely hear the passenger. "Hey, Studley, what's up, dawg?" I couldn't make out the guard's response. "We've got the last of the stuff from Safe House Five. . . . I know, right?" There was laughter.

"*Interior guard is waving them past. You're inside.*" Then music started playing in my earpiece. It was some techno-remix of the *Mission: Impossible* theme.

"Turn that shit off," I hissed.

It stopped. "*Sorry, just trying to set the mood.*"

The brakes whined as we rolled to a stop. The smell of diesel was strong in the air. The engine died with a gurgle, and the doors slammed. I heard voices speaking in English, somebody laughed, and then it was quiet.

"*They're walking away from the truck. You're parked just south of Building One.*" I had memorized the overhead layout of the place, and we had numbered every structure inside. "*You've got somebody on the wall directly above you. Hold on a second—I'll warn you when you're clear.*"

I scurried around until I could see out the back. The interior of the fort was getting darker by the minute. There were only a handful of exterior lights scattered about, and luckily most of them were low wattage. Once it was fully dark, this place was going to be my playground.

I'm coming for you, Valentine.

♠
Chapter 18:
Civil War

VALENTINE
1955

As darkness fell on the tiny Gulf emirate, the Zubaran Civil War began in earnest. Fighting had broken out all across the city as forces loyal to the Royal Family clashed with the numerically superior forces of General Al Sabah. According to news reports, there was heavy fighting near the palace. As expected, the Royalists attempted to retake Zubara's seat of government.

By now, most everything we were taking with us was packed onto pallets, ready to be loaded onto the boat when it arrived. Everything else was being systematically destroyed. We were leaving nothing behind for the Zubarans to capture.

A lot of us didn't have anything to do. Everything had been broken down and packed away, so we didn't even have a television to watch. We ended up gathering on the roof of the dormitory, where we had a pretty good view of the city, to watch the fighting.

It was like a grim fireworks show. The occasional stream of tracer fire arced into the darkened sky. We could see flashes and hear distant rumbling as both sides shelled each other with artillery. Jets roared overhead, and ancient air-raid sirens screamed throughout the city. Several large fires had broken out. Volleys of rockets were exchanged. We watched in awe as a Zubaran jet, engulfed in flames, plunged into the bay.

I sat on an old metal bucket and played my harmonica. I was rusty, but I'd been pretty good back in the day. I played a sad, lilting tune. I didn't know what it was called, but no one seemed to mind me setting things to music as we watched Zubara burn.

"We caused this," Anita King said. She stood near me, arms folded across her chest, looking off into the distance. "We destroyed this country."

"We were trying to prevent this," Holbrook said, looking through a pair of large military binoculars.

Tailor's face was briefly illuminated as he lit a cigarette. "This was bound to happen sooner or later," he said, snapping the lighter shut. "There was no way a handful of guys was going to come in and change the course of this country."

"Then why did you sign up?" Holbrook asked.

Tailor shrugged. "It was something to do. I was bored." He cracked a smile, and Holbrook shook his head.

Frank Mann, the armorer, was with us. "It's been nice working with you guys," he said. "You didn't abuse my weapons. I appreciated that." We all chuckled.

"You know what really pisses me off?" Holbrook asked. "You know they'll try this again."

"Who?"

"Whoever the hell we work for. These black-ops guys. Project Heartbreaker failed. But you know they're going to try this again somewhere else. Might be a year from now, might be twenty years. But they *will* try again. And a handful of guys will die trying to accomplish a mission an entire army would have trouble with."

He was right. If Gordon Willis was representative of whatever shadowy organization he worked for, I knew they'd try something like this again. Our employers had no regard for human life, neither ours nor those of civilians caught in the crossfire. They would do anything, no matter the cost, to accomplish their ambiguous and convoluted goals. We were the ones that paid the price.

Whoever they were, they were powerful, well-funded, and connected. And they were arrogant. I had no doubt in my mind that they'd try again someday. A strong wind gusted from the ocean. A storm was coming, unseasonably late in the year.

LORENZO

I hung from the underside of the stairs of the big forties-era structure we had christened Building Two, sweat rolling down my face and stinging my eyes. My grip was tight on the hot metal bars, and I prayed that the Dead Six personnel standing ten feet away would hurry up and find a better place to be.

"*Aqua Teens* is way better than *Venture Brothers*," the first argued. There were some clicking sounds, and then a lighter flame appeared, briefly highlighting the two men. I could hear him take a long drag. The nearest light was burned out, and it was dark enough that I could only see the glowing red embers.

Using the thermal camera on Little Bird, Reaper had warned me right before the Dead Six men had turned the corner. My awkward perch was the best that I could come up with on short notice.

"Dude, you're stupid," the second replied. "*Venture Brothers* has Brock Samson. *Brock Samson*, man. All you got is a milkshake. Quit hogging that."

Who argues about cartoons in the middle of the night? Ignoring the growing pain in my arms, I contemplated shooting them and getting it over with, but it was too damn hot to have to drag their bodies to a hiding place. Luckily, after a few minutes the two super geniuses decided they needed some munchies and went back inside. The smell from Building Two's open door told me that it was the chow hall.

I slowly lowered myself to the floor, careful to settle my weight without making a sound. Checking my watch, I cursed the delay. I didn't know what was going down at midnight, but I didn't want to be here to find out. I'd crept around the first few buildings now and I still hadn't seen Nightcrawler. My best bet was to isolate him and find out where the box was. If he had any clue how incredibly valuable it was, he had more than likely kept it for himself. If not, I could certainly carve the box's location out of him.

Building Three looked liked like the living quarters, so that's where I'd start. I could stick to the shadows under the wall of the old steel building all the way there. It took nearly twenty minutes, since I had to low-crawl through a few narrow patches between rays of naked light, but this was my element, I was a ghost, I was a predator. Move . . . stop, wait, listen . . . move. Every time I heard Reaper's voice I would freeze and wait until the danger passed. There was one final wide space to cross, but it was relatively dark and scattered with miscellaneous barrels and bits of cover, and then I was in place.

Building Three had a covered stairwell on both ends. Reaper's thermal camera couldn't help me once I was under a roof. I heard the footsteps coming and unconsciously calculated where they would be looking as they descended. I pulled into the darkest corner, hand coming to rest on my Greco Whisper CT. The 5 ° inch blade came out slowly, not making any noise, and I held it in against my body. A bearded man came down the stairs, whistling. *If his eyes so much as flick in this direction . . .*

Knives aren't for fighting. Knives are for *killing*. I was already visualizing his death, when luckily for both of us, he just kept going, opened the door, and walked out. I started breathing again and sheathed the blade back under my vest.

The second floor. *Hall clear.* I couldn't believe it. Their names were actually *written* on the doors. The first door said McAllister. The next door read Valentine and had a stupid heart with an arrow through it. Jill had thought that she'd heard Nightcrawler called Val back at the Hasa Market. The door was locked, but I picked it in under five seconds. I drew my 9mm, screwed the suppressor on, and entered the room without hesitation. Thankfully the hinges did not squeak.

The nearest exterior lights of the compound provided enough illumination to see by through the open balcony door. The balcony was empty. The bed was unoccupied. I checked the bathroom. The shower was damp, and there was still condensation on the mirror. He had not been gone long. Music came from the other bedroom attached to this bathroom. I had to hurry. I closed the door. If anyone returned, it would at least give me a brief warning.

Some weapons were thrown on the bed. There was a disassembled 7.62mm SCAR sitting on top of some armor. The armor itself was stained with dried blood and had a bullet impact on the trauma plate. I could not help but notice the oddball sidearm still holstered on the green web gear, a weird, customized S&W .44 Magnum. That was probably the same gun that had blasted a hole clear through Hosani and into me. I'd found the right room.

I began to ransack the room, going through the footlocker and checking the contents, trying not to disturb the scene. If the box wasn't here, I was going to hit the main building next, and the last thing I wanted to do was raise an alarm in this ant's nest. Clock was ticking. The shooter was bound to be back any minute. Nothing of interest so far. Closet next. Random gear and clothing had just been dumped in here. He must have known that this was temporary.

On the floor was a plain duffel bag. Unzipping it revealed a whole bunch of money. I was positive that some of the rubber-banded stacks had come from me. *Bastard.* But on top of the money was a small wooden box. *Could it be?* I picked it up. It felt exactly like the replica I had left to be mangled in Adar's house fire.

YES! YES! YES!

"I've found it," I whispered into the radio. The others, even Carl, actually cheered. Leaving the money, I stuffed the box into my vest. All that cash . . . It would just slow me down, though. The oldest, scariest part of me was really tempted to stay there until Nightcrawler came back, just so I could murder him on general principle, but it was time to go. "Prepare to extract. Reaper, how's it look out there?"

"Compound looks clear right around you, but I can't see under the overhangs."

"Military vehicles? Lorenzo," Carl's voice sounded urgent. *"There's something weird going on down here."*

"What've you got?" Something moved in the corner of my vision. "Wait—"

Lights flashed inside my skull, and the world exploded in pain.

VALENTINE

My hand hurt. I hadn't busted anybody in the head like that in a long time. The stranger in my room flopped to the floor like a sandbag. My mind raced as I tried to figure out what was happening. *Who is this guy? Are the Zubarans coming after us?*

I'd crossed over from Sarah's room by hopping the balcony. I'd left my balcony door open, so the guy hadn't noticed when I came in. He'd been huddled over by my closet, holding something in his hand. I was on top of the guy immediately. I didn't give him time to breathe. I slammed my knee into his spine, putting all of my weight on it, while I checked him for weapons. I found some kind of fancy 1911 pistol, a boxy custom job with a wide-body frame, tucked in a holster on his right side. I had a hard time pulling the pistol out, since there was a long suppressor screwed on the end. My own gun was still in its holster, sitting on my bed across the room. I swore at myself for leaving the room unarmed. It was a stupid thing to do, given the circumstances.

I swiped off the safety of the stranger's gun as I stood up, and kept it pointed at him. My eyes darted to the gun in my hand, and something clicked in my brain. I stepped around the splayed-out intruder and hit the light switch.

"You!" I snarled. "It's you!" I couldn't believe it. It was the guy from Hasa Market. Lorenzo, the girl had called him. "What the fuck are you doing here?" I said and kicked him in the ribs as hard as I could. He gasped in pain, and I kicked him again. He flopped over onto his back. "What did you think was gonna happen here, asshole?" I asked. "Huh? You got some balls, man, I'll give you that." I tried to kick him a third time. He was ready for it. He spun around on his back, feet moving so fast I couldn't keep up. He kicked the pistol out of my hands. It flew across the room and slid under my bed.

Lorenzo tried to scramble to his feet, but I was on top of him. I grabbed his tan vest, hoisted him up, and slammed him against the cinder-block wall. He was still disoriented. I reached behind him and clamped onto his vest again. I was a lot taller than Lorenzo. I pulled his vest up from behind and down over his face. I leaned into him

then, punching him in the head over and over again,
hockey-brawl style.

I thought I heard Lorenzo say something, but I couldn't
understand him. Then the building was rocked by an
explosion outside.

LORENZO

My brain must have really bounced off the inside of my
skull, because I couldn't remember how I'd ended up on
the floor with a mouth full of blood. My earpiece was lying
next to my head, and I could barely hear Carl screaming
about something.

Someone was talking, angrily asking me questions. The
kick that landed in my ribs was unbelievably hard. The
second was even worse. It was that son of a bitch,
Nightcrawler. There was a gun in his hand. My gun, *damn
it*! He tried to kick me a third time, but I reacted and
kicked my gun across the room. Strong hands grabbed
me, jerking me to my feet and hurling me into the far wall.
He pulled my vest over my head and was on me in a
second, knuckles slamming into my face repeatedly.

I slid down, shaking my head, trying to focus, which is
difficult when you're getting punched. I couldn't hear
Carl, but he could still hear me through my throat mike. I
needed a distraction. "Carl, hit it."

A concussion shook the room as Carl radio-detonated
the Semtex plastic explosive I had left in the Mitsubishi.
Nightcrawler spun, surprised by the noise. I shoved myself
upright as he turned back to me. I kicked him in the chest.
Dust flew from my boot as he crashed back into the wall

next to the bed. I moved in while he was off balance and threw a knee to his side. He grimaced but stayed up. I followed with an elbow to his face, but he blocked it with his forearm and then used his size advantage to shove me back with one big meat hook against my sternum.

The kid was bigger and stronger, but I was faster. He was using a form of Krav Maga, but he was rusty. He didn't practice much, I could tell. I locked up on his arm, spun inside of it, and slugged him in the kidney, then put my foot on the inside of his knee and forced him down. I jerked up on his arm, trying to snap it at the elbow. He crashed into the shelf, snapping boards and sending things flying. He shouted incoherently as his other arm came around with something shiny and metallic and caught me on the side of the head. *Thunk!*

I must have gone out for a second. I was down, blood spewing from my mouth. The room spun as I refocused, again on the floor, and at the blood-stained Korth revolver that he'd just hit me with.

I rolled out of the way as his foot kicked through empty air. I was back up in a split second, trying to make distance until I could see straight. I was dizzy, but my blade appeared in my hand, like I had willed the Greco there with anger alone. His hand came out of his pocket, and a switchblade opened with an audible *snik*. Time slowed down as we focused on each other.

"Oh, it's on now," he said as he pointed the knife at me, chest heaving, gasping for breath.

I spat out a bunch of blood. "On like Donkey Kong, motherfucker."

We charged.

VALENTINE

I had to finish this. The warning klaxon was screaming, and I could hear people shouting outside. Lorenzo had a hard gleam in his eye, and I knew he meant to kill me.

He lunged. I dodged to the right and tried to slash at him with the Infidel automatic knife in my left hand. His hand arced around and put a gash up my left cheek, barely missing my eye. It wasn't deep, but Christ it was close. I slashed at his abdomen as he pulled away and managed to clip him.

Lorenzo only took a moment to recompose and came at me again. I could tell he was a better fighter than me. He fought like a wounded animal and was extremely fast. This guy was dangerous. But he was injured. I still had the advantage.

He slashed at my face. I leaned back and dodged it, but just barely. I tried to stab him in the abdomen. He moved to the right, avoiding the thrust. His right hand came back down, trying to cut open my left arm. I twisted to the left at the last second. He sliced upward, nicking my arm.

He didn't let up. As I recoiled in pain, he brought his left elbow up and smashed it into my face. Lights flashed in front of my eyes. I dropped my knife. Lorenzo then snap-kicked me in the chest, sending me crashing to the floor.

He was on top of me in an instant. I kicked out, nailing him in the groin. Lorenzo grunted and gasped for air, face turning red. I turned around, fumbling for any kind of weapon. My hand found the rock I used to prop the balcony door open. Grasping it, I sat up and threw it at Lorenzo as hard as I could. His hands flew up to cover his face. The white, softball-sized Zubaran rock hit him in the forearms. He reeled back.

I only had a second. I sat up and dove toward my bed. I desperately grasped for my holstered revolver sitting on my armor. Lorenzo reached me before I could reach my .44, trying to plunge his blade into my back.

LORENZO

It should have been over by now. I should have been able to take him, but those initial hits had left me disoriented, sluggish. Before I could drive my knife into his spine, his enormous boot hit me in the stomach. My abs absorbed the hit, but I staggered back, gasping for air. The kid was pulling that big .44 now, the muzzle swinging toward me.

I stepped into him, knife humming through the air. He raised his right hand to hold me off and I opened his forearm, splashing the walls with red droplets. The kid screamed as the blade struck. But I was too late, he swiveled the big revolver into me from a low retention position.

The concussion was deafening in the little room. The mammoth slug hit me square in the chest. My armor stopped it, but I couldn't breathe. It was like being hit with a bat. Fire washed down every nerve. It took everything I had to stay on my feet. We locked up, me trying to keep that gun away and his blood-slick hand wrapped around my wrist to keep my knife at bay.

I got my fingers around the cylinder of the Smith and wouldn't let it turn as he squeezed the trigger. I could feel his other hand slipping off my knife, and as soon as he let go I was going to plunge it into his neck. We spun around, shoving and grunting, stumbling over the junk on the floor. He was shouting in my ear.

All coherent thought had ceased. It was kill or be killed. No time for fear, no time for pain. I kept throwing knees, trying to tear him down. He head-butted me in the face, smashing my nose, but he stumbled back as well. My eyes filled with involuntary tears, and my hand began to slip from the cylinder.

Desperate, I dropped my knife, reached across his torso, and got my thumb under the hammer of the Smith just as it fell, blocking the shot. His wounded hand now free, the kid swung for my face. I ducked, pushed the gun away from me, and hit him repeatedly, forearms, fists, elbows, knees, every time that gun came back around, I hit him again. He went to his knees, still trying to shoot me. I stepped back and snap-kicked him in the face.

He landed flat on his back with a huge crash.

That had to do it. I bore down on him, ready to beat his head in. He jerked the gun up.

BOOM!

There was a flash of light as he fired, so close that fire engulfed my vision. He missed, but pain like nothing I had ever felt before pierced the right side of my skull. The bullet skimmed past my head and blew a chunk from the ceiling, but I was already falling, clamping one hand over my bleeding ear.

My balance was just gone. I could barely think. I wanted

to vomit. All I could hear was this terrible grinding noise as my eardrum died. He was rising, wobbly, seeing two of me. Then I saw tiny green lights under the bed, the night sights from my 9mm. I snatched it into my hand, rolled over and stood, gun punching out, finger already on the trigger.

I was staring down the barrel of his .44. The suppressor of my gun was inches from my opponent's face, centered on the bridge of his nose. Our fingers were on the triggers, both of us just ounces of pressure away from oblivion.

We glared at each other. Each of us battered, cut, bleeding, and pulped. I was blowing frothy blood bubbles every time I exhaled. He moved his mouth. He was talking. *Holy shit, I'm deaf!* I could barely understand him. "What the hell are you doing here?"

Careful not to let my gun move, I reached into my vest, grimacing as my hand brushed the area that was now one massive spreading bruise, and pulled out Adar's box. "I've got what I came for."

Nightcrawler was confused. "That? I don't even know what that is!"

"I'll be going now," I said.

He was shaking badly, and blood was dripping from his forearm, but it wasn't pumping like I'd severed the artery. *Too bad.* "I don't think so."

I didn't hear the door open behind me, but I did feel the terrible impact as they smashed a rifle butt over my head. I ended up on the floor. The last thing I remember was looking at the ceiling, surrounded by angry shadows pointing guns at me. I couldn't understand a word they were saying over that damn *ringing*, and then everything faded to blessed black.

Chapter 19:
Best Laid Plans

VALENTINE

It was like an old John Woo movie. Lorenzo and I stood in my little room, not six feet from each other, guns drawn. Neither of us fired. I don't know why. My arm was bleeding badly and burned with pain. I was dizzy and felt sick. It hurt to breathe. Only *the Calm* kept me focused enough to stay in the fight. I barely noticed the pain, and even though I was terrified, I felt no fear.

He was so focused on me that he didn't notice the door opening behind him. Tailor, Hudson, and two of Hunter's security guys came rushing in, weapons at the ready. I lowered my gun just as Hudson bashed Lorenzo in the head with the buttstock of a carbine. The intruder's gun clattered to the floor as he collapsed. He lay there for a second, staring bleary-eyed at the ceiling before losing consciousness.

I stepped back, setting my revolver down on the bed, and clutched my bleeding arm. *The Calm* was wearing off, and I was beginning to notice the pain. And holy crap did it hurt.

"Michael!" Sarah said, pushing her way through the men in my room, holstering her Sig .45. She threw her arms around me and hugged me tightly. "What happened?" she asked. "Your face! You have a cut on your face! I was walking back to the dorm when I heard the shots. Oh my God! Your arm!" She turned to yell at Hunter's men as they picked Lorenzo up off the floor. "Get a medic up here right now! He's injured!" Shouts went out for the doc.

"Val, what the fuck happened up here?" Tailor asked. He lowered his carbine as Hunter's two security guys dragged Lorenzo away.

"That's the guy from Hasa Market," I said, wincing with the pain.

Nervously, Tailor looked around for anyone who wasn't in the know. "Did he come back for his money?"

"He was in here looking for that puzzle box I found in Adar's safe. I jumped him. Son of a bitch is a hell of a fighter. If I hadn't got the drop on him he'd have sliced me open." I said, straining. "Where the hell is Hal? Christ, I'm bleeding like crazy here." I wiped the blood from my cheek, smearing it across my face.

"Stop being a pussy," Tailor said. "Focus. You sure he wasn't after the money?"

"He only seemed to care about the box."

"Tailor looked thoughtful. "Shit. We need to tell Hunter."

"You're going to tell him about the money?" Hudson asked, concern in his voice.

"No. Especially not this dude's cash," Tailor said. "We found that box and a bunch of money in Adar's safe. We'll just tell Hunter about the box and shut up about the rest."

"Damn." Hudson whistled. "You guys find a lot of money laying around, don't you?"

A moment later, Hal, the medic, came rushing into the room, carrying his jump bag. Tailor gave everyone the eye so there would be no more talk about the money. "Everybody get back," Hal said. "Let me see him. Sit down on the bed, Valentine. Goddamn, you got yourself all cut to shit, didn't you?" He looked me over, illuminating my wounds with a small flashlight. "Yeah, that one on the cheek is going to leave a nasty scar. Not too deep, though. Let me see your arm. Wow, yeah, you're going to need stitches on this." I winced as he poked and prodded the bleeding gash. "Quit being a little girl," Hal chided. "Holy shit, you're lucky. Any deeper and this would've severed your radial artery."

"Just patch me up, Doc. Was anybody hurt in that explosion?"

"I don't think so," Hudson said. "I was outside when the truck blew. Nobody was nearby. Did that guy have something to do with that?"

"I think so. Hal, please hurry. I need to talk to Hunter right away."

"Just hold still," Hal said. "This is going to hurt."

He wasn't kidding. Hal expertly stitched up the long gash on my arm without bothering with anesthetic. He then bandaged my face and stuck cotton balls in my nose to stop the trickle of blood. Lorenzo had elbowed me pretty hard, but my nose wasn't broken.

I turned to Sarah as Hal applied the last of my bandages. "Go get your body armor on and tell Hunter I'll be there in a minute. Tell him that the guy we caught is the same shooter from Hasa Market. They call him Lorenzo. Bring the puzzle box to him, too. We have a major security breach here. Somehow this guy was able to track us back to the fort. If he found us, Al Sabah's forces might have, too."

"Okay," Sarah said. She picked up Adar's puzzle box and turned to leave the room. She paused by the door and looked back at me.

"I'll be right there," I said. "Don't worry." Sarah flashed me a worried smile and was out the door.

It wasn't until after she'd left that I remembered that the key Sarah was wearing on her necklace had been inside that box.

LORENZO

I woke up in terrible pain. "What time is it?" I asked.

"Time for you to start talking," a voice said. The screeching banshee death wail in my right ear had calmed down enough that I could hear, but I had the worst headache ever. Waves of throbbing suffering cascaded through my skull with each heartbeat. Every bit of me hurt.

There was a blinding light aimed at my face. The light moved away, and I blinked in confusion. It had been a flashlight. "All yours, sir," a young man said. "He'll live as long as you want him to."

"Thank you. That will be all, Hal," said the man with an eye patch. He was probably sixty but looked tough for his age. The medic picked up his bag and left us. We were in an old room. It smelled of mildew and decay. The walls were made of rough, crumbling brick, and down the center of the room was a line of rusty iron bars cemented into the floor and ceiling. *A jail?* On the other side of those bars were two other men, both armed and watching. I was sitting on the floor, back to the damp wall. When I tried to move, a chain clanked. My left arm had been handcuffed to a bar.

The old man was sitting on a folding chair, just out of reach. "This was the original brig for Fort Saradia. Appropriate right now, don't you think?" He took his time lighting a fat cigar, finally blowing a pungent cloud of smoke in my direction.

I took stock of the situation. I couldn't have been out long. My vest was gone. My shirt had been torn open, and there was a spreading black and purple blotch over most of my chest and stomach. Something was packed into my ear, and the blood that coated my neck and chest was still slick. I tugged on the cuff. The bar was rusty, but solid.

He got tired of waiting for me to answer. "Why is this important?" he asked, cigar in one hand, Adar's box in the other. "It's an Arabian puzzle. Very old from the looks of it."

"I'm into antiques." It hurt to talk. My face was too swollen. I bet I looked like a mess.

The old man smiled, only there was nothing friendly about it at all. This dude was dangerous. "I don't think you realize the world of shit you've gotten yourself into, boy, or maybe you do. Maybe you know exactly who you're messing with."

I recognized the voice now. I'd heard him on the radio. "So, Big Boss . . . How's Nightcrawler?" I chuckled. "Did I manage to take his arm off? You Dead Six guys get good medical, right?"

Big Boss scowled. That had gotten his attention. "Mr. Valentine will be just fine. You, I'm not so sure about." He didn't seem concerned to drop actual names, which meant he wanted me to know I was dead, no matter what. The only question was how much it was going to hurt first. "I'll ask you, just one time, who you are and who you work for. You will answer me truthfully, or I'm going to make you suffer in ways you can't even imagine."

That's where he was wrong. I had one hell of an imagination. And I just had to keep these people occupied until whatever apocalyptic thing the Fat Man had been talking about happened at midnight. "I'm not telling you shit. I'll only talk to Gordon. I don't have time for his flunkies."

Big Boss nodded. "I see. Either you know what you're talking about, or you're full of shit and I know where that missing radio wound up. Speaking of radios, who were you talking to on yours?" Big Boss pulled my radio out of his shirt pocket. "I tried to be polite, but someone just started calling me names in what I believe was Portuguese. They're not answering now, for some reason."

"They're picky like that."

Big Boss paused to address the two men who had been watching. "Conrad, Walker, come here for a minute. And remove your sidearms. I'm afraid this one's tricky." The two men drew their pistols and placed them on a table, then came through the bars. The gate had probably been missing for years.

One was a taller dude, and he accidentally bumped his head on the only light bulb, sending it swinging wildly back and forth, casting crazy shadows in the old brig. The other was about my size, with sunglasses perched on his head, who looked like he knew his way around the intricacies of hurting people. They grabbed on and smashed me into the wall.

"To warm up, I want you to take our friend here and break every one of his fingers." Big Boss paused as the door opened.

A woman entered. Young, auburn hair tied back, and rather cute, she was totally out of place in this dismal setting. She seemed a little ruffled when she saw the two goons holding me. It was pretty obvious what was about to happen. "Colonel, we've sighted the boat. It'll be at the dock in a few minutes."

Big Boss glanced at his watch. "They're early. Spread the word and start loading. I'm on my way down."

The two thugs were dragging me to my feet. I didn't resist and the handcuff scratched its way up the bar until I was standing. The girl's voice sounded familiar too. It was worth a shot. "Hey, Sarah." She twitched in surprise. *Yep, that was her.* "Sorry about cutting up your boyfriend."

"You bastard," she spat. "I'll—" Then her eyes flashed as she changed her mind. She crossed quickly into the cell, apparently surprising the men holding me. She cupped her hand and smacked me upside the head, right across my bandaged ear.

The pain was nauseating. I grunted, but forced it into a laugh. "What kind of limp-dick carries a gun like that anyway? He's compensating for something." I forced myself to laugh so hard I started wheezing. It actually hurt. And that's when I saw the briefest flash of a metallic trinket hanging inside her shirt. The necklace looked familiar. *No. That's impossible.* But then she was backing away, hands balled into fists, and it was out of sight.

She was *really* pissed off now. She was about to come at me again when the old man spoke up. "That'll be *all*, McAllister," he said gruffly. Sarah gave me one last defiant look before leaving.

Big Boss then turned his attention back to me. "Don't worry, friend. This won't take too long. I'll have you singing like a bird by the time my men get packed. I was interrogating Communists when your mommy gave your daddy the clap for the first time." Big Boss strode out, pausing just long enough to drop the box and my radio on a table by the exit.

"Don't hurry on my account," I called after him.

He paused and smiled. "Oh, don't worry. You don't have to wait up for me. Walker, start with the pinky."

Oh hell.

"Yes, sir," said the shorter one cheerfully, obviously excited. The other dude slammed his weight into me, pinning me into the wall. I thrashed, but with my wrist handcuffed, it wasn't like I had a lot of maneuverability with that hand. The one called Conrad punched me in the stomach, which got my attention just long enough for Walker to latch onto my fist. While I struggled, he pried

my pinky loose and yanked it back. I screamed as it broke
with a sick crack.

VALENTINE

Goddamn it, I thought to myself bitterly. *I knew it was
too good to be true.* I cursed myself for staying with
Dead Six. We should've used the confusion of Project
Heartbreaker being terminated to sneak out and link up
with Ling's people. We could've slipped away, and with
everything being packed up and shipped out, they'd
have had no time to try to find us. It would've been
perfect.

Instead, here I was, decked out in full battle rattle with
a rifle slung across my chest and a bandage on my arm.
The fort was on full lockdown. Everyone healthy enough
to hold a weapon was kitted up and told to be on the alert.
Despite Hal's painkillers, I hurt, and my face was bruised
and swollen. Worse, the sky had clouded over. Thunder
rumbled overhead; it was threatening to rain.

Most of us were standing by on the docks at the north
side of the fort. They sat just beyond a huge stone arch in
the old wall of Fort Saradia. Colonel Hunter had ordered
patrols of the compound as well. Every person that could
be spared hurriedly loaded equipment onto the dock.
Word was Hunter was going to try to get the boat to come
sooner. My own personal gear, including a backpack full of
money, was still in my room. I *really* hoped I'd have time
to get it before we had to board the boat.

We were prepared for the worst. We'd emptied the

armory and broken out all of our heavy weapons. We quickly set up defensive fighting positions covering both the gate and the docks, backed up with machine guns, RPGs, Javelin missile launchers, and everything else we had lying around. If the Zubarans came looking for a fight, they were in for a big surprise.

We couldn't take everything with us. I was shocked at how much weaponry they'd stockpiled in our armory. Most of it had been locally acquired, either captured or given to us by the Zubarans. There was a lot of Chinese and Russian hardware. We'd rigged the supply building, where the armory was, with explosives. As soon as we cleared out, we'd blow the rest of it in place so General Al Sabah's troops couldn't make use of it.

Sarah was with me. Her hair was pulled back into a ponytail. She'd put on her body armor like I asked. It was soft armor, useless against rifle fire. We couldn't find any regular armor that would fit her. She carried a Mk. 16 5.56mm carbine in her hands and had her Sig .45 on her hip. Sarah had a serious look on her face as she kept watch over the harbor.

God, she's beautiful.

"I've got a boat in sight!" someone shouted. He was looking out over the bay with a pair of night-vision binoculars. "It's a ways out, approaching slowly."

"Is that our ride?" someone else asked. "Did the colonel talk them into showing up early?"

"Sarah, go tell Colonel Hunter we have a boat in sight," I said. Most of our radios were packed away, and our network had been dismantled. We had to communicate the old-fashioned way.

"Okay. I'll be right back." Sarah trotted off, disappearing from sight.

The group was smoking and joking, eager to head for home. Holbrook, the only surviving member of Singer's chalk, was telling everybody that the beers were on him as soon as we got to a non-shitty country. Now I could see the lights of the boat. They were growing quickly.

"Gimme those." Tailor stole the binocs from the guy using them. He scowled. "Val, that boat looks too small. . . ."

There were several quick flashes from the boat. I could see them clearly without night vision. The sound came an instant later. "Get down!" I screamed, pulling Tailor to the ground. The tracers were high, hitting the fort wall behind us, showering us in dust and debris. But then the gunner adjusted fire and walked the bullets into the dock. Chunks of concrete and wood went flying as heavy rounds punched through walls, equipment, and men. Two streams of tracers zipped from the boat as it hosed our position with twin fifty-caliber machine guns.

"Return fire!" Tailor yelled, trying to make himself heard over the chaos. A fire erupted behind us as the boat's armor-piercing/incendiary rounds ignited something flammable. "Take that boat out! Somebody grab a Javelin!" Fillmore and Chetwood ran for the missile launcher.

The boat was still hundreds of yards out. It gunned its engines and sped up, continuously firing on our position. Several men were able to bring their weapons to bear and return fire, but to no effect.

Through the three-and-a-half power magnification of my ACOG scope our attacker looked like a patrol boat of the Zubaran Coast Guard. Leaning around the barricade of sandbags I was using for cover, I squeezed the trigger, popping off shot after shot at the incoming boat. It strafed the dock again, twin tongues of flame tearing into our position with lethal results.

"Where is that goddamned Javelin?" Tailor screamed again, firing his weapon as he did so. I looked around, trying to figure out what happened to our missile crew. They were on the other side of the entrance to the dock, about twenty-five meters from my position. Fillmore and Chetwood were lying behind a pile of sandbags, blood everywhere. Chetwood had been decapitated. Fillmore was missing an arm and screaming his head off. *Christ* . . .

"I got it!" Holbrook shouted. He slung his weapon behind his back and ran into the open just as the incoming patrol boat opened fire again. I watched in horror as a heavy .50-caliber round smacked into him, punching through his body armor like it wasn't there. The bullet exploded out his side in a spray of blood, guts, and bits of shattered ceramic. Holbrook didn't make a noise as he went down.

If we didn't get that missile, we were all dead. "Tailor, I'm going," I said, feeling no fear as *the Calm* pushed all emotions aside. Without hesitation, I sprinted for the other position and jumped over Holbrook's body. I made it across. I dropped to the deck and slid to a stop on my knees. I roughly pushed aside Fillmore and picked up the Javelin launcher. Shouldering the heavy beast, I looked through the sophisticated sight and pointed the weapon toward the Zubaran patrol boat.

The Javelin achieved missile lock. I pressed the firing

stud. The missile's expelling charge caused it to belch out of the launcher. A fraction of a second later the rocket motors ignited, sending the missile roaring up into the night sky on a column of smoke. It took the missile a few seconds to arc through the sky. It came screaming down, slamming into the boat from above and detonating. The hull was ripped in half in a flash of light.

My comrades on the dock stood up and cheered, holding their weapons in the air while the sinking boat burned. For my part, I simply dropped the Javelin launcher and exhaled heavily, taking stock. Fillmore was already gone. My pant legs were coated in the blood of my dead teammates. The patrol boat's strafing run had killed several of us, and the screaming told me others were wounded. Thunder rumbled overhead again, and the rain began. Within moments it was pouring.

Seconds later something shrieked overhead and detonated inside the compound. Then there was another, then another. The ground rumbled as mortars struck the armory and the admin building. My heart dropped into my stomach. *Sarah!*

"Val, where are you going?" Tailor shouted as I took off at a run.

"I have to find Sarah!" I said, not looking back.

LORENZO

The big lump of meat, Conrad, let go of me, and I sank to the ground, retching. Walker didn't just snap my finger bones, he broke them slowly, grinding away, joint on joint, until he was sure he'd hit every nerve bundle. He was a fucking *artist*.

"Two down, three to go," Walker said. "And I'm just getting warmed up on this one. This is going to be a long night. You really shouldn't have come here. You're my bitch now."

"No shit," I gasped. I had no weapons. They'd searched me, disarmed me, and I was already hurt and handcuffed to a wall. Options were limited. There was no room for error. I had to kill both of these men. I felt around the wall behind me. *This place is old and crumbling. There has to be something I can use. There.*

"Ready for the next one, Stan?" Walker asked.

Conrad shrugged and started in. "Sure, but I don't get off on this like you do." He grabbed me around the back of the neck and dragged me up the wall, loose brick scraping my back. He slugged me in the stomach again, hammering the tissue that had already been pulverized by a stopped bullet. It hurt so *bad* that I just wanted to curl up into a ball and die, but that's why I did all of those damned sit-ups. I took it. I had to let them think I was helpless, but I still had one hand free, and I clutched the chunk of brick tight.

There was a burst of noise from outside. Walker and Conrad glanced at each other. "Gunfire? Who's shooting?" Walker queried. My hearing was still all buggered up. I had no idea. "Check it out," he snapped. Conrad let go of me. This was my chance. I slid to floor, limp, gagging, as if that last punch had leveled me.

"Okay," Conrad said, jogged toward the exit. I waited until the door closed.

But Walker wasn't stupid. He'd stepped out of arms' reach to wait for his backup. *Chicken shit.*

I crawled to my knees. I had to make this count. "Wait? You hear that?" I gasped, looking toward the door.

Unconsciously, he turned. "Wha—" But was cut off as I hurled the brick as hard as I could. His glasses flew off and he stumbled back, hands clutched to his face, screeching in pain, one eye obliterated. I scrambled for him, but the cuff chain snapped tight, just short, just out of arm's reach. *Shit!*

"Help!" Walker, blinded, was tripping, stumbling, but getting farther away. "Conrad! Help!" he cried.

His aviator shades were at my feet. I snatched them up, ripping them apart, knocking the remaining lens out. I bent the wire spine straight and went to work on the cuffs. Men like me have an instinctive fear of being in hand-cuffs, so I had practiced this a few hundred times. I could pick a handcuff with a toothpick. "Maybe Big Boss will lend you an eye patch, asshole!"

The door flew open and Conrad ran back in, shouting, "We're under attack! It's the army." Then he collided with his bleeding friend. "What the hell?"

"My *eye!*" Walker screamed. "He put out my eye!"

The cuff clicked loose and I ripped my damaged hand out, leaving a lot of skin behind. I crossed the cell, reaching up and swatting the lone light bulb, shattering it and plunging us all into darkness. They never saw me coming.

I kicked Conrad's ankle out from under him. The bone splintered and he toppled down to my level, where I ridge-handed him brutally in the throat. Conrad choked, gagging, still confused as to how I got all the way over here. I grabbed him by the hair and slammed his face into my knee, knocking half his teeth out. He was down.

Walker was groping about, searching for his gun. They'd left them on the table by the door. He found the table just as I found him. My arm slid around his throat, injured left hand putting pressure on the side of his head as I cranked back, taking us both to the ground. He thrashed, kicked, elbowed me in the side, but once I'd cut the flow of oxygen off to his brain, he was out in ten seconds. The elbow hits got weaker and weaker, then finally stopped. When I was convinced the struggle was over, I rolled his unconscious form off.

Gasping, I struggled to my feet. There were flashes of light coming through the narrow windows. A high-pitched whistle terminated in a explosion against one of the walls. The compound was under attack. I had to get the hell out of here. I ran my good hand over the dark table until I found what I'd come here for. The box went into one pants pocket, radio into the other. I kept Walker's gun.

The two men were groaning, stirring. I could have just put a bullet into both of them, but I might need the ammo. I booted Conrad in the head once more to be safe, then rolled Walker over, stripping him of two spare magazines. Blood flow restored, the man was starting to come to.

Being an asshole, I just couldn't help myself. Squatting down, I grabbed all the fingers on Walker's right hand. "Wake up." Then I cranked them back so brutally hard that they touched his wrist, breaking every one of them so fiercely that the skin of his palm split open. He sat up, screaming, so I smashed him in the face with his own gun.

It was time to go.

VALENTINE

Fort Saradia was in utter chaos as mortars rained down on us. I left the relative safety of the stone archway that led to the docks and ran into the open, desperate to find Sarah. She was probably either in the admin building or the old brig, where they'd taken Lorenzo.

The admin building was easier to get to, and it was where Hunter's office was, so I started there. Hearing the screams of more incoming shells, I huddled by the wall of the closest building and covered my head. Two big military trucks, wearing Zubaran Army markings, were parked by the north wall of the supply building. Those trucks had been sitting in the compound since day one, but we hadn't used them. I hoped they'd protect me from fragmentation.

Five more mortars exploded in the compound. The first one didn't hit anything. The second struck the admin building. The third hit the dormitory building and destroyed several rooms on the top floor. The fourth hit the big gas tank directly west of my position. Hot wind blew across my back as the fuel tank erupted in a huge fireball and burned. I didn't see where the last mortar hit, but it was close. The barrage ended. An assault was coming, and we were undoubtedly outnumbered. Through the torrential downpour, I saw the survivors from the docks running back into the compound, toward my position, as they prepared to make a stand.

I had my own mission, though. Clenching my MK 17,

I took off at a run again, rounding the east corner of the supply warehouse. One of the shells had struck the ground right next to the building, making a small crater and collapsing part of the wall. I didn't stop to see if anyone was hurt inside. I jumped over the crater and continued running.

A loud crash echoed across the compound. I stopped and took cover. A French-built Leclerc tank smashed through the front gate, busting the heavy metal doors open. The turret had been turned around to keep from damaging the barrel. As it cleared the gate, it began to swing its gun around, looking for a target.

A few seconds later, a Javelin missile shrieked down onto the tank and slammed into the top of the turret. The missile hit with a loud metallic *BANG,* sounding like someone hitting a metal plate with a sledgehammer. The tank rumbled to a stop just inside the gate, burning. Brilliant flames shot out from under the turret as the ammunition inside cooked off and burned.

The destroyed tank effectively blocked other vehicles from entering the gate, but that didn't stop the onslaught. Armed troops began pouring into the compound, coming around the tank on both sides. They were a mix of Zubaran Army regulars, with their desert-camouflage uniforms and helmets, and irregular militia, who wore black fatigues and masks over their faces.

Holy shit. There's a lot of 'em. I backed up and dove into the mortar crater and used it for cover. I acquired a target through my ACOG scope, a militiaman with an RPG, and popped off a shot. He dropped to the muddy ground. I shifted my carbine to the right and fired three shots at another cluster of soldiers, Zubaran regulars. One went down, but the others took cover behind the tank.

They just kept *coming*. To my left, my teammates had gotten a couple of machine guns set up. They tore into the soldiers as they filed in past the tank, but the enemy was relentless. I fired continuously, pausing only to change magazines. I don't know how many I hit. More than a dozen Dead Six operatives were all firing into the same enemy position, mowing down the Zubaran soldiers, but there were too many of them. Rounds began to strike the dirt around my little crater, and the wall behind me. I suddenly felt very vulnerable. Taking a chance, I came to my feet and ran for the admin building, bullets snapping past me as I went. I hugged the wall, hoping the hostiles wouldn't see me through the rain.

Thunder clapped overhead, barely audible over the roar of the battle as I reached the admin building. My heart sank when I saw the damage. A mortar had struck the roof, partially caving in the second floor. Hunter's office was on the second floor. *Oh God, no . . .*

My *Calm* began to fail. I was nearly in a panic. I busted the ground-level door open and entered the building, heading for the stairs.

"Sarah!" I shouted, hoping she would hear me. It was dark inside. The impact had knocked out the main lights. The emergency lights had kicked on, but they didn't provide much illumination. I switched on my weapon light as I vaulted up the stairs two at a time. "Sarah!"

I made it to the second floor and shined my light down the hallway. The roof had caved in at the far end of the hall where Conrad's office was. A small fire burned within, and the hall was quickly filling with smoke. Hunter's office was closer. The door had been knocked off the hinges, and the ceiling was cracked all the way down the hall, but the roof hadn't caved in yet. The old building's solid construction was the only reason it had been able to withstand two direct mortar hits.

"Sarah!" I shouted, growing desperate.

"Here!" Sarah replied, her voice resonating through the low-pitched roar of the battle outside.

"Sarah, where are you?" I shouted, running into the hall.

"I'm—" She coughed. "I'm in here!"

I followed the sound of her voice to the first room in the hall. The door was open. A smear of blood was on the floor, leading into the dimly lit room. I found Sarah sitting on the floor. She was holding Anita King in her arms. Anita was dead.

"Oh God, are you alright?" I cried, dropping to my knees and throwing my arms around Sarah. She had a few cuts and bruises. Blood trickled from a scrape on her arm.

"She's dead," Sarah said. "She . . . she was in the hall when the shell hit. She got hit by shrapnel or something. She wasn't wearing her vest. I . . . I just stepped in here. I was knocked down. Anita died."

"Sarah!" I shouted, shaking her. "Hey! We can't stay here. I need you to focus, okay? Are you hurt?" She was shell-shocked.

"I don't think so," she responded, still sounding distant. "I just fell down when the shell hit. I think I hit my head on the floor."

"C'mon, we gotta go," I said.

DEAD SIX467

"I can't leave Anita."

"We have to. She's dead. There's nothing you can do for her now. Come on now, *please*!"

Sarah took a deep breath and jerkily nodded her head. She gently lowered Anita's body to the floor, and I extended my arm. Sarah grabbed it, and I pulled her to her feet.

"Come on, we have to get out of here," I urged. "Are you sure you're okay?"

"I'm fine," she answered, sounding more collected. She brought her slung carbine around and grasped it in her hands. "I'll be okay. Let's go." I nodded and led the way back into the hall, heading for the stairs.

"Wait!" Sarah cried. "The Colonel! He was in his office!" She turned and ran down the hall to Hunter's office without waiting for me. I swore aloud and followed.

Hunter's office door was lying on the floor in the hall. Sarah stepped on it as she crossed into the room. I coughed in the smoky air as I followed. The office was smashed. Part of the ceiling had collapsed and fallen right on Hunter's desk.

"Mike!" Sarah was kneeling on the floor next to the pile of rubble that had come from the ceiling. Colonel Hunter was trapped under the debris. It had all come down right in his lap, smashing his chair to the floor and crushing him.

"Colonel!" I crouched down next to Sarah. "Jesus," I said, surveying the damage. It was bad. Hunter was broken and bleeding. A massive pile of blocks and rebar had landed on his abdomen. Only one of his legs was visible under the rubble.

"Valentine?" Hunter asked weakly, blood tricking from his mouth.

"I'm here, sir," I said, leaning in so I could hear him over the noise of the fighting outside. "We're gonna get you out of here. Hang on."

"Bullshit," Hunter wheezed. "I ain't goin' nowhere. You . . . you get her out of here, you hear me, boy?"

"Yes, sir," I replied solemnly.

Hunter coughed up a small amount of blood. "You know I was supposed to leave last night? All of us were. Not you guys, but the support staff. I said no. I told Gordon I wasn't leaving until all my guys got out. I think maybe that wasn't such a good idea," he said, somehow managing a raspy laugh.

"What happened, Colonel? That boat was a Zubaran gunboat. It strafed the docks, killed a bunch of us." Sarah gasped as I told them that. "What the hell is going on?"

"Gordon Willis sold us out," Hunter said quietly. "He . . . he told the hajjis where we are. Made a deal with somebody. Same thing with that raid on Montalban's yacht. That was his own idea, not a sanctioned hit. Gordon's playing both sides. Son of a bitch sold us out."

My eyes narrowed, and my hands clenched into fists. I was so angry I was shaking. I closed my eyes for a second and tried to remain focused.

"Take this," Hunter said. He pushed a small object into my hand. It was a thumb drive. "Everything on Project Heartbreaker is on here. I've been doing some homework. Everything I found out about Gordon's double-dealing is on here, too."

"What do I do with this, sir?" I asked. The thumb drive had Colonel Hunter's bloody thumbprint on it.

"Give it to the right people," the colonel replied. "Find someone you can trust. Be careful. This is a lot bigger . . ." Hunter's voice trailed off. He coughed up more blood.

"Colonel! Stay with us!" Sarah cried.

"This is bigger than you know," Hunter whispered, his one eye staring at me intently. "There's something else, too, not on the drive. Another project. Like Red, only bigger this time." Hunter trailed off again. His breathing was ragged now. Blood bubbled out of his nose. "Project Blue's ready. You've got to . . ." His words tapered off, too faint to hear.

Hunter was almost gone. "I can't hear you. What?" I asked urgently.

Suddenly he grabbed my armor and pulled me close with surprising intensity. *"Evangeline!"* he hissed. Then his grip relaxed. His eye unfocused. "Find—" He coughed, painful and wet, gasping for air as his body shut down.

Colonel Curtis Hunter died before he could finish that sentence. I quietly swore to myself before gently closing his eye. I pocketed the thumb drive and stood up.

"What was he trying to say?" Sarah asked.

I shook my head. "I hope it's on this drive. I hope it's not for nothing." I stepped across the room and looked out the window. My remaining teammates had fallen back to the supply building behind my position. They were being pushed back to the docks. Enemy troops continued to pour in around the disabled tank, spreading out through the motorpool as they entered the compound. There was literally a heap of dead Zubaran militiamen all around the tank, but more kept coming, stepping over their dead comrades. General Al Sabah was using the local radical militants as cannon fodder.

Sarah huddled close to me. "What are we going to do?" There was fear in her voice.

"I still have the phone Ling gave me." I was scared too. "If we get out of the compound, we can contact her. She said the deal was still on if we needed her help. We can—"

Before I could finish that thought, the entire compound was rocked by a huge explosion. The concussion hit my face through the shattered windows. A section of wall just down from the gate was blasted high into the air. I turned and shoved Sarah to the floor, covering her with my body as pieces of the wall rained on the compound.

I risked another look out the window. Through the new hole in the wall, dozens more soldiers streamed into the compound, a lot more Zubaran regulars, supported by some kind of wheeled armored car. They had to be hitting us with a company-sized element, if not bigger.

Sarah shook her head. She grabbed my hand and held it tightly. "We're . . . we're going to die here, aren't we?"

I stood there helplessly watching as the Zubarans pushed my remaining friends back even farther. The compound was being overrun, and they weren't taking prisoners. I looked down at the floor, then over at Sarah. I nodded slowly as my last hope died.

Sarah closed her eyes for a second while she took a deep breath. "Promise me you'll stay with me until the end," she said, looking into my eyes.

"I promise," I replied. "I won't leave you. No matter what." Tears welled up in Sarah's eyes as she leaned forward and kissed me. I stepped back and steeled myself. "Are you locked and loaded?"

Sarah pulled back the charging handle on her carbine slightly, checking the chamber. "I'm ready."

"Stay behind me. Stay low. Move when I move, stop when I stop. We're going to circle around the backside of the building and link up with our guys on the other side. Let's go," I said, leading the way out of Hunter's office. Zubaran soldiers were running past the admin building, one floor down from where I was. I didn't have much time before they entered the building. It's a strange feeling, knowing you're running off to your own death.

I didn't make it three steps before my phone rang.

Chapter 20: Rain

LORENZO

It had begun to rain, giant, stinging drops falling like some sort of biblical vengeance.

I was pulling myself around the back corner of the brig when a Zubaran armored car came through a breach in the wall. Soldiers in desert camouflage scurried through behind it, firing wildly at anything that moved. Muzzle flashes were coming from everywhere as Dead Six returned fire.

Really. Not. Cool.

Deaf in one ear, every inch of me hurting, and with two broken fingers, I crouched in the shadows and called for help. "Reaper! Come in Reaper! This is Lorenzo. Come in, damn it!" I shouted into the radio.

"Lorenzo! You're alive! Get out of there. The army is attacking!"

No shit. "Status?

Carl responded. *"The road's blocked. I can see five*

armored cars. There's a company-sized element hitting the compound now, mix of regulars and militia. You've got an unknown number of troops sitting in reserve about a click off the gate."

"What about the dock?" If I could get out the back way, I could swim for it.

Reaper came back. *"There's a couple patrol boats out there now.*"

Something whistled off to the side and exploded against Building One. The army was launching RPGs. I ran a few feet to the side and took cover behind a low wall. Hunkering down, I watched the battle between Dead Six and the army unfold. The Americans were putting up a fight, taking defensive positions around the buildings, but there seemed to be an unending stream of fanatical fighters pouring in. Bullets were flying in every direction, some leaving visible trails, the rain was so thick. A few Dead Six ran past, carrying heavy weapons, but they were too preoccupied to notice me hiding in the mud.

"What's your status?" Carl demanded.

I had broken at least one rib, if not more, and one lung felt like it was full of burning hydrogen instead of air. "Oh, I'm doing just *swell*. But the exit's blocked." Just as I said that, the armored car exploded, lifting and flipping its turret on a pillar of fire and throwing fragments fifty feet into the air. "Damn! Really blocked. I'll think of something."

"Lorenzo, be careful." It was Jill. She sounded terrified.

"Get off the line!" I snapped. There was no time for sentimentality. Off to my right, several grenades exploded around the parked cars, shredding some of the Dead Six personnel. One of the Americans, badly injured, stumbled, confused, in the direction of the enemy, raising his empty hands in surrender and was shot dead on the spot. They weren't taking any prisoners. "Reaper, can you keep L.B. in the air in this weather?"

"Yeah, chief. It's all-weather capable."

"I need you to be my eyes. I'm at the east wall, by the old brig, uh, Building Six."

"Lots of heat blooms from the explosions. Wait. I see you."

I had to get out of here. The army was bottlenecked with that APC blocking the hole in the wall and a tank burning in the main gate. As long as they kept trickling through, Dead Six could hold them, but I didn't want to be out here in the open when either side started getting desperate. Dead Six personnel had moved out of the dorm to hold the gates, so they should be empty. "I'm going to take cover back inside the apartments. Let me know when I've got company." Both sides of this battle would kill me, so it was time to do what I do best in situations like this. *Hide.*

Slipping through the rapidly growing puddles, I had just reached the dorm when I was forced to dodge into a doorway to hide. Some more Dead Six men ran past, guns held high, faces grim. Once they were gone, I ran up the stairs, sprinted down the hall, and ducked back into the Valentine's room. At least it was familiar, and I really didn't want to participate in the war unfolding outside.

"Reaper, status?"

"Dead Six is fighting like crazy, but more Zubarans are inside. You better think of something fast, boss, because they're coming in force now."

Plan. I needed a plan. The rain drumming the roof was louder than the gunfire. My eye landed on the bug-out bag filled with *my* money.

VALENTINE

I looked at my cell phone like I'd never seen one before as it beeped and buzzed in my hand. Tailor was calling.

"Hello?" I said awkwardly, pressing the talk button.

"Where the *fuck* are you?" Tailor screamed in my ear.

"I'm in the admin building," I hissed, trying not to make too much noise. "I found Sarah. Hunter, too. Hunter's dead."

Tailor swore. "You have to get back here, right now!"

"Get back *where?*" I asked, exasperated.

"The north side of the supply building. We've . . . shit, choppers inbound! I'll call you back!" The line went dead.

"What is it?" Sarah asked. As if to answer her question, a Zubaran Army Mi-17 helicopter came in low over the compound. It slowed and came to a hover between the admin building and the dormitory. It was so close I could see up into the open back door. I pushed Sarah to the floor and lay on top of her, hoping the troops in the back of the helicopter couldn't see down into the window.

"Stay down," I told Sarah over the roar of the chopper's rotor. I poked the top of my head over the bottom of the shattered window frame so I could see. The door gunner on the left side was constantly firing. The chopper's hull was pinged and dinged by bullets as my teammates returned fire.

Ropes dropped from the chopper's open back door. Zubaran Special Forces soldiers, clad in their distinctive blue camouflage fatigues, began to fast-rope to the ground. They were inserting them right in the middle of the compound.

Four soldiers had reached the ground when an RPG rocket punched into the chopper's front-left quarter, right behind the cockpit, and exploded. The chopper spun wildly once, flinging a soldier out the back door, before going nose down and slamming into the dirt. Pieces of the chopper's rotor shot across the compound as it landed right on top of the troops it had just inserted.

My phone buzzed again, and I ducked back down. "Tailor!" I said, pushing it to my ear.

"Listen," Tailor said. "You have to get to the north side of the supply building. We wired up the west wall with explosives. As soon as it blows, we're going to make a break for it. We've got those two trucks, the Army ones. We can't wait. Another APC just came in through the hole they breached. The chopper wreck will hold up the armor for a minute, but they'll get around it." The Zubaran vehicles had to go up the narrow corridor between the admin and supply buildings and the dormitory. The west side of the compound was blocked by the remains of an old stone wall that was part of the original British fort.

"Okay, we're moving," I said.

"Val, we can't wait," Tailor repeated. "If you're not here in a couple minutes . . ."

"Leave without me. If I'm not there in a minute, it means I'm dead. Good luck, bro."

"Good luck."

Stashing the phone, I quickly outlined the plan to Sarah.

"That's crazy!"

I agreed. "But it's the only chance we've got. Come on, we have to go. It's not far." We had one shot, and we were going to take it. I checked out the window. The Zubarans were still advancing. It was too risky to go back the way I'd come in. Cautiously, I led the way as we entered the stairwell, hoping we could make it to the first floor unnoticed. The admin building only had one set of stairs, and they landed on the first floor right by the east-side door.

We were on the landing between the first and second floors. I held my hand up, signaling Sarah to stop, and peered around the corner. The ground-floor landing appeared to be clear but was illuminated from the outside. Problem was, a squad of Zubaran soldiers had hunkered down by that door to shoot at my comrades.

The door was still open to the outside. There was no way we'd get by unnoticed. *Shit.*

"Hang on," I whispered to Sarah. "Cover your ears." I pulled a grenade from my vest and grasped it tightly in my hand. I peeked around the corner again and, sure enough, saw movement and shadows. The enemy troops were still there. I pulled the pin, leaned around the corner, and tossed the grenade down the stairs.

BOOM! The concussion was deafening as the grenade detonated. We had no time to waste. I slapped Sarah on the shoulder and quickly made my way down the stairs.

On the ground-floor landing was a dead solider. As I came down the stairs, another man entered the building,

G3 rifle held at the hip. I snapped off a shot at point-blank range, aiming high so my shot would clear his body armor. The bullet tore through the soldier's throat. Before he hit the floor, I was on the landing. Just outside the door was another wounded soldier. Two of his comrades were leaning over him, tending to his wounds. One was looking up at me as I appeared in the doorway. I shot him in the face, shifted over, and shot the other before he could react. I left the unconscious Zubaran alone and rounded the corner, heading deeper into the admin building.

We entered the operations center. It had been gutted, with all of the valuable equipment removed or destroyed. Crossing the ops center, we cleared its back door and entered the short hallway that lead to the north door. Sarah watched our backs. With the noise of the battle going on outside, I couldn't hear very well. For all I knew another squad of Zubarans was parked just outside. I decided to crack the door as quietly as I could and take a peek.

The door was stuck. I swore aloud.

"Mike, they're coming!" Sarah said. She had the door to the ops center cracked and was watching the way we'd come in. Before I could say anything she stuck the muzzle of her carbine through the door and fired off a long burst. "I got one!" she shouted.

"Get down!" I screamed as bullets punched through the metal doors and zipped down the hall. Sarah ducked to the floor, stuck her carbine through the door again, and fired off the rest of her magazine on full auto.

She looked over at me. "What are you waiting for?"

"Reload, reload!" I shouted. "The door is stuck! I can't get it open!"

"Kick it or something!" Sarah yelled, fumbling as she tried to insert another magazine into her weapon. "I'll hold 'em off!"

"Short, controlled bursts!" I shouted, then turned back to the door. I kicked it as hard as I could. It budged a little. More shots punched through the door and came down the hallway. One buzzed right past my ear. "Fuck this," I said to no one in particular. I backed up, stuck my right shoulder out, and charged at the door, yelling like a madman as I went barreling down the hallway. I hit the door, and it popped wide open. I flew out into the rain, tripped, and landed face-first in the mud, right on top of my weapon.

I grunted and pushed myself up. A Zubaran militiaman stood behind me, to my left. He was standing against the wall of the admin building, rain drizzling off of the mask he wore. He was pounding on his M16 in a vain attempt to clear a jam. He looked up at me, eyes wide. It was too late for him. I rolled to my right and yanked my revolver out of its holster. Extending my arm, I snapped off a shot. The .44 roared in the narrow alley. Blood splattered on the wall behind the militiaman and he crumpled to the mud in a wet heap.

I reholstered my gun and pushed myself off the ground as Sarah came running out the door. "Mike, they're coming!" she warned, pressing herself up against the wall. "Are you okay?"

"Good to go!" Swinging my rifle around, I leaned around the door frame and popped off four or five shots down the hallway, scattering the Zubaran troops advancing through the ops center. The door at the end of the hall was open. My middle finger moved to the trigger of my under-slung grenade launcher and squeezed. The weapon bucked under my arm, launching a 40mm high-explosive round with a loud *POOT!* Before I could finish ducking out of the way, the round exploded in the ops center, right in the middle of the cluster of enemy soldiers.

"Watch the door, watch the door!" She shouldered her weapon and covered the hallway as she crossed. It was clear. "Let's go!" I grabbed her by the arm and pulled her close to me. Sarah covered to the east while I risked a look round the west corner.

"Shit!" I said, pulling back just in time. Several rounds snapped past me. Maybe a dozen Zubaran regulars were creeping up the side of the admin building. "We can't go this way."

"Over here!" Sarah said, pointing to the chopper wreck with her carbine. I removed my last hand grenade from my vest and lobbed it around the corner, up the west side of the building. Sarah and I bolted for the chopper. The grenade detonated behind us a few seconds later.

We dashed into the open, running past dazed, wounded, and surprised Zubaran troops around the wreck of the Mi-17. We turned north and ran alongside the supply building. It wasn't that far. I could feel my heart pounding in my ears as I sprinted with sixty pounds of gear on. Thunder crashed again. The rain was pouring harder than ever. Tracers flashed by, but we kept running. There were bullets buzzing from every direction. Rounds splattered into the muddy ground ahead, barely missing Sarah's legs. *Smack!* My leg came out from under me. I stumbled and fell into the mud. It burned. Blood leaked from a gash in my calf. I grunted in pain.

"Mike!" Sarah cried, looking back. She stopped running and turned around.

"No, Sarah, don't stop!" I screamed. "Keep going!"

But she didn't listen. She started toward me. A hole was torn in her vest as a bullet punched right through it. A second bullet hit her a little lower, in the stomach. A third went into her side. Sarah's face went blank. She collapsed to the muddy ground.

"*Sarah!*" I screamed. My voice sounded like it was coming from far away. I couldn't feel my wounded leg anymore. I pushed myself up off the ground. Bullets zipped past me as I limped to her. My left leg buckled. Every time I put weight on it, I began to fall. The wind was knocked out of me as a bullet struck me in the back, cratering on the ceramic plate in my vest. It felt like I'd been hit with a sledgehammer. I fell again.

I crawled through the mud, bleeding, dragging my weapon on its sling. On my hands and knees, I reached Sarah and lifted her head up. She was completely limp, nothing but dead weight. Her pupils were dilated. Her beautiful face was smeared with mud. I held her body close to me as blood poured from her vest. I couldn't breathe. I couldn't move. The rain poured down relentlessly. Sounds began to fade out. Everything sounded muffled, like I was underwater, except for my own ragged breathing and the pounding of my heart.

I was being shot at. I ignored it. The strange key I'd given Sarah was hanging around her neck, drenched in blood. I grasped it in my hand. There was a concussion. Then everything went black.

My eyes opened. I don't know how long I was out. I

was lying on my back, staring up into the rain. Sarah's key was still in my hand. My ears were ringing, and I could barely feel anything. I couldn't see out of my right eye. Warm blood, my blood, was pouring down my face.

I saw Sarah out of the corner of my eye. She was just a few feet away, but out of my reach. I couldn't sit up. I was bleeding badly. I was about to die. Holding my last breath, I stretched my hand out and reached for her.

Then she was out of reach altogether. My last conscious thought was the realization that I was being dragged away.

LORENZO

"Squad of soldiers is heading right for your building. Eight of them."

Carl's voice now. He had a laptop in the van and could watch the videos, too. "The dorm's a good position for them to take. Gives them cover and elevation against Dead Six. They'll use the windows on the west-facing rooms." Carl knew, because that's exactly what he would have done in this situation, and he had a lot of experience leading infantry in combat. Unfortunately, that was the building I'd picked to hide in.

I grabbed the bag of money. I'd slip out the north stairs. I'd just reached them when a sudden rhythmic beating rocked across the compound. "What's that?" I shouted.

"*Helicopter incoming!*" Reaper answered. "*Where'd that come from?*"

The stairs were exposed to the open air. Suddenly a

chopper appeared through the rain, slowing to a hover thirty feet off the ground, rotating as the door gunners blasted the living hell out of Building One with belt-fed machine guns. Ropes spilled from the open doors, and blue-camouflaged Zubaran Special Forces started fast-roping down. These guys were everywhere.

Then there was a terrible bang, like a clap of thunder. The side of the helicopter seemed to collapse into itself, belching smoke and launching one of the soldiers out the open rear door. The chopper fell from the sky. The rotors hit, hammering the mud into a circular plume before fragmenting into thousands of lethal bits. Fire, blood, oil, and flesh sprayed in every direction. I ducked as a chunk of the broken rotor screamed past and hit the stairwell just over my head.

Looks like I'm not going that way. I ran back inside the dorms. I needed a way out. The weight of the money gave me an idea.

"Soldiers are in your building," Carl insisted. *"Whatever you're gonna do. Do it quick!"*

"Roger that." I picked a west-facing room, whose door was unlocked, and hurried inside. It was a mirror image of Valentine's room. I dumped all the cash on the bed and spread it around, trying to make the money look as tempting as possible. That was one expensive distraction. Walker's gun was still in hand, a .45 Sig 220. I pulled the slide back slightly. There was already a round chambered.

There was a crash as another dorm door was kicked in, followed by automatic weapons fire and a scream. I entered the small bathroom, shoved the pistol in the back of my waistband, and stood on the toilet. I placed my hands on the opposite wall and slowly levered myself into position, "walking" with my hands until I was above the door frame. Every bit of pressure against my left hand caused unbelievable agony. Palms pushing out and boots pushing back against the opposite wall, holding myself there by muscle tension alone, I was now out of view of anybody looking through the bathroom door.

I knew how third-world armies cleared rooms and you did not want to be at ground level.

Drops of blood fell from my lacerated face and hit the floor. My arms began to vibrate from the strain of holding myself there. My swollen, broken fingers throbbed. More gunfire ripped through the dorm. They were spraying down each room as they kicked in the doors. *Hurry up.*

There were shouts in the hall, someone barking orders, and then they were here. The soldiers fired, bullets shredding through furniture. Dust erupted below as projectiles shot through the bathroom walls. I held my breath as a rifle barrel appeared through the doorway under me and shot the shower square into porcelain shards. The muzzle blast pounded upward. Flinching, I slipped a bit, biting my lip and praying for gravity to fail. I held on. The rifle disappeared.

Persian. "Look at all this money!"

"Praise be! It's a fortune, Mohammed."

Arabic. "What's all this? You two, keep moving."

"But, sir!"

"Move, dog. That is an order. And close the door."

The stomping of boots. *Wait for it.* Gunfire in the next room. Give him a second. I drew the Sig in my blood-soaked right hand and cocked the hammer, only one handed on the wall now, injured and too weak to hold me, slipping. The others were still shooting.

Go.

I dropped, landing feet first in a crouch. One soldier, an officer in the desert camo of a Zubaran regular, was standing at the bed. He looked up, both hands filled with rubber-banded stacks of currency, surprise registering on his face just as the front sight covered it. Masked by the cracks of rifles in the next room, I fired.

The bullet hit him in the sinus. He went down with a spray of blood and snot painting the wall. I de-cocked the Sig and shoved it back in my waistband as I moved. This was my ticket out. I pulled off the ragged remains of my shirt as the gunfire continued and more explosions ripped through the compound.

The officer was dead, eyeball dangling on a bloody cord from the shattered orbital socket. That's what he got for being greedy. He had a captain's insignia on his collar. I unbuttoned the bloody uniform jacket, tore it from the twitching corpse and put it on. He was much shorter than me, and my wrists dangled naked from the sleeves. There was more stomping of combat boots outside the door now. This building was clear. I didn't have much time. I tugged on the officer's blue beret.

One problem, he didn't look anything like me at all. *Shit.* It was dark, but I couldn't bank on that. I needed a distraction. They couldn't see my face.

"Sir?" someone shouted through the door in Arabic. "The colonel says we need to fire from these windows at the Americans." They started banging.

I saw the dangling eyeball and had an idea.

Falling into the hallway, I pressed the blood-soaked pillowcase against my face. "Aaaiiiii!" I screamed, my voice unnaturally high pitched, as I had no idea what this officer sounded like. "Booby trap! Booby trap!"

"Captain!" one of the soldiers shouted. "Are you all right?"

"My eye! My eye!" I held out my hand with the officer's eyeball in it and showed it to him. "Aaaaiiii!"

"Merciful Allah!" the soldier screamed, recoiling. "Get him out of here! Medic!"

Hands grabbed me by the arm and pulled me along, I kept my head down and weaved, crying and sobbing. Then we were outside, the rain pelting us mercilessly. The black night was lit by hellish fires, and smoke obscured everything. Good for me, as I was only partially in the enemy's uniform. The Zubarans were in the middle of a coup, most of these guys were Sabah's irregulars, so hopefully there were a lot of new faces. We were heading for the breach in the wall.

I looked back over my shoulder as I was pushed past the burning APC and into the rift. A couple Dead Six were leapfrogging their way toward the gate, firing at this position, their only hope for escape. Desperate and stupid, they were cut down one by one. The soldiers passed me off to other waiting hands outside the wall and returned to the fight. I discreetly tossed the eyeball in a puddle.

"Hang on, Captain. I've got you," someone shouted. I couldn't see him, as I was still covering my face with the pillow. Strong hands shoved me down. There was a lot of screaming and crying around me. The army had taken an absurd number of casualties. "I'll be right back," the medic said. All he saw on me was a head injury and it wasn't squirting. He had more important things to worry about right now. Lifting the bloody rag, I saw the medic kneeling next to me, up to his wrists in another soldier's pelvis, trying to clamp off a severed femoral artery. He was shouting for assistance.

Through the jagged breach in the old wall, I could see Dead Six, still fighting. There were fewer of them, and they were taking fire from multiple directions now. Most of the buildings were on fire, the rain pummeling giant clouds of steam into the air. Some Dead Six were fighting their way past the helicopter crash, using whatever cover was available. There was the kid, Valentine, and he was making a mad dash away from a bunch of pursuing soldiers. The girl, Sarah, was right behind him, as they headed for the back wall.

Seeing Sarah reminded me of what I'd noticed briefly in the brig, but that was impossible. That couldn't have been the key. I'd gone through hell for this thing. I pulled Adar's box out of my pocket and tried to work the puzzle, but it had been *broken*. The pieces had just been stuck back together. The box slid open, revealing . . . *absolutely nothing*.

Well, fuck me. I jerked my head up. Sarah was forty yards away, running for her life. Valentine's leg was shot out from under him. Sarah turned, screaming, and went back for him. Then several bullets struck, and Sarah fell in a fog of blood.

I stood. I had to get that key. The medic was screaming at me to get down.

There was the kid. He got up, fell, got up again, got

shot in the back, went down, but starting crawling to his girlfriend. He reached her, shell-shocked, looking for something that wasn't there, oblivious to the inevitability of his death and the carnage around him. Several grenades exploded between us, temporarily hiding him from view. The gunpowder cloud was gradually crushed by the rain, revealing Valentine on his back.

"Cover me!" I bellowed in Arabic. Back through the breech, I sprinted through the rain, bullets screaming past in both directions as the last of Dead Six retreated, water geysering up as the newly formed puddles were struck. I slid in the mud, sprawling down next to Sarah.

Sarah was dead, eyes open, crimson stream trickling from her mouth, white shirt soaked by rain and blood. She was wearing a few necklaces, and right in the middle, riding on a fragile chain was the *key*. Grabbing the chains and ripping them off, I held it up to the light of the fires, other trinkets dangling below. Unlike its last holder, the key was undamaged.

I glanced at Valentine. He was badly injured, blood pouring from his head, staring, incoherent, smoking shrapnel embedded all over his armor. He'd be gone soon. I shoved Sarah's jewelry into my pocket. The main fight was heading past me. There was a roar as Dead Six breached the west wall. Soldiers were swarming after them. I turned to leave.

Valentine stirred. He was dying, but he only seemed to care about the dead girl. He reached one blood soaked hand plaintively for her. It was the arm that I had slashed, red stain soaking through the bandage.

He was reaching for Sarah, but it felt like he was

asking for *my* help. It was crazy. He was too out of it to know I was there.

Compassion. Criminals aren't supposed to have any.

Screw him. But still, I hesitated. *He deserves to die. But not today. Not like this.* "Damn it." I didn't know why, but I grabbed the drag handle on the back of his web gear and jerked. Agony tore through my injured torso. I pulled him through the mud, back toward the hole.

It took the last of my strength to drag his unconscious weight through the breach. The Army had seen me run out, and not realizing who I was, welcomed me back. Dozens of Zubaran Army regulars were leaping from the backs of trucks, running into the compound to mop up the slaughter. I was so covered in blood, filth, and mud that I was utterly unrecognizable at that point.

Somebody saw the insignia on my collar. "Captain!" a soldier shouted. "What are you doing?"

"We need this one alive. Get him in the truck," I ordered.

The American kid was unconscious on the seat beside me. A medic had done a competent job stopping his bleeding before we had departed, supposedly for the hospital. I had waited until we were out of sight of the compound and past several other APCs set up as a road-block before I clubbed the driver and tossed him onto the road. I was kind of making this up as I went along.

"Reaper, I'm back."

"Where are you?"

"I'm driving a Zubaran Army pickup south on the main road. What's left of Dead Six?"

"Okay, I'm pulling back for a better view." Reaper's voice was intense in my good ear. *"The last of them blew a hole in the west wall of the compound and moved south through the shanty town past the roadblocks. Looks like they're in two army trucks. No sign of pursuit."*

They had to be going to a safe house. "Track them," I ordered.

"They're heading south on Balad." He continued to give me directions as I drove like a madman, keeping the hammer down and blowing through roundabouts like they weren't there. The windshield wipers couldn't match the intensity of the deluge, and I could barely see. Headlights flashed behind me. Carl and Jill had caught up.

Valentine moaned. He didn't look good, pale and shaking from blood loss, and I wondered if my act of kindness/stupidity would have been for nothing. Reaper informed me as the Dead Six trucks pulled into the back of a slaughterhouse a mile south of here.

"Lorenzo, what are you doing?" Carl asked. *"Do they have the key or something?"*

This was idiotic. *I am an idiot. Why am I doing this?*

I didn't know, but it was too late now.

"No, Carl. I've got it. Just hang on." I looked down at Valentine. "You owe me," I whispered, even though he couldn't hear. "You owe me big."

I arrived a moment later. The garage door of the slaughterhouse was still closing, light leaking out from beneath. I laid on the horn, and after a moment the door stopped and then reversed its motion. Leaving the kid behind, I bailed out of the cab, and hobbled toward the headlights of Carl's van. Armed Americans came out of the slaughterhouse and approached the still-running Army truck.

I slid into the passenger seat of the van, and it was moving before the door closed.

No amount of rain could wash Zubara clean tonight.

Chapter 21:
Nefarious Master Plan

LORENZO
May 12, 2008

The light streaming through the window was blindingly bright. Cringing as the bandages around my chest tightened, I raised one hand to block the sun from stabbing through my eye sockets.

"So, you're awake." Jill Del Toro smiled as she opened the curtains. "How do you feel?"

That was a stupid question. "Ever take a contact shot to the chest with a .44 Mag?" I asked rhetorically. My voice sounded funny. Sadly, I already knew that as bad as my ear was ringing, I had done some serious damage. When that ring went away, I'd have lost a range of hearing forever.

"Uh . . . nope. Can't say that I have."

"What time is it? How long have I been out?" After getting patched and stitched from the Dead Six gig, I had gone right into a fuzzy, painkiller-induced sleep.

"It's five in the afternoon. Don't feel bad. You looked like hell."

I studied my left hand. Carl had taped all the fingers together. He was a decent doctor. He had certainly gotten enough practice on me over the years. "Well, I got pistol whipped with a ten-thousand-dollar Korth. Funny, it felt the same as getting pistol whipped with a Ruger. Who would have thought?" I looked under the sheets. I wasn't wearing any pants. "Please tell me Carl's got the key? Really intricate antique thing?" Jill nodded. "Oh, thank you."

I'd done it. After all that, we'd gotten the key.

The gloating almost made up for the physical suffering. Good thing painkillers tipped the scale in gloating's favor. "Has there been any backlash from our little escapade?"

"It's all over the news. The police are saying it was a terrorist group and that they've been eliminated. The emir was murdered last night. General Al Sabah is getting all the credit for tracking the assassins back to Fort Saradia and eliminating them."

I nodded. So, just like that, the bad guys had won.

She slowly sat on the edge of the bed, her manner serious, her voice somber. "I watched the video from Little Bird. I saw them die. I saw them all die."

"Those kinds of things happen in this world."

"Dead Six ruined my life. They murdered my friends. I didn't think I would mind seeing them all killed, but that . . . I just don't know." She trailed off. "That just seemed so *wrong*."

I could tell she was really upset, just trying not to let it show. "Well, it wasn't really the trigger pullers' fault. They were probably kept in the dark and just given orders. It was that one guy from the embassy that wanted you dead."

"Gordon," she sighed.

"I don't think he was there," I said. "Sorry."

"Now him, when he gets his, I want a front-row seat. That last girl, though, when she got shot, and he tried to protect her? That was the girl from the radio, wasn't it?"

I nodded. "His name is Valentine. Her name is . . . was . . . Sarah."

Jill bit her lip. "That was the saddest thing I think I've ever seen. But I have to know. Why did you go back for him?"

I'd gone back for the key, but I'd taken him with me, and I didn't even know why. The bedroom door opened. "Because Lorenzo's an idiot," Carl said as he entered the room with a sandwich on a plate.

"Hey, you brought me some dinner. Thanks."

"Get your own," he responded as he took a bite. "Why the hell did you save him anyway? That just complicated everything. Lucky you didn't get shot. You just can't stick to a plan, can you? Why do you keep screwing up simple things?"

Jill gave him a look that would have killed most men with a soul. "I thought it was brave, and if it wasn't for Lorenzo *screwing up* I'd be dead."

Carl ignored her and chewed his sandwich. "Last time I checked, we're not the good guys."

I shrugged, not really knowing the answer myself. "Must have been the blood loss. I was kind of out of it. I wasn't thinking clearly." That seemed to placate Carl, though Jill's expression indicated she knew I was lying. "Well, at least we got the key, which means Phase Three is a go." That reminded me, I had better call the Fat

Man before he got jittery and started eating my family members.

"Can I know what that is now?" Jill asked. We both looked at her, but neither responded. "This *Phase Three*. I think I've proven my worth around here. You got your stupid box, so what's the deal? I can't believe what you went through to get it, either. Not that it hasn't been fun, but I would like to get back to someplace without terrorists and mercenaries and crazy people."

I had been giving this some thought, and now was as good a time as any. "Okay, but do me a favor first. There's a big freezer in the garage. Could you get me an ice pack out of there first? My face really hurts."

"Okay, sure," Jill said as she left.

Carl raised a single bushy eyebrow as I rolled out of bed and winced as my feet hit the floor. "Are you crazy?" he asked.

"Well, I'm thinking about offering her a real job. We need to see if she's up for it," I explained as I walked gingerly to the mirror. My equilibrium was off, and it hurt to inhale. "I think she's tough enough. Dude, just trust me."

"Okay. Whatever. But I'm getting worried. Lately you've not been yourself. This job's affecting your brain. We're not in the helping business. Survival first. Everything else, second. You can do good deeds on your own time. I'm here to keep Big Eddie from skinning me alive. Other than that, I don't give a shit."

I examined my battered face in the mirror. I had really taken a beating. Nobody would ever accuse me of being pretty, but once the swelling went down, I would probably be back to my forgettable average self, just how I liked it. "Have I ever been wrong, Carl?"

"Constantly," he replied. There was a frightened scream from the garage. "See."

So Jill had found the freezer. "All part of my nefarious master plan. Come on."

I ran into her on her way out of the garage. Jill nearly took me down as we collided, causing me to wince in pain. "Somebody want to tell me why there's a dead guy in the fridge?" she shrieked.

She was actually taking it pretty well.

"Why is there a dead body in the freezer?" Jill shouted. "That scared me!"

Taking it well . . . relatively speaking.

"Hey, it worked for Walt Disney." I opened the freezer door wider. Carl and Reaper were leaning on the van, enjoying the show. "Jill, allow me to introduce you to Ali bin Ahmed Al Falah, terrorist financier, evil genius, slave trader, gun runner, and huge Streisand fan. Seriously. I can't make this stuff up." Falah's body had been crammed into the freezer. Skin gray, beard flecked with ice, his frozen eyeballs were staring at us.

"His pictures are all over the living room," she asked suspiciously. "What kind of sick game is this?"

"Mr. Falah here was a *very* bad man. I've got pictures of him hanging with Osama. Phase One of this job consisted of me following him, watching him, learning his habits, how he talked, how he sounded. I took on the persona of a man named Khalid. I actually bought Falah's social club so I could get into his circle of friends."

"Why?"

"Because I need to be able to impersonate him so well that people who've known him for years wouldn't be able to tell. Freeze pop has a standing appointment for a party that I need to crash. Plus, we needed his cash. This James Bond crap is expensive."

"I do like my toys," Reaper explained. "It is hard to hack half of the Zubaran government with sucky equipment."

"Did you really need those big speakers, though?" Carl asked him.

"Helps me get in the mood."

"Anyway, I arranged a meeting between Falah and some imaginary Russian arms dealers to take place at my club. The plan was to get him inside, make him disappear, and I replace him. Nice and simple."

The idea didn't seem to shock her. "And that got screwed up when Dead Six assassinated him?"

"Exactly. When they put a bullet in his heart, we had to improvise. Luckily, all of his guards got killed, too, so though there were witnesses to the shooting, none of them were real chummy with Al Falah." I gestured at the dead fat body wrapped in plastic. "I had planned on making him go away, nice and quiet. The ground work was already laid—now it was just messier. I made some calls as if I was him, telling his associates that I had faked my own death to go into hiding." I left off the fact that I had even sent hand-forged letters to his children and wives. That seemed a bit grim. "Reaper had already taken command of all of his e-mail addresses—"

"I'm like the grand pimp mack daddy of identity theft," Reaper said proudly.

"So as far as the terrorist world knows, Al Falah is alive and well and living incognito, hiding from the Americans. Since he was in such mortal danger, he asked for his dear old friend, Adar Al-Saud, to come and assist him. Adar's a psychopath, but he's one very special psychopath."

On cue, Carl reached into his shirt and pulled out the key. It was still riding on Sarah's chain. It spun, reflecting the light. "Adar's daddy was an important man. Not many folks get access to the place we're going. They sure don't make them like this anymore."

Reaper took the key from him. He twisted the base slightly, causing dozens of perfectly carved, delicate pins to extend in various directions. It was remarkably complex. "They *never* made them like this. I'm telling you guys, man didn't have the mechanical ability to design something like this a thousand years ago. This would be tough to do with modern CNC machining." Carl quickly took the key back before Reaper could suggest something about space aliens.

"So, you need to pretend to be Al Falah for Phase Three? Do you really need to keep him in the freezer, though?" She looked ill. "That's just gross."

I nodded. "All part of the plan. Mr. Falah here still has one last job to do." I patted him fondly on his frozen shoulder. "He's going to throw the hounds off the scent long enough for us to get away."

"Okay, I get it. I get it . . . That's a lot of effort to steal . . . what?" Jill asked. "What could possibly be so important? Zillions of dollars? Somebody's Faberge' egg collection? The Holy Grail?"

My crew traded glances. This part was hard to explain.

"We don't actually know *what* it is, just *where* it is," I said slowly.

"Look, if you feel the need to keep me in the dark still, that's fine, but don't treat me like I'm stupid."

"No, really." I raised my hands in surrender. "They said that it would be the only thing there, it's portable, and that we couldn't miss it. They drew a rough sketch of it, but I don't have any idea what it's supposed to be." I held my open hands about two inches apart. "All I know is that Eddie wants it very badly."

"I can't even find it on the *Internet*," Reaper exclaimed, because, you know, that's the source of all knowledge in the universe.

Jill was incredulous. "All this . . . and you don't even know what you're stealing? You guys are nuts."

"No, Eddie's nuts. We're just too good at what we do."

"Man, close the fridge. That's freaking me out," Carl said.

After briefing Jill on the highlights of the utterly insane and possibly suicidal plan, we took a little drive in the van the next morning. I did not tell her where we were going and once again made her wear the blindfold so that she would not be able to lead anyone back to our hideout. She was quiet as we drove through the streets of Zubara, probably thinking about what I had told her. I didn't speak either, mostly because my face still really hurt. Carl was a decent medic, but having a mercenary smash your nose back into place and pull a broken tooth with a pair of pliers didn't exactly qualify as quality medical care.

The streets were relatively quiet. Supporters of the

emir had seen which way the wind was blowing. The ones that had enough money to cause trouble were on their way to Europe or Saudi Arabia. General Al Sabah owned Zubara now, and he was an astute enough man to not rock the boat more than he needed to.

Once I was sure that we had taken enough turns, I told Jill she could take her blindfold off. She rubbed her eyes as she adjusted to the light. The ocean was a brilliant blue out her window.

"So, where are we going?"

I didn't answer. "Now that you know about the job, and you know how dangerous it's going to be, I'm giving you an option." She waited, watching seagulls spiral over the passing beach. "This next part is going to get complicated and I don't normally recruit interns from the Department of Agriculture. This is a job for professionals, and I'm going to need a professional, not an amateur."

"I never claimed to be anything I'm not."

"True." I parked the van at the end of a long wooden pier. There was a fifty-foot boat moored at the end. "Look, I promised that if you helped us, I would get you out of the country safely. And you've held up your part of the bargain. It was like you were part of the crew over the last few weeks. So now it's time for me to hold up mine."

She looked at the boat and then back at me. "I see . . . I thought you were going to ask me to keep help you with Phase Three."

"Yes, I am. But if you want out, now's your chance. That boat is headed for Bahrain. I know the captain. He's a decent man, and he'll take you to another friend of mine. From there, you'll board a plane and take a circuitous route back to the US. Tickets and instructions are in the bag."

"I can't go back to the States. Gordon's people will kill me."

I patted a leather bag on the seat beside me. "There are some new papers in here. Forged passports, driver's licenses, social security numbers, birth certificates, everything you need, all clean, courtesy of Reaper, on the house. His work is as good as you'll ever find."

"He's really sweet," Jill said simply. "Squirrelly, but sweet."

"I've left contact information for an old acquaintance of mine. I've already spoken to him. He's agreed to help you get a new life set up. He's done this kind of thing before, and he owes me a favor." He hadn't been the first person I'd thought of, but as I'd gone down my list of other contacts in the States, most of them were either dead, in prison, or way too untrustworthy to send Jill to. Even though our last parting hadn't been friendly, at least the old guy was honorable, so Jill would be in good hands.

"You will never be able to go back to where you're from. You can never let your picture show up in the newspaper. Don't end up on TV. And never get in trouble with the law. You get fingerprinted, and Gordon's people will find you and kill you. You will never be able to let anyone know that you're alive. You can never contact any family or friends."

Jill sighed. "I told you, Lorenzo. My family is all dead. . . . Maybe that's for the best. Look at the mess it's gotten you guys into."

That was a bleak way to look at it, but probably true.

"You'll have to start over. I can tell you right now that it'll be extremely hard." Pushing the bag over, I continued. "If you choose to go home, you can't be Jill Del Toro ever again."

She opened the bag and pulled out some passports. "Peaches LaRue? Delilah B. Sweet?" she said incredulously.

"Reaper has a thing for strippers. Take it as a compliment." I shrugged. "There's a couple thousand dollars in cash in there and a bank card to a Chase Manhattan account with a hundred and fifty thousand in it. That's from me. Use it to get your new life started, but spend it gradually so it doesn't attract a lot of attention. Consider it a going-away present." I nodded at the boat. "All you need to do is get on there, and never look back."

She glanced at the boat, at the bag, and then back at me. "You said you were giving me an option. What's behind door number two?"

"I won't lie. Carl thinks I'm insane to offer you a job, but I've got a good feeling about you. I think you're sharp and tough. Plus, a pretty girl does come in handy."

"So, you think I'm pretty?" Now she was just being coy.

"Well . . . duh. I think you'd work out well. You help us complete Phase Three, and I'll make you a full partner. The money is good. You get to live a crazy life, bouncing around the Third World, robbing and conning assorted warlords, terrorists, scumbags, and lunatics, until eventually one of them catches and tortures us to death, or we're nabbed by some government, that'll just throw us in jail forever."

"Gee whiz, what's the downside?"

"You don't want to be around Carl on casual Friday."

She studied the contents of the bag. I did not envy her choice. Both options required her to give up her entire life. Jill bit her lip as she studied one of the driver's licenses. "How long do I have to decide?"

"The boat leaves in ten minutes." I glanced at my watch. "Make that seven. I talk too much."

"I've got a few questions. . . ." She paused, then gave me a dangerous look. "And don't you dare bullshit me. I want the truth. Why do you do this, Lorenzo?"

"This job? It's for my family, and I'm working on a way to make sure Big Eddie won't ever threaten them again."

"No, I know about them. Why do you do *this*?"

I studied the wheeling birds and the sparkling water. Why did I do it? It had all started as some sort of game, a challenge, a competition against the world. I had been the juvenile delinquent, the black sheep, the rebel. The first to fight, the first to cheat, the one that had to win, even though it didn't matter what I was winning, or what I was losing in the process. One day I had just walked away, fell off the grid, disappeared into the stinking underbelly of the world. I had become a predator of the predators, the ultimate rush, the perfect challenge.

Now I was just tired. And I didn't want my family, who were just normal, decent people, to pay for my sins. But even once this job was done, and even with Big Eddie either satisfied or dispatched, I couldn't imagine myself doing anything else.

"Hell if I know. It's what I do." She nodded as if that made perfect sense. "Boat's about to leave," I pointed out.

"Do you do a lot of bad things?" she asked.

"Depends on your perspective."

"I know I can do it if I have to, but I don't like to hurt people," she stated.

"I don't, either. But most of the things I deal with don't rank as people."

Jill turned her head, like she didn't want to look at me. "Is that the only reason you want me to stay? Because I might come in handy?" She was fishing for something.

God, she was beautiful. She was good and decent and strong. She deserved better than this, better than me. "What do you want me to say, Jill? I don't think I'm the man you think I am."

"And . . . I know you're wrong. I can see it. I just wish you could too." Jill turned back. Her eyes were full of moisture. She kissed me gently on my battered lips. She slung the bag over her shoulder, opened the door, and stepped onto the sand. She had a beautiful smile full of perfect white teeth. "Thank you for saving my life, Lorenzo."

"You're welcome."

"I just don't think I could do the kind of things that you do. It's nothing personal, but I just don't know if I could live in your world."

So that was it.

I held out a slip of paper. "That's a number I check periodically. If you ever change your mind, or if you ever need me for anything, leave a message. don't use any names. I'll know who it is."

She took the paper from my outstretched hand. "Thanks. You know . . . if things were a little different . . ."

"Things will never be different." I smiled. "If you

change your mind and decide to come with me, you don't have to wear the blindfold back to base."

"Goodbye, Lorenzo," she said softly. "Good luck. Thank you for everything." Jill closed the door and walked down the pier.

I watched her climb onto the boat. She never looked back.

♠

Chapter 22:
Casualties

VALENTINE
Location Unknown
Date/Time Unknown

Someone was singing. It was a woman's voice, soft and warm. It seemed to fade in and out. I couldn't tell where it was coming from. I couldn't see anything or feel anything. That voice was the only thing I had to focus on as I tried to collect my thoughts. It was like a dream.

I don't know how long it took, but eventually I was able to open my eyes to find an unfamiliar gray ceiling. The singing continued, but now I could hear it clearly. I wasn't alone, wherever I was. The room I was in was small. The walls appeared to be metal. Against the far wall was a small desk. A woman sat at the desk, facing away from me, hunched over a laptop. She had long black hair.

My mouth was so dry I couldn't speak. My throat was sore. All I could manage was a hoarse, raspy cough. The woman in the chair perked up and turned around, pulling small white earbuds out of her ears as she did so. *Ling?*

Ling stood up and quickly crossed the room. "Mr. Valentine!" she said. "My God. You're awake." I struggled to sit up. Ling helped me. I pulled an oxygen line from my nose. I had all manner of tubes, hoses, and IVs stuck in me. A cardiograph rhythmically beeped with the beating of my heart. "You should leave those in," Ling said.

"Where am I?" I croaked. "What happened? How . . ." I trailed off, coughing again. It hurt to talk.

"Hold on," Ling said, hurrying to the door. "I'll get the doctor!" She was gone, and I was alone again.

A minute later, several people rushed back into the room, including a man who strongly resembled Albert Einstein. He had a bushy mustache and a wild shock of white hair. He was wearing a lab coat. He put a hand on my shoulder and asked me to look at him. I slowly turned my head, only to have a flashlight shined in my eyes. I flinched; it was so bright it hurt.

"I'm sorry about that, Mr. Valentine," the doctor said. He had a German accent. "You've been in a coma for more than a week. Oh. Forgive me. I am Dr. Heinrich Bundt."

I took several deep breaths. "Where am I?" I asked again.

"You're on the *Walden*," Ling explained. "It's an Exodus ship. You're safe here."

"How did I get here? Why . . . ?" I trailed off again. My head hurt.

"You were very badly injured," Ling said. "We almost lost you."

Dr. Bundt straightened his glasses. "Mr. Valentine, I'm afraid you sustained a coup-contrecoup injury. That is to say, a traumatic brain injury affecting both your frontal and occipital lobes."

"Brain injury?" I muttered, suddenly very worried about my aching head.

"That's correct. You had a subdural hematoma to both the front and back of your brain. We were forced to place you in an induced coma after neurosurgery. Given the—"

"Wait, wait, wait," I said, interrupting. "What the hell did you do? Drill a hole in my head?"

"That's correct," the doctor said, sounding very reassuring, all things considered. "It was necessary to drain the hematomas to reduce the pressure on your brain. You should consider yourself very lucky that you suffered no permanent brain damage, given the time that elapsed between when you were injured and when we were able to treat you."

"So . . . am I going to be okay?"

"Time will tell, but I believe so."

I rubbed the sides of my head. "Where's Sarah?" The room suddenly got very quiet. Ling, the doctor, and a couple of orderlies just looked at each other stupidly.

"Where is Sarah?" I demanded, sitting up.

"Mr. Valentine, *please!*" Dr. Bundt said.

"Let me talk to him," a familiar Tennessee twang said. "Give us a minute." The doctor, Ling, and the orderlies left the room, leaving me alone with Tailor. "Hey, brother," he said quietly.

"Tailor, where the hell is Sarah? What happened?" I was getting scared.

"Christ . . . You don't remember, do you?"

"Remember *what*, Tailor?" I asked, a pit forming in my stomach.

"Sarah didn't make it, bro."

I looked at Tailor for a few seconds, then closed my eyes. My stomach twisted into a knot. I rubbed my head again, struggling to remember. Images flashed in my mind. I fell into the mud. I was hit. Sarah turned around. She came back for me. I was screaming at her to keep going, but she didn't listen. She was hit. She went down. She died.

"Oh God," I said, burying my face in my hands. "Oh my God." The knot in my stomach began to hurt. My chest tightened. It was hard to breathe.

"Yeah," Tailor managed. "Bad op, man."

"Bad op," I repeated, my voice wavering. "What the hell happened? How did I get here?"

"You were hit," Tailor said. "So was Sarah. A grenade went off near you. Hudson saw you go down, then lost you in the smoke. There was a lot of shooting. Then the charges on the wall went off. We had to go."

"Why did you come back for me?"

"We didn't. I told Hudson to get in the truck. We took off. I thought you were dead."

"Wait," I said, rubbing my eyes. "How did I end up here, then?"

"We managed to get out of the city, just by pure luck," Tailor explained. "We went to that contingency safe house south of the Al Khor district. You know, the one Hunter told us to never use unless it was a dire emergency. We made it. Somebody else knew about it, though, because after we got there a truck rolled up, dumped you, and took off."

"What?"

"I'm serious," Tailor said. "Someone pulled you out of the fort, tailed us to the safe house, left you, and disappeared. I have no idea who."

That didn't make any sense. "Was it the Exodus guys?"

"They say they don't know anything about it. That's what I'm telling you. I have no idea how you made it out of there alive. Anyway, I used that phone Ling gave you, got a hold of her. Took some doing, but I was able to talk her into getting us out. Told her you were wounded. That seemed to work. I think she likes you."

"Who's left?" I asked.

"You and me," Tailor replied. "Hudson. Frank Mann. That Nikki chick that translated the documents. One of Hunter's security guys. Baker's entire chalk. Hal the medic. Couple other guys. Eleven total. Would've been twelve, but Cox bled to death in the truck."

"Eleven," I lamented. "Jesus Christ."

"Hey, man," Tailor said, trying his best to sound consoling. "At least that many got out. Could've been a lot worse. We're still alive."

"Still alive." I looked up into my friend's eyes. "Tailor, I . . . Sarah's dead. She . . . I promised her I wouldn't leave her. I don't know what I'm going to do now."

Tailor's brow crinkled with concern. "You're going to get some rest, bro," he said. "I'm going to get the doc. Don't worry about anything. We'll talk later. Okay?"

I didn't respond. I just closed my eyes again.

VALENTINE
Exodus Ship *Walden*
Port of Mumbai, India
May 16
0700

I was alone in my little metal room, picking at my food, when Tailor came in. "How you doing, Val?" he asked.

I shrugged. "I walked all the way to the galley and got this food," I said. "I'm mobile again, anyway." The wound to my left calf had gone deep, but it hadn't shattered the bone or cut anything vital. It was slowly healing.

"That's good," Tailor said. "I need you mobile. We're pulling into port right now. The crew says we should be at the pier in less than an hour."

"So?"

"So, we're leaving," Tailor said. "I collected your stuff for you. It's in a bag ready to go. Hudson's trying to find you some fresh clothes. You're hard to fit, you big son of a bitch." I was five inches taller than Tailor, and that always seemed to piss him off just a little.

"Where in the hell do you think you're going to go?" I asked. Tailor's plan sounded ill-thought-out to me.

"Val, listen. Between me and Hudson we've got three hundred and seventy-five grand, okay? We have plenty of money. It's enough for all of us to find room and board for a while, get some supplies, and lay low."

"Lay low?"

"Right, until things calm down. Then we can start thinking about going home, if it's safe. Now come on. You gonna be ready to go? You feel okay?"

I gave Tailor a hard look for a long moment. "Tailor, I'm not going anywhere," I said flatly.

"What are you talking about? We know for a fact that this ship is going to dock in Mumbai. We're getting off here. We don't know where in the hell they're going after this. We need to go while the going's good."

"Tailor, I'm not running away to India. I'm not going to go hide in a dirty safe house somewhere. I'm staying right here."

"Goddamn it, Val," Tailor said, anger rising in his voice. "Don't argue with me. You're not thinking clearly right now. Trust me. Get your shit and get ready to go."

"*Trust* you?" I said. "Trust you? Tailor, trusting you is how I ended up in Zubara in the first place!"

"Well, shit happens!" Tailor said, louder still. "I didn't force you. You wanted to go just as bad as I did, and you damn well know it. Now we need to get off this boat before these Exodus nut-jobs drag us off someplace and we disappear!"

"No, goddamn it! I'm sick of your shit! These 'nut-jobs' have saved our lives *twice* now. Maybe you didn't notice that they didn't charge you for getting out of Zubara? They helped us even though they're not getting anything out of it!"

"That we know of," Tailor interjected. "You don't know what they're planning. You can't trust these people. You don't know them. You need to listen to me. We both know I'm right."

"Listen to you? *You* were ready to take Gordon up on his offer!"

"What? Val, I—"

I cut Tailor off. "Shut up! If I hadn't been ready to shoot him, you would've probably signed up and left the rest of us behind! I know you, man. I *know* you. You just can't pass up an opportunity like that, can you? You know what the difference between you and me is? I don't know why the hell I do it. You, you do it because you're addicted to it. You're a goddamned war junkie!"

"You're about to piss me off, Val," Tailor warned, pointing a crooked finger at me.

"I don't give a shit!" I shouted. "Go ahead, get mad! What the fuck are you going to do? *Huh?* I have *nothing left*, Tailor! So hit me! Shoot me! I don't care! You'd be doing me a favor!"

Tailor's harsh expression softened just a little. "Val . . . ," he started.

I interrupted him again, much more quietly this time. "Tailor . . . I'm just tired. I can't do it anymore. Hell, it's all I can do to get out of bed. I've spent the last three days trying to think of reasons to bother, and I keep coming up short. I'm not going."

"I've already talked to the others, Val. We're going."

"I know. I understand. It's okay. If you guys want to go, then go. I know how it is, man. Don't worry about me. I can take care of myself."

"I've gotta go get ready," Tailor said. He turned to leave, but paused by the door. "I'll see you around, man," he said, and was gone.

VALENTINE
Exodus Base
Somewhere in Southeast Asia
May 20

Strange music echoed in my ears as I pushed open a heavy wooden door. I crossed the threshold and entered the room beyond, despite the suffocating sense of apprehension that squeezed my heart. Directly across from the door was an ornate four-poster bed. A painting hung on the wall above it, but I couldn't make it out.

Slowly I turned, looking across the room I was in. It was familiar; I'd been here before. At the far end of the room a woman hung from the ceiling, her hands bound above her head. I approached her, unsure of what was compelling me onward. The apprehension was turning into dread. My skin began to crawl.

I looked up at the girl as she hung from the ceiling, motionless. Her body had been cut open, her organs removed. Black hair hung down over her eyes, and her face was shrouded in darkness. I tried as hard as I could to focus on her, but I just couldn't make out her face.

I couldn't stand it anymore. I was overwhelmed by fear and confusion. I knew where I was, but I couldn't remember where that place was or why it was important. I didn't know how I got there. I turned to leave.

Something clamped down on my arm as I turned around, and squeezed. The girl was now standing behind me, grasping my arm with her hand. She lifted her head, the dark hair moving aside. It was Sarah. Her eyes were gone.

"You said you'd stay with me."

My eyes snapped open as I was wrenched back to consciousness. I sat up in bed, looking around the room, trying to remember where I was. It was dark. I nearly knocked my lamp off the table trying to turn the light on. The little fluorescent bulb flickered to life, and the room was illuminated with pale light.

My heart was pounding so hard I could feel it in my ears. I sat in bed for a few minutes, breathing through my nose, trying to calm down. I'd had that nightmare before. I had a nightmare every time I went to sleep.

I sighed and rubbed my face with my hands. The clock on the wall told me it was just after three in the morning. There would be no getting back to sleep tonight. Resigned to that, I swung my legs off the bed and stood up.

Exodus had housed me in a small metal Quonset hut that, despite its utilitarian appearance, was actually pretty comfortable. It lacked a kitchen but had its own bathroom. (In any case, I'm a terrible cook; I was more than happy to get my meals from the nearby cafeteria.) I headed into said bathroom to take the first leak of the day.

My heart was finally slowing down as I washed my hands. I missed Sarah so much it hurt. I knew her death wasn't my fault, but that didn't make it any better. She died because she came back for *me*. Worse still, *she* died and *I* lived. That was so unfair it made me sick.

Sarah was one of the kindest people I'd ever known. I, on the other hand, had spent most of my adult life shooting people for money. I had blood on my hands, and

I knew it. If anyone deserved to die, it was *me*. Worst of all, I'd broken my promise to her. I told her I'd stay with her until the end.

Looking down at my hands again, I realized I'd been washing them for several minutes straight. I got lost in thought like that once in a while, especially since I'd woken up on the *Walden*. I wondered if it was a side effect of them drilling holes in my head.

I turned off the water and looked at myself in the mirror. I barely recognized the man that looked back at me. My hair was buzzed short, military style. There was a horizontal cut across my forehead, just above the hairline over my right eye. This had been from a Zubaran grenade, I think. Another gash went from my left cheek up my face, splitting my eyebrow in two. Lorenzo, whoever the hell he really was, had given me that one. Missed my eye by a fraction of an inch. My right arm had been similarly carved up.

There were more still-healing scars from where Exodus doctors had treated my injuries. There was the mark on my shoulder from where a bullet grazed me after we assassinated Al Falah. Yet another one cut across my left calf, where a Zubaran bullet had winged me and caused me to fall on my face. Small frag marks peppered my arms and legs. I frowned at my reflection in the mirror before turning off the bathroom light.

Later in the morning, I found myself sitting on the bed, digging through the backpack that served as my bug-out bag. Inside were all the things I thought I'd need for a quick escape, or if I had to be on the go for a while. I'd had it with me when I'd been hit at Fort Saradia.

I laid several stacks of bills on the bed, my half of the money we'd taken from Adar's safe. It was a shame I'd lost my share of Lorenzo's money. I found a zippered pouch. Inside were my driver's license, passport, concealed firearms permit, and other personal identification documents that had been confiscated from me. I wondered if it was safe to use any of these documents. Were they looking for me? Did they think I was dead? Would I get flagged at the airport or something?

Hidden beneath a box of .44 Magnum ammunition was an envelope. I'd tried several times before to open it, but hadn't been able to bring myself to do it. But this time I succeeded. I carefully opened the envelope and removed the pictures inside.

These were the only pictures I had of Sarah. She'd gotten her hands on one of the cameras we had and used the equipment in the lab to print out photographs before clearing the camera's memory.

The first was one of me. It was an awful picture. I wasn't even looking at the camera. I was standing by a building, sunglasses up on my head, mouth open. I'd been halfway through a sentence when Sarah jumped me with the camera. It was a completely natural picture. The next one was of the two of us together. I had my arm awkwardly around Sarah's waist as she pulled me close to her. She had a bright smile on her face.

My God, she was so beautiful. I stared at the pictures for a long time. My hands started to shake. I set the pictures down and buried my face in my hands as my chest tightened. There, alone in my room, I sat on my bed and wept for the first time that I could remember.

Some time later, I noticed something else in the bag as I put the pictures away. It was Colonel Hunter's flash drive, with his bloody thumb print still on it. I had forgotten completely about it. I held it in my hand and struggled to remember, there was something important about what was on here. Information he wanted me to see. I had to take a look.

I made my way across the Exodus base in the early morning darkness. The base was a walled compound that seemed to have sprouted out of the jungle, big enough to house a couple hundred people. The low, utilitarian buildings were interspersed between huge trees and thick vegetation, permanently shrouded in shadow by triple-canopy tree cover overhead. Misty shafts of light would poke through the trees during the day, giving the base a very ethereal look, but right now it was dark.

The compound sat on a flat spot between thickly forested hills and a rocky beach. The dense tree cover probably made the place difficult to study from the air or by satellite. I could faintly hear the low rumble of waves over the constant din of nocturnal animals and insects, generators, and a few vehicles.

Across the rocky beach was a dock big enough to service a ship the size of the *Walden,* though that ship was long gone. On the other side of the compound, in a narrow clearing, was a short airstrip, and planes would occasionally come and go. Only one road led out of the compound. Out the gate, the gravel path wound its way through the hills until it disappeared.

Many areas of the small base were off-limits, at least to

me. An armed patrol roved the facility, and guards were posted at the entrances to a couple buildings. These areas were fenced off from the rest of the compound, even. Vehicle traffic was sparse, but there was a motorpool.

I'd been here for a couple of weeks, but hadn't ventured out much without Ling. While everyone I met was exceedingly polite, I was regarded as an outsider. No one spoke to me unless I engaged them in conversation first, except for Ling and Dr. Bundt. But I'd been around enough to know where to find a computer.

There was an Internet cafe in the compound, apparently for use by transient Exodus personnel who needed to check their e-mail or something. I'd been past it several times before, but had never gone in. What did I need to get on the Internet for? I was scared to even check my e-mail, lest the people behind Project Heartbreaker realize I was still alive. I suppose I could've at least checked the news or something, but honestly, at that point I didn't give a good goddamn what was happening to the rest of the world.

Entering the café, I noted that it was all but deserted at this early hour. Out of fifteen computers, only two were occupied. A squat Asian man sat behind a desk near the door, reading a newspaper in a language I didn't recognize.

I approached his desk. "Uh, good morning," I said awkwardly. "I need to use a computer."

"You come right place," he said with a thick accent, not lowering his paper. "This Internet place. Many computers. Here." He began to slide a laminated card across the desk to me, but stopped. "Wait. You guest. You can't get on Internet. Information security rules, okay? Sorry!"

"Listen, I really need to use a computer."

"No Internet, okay? Sorry!" he said, sounding testy.

"Listen. I don't need the Internet. I just need to use a computer. Please."

The clerk folded his newspaper in a huff and thought for a moment. "Okay. Use computer ten. Internet not work. Okay?"

"Uh, okay," I said. "Um, thank you." I turned on my heel and headed for computer number ten.

The computer, like most Internet cafe machines, was a few years old and was pretty beat-up. But it would do for my purposes. I fished Colonel Hunter's thumb drive out of my pocket and plugged it into a USB port. It took a few seconds for the computer to read the drive, then a window popped up displaying all of the available files. It wasn't even password protected; Hunter had put this together in a hurry.

There was more information on the drive than I could've imagined, hundreds of files. One was an initial proposal, more than five years old, describing the theory behind Project Heartbreaker. It was written by someone named Walter Barrington and was vague, at best.

> *The use of a DEAD unit would accomplish overall regional goal, but with limited chance of blowback to core elements. See success of D2 and D3 in completion of Project Red in China. The failures of D4 in Chechnya and the eradication of D5 in Mexico were unforeseen setbacks, but in no way undermine the viability of the DEAD program as some program administrators have alleged. I am*

certain Zubaran security could be achieved with a
limited expenditure of resources.

They had done this before.

There were personnel files for every member of Dead
Six, including our field leaders. I found mine. It proved to
be a fascinating if vaguely surreal read. It was almost
frightening how much they knew. My Air Force service,
details of my time with Vanguard, bank statements, phone
records, everything about me up until my recruitment.
After that were newer entries about my performance in
Zubara, evaluations, even notes regarding my relationship
with Sarah. Apparently, I had gained Hunter's admiration,
though he'd suspected I was a flight risk.

There were bios for every one of us, nearly clinical
assessments of our suitability. There was one common
thread in the pre-recruitment section. Nobody of importance would notice if we were gone.

The meat, the part that Hunter had entrusted me with,
came from his personal logs. There were two sections,
official daily entries reporting back to some unknown over-
seer about our operations, successes, goals, and losses.
April 1—Successfully neutralized terror cell in city. 20+
kills. No losses. It was all very professional. In addition to the
official entries, though, were his notes, almost like personal
journal entries. Apparently these had not been sent in
with his reports. *April 1—Tailor's chalk hit a club. Murdered*
a bunch of them. Burned it down. Sent a real message.
Good op. Not getting support from above. Logistics are a
nightmare. I've got a bad feeling about this one.

I began to skim.

April 15—Tailor and Valentine eliminated Adar. Gordon screwed them, sent just the two of them. Said he wasn't authorized more, but I think it was a test. I think he's eyeing them for Direct Action jobs. They got the job done, though. Chalks are running without enough support. Intel is shit. They're lucky to be alive. Two chalks have taken casualties now because of Gordon's bullshit. I don't know what he thinks he's doing, but nobody will answer my questions.

It seemed that Colonel Hunter had grown increasingly disaffected with the project as time went on. He distrusted his superiors, especially Gordon Willis.

April 18—I got confirmation today. The hit on the assistant ambassador was Gordon's call. Anders pulled the trigger. That was unnecessary. They were being evacuated anyway. They were no threat to OpSec. This was not part of the plan. This is not what I signed up with the organization for. Things have changed over the last twenty years, and not for the good.

Frustratingly, there was almost nothing *about* his organization on the drive other than a few scattered opinions. It was, however, pretty clear that whatever the late colonel's organization was, it was powerful, it operated strictly behind the scenes, and it had been around for a long time.

April 21—Singer is dead. Two chalks took heavy casualties. Gordon didn't give two shits, and now I know why. Gordon secured another asset for Project Blue. Blue is so much bigger, but still. As much as I dislike Gordon, I can't believe he'd compromise this entire operation just to boost his career.

That was one of the few mentions of Project Blue, but there was a lot more about Gordon. I learned a great deal about the man. Hunter had despised him and didn't trust him in the least.

May 5—We're done. I've not got the order yet, but I can read the writing on the wall. Project Heartbreaker is Gordon's baby, his ticket to upper-management. He lobbied for a DEAD op in Zubara. But by last month our superiors knew we were done. Zubara has spiraled out of control and I simply don't have the manpower to do anything about it. Too much reliance was placed on indigenous assets. The Emir is too weak. The best I can hope for is that we can kill a few more of these assholes before we pack it in. Gordon's withdrawn. He knows his career is shot.

By May 7, Gordon Willis had received orders to wrap up Project Heartbreaker as quickly and quietly as possible and prepare to withdraw all assets from Zubara. The hit on Rafael Montalban had taken Hunter by surprise. Even his official report had plainly stated that Gordon had ordered the op over Hunter's objection.

May 10—Gordon is up to something. Orders were hands off on anyone from the Rivals. Montalban was not on our list. Moving on someone as high up on their hierarchy as Rafael Montalban is an act of war. Gordon had to have cut a deal with somebody. This puts us all in danger. Our organization isn't ready for that kind of fight. The bastard. He'll hang for this.

The lack of details about Montalban's rival group was also frustrating. It was as if Hunter had expected whoever read this to already know about them.

I sat back from my computer and pinched the bridge of my nose, closing my eyes tightly for a moment. I realized I'd been reading for two hours and had scarcely learned a thing. What did he expect me to do with the information on this drive? Who could I give it to that would make a difference? Who would even believe me? I'd have a hard time proving that I'd been in Zubara at all, much less that there had been some kind of international conspiracy afoot there. Still, I wasn't ready to give up just yet. I rubbed my eyes and continued to read. There was only one entry left, dated the morning of Dead Six's betrayal.

May 11—Preparations for the evacuation have been made. I pushed for one last mission targeting General Al Sabah, hoping that maybe we could leave this country a little better off, but was denied. Gordon Willis left ahead of the rest of us. Probably hoping for a head start so he can try to explain this all away before I can file my official report. I think I know what he's up to. Turns out Rafael Montalban's second-in-command was his younger brother, Eduard. I've gathered some evidence that Eduard has been in contact with Gordon. I think the Montalbans just had a coup, only our organization will get the blame. I don't know why Gordon did it. He either got paid off by Eduard, or worse, he's more ambitious that I thought. Worst case scenario, he's trying to force us into a war so we can initiate his precious Project Blue. Even Gordon can't be that crazy.

I could figure out the rest. Instead of waiting for Hunter to burn Gordon to their mysterious organization, Gordon had turned the tables and sold us out to General Al Sabah.

Recording any of this is a direct violation of OpSec, but I have a bad feeling about tonight. This file is my insurance policy. The first DEAD unit was stood up thirty years ago. Detachment One, protecting the world from communism. I was on D1. We accomplished a lot of good, killed a lot of bad guys, saved a lot of lives, but things changed. We've changed. The organization has gone bad, turned rotten. I don't recognize it anymore. Men like Gordon Willis run it now. I used to be proud of what I did, but not anymore.

> *The plan is to evacuate by ship. A handful of*
> *D6 have been approached and accepted perma-*
> *nent positions with the organization.*

Gordon had tried to hire me and Tailor, and I had
nearly shot him. The personnel files were still open in
another window. It looked like some of us on the chalks
had been approached, and it appeared several had agreed.
Sarah hadn't been approached, though; neither had Anita
King. In fact, there was a note on all the support-staff files
that they were *unsuitable for recruitment.* Curious, I
continued with Hunter's final entry.

> *The recruits and I will rendezvous with a*
> *chopper in the gulf for transport home. As for the*
> *rest, once out to sea, the evacuation ship will be*
> *destroyed, terminating the remainder of D6*
> *deemed to be security risks.*

Shocked, I stopped reading. I must have made a noise,
since the man running the café gave me a disapproving
look before going back to his paper.

> *It pains me. These boys fought and died*
> *thinking they did it for their country. I was the*
> *same way once. But most of these boys were dead*
> *before they left the States. They didn't even know*
> *it. It was Gordon's suggestion to our superiors*
> *when this mission started to go off the rails.*
> *Anyone who might talk about our operation was to*
> *be eliminated. The control staff especially knew too*

much. Gordon decreed that they were to be on that boat, no matter what. I disagreed, but he outranked me. Too dangerous, he said. Deniable and expendable, he said. Then, when command agreed with Gordon's plan, I knew for sure that this outfit had gone straight to hell.

I'm amazed that command went along with this. I'm fighting to get the order rescinded. I volunteered to stay, to try to force their hand. Majestic used to mean something. I can't let this stand.

Majestic? Was *that* who I'd been working for? I'd heard the name before, but only on *From Sea to Shining Sea.* I thought they were just some ridiculous conspiracy theory. It seemed less ridiculous now that I'd ridden in a few stealthy black helicopters.

But there it was, in black and white, right in front of me. I had worked for Majestic. And not only had Gordon Willis betrayed us, but he'd apparently betrayed them as well. More importantly, he had personally and deliberately orchestrated Sarah's death. If the Zubarans hadn't killed her, then Majestic would have.

I sat there staring at the screen. My heart began to pound so hard I could feel it in my chest. My hands were shaking. A pit formed in my stomach. I felt something well up inside of me that I hadn't felt since the morning my mother was murdered. My eyes narrowed slightly, and I scrolled back through the documents to confirm something I'd seen. Yes, there it was. Gordon Willis's home address.

I stood up from the computer and shoved the thumb drive back into my pocket. I left to find Ling; I needed to talk to her. It was time for me to go home.

Ling was teaching children to fight.

I found her near the docks, working in a large structure with corrugated steel walls and a dirt floor. It had been a storage building once, but it had been turned into a training dojo. Ling was standing in front of twenty kids, boys and girls, the oldest maybe sixteen, the youngest approximately twelve, while she yelled at them in Chinese. Though I hadn't made any noise, she turned when I entered, giving me a small nod, as if to say *give me a moment*.

Turning back to her class, she continued shouting. There was nothing gentle about her commands. I only knew a handful of words in Chinese, but I gathered that she was not pleased with their efforts. The children were all barefoot, wearing shorts and T-shirts, and every last one of them was drenched in sweat. At Ling's command the kids broke into pairs and immediately set about trying to murder each other. It wasn't the sort of sparring you'd expect from children being taught martial arts. They fought each other viciously. The soft dirt floor had seemed odd at first, but as I saw a teenager go bouncing across it on her head, I could understand the logic.

"Shen?" Ling asked. "Would you continue the lesson?"

There was movement in the doorway I'd just come through. A short Asian man wearing green fatigues passed by. I had not heard him at all. He dipped his head, giving me just the briefest acknowledgment as I jumped in surprise. He took Ling's place in front of the class as she approached.

"How long has he been following me?"

"Since your arrival," Ling explained. "Shen is very good at what he does." Shen caught one of the teenage boys by the wrist, mid-punch, and began to berate him for something in Chinese. He proceeded to demonstrate by putting the kid in an arm bar and then tossing him on his face until the kid desperately tapped the dirt for mercy. "We meant no offense, but you are a stranger here. Some were nervous about your presence. Your status has allowed some leeway, but I needed to placate others. My apologies. You are looking well," she said, sounding slightly less serious. "Are you feeling better?"

"Much." My health was improving, but my mood wasn't. Shen kicked a girl's legs out from under her. "He was in Mexico with you, wasn't he?"

"Yes. He is alive because of you. All of us from that day are."

I shrugged. The attention made me self-conscious. "I just did what anyone would have done. It was nothing."

Ling shook her head. "No. It is the reason you are here. Your actions in Mexico earned our gratitude. You alone risked your life against impossible odds to ensure our survival. Exodus does not take its debts lightly. You are a bit of a legend in some circles."

That explained some of the odd looks I'd gotten while I'd been here. These Exodus people were a strange bunch. "Hey, how is . . . you know, *the girl*? The one we rescued? Is she here?"

Ling smiled at me. "She will be disappointed to learn

that she's missed your visit, assuming that she doesn't already know. I'm afraid she's not here. She is well."

I had about a thousand more questions about the mysterious girl we rescued in Mexico, but the look on Ling's face and the tone of her voice told me she wouldn't answer any of them. My thoughts were interrupted when one of the kids screamed when a punch landed way too hard. "That's pretty rough," I suggested. "Aren't they a little young for this?"

Ling thought about it for a moment. "And how much older were you when you killed the men who murdered your mother?"

How the hell had she known that? I was sick of everyone knowing more about me than I did about them. It was none of her damn business. When I didn't respond, Ling continued. "It takes dedication to become a member of Exodus."

"You're teaching little kids to kill."

"I'm teaching them how to *survive*. They are all volunteers. These *children* have seen horrors that even you cannot imagine. Yes, we teach them to fight, to kill, and when they're older, someone like me will lead them into battle. Several of these children have already seen war. Others, like that young man there, were forced to watch as their family was murdered by the agents of a genocidal tyrant. That girl was abducted from her home and sold into slavery. They were all forgotten by the world and survived their ordeals only by the grace of God. We teach them the skills they need to not only survive, but *prevail*. They will go from being helpless to being able to help others."

This was very personal for her; I could hear it in her voice. "You went through something similar yourself once, didn't you?"

The look she gave me was cold. "I'm assuming you did not come here to judge my organization or my beliefs. So, what is it that I can do for you, Mr. Valentine?"

"I need transport back to the States."

Ling studied me with her dark eyes as she thought about my request. "There is nothing for you there now."

I answered without hesitation. "There's one thing."

"Of course." Ling thought about it for a moment. "Walk with me, Michael."

There was a rocky path down the shore. Ling led the way. Walking was still difficult, and after a few minutes of exercise, I'd developed a terrible headache. Ling sat on a big chunk of volcanic rock and gestured at a spot for me to sit. "I apologize. I just wanted someplace private to talk. It is easy to forget you recently underwent surgery."

"I'm fine," I insisted, carefully making my way across the rocks before sitting down. The sun was climbing into a brilliantly blue sky over the jungle behind us as incoming waves gently rolled in. It was quite a view.

Ling was quiet for a few moments. She brushed a loose strand of her long, black hair out of her face as she looked out over the ocean. I couldn't guess what she was thinking; I'm pretty perceptive, I think, but this woman was impossible to read. Before I could say anything, though, she asked me a question. "What changed?"

"What do you mean?" I asked.

"You've been with us for quite a while now, and seemed content enough with our hospitality. Until this morning, that is, when you suddenly decided you need to return to the United States. I don't need to tell you how risky that could be for you. Your former employers are not people to be trifled with. Right now they most likely think you're dead. Is it not better to go on letting them think that, rather than to risk being tracked down?"

Ling knew more about Project Heartbreaker than she let on. Once again, the Exodus operative seemed to know a lot more about what was going on than I did, and I was getting sick of it. I'd had enough of being the last one to know everything.

"Look," I said, trying to be firm without being rude. "I don't really want to get into it. Nothing personal. I just thought about it last night, and I think it's time for me to go home. I mean, I can't stay here forever."

She raised an eyebrow at me. "I see." She sounded dubious. "I take it you learned something new while using the computer this morning?"

I took a deep breath before I said anything. I hated being spied on, but there was nothing to be gained by getting angry with Ling. I needed her help. "Yes, I did, but I don't want to talk about it. I'm sorry to impose on you again. And please don't think I'm not grateful for everything you've done for me. You saved my life, and the lives of my friends. But I really can't stay here."

"When I was thirteen," Ling began casually, looking out over the ocean again, "my parents were arrested by State Security. They were Christians and tried to flee with me to the South when the war started. I was sent to a Communist Party School to be reeducated. I never saw them again."

"That's . . . awful, I said hesitantly. "I didn't know."

"Four years later I was conscripted into the Women's Auxiliary of the People's Liberation Army. I was wounded in the Third Battle of Shanghai later that year. Our forces were in complete disarray after Shanghai was destroyed by a nuclear weapon. A corrupt officer sold me and a dozen other women to a band of human traffickers from South China in exchange for the equivalent of five thousand dollars. I spent the next two years in hell before I was rescued by Exodus. Like the children you met this morning, I immediately volunteered. I've been here ever since."

"Why are you telling me all this?"

"I realized that I know everything about you, Michael," she said, casting me a sidelong glance, "and you know nothing about me. I can tell that bothers you. I will arrange for you to return to America if you wish. But will you please tell me why?"

My expression hardened as I carefully chose my words. "They told me I was doing a great thing, that I was serving my country. We went over there for that reason. For many of us, it was a second chance, an offer of redemption. They sent us on missions that were so dangerous it was a joke. Many of my friends died in the process. We never quit. Not a single one of my teammates asked to go home."

"Until you contacted me," Ling injected.

"It wasn't about me anymore. It was about Sarah. And I saw the writing on the wall. I didn't trust the people I worked for. I was worried they'd leave us hanging if things went south." I shook my head bitterly. "I hate it when I'm right."

Ling gave me a faint smile. "Michael, I could tell that the night you and your friends met me in Zubara. I knew right away it was about her."

"We went over there trying to do the right thing. No matter what they asked of us, we did it. We accomplished the impossible. I did terrible things, killed so many people, because they told me it was necessary. They told me I was protecting my country. And what did we get for it? They turned us over to the people we'd been fighting and left us all to die. Their brilliant plan didn't work the way they thought it would, so they made a deal with the enemy because suddenly we were inconvenient."

"And who is 'they'?" Ling asked.

"They're called Majestic, but it's just a name. I don't know if it really means anything. I was given a lot of information by my boss before he died, and even with all that, I don't really understand everything that was going on. There are too many layers to know who's really pulling the strings, you know? But I do have one name. Gordon Willis. He was the guy that recruited me. He's the one that sold us out. He's the reason Sarah's dead."

Ling gave me a hard look for a few seconds. "I see," she said at last. "It is as I thought. I could see it in your eyes when you found me this morning."

"See what?"

"The hatred, the anger, the desire for revenge. I know these things very well. These are the things that motivated me to join Exodus in the beginning. I volunteered with the idea that I would eventually track down the PLA officer that sold me and my comrades to the slavers. I fantasized about that often when I began my training. And when I was done with that corrupt officer, I was going to go after the Communist Party running dogs that took me away from my parents." Ling actually chuckled, as if telling a silly story about her petulant youth.

"I take it that didn't work out?"

"Of course it didn't. I don't know the name of the officer that was responsible for what happened to me, even if he survived the war. Exodus doesn't have the capability to overthrow the Communist government of North China. And operations aren't planned around the angry wishes of eighteen-year-old new recruits. People who join Exodus only to seek revenge don't last very long."

"Ling, I see where you're going with this, but I don't—"

"*Do* you now?" Ling said sharply, interrupting me. "I told you all this because I want you to know that I understand how you feel. I know too well the bitter taste of betrayal, the frustration of being powerless to change a vile injustice. I understand the desire to avenge your dead comrades and bring justice to those responsible, probably better than you do. I'm not trying to talk you out of doing what you think you need to do."

I said nothing. Now I was just confused.

Ling smiled. "Surprised? Exodus's reason for being is to fight for those who can't fight for themselves, to avenge those that the world has forgotten, and speak for those who have been silenced. Look around you. The world teeters on the brink of the abyss; civilization dangles by a thread. On every corner of the earth there is oppression, injustice, slavery, and tyranny. In far too many places freedom is being stamped out under a jackboot. In other places, people are slaughtered wholesale for being the wrong race or religion. Meanwhile the so-called *civilized world* blithely ignores these horrors so long as they don't interrupt the latest reality-television program."

I was taken aback. Ling was one of the most reserved people I'd ever met.

"For six hundred years," she continued, "Exodus has stood alone against the darkness. For six hundred years, we've fought for the dignity and the freedom of the individual. For generations we've fought, and died, for the idea that every human life has value, and that the individual is as important as the kingdom or the state. We fight for the idea that every person is accountable for his actions, no matter how powerful or exalted he may be."

My God, I thought. *The woman is a fanatic.*

Ling straightened her hair and blushed slightly. "I apologize, Michael. I get carried away on occasion. I am very passionate about this, I'm afraid."

"I can, uh, see that," I managed. *Crazy,* I didn't add.

"I do have a point," Ling said, obviously a little embarrassed. "As I said, I'm not trying to talk you out of doing what you think you must do. My whole life is dedicated to bringing vengeance to the corrupt and the wicked. I am in no position to lecture you about doing the very same thing in your own way."

"I don't understand," I said. "Why did you bring me out here?"

"Really, Michael, I just wanted to talk to you. You obviously had something on your mind."

"So . . . you'll help me go home, then?"

"Yes, of course," she said. "It might take a little time,

but we will find you a safe way to return to the United States, if that's what you really want. We'll be sorry to lose you, but I'm not going to stand in your way." Ling's expression hardened. "I do have some advice for you. There's a very fine line between avenging those who have been wronged and seeking revenge for your own gratification. It's easy to stray from one side to the other. Once you start down that path, it becomes harder and harder to turn around. There's no telling where it will lead you, and you may not like where you end up. You may find yourself digging your own grave in addition to your enemy's. Are you prepared to deal with the consequences?"

"I don't know," I said honestly, looking out over the ocean. "But I don't have anything to lose. They took everything from me. My life, my friends . . . Sarah. What else can I do?"

"Would Sarah have wanted you to make this choice?"

Ling stared at me for a few seconds. I really didn't have an answer to that. The question made me uncomfortable. After a moment, Ling's expression softened. I could almost see the gears turning behind her dark eyes, but as usual she gave no indication of what she was thinking. I was taken by complete surprise when she grabbed my hand and squeezed it tightly.

"Walk with God, Michael," she said. "And please be careful." She let go of my hand, stood up, and turned away. She paused after a few steps and looked over her shoulder. "It will take me a few days, maybe a bit longer, to make the preparations. I'll come get you when it's time."

Ling then walked away without looking back.

♠

Chapter 23:
The Heist

LORENZO
June 15

Countdown to D-Day.

The radio was on in the background. Just as I had expected, General Al Sabah's true colors were showing. All of Zubara's major industries had been nationalized, and if you didn't like it, too bad, please line up against that wall and wait your turn. The brain drain of the upper-class fleeing was already starting to affect the running of the country. People who had cheered the general's rise to power a few short months ago were cursing now as their property was confiscated. The university had been closed down, the remains turned over to the craziest mullah he could find. The Zoob was toast.

People never learn. It made me kind of melancholy. I had liked this city. But it didn't matter, we'd be leaving for our meeting in Saudi Arabia shortly, and I didn't plan on ever coming back. I'd had some good times here. Shaking my head, I went back to work comparing three different shades of brown contact lenses so that I could match Falah perfectly. *Good times?* I was just being stupid. Carl shouted for me from the garage.

"What do you think?" he asked proudly when I came down the stairs. He was gesturing at the massive black car that filled the entire space. "No more of that pussy van. This is *class*." It was a Mercedes-Benz 600 luxury car, built in 1968. When I had explained the plan to Carl, he had been very specific about what kind of vehicle we would need. "six point three liter V8, single overhead cam, Bosch *mechanical* fuel injection, hydraulic suspension, sweet mother of God, it has hydraulic windows and trunk lid."

"You're starting to sound like Reaper," I said.

Carl shook his head at my apparent lack of appreciation for automotive excellence. "No soft electronics, genius. I've worked this baby over. She's cherry. I don't know where Hosani found her, but damn." He whistled.

"Maybe he bought it off Fidel Castro?"

Reaper was in the backseat, bolting Starfish down. Our testing yesterday out in the boondocks had shown it was ready to go. He chimed in. "Pol Pot, Kim Jong Il, and Ceaucescu drove one of these, too. Idi Amin, Ferdinand Marcos, all the real bad asses. This is the ultimate dictator dope-ride."

"Don't forget Elvis Presley," I added. "And the Popemobile."

"See," Carl insisted. "Those guys *know* class." He turned back to the car sadly. "Too bad we've got to trash her."

"Every mission has casualties. We're sacrificing her for

the greater good." I put my arm over his shoulder. "Dude, we live through this and I'll buy you *two*."

Carl patted the hood fondly. "I'm gonna hold you to that, Lorenzo."

LORENZO

East of Riyadh, Kingdom of Saudi Arabia
June 18

Phase Three begins.

The palace compound rose out of the bleak desert like some ancient monument. It was the only human habitation for miles, with nothing but sand stretching in every direction as far as the eye could see. It had once been an oasis and was now a self-contained miniature city. Isolation was the complex's first layer of defense. There was no way to sneak in. If you wanted to get through those walls, you needed an invitation.

Behind the walls lived a staff numbering in the hundreds, and only a select few of them were ever allowed to leave. Every inch of the interior was constantly monitored. The security here was so unbelievably tight that only once a year were outsiders allowed into the inner sanctum.

The temperature outside was so bad that the window glass of the limousine was scorching hot to the touch, but the overburdened air conditioner kept me semi-comfortable in my traditional robes and additional fake fat padding. Starfish was sitting on the floor next to my legs, black and ominous. "Reaper, is this thing going to give me cancer?"

"Probably not. Now back to quizzing. Third wife's name and birthday?" Reaper spoke from the front seat. He looked much different with his hair in a neat ponytail and wearing a suit. Both he and Carl were sporting the black-sunglasses bodyguard look.

"Sufi. August twentieth, 1985," I answered, switching back to Arabic. I tugged on the fake beard that had been weaved into the real one I'd grown out over the last two months and dyed gray. "She is a shrill little harpy, who will give a man no rest."

"What do you think about football?" Carl asked.

I checked the glued on latex attachment on my nose. It itched horribly but looked perfect. "It is a pathetic distraction that takes our young men away from more important pursuits, such as jihad or reading the scriptures," I replied, knowing that my tone and inflection was a perfect match to the hours of recorded tapes of Falah's conversations. Then in my own voice in English, "But I think Al-Nasiffia will take the regional championships."

"Quit screwing around, you need to be in character." The palace was growing larger through the window. We were close now. The walls were forty feet tall and thick enough to withstand anything short of 105mm direct fire. FLIR cameras swiveled downward to examine us. The massive front gate hydraulically opened as we neared.

I cleared my mind. For the next few minutes, I needed to think and act as if I were Ali bin Ahmed Al Falah, terrorist scumbag. We passed through the tunnel in the wall and entered the Garden of freaking Eden. A paradise waited inside the walls. It had trees, orchards, a lake with spiraling fountains, and behind that was the palace itself.

The small model in our hideout had not done the thing justice. It was *huge*.

But I wasn't here for the palace. I was after what was *under* it.

My trained eye picked up the multitude of cameras and guard posts watching us. We stopped at the base of the palace, and I prepared myself as my "bodyguards" exited and opened my door. Carl extended a hand and helped me out. The heat was like a blast furnace.

I was in character now.

A hulking brute of a man approached, with four rifle-armed guards trailing behind him. He looked awkward in a suit. "Ali bin Ahmed Al Falah, my name is Hassan, and I am the director of security for Prince Abdul."

"What happened to Adar?" I asked suspiciously. "He was in charge of security the last time I was here."

"He left for other opportunities," Hassan replied without hesitation. In reality he had left for Iraq, where there were more opportunities to hurt people, until Falah had called him to Zubara.

"Of course. I had not heard from my old friend recently. I've been worried about him."

"Please come with me, sir. The other guests have already arrived."

I followed Hassan up the stairs, Carl and Reaper behind me, and the four guards behind them. I spotted at least one sniper on the roof. There were two helicopters parked on a nearby pad. Several other limos and expensive super-cars were parked just forward of mine. Through the steel-reinforced twelve-foot front doors, cold air washed over us as we came into the entryway that was bigger than the largest house I'd ever lived in. A solid gold chandelier was overhead, and the best word to describe the interior of the palace was opulent. Paintings and statues that would have been centerpiece attractions at the finest museums in the world lined the walls, mere trinkets here. The prince had some cash.

Hassan gestured toward a metal detector manned by two more guards. Adar's box was safely concealed inside my padding. Whatever metal the key was made out of didn't trigger metal detectors, we'd already checked. I stepped through, clean, followed by my crew.

Nobody brought weapons anywhere near the prince.

It beeped as Carl stepped through. The four guards lifted their guns slightly. Carl raised his hands. "I got a piece of metal stuck in my back," he stated. Two other men appeared and immediately led Carl aside for a more invasive search. As a VIP, I knew that I would be spared such indignities.

Hassan held up one gigantic hand to stop me. "I apologize for the inconvenience, but surely you must understand, with all the questionable activity concerning your disappearance and the resulting confusion, I need to be sure of your identity before I allow you into the presence of Prince Abdul." He held a small box with a scanner window in his other hand. It had two lights on it. One red. One green.

"But of course," I replied. Without hesitation, I put my right thumb on the window.

Reaper had spent hours testing the prosthetic attachment. It was a relatively new technology, and the single, tiny piece of etched, synthetic flesh glued to my hand had cost a ton, and just to be on the safe side, I was wearing one on each finger. Micro engraved with pre-programmed whirls and ridges, it was the most practical way to fool a fingerprint machine. The machine would only read Falah's fingerprints.

The red light lit up.

Not cool. A single bead of sweat rolled down my back. The guards shifted, spreading out around me.

Hassan shook his head. "Technology, it never works right. Please try again, sir."

I put my thumb on the glass. Hassan nodded at the guard behind me. If this didn't work, we were going to die. Horribly. Turn green, you little bastard.

Green light.

"Ah, excellent. I apologize for the inconvenience." Hassan smiled. His teeth looked slightly pointed. "There is just one more thing. I have someone who wishes to speak with you, an old friend who was most shocked by your sudden disappearance." He clapped his hands.

"Please hurry," I said with some exasperation. This was not good. We had not planned on anyone close to Falah being at the palace. He was known to these people, but only because of an annual meeting. Conning a close associate was a thousand times more difficult than mere business acquaintances. "I do not wish to be late."

A young man in a gray guard's uniform came around the corner. "Al Falah!" he exclaimed, his face lighting up. "Oh, I was so sure you had been murdered."

Flash back to the apartment, hours spent going over the cards, each card a picture of one of Falah's people, with a name and a description on the back. Carl had quizzed me mercilessly, hammering these strangers into my brain. "Rashid!" I exclaimed. "What are you doing here?" *Really, what was he doing here?* Rashid was one of the bodyguards that had supposedly been killed during the hit. He had been in the chase car that had taken off after the sniper. This was way too close.

I'd been practicing for weeks, talking like Falah, moving like him, watching videos, listening to phone calls, and then finally watching him in person in the club, conversing with the man, playing games of chess against him, all coming down to this.

"I saw you get shot, and then we chased the assassins. They crashed into our car. I was the only one who lived. I woke up, and there was this tall American standing over me. He pointed this huge revolver at my face. I prayed for my life. He fired, but the bullet only grazed my head." He eagerly indicated a long scar going down the side of his head. "I thought I was dead, but Merciful Allah spared me!"

Valentine, you cock-fag sack of shit monkey-humping pus ball!

I smiled broadly. "How fortuitous."

"But how did *you* live?" He studied me carefully, obviously suspicious. Apparently he'd shared his concerns with Hassan also, because the tall man had that look in his eye that suggested he was ready to break me in half at a moment's notice.

"I hired Khalid, from the club, to stand in my place. I had heard rumors of Americans operating in the city, and it worried me. Allah smiled upon me, as I had been wise to do so. Rashid, I'm so very glad to see that you are alive."

I spoke as he spoke. I moved as he moved. I was Ali bin Ahmed Al Falah.

"As am I to see you." He grinned, buying the act, then nodded at Hassan. "I am working for the prince now, but I would be honored to serve you again, should you ever need me."

"Of course. Thank you, my son."

Hassan gestured toward the epic marble staircase. "Right this way, sir. The meeting is about to start. Your men will stay here, and we will provide them refreshment." I nodded at Carl and Reaper. They knew what to do.

There was an elevator shaft in the center of the staircase. Hassan and I traveled up several floors. The motors were utterly silent, and it was the smoothest elevator I'd ever ridden. The control panel was encrypted, and the basement levels couldn't be accessed without authorization from central control. Even the carpet inside the elevator was so thick that I left footprints.

"The prince respects you a great deal," Hassan said, attempting small talk. "He was worried that you might have been hurt in the recent unpleasantness."

"I am only sorry that so many of our brave brothers gave their lives to the cowardly Americans," I answered. "And I'm greatly troubled that I would have caused a man as noble as Prince Abdul any distress. I do hope that he will accept my humble apologies."

The door whisked open at the top floor. We exited into a long hallway, and Hassan led the way into a meeting room the size of an aircraft hangar.

It was only because of Big Eddie that I knew anything about this meeting which was conducted annually in extreme secrecy. By special invitation only, it was a gathering of the region's movers and shakers, and a handful of special guests from the rest of the world. Businessmen, politicians, scions of powerful families, royalty, and propaganda masters, some of the most important string-pullers on Earth were gathered here. Unspeakable things were planned in this room, agendas set, and massive checks written. This was where the real behind-the-scenes action took place.

Reaper's conspiracy-theory radio would have a heart attack.

The guests were milling around, eating endangered species off a buffet table that could feed Ecuador for a year, mingling and waiting for their host to arrive. I recognized many of them from the flashcards, others from the news. I stayed in character, passing through the room, looking for familiar faces, watching for anyone who might know the terrorist financier that I was pretending to be. In this crowd, Falah was a low-level player. He barely ranked an invite only due to his many contacts. If a bombing was going down within 1,500 miles, Falah probably knew about it beforehand.

The prince had not arrived yet. In a country with 4,000 members of the royal family, he was not even close to being the heir, but through malicious use of his fortune, Prince Abdul had carved a place for himself as the ultimate arbiter of power in the Middle East, and since the world's economy had stupidly become dependent upon this region's resources, the decisions he made affected every person on the planet. He had his fingers in everything, oil, war, politics, even entertainment. Nothing happened here unless the prince had knowledge of it. OPEC was his bitch.

The annual meeting was held for two reasons. First, so the prince could set his agenda for the next year, and coerce or bribe the various VIPs to work together to accomplish his goals. Second, it was to stroke his massive ego. He liked being so important that presidents and dictators jumped at his command. Factions that absolutely hated each other came together for this meeting, all evil but each hoping to be the side that curried the prince's favor this year. This must be what Satan's throne room was like.

Of the hundred or so guests, there were maybe a dozen Europeans, a few Asians, and a handful of Africans. I recognized one American, a former senator who was surely here lobbying on behalf of something nefarious.

There was one man standing to the side that I knew immediately, not from the flashcards but from the protestor's signs. General Al Sabah had come himself to pay respects to the ultimate Godfather. He looked a little uncomfortable. Maybe his ascension hadn't had the prince's blessing, but he'd earned his way in through ruthlessness. I'm sure he'd fit right in.

Flash back to the model. Remember the layout. Focus on the mission.

A hand fell on my shoulder. I slowly turned. It was one of the Europeans. "Ah, Mr. Al Falah. What a pleasure to meet you," the man said. He didn't look like much.

Falah's English was rough, halting, and so was mine. "The pleasure is mine . . ." I did not recognize him from the flashcards. "Mister?"

"Montalban. Eduard Montalban." He smiled, but his eyes were pools of nothing. I had looked into serpent's eyes that held more soul. He leaned in close and hissed in my ear, "But for you, Lorenzo, my friends call me Big Eddie."

I couldn't speak. Big Eddie was *real*.

His accent was British, and his manner was effeminate. His nails were manicured, and each finger had some form of expensive jewelry on it. Probably only in his thirties, with Flock of Seagulls hair and dark circles under his eyes, he looked skinny and weak. He even spoke with a bit of a lisp.

All this time, I had been picturing Lex Luthor, and instead I got Carson from Queer Eye. It was a bit of a shock. As Carl would say, Big Eddie was a *poofter*. This really wasn't what I had expected.

But I would be a fool to underestimate him. I knew for a fact that he was directly responsible for hundreds, if not thousands, of murders. He was a pure killer. This man had more blood on his hands than anyone could ever imagine.

"Nice to meet you, Mr. Montalban. I do not believe that I've seen you at this meeting before." It was difficult to stay in Al Falah mode and not just snap his neck. The room was lined with guards, and I wouldn't make it ten feet. I could live, well, die with that, but it would seal my crew's fate as well.

"No. You would be correct. This is my first year. Normally my half-brother represents the family interests." Eddie did not blink as he appraised me. My initial take had been correct. There was no soul in there. He was empty.

"It is unfortunate that he could not make it."

"Yes. His boat exploded. Bloody sad bit of business,

that." He glanced over his shoulder at the American delegation. "That Senator Kenton is a batty shit, isn't she? Hag just won't shut up. Her people are a constant pain in my arse."

"Indeed. Filthy Americans," I responded. *What was he doing here?* I struggled to be polite while the wheels in my brain were turning. "So, what is it that you do, Mr. Montalban?"

"The family business." he waved his hand dismissively. "Shipping, mostly. All the oil in the world won't do any good if they can't move it, you know. I don't trouble myself with the details." Then Eddie leaned back in and whispered into my good ear. "Just a slight change of plan, chap. You just keep up the good work. Pretend I'm not here." His closeness made me cringe.

"This wasn't part of the deal," I whispered.

"I make the deal. You do what I say." He must have caught the murderous glimmer in my eye. "That would be a mistake, my friend. Even if you succeeded in taking me out, your family would still die."

"What do you want?"

His breath stank of menthol lozenges. "Why, you're a legend. The family wouldn't be where it was today if it hadn't been for you. I just wanted to meet you in person." He reached up and tugged on the end of my beard. "I'd say face-to-face, but this is close enough. You're probably the best employee I've ever had. When you quit, I was simply *heartbroken*."

I had been warned back then. Nobody left Big Eddie's service. *Nobody*. "Yeah, me, too."

"Do your job. Now get back to work." Eddie adjusted

his silk tie as he walked away, waving foppishly at someone else, returning to the party.

Focus on the plan. Deal with Eddie later. It took me a moment to compose myself. Why had he bothered? It didn't make any sense. *Shit.* He'd told me his name. He was going to kill me.

Servants in tuxedos began to usher the guests away from the buffet and toward a rectangular table the size of a basketball court. Bummer, since the harp seal looked delicious. The meeting was about to begin. I could only hope that Reaper and Carl were ready. I checked Falah's Rolex, the meeting was exactly on schedule. It was time.

Hanging back, I waited for the group to begin to sit in their assigned places around the giant table. The room gradually darkened; projectors came out of the ceiling and displayed images and maps on the walls. The prince entered the room, and the power brokers politely clapped. Prince Abdul was one of the richest people in the world. If he woke up with a tummy ache, gas prices would go up fifty cents a gallon by lunchtime, so you damn well better believe they clapped.

While the main attention was elsewhere, I grimaced, stumbled, and caught myself on the edge of the buffet table. There was a servant by my side almost instantly.

"Are you all right, sir?"

"My arm hurts. Oh, my chest." I gasped and wheezed, doing my best to contort my face. The servant was on a radio, and I had a guard on each arm helping me toward the exit within seconds. In the background, the prince was giving his opening comments. Most of the power brokers did not notice my exit. Big Eddie winked.

♠ ♠ ♠

We had memorized the layout of the palace. Every room and corridor was known to me. I knew exactly where I was as the guards pushed my wheelchair down the marble hall. The infirmary was the tenth room on this wing. The guards chattered into their radios, asking for one the prince's physicians to meet them.

"Oh, the pain." I was really milking it. "It is my heart again. Summon my men; they have my special medication."

"Do as he says!" one of the guards ordered as he rolled me into the white-walled room filled with state-of-the-art medical equipment. They gently lifted my padded bulk onto a padded table. There were two guards in the room now.

This was right where I needed to be. The building plans indicated that the infirmary backed up to the secondary security-control station. They shared the same wiring conduit behind the walls. The plans said that the access panel was ten feet from the northwest corner. Reaper figured that it would look like a half-size metal door with electrical warning stickers on it. *There.*

"Dr. Karzi, it is Al Falah, one of the guests. He has fallen ill. He says it is his heart," one of the guards exclaimed as an older man entered the room, pulling a white smock over his starched shirt and tie. He rudely pushed the guard aside and pressed his fingers against my neck. He scowled.

"That is odd," he muttered. "Describe your pain."

"It hurts." I held up my arm and risked a glance at my watch. I had been playing sick now for three minutes, which meant Carl had probably tripped Starfish's timer by now. "I need my men . . . my medicine . . ." On cue, Reaper appeared, being led by a third guard. He gave me an imperceptible nod.

The doctor began to open the front of my traditional dress. "Your heart rate is only forty beats per minute. Something is abnormal." There were some downsides to having ice water running through your veins.

"I have his medication," Reaper said, holding up the briefcase he had been allowed to obtain from our car. Sadly, there were no guns in it, because we had been certain that even in this scenario, they would probably still give it a cursory check. He opened the case.

The doctor was going to figure out something was wrong any second now. The guards looked more concerned for my health than for any trickery. Well, they should be concerned; Al Falah was buddies with every badass terrorist in the business. I was the equivalent of a rock star to these guys.

Several stories below, Starfish was counting down to firing. I was technically illiterate, but Reaper had done his best to educate me. Starfish was a NNEMPD, a Non-Nuclear Electromagnetic Pulse Device. When Starfish's timer hit zero, it was going to use a small amount of explosives to cause a compressed magnetic flux. It would nail every electronic device within a couple hundred yards with the equivalent of getting struck by lightning ten times in a quarter of a second.

Reaper came out with a syringe full of amber liquid. He tapped it and squirted a bit out to remove the air bubbles. The doctor glanced at him. "This isn't a coronary. What is his condition?"

The lights went out, plunging the room into pure black.

"Just plain mean," Reaper answered.

I nailed the doctor with an elbow to the face and then sprung off the table, moving in the direction of the three guards. I couldn't see, but I had been expecting this. They were caught by surprise. A shape moved in front of me. I kicked straight out, low and fast, and caught someone in the knee. There was a scream. A hand grabbed my thobe and pulled. I grabbed the wrist, twisted it, and levered it down, snapping bones. I palm-struck that guard in the throat and put him down.

The emergency power kicked on a second later. The place was certainly efficient. The third guard was down, Reaper's syringe in his neck. The man with the broken knee fumbled with the strap over his pistol. I snap-kicked him in the face, and he was done.

Reaper retrieved the briefcase and sprinted to the access panel. He opened it, revealing a twisted pillar of wires and fiber-optic cables. He immediately went to work. Starfish wasn't powerful enough to destroy everything, just the unshielded electronics that were close to it. It was at ground level and wouldn't travel very far. Inside the palace, it would have fried a lot of stuff, but the main security system would be shielded. But that was okay. We didn't want to take it out; we only needed to give them a surge hard enough to force them to restart.

I pulled the syringe out of the guard, moved to the next one, and poked him in the side, careful to only give him a few CCs of the powerful horse tranquilizer. The doctor moaned and crawled toward one of the guard's squawking radios. "Nighty night, Doc." I stuck him in the arm and gave him the last of the drug. He sluggishly rolled over, smiled stupidly at me, giggled, and was out.

"System report. What caused the power surge?" It was Hassan's voice on the radio. I picked it off of the guard's belt. Apparently it hadn't been hot enough to fry these.

"Unknown, sir," someone else responded. *"The system has gone down. We'll have it back up shortly."*

"Find out, or I'll have you fed to the tigers," Hassan snapped. *"Taha, report."*

The line was quiet.

"Taha. What's the status of our guest?" Hassan sounded angry. He did not seem like the kind of person I wanted to deal with when he was angry. I had to assume that one of these men was Taha.

I made my voice as neutral as possible. "Dr. Karzi says that it was just gas. Al Falah is resting." I began to remove weapons from the guard's duty belts. FN FNP 9mms, good guns.

"Fine. Get him back here as soon as you can. Hassan out."

I checked my watch. "Forty seconds," I said to Reaper.

"Working on it." He was flipping through wires like a man on a mission. "Get my computer." I pulled the laptop out of the briefcase, opened it, and waited for his next command. It was already running and on the correct screens. We had practiced this a few times. This was his gig now.

From Big Eddie's intel we knew that the palace compound was a closed system. There was no way to hack into the security from the outside world. If you wanted to take over, you needed to be in the belly of the beast. The design parameters told us that we had one minute from a power outage for the system to reset, and then we'd be locked out. It was a narrow window, but it was all we had.

Reaper picked a fat yellow cable and did his magic to it, clamping some sort of ring around it. He plugged a USB cable into his machine and then pushed me rather rudely out of the way.

"Thirty seconds."

"I know. I know," he muttered. Screens flashed by as he paged through them. "Come on, baby, come on."

I stuffed two of the FNs inside the thobe and left the third on the countertop by Reaper. I stuck four extra magazines into my pockets. Might as well be ready, because if he couldn't get us into their system, we were going to have a whole lot of explaining to do. And when I said explaining, I meant shooting. I also took one of the radios.

"Twenty seconds."

Numbers were scrolling through a box on the screen. Another box was gradually filling up with asterisks below it. This was hard to watch, and my stomach felt sick at the tension. The computer beeped.

"Ten. Why did it beep?"

"Shut up, Lorenzo!"

"Five."

The screen changed color, and Reaper clapped his hands together above his head. "I so rock! We're in. I think I should be the new sysadmin." Reaper began to tab through windows. Alarm systems, cameras, laser arrays, surface-to-air missiles; you name it, we had it. He immediately found the camera for the infirmary. It was a black-and-white image of the two of us standing over the computer, with a bunch of people lying on the floor. He fiddled with the track ball, and the camera rotated until it was looking at the far wall. Now it was an empty room.

"I'm going," I said. I reset the timer on my watch. "Mark, ten minutes. Then we blow this sucker." From our best estimates, that was how long we figured we had before system command figured out that they were compromised and the whole place locked down on red alert.

"I know the drill," he replied, not taking his eyes from the screen. Of course he did. We had practiced this a hundred times. He was already screwing around with the palace's communications. In a few seconds, the only people who were going to be using the radio net in this place were the ones Reaper was going to allow to do so. He didn't need to do anything to the outside equipment; Starfish had destroyed most of that. So now he was randomly closing down interior systems. Hopefully they'd think that it was some sort of equipment malfunction and not that they were being violated by people like us.

At ten minutes, I exited, took a quick glance down the hallways, and then walked purposefully toward the main elevator. Some servants noticed me, but I smiled at them like I belonged there, and they let me pass. I entered the elevator and waited for the doors to close.

Nine minutes left. The elevator was secure and plated in gold and polished mirrors. You needed a card key to access anything other than the main floors. Only a handful of the staff here had the card necessary to do so. I didn't even press any buttons, and the car began to move smoothly down. A digital display counted rapidly into the negative numbers as we headed deep into the bowels of the palace.

My radio beeped. I pulled it out. "Go."

"I'm in control now. I've locked out everyone else. They're confused, blaming it on the surge. You've got two guards standing at the base of the elevator shaft, and you're going to walk right into them."

"Put me through to them," I said, then cleared my throat. I had only spoken with him for a moment, but I needed to do a real convincing Hassan, real quick.

"You're on," Reaper said, and the radio clicked.

"All guards on basement six report to the level command post." I could only hope that those were the correct terms, as that was what they had been labeled on Big Eddie's stolen plans. "I want you there immediately."

"But, sir, you said not to leave our—"

"Tigers! I will feed you to the tigers! Hassan out." I shouted.

"They're moving, Lorenzo," Reaper said.

At seven minutes the elevator slid to a halt at negative six and the doors whooshed open. This was the lowest floor, chiseled out of the solid rock and containing one very secure vault. The hallway was empty. The concrete floors echoed as I walked down them. The level command post was just around the corner. I needed to get past it to get to the vault room.

I slid along the cold wall. Even the desert heat couldn't reach this deep into the Earth. I carefully took stock of the command room. I could see at least a half a dozen men through the glass doors, most of them standing, looking around nervously, waiting for Hassan to arrive.

I checked my watch. Six minutes. There was no way I was going to get past there without getting spotted. I pulled out the radio. "Need a distraction at the guard room."

"I'm looking through the menus. Hang on."

The clock was ticking. I was going to give him thirty more seconds, and then I would try to sneak past on my own. Knowing that I was probably going to get spotted, I pulled one of the pistols and checked the chamber. No time for thought, once you pick a course of action, you were committed, and you'd damn well better see it through.

"Got it."

The guards shouted in confusion as the fire sprinklers came on. I was immediately drenched in the downpour. I moved quickly while they were either looking up or covering their heads. I ran, splashing down the hallway, and pushed my way through the heavy double doors at the end. Once again, I didn't even have to swipe a card.

"Oh shit. I screwed up, chief."

"What?" I stared at the mighty vault door. It was enormous, a circular stainless-steel ultra-modern monolith to security engineering. To a thief like me, it was the most intimidating thing I had ever seen. Multiple combination locks ringed the device, over a dozen giant bolts were compressed into the tempered steel at different angles. The fact that the sprinklers in here were dumping water everywhere made the scene slightly surreal. On the other side of that vault were the greatest treasures in the world, wealth beyond all comprehension.

But that wasn't what I'd come for.

"That command turned on all the fire sprinklers in the palace. I'm watching the cameras. Everybody is freaking out!"

I continued down the hall. The carved stone became rougher and rougher and the passage started to trend sharply downward. I was now in the ancient tunnels that predated the construction of the palace. There were no sprinklers here, but their water flooded in a fast trail past my feet to disappear ahead of me.

"The IT guys know something is up," Reaper exclaimed. *"Hurry."*

They were ahead of schedule. Why was it that nothing ever went according to plan?

The tunnel opened into a larger room. A string of lights had been bolted into the ceiling. The room was perfectly square, every surface covered in carved writing. I didn't recognize any of the words; everything was too archaic. There was a circular indentation on the floor. The room felt *ancient*.

And it should. This space had been carved over a thousand years ago by unknown hands. Discovered by Saladin's armies, it had been used to house his most valuable possessions. Or so the Fat Man's report had said. All I knew was that the thing I sought was under my feet.

There were only a handful of these keys still in existence, passed down from fathers to whoever was the best warrior among their sons for hundreds of years. Over time they had gained something of almost religious significance. It was prestigious to be the bearer of the key, even though the reasons had long since been lost to the sands of time. Eddie's file had said the prince didn't understand what he was sitting on, except that it was prestigious and therefore had to be hoarded.

I found the keyhole in the center of the floor, a bizarrely geometric shape, going straight down. Standing in the indentation, I took the key out. I had to turn the base slowly until the protruding spines lined up with the hole. I inserted it until it clicked into the lock. As I twisted the base back, there was a cold hiss of air around me and the stone under my feet began to shudder. Steps appeared one by one as the floor sank. I leapt back in surprise. I had expected a simple door or something, not an elaborate construction that seemed to work like oiled silk even though it was a millennium old.

Holy shit, that's cool.

Within thirty seconds a narrow staircase had materialized, shooting straight down into the darkness. The steps were tiny, brutally steep, and made for feet far smaller than mine. I went down, and after a few steps I made out a faint glow. The stairs terminated in a stone wall carved with a three-foot skull. The skull had curving ram's horns. The light was coming from inside the skull's open mouth.

There it is. Whatever it is. It was sitting in the alcove formed by the mouth. It was vaguely Egyptian looking, almost like one of those beetle things they carved on the pyramids. A scarab, I believe they were called. It was only two inches of intricately carved black metal wrapped around a gold blob. At first I thought the center was glass, but it was different somehow, almost like crystal. With a shock I realized that the center was actually where the light was coming from.

I was scared to touch it. Maybe it was *radioactive.*

"Shit," I muttered. I didn't have time for this. I reached inside the alcove and scooped up the thing. It was surprisingly heavy. I froze as I felt it shift in my palm, for an uneasy second thinking that it was alive, but it was the golden interior. It was some sort of dense liquid shifting about sluggishly. I felt incredibly nervous, like I was a child screwing around with something that I really shouldn't be. There was an unbelievable temptation to just put it the hell back.

This thing wasn't natural. It was somehow *wrong*.

Reaper pulled me back. *"Time's up, Chief."* I looked at my watch, I had only been down here for ten seconds, but it had felt like forever in the dark. *"I gotta go. I've set the system for our getaway and crashed everything else. I locked the sprinkler controls. I've opened every gate except for the one that leads to the water main. I'm going to pump half the Gulf in here before they get that door breached, punk-ass newbs tried to mess with me. Elevator is running freely now. The guests are trying to get out. All hell's breaking loose. Shit. Some guards are coming this way, gotta run."*

"Go, I'll meet you at the car," I said, stuffing the scarab inside my clothing. I didn't have time for metaphysical bullshit. I had a job to finish. I ran back up the stairs, reached the top, twisted the key free, and sure enough the stairs began to rise, one by one. I knew that within seconds it would be like I had never been here.

There was no way that stealth was going to work now. I drew one of the FN pistols and kept it low at my side as I hurried up the tunnel. The sprinklers were still pumping. One of the guards stepped into the raining hallway from the control room, shouting into his blocked-off radio. He heard my footfalls and turned just in time to catch a face full of steel slide. The shock reverberated down my arm, and the guard rebounded off the wall. I was past him, in a full-on sprint now. Voices shouted behind me. I extended the 9mm as I ran, not even looking as I fired wildly down the corridor, just trying to keep their heads down.

Bullets whizzed past. I spun to the side as I slid into the elevator. Projectiles impacted the wall, shattering the polished glass. Mashing the up arrow repeatedly, I leaned the gun around the corner and cranked off wild shots until the slide locked back empty. The door slid closed, bullets clanging off the exterior.

I dropped the spent mag on the soggy carpet and reloaded. The elevator car vibrated slightly as pulleys lifted me toward safety. I pushed the button to stop at the lobby floor. The doors opened onto pure pandemonium. Water was pouring down the walls, collecting in chandeliers, and ruining antique furniture. Billionaires were pushing to get out the entryway, and the prince's men were trying to stop them. A fight had erupted between one of the big-wig's security detail and some of the gray-uniformed guards.

I collided with a fat, bloated slug of a man. He glared stupidly at me with little pig eyes and tried to push his way into the relatively dry elevator. "Hey, you're bleeding," he said nasally in American English as he pointed at my robes. "What happened in here?" Not seeing any guards looking in my direction, I grabbed him by the throat, yanked him into the car, broke his nose with a head butt, kneed him hard in the crotch, and then slammed his face repeatedly into the wall. He collapsed in a whimpering heap in the shell casings and broken glass.

Nonchalantly as possible, I stepped into the indoor rain and pushed through the chaos. Carl magically appeared at my side. "Wow, you really kicked Michael Moore's ass," he whispered. I turned back briefly. It had kind of looked like him . . . *Naw.*

There was Reaper, also heading toward the door. Hassan was blocking the door with his bulk, shouting for order and begging the VIPs to calm down. I saw Eduard Montalban at the foot of the stairs, a grinning caricature of a human being. In sharp contrast, the Fat Man stood behind him, holding an umbrella open over his employer. Big Eddie golf-clapped for me.

Hassan finally relented, surely not willing to risk the prince's wrath, and let the sodden guests through the door. We shoved along with the rest of the sheiks, royalty, CEOs, and scumbags into the scorching desert air. Hassan was too busy screaming into his nonresponsive radio to notice me exit. Steam immediately rose from my man-dress as we headed for the car.

The crowd was spreading when the first explosion went off. It was at the opposite end of the compound, but it sent the group into an even bigger frenzy. Reaper had set the mines along the opposite perimeter to detonate randomly. He was grinning from ear to ear, enjoying the up-close view of his handiwork.

The radio under my thobe began to speak. It was my voice in panicked Arabic, the audio file recorded back at our hideout and set to play on the radio net as a final distraction. It was going to repeat every thirty seconds, and it was the only thing that was going to broadcast over their intercoms and radios. *"We're under attack. Forces are breaching the north wall. All guards to the north wall. Evacuate the guests. The prince does not want them found here. Let everyone out the gates!"* I opened the door and slid into the backseat of our Mercedes. Carl and Reaper jumped in the front.

Around us, other drivers were attempting to start their expensive cars to no avail, their modern electronics all hopelessly fried by Starfish. "Go!" I shouted. We were spinning tires and leaving rubber on the pavement in an instant, zipping through the gardens, through the tunnel under the wall, and then we were out into the blinding desert. The acceleration sucked, but within a few minutes our land-yacht was doing a hundred.

We had done it. We had pulled it off. The palace was shrinking in the distance. All three of us began to whoop and cheer wildly. Carl screamed out happy profanities. Reaper punched the ceiling. We had done the impossible. Phase Three was done. This suicide mission was done. *Screw you, Eddie. We got your stupid treasure.*

Then the adrenaline began to subside, and my hands began to shake. That is when I noticed the blood and felt a burning sensation in my back. I stuck one quivering hand under my thobe and probed around. It came back slick and red.

Nothing ever goes according to plan.

"Ow! Carl, careful!" I snapped. "That hurts."

"Quit your crying. Here you go." He waved a bloody Leatherman multitool in front of my head with something held in the pliers. I opened my hand and he dropped a bullet fragment onto my palm. Carl poured something stinging on my back then started to tape down a bandage. "That's it. Must have bounced off the elevator wall and got you. I thought the way you were whining you might actually have gotten hurt or something."

The limo was still cruising across the bleak desert. Reaper was driving now, so Carl could play medic, and had taken us off the main road and deeper into the dunes. The car kicked up a massive sand plume behind us. "We're almost there," he shouted into the back compartment.

"Good," I answered as I threw the waterlogged and bloodstained man-dress on the floor. Carl handed me a T-shirt. "As soon as we stop, you guys grab Al Falah out of the trunk, shove him back here, and we'll light this sucker. I'll get the van ready."

"What, you get one little hole in you and you think you don't have to lift the fat guy?" Carl asked with a grin. Even a bitter and angry fellow like Carl had to be in a jovial mood after pulling off a heist like this. He started to undo his tie. "At least he'll be thawed. When he wouldn't bend, it was a hell of a time getting him in the trunk."

They'd identify the burned corpse as Al Falah, probably assumed murdered by his co-conspirators, which would totally point the investigation in the wrong direction at first. Eventually an autopsy would show that he'd been dead for a long time, but by then we'd be well out of the country.

I tried to turn serious for a minute. "Guys, I've just got to say. You were amazing back there. The EMP was awesome. You took down security in record time, everything. That was damn near perfect . . . except for the sprinklers."

"Yeah, what the fuck was that?" Carl shouted before he called Reaper something unpronounceable in Portuguese and threw his tie at the driver.

"Hey, I had to improvise," our techie answered defensively. "Next time, you do the computer stuff and I'll do the kung-fu ninja stuff. How hard could it be?"

"Well, either way, we're done." I pulled the scarab from my pocket. It still made me uncomfortable. "We got his damn . . . whatever."

"Rub it and see if it grants three wishes," Reaper suggested.

"Whatever, Aladdin, Big Eddie will be in contact and we can arrange a handoff. And I didn't get the chance to tell you—I met Eddie. He was there at the meeting."

"No way," Carl said. "Was he there because of us?"

I shrugged. "I don't know. But he felt the need to talk to me in person, which can't be good."

"Do you think our families are off the hook?" Reaper asked quietly.

"I think I've got an idea to guarantee Eddie sticks to his word. I'll fill you guys in on the way to the border."

An ancient oil rig appeared ahead of us. It had long since fallen into disuse and was slowly decaying back into the desert. There was a wooden shack behind it where we had stashed our van. A few minutes to destroy the evidence, and we'd be on our way toward the border. We parked near the dilapidated shed. Old canvas tarps whipped in the wind.

I stepped into the searing heat, savoring the *freedom* of it, and went to unlock the padlock we had left on the shed. Carl pulled out a pair of binoculars and scanned the desert we'd just traveled. "Lorenzo, we've got dust behind us. We're being followed."

I shouted back as I unlocked the door. "How far?"

"We've got maybe five minutes," he responded. "How'd they find us?"

I'd hoped that Starfish would have bought us more time. "Eddie probably had a bug stuck on our car during the meeting," I shouted. Well, it was either Eddie's goons or the prince's men. Eddie must have decided he couldn't trust us to hand off the goods, that double-crossing bastard, and heaven help us if it was Hassan. I shoved the door open. The white van was a welcome sight. "Hurry up and move that body! We've got to roll."

I was getting into the van, looking for the ignition key, as Carl was unlocking the limousine's trunk. Reaper was getting out of the driver's seat.

"They won't be able to catch us, Lorenzo. Nobody can catch me," Carl said as the trunk lid opened.

CRACK!

I jerked my head in surprise, jolted by the unexpected noise, dropping the keys to the van's floorboards.

Carl's beady eyes narrowed in momentary confusion, bushy brows scrunching together as he looked into the trunk. The first bullet had struck him square in the chest, leaving a red hole on his white dress shirt. The second concussion came a split second later. Blood spurted from Carl's neck, his hands flying reflexively to his throat as he fell sprawling into the sand.

Time jerked to a screeching halt.

"*Carl!*" Reaper screamed. Someone was crawling out of the trunk.

I was moving, the FNP coming out of my waistband.

The man twisted to the side, one foot hitting the ground, the other still bent in the trunk. He extended a small B&T machine pistol in one hand, seeking Reaper.

"Down! "Down!" I pushed around the van door, punching the FN out, the front sight moving into my field of vision, finger already pulling the trigger back.

Too late.

The submachine gun bucked, brass flashing in the sunlight. Reaper jerked violently to the side, spinning, crashing into the limousine's hood as the window beside him shattered. I fired, the 9mm in my hand recoiling, the front sight coming back on target, firing again.

The man dove from the trunk, rolling in the sand on the other side of the limo. I moved laterally, gun up, tracking, searching, looking for another shot. He opened up from under the car. Bullets stitched across the shack behind me, flinging splinters into the air. Metal screeched as something struck the van. I was running now, not even thinking about it, trying to flank around the side of the car.

He rose, looking for me, glaring over the top of the limo, stubby black muzzle swinging wide. He was a tiny, dark-skinned man, drenched in sweat. Still moving, I saw him first, centered the front sight and fired. His head snapped back violently, visible matter flying as I shot him in the face. I hammered him twice more before he disappeared.

I lowered the gun. Multiple dust plumes were closing in the distance. Reaper was dragging himself up the car hood. He screamed as the pain hit him. I grabbed him as he started to fall again. "Can you move?" I shouted.

He grimaced, biting his lip, tears running down his cheeks. "Yes."

"Get in the van. Hurry!" Reaper lurched away. I ran for Carl.

My friend was gasping, shaking, blood streaming between his fingers as he kept pressure on his neck. He focused on me as I knelt beside him. "Get him?" he wheezed. There was a massive quantity of blood already spilled on the sand.

"Yeah, I got him. Hang on, man, I'm gonna get you out of here."

Carl closed his eyes. He grabbed my hand and squeezed.

Then he was gone.

"Carl?"

The cars were closer now. I knelt by the body of my friend, pistol dangling from my numb fingertips. I wanted nothing more than to stay here and wait for them to arrive.

Then all of this would have been for nothing.

I stood, dragged Carl's body to the limo, gently set him in the driver's seat, then went to the trunk. Falah's body was still cold. It was probably the only thing that had kept the assassin alive in the heat, lying on that ice block, waiting for his chance. He must have gotten in while we were at the palace. I retrieved the white phosphorus grenade from under Falah, pulled the pin, and tossed it into the Mercedes. It ignited behind me in a billowing wall of chemical flame.

Carl would have liked the Viking funeral.

Reaper was sobbing when I got into the van. "Dude,

the fuckers killed him." He was cringing from the pain, holding his hands tightly to his wounded side. "Eddie did this. Bastard's gonna pay."

I found the keys on the floorboard. The goons were inbound. It was going to be a race to the border now.

Chapter 24:
Welcome Back,
Mr. Nightcrawler

LORENZO
June 18

I was certain we had lost them after we had crossed the border. A gentle breeze had calmed the raging temperature. The sun was setting over the desert, and if it hadn't been such a terrible day, I would have thought it was beautiful. I cradled the rifle in my arms and scanned the horizon.

Part of me was secretly praying for cars to appear on the road. Carl had been my best friend.

The village was small, consisting of a few small compounds and some outlying buildings. The van was well hidden. I sat in the shade beneath an awning, gun in hand, black and gold scarab in a pouch I'd tied around my neck. In the distance dogs barked and children laughed.

It had been my fault. I should have seen it coming. I should have done *something*.

There was movement in the doorway behind me.

"Your friend will live. He was struck twice, but the wounds were superficial. Given time to heal, he should have no permanent disability."

"Thank you, doctor," I replied, never taking my eyes off the horizon.

"I'm afraid I'm no Doctor," the Qatari answered. "I failed from an American veterinary school."

"Good enough." I lifted the rubber-banded stack of money above my head. He took it. This particular establishment had a reputation within the criminal element of the region. "When can I move him?"

"I would not move him until morning. You may sleep in the guest room. I shall have my servants prepare it." He turned to leave.

"We were never here," I stated.

"But of course."

Carl's duffel bag was open on the bed. I found the manila folder with the mission details and dialed the Fat Man's number on my untraceable cell phone.

I had checked on Reaper before retiring to the guest room. He had been asleep, and had looked terrible, even paler than normal, with bandages all over his skinny chest, and buried beneath IV bags. A heart monitor kept a steady pace. He would be fine, but the sight of what was left of my crew filled me with rage.

"Yes," the Fat Man answered on the other end of the line.

"I want to talk to Eddie."

There was a pause. "Mr. Lorenzo, Big Eddie does not speak with the help. I am his intermediary and—"

"Put him on or I toss the scarab in the ocean," I stated calmly.

"Think of your family before you make any rash decisions."

Part of my family had been shot in the throat this afternoon. I was not in the mood to play games. "Do it."

There was a moment's hesitation. "Please hold."

I rummaged through Carl's bag while I waited. We had worked together for so long that it still hadn't sunk in that he was really gone, corpse burned to ashes on a Saudi dune. Death was always a possibility in this business, but you never really got used to it. I found another folder in the bag. It had *Carlo Gomes* written on it in black marker. It was the information about his family that the Fat Man had originally given us in Thailand.

I opened Carl's folder. The man had never talked about his people. There were a handful of photographs. They were marked Island of Terceira. The pictures were all very old. Beneath each person's photo had been handwritten the word *deceased*.

Carl had no family left. Eddie had never held leverage on him . . .

Carl had done it for us.

"Ah, Mr. Lorenzo. Good to hear from you." The oily sound of Eddie's voice uncorked a clot of rage in my soul.

"Why did you do it, Eddie? Why'd you try to kill us?" I hissed.

"Just business. I'm sorry about that. I saw the opportunity at the meeting. I realized what you had done. Brilliant move, I must say, but with the cameras around the cars disabled, I sent one of my men to accompany you. I thought I would tie up some loose ends."

I was a *loose end*. He did not even sound defensive. That was just what our lives were worth to him.

"I was going to give it to you."

"It was a calculated risk."

"I should just destroy this thing and walk away," I said, trying to keep my voice as neutral as possible.

"Do so and you will have a much shorter Christmas card list. The original deal is still in place." He laughed. This was amusing him. "See, Lorenzo, you're a pawn."

"I guess that makes you the queen."

"Fair enough. But you will bring me that phylactery, or I give the order and your loved ones get fed to the sharks. Listen to me carefully, chap. You do not have any idea what you have. The contents of that thing are more important than you can even imagine. I've strangled children for far less, and I sleep very well at night. You will give it to me or you will have—"

I cut him off. "Now you listen to me. You harm any of my relatives and I'll give this thing back to the prince and tell him who hired me to steal it."

Eddie let out a long breath. "You bloody fool."

"No, you're the fool. You screwed up. I know who you are now," I snapped. "Mr. Montalban."

"I suppose that was a mistake. You know what they say about hubris," Eddie said slowly. Whatever stupid bit of arrogance had caused Eddie to reveal himself to me at the meeting was going to be his downfall. "Let's be reasonable, Lorenzo."

"Reason went out the window when your boy crawled

out the trunk. You'd better pray that none of my nieces falls down and scrapes a knee, because I'll assume you were behind it." I seized the moment. I was tired of being pushed around, and now it was time to push back. "We trade. You get your bug right after you transfer twenty million dollars into my Swiss accounts. Then you walk the fuck away. You ever contact me again, I call the prince. If I die of anything other than old age, I'll have somebody else contact the prince. You ever look at my family cross-eyed again, I call the prince. If one of my brothers gets prostate cancer, I'm going to hold you responsible."

"And call the prince, yes, yes, I get it. . . . You know, Lorenzo, I never took you for a tattletale. But that's why you were always my favorite. You'll do anything to get the job done. Very well, I can deal. Fair enough." I could tell that he didn't think it was fair at all. Fair was not a concept a man like Big Eddie understood. Someway, somehow, he would find a way to kill me. There was no turning back from this point. For this to end, one of us had to die. "When can I have it?"

"I'll be in touch." I hung up.

I awoke with a start. It was dark, and I lay there for a second, heart pounding. The house was quiet, but I snatched up my rifle and went to the window anyway. There was no movement outside. No dogs barking. *All clear.*

But I stayed there, watching, waiting, too wired to return to bed. I was letting this get to me, letting it affect my judgment. There was a cough from next door. *Reaper.* That's what had startled me awake. I put down my rifle and went to check on him. Surprisingly enough, he was awake too. Sitting up in bed and looking out the window, white bandages reflecting the moonlight.

"How you feeling?" I asked.

"Carl's gone, man," Reaper said as he wiped one hand under his nose. "Holy shit, I didn't think Carl could die. He was too *angry* to die. It's dumb, but like if he got shot, he'd just get more pissed off . . . Shit . . . That sounds stupid. He wasn't the Hulk."

I pulled up a seat. "I know how you feel."

He got really quiet for a while. This was hitting him worse than me. "Man, it's been so long. . . . Carl was always there for me. I don't know if I ever told you, but when I met you guys . . . I was really scared." He said that as if it were some kind of revelation, and maybe to him it was. "I was all alone. I didn't know where to go, and you gave me a job, gave me a *mission*. You know, I never fit in back home."

I nodded, as if that were a surprise. "Me, either."

"Okay, this might come as a shock, but I wasn't as tough when I was a kid. I was kind of a nerd," he said, like he was admitting something shocking. "I got picked on a lot. I was always the smartest kid, but I was so much younger than everybody else, so I was like a weirdo."

"You were like Doogie Howser."

"Except straight. Totally straight," he corrected me. "Then my mom got remarried, and my stepdad was like this super tough-guy fucking lumberjack or something, and my step-brother was Johnny Football Hero, and he got all the chicks, and there I was, this little scared dork *weakling*. . . . I could never live up to their standards. I *hated* them."

I wondered if this was how some of the genius super-villains from the comic books started out. I just kept nodding.

"So I showed them. I'd be way more bad-ass than they could ever be. It was time to Fear the Reaper, you know what I'm saying? I had *skills*, man."

"Two hundred felony counts is pretty damn impressive for a teenager."

"Well, I wasn't as clever as I thought I was back then." Reaper smiled sadly. "I scared the shit out of the government, though! I crashed a bank and turned off all the lights in Boston, just because I *could*. They wanted to make an example out of kids like me. Mom was heart-broken, and you know what the weirdest thing was? My stepdad, the *asshole*, he's the one that helped me the most. He gave me a plane ticket to a place with no extradition and told me it was 'time to be a man' . . . that was the nicest thing anybody had ever done for me."

Shit. If Reaper started crying, I wouldn't know what to do.

He started crying. "You guys took me in after that. You were my family. *Family* . . . But now? First Train, now Carl. They were my *brothers*. We're all that's left, and look at me. They almost got me. I've never been shot before." He blinked the tears away. "This shit just got *real*. Eddie's going down. Eddie and that fat fucker in the white suit, both. I'm gonna kill them, Lorenzo, I swear to God, I'm gonna kill that fat bastard if it's the last thing I do. I'm gonna wipe that smile off his fucking face."

I patted him on the arm. I had a hard time with emotions, but revenge, that I could understand. "That's the spirit."

"They're gonna *fear* the Reaper," he vowed.

VALENTINE
Quagmire, Nevada
June 21
1500

The Nevada sun blazed overhead as I hiked up the road from the Greyhound bus station. Quagmire's bus station wasn't really a bus station. It was a tobacco shop and party store that the Greyhound bus occasionally stopped at. Hawk knew I was coming, but he didn't know what time I was getting in. No one was waiting for me.

I thought about calling him. I had a prepaid phone that I'd purchased after I landed in the States. I decided I'd just walk. I was probably being paranoid, but I was very leery about using a cell phone still. It was a good hike to Hawk's ranch, but I knew the way. I shouldered my duffel bag and started down the road.

I was walking up Main Street in Quagmire when a big Ford pickup, adorned with an NRA and a US Marine Corps window sticker, slowed to a stop next to me. The driver, a crusty old guy wearing a NASCAR hat, rolled down his passenger-side window and got my attention. I immediately tensed up. I was unarmed, save a pocket knife I'd bought at a Wal-Mart. My left hand slid down to my pants pocket, where the knife was tucked away.

"You need a lift, son?" he asked. I had a big green military duffel bag, and my hair was still buzzed short. He probably thought I was a vet coming home. *Close enough.*

I relaxed some and moved my hand away from my pocket. "If it's no trouble," I said, stepping closer to the pickup.

"Where ya headed?"

"You know the Hawkins place? It's on the north end of town."

"Oh hell," the man said, grinning. "I know Hawk. C'mon, get in. Toss your bag in the back. I'll give you a lift. It's no trouble." I thanked the man, threw my heavy bag into the back of his truck, and jumped in.

We rolled past the limits of the town, following a well-worn dirt road. About half a mile down it, we passed through a gate that had been left open, ignoring the NO TRESPASSING signs that were fading in the desert sun. The truck left a cloud of fine dust in its wake as we neared the house at the end of the road.

It was a modest-looking two-story ranch house, very unassuming and unremarkable in appearance, just like its owner. There was more than immediately met the eye. The old man stopped his truck by a well-used, dusty Dodge turbo diesel pickup. I thanked him and got out. As soon as I grabbed my bag, the old man turned around and headed up the road again, leaving me standing in his dusty wake.

The sun was intense overhead. I squinted even through my sunglasses. I slowly walked toward the house, bag in hand. On the porch, in the shade, Hawk sat in a rocking chair, reading a newspaper and sipping ice water. "Hawk," I said, stepping onto the porch. He didn't get up, but I knew he recognized me. If he hadn't, I'd have been staring down the barrel of a .44 Magnum before I even got close.

Hawk folded his newspaper and set it aside. "Good to see you, kid," he said simply. "I was glad to hear from you. I kind of figured you were dead."

"You were almost right," I said levelly.

"Where's Tailor?"

"I don't know," I replied truthfully. "He was alive last time I saw him. It's a long story."

Hawk nodded and stood up. "C'mon in." He led the way into his house. It was air-conditioned and mercifully cool inside. I was immediately greeted by a pair of big mutt dogs that wanted to be petted. Their tails wagged back and forth as they sniffed me. I smiled and set my duffel bag down.

Hawk shooed the dogs away and led me to his kitchen. He motioned for me to sit down and went to the refrigerator.

"Want a beer?" he asked.

"No thanks," I said quietly.

"Ah," he said thoughtfully. "Didn't think you would. Here." Hawk turned around and placed a ice-cold can of Dr. Pepper in front of me. The man knew me well. He then pulled out another chair and sat down, popping open a can of beer. "So, where ya been?"

I didn't answer at first. I took off my baseball cap and sunglasses. Hawk got a good look at the scars on my face for the first time. He just nodded.

"Start talking, kid."

I sat in Hawk's kitchen and told my story for more than half an hour. Where I'd only told Ling a little bit about what had happened, I poured my guts out to Hawk. I knew I could trust this man. I told him everything.

Gordon Willis. Project Heartbreaker. Zubara. The fighting, the killing, the loss, all of it.

My voice wavered a little as I recounted the night Sarah died. He sat back in his chair, rubbing his chin when I told him about the man called Lorenzo that had showed up in my room. He raised an eyebrow when I told him about how I'd first encountered him, and nearly captured a woman named Jillian Del Toro, but he didn't say anything.

Hawk's eyes narrowed a little when I described Sarah's death and explained that I didn't know who pulled me to safety. He would just nod and sip his beer, not saying anything, until I finished.

Hawk looked thoughtful for a moment. "Bad way, kid," he said simply. "So you haven't heard from Tailor?"

"No. He has no way to contact me."

"He hasn't called here," Hawk said. "Eh. No worries. Tailor can take care of himself."

"Did you get the package I sent?"

"I got it," Hawk said. Ling had helped me ship my revolver and my knife to Hawk. They were both disassembled and placed in a box full of random machine parts I found. They apparently made it through customs. "Your .44 is all cleaned up and put back together. They're up in the room I made up for you. I put your other guns up there, too. Figured you'd wanna go shooting while you were here."

"Thank you," I said, looking down at the table. I didn't know what else to say.

"No sweat, kid," Hawk said after a moment. "You know you always got a place here. Now listen. I need to go water the horses. You can come help if you want, but you're probably tired."

"If it's okay, I'd like to go upstairs and lie down. It's been a long day."

"No problem," Hawk said, standing up. "Your room is first one on the right upstairs." I thanked Hawk again and made my way up to the room he'd prepared for me. I opened my duffel bag, found some comfortable clothes to sleep in, and crawled into bed. I was asleep in minutes.

It was dark when I awoke. I sat up in bed, sweat beading on my face. My heart was racing. I fumbled with the lamp next to the bed until I got it turned on. My eyes darted around the room. I was breathing hard. There was nothing there. I was safe in bed. Exhaling slowly, I rubbed my face with my hands. The clock said it was just after midnight. My mouth was so dry it felt like my tongue had swollen up. I climbed out of bed and headed down to the kitchen.

It was cool in Hawk's house as I padded down the stairs. I was only wearing a pair of shorts. It was quiet. Hawk was undoubtedly in bed already. I made my way into the kitchen but didn't turn on the light. I grabbed a cup and opened the fridge, pouring myself some water from the filtration pitcher.

I stood upright as a key hit the lock on the front door. I could hear the door swing open, then close again. It was then locked. I relaxed a bit. Hawk must've gone out late or something. No one breaking in for nefarious purposes would have a key and not even try to be quiet. I stepped away from the refrigerator, cup of water in hand, and stepped toward the door to the front room.

"Hawk?" I asked, squinting into the darkness. A moment later, someone appeared in the kitchen doorway and switched on the light. A woman stood not five feet from me with a blank look on her pretty face. She wore a short pink jumper, like a waitress uniform, and tennis shoes. She carried a purse under her arm.

Her eyes went wide when she saw me standing there in my shorts. It hit me then. I recognized her. It was Jillian Del Toro. *Jesus Christ. It can't be.*

I think she recognized me, too. Dropping her purse, her hand flew behind her back. Before I could say anything, she'd produced a Smith & Wesson M&P compact pistol and leveled it at my face. Her nametag said Peaches.

She sure as hell didn't *look* like a Peaches. She had an intense gaze; it was a mix of obvious fear and anger. I looked back down at the pistol in her hands. It was shaking slightly, but it was close enough that I could see the rifling in the barrel. It was a 9mm.

I dropped my water cup on the floor and slowly raised my hands. "Please," I said. I was very calm. "Put the gun down. I'm just as confused as you are. I'm not going to hurt you."

"You shut up!" she said fiercely. "I know why you're here!" Her grip on the pistol tightened.

"I'm getting a cup of water," I said, nodding to the puddle on the floor. "I'm standing here in my *shorts* for Christ sakes." *The Calm* was wavering as I became agitated.

"Shut up!" Jill shouted. "You're Dead Six! You're here to kill me!" I visibly halted when she said the words "Dead Six."

"Dead Six is done now. I barely got out alive."

"I know that! But what are you doing here?"

"I was *getting* a God damned cup of *water!*" I said, almost shouting now. "What do you think, I came to Nevada and infiltrated Hawk's house in my fucking underwear so I could kill you?"

"Just shut up!" Jill snarled. She shifted her weight forward slightly. Her pistol was in arm's reach. *Close enough.*

Moving quickly and following through, just like I'd been trained, my hand shot up and grabbed the pistol. I forced it upward, yanking both of her arms up with it. I was taller than Jill, and stronger. I twisted the pistol in her hands and slammed my other arm into her sternum. There was a chance she'd pull the trigger, but it wouldn't hit anything but the ceiling. The blow knocked her off balance. She stumbled backward and lost her grip on her gun.

I have to give her credit. She didn't stay down. She immediately got back up and came at me. In one smooth motion I shifted the pistol to my right hand, grasped the slide with my left, and racked it as I extended my arm. An unfired cartridge ejected and bounced off the floor. Jill froze as I pointed the S&W at the bridge of her nose. Her eyes were wide with terror, but she didn't blink and didn't cringe. *Ballsy.*

"Now that's *enough*," I said firmly but calmly. I side-stepped to the left, shifting the pistol to my left hand then gripping it with both hands. "Just calm down, okay?"

"What the *hell* are you doing, boy?" Hawk's gravelly voice boomed. I froze, and my head snapped around.

Hawk was standing in the other doorway to the kitchen with a Remington 870 shotgun in his hands.

"Hawk!" Jill cried. "He's from Dead Six! They found me!"

"Hawk," I said. "This is the girl I told you about! She was over in the Zoob! She shot me in the back!"

"You pointed a gun at my face and took me hostage!" Jill snapped back.

I was pissed off now. "Well, what the hell—"

"Both of you shut up!" Hawk said, lowering the shotgun. "Damn it, Val, you give that girl her gun back. Jill, you holster that gun and calm down." Giving Jill a dirty look, I dropped the magazine out of her gun, locked the slide back, and handed it to her. She snatched it out of my hand. I gave her the magazine a second later. She didn't reload it.

Hawk sighed. "Both of you relax. This is my fault. I guess I should've told you about each other. Val, I was gonna say something to you when you got up. You're both guests in my house, though. I expect you to behave yourselves. Now you damn kids go to bed. We'll straighten this all out in the morning." Hawk turned and left the kitchen, leaving Jill Del Toro and me alone. She folded her arms across her chest and looked at the floor. I shuffled my feet. Neither of us spoke until we heard the door to Hawk's room close.

Jill glared at me. "It's *your* fault."

Hawk roused me out of bed at six in the morning and told me to go feed the horses, reminding me that he wasn't running a bed-and-breakfast. Half an hour later I was in the barn, carrying big bales of hay from the loft out into

the field. The horses were already happily munching on
their grain in their stalls. I was going to spread the hay
around outside to keep them busy while I got to cleaning.
See, I had to shovel the horse shit after I fed the horses.
Living on a ranch is a lot of fun, let me tell you.

I hauled another hay bale through the barn, this one
for Hawk's ill-tempered stallion. I was wearing leather
gloves. My .44 was holstered on my left hip, out of habit
more than anything else. After everything that happened,
I really didn't like going around unarmed.

Jill Del Toro was standing in the barn, dressed in jeans,
a T-shirt, and work gloves when I came back in. She carried
a pitchfork and a shovel in her hands.

"Hey," she said, sounding much more amicable than
the night before.

"Mornin'," I said, nodding at her. "Hawk drag you out
of bed too?"

"What? No, I worked swing shift last night. He lets me
sleep in on my days off."

"Must be nice," I grumbled.

"Look," Jill said awkwardly, "I'm sorry about last night.
You know, for trying to shoot you."

"Well . . . I'm sorry I hit you," I said.

"It's just that I saw you, and I remembered from
before, when you grabbed me, you know, and I kind of
freaked, and—"

I held up my hand. "Hey, it's cool. I know what it's like
to be twitchy." We both fell silent for a few uncomfortable
seconds.

Jill looked me in the eye. "Can I ask you something?
How . . . *whoa*. Your *eyes* are different colors!"

I rolled my mismatched eyes and sighed.

"I'm sorry!" Jill insisted, embarrassed. "I've just never seen anyone like that before. I can't believe I didn't notice last night."

"What were you going to ask me?"

"Oh, right. How did you end up here? Where do you know Hawk from?"

"I was going to ask you the same thing," I said. "I know Hawk from way back. I used to work for him. Hell, my stuff is stored here. My Mustang is still in his garage. Unless he sold it. The question is, what the hell are *you* doing here?"

"We were in Zubara after that night. You know, when the fighting started. Lorenzo got hurt pretty bad dragging you out of there. He—"

I interrupted her. "Whoa, whoa, whoa. Stop. Hang on. Back up the truck. What the hell do you mean, *Lorenzo dragged me out of there*?"

"Oh . . . you don't know?"

"No, I don't know! The motherfucker showed up in my room, pulled a knife on me, gave me *this*," I snapped, pointing to the scar on my face, "and *this*," I added, indicating the scar on my arm, "and I still don't know what he was after. Now you're telling me he *rescued* me?"

"Hey!" Jill said. "Your friends broke his fingers. They were torturing him!"

"What the hell was he doing in our compound in the first place?"

Jill deflated a little. "That's, uh, that's a long story," she said.

"We've got a lot of shit to shovel," I suggested.

"Fair enough," Jill replied. We spent the next two hours doing various farm chores as Jill told me her story. She'd been an intern at the US Embassy when she had a run-in with Gordon Willis. Gordon had some embassy staff murdered. She went on the run, was kidnapped, and was eventually rescued by Lorenzo, in the very house where I'd blown Adar's head off. The whole thing made my head spin.

I told her parts of my own tale as well. She laughed nervously when I explained that Gordon had described her as a dangerous traitor.

"I'm sorry about Sarah," Jill said eventually.

"How did you know?"

"We had one of your radios for a while. and I was watching on camera when she . . .when it happened. Lorenzo has this little drone airplane."

I exhaled. "Thank you. I'm doing okay, all things considered. So . . . where is Lorenzo now?"

"Honestly?" Jill said. "I have no idea. I haven't tried to contact him. He could be anywhere."

Chapter 25:
Undocumented

LORENZO
June 22

This part of the Red Sea was really more of a dirty blue.

The boat rocked in the mild waves, Saudi Arabia behind us and North Africa somewhere over the horizon. The air smelled of fish and diesel fuel. I leaned against the railing, contemplating our next move.

Reaper was sleeping in one of the passenger cabins. It had only been a couple of days since he'd been shot, and he was still looking haggard. My back still ached from the ricochet that I had picked up in the elevator, and the last member of my crew was dead. Right now I wanted to get as far away from this damnable place as possible. Our next stop would be Egypt. There was a safe house in Cairo that we could hole up in while we formulated a plan to deal with Big Eddie.

Eduard Santiago Montalban. Half brother to the billionaire businessman murdered recently in the Gulf.

Raised in Hong Kong, educated at Eaton, and as far as the world knew a useless fop that lived off the family wealth. He was all over the high-society pages, philanthropist, humanitarian, playboy, all that bullshit.

In actuality, he was the one that took care of the dirty side of the Montalban family business: murder, extortion, bribery, money laundering, slave trading, you name it, Big Eddie was involved. All the years that I had worked for him, I would never have guessed who he was. At times, I'd thought that he was imaginary, a name put onto some cartel of powerful individuals. Surely, one man wouldn't be capable of that much evil.

Allowing me to find out his true identity would be the biggest, and last, mistake that Eddie would ever make.

We would arrange a handoff for the scarab to string him along, but I planned on getting to him first. He was so fixated on getting it that a preemptive strike would be the last thing that he'd expect.

And what was in there that made it so valuable? The metal was something hard and black that I couldn't recognize. The glowing amber liquid was a mystery. Nervous that I'd had it next to my skin for so long, I'd had Reaper check it with a Geiger counter. It wasn't radioactive, and he couldn't recognize it, so Reaper had hypothesized that perhaps the glow was some sort of bioluminescence. In other words, it might be alive.

Maybe it was some sort of bio-weapon? But its setting didn't make any sense for that. Reaper, being absurdly inquisitive, had wanted to crack it open so he could get a sample to test. I'd shot that down, because I was afraid that opening it would kill us all. I just wanted to get rid of it as fast as I could. Maybe I was psyching myself out, but it made me uncomfortable just looking at it. All that we knew for sure was that it was more valuable than all of the other treasures in the prince's vault and that Eddie was willing to kill crowds of people to get it.

My cell phone began to vibrate in my pocket, interrupting my thoughts of revenge. Glancing around, I made sure that there were no other passengers along the railing, just a couple of filthy seagulls. It was a forwarded voice mail from another one of my numbers. Suspicious, I punched in the security code. I did not give that phone number to very many people.

"You said not to use any names, so I hope you recognize my voice." It was Jill Del Toro. "I hope you guys are doing okay with that thing you were working on. The date's passed. I'm settled in pretty good here, thanks to you." I was embarrassed to find myself grinning stupidly, not the way a cold-blooded criminal was supposed to act, but it was good to hear the recording of her voice. "You said to contact you if I needed help. There is something going on, something related to what happened before, from when you found me. I don't know who else to turn to. Lo—" She caught herself then continued. "Please call me."

She rattled off a phone number and the message ended. I dialed the number; it had an American area code, but I didn't know which state it was for. An answering machine picked up.

"Hi, you've reached Peaches. Leave a message." It was Jill's voice; damn Reaper and his stupid stripper-name fake IDs.

"Got your message. I, uh . . ." What was I supposed to

say? It wasn't like I didn't have more important things going on. Eddie needed to be dealt with. I had a mystery bug full of something glowing and apparently alive, and a crown prince who would have me fed to his tigers if he found out I'd been the one to steal it. My family was still in danger, and the only surviving member of my crew was healing from multiple gunshot wounds.

She had never even been a real member of my team. Like Carl said, she was just some stray that I had saved from Adar's goons. She had even turned her back and walked away, so as not to sully herself in my gritty illegal world. I was a hardened, professional criminal. I didn't have time for helping people out of sentimentality.

"I'm coming. Call me when you get this and let me know where to meet you." I folded the phone and stuck it back in my pocket. "Fuck!" I shouted. The seagulls scattered, squawking at my vehemence.

Screw it. I was running out of friends. I could arrange a meeting with Big Eddie in the States just as easy as I could meet him in Egypt.

Change of plans. I was going home.

LORENZO
Santa Vasquez, Mexico
June 24

The chubby man wiped his brow as he entered the little office. Massive sweat rings had pooled in his armpits. He'd been working outside on the tiny airport's asphalt runway, and it was over a hundred degrees. He dropped the bag containing his lunch on the desk and immediately turned on the oscillating fan, sticking his face directly in front of it. He never heard me rise from behind the filing cabinets.

I wrapped my arm around his throat, other hand clamping over his mouth, locking him right down. "Make a noise and I'll snap your neck," I whispered. He nodded slowly. "Good. Don't reach for the gun in your desk. I've already taken it. Go for the knife in your pocket and I kill you. Comprende?" He nodded again. I removed my hand slowly but kept up the pressure so he could barely breathe.

"What do you want?" he whispered, terrified.

I slowly reached down and lifted his lunch bag from the table, bringing it up to our faces, and smelled it. Ham, eggs, bacon, guacamole, jalapeños, on fresh baked bread, *oh yeah* . . . I hadn't eaten since the flight. I was starving. "I want your lunch. Dude, *Lomitos Argentinos*? This stuff is going to kill you. I see Juanita's still trying to fatten you up. It's working." I patted his gut.

He hesitated. It had been years. "*Lorenzo?*"

I let go of his throat. "What's up, Guillermo?"

He spun around, eyes widening in shock. "*Pendejo!* You scared the piss out of me!"

I put my finger in front of my lips, signaling the need for quiet. "I snuck in. I didn't want anybody else in your outfit to know I was here. What's up, man?" I grinned.

He crushed me in a hug. "You always were a scary bastard," he said as we clapped each other on the back. Guillermo let go and studied me. "But what're you doing here? I thought you guys were in Thailand? Where's

Death Train? Where's Carl? The asshole still owes me money."

Guillermo Reyes and I went way back. I shook my head. "Big Eddie killed them."

"Oh, shit. Sorry, man," he said. "That sucks. They were good men, honorable men. I hadn't heard . . ." Realization dawned. "Hey, man, I don't do *nothing* with Big Eddie anymore. He's too crazy. The money's not worth it. That man gives me nightmares."

"I know," I said quickly. "I don't want you to get involved."

It was obvious that was a relief. "Well, thanks for sneaking in. Last thing I want is being seen with somebody Big Eddie's looking for. I like not getting my house burned down with me in it, know what I mean?"

"I need a favor."

Guillermo scowled. He knew exactly what kind of favor somebody like me probably needed. "I'm a legitimate businessman now."

"Legitimate my ass. That's why this dinky airstrip has fifty flights a day taking off? Sightseeing?"

He smiled; once a crook, always a crook. "Smuggling is a legitimate business. All right, I still owe you a favor."

Once upon a time—well, about eight years ago— Guillermo had pissed off a certain group of drug dealers. They'd decided that for his disrespect the lovely young Reyes family needed to die. But before that could happen, Carl, Train, and I had made all those bad men go quietly away forever. We'd staged our own little *Dia De Los Muertos*, only with real dead people, *and* kept their money. Good times.

"A favor? You owe me like five." He had three kids, so he knew exactly what I was talking about. "But I'm not picky. I just need intel. It's been a really long time, and I need to cross the border tonight." It would have been nice to fly directly into the states, but since I had no idea what the mystery item in my possession was, I had not wanted to try to bluff my way through US Customs. Those guys were actually really good at their jobs. The officials at the Mexico City airport were a lot easier to work with once you passed over the *mordida*. Reaper was still in Cairo recuperating. Once I had a clue where I was going, he would just fly directly there to meet me. Travel was much simpler when you weren't smuggling glowing beetle vials.

"Whoa. Lorenzo is going back to the States? Are you loco? You need a place to hide, I can help you. I've got a little place back in the mountains. Beautiful. You stay there as long as you want."

"No. I've got to do this. I just need to know where it's safe to cross." The last time I'd been here, Mexico still had a semi-functioning government. I didn't know what the border was like anymore. For all I knew, the Americans had actually secured it since then. "I only need to get into Arizona."

Guillermo plopped into his seat and opened his lunch. He pulled a giant knife from his pocket, flicked it open, and sliced his messy sandwich in two. He passed me the smaller side. "So, you were thinking that with a full-on revolution south of the border, your countrymen would actually be paying attention?" He laughed. "Man, you worry too much. Paying attention would cost money and be *racist*. Some movie stars said so. The military is for rent in this State. You got some extra money and I'll send you across with an army tank if you want."

So, just as lax as usual. *Figures.* "No tanks."

"Seriously, man. It's so open that it's getting bad for business. I'm a professional, I run a *clean* outfit, but now I've got to compete with every coked-out asshole who's just itching to shoot up innocent bystanders. And those UN *pinche* faggots—gotta bribe them more often than I did the old *Federales*. And you won't believe this. I've got rag-heads sneaking across the border to blow shit up. Hell, about once a week now I get some dude named Achmed, pretending to be Mexican, crossing the border with bombs or poison gas or some scary shit. You know me, I kill those *putas* on sight."

"That's mighty nice of you, Guillermo."

He snorted. "They start blowing up schools in Happytown, USA, and it turns out they crossed here, and then the US overreacts once the shit's already blown up, and it'll kill business for us regular guys. It'll go from one Border Patrol per hundred square miles to a thousand Navy SEALs. I know how you Americans do it. You love to lock the barn after all the horses are gone. It's getting bad lately. The world's getting crazier, I tell you."

It was kind of sad when smugglers were our first line of border security. The food was amazing. Juanita was still a great cook. "Got a map?"

Santa Vasquez *stank.*

The smell was a combination of chemicals, garbage, open sewer, and crowded humanity. I had been all over the Third World, and this town had to be in the middle of the list of olfactory offenders. It was worse than Afghanistan, where the stink of dried human waste was embedded into the dust, but it was far better than the shallow-grave smell of Bosnia back when everything fell apart there.

The town was on the other side of the sagebrush-covered hillside, but the prevailing winds still carried the funk toward the Arizona border. It was night and dark enough that I could barely make out the rest of the group stumbling northward. During the day illegals tended to walk in bunches, but at night they unconsciously strung out into a single-file line. I could hear the sloshing of the milk jugs of water that everyone else was carrying. The ground was rough, uneven, and strewn with trash.

I was dressed like the other border jumpers. Rough jeans, a button-down work shirt, and a ratty ball cap. I was unshaven and had not bathed since my flight had landed in Mexico City yesterday morning. I was traveling light, just a small pack and some water. The drug mules were the ones with the burlap forty-five-pound backpacks, and their tracks tended to leave deeper heel prints. Those were the ones that the Border Patrol paid extra attention to, and those boys knew how to track. Once I split off from the herd, I didn't want my footprints to stand out.

It was late June and hot, but my body was acclimatized to the Middle East. This was pleasant by comparison. We were 5,000 feet farther above sea level than I was used to, so I was a bit out of breath. The border was a hundred yards away, and Guillermo said that the terrain was rough enough and covered in ocotillo that it was a rare occurrence to have Border Patrol vehicles in the area.

Since I wanted to be discreet, Guillermo had pointed me to this section. The path was through a rough, hilly area. If any of my fellow travelers got picked up by the USBP, they would be detained, given a Capri Sun drink and a picante-flavored cup of noodles, fingerprinted, and bussed back across the border. For me, I was armed, smuggling something priceless, and had no idea what kind of flags my fingerprints might raise in America, so better safe than sorry.

Jill had not called me back yet, and it was beginning to worry me. I had left a message with the Fat Man to tell Eddie that I would arrange a drop-off within the week. The last thing I wanted was for him to get jumpy. When Eddie gets jumpy, people get burned.

There was movement in the sagebrush ahead. Instinctively, I took a knee and crouched low. The other illegals—technically I suppose I was an illegal, too, even if I was an American citizen—kept walking. They were talking, laughing; a few had ear pieces in and were listening to radios or iPods. I had the impression that most of them had done this before. Pulling the night-vision monocular from a pocket, I pressed it to my eye and scanned the horizon.

Vehicles at the border. *Damn it, Guillermo.* Staying low, I moved off to the side. Thousands of people walk across this border every day, and I have to blunder into a section that was actually covered by *La Migra*. We were in a natural gully with rocky hills surrounding us. It looked like it would be one heck of a climb. I sighed. Apparently I would be taking the high road.

Twenty minutes of hard scrambling later, I was on the

top of the rocky hillside. The terrain up here was horrible, but I was certain that I wouldn't run into any more inconveniences. Only a crazy person or somebody who really wanted to avoid getting spotted was going to take this path into Arizona.

Somebody was coming.

Give me a break. I settled myself into a depression in the rock beneath some prickly pear and scanned through my monocular. Three men were on the steep hillside above, moving through the shadows. They were dressed similar to me, each carrying a heavy pack, and were having a tough time moving through the thick brush and cacti. Probably drug runners. I stayed hidden. Most mules were unarmed, just regular Josés roped into carrying the packages in exchange for passage, but in every group there was usually one actual bad dude with a gun.

I watched them pass. Two of them had long tubes strapped to their packs. They paused just past me at the lip of the hill and examined the trucks parked below. One of them pointed and spoke. It wasn't in Spanish. My ears perked up. I recognized the language. *No way.* I crawled forward slightly, careful to not shift any of the rocks. Scorpions crawled under my body. The man said something else before turning toward the border and continuing on.

What the hell were Chechens doing crossing the American border?

Guillermo hadn't been kidding. It was getting crazy around here. I refocused the monocular and took a closer look. Those tubes looked suspicious.

Oh, wow.

I pulled my STI 9mm from my holster, the Silencerco

suppressor from my pocket, and began screwing them together. *Not in my country, assholes.*

A few hours later, I stood inside a gas-station phone booth in a town north of Nogales, Arizona. It was close to three in the morning and the little desert town was utterly silent. A stray dog watched me from under the gas station's neon sign. Loud insects buzzed around the glass.

"Sheriff's Department."

"Listen to me very carefully," I said, adding a Mexican accent to my voice. "There are three dead men on the American side of the border, just north of Santa Vasquez."

"Okay, and who is this?" The deputy sounded almost bored. Apparently multiple dead bodies were not that strange of an occurrence on the border.

"I'm the man that killed them."

"Wait, what?" *That* got his attention.

"The men were crossing the border. They were Chechen terrorists." I was careful not to touch anything in the booth in a way that would leave fingerprints. My rough clothes were splattered with dried blood.

"Chechens, like from Chechnya?"

"Yes. Write this down." I rattled off the GPS coordinates. "That's where you'll find the bodies. There's a missile hidden under some rocks ten meters east of the bodies."

"A missile?"

"Look, I'm just a coyote," I lied, "but I don't want guys like that shooting down airliners, you know what I mean. I'm calling because one of them talked before he died. There will be a second group crossing the border in the same area just before dawn."

"Sir, I need—" I hung up the phone and quickly walked to the still running Ford Explorer. The last Chechen had talked all right, encouraged by some expedient use of my Greco knife. There had been a vehicle waiting for them, but I didn't feel the need to tell the deputy about where I had left the driver's body. Besides, I had needed a ride.

I had dealt with people like them before, bloodthirsty fanatics who just plain liked to kill innocent people. The average American had no idea what was waiting for them out in the world, and there was some serious badness crawling across the country's soft white underbelly. At first I had assumed that it was just random chance that had allowed me to bump into those men, but I had a sneaky suspicion that Guillermo might have put me on that particular path for a reason, and probably saved him some work, the sneaky bastard.

Warning the cops about the second group of Chechens would count as my good deed for the day. Never hurts to put a check in the positive-karma box. I wiped some of the dried gore from my hands with a rag as I drove north. That third terrorist had been pretty tough, but everybody talks eventually. In the back seat was the second portable Russian surface-to-air missile launcher. I figured it might come in handy.

Flagstaff was my next stop. If my attempt on Eddie failed, then I knew he would kill my family purely out of spite. They deserved a warning. And there was only one person I could think of who might be clever enough to reach them all without Eddie's goons finding out.

Too bad he was an FBI agent. I bet you thought *your* family reunions were awkward.

LORENZO
Flagstaff, Arizona
June 25, 2008

My brother's house was in the suburbs. It had been easy enough to find with the address written in Eddie's folder. The sun had been coming up by the time I found the place, so I had just done a quick drive-by. I had no way of knowing if or how Eddie was monitoring them, so I didn't want to risk a visit during the daytime. Plus, I looked like I was here to pick fruit, smelled horrible, and was still splattered with at least a pint of Chechen.

I checked into a cheap motel, cleaned up, shaved, and slept until sundown. My dreams were strange and featured those dancing hippos from the old Disney movie until they were violently torn apart by an alligator with an effeminate English accent. I woke in a foul mood. Jill still hadn't called back, and frankly that was really beginning to gnaw at me. I called in an update to Reaper before leaving for Bob's place. At least he was sounding healthier, eager for revenge, and was ready to fly out as soon as I needed him.

There was another Ford Explorer in the motel parking lot. Using my Leatherman, I swapped license plates then headed back to the suburbs.

Bob had a great security system. It took me almost three whole minutes to figure out how to circumvent it after I'd climbed over the back fence. Luckily he didn't have a dog. He was allergic to them.

It didn't seem right to break into my own brother's house, and it certainly wasn't the best way to make an impression, especially considering that I hadn't seen him for years and he had no idea what I actually did for a living. But I couldn't risk just knocking on the door in case Eddie was watching the place. The last thing I wanted to do was contact him at work while he was surrounded by other Feds. I've got an aversion to cops. Nothing personal, mind you, just that our philosophies on life tended to diverge rather abruptly.

It was nearing midnight as I crept through the house. There were kids' toys scattered across the carpet and dozens of pictures on the wall. The kitchen was empty, and there were crayon drawings held onto the fridge with magnets. It was a really nice house. Clean, organized, but with that little bit of chaos that healthy kids always managed to bring. It reminded me a bit of Gideon's house, and that thought brought back memories. Gideon Lorenzo had been a good man to take me in. Compared to how I'd grown up, their house had seemed so warm, and I never had to worry about being hit with randomly thrown beer bottles.

Suddenly the room was bathed in scalding light, blinding me. It had to be one of those eyeball-melting police flashlights. "Don't move!" a deep voice bellowed. It was a command voice that was used to being obeyed. I slowly raised my hands to the surrender position.

"It's me, Bob." Hands open, I turned toward the giant in the doorway. "Shoot me, and Mom will be pissed."

The brilliant light moved to the side, leaving white ghosts floating in my eyeballs. "Hector?"

It had been a long time since anybody had called me that.

Robert Lorenzo was big man, six and a half feet tall, broad and barrel-chested. He looked nothing like me at all, which wasn't a surprise, considering that I was a foster kid.

The Lorenzos were good people. I'd never really felt like I had fit in, no matter how hard I'd tried, but they had loved me as if I were one of them regardless. They were hard-working, honestly religious, salt-of-the-Earth decent folks. My real father had been a petty criminal, crackhead, piece of filth, and Gideon Lorenzo was the judge who had finally sent him away for murder.

Gideon had never confided in me the logic behind taking me in. I just remember him staring down at me from that tall judge's seat while I had been giving my eyewitness testimony against my real father. His kind eyes had filled with involuntary tears as I'd talked about how I'd watched my mother get her head kicked in, even after I had tried to defend her by stabbing my father with a fork. I had been twelve.

Four years. For four years I had lived with the Lorenzo family. Then something terrible had happened, popping the happy bubble where I'd briefly gotten to live like a normal person. I had violated Gideon's deathbed final wish, but my services had been needed to make things right, and I did what I had to do.

While in their care, I had never officially taken their last name. After I dropped off the grid, I'd lived under many different names, changing identities like clothing.

Eventually I'd started going by Lorenzo. It had seemed like the thing to do at the time. It had seemed *right*. If only I had realized that it would eventually come back to haunt me.

"So, you want to tell me how you broke into my house?" Bob asked as he settled onto his couch. He put his bare feet up on the coffee table. His Remington 870 was leaning against the arm of the couch.

"Always right to the point with you, wasn't it?" I dodged. "Where's the wife and kids? How's Gwen?"

"Visiting her mom. You'll like her. She's nice. Now back to the B and E." Bob looked like Dad before he had died. The resemblance was almost eerie. The last few years had rendered him totally bald, but that wasn't a surprise, as he'd starting losing his hair at sixteen. "You could have knocked. I almost plugged you back there. I'm a light sleeper."

Real light, apparently. I had been in full ninja mode. "The door was open," I lied.

"No, it wasn't," Bob said with finality. "It was locked, and the alarm was armed. It's been forever since I've seen you, and you sneak into my house in the middle of the night. Why?"

I had to be careful here. He was my older brother, and he was damn smart. I had known him very well once, but we were almost strangers now. "I need your help."

"What's going on, man?" Just like his father, there was no way I was going to be able to lie to this man and get away with it. I just hoped that he wouldn't try to arrest me. That could get messy.

"I had to sneak in because there are people watching

your house. You're in danger, the whole family is in danger, because of me, and I'm here to warn you."

Bob laughed. "You always were a hoot. No, serious, what's going on?" After a moment of studying my grim expression, he realized I was for real, and then there was a hint of anger in his voice. "What have you gotten into?"

The Lorenzos had always been a real law-and-order bunch, except for me, obviously. I leaned back on the comfortable couch and groaned. This wasn't going to be easy. "Do you know what I do for a living?"

"You work for some international-relations firm. That was what the last Christmas card said, which, by the way, is the only reason any of us even realized you were still alive. You've only visited Mom, what, once since you ran off and joined the Peace Corps." He said that with just a hint of disdain. Bob had joined the Army.

"About that . . ." We had been close once. He was only a couple of years older than me, and after Dad had died Bob had become the family rock, while I had run off. This was a lot more difficult than I had thought it would be. "I'm not a businessman. I was never in the Peace Corps. I think they're a bunch of hippies. Look . . . I'm . . . I'm a crook."

"Crook? Like a criminal?" The last little bit of a smile faded. His normally jovial face grew hard, and now he really reminded me of Dad. "What kind of crook?"

"A very good one. Ever hear of the Cape Town diamond-exchange robbery?" I asked. He slowly nodded. I was sure the FBI had passed around a memo about that one. It had been rather impressive. "That was me. Bangkok National. *Me*. Bahrain Museum of Antiquity. *Me*. Vladivostok gold-train heist, all me." Bob's eyes grew wide. Of course he had heard of those. They were some of the more infamous robberies of our generation. "After that, I decided I didn't like robbing normal people and I started to rob from other bad guys. Those jobs you probably haven't heard about, but I'm pretty good at this stuff."

"You can't be serious," he stated.

"I worked for a man called Big Eddie for a long time, the crime lord who has a piece of everything in Asia. I'm assuming the FBI's heard of him?"

"Of course. The organized-crime guys have a task force dedicated to just that group. Personally, I thought he was a fairy tale."

"Oh, he's real." I tossed the manila folder from Thailand on the coffee table between us. Bob picked it up and started to leaf through the family pictures. "He had one last job for me, and he gave me this to assure that I'd do it. I know he'll hurt every single person in there, and I need you to get to them first, as quiet as you can."

My brother crumpled the edges of the folder as he read. I could see the realization that I was telling the truth dawning on his face. "I can't believe this. This . . . this is nuts. Sure, you were always pushing the boundaries, petty theft, joyriding cars, stupid crap, but this?"

"Bob, I know this is a shock, but listen to me. You can't be obvious. Big Eddie will find out. You can't bring in the FBI. Eddie has men on the inside. He will find out. This man sits on Satan's right hand. You have no idea what he's capable of. I need you to help me stop him."

"I can't believe you're some sort of international super thief, I mean, come on man, you were such a . . ."

"Dork?" I offered. It was true. Bob had been the tough one.

"No offense, but heck, when we were kids, when I played football, you did *gymnastics*."

"It comes in handy. I'm a good second-story man."

"You were in the *drama* club. You were really good at it too, before you dropped out."

I shrugged. "Playing pretend comes in handy," I answered, my voice a nearly perfect impression of his own. I'd always had a gift for being someone else. Compared to some of the cons I had pulled off, sophomore-year *Hamlet* was a piece of cake. "Do you believe me?"

He rubbed his face in his hands. After a long pause, he looked me in the eye. "Yes. I can see it. You always were the crazy one." I could tell that this was breaking his heart. He had always looked out for me, like a good big brother. "Hector, you've got to come in with me. The FBI can protect you. *I* can protect you. You can testify against this Big Eddie. I can get you into the witness-protection program."

"Bob. This is bigger than that. Way bigger." I stood. "Please, just get everybody to safety. You don't have much time. And you've got to keep it low profile. Nothing official, because he *will* know. You're the only one that can do this. Eddie tried to kill me. He shot one of my friends and murdered the others. He cut one's *head* off. I've stalled him for now, but the man is a snake, and he'll bite soon. It's his nature."

My brother stood, too. He towered over me, and his face was dark, clouded with anger. The shotgun was still leaning against the couch.

"You gonna try to arrest me?" I asked. Bob was a good and honorable man, and I did not know what I would do if he tried. "If you do, then you're signing our family's death warrant. As soon as Eddie finds out I've made contact with you, they're all dead."

"What do you plan on doing?" Bob was seething.

"I'm going to kill Eddie first."

"You're a murderer, too?"

No point in beating around the bush. "Bob, I shot three Chechens and tortured a fourth one to death before I ate breakfast this morning. What do you think?" I answered, hard and low.

He was taken a back. "That was you? I saw the bulletin about the SAM and the bodies. ICE nailed some more coming over at dawn with missiles because of an anonymous tip. The report said that one of them had been cut to ribbons, bullets in the other one's heads, execution style. . . . I can't imagine my little brother doing that." Bob slowly sat back down. "What have you become?"

"I'm a monster," I answered truthfully. "But I'm still your brother. Protect them, Bob. It's up to you." I turned and walked for the back door. I'm sure this was a lot to take in.

"Hector."

I stopped, hand on the doorknob. He sounded broken. It tore my heart open. "Yeah, Bob?"

"Be careful, little bro."

"You, too," I answered as I slipped out the door and into the night. I had to pause to wipe my eyes before scaling the back fence.

Chapter 26:
Qagmire

VALENTINE
Quagmire, Nevada
June 28
0500

The sun wouldn't be up for a while, but the little diner where Jill worked opened at five. The place opened at oh-dark-thirty so the local ranchers could get their breakfast and coffee. She was on early shift today and was probably getting ready for the early birds. At this hour, she'd be the only one there, doing both the cooking and the serving. The regular cooks and waitresses came in later in the morning.

I hadn't planned on being up that early, but I still had terrible nightmares sometimes. Once I woke up from one of those, I was up for the day. Hell, I didn't want to go back to sleep anyway. I was hungry, too, so off I went to the only place in town where I could get breakfast at that hour without cooking it myself.

A few days earlier, Hawk and I had pulled my Mustang out of his shed and dusted it off. He'd taken very good care of it. The oil had been changed, the tank was full, and the registration fee had been paid for me. I'd missed my car, and it was nice to have it back.

The diner Jill worked at was called Shifty's, which I thought was hilarious. The place had been a staple of Quagmire life for forty years. The food was good, too. I'd eaten here every time I'd returned to Quagmire over the past few years. It was a decent place for Jill to work while she tried to figure out how to start her life all over again.

Really, I was in the same situation. After being gone for months, I was back in the United States, home sweet home. Nothing had changed. The fall of Zubara had been pretty big news while it was happening, but the press had no idea there was direct American involvement. The only ones that even suspected that were conspiracy nuts like Roger Geonoy and the kooky guests on *From Sea to Shining Sea*. I began to wonder if any of their other stuff about aliens, ghosts, and demons was true, too.

Anyway, I was in an interesting situation. It was as if the last six of months of my life had never happened. Save for the scars on my body and the ache in my heart, it would've been easy to pretend that all was well and that everything was normal.

And let me tell you, it was tempting. Back at the Exodus base I had been so filled with rage that I was ready to track Gordon Willis down and murder him. That had been my primary motivation for returning home, after all. But now that I was here . . . well, let's just say that reality had sunk in a little bit.

Having a quiet life and working on Hawk's ranch had done me a lot of good. My mom used to say that taking care of animals, especially horses, was good for the soul. She was onto something, I think. Hawk wouldn't come out and say it, but I think he really enjoyed having Jill and me around. He was old enough to be our father, and had lived alone since his wife, Elaine, died.

Seeing Jill every day had been nice, too. The girl was an absolute sweetheart, and she was beautiful too. After losing Sarah, I was completely disinterested in any kind of romantic pursuits, but . . . well, Jill was easy on the eyes, especially in the little cutoffs and tank top she wore when working in the garden. If things had been different . . . But they weren't.

In any case, I wasn't ready for anything like that, and Jill was still going on and on about how dreamy Lorenzo was. I felt bad for the girl. She was young and, despite everything she'd been through, naïve. Lorenzo wasn't coming back for her, period, end of story. I don't care if he did save my life; it was plain to see what was going on. I just didn't have the heart to tell her. She'd figure it out eventually. Probably better that she came to the realization on her own.

The question remained, though: What in the hell was *I* supposed to do? Aside from Hawk and Jill, I didn't really have any friends. I had nowhere else to go. And what was I going to do, go find a job? I didn't have a fake ID or alternate passport or anything. For all I knew, the moment I popped up on the radar, Gordon Willis's organization would come swooping down in their stealthy helicopters and make me disappear into the night. I was scared to drive my own car anywhere beyond the bounds of Quagmire.

I had thousands of dollars stashed away, so I wasn't hurting for money at the moment. I wasn't about to try to access my old Las Vegas Federal Credit Union account, and I doubted I'd ever been paid a dime for my service in Zubara. But I still had access to my old offshore account with the Bank of Grand Cayman. As far as I knew, my former employers had never found out about it. They probably didn't look real hard, considering they were planning on killing me anyway.

But I couldn't stay in Quagmire forever. It was a small town in the middle of nowhere, which seems like a good place to hide, but it's really not. People noticed a new face in Quagmire, especially one as scarred up as mine. Sooner or later somebody would notice me, and being noticed could get me killed. Not just me, either, but Hawk and Jill also.

Besides, I wasn't about to just stay in Hawk's spare bedroom, mooching off his hospitality until my savings ran out. I was determined not to be a burden on him or put him at risk. I had to leave Quagmire, and soon. But where would I go? My original plan of hunting down Gordon Willis seemed, as Ling suggested it would, silly now. The injustice of what that man had done still burned a pit in my stomach, and I hated him all the more for being powerless to change it, but what could I do? Even if I could get to him without getting picked up, would killing him change anything?

Sighing, I shook my head. Five o'clock in the morning was no time to be making big life decisions, especially not on an empty stomach. I pulled into the empty parking lot of Shifty's and parked my Mustang. Jill liked to walk to work. It appeared I'd be her first customer.

The place was dark. *Weird,* I thought. *Where is she?* Jill should've been there for at least half an hour already, but the diner was still locked up. No one had been in.

Suddenly worried, I looked around the parking lot. Jill had left Hawk's house an hour ago. It didn't take that long to walk to the diner. I hadn't seen her anywhere along the way. It's hard to miss the hottest girl in town in a pink miniskirt jumper and white sneakers, after all.

I couldn't see anything out of the ordinary. I was so upset I was on the verge of panic. If somebody had just driven up and grabbed her on the way to work, how would we ever know? *Oh, God. Oh, God, no . . .*

Something caught my eye then. A faint glow in the darkness, coming from the weeds across the parking lot. It was only there for a moment, then disappeared. I broke out into a run, pulling a small flashlight out of my pocket as I did so. It had come from near the entrance to the parking lot. There were some scrubby little weeds near the edge of the sidewalk.

There. On the ground was Jill's cell phone. The screen had illuminated for a moment and I was lucky to have seen it. Nearby was her purse, its contents spilled out onto the ground. A little bit farther away from the sidewalk I found Jill's gun.

Picking up the little S&W compact, I checked the chamber and magazine. It hadn't been fired. She'd either drawn it and been disarmed or it had been found and tossed. Jill had been taken. There was no doubt about it.

They'd snatched her off the side of the road. I lifted her phone, intending to call the sheriff. Jill had been kidnapped, and there wasn't any time to worry about that.

It hit me then. What if they were looking for me? What if they took her because they thought she could lead them to me? A knot formed in my stomach. It didn't make any sense, but what else could it be? Why would anyone kidnap a waitress in Quagmire freaking Nevada? It couldn't be a coincidence. I couldn't call the sheriff. They'd be waiting for me. But if I didn't call, how would I ever find Jill? I had to do something. They were going to hurt her, or kill her. *Damn it! What do I do?*

I noticed the screen on her phone then. It was open to her address book. There were only two entries, and one of them was Hawk. The other . . . *well, holy shit.*

The phone rang six times before it was answered. On the other end of the phone was a voice I'd not heard in a long time.

"Jill?" he said.

"Guess again, Lorenzo."

LORENZO
Somewhere in Arizona
June 28

I had just hung up on the Fat Man. The meeting had been arranged for a few days from now.

Reaper's snooping had shown that Eddie, like all good international playboys, had a penthouse in Vegas. I had arranged the handoff for some innocuous shopping center with plenty of eyewitnesses, just like they would have expected. My gut told me that though Eddie wouldn't dare show his face at the handoff, he wouldn't be able to wait to see his treasure. So it seemed logical that he would be staying at his local residence.

And the night before the handoff, I was going to break in and take care of business. The place wasn't in his name, rather owned by one of the Montalban family's shell corporations. Reaper, more dedicated than I had ever seen him, had been doing a lot of digging and had compiled quite the list of properties, from private islands to penthouse suites spanning the globe; Big Eddie certainly got around.

The Fat Man had sounded suspicious. They'd probably thought I would have still been somewhere in the eastern hemisphere. Screw them. Las Vegas seemed like as reasonable a place for a drop as any. I could have picked a hundred other cities in twenty countries and Eddie probably had a place there, too.

He wouldn't be expecting me to take the fight right to him. Reaper was en route, and the plan seemed to be coming together. Plotting revenge gave me a feeling of smug satisfaction.

I would be in Vegas before lunch, leaving me with plenty of time to scout the place, take care of some business, catch up on some sleep, and get some Thai food. There was this one little hole-in-the-wall place off the strip . . . My phone rang. I was expecting Reaper, but the caller ID was a surprise. I stared at it for a moment. I had arranged for the drop to be in Nevada once I had figured out that was the prefix from Jill's phone, but now with the handoff arranged . . . *She sure has lousy timing.*

I flipped the phone open. "Jill?" I asked.

"Guess again, Lorenzo."

It definitely wasn't Jill. The voice was familiar . . . from Zubara. *It can't be.* "Valentine?"

"Yeah."

It took me a long moment to wrap my brain around this. How had Dead Six found her? Valentine, the killer with the .44 Magnum, and he was only alive because of my stupidity. I should have killed him when I had the chance. "If you hurt her, I swear I'll—"

He cut me off. "Shut up. Listen to me."

"No, *you* listen to *me!* I'll cut your eyes out if you don't put her on," I shouted into the phone.

"Goddamn it, if you want that girl to live, *listen to me.*"

"What did you do with her?" I asked before he could say anything else.

"For Christ sakes, I didn't do anything with her. Somebody else did. They took her."

"*Who* did? Where?"

"I don't know. Who else have you pissed off?"

Answering that accurately would require a lot of time and thought. "Where was she taken?"

"Quagmire. It's in Nevada."

"I've never been there, but I know where it's at. I'm a few hours away," I said, stomping on the gas. The terrorists' Ford wasn't built for speed, but I would make it work. "What happened?"

"They grabbed her on the way to work. I was going to stop in and say hi, get some breakfast, but she never made it. I found her stuff on the ground in the parking lot."

"Wait, what are you talking about? What's Jill doing hanging around with *you*?" My hand tightened on the phone so hard I thought it was going to break.

"She was in Quagmire when I got there."

"Then what are *you* doing in Quagmire?"

"None of your goddamn business," Valentine said. "Try to keep up. I was in Quagmire. I met the girl there, your little sidekick that shot me in the back in the Zoob. Something happened. She was taken. I don't know who did it. I found her phone. I called you. Still with me?"

"Yes," I said, trying not to let my frustration bubble over into anger. "Could it have been Gordon? Jill told me about a run-in at the embassy with somebody named Gordon Willis." There was no response. "Valentine?" I wondered for a moment if the line had gone dead.

"Yeah, you're right. I thought they were looking for me. But I think they were looking for *her*. They're good at cleaning up the loose ends."

"You know this Gordon Willis?"

"Long story. Look, if they have her, they're going to make her disappear. We don't have any time."

"That's not going to happen. I'll be there in a few hours," I repeated.

"Can I ask you something?" Valentine said after a long pause.

"What? Go ahead."

"Is it true that you pulled me out after I went down? In the fort, I mean."

"Yeah, I did."

"Why did you do that?" he asked.

"I . . . I don't know. You don't sound very grateful."

"I'm *not*," he said harshly. "Call me when you get here."

The line went dead.

LORENZO

Quagmire, Nevada

Quagmire was a typical, pissant desert town. The only things that looked new were the McDonald's and the slot machines. Nothing interesting ever happened in towns like this. It wasn't the kind of place that attracted rogue government operators, that was for sure. This should have been a great place to disappear.

You would think.

Valentine had given me directions to a small ranch on the outskirts of town. Even in the middle of the day, the roads were mostly deserted. If this was a setup, I was walking right into it.

The house was far enough out of town and away from any neighbors that there could be a ton of gunfire and nobody would notice. It was rather isolated on its own gravel road, surrounded by barbed wire and trees. Some horses studied me stupidly. I hate horses.

The weight of the STI on my belt was comforting, but if this was a professional trap, it wouldn't do me a bit of good. Somebody would snipe me from the trees or a SWAT team would toss flash-bangs and then swarm around every corner. I walked up the porch, knocked, and waited. If I was the hitter in this situation, this is when I would just shoot them through the door.

There was a noise as the door was unlocked. Then it creaked open.

Valentine.

This was the first time I'd seen him in person without immediate violence. He was just over six foot. Dark hair, a face that made him look too young, muscular, but he really didn't look like much. Yet I had already gotten my ass kicked once by this guy, so I knew that looks could be deceiving. His face was still healing from where I had cut him, and that wasn't the only scar visible. Valentine looked older now than when I had met him before, tired and run down. Zubara had taken a lot from him. His eyes were different colors. I'd never noticed that before. It was weird. It made it a little unsettling to look him in the eye. It kind of pissed me off.

"Hey."

"Hey." He leaned his head out of the doorway and looked around the gravel driveway. I don't know what he was expecting to see. It wasn't like I would need to bring friends if I was going to waste him. Valentine regarded me warily, like most people would look at an unfamiliar dog. Finally he turned into the entry, nodding his head for me to follow.

The living room was vaguely rustic, with antlers mounted on the walls and a few pictures over the fireplace. It didn't feel like his place. It was an awkward moment. Neither one of us offered to shake hands. I stepped inside and he gestured toward a chair.

"No thanks. I'll stand." It was slower to draw from a hip holster while seated and I didn't trust him as far as I could throw him.

"Suit yourself." He closed the door.

"Anything new on Jill?"

"Nothing. There's not much to Quagmire, so she's probably not here. I don't know where they've taken her. We didn't get the authorities involved. Hawk called her boss at the diner and said she had to leave for a family emergency, so no one in town is suspicious."

"The cops can't do anything I can't," I said. The FBI handles all kidnapping cases, and I really didn't want *them* involved in this. Especially not my brother.

"Like I said, they must've grabbed her on the way to work. I found her purse, her phone, and her gun lying on the ground. She didn't get a shot off or anything. I have no idea who would've taken her."

"Maybe they were looking for *you*," I snapped. "What the hell are you doing here anyway?" It infuriated me that Jill might've gotten caught up in Valentine's mess. I swear this kid destroys and ruins everything he comes into contact with. He was the bane of my existence, and it was all I could do to not punch him in his stupid face then shoot him between his stupid mismatched eyes.

"Maybe they were looking for *you*," he retorted. "Or did it never occur to you that hanging out with a guy like you could be bad for your friends' health?"

My muscles tightened. My fists clenched. A vein bulged in my forehead. Valentine didn't know about Carl or Train, but that was about the worst possible thing he could've said to me. I was very close to pulling out my STI and putting a bullet in this asshole.

He must've read my body language. The expression on his face subtly changed. "Go ahead," he said, staring me down. "*Pull* it. You better be quick, motherfucker."

"You don't know when to quit, do you?" I growled, tensing up.

"Because you know what will really help you find Jill? Shooting *me*. Assuming you're faster than me, which you're not. And then if you do get her back alive, you can explain to her how you murdered me in a tantrum because I said something that made you mad. After she's spent days telling me what a great guy you are, I'm sure she'll understand."

I grudgingly had to admit to myself that he had a point. This pissing contest was getting us nowhere. Jill's life was in our hands. I exhaled heavily and tried to force myself to relax. Valentine did the same. "Sorry . . . I've been driving all day." I relented and sat in down in a chair. "Why did you call me, Valentine?"

"Jill's a nice girl. She told me her story, you know. She was doing fine until she got caught up in the crap that we got caught up in. You and I, and the people we associate with, came into that girl's life and screwed it up royally. And now, either because she knows me or because she knows you, her life is in danger. *Again*. She deserves better than that. I don't want to see anything happen to her. And I didn't know who else to call. What are the cops gonna do? The people that might be after us are more than the sheriff can handle. Also . . ." Valentine trailed off for a moment. "Jill told me you saved my life. There've been times when I wish you'd have just left me there, too. But debts have to be repaid all the same. We owe her a debt, too. We brought this on her. So you and I, we need to make this right." He was quiet for a moment. What he'd just told me had obviously been hard for him to say. "You know, I honestly don't know what she sees in you."

"Hell, me either," I said, but really I was just trying to be agreeable. I happen to think I'm a pretty amazing guy.

In all of my life, no matter how bad things got, I never once wished I was dead. My survival instinct is too strong. I know I'm not going to live forever, but damn if I'm not going to try. I don't give up. I don't quit. And I'd kind of assumed Valentine was much the same. I'd seen him in action, after all. He was a hardened killer, the man that had thwarted me at every turn, my *nemesis*, but all I saw was a broken young man who'd watched his girlfriend get shot to death right before his eyes. He couldn't have been much more than twenty-five, and he acted as if his life was over. They'd taken everything from him. That's when it hit me, slapped me right in the face. I finally understood why I had dragged him out of Fort Saradia.

I'd felt *sorry* for him.

I hadn't known that I was capable of pity. I shook my head, and then it was gone. Men like us didn't need pity, just a balancing of the scales. As far as I could see, what Valentine needed was a cleansing vengeance, but there wasn't time to ponder on his questionable mental state. We had work to do. "Do you know how they found her?

"I don't know. She's been here longer than me. She works at a little diner in town called Shifty's, but lives under an assumed name, Peaches."

"Right."

"It seems we have a mutual friend here. Everyone in town thinks . . . well, thinks Jill is Hawk's illegitimate daughter that he was reunited with. Hawk didn't try to dispel the rumors. Thinking she was Hawk's daughter kept horny ranch hands from sniffing around, and it was better than the town thinking he'd shacked up with a woman young enough to be his daughter, I guess. Hawk's been letting me crash here, too."

Hawk? I looked around the living room. Suddenly everything seemed to fit. I knew this wasn't Valentine's house. It was *Hawk's.* I knew that Hawk would take care of her when I sent her to him. I never imagined she'd end up living in his house.

"How do you know Hawk?" I asked. "And what are you doing living over his garage like the Fonz?"

"You making a scrapbook?" Valentine retorted. "That's none of your business. And no, he wouldn't tell me anything about you, either."

Of course. Hawk was a professional. "Let's keep it that way. Where is he?"

"He's out in town talking to some people, trying to find out if anyone saw anything. He'll be back soon. But money says she's long gone by now. I wish I had more to tell you."

"I've called in some help. My associates will be here soon." It sounded more important to say *associates* rather than lone techno-geek. "They're good at shaking the trees and seeing what falls out. Right now your buddy Gordon Willis is the only lead we've got. He's a federal employee of some kind, right? It's a start." There was the outside chance that Bob might know of him, too, but I didn't say that.

My phone rang. "Hang on." I was hoping that it would be Bob with good news about how he'd arranged to get the family to safety, but I didn't recognize the number.

"Mr. Lorenzo." The voice was electronically distorted, drastically deep.

"Yes?" My frown must have indicated to Valentine that something was up. He stood, looking nervous, and peeked through the blinds.

"We have your friend, Jill Del Toro. If you ever want to see her alive again, you will do exactly what I say."

"I'm listening," I replied calmly. Inside I was raging, wanting to kill, to murder, to drive my knife through someone's trachea and shower in the arterial spray. "What do you want?"

"You have two videos of Americans in Zubara. One video of two Americans executing a man. A second aerial video of a gun battle between Americans and the Zubaran army. You will deliver those to us. You will do so in person. If you do not, Miss Del Toro will die."

Videos? I hadn't even thought of those since getting the key back. As far as I was aware, Reaper had them on his laptop. Jill must have told Gordon's men about them while being interrogated. "Let me speak to Jill so I can know she's okay."

The line was silent for a few seconds. Then Jill's voice, desperate, "Lorenzo! It's a tra—" Then she was gone.

Of course it was a trap. Why else would they want me in person? I could easily have made copies. The videos were just an excuse. They wanted the witnesses dead. Back to the distorted voice; the speaker sounded vaguely demonic. "Where are you now?"

"Maine." My cell phone was untraceable.

"You have twenty-four hours to get to Nevada. We will contact you then."

"I want to see her in person or you don't get the videos."

"Of course." The line went dead. I resisted the urge to chuck the phone across the room.

Valentine scowled at me. "They'll be waiting for you. You know it's a trap, right?"

I nodded. "They won't expect *you*, though. Feel like making some trouble?"

Valentine actually grinned. It was an unpleasant, predatory expression, like a wolf eyeballing a rabbit. "I need to break in my rifle anyway."

"We need to make a plan."

"How about we drive there and shoot everybody?"

"Except for Jill," I corrected. "But that'll do." We were going to need a little more finesse than that, probably, but that was pretty much what it amounted to. Valentine held out one hand. I didn't trust him. I didn't like him. But I knew he could fight, and he was the best option Jill or I had right now.

We shook on it.

Chapter 27:
Last of the Gunslingers

VALENTINE

Once again I was in the middle of somebody else's fight. The story of my life, right? Well, not so much this time. I had reason to believe that Gordon's group was behind the abduction. It wasn't really through any desire to repay Lorenzo for saving my life, because *fuck him*. But I liked Jill. And like I told Lorenzo, she didn't deserve to die because of her association with *us*.

As for Lorenzo . . . he was a strange one. He was constantly on edge, with a sort of angry nervous energy. I didn't trust him, though I really didn't think he'd try anything while Jill's life was on the line. Frankly I couldn't see how somebody with a heart of gold like her could fall for such a prick.

Lorenzo was hard to describe. He was short, six inches shorter than me at least. I couldn't tell what ethnicity he was. His skin was a pretty indistinct shade of brown that could've originated from dozens of countries. His black hair was cropped short, and he had some kind of permanent stubble thing happening on his chin. His eyes were like knives, and I swear he was always watching you.

He had gone into the other room to make a phone call, muttering about "gathering intel" or something. I listened to his half of the conversation through the door all the same. Some guy named Bob had been pissed about something but had known right away who Gordon was. The conversation had ended abruptly after that.

A couple hours later, Lorenzo's so-called associates arrived. His associates consisted of exactly one skinny Goth kid dressed all in black, carrying a laptop. He had a big hockey bag slung over his shoulder.

The kid was a trip. Black fatigue pants, combat boots, black Rob Zombie T-shirt, black trench coat, and his hair hanging in front of his eyes. He had piercings in his nose and ear. He had tattoos on what small amount of his pasty white skin could be seen.

He looked surprised when he noticed me sitting against the far wall.

"Who the hell are you?" he asked.

"Who the hell are *you*?" I retorted.

"Wait . . . it's you! You're that guy!"

Raising my eyebrows, I looked over at Lorenzo. *Seriously?* Lorenzo just shrugged.

"What are you doing here?" the kid asked.

"I'm going to help you get Jill back so I can get on with my life," I said, going back to my cleaning. On a table in front of me was my disassembled DSA FAL carbine. It had a short, sixteen-inch barrel, a folding stock, and rail hand guards. It was equipped with an ACOG scope and a weapon light. It was nearly identical to the carbine I'd carried while on Switchblade 4. Also on the table was my beloved .44, a S&W Performance Center Model 629 Classic. It had a five-inch heavy barrel, a smooth, stainless-steel cylinder, and a black Melonite finish on the rest of the gun. Lorenzo had given me a dirty look when I pulled it out. I just smiled at him in return.

Lorenzo addressed his associate. "Reaper, this is—"

"I know who he is," the kid interrupted. "Is he for real?"

"He's for real," Lorenzo replied.

Reaper, I guess his name was, stared at me. "Dude, what's wrong with your eyes? They're like totally different colors. That's fucked up."

Lorenzo ignored him. "Let's get started. How are we gonna do this?"

"I'm still on board with the 'go in and kill everybody' plan," I said. "Or did you get enough information to make a better plan than that?"

"No." Lorenzo frowned. "We need to find Jill first. We still need more information. Their *meet* will be a turkey shoot. I called somebody earlier who might know. He's working on it now." Reaper raised an eyebrow, but Lorenzo didn't elaborate about his mysterious phone call.

"I don't think we have a lot of time," I said. "We don't know what we don't know. We'll just have to go in and play it by ear."

"Not really my style," Lorenzo said.

"Mine, either," I confessed. "But nobody ever tells me what the hell is going on, so I just roll with it. You guys got weapons?" If they didn't, Hawk sure had a basement full of them.

"Hells *yeah*, we got weapons!" Reaper said. He picked up the hockey bag and dumped it out onto a table. Lorenzo rolled his eyes as weapons, magazines, radios, body armor, and night-vision equipment came clattering out of the bag, landing in a heap on the table.

So *this* was the crack team that had managed to track down Dead Six and infiltrate our compound. I shook my head and went back to my cleaning.

Reaper handed a carbine to Lorenzo, who proceeded to check it. Some kind of short, select-fire AR-15, with a twelve-inch barrel and a suppressor. Reaper pulled from the bag a Glock 17. He inserted a magazine, chambered a round, then stuck the pistol in a shoulder holster under his trench coat. On his belt he had more magazines. He then picked up what I assumed was his primary weapon.

"Benelli M1," Reaper said proudly as he started stuffing 12-gauge shells into every available pocket. "Semi-auto, short barrel, badass all the way."

"That's actually a Benelli *M2*," I corrected. Reaper frowned. I wondered how well Reaper could use his shotgun, though. He looked like an extra from *The Matrix*. Reassembling my rifle, I watched the two of them get suited up. I could tell they'd been working together since . . . well, probably since that kid graduated from high school, which couldn't have been all that long ago. Still, for old friends, they didn't talk much. It might've been because of my presence, but then, professional thieves probably have some weird interpersonal dynamics going on.

Like I've got any room to talk, right?

Hawk came home while we were still playing dress up.

He scowled first at the strangeness that was Reaper, then at me, then finally gave Lorenzo a silent nod. "Been a long time."

"Hawk," Lorenzo responded uncomfortably.

The two stayed, exchanging a look that I couldn't decipher. There was a lot of history there, and I couldn't tell if they were friends or enemies or maybe somehow both. Finally, Hawk spoke. "No sign of the girl. No one in town knows anything."

"I guess we keep waiting," I said.

Lorenzo reached into his pocket as his phone vibrated. "Yeah?" He listened for at least a minute straight. "Okay, I got it. Thanks. I'll be in touch."

Hanging up the phone, he looked at me.

"What's the word?" I asked, fiddling with my thigh holster like a woman adjusting a stocking.

"Our next stop is a closed rest stop down the highway. Out past it is an abandoned prison work camp. That's where they're holding her."

"You're sure of this? Can your friend be trusted?"

"Oh, I'm sure. He's like a brother to me."

LORENZO

The four of us were still in Hawk's house, readying equipment. We would be leaving in a few minutes. At one point I caught Hawk studying me. He motioned for me to step aside to speak. I stopped loading magazines long enough to follow. He had aged a lot since I had seen him last. I knew Hawk was at least a decade older than I was, and there had apparently been some hard years in there. His hair was grayer, his face lined and creased by the sun and wind of several continents, and he'd picked up a limp at some point.

When we were out of earshot, Hawk began to speak. "You know, I thought you were dead. Everybody from the old crew thought for sure those Cubans had got you in Sweothi City."

"It was better that way," I answered. "Some of us didn't part on the best of terms. I figured it would be easier for everybody if Decker assumed I was dead."

Hawk nodded sagely. "That was probably smart. Adrian wasn't the kind of man that I'd want holding a grudge against me, so I suppose it was for the best. Well, I was glad to hear from you. I always hated losing men. I just wished you would have called sooner, because that's one less thing I would have had gnawing at me, Ozzie."

It had been a long time since I had gone by that name, just one of many in a long line of aliases. "I go by Lorenzo now."

"That's what Jill told me. That girl wouldn't shut up about you. She's got quite the fondness for you. She talked a lot, but I'll admit, it was nice having a young lady around. You've changed more than your name, *Lorenzo*. You're a different man than you were back in Africa."

"What makes you say that?" I asked slowly.

"The man I knew back then was a stone-cold killer who only thought about himself and back-stabbed anybody who got in his way, unless you just happened to somehow become one of his friends, and he didn't have hardly any of those. A man so twisted up inside and scary driven that it even got to worrying somebody like Decker. Why do I think you changed? Because for a woman that good to take a liking to you, you're either a better man than I remember, or you're a whole lot better con." The old mercenary gave me the smallest bit of a grin. "And Val might not think so yet, but you did the right thing helping him. That boy's like a son to me. Don't you tell him I said that."

"You don't have to come with us, Hawk."

He was solemn. "True. I don't. I'm retired. I've got a nice place, just how I like it. Comfortable, I suppose. But you know, I think I took a liking to that girl too. Hell, Val and that little lady damn near killed each other in my kitchen when he first got here. Had to separate 'em like a couple of squawkin' kids." Hawk let out a raspy laugh. "He's sure got a soft spot for the females. And they're about the same age. They got along after a while. Gave her someone else to blab about you to. I was getting tired of it."

I laughed along with him. We'd overthrown a country together once. Hawk was the last of the gunslingers, and there was nobody alive I'd rather have at our side.

Valentine appeared in the doorway. "It's time." He was dropping rounds into his revolver and snapped the cylinder closed. Well, maybe Hawk wasn't the *last* of the gunslingers.

VALENTINE

It was a long drive out of Quagmire to the rest stop, following a lonely two-lane highway with sparse traffic.

We were far away from the nearest interstate, and there wasn't much going on out here. The rest stop itself was closed, but you could still pull off into the parking lot. Sitting in that parking lot was a nondescript black Suburban. I watched Lorenzo get out of his car, and I could tell he was surprised.

Anxious, I got out myself, my hand hovering over my pistol. All four of us had on body armor and other assorted battle rattle. I hoped like hell it wasn't a cop. At best, he'd think we were a bunch of militia nuts or mall ninjas. Or maybe we could pass ourselves off as airsofters. Anyway, I doubted most militia nuts were nearly as armed and dangerous as we were.

From out of the Suburban stepped a big guy, tall, barrel-chested, and muscular. He and Lorenzo were exchanging words as I approached, and the bald man seemed none too concerned that Lorenzo was dressed in full tac gear. I could tell they knew each other. Was this the "Bob" guy Lorenzo had been talking to on the phone? Why would he be here?

That's when I noticed the government plates on the Suburban. "Well, fuck me," I said to myself. There were Feds here. Lorenzo had called a Federal Agent. Was this a setup? Had this entire thing been some overcomplicated scheme to turn me over to the government? It didn't make any sense. My mind raced. Adrenaline surged.

"Lorenzo, you need to tell me what the hell is going on here," I said calmly. My right hand had reflexively found its way to my chest, resting on my plate carrier. My left hand was on the butt of my .44. "Why is there a Fed here?"

"No! It's cool! It's cool!" he said excitedly. "This is my brother, Bob. He's—"

I unsnapped the retention device on my thigh holster.

"Listen to me!" Lorenzo insisted. "It's not like that. He's my *brother*. He wasn't supposed to *be* here. He's supposed to be getting his *family* to *safety*!" Lorenzo glared at the other man.

"So," I said, *Calm* wavering as I grew angry, "you called a *Fed*. Your brother the *Fed*. You idiot! Why in the hell didn't you just have me call the cops if you wanted the Feds involved? Jesus, why don't we just the ATF and the Secret fucking Service while you're we're it! Hell, we can get the DEA and the Coast Guard in on it, too, and have a giant fucking federal law-enforcement jamboree!"

"Look, kid," the big man said, "I don't know who you are and I don't care. I'm here to help my brother get his girlfriend back."

"She's not my girlfriend!" Lorenzo sputtered. The big man grinned. I relaxed slightly. Though they didn't look anything alike, they sure acted like brothers.

"This is Bob," Lorenzo sighed "Bob, this is—"

"Don't you *dare* tell him my name!" I yelled, wheeling around.

Lorenzo laughed. "I'm just kidding, relax."

It was going to be a long night.

LORENZO

Valentine stomped away, muttering and swearing. I turned back to Bob and whispered, "What're you doing here?"

"I've got a contact in Vegas I was going to see. Let's just say he's *outside* my chain of command, but he's really good at hiding people. Don't worry. I've got things moving to protect everyone from your boss." My giant of a brother nodded after Valentine. "Your friend seems a little tense."

"He's wound kind of tight. But back to the question, what are you doing here? What about the family?"

"The family will be fine. I've put some things into motion. You should have come to me sooner." Bob shaded his eyes and scanned the horizon. "Look, Hector, this Gordon Willis you asked me about, he's not just a low-level chump. He's more important than that. I don't think you realize just who he works for, but it's bigger than you can imagine. If he has your friend, she's in big trouble."

"You can't do this, you're the law. You're a *cop!*"

"I won't be for long if anybody ever finds out about this," he answered. "Maybe we can share a cell."

"But these are *your* people."

He raised his voice. "These are not *my* people. My people take an oath to defend the Constitution, and I'm sick of watching men like Willis shred it. People like him work in a different kind of government than the one I signed on to. Black, secret, unaccountable. We're not even supposed to ask questions about his operation. He's had suspects taken in, no evidence, no investigation, no trial, and they just disappear into thin air, forever. These aren't even bad guys they're rolling up. They're regular folks who've asked too many questions about the wrong powerful people."

This was kind of a scary paradigm shift. Bob had always been the good one and I had been the bad one. *Simple.* "But you've always been so . . . law-abiding."

"There's a higher law, and it's time that these men had to answer to it." Bob was truly angry, red-faced and nostrils flaring, like the very idea of Gordon's outfit offended him to his core. "I'll take the risk."

"You're familiar with them?"

"You have no idea," Bob stated coldly. "Let's just say that you don't know as much about me as you think you do and leave it at that. I can't let you go in there with just these guys." He gestured at the other three. "Who are they, anyway?"

"You can call the big kid *Nightcrawler* since he's so worried about me telling you his name. The old guy is Hawk. The other kid goes by Reaper."

"Okay, then I'm Colossus and you can be Wolverine. Doesn't anybody have a normal name in your business?"

"Actually, I go by Lorenzo," I responded, slightly embarrassed.

Bob just stared at me. "Seriously? Wow, man, that's *devious*. And what part came as a surprise when Big Eddie found his way past your masterful secret identity? You were only raised by Lorenzos."

Reaper walked up. "If we've all got superhero names, then Jill should be Aquaman since she's been kidnapped twice." I just looked at him like he was stupid. "What? Didn't you ever watch *Super Friends*? Aquaman . . . you know, always got captured? Never mind." Reaper wandered off.

"*Super Friends* was off the air before that kid was born," Bob said.

"I know, but he spends a lot of time on the Internet."

"You guys done screwing around?" Valentine growled as

he approached. "Let's get going. We're kind of conspicuous hanging around in all of this crap," he said, indicating the pouch-laden plate carrier and battle belt he wore.

He was right. We needed to get going. "We're not here to arrest them," I warned Bob.

My brother shook his head sadly. "Willis's men aren't the type you can arrest. They're a bunch of professional killers. Castoffs who've gotten kicked out of every reputable organization there is because they're too violent, too crazy, or too corrupt. Operations like his attract them like flies."

"How do you know all this?" Hawk asked suspiciously. Switchblade hadn't always been a respectable mercenary company, so Hawk had developed an appropriate paranoia about the law.

Bob shrugged. "A man has to have a hobby. Mine is collecting trivia about scumbags." My brother was being evasive. Somehow he knew exactly who Gordon Willis was, knew something about his organization, and apparently hated them with a passion. "The old work-camp is over that rise. We used to use it to hole up Mafioso witnesses out of Vegas. Word is that Willis's men are using it for something now."

"Let's get these cars hidden, then sneak up on the camp and see if we can spot Jill," I suggested, hefting my AR-15. "If we're lucky, maybe we can get her out with minimal shooting."

"I wouldn't bet on that." Bob turned, opened the back of his Suburban, and pulled out a long black Remington 700 sniper rifle, with a suppressor, bipod, and US Optics scope. He worked the bolt and chambered a round. He put the heavy barreled rifle over one shoulder. Bob almost seemed to be looking forward to this. Maybe I *didn't* know him as well as I thought I did. "When the shooting starts, take them hard and fast."

"That's what *she* said!" Reaper quipped.

"You. Stop talking," Valentine ordered.

Reaper grinned, gesturing with his stubby shotgun. "Then let's go." The bravado was forced. The kid was tough, but he wasn't a warrior like the rest of us, but God bless his techno-geek soul, he was ready. "Let's smoke these fags."

Hawk adjusted his old South African army vest. "Yep." Then he spat on the ground.

Valentine raised an eyebrow. "Smoke these fags?" he asked, looking at me incredulously. "What have you been *teaching* this kid?" I held up my hands in surrender. A general has to fight with the army he's got.

The five of us climbed the sagebrush-and-scrub-tree hill. The sun was rapidly setting. I suggested we track farther to one side so that we could attack out of the sun. Valentine didn't seem to care one way or the other, Bob and Hawk thought it was a good idea, and Reaper was used to following my orders.

We picked our frequencies and checked the radios on the walk in, and they worked fine. We had no plan and no intel. Our group had never worked together before, and there wasn't a lot of trust.

"So why do you guys use those old Belgian rifles?" Reaper asked Hawk and Valentine at one point, displaying his ignorance. "Those are the same kind as those rusty poacher guns from all over Africa, right? Why don't you get something *new*?"

Hawk grunted. "They're all over Africa because they still work, kid. Besides, you can dress 'em up if you want. Look at his," he said, indicating Valentine's railed-up FAL. "You can bolt ten pounds of crap on it if you want." Valentine's rifle was fitted with a Tijicon scope and had a flashlight bolted to the hand guards. It looked heavy, but he didn't seem to mind. "And it's at least a manly thirty caliber, unlike Lorenzo's pussy twenty-two."

I paid Hawk's opinions on terminal ballistics no mind. I'd lost track of how many people I'd killed with a short-barreled 5.56 over the years. I preferred lots of little bullets to a few big ones, but then again, anybody worth shooting once was worth shooting five to seven times.

"M-16s are poodle shooters," Hawk said. "That's all they're good for."

"I'm pretty good with a FAL," Valentine answered Reaper, not looking up from the trail through the sage-brush.

"How good is pretty good?" Reaper asked. The kid just didn't know when to quit.

"Look," Valentine said levelly, pointing the knife-edge of his hand at Reaper. "This isn't a *game*, okay? You need to focus, or you're going to get yourself *killed*. Now either lock it up or go wait in the car!"

Reaper seemed taken aback by Valentine's harsh words. "Okay, okay! Sorry. I miss a lot. That's why Lorenzo makes me use the shotgun."

"Super," Valentine muttered. "You know, we really ought to be quiet."

"Kid's right. Quiet down. They might have sentries posted at the top of the hill," Hawk suggested.

"They won't," Bob replied. "They've been operating above the law so long, they think they're untouchable. The idea of us coming to them will never even enter their minds."

"I hope you're right," Hawk muttered.

After half an hour of walking, we hunkered down in the rocks overlooking the old prison work camp. It looked like a ghost town out of an old western movie. There were several wooden buildings, in two horizontal rows heading away from us, paint long since peeled, signs long since faded. One larger building was directly below us, newer, built out of cinder blocks; it looked like it had been a truck stop or some sort of garage back in the days before the freeway bypassed this little settlement. Fence posts stuck out of the ground like random teeth in a broken jaw, the barbed wire mostly rusted away.

There were several vehicles parked on the broken asphalt around the garage, new vehicles, black sedans, a Chevy passenger van, and another G-ride Suburban. There were a couple of men standing around the cars, smoking, talking, long guns visible slung from their backs.

"Damn, there's a lot of them," I said.

Bob extended the bipod legs on his sniper rifle and hunkered down, scanning through his scope. "I've got three in the parking lot. At least one moving inside the garage." After a moment he stopped, then cranked up the magnification. "Hector, take a look at the window on the left."

"Hector?" Reaper laughed. "Your real name is Hector?"

"Shut it . . . *Skyler*," I answered. Reaper was immediately silent. Valentine snorted as he tried to suppress a laugh.

"Yeah? Well, what the fuck kind of name is *Nightcrawler*?" Reaper asked defensively.

"It's French," he replied, looking through the scope on his rifle. He then turned to my teammate. "You know that's not actually my name, right? Just like you. Reaper isn't your real name. *Skyler* is your real name, and I think it's pretty." Valentine cracked a smile again.

I shushed Reaper before he could retort. Bob moved aside and I got behind the Remington. It took a moment to find the right window on 14X magnification. The glass was gray with filth and hard to see through. "That's her." Jill was slumped in a chair, long black hair obscuring her face. Seeing her there filled me with fresh anger.

The terrain leading up to that window was rough enough that it gave me an idea. I didn't want to endanger the lives of these men any more than I had to. I moved into a crouch and examined each of them in the fading light. "Okay. Here's the plan. I'll sneak up on that building, break in, and secure Jill. If everything works out, I can get her out of there before they ever even know we were here."

"That's just stupid," Bob said. "There's no way you could sneak in there under their noses."

Reaper just looked at him and grinned. "Dude, you have *no* idea. Your brother could steal cookies from the Keebler elves."

Hawk reached over and tapped Valentine on the arm, gesturing down the hillside. "Check out that ravine," he said. He'd always had a good eye for terrain.

Valentine nodded. "While you're crawling through the weeds, we'll take Marilyn Manson here and head down that way. It'll put us closer so we can back you up if this all goes to shit." He looked to Bob. "You good enough with that rifle to give us some cover?"

My brother nodded. Before I had dropped off the grid, Bob had already been a champion rifle competitor. When we were teenagers, I had spent my free time boosting cars, while he had shot coyotes for the local farmers. Bob was better than me at most things, and shooting was probably toward the top of that list, and that was before he had joined the Army and become some sort of Green Beret or something.

"He'll do fine. We all will." This was it. This wasn't a heist, it wasn't a job. These men were here to help me. This was a rescue mission. I'd led many crews, but usually for money. I didn't know how to motivate people with pure intentions. Awkwardly, I put my hand out, palm down. "Thanks, guys."

Reaper enthusiastically put his on top of mine. "Anytime, chief!"

It took a moment before Bob followed suit. "No problem, bro."

Valentine looked at us incredulously. "Are you guys for real?"

"I'm not really good at saying thank you, okay?"

Valentine glanced over at Hawk, who just shrugged, then back at us. "You guys are so *gay*."

Reaper yanked his hand back, embarrassed. Okay, so maybe it was corny. I took one last look at my friends—and Valentine—nodded, and disappeared into the weeds.

♠

Chapter 28:
The Calm

VALENTINE

Lorenzo's little buddy tagged along as Hawk and I made our way down the ravine, practically crawling along as we went. There were several cars parked outside of the building that Jill was being held in, and there were armed men standing watch outside. They didn't seem particularly alert, but it wasn't quite dark yet and I didn't want to blow our cover.

I was most worried about them spotting Reaper. Where Hawk and I were dressed in earth tones and flat colors, Reaper was dressed entirely in black. Black sticks out pretty clearly against a dusty brown hillside in the Nevada desert. Worse, the kid just didn't know how to move. We had to crawl along more slowly than we would have otherwise, making sure Reaper utilized available cover and concealment.

Lorenzo, on the other hand, moved like a ghost. I tried to track him as he crept down the hill parallel to us, but quickly lost sight of him in the sage. Grudgingly impressed, I had little doubt Lorenzo would make it all the way down without being spotted.

LORENZO

There was probably only a few minutes of weak daylight left coming over the hills by the time I crept up on the cinder-block wall. My load-bearing equipment was coated in dirt, twigs, and dead sage. I hadn't been seen.

"*Looking good,*" Bob's voice said in my ear. "*Guards are leaning on the cars out front. I don't see any movement in the back room. There are a few men inside the next room.*"

Crouching below the window, I cradled my nose-heavy AR in my strong hand and reached up and tested the window. It was the multi-paned, hinged type. It moved slightly. It was unlocked. Just then my phone began to vibrate. I pulled it out of my pocket, glanced both ways, still clear, and flipped it open. "Hello?" I whispered.

"*Mr. Lorenzo.*" It was the digitally altered voice. I could hear the real voice through another broken window fifteen feet away. "*Where are you?*"

"I'm going through Las Vegas now," I whispered. "Bad reception here."

"*You will proceed to Quagmire, Nevada, and wait for further instructions.*" The normal human voice came through the window a split second before the distorted voice.

"Sorry, you're breaking up." I closed the phone and put it back in my pocket.

"Lost him. He says he's in Vegas," the voice said. "Send the strike team to Quagmire."

"Should we take the girl, sir? He said he wanted to see her alive."

"They all say that. Keep her alive long enough to talk on the phone if we need her. Then put a bullet in her. Remember, we want this Lorenzo alive. Eddie won't give us anything for him dead."

Eddie? How could Gordon the government guy be involved with Big Eddie? This didn't make any sense. Valentine must have picked that up from my microphone. *"I recognize that voice. Gordon's here. You don't touch him. He's mine."*

"Let me get Jill first. Then you can go on a killing spree," I whispered.

"A bunch of men in SWAT gear are loading into the passenger van," Bob noted calmly. There was the sound of a door sliding shut, and then a large engine revving. They were going to set up an ambush for nobody. I crouched lower as the headlights briefly swung past the cinder-block wall.

This was as good as it was going to get. "I'm going in." I sprung up and took a quick look through the dirty window. Jill was still slumped in a chair. There was nobody else in the room. The room was filled with old trash, rusted metal, and broken bits of wood. Thick spiderwebs clouded the corners. I pushed the heavy panes open slowly, rust binding in the hinge, begging to let out a screech. I gritted my teeth, pushing, praying for silence. Finally it was open wide enough to scramble through.

The door to the back room opened. I slid back down

the outside wall. A man was coming into the room. He was wearing a suit, and a cigarette dangled from his lips. He was small, weasel-like, and had an MP5 slung over one shoulder. "Hey, baby. The boss man says we don't need you much longer."

Jill raised her head for the first time. There was duct-tape over her mouth. Having held her against her will once myself, I could understand the need for the tape. She struggled against the chair. The fierce anger in her eyes was very familiar. The man closed the door behind him. "See, the way I figure it, I'm your only hope right now. You do me a little favor, and maybe I do you a little favor, know what I mean?" If he was any more of a slimeball he'd be leaving a trail.

The man leaned the MP5 against the wall. He took his suit coat off, threw it on top of the gun, and began to loosen his tie. "You know you want it anyway, baby. Make this good for me, and I can talk the boss into letting you go." Jill just glared at him.

I found the small dowels in my pocket, palmed them in one hand, then slowly put my hands on the windowsill and began to lever myself through as silently as possible. If I could take this guy out quietly, we still had a chance.

The man had his back to me, distracted as he ran one hand through Jill's hair. She jerked her head away. "Fine, you wanna be a bitch, whatever. I like it when they fight." He laughed.

What happened next was a surprise. Jill's hands came around in a blur, bloody tape still tied around her wrists. She must have been working those against the back of the

chair for hours. She slugged him right in the throat. He
made a terrible *gahhwk* noise and stumbled. Then Jill
stuck one thumb into his eye and locked the other hand
around his larynx. The man started to scream, but she
cranked down on his throat and choked it off. Her knee
found his crotch, so violently hard that I cringed.

He punched her in the side, she cranked down harder,
crushing his windpipe, forcing him to his knees. I pushed
myself through the window, landing on my hands and
rolling. The would-be rapist was on his back now, with Jill
bearing down on his throat with both hands. He grabbed
her by her hair and jerked her down, but she kept cranking
on his neck.

The door opened. I stepped behind it without thinking,
a dowel in each hand. "Davis, what the hell are you doing
in here?" the second man asked. He stepped into the dark,
his imagination filling in the blanks about the struggle
before him, drawing all the wrong conclusions. "Can't you
just keep it in your—" I kicked the door closed after he
stepped through, the length of piano wire stretched
between the two dowels coming down over his head. I
crossed my arms and tugged with all of my strength.

He never knew what hit him. The second man struggled,
leaning forward I followed, all my weight dragging the
wire inexorably through his flesh. The wire grated against
vertebra in a matter of seconds, and we both fell to the
ground in a spreading puddle of red. His head was barely
attached.

I rolled off the twitching body and moved to assist Jill,
but she didn't need any help. She leaned back, shaking.
The man's eyes stared blankly at the ceiling, his tongue

almost bit off between his teeth. Jill stood, angrily ripped
the tape from her face, and kicked the body once.

"Jill? Are you okay?" I whispered, the sound of
conversation barely audible on the other side of the door.
The rest of Gordon's men hadn't heard. She fell into my
arms and sobbed. "It's okay. I've got you."

"You came for me." She was trembling. "I thought I
was dead. . . . I've never killed anyone before."

"It's okay; he deserved it. Let's get out of here."

We weren't out of the woods yet. The radio crackled.
"Lorenzo, did you get her?" It was Hawk.

"Yeah, we're coming out. Two down."

"Hold on. There's more vehicles coming in," Bob said.
"I've got an SUV and a couple of sedans." Headlights came
through the window. Our escape route was illuminated.

"Are they holding a convention?" Hawk asked.

*"Lots of men moving now. These new ones seem to be
paying attention. Don't move,"* Bob insisted. *"These aren't
government."*

"What's wrong?" Jill asked desperately. She was wearing
some sort of pink waitress outfit, but it was filthy and blood
splattered. She looked exhausted. "Is that Carl on the radio?"

She didn't know. It just strengthened my resolve. I had
to get her out of here. "We can't sneak out. We're stuck.
We might have to fight our way out."

"Lorenzo, we're in position. Just say when," Valentine
said. His demeanor had changed. He wasn't the sarcastic,
nervous asshole he'd been before. Now he sounded utterly *calm.* I'd seen him in that state before. I could only
imagine what kind of childhood he must've had to have
gotten so messed up.

Jill knelt by the nearly decapitated man and removed a
Glock from his belt. She checked the chamber then stuck
it into her waistband. "There's a subgun under that coat."
She followed my pointing finger and nodded. I leaned
against the door and listened. There were more voices on
the other side now.

"So what do you want, Gordon?" Oily, British accent,
effeminate. "I've got important business to conduct. I
don't have time to drive out to middle of the bloody
desert. I had to fly into a pathetic little airport in the middle of this dreadful desert just to get here. And it was
closed. There was nothing there but an empty hangar! I
had to land at a closed airport like . . . like some kind of
vagrant!"

Eddie?

"I would think by now you would trust me." The voices
were muffled through the ancient wooden door, but that
had to be Gordon. "Why the entourage?"

"Associates of mine from Las Vegas. I had them pick
me up. But I didn't bring them just because I don't trust
you. I also have some personal business to conduct in the
area." In other words, these were the men that he was
planning on using to kill me at the scarab drop.

"Well, Mr. Montalban, as for your personal business, it
turns out that there might be another favor I can do for
you."

"Removing my brother from the equation did improve
my affairs rather immensely. But all part of fulfilling
Project Blue, to the benefit of your employers, of course.
And in addition I paid you rather handsomely, so I would
hardly call it a favor."

"As was part of the agreement. My partner is at the Alpha Point for Blue now."

"I always keep my promises, Mr. Willis. So tell me why you dragged me out here to this filthy, dreadful little place."

After all of this, Eduard Montalban was in the next room. He'd killed my friends, tried to kill me, and had threatened my loved ones. All thoughts of escaping quietly were dismissed. There was no way he was getting out of here alive. I looked to Jill, eyes wide, stubby machine gun shaking in her hands, and she understood. I pulled a frag grenade from my vest and put one hand on the door knob. "Get ready," I whispered into the radio.

"This thief, Lorenzo, that you asked me to keep an eye out for—"

Eddie cut him off. "Lorenzo is why I came to America in the first place."

"How much would he be worth if I was able to deliver him into your hands?" Gordon asked.

Eddie didn't hesitate. "Though a challenging diversion, he's worth nothing; But he has something in his possession, an antique piece of *jewelry*. For that, I'd give you ten million."

"What if I told you that a person of interest we were looking for was picked up by facial-recognition software while passing through Las Vegas? Once flagged, SIGINT eventually pinpointed her in Quagmire. Surprisingly enough, under interrogation it turns out she's friends with this Lorenzo of yours. My men will be picking him up shortly, right down the road. And for you, a special deal. I've *neglected* to mention any of this to my superiors."

"Of course. But if your men screw this up and I don't

get my property back, I'll hold you responsible." A small dog began to bark in the next room. Who the hell brings a dog to a meeting like this?

"It's already in motion," the government man said. Somewhere, an armed squad was lying in ambush for us. They hadn't the faintest idea where we actually were.

"I hope you realize who you're dealing with, Gordon. Underestimating a man like Lorenzo can be fatal."

Damn straight.

I opened the door.

VALENTINE

My blood had run cold when I'd heard Gordon's voice. Then *the Calm* had washed over me, and suddenly I felt very detached. I couldn't believe it. I had all but resolved myself to disappearing quietly. I had convinced myself that getting to Gordon was impossible, that it was just an angry fantasy. Now Gordon had been dropped right into my lap. He'd injected himself back into my life and screwed it up all over again. Beneath *the Calm,* at the outermost limit of my perception, I was seething with anger. He wasn't going to get away this time. He wasn't going to do this to me *twice*.

Reaper and I were in a shallow ravine that was about two-thirds of the way down the steep hill we'd come from. Hawk had crawled another twenty feet to a better position of cover. At the top of the hill was Bob with his rifle. At the bottom of the hill was the cinder-block building where they were holding Jill.

"Reaper, keep your head down," I said. The nearest visible bad guy was far out of range of his stubby shotgun. "I'll tell you when to move. Stay alert."

There were two parties of men hanging around outside. One was presumably from Gordon's group, since they had been driving the government Suburbans. Only three of them remained outside, doing a very poor job of keeping watch. The rest, more heavily armed in SWAT gear, had piled into a van and left. I figured that was the group that was supposed to be ambushing us at the arranged meeting point.

But several other cars that had just arrived, and these new guys were anxious. A handful of men got out and entered the building, including one of the biggest, fattest men I'd ever seen. This giant whale of a man was probably close to seven feet tall and had to weigh four hundred pounds.

"Who's the fat guy?" I whispered into my radio.

"*Unknown,*" Bob tersely replied.

"Fat guy?" Reaper asked, suddenly sounding even more anxious. Before I could stop him, he poked his head over the ravine to see. A shocked look appeared on his face, and he immediately dropped back down.

"What is it?" I asked. But Reaper wouldn't tell me anything. He just whispered into his radio that "the fat man" was here. Lorenzo clicked his microphone in reply.

Bob had said over the radio that these new arrivals were more alert, and that was definitely true. Compared to the government suits, the new guys looked like they belonged in a European fashion magazine, and they were all openly carrying weapons. Some had MP7 submachine guns, some had G36C assault rifles, and all were alert.

I was startled by the sound of a muffled explosion. The windows of the cinder-block building blew out, and the prison camp suddenly came alive.

The men outside were all startled by the blast. I put my aiming reticle on the upper chest of one of the new guys. He was hanging back by a sedan, his carbine shouldered, obviously providing rear security. I swiped my selector switch to the fire position and squeezed the trigger. I hit the man in the sternum, and blood from the giant exit wound on his back splashed onto the car door. He crumpled to the ground, landing in a small cloud of dust.

One of the others running full tilt toward the building caught a round in the chest and almost did a cartwheel into the dirt. With my hearing protection in I couldn't hear the distant crack of Bob's suppressed rifle, but I knew it was him. Another shooter, one of Gordon's men, had drawn his pistol and was about to open the door to the cinder-block building. Before I could drop the hammer on him his head exploded into a red cloud, and down he went. Bob again. *Damn. Dude knows how to shoot!*

The others had turned around and were running back toward their vehicles. I fired at one of them and missed, leading him too much. But he froze when he saw the bullet impact the dirt, like a deer in the headlights. I squeezed the trigger again, and down he went. Scanning through my scope for targets, I lined up one of the new guys just in time to see a muzzle flash. Sand and tiny pebbles hit my face as his bullet impacted the dirt a few feet from me. I ducked back down into the ravine and was out of his line of sight, but more and more bullets snapped overhead and hit the rocks around us. Off to the side, Hawk slid into the gulley, calmly rocking a new magazine into his rifle.

Reaper was to my left, trying to become one with the earth. His already pale skin had gone white, and he had a death grip on his little shotgun. I could tell that this really wasn't his cup of tea. Honestly? I wasn't exactly having the time of my life, either, but there are worse ways to spend your time.

I got on my radio. "Bob, they got me pinned down. Help me out here."

"Roger," was all Bob said in response. A moment later, he spoke up again. *"Hey, Nightcrawler . . . I got another one, but the rest are hunkered down pretty good. If you follow that ravine, it works its way down the hill and it'll get you closer."* I signaled Hawk and used my hands to indicate for him to cover us. *"It looks shallow as you get to the bottom, but there are some big rocks down there that'll give you cover. You'll come out pretty close to the corner of the building. Just make sure you watch both sides. Guys could come around the building either way. You up for it? I can't get Lorenzo on the radio."*

"Roger. Moving." I looked over at Reaper. "You ready?" He looked back at me, eyes wide but full of surprising determination. He nodded. "Alright, then. Follow me."

Hawk popped back up, firing, trying to keep the bad guy's heads down as Reaper and I moved. We snaked our way down the ravine, trying to stay out of sight. I could barely hear the occasional snap of a rifle bullet coming from Bob's position, always followed by sporadic, sometimes automatic, weapons fire in response. They didn't know where he was, and he was picking them off one by one.

We made it to the rocks at the bottom of the hill. We had to crawl from the end of the ravine, little more than a shallow gulley at this point, to the rocks. Reaper followed close, breathing hard and sweating heavily in his black trench coat. I crawled to the far left edge of the rocks, still in the prone. I was very close to the cinder-block building, and there was only one door on the side that was facing me. I also now had a clear view of the men taking cover behind the SUV, busily shooting at Hawk's position.

I snapped off a shot, and one of the men fell. The other surprised me by how quickly he reacted and returned fire. I pushed myself back behind the rocks while he popped shot after shot off at us. He suddenly shifted his fire back toward Bob's position after a near-miss from my sniper overwatch. I rolled out from the side of the boulder and fired twice. "He's down," I said into my radio.

I was about to make a dash for the door when one of Gordon's men came around the corner of the building to my left. He fired a burst at me. The bullets impacted the rocks, sending dust and debris flying. I let myself fall to the ground and scrambled behind cover. A second burst narrowly missed me, and a third one peppered the rocks I was now hiding behind.

I moved to my right and came up firing. My rounds hit the ground and the wall near the government guy just as he disappeared back around the corner. I held my fire but kept my sights on where he was. He'd either come back out or circle back around the building. Hawk was covering my right flank, so I wasn't worried about that. Sure enough, he did a quick peek, broadcasting to me where he was. As soon as he stepped around the corner, I opened up on him. At least three of my rounds tore through him.

I ducked back behind the boulder. "How are you doing?" I asked Reaper as I removed the nearly spent magazine from my rifle. He just nodded at me as I pulled another one from my vest and locked it into position. "Okay," I said, "head for the door."

I dashed from behind the rocks with Reaper right behind me, running so fast that we smacked into the wall. I pointed down the wall of the building, indicating to Reaper that he needed to watch that corner. Reaching down, I tried the handle. The old door wasn't locked, but it was stuck.

Subtlety was never my strong point. I nodded at Reaper and kicked the door in.

LORENZO

I threw open the door, taking in the scene in an instant. There was Eduard Montalban standing in the filthy abandoned garage. Next to him was the hulking Fat Man, who looked like Moby Dick in his white suit. Eddie was wearing a silk shirt, Flock of Seagulls hair combed high, little yippy white poodle-dog under one arm, the smirk on his face turning to disbelief as he saw me. Gordon and one of his men had their backs to me and were just beginning to turn as they saw Eddie's shock. Both sides had several goons arrayed across the room, but none of them would be fast enough to stop me.

The grenade left my hand, spoon popping off in

mid-flight. "Hey, Eddie," I stated as the grenade struck the concrete floor, bounced, and spun between Gordon's legs.

"Bloody hell!" Eddie shrieked. The poodle started barking.

Chaos. The Fat Man was far faster than he looked. He spun about, one massive arm sweeping Eddie up, lifting his employer and shielding him as they dove away. Gordon acted in pure instinctive self-preservation, one hand coming up, grabbing the government man next to him by the necktie, and yanking hard. The man, taken by surprise, toppled over on top of the grenade as Gordon hurled himself into the old oil pit.

I ducked back around the corner.

THUMP.

I felt the pressure in my teeth. Gordon's guard absorbed most of the blast and saved the others. The walls were sprayed like a red Jackson Pollock. Decades of dust and cobwebs were dislodged from the ceiling, obscuring everything.

Jill pulled her fingers out of her ears and actually smiled at me. I motioned for her to stay put before taking a quick peek through the doorway. The windows had all been shattered. Dust whirled. One of the goons was screaming. There was gunfire coming from outside.

Something moved in a pile of dust. *The Fat Man.* The back of his white suit coat was shredded and burned. Small spatters and trickles of blood covered his back. He pushed himself up with one arm, Eddie still held protectively beneath him. I raised my AR, taking the safety off, finger moving onto the trigger, red dot settling on the Fat Man's back.

The wall next to me exploded in a shower of cinder fragments, and I jerked the trigger as I cringed, missing my target entirely. Something sliced hot across my cheek and I fell into the back room, bullets screaming through the doorway overhead. I scrambled to the side as the floor erupted into dust.

"Lorenzo!" Jill shouted as I rolled toward her. She raised the MP5 and fired out the doorway. A man cried out in pain.

Still prone, I leaned around the doorway and spotted a government man moving through the dust, firing his M4 at us. Jill shot again, and the man stumbled. "They've got vests on!" I shouted as I put the Aimpoint on him and cranked off several quick shots. Soft armor would stop her 9mm, but not my 5.56. He fell to his knees and Jill's third shot hit him in the bridge of the nose. I scrambled farther out, searching for Eddie.

The spot where the Fat Man had fallen was empty.

"Shit!" I shouted. More shapes were appearing in the dust. I fired at anything that moved. That damn poodle was still barking. Bullets impacted our wall, digging fierce pits into the cinder-blocks, or skipped across the concrete and smashed our room into debris.

Flipping the selector to auto, I emptied the rest of my magazine into the confusion, then rolled inside, fumbling at my vest for a reload. There were a lot more bad guys than I had expected, but they were being hit from multiple directions. Jill was crouched behind me. I made eye contact and gestured violently toward the window. We had to get out of here. "I'll cover you," I said as I slammed the magazine home and slapped the bolt release.

"Quit shooting! Stop it!" Eddie was screeching. The random gunfire tapered off and died. "I need him *alive!*"

"Go!" I shouted to Jill, leaned out, and fired in the direction of Eddie's voice. There was a rusted truck parked near the main door, and it sounded like he had come from behind it. I stitched a line of impacts across the truck body, the clang of hot lead on metal louder than my suppressor. Jill sprang up and pushed her way through the window. Within seconds, multiple rifles opened up on my position. I fired until she disappeared, going clear through my second magazine.

"Damn it!" Eddie shrieked. "I said quit *shooting*! Next one of you wankers shoots at him and I'll slit your throat myself! Lorenzo!" I pulled back, reloading again. I could feel the heat rising from my rifle. "Listen to me carefully. I just want what's mine. I don't care about you."

Red laser dots flashed on the far wall. Bright flashlights illuminated the doorway. If I tried to move, I was dead. Rather than fire and maneuver, I'd allowed myself to get pinned down. At least Jill had gotten out. "Bob, the hostage just went out the window. Cover her. I'm stuck," I whispered. There was no response. I grasped my radio. The box had been smashed by a round. *Damn*.

"I'm listening, Eddie," I shouted back. The gunfire outside continued. It sounded like the others were busy. "What're you offering?"

"Give me the scarab, you and all your people walk, and I pay you *double*."

"Sounds tempting," I lied. We were dog food the second he had it. I didn't dare stick my head around the corner, and I couldn't try to move across the doorway.

There was a large piece of broken mirrored glass on the floor. Grabbing it, I held it up and used it to peer around the corner.

"Yes, it is tempting. We both know you're stuck, and it won't take too many bullets to carve through that wall. My associate is setting up a belt-fed as we speak. . . ." There was a sudden burst of much louder gunfire, and the wall above me exploded into shrapnel. The sound was horrendous. The gun fired so fast it was like a buzzsaw. I covered my head and tried to make myself as small as possible as I was pelted with jagged bits. The poodle yelped. "Hush now, Precious, the bad man won't scare you anymore," Eddie soothed. "You've got ten seconds, Lorenzo."

Moving the broken shard of glass, I scanned the garage. Multiple bright weapon-mounted lights shined back at me, and there was the Fat Man, a terrifying German MG3 machine gun on a bipod resting on the old truck hood, pointed right at me. I coughed as more dust settled onto my face. Hopefully Jill and the others would make it out of here, because I didn't think that I would.

But at least I could take Eddie with me. "I've got to know. What is it? Why is it so important?" If I could keep him talking, maybe I could figure out where he hiding.

"Is Willis around?" Eddie asked. "Or any of his men?"

"No, sir. He took off running into those old buildings," a voice behind one of the bobbing weapon lights answered.

"Well, chap, you might as well know. Gordon and I may be from rival organizations, but I'm helping him accomplish something for his employers, and in turn he's helping me get the position I so rightfully deserve among my peers.

And you are going to help keep me there. The thing you stole? It isn't even for me. There's a certain individual, who even I am scared of, and he'd do *anything* to get that scarab. Now quit stalling. Time's up, Lorenzo. Where . . . is . . . *my* . . . *property?*"

The scarab was sitting in a Velcro pouch on my armor. I held the AR tight and did one last pass with my makeshift mirror: three lighted weapons trained on my position, and a belt-fed machine gun. It was Butch and Sundance time.

Then there was another reflection shifting in the glass, the flash of a pink waitress dress creeping up behind the Fat Man.

Oh, please no.

No time to think. I sprang up, muzzle rising as I heard the *brraaappp* noise of the little MP5 in Jill's hands on full-auto. The Fat Man jerked as her bullets stitched up his side. The MG3 fired wildly past me, tearing a gash of dust and pulverized cinder block up the wall. My Aimpoint settled on the first weapon mounted light and I fired twice, shifting immediately to the next light and firing again.

I was blinded by the scalding beams, burning bullets zipping around me, through my clothing, feeling them parting my hair, buzzing past like angry bees. There was the third light, dancing with muzzle flashes, and I pulled the trigger twice more. Jill was shouting as she fired.

One of the lights was weaving, a shadow appearing behind it. My gun moved back toward him, but I tripped on some debris, sprawling forward, jerking the trigger as I went, supersonic lead filling the empty air where I'd just been. The other light swung upward, briefly illuminating the bloody ceiling as the man holding it went down. The Fat Man grunted under the impacts as Jill shot him again, and finally he and the heavy machine gun disappeared behind the truck.

There was only one weapon light shining now, swinging wildly toward Jill. We fired at the same time. The bulb shattered.

The room went dark

I gasped for breath as the filthy dust stirred. My good ear was ringing from the gunfire, but above that I could hear a man crying and the sounds of someone breathing froth through a torn-open chest.

This time the flashlight piercing the darkness was mounted to *my* gun. "Jill!" I shouted. I only activated the light for a split second to find my way, then it was back out to avoid being a target and I was moving to the truck and the last place I'd seen her.

"Lorenzo!" she hissed at me. "Over here."

I found her in the dark, kneeling behind some rusted junk. The empty MP5 had been tossed, and she had a pistol in her hands. She flinched as my hand touched her shoulder, but at least she didn't shoot me.

"Are you okay?" I whispered, crouching beside her. I didn't know who was still alive in the garage.

"I'm okay." She gestured at the Fat Man, his massive, sprawled, white-clad form standing out in the dark. "But he's not. Shot him like ten times."

I didn't know why, but I hugged her then, held her tight, my face pressed into her soft neck, her dark, blood matted hair pressed against my cheek. That lasted for a few seconds as there was more high-powered rifle fire nearby, several back and forth volleys. The others were still fighting.

Back to business . . .

"Did you see which way Eddie went?"

"The one that looked like he came from an episode of *I Love the Eighties*, with the poodle?" I nodded, somehow in the dark she could tell. She pointed out the large front door. "He headed for those old buildings."

I couldn't let him get away. I stood, dropped my partially expended magazine, and drew a new one from my vest. "Head for the hills to the west. I have a friend out there. He'll get you out of here."

"I'm coming with you," she answered defiantly.

"This isn't a democracy. You're—" Something stirred behind me, gliding into the garage, a shape with a weapon. I turned, pulling the rifle to my shoulder. The man was in my sights, but I knew I was too late.

We both froze. Guns raised, death only a tiny bit of pressure on a trigger away.

"Valentine," I acknowledged, relieved, and lowered my carbine.

Valentine's FAL hovered on me for just a fraction of a second. *That son of a bitch,* I thought. *He's actually thinking it over.* I glared at him for an instant, daring him to pull the trigger. His expression changed almost imperceptibly and he lowered his weapon. "Is Jill okay?"

Before I could answer, Reaper swept into the room, trench coat billowing like something out of a bad vampire movie. Man, I hated that stupid coat. He grinned when he saw us. "I'm glad to see you guys. I've been trying to get you on the radio. Bob says that that van full of SWAT dudes has turned around and is on its way back. We've got to go." Reaper shone his light around the room, seeing the multiple bodies and blood still dripping from the ceiling. "I love what you've done with the place."

Valentine was all business. He quickly scanned the dead. No quips. No jokes. Only: "Where's Gordon?"

"He went that way." I nodded toward the ghost town.

"Then let's go."

VALENTINE

I turned to leave, but paused. I looked back at my . . . companions? I don't suppose we were friends. Standing close to Lorenzo was Jill, a gun in hand, her hair a mess, blood-stains on her pink jumper.

"You alright, darlin'?" I asked of Jill. She nodded at me but said nothing. She was hovering close to Lorenzo. I managed half a smile for her, then put my game face back on. Gordon was out there somewhere, and he wasn't getting away.

"*Val, what's your status?*" Hawk asked over the radio.

"Cover the entrance. I'm coming out."

"What's the plan?" Reaper asked.

What is it with these people and their stupid plans? A plan is just a list of things that don't happen after the first shot is fired, and the situation had already gone straight to hell. "Gordon's back there somewhere," I said, gesturing to the door. "I'm going to find him and kill him." My blood was running cold.

"That's it?" Jill asked, speaking up at last. "You don't

know how many of them there are! You're going to get yourself killed!"

"The van full of SWAT guys is coming back," Reaper said again.

"This is gonna get interesting." I moved forward and opened the door. It was mostly dark outside now, and only the last bit of sun crept over the hill to illuminate the interior of the long-abandoned prison camp. There was a row of buildings along each side of a gravel road. Barracks, mostly, but utility buildings, a mess hall, things like that. The tall fence that had once surrounded the place was falling down, and several of the structures had been vandalized.

I moved out the door. Lorenzo stepped out behind me, with Reaper behind him. He made Jill stay inside. *Good*, I thought. I didn't want her to get hurt, especially after all this.

I moved to my right, edging towards the corner of the building. It was shadowed here, and I was thankful for that. The next building over didn't have any windows facing my position, but others did, and I was exposed.

Hawk came over the radio. *"Val, I'm moving up on you. Cover me."*

I leaned around the corner. The road that led into the camp was lit up by the headlights of the van. It was rapidly approaching our position, leaving a long dust cloud behind it.

"You see the van?" Lorenzo asked. He was now right behind me.

"Got it," I said.

"We should move over there," he said, pointing to the

next building. "Find some cover and light 'em up as they come out. We—"

His voice was cut off by the loud bark of my carbine. He hissed an obscenity, but then opened fire as well. Hawk joined him an instant later. I couldn't see anything but the dark mass of the van beyond the blinding headlights, but that was enough. The glowing red reticle of my scope was centered on it, and I let go. I fired as rapidly as I could, my rounds tearing into the van, my face illuminated briefly by each muzzle flash. The van skidded to its right and crashed into the far corner of a building. My bolt locked back, and my rifle was empty. I looked back at Lorenzo as he dropped the magazine out of his carbine.

"Let's go. I couldn't have gotten them all."

LORENZO

Valentine ejected the empty magazine from his rifle, flinging it away from him as he rocked it out, and locked a new one in place. The bolt flew forward with a clang.

"Let's get them," Jill said. I turned. She was right behind me, one of Eddie's goon's G36 carbines in her hands. Before I could even tell her to go back, she snapped, "Shut up, Lorenzo, I'm coming." Her tone suggested that there wouldn't be any arguing.

Valentine grinned at me. *Asshole*. I shook my head while walking quickly toward the smoking wreck. "Stay low. Hawk, cover us. Valentine and Reaper, flank right. Jill, stay behind me. That little pad on the front grip activates your flashlight. Leave it off until—"

"I'm not retarded. I can use a stupid light. Come on already," she hissed. "Gordon's going to get away."

Fair enough.

There was no discernible movement around the van. Steam was rising from the smashed-open radiator. I sprinted the last few feet and stuck my muzzle through the driver's side window just as Valentine threw open the rear doors. The driver was dead, his face mashed against the wheel, blood leaking from his ear. The passenger's brains were sliding down the dash. The back was empty, but there was some blood. The others must have bailed out.

There was a raised wooden walkway on both sides of the rectangular barracks. Reaper's boots echoed hollowly on the wooden planks as he walked toward the open doorway. Suddenly, he and Valentine both crouched down. I stood there stupidly for an instant before realizing that they were still in communication with Bob. I grabbed Jill by the wrist and pulled her down beside the van.

A supersonic crack whistled overhead, and someone screamed inside the darkened barracks. Reaper threw himself flat as the SWAT team inside fired wildly through the plank walls in response. Valentine disappeared in a flash, moving to the building's corner. Jill and I were in the shadows, and the SWAT guys were firing at nothing.

"Reaper, stay down!" I had one frag grenade left. I pulled it from its pouch, yanked the pin, and chucked it through the barracks window. A few seconds later, the barracks shook and bits of jagged metal hummed through the air, seeking flesh.

"Now!" I shouted. Reaper popped up, turned on his

Surefire light, and leaned across the barrack's window. The stubby 12 gauge belched fire three quick times. You didn't need to be a good shot at conversational distance. Off to the side came the thunderous crack of Valentine's .308.

"Clear!" he shouted.

"Scratch two more assholes," Reaper responded.

But how many did that leave? I sprinted toward the barracks, vaulted over the railing, and landed beside Reaper. Hawk was running up behind us. The railing next to my head made a hollow *thunk* noise as a bullet smashed into it. I pressed tighter against the wall. Jill was still prone by the van. "Everybody down! That came from the water tower!"

"Bob, sniper on the water tower. Take him out," Valentine ordered as he walked calmly into the barracks. "Hey, Lorenzo. We've got to keep moving."

I scanned the town. There were only intermittent patches of amber lighting, and most of the ramshackle buildings were deadly ambushes waiting to happen. I pulled out my night-vision monocular, pressed it to my eye, and scanned around the corner.

Through the NVD I could see a man with a rifle standing at the top of the water tower's ladder. There was another crack, and the man toppled from his perch, fell two stories, and landed lifelessly in a cloud of dust. My brother was a damn fine shot.

Hawk clambered up the steps and took cover next to me. "Val, if that G-man's running from you, he's probably holed up in that last big building." It made sense, it was the easternmost position they could fall back to. To get back to their vehicles they would have to either fight past us through the southern row of buildings, or they'd have to try to cross back between the buildings on the north side. Each time they left cover, we could engage them, and to reach a car they'd be visible to Bob. Holing up to wait for reinforcements would be the smart thing to do.

"The mess hall? I'm on it. Come on." He disappeared into the shadows of the barracks, heading for the back door.

"Doesn't he ever plan anything?" I grunted. There couldn't be many of Eddie's goons or Gordon's men left, but the element of surprise was gone, and they would be waiting for us somewhere in that twisted labyrinth of junk and jagged wood. The four of us stood and followed Valentine into the darkness.

Chapter 29:
Dropped Call

VALENTINE

Gordon. I was so close now I could taste it. I could sense his presence. I can't remember ever being more focused, more intense, yet so detached. *The Calm* had never been this overwhelming before. My survival instinct had been turned off. This was *it*. I only had to live long enough to kill Gordon. After that it didn't matter.

I entered the darkened barracks, stepping over the bodies of Gordon's men. It was a mess in there; Lorenzo's grenade had done the trick. The rest of the building was virtually empty, with little more than old frames for bunk beds. At the far end was another door. That's where I was going. Gordon was hiding in this camp, somewhere, and I was going to find him.

I slowed to a fast walk as I approached the far door, my rifle up and at the ready. There were no windows on the ends of the buildings, just narrow ones along the walls. Moving to the right side of the door frame, I pulled the door open and peeked out. It was about twenty feet to the next barracks building, and its door was closed. There could be shooters on the buildings across the road, so I'd have to be careful. I looked back at Lorenzo, and with hand signals told him to cover that direction. He shifted his carbine to his left shoulder and stacked behind the doorway.

I dashed across the gap between the barracks. On the other side, I pressed myself against the wall and crouched down. At the same time, Lorenzo was leaning out of the door, his weapon covering across the road.

Flipping around, I pointed the muzzle of my rifle at the door and reached for the handle. It was locked and made of metal. It looked too solid to kick down.

"Reaper!" I hissed, trying not to make too much noise. "Get up here with that room broom! I need you to bust a lock!" The kid came running out of the barracks in a crouched jog, weapon in hand. He didn't even stop to look at the buildings across the way. He obviously had complete confidence that Lorenzo would cover him. The kid pressed himself against the wall on the left side of the door frame, opposite me.

"Use that shotgun to blow the lock on this door so we can keep moving!" Reaper pointed the stubby muzzle of his weapon at the door's handle and flinched as he pulled the trigger. The shotgun roared, and the door handle exploded.

There was no time to pause. Reaper turned away, and I booted the door in. A man was crouched about halfway through the building. I snapped off two shots at him, then ducked back out of the doorway, crouching down in case he fired through the wall. He fired two more shots through the doorway, then it was quiet. I leaned in and saw him, slightly magnified through my rifle's scope. One of my rounds had gone through his abdomen, and he was now slowly crawling toward the far door, leaving a thick trail of blood in his wake.

I walked up quickly and stomped down on his back. He shrieked in agony. "Where's Gordon?"

"I don't know who that is!" he cried, blood pouring out of the exit wound beneath my boot. I shot him in the back of the head, shattering his skull like a watermelon with a blasting cap in it.

"Clear!" I shouted. The room was suddenly quiet. The air stank of burnt powder and dust. We crossed the room and opened the door at the far end. The doorway to the next barracks was closed, and again we had to contend with the gap between the buildings.

I peeked outside and nearly lost my head. The shots were coming from the barracks building across the way. I fell back inside the doorway just in time to avoid being hit. The shooter then began to pepper the wall with rifle fire. Bullets tore through and snapped angrily overhead.

"Everybody down!" Hawk shouted. Lorenzo furiously started low-crawling toward the back of the building. I crawled forward and got as close to the door as I could.

The shooter was still firing through the wall, about one shot every second. He was focusing on our end of the building, though. Looking back, I saw Lorenzo pop up and fire off a long burst from his carbine. The suppressed weapon sounded like a rapid series of hissing pops as it fired.

Still in the prone, leaning out of the doorway, I began to fire at the building across the road. Lorenzo's bursts of fire had shattered the windows and stitched the wall, but the shooter was nowhere to be seen. We both paused for a moment and waited. A second later, he popped up again in the exact same spot. Both Lorenzo and I lit him up. I don't know how many rounds the shooter took, but he fell from sight and didn't appear again.

"Keep moving," I ordered, scrambling to my feet and heading for the next building. I took up position on one side of the door, and Lorenzo was on the other a second later. Hawk wasn't looking so good.

"You okay?" I asked.

"I'm too old for this shit," he answered.

"Do you have any more frags?" I asked. Lorenzo shook his head. *Damn it*. We were going to have to do this the hard way. I reached down and opened the door. We were answered with weapons fire, only this time there were multiple shooters. Lorenzo and I both leaned in and returned fire. Lorenzo mashed himself up against the fence that connected the buildings as one of the shooters inside returned fire through the wall. There was no way we were getting through that door without getting killed.

I decided to take a chance and flank them. I took off at a run up the right side of the building. Gunfire echoed through the camp as I made my way along the wall. I stopped about three-quarters of the way down and began to fire through the wall into the barracks. This way, my companions wouldn't be in the line of fire and there was a chance I'd actually hit one of the bad guys. If nothing else, it'd distract them long enough for the others to make a move. I burned off the rest of my magazine as fast as I could pull the trigger.

My rifle's bolt locked open. I began to jog back to the rear of the building, reloading as I went. A tiny bit of movement in the periphery of my vision alerted me. I spun around, seeing a man in a dirty suit, limping badly, blood pouring from wounds on his arms and legs. He raised a handgun. I turned toward him, reaching down for the revolver on my thigh. I felt a thump as a round smacked me in the chest plate. I lost my balance and fell.

The shooter aimed unsteadily, pistol wobbling in one bloody hand, just as my .44 cleared its holster. I took a bead on him and fired between my knees. His head snapped around in a pink cloud. Rolling back to my hands and knees, I scrambled ahead, heading back to the others.

The others were behind cover in the entrance of the final barracks. Lorenzo was nowhere to be seen. Rifle still slung across my chest, revolver held at the ready, I jogged down the length of the barracks, passing Reaper and Jill and stepping over dead bodies. It looked like I had managed to plug somebody through the wall after all.

"Everybody okay?" I got a chorus of nods in response.

I looked out a window just in time to see Lorenzo enter the mess hall building.

"Where's *he* going?"

"I don't know," Reaper said. "He just took off."

"Let's go!" Jill said, a fire in her eyes.

Holstering my Smith & Wesson, I pulled a fresh twenty-round magazine from my vest and locked it into my FAL's magazine well. I looked back at my companions and was out the door.

LORENZO

Valentine was a killing machine.

The last of Gordon's SWAT team were gone, shot to death through the barracks walls. Bodies twisted into unnatural positions, hands curled into claws, staring blankly at the beams overhead. I stepped quickly through the mess, shell casings spinning away underfoot. Hawk had been firing from the window, hammering his Para FAL at someone in the northern buildings. Reaper and Jill were back toward the entrance.

I crouched near the rear door and scanned the last building. There was no visible movement, but there had been earlier, and none of the men that we had killed were Eddie or Gordon. Process of elimination left that one.

Elimination. Sometimes I make myself smile.

There was a noise, high pitched and repetitive over the ringing in my ears. It was coming from the cafeteria. The noise seemed out of place in the ghost town.

Barking. It was Eddie's poodle.

I'm by nature a cautious man. You do not live long in my business by charging into situations, but caution went out the window when I heard that sound. Eddie's presence here tonight was like a gift from heaven, and I wasn't going to leave without sending him to hell.

"I'm going in," I said into my radio, took a quick look, didn't see any obvious threats, then sprinted for the cafeteria, realizing halfway across that I didn't have a working radio. Too late to turn back. I covered the last bit of distance and slid to a stop in the gravel next to the open doorway.

The old mess hall was a huge building. I rounded the corner and activated my flashlight. The interior was a mass of old tables, most of them broken and sticking up at odd angles. The light created horrific shadows dancing on the walls. Nothing moved, but you could have hid an elephant in here and I wouldn't have seen it.

That annoying barking came again, a high-pitched yipping, louder now, off to the side. My light illuminated another door, probably to the kitchen. I moved through, using what cover was available, ready to shoot at any second. The kitchen was empty also, just some dust-coated countertops, old bottles, and a rusting industrial-sized stove. There was another door, and the barking was coming from inside.

I kicked the door open, the old bolt tearing right through the age-softened wood. Rickety stairs descended into the darkness.

Man. What I'd give for another grenade.

The yippy dog was really freaking out now. I cracked the vertebra in my neck. This was it.

I swept around the corner, light stabbing into the darkness. Below was a small pantry, filled with empty shelves, probably sunk into the ground to keep the food from the desert heat. Eddie's poodle was in the center of the room, its leash tied around a beam.

The dog was snarling at me. I moved the light around, but there was nobody else in the room. There was a dusty tarp hanging in one corner, big enough to conceal a man.

I started down the steps, gun up, finger on the trigger,

Aimpoint dot floating on that tarp. My heart was pounding. Was that Eddie behind there? I took aim and stitched a line of shots up it. The AR moved slightly under recoil as something shattered and fell behind the tarp. The poodle yelped in surprise and whimpered.

If Eddie was hiding in there, he wasn't happy.

The first gunshot struck me low in the back. I stumbled forward, accidentally discharging my weapon as another round tore down my arm. I tried to turn back toward the kitchen, but as my boot landed on the next step, the ancient stairs broke and gave way under my weight. Windmilling, off balance, another shot sparked off my AR's receiver and I crashed halfway through the stairs, legs dangling over the pantry, jagged wood stabbing into my arms. The door to the giant stove was open now and a hand with a pistol extended out of it. I saw the muzzle flash, and something tore along the side of my scalp, snapping my head back. Another shot thudded into my armor as the rest of the staircase collapsed around me.

The air exploded from my lungs as I landed hard in a pile of dust and wood. I lay there for a split second, lights exploding behind my eyes. I had walked right into it, focused on the noise, and waltzed right past Eddie's ambush.

Choking, gasping, I pushed myself deeper into the corner under the broken stairs as I drew my pistol. My body was on fire with pain, and blood was running out of my hair and into my eyes. My protesting lungs wouldn't fill with air at first, but I forced back the rising tide of panic. The bag containing the prince's treasure had somehow spilled free and was resting on the floor a few feet away, just out of reach.

"Lorenzo, I thought you were supposed to be good at this," Eddie said from above. He peered over the edge at me, smiling, H&K P7 in one hand, his silk shirt filthy with old rust, puffy hair matted with cobwebs. He moved back over the threshold as I raised my gun and fired. The bullet smashed into the ceiling.

I kept the shaking front sight aimed at that doorway and tried to breathe. The basement was dark. My AR was smashed on the ground beside me. I had no cover. At least that dog had shut up. I glanced over at the Precious's last position. It looked like I'd accidently shot the poodle before the stairs had fallen on it. *Ouch.*

"You know you're not the first one to come after me. Did you really think it would be that easy? You probably did. I try to cultivate a certain manner. It tends to cause men like you to underestimate me." Eddie's effeminate voice was safely out of sight above. "Where's the scarab, Lorenzo?"

"Sorry about your dog." I coughed and used my sleeve to wipe the blood out of my eyes. If Eddie was going to finish me, he needed to stick his gun over the edge. So I only had one shot. The STI slowly quit shaking. Blood trickled down my lacerated arm and pooled inside my armor.

"I'll buy a new dog. The scarab is irreplaceable."

Come on, Eddie. Just a peek. "It must be worth a fortune."

"It's not the money. It's the *sentimental* value. The man that wants that thing is far more dangerous than me. He'd crush the prince like a bug. But if I have it, he'll do anything I ask. You have no idea how important that bloody thing is. This is your last chance, Lorenzo. Where is it?"

It was sitting right there in the dust, but I wouldn't give him the satisfaction. "Someplace you'll never find it," I answered, and it wasn't a stretch of my acting ability to sound injured. "So let's get this over with."

Eddie was quiet for a moment. "You realize, of course, that I'm still going to kill your family. It's a matter of principle now."

"Of course," I answered as I blocked out the pain, the throbbing in my head, the ringing in my ears, the blood in my eyes, and focused on that glowing front sight. *One shot. Just one shot.*

Then there was a gunshot, not from a handgun, but the thunder of a .308 round, followed by several other deep booms from Reaper's Benelli. They were close.

"Sounds like your mates are here. I'm afraid our time together has come to an end."

"Yeah, that's too bad." *Front sight. Front sight. Come on.*

"Farewell, Lorenzo."

I was waiting for it. *Please, God, just one shot.* But Eddie didn't appear at the edge. Rather, there was a scratchy clicking noise. *A lighter?* Then a glass bottle with a flaming rag stuck in the top flew through the doorway. I watched in horror as the Molotov cocktail sailed across the room and shattered against the far wall. The liquid inside spread across the walls and wooden shelves, ignited, and bathed the tiny room in heat and flames.

I pushed myself to my feet, scrambling, searching for handholds to get out of the deathtrap. The fire was spreading, eating up the dry wood, leaping up the walls, licking at me, singeing my clothes. The heat sucked the moisture from my eyes, and the poison smoke billowed into my lungs.

Eduard Montalban chortled like a deranged schoolgirl as he fled the kitchen. I screamed as the flames tore at me.

VALENTINE

The smell of smoke hit my nostrils as I reached the mess hall. The door was already open. I crouched and studied the darkened interior. Hawk crouched across from me and shined his flashlight into the room. Smoke was drifting up through the floorboards, obscuring everything.

Hawk killed the light and glanced at me. "What do you want to do?"

Jill and Reaper were still shadowed in the safety of the barracks. I keyed my radio. "I don't see Lorenzo, I—" I froze. Something moved quickly at the far end of the room, headed for the door. I flashed my weapon light, and there he was.

Gordon.

My former employer flinched in the blinding light, his normally expensive suit covered in dirt and rust. He had a handkerchief pressed to his mouth because of the rising smoke and had just reached the back door. He looked back at us for an instant, then dove through the doorway. I opened fire, rattling off half a magazine at where Gordon had been, then firing through the wall at where he might be. Before Hawk could stop me, I took off in pursuit and disappeared into the smoke.

LORENZO

The world was engulfed in flames. Fire moved like a living creature, consuming everything around me. I reached for the scarab, but the fire drove me back. There was no time to retrieve it, and I stumbled away. The heat was unbearable, my exposed skin was burning. My mind swam through incoherent thoughts as my lungs pumped poison gases into my brain.

Not like this. I can't go down like this.

The fingernails of one hand tore off trying to pull myself up the wall to reach the doorway. It was only about a dozen feet, but it seemed a million miles away.

Calm down. Hold your breath and fucking climb.

I unsheathed my Greco knife and stabbed it into the planks high above my head. Driven with the strength of desperation, the blade stuck deep. I only had one chance. With my clothing burning, driven by adrenaline, I pulled on the knife while I jumped, boots scrambling for purchase, bloody fingers tearing at the boards above. The remaining cartridges in my AR began to cook off, sounding like firecrackers inside the conflagration.

Somehow I found purchase, dangling by my fingertips. I was halfway there. *Shit, it hurts.* I jerked the knife out, raised it overhead as I began to slip, and slammed it home again. The next few seconds were a blur of pain, tearing muscles, and fire, always the fire. Finding fingerholds when there were none, I reached the jagged broken top step, got one hand onto it, and pulled myself upward. By a miracle, it held.

I crawled onto the kitchen floor. Black smoke billowed through the doorway over me, filling the room. Face on the ground, I opened my mouth and inhaled. I immediately began to cough, violent spasms that were like vomiting pain.

"Lorenzo!" someone shouted. Hands grabbed me by the straps on my armor and pulled me across the kitchen. Black combat boots stomped ahead of me. Reaper. "Holy shit! You're on fire!" He whipped off his giant coat and covered me with it, beating at my back and legs.

Finally I rolled over and gasped, precious air filling my lungs. He was pulling me outside the burning mess hall. It took a moment for my head to quit spinning. Jill was staring down at me, her hands on the side of my face. She was saying something.

"I'm okay," I rasped, trying to sit up. Pain like electric current moved through my limbs.

"You know fuck-all about okay." She pushed me back down. "Hold still. You're hurt."

Pain was replaced with anger. Anger was replaced with rage. I grabbed her arm. "Where's Eddie?" I snapped.

"I don't know," she cried. "You're hurting me."

I immediately let go. "Sorry." I left a soot-black, blood-stained handprint on her arm. "Help me up," I ordered. Jill and Reaper both took an elbow and helped me stand. Reaper pushed me a small bottle of water, and I sucked at it greedily. It burned going down my parched throat. After a few seconds, I had to stop and puke the water and a bunch of soot up, then I went back to drinking. They both wore looks of shock as they studied me. I had to look pretty bad.

"Screw it. I'll live," I wheezed as I tossed the bottle, sounding like a ten-pack-a-day smoker. "Status?"

"Bob's pinned down. Somebody got back on that machine gun. Valentine saw Gordon. He and Hawk went that way." Reaper pointed toward the garage. "We haven't seen Eddie."

The scarab was still down there, lost in the flames, probably melted. Whoever wanted that thing so badly was probably going to be pissed. I patted my side. At least I had stuck with my training and reholstered my pistol even while standing inside a fireball. I pulled the gun now and let it dangle at my side.

"Quit staring. Let's go help my brother."

VALENTINE

Gordon was not going to get away. *The Calm* was failing, replaced with rage. I was hunting him like an animal, and I'd never felt more alive. I think I actually had a smile on my face.

"Val! Wait!" Hawk shouted, struggling to keep up.

It was dark. The air was filled with smoke. My eyes welled with tears, and my lungs ached. My focus was on the back doorway and the pitch-black space that Gordon had escaped into.

Bob was saying something over the radio, sounding scared, but I couldn't understand him over the beating pulse in my head. Gordon had to die first; then I could care about everyone else's business. I reached the doorway. I pulled up against the frame and flashed my weapon light before stepping through. *Clear.*

I stepped forward and was immediately cracked across the chest with a 2x4. I lurched back, disoriented, and fell to the ground. The man was on top of me in an instant. I raised my hands to protect my head as began to bludgeon me with the board.

My attacker swung again. The board struck my arm, and shocking pain flooded all the way to my shoulder. My arm went numb. I struggled for my pistol, but he slammed the board down on me again. The man raised the 2x4 over his head, meaning to swing it down on me like a sledge-hammer. He left an opening. I planted a size-twelve boot right in his nutsack.

He stumbled back, giving me a moment of respite. Before he could recover, someone jumped over me and dove into my attacker. I was dazed. My head was swimming, and it felt like my skull had been split open. I was too dizzy to rise.

I could barely see what was going on. Two men fought viciously in front of me, moving so fast in the dark I couldn't tell who was who. I then heard Hawk grunt in pain as the two shapes moved apart. There was sudden flash of steel as a knife darted between them. I raised my gun as one of the shapes tottered forward, went to his knees, and fell face-first to the floor.

"Hawk?" I asked. "You okay?"

It took him a second to respond. "Fine," he grunted as he emerged from the shadows, holding his old Randall knife in one hand. His other hand was clamped against his side. "He stabbed me. Not too bad, though." Despite his injury, Hawk helped me to my feet. I wobbled but was able to stand.

Is it Gordon? My deceased attacker was wearing a suit and was about the right size. I swung my rifle around and thumbed on my flashlight. I don't know who the man was, but it wasn't Gordon Willis. Probably one of his flunkies. The side of his neck had been split open from his collarbone to his ear. *Damn.* Hawk spat.

Gunfire echoed from the direction of the garage. Beyond that I could hear the noise of an engine turning over.

Gordon was getting away.

LORENZO

Reaper was in front now as we hurried back toward the garage, trying to stay in the shadows as much as possible. We could see a stream of tracers flying from the side of the garage up into the hillside where we had left Bob. I stumbled along, one arm over Jill's shoulder as she kept me upright. The mess hall was burning bright, and the flames had spread to the surrounding buildings. The camp was coming down.

I avoided taking a mental inventory of my injuries. Nothing seemed to be bleeding very fast.

We all instinctively ducked as we were suddenly illuminated by car headlights. Somebody had made it back to the vehicles. There was a sudden roar from a powerful engine, and one of the Suburbans sprayed gravel as it turned around and tore away from us.

That's when I saw Valentine emerge from one of the buildings on the other side of the horseshoe. *"Gordon!"* he screamed, running right into the middle of the road, oblivious to danger. He snapped his FAL to his shoulder and fired at the Suburban. Several holes were punched in the back of the SUV before Valentine's bolt locked back. He rapidly reloaded, once again flinging the empty magazine away and rocking in a new one, but it was too late. By the time he dropped the bolt on a live round, the Suburban had dipped into a gully and disappeared from view.

Valentine slowly lowered his rifle. He stood there quietly, seething, staring at the horizon as if he could will the Suburban to come back. Hawk appeared behind him, limping badly. His rifle was slung, his .44 dangled from one hand, and his other hand was pressed against a wound on his side.

Hawk caught my look. "Keep moving! I'm fine." Another burst of machine gun fire tore into the hillside. All of us flinched in that direction. *Bob.* I was running now, the others right behind me. Valentine saw us and followed. My 9mm was at the ready as I moved around the corner of the garage.

The MG3 was braced over the hood of a sedan. A giant white shape was manning the gun, firing short bursts onto a patch of darkened mountain where my brother had gotten pinned down. It was the Fat Man. The back of his white suit was shredded from my grenade. Blood ran from dozens of injuries. Maybe he had on some kind of body armor, or maybe he was just that tough, but somehow the son of a bitch was still alive. I could feel the others behind me, five of us in a row now. I settled my front sight on him and fired, still walking forward.

He grunted, raising the machine gun off the hood of the sedan. I fired again. Valentine's rifle bucked off to the side. The Fat Man began to turn, surprisingly enough, a strange smile on his face even as our bullets struck home. Jill was shooting her pistol now, cranking off shots as fast as she could pull the trigger. I kept shooting, but impossibly the Fat Man stayed on his feet as bullets puckered into his bloated frame, tearing him apart. Reaper's buckshot rocked him slightly, sending the MG3's muzzle into the dirt. I kept firing, front sight tracking back down; now I was shooting for his head. One of Hawk's .44 slugs erupted through his cheek, and he spit teeth but stayed upright. Still closing, Reaper hit him again, the buckshot in a tighter pattern now, taking the Fat Man's kneecap off.

His ponderous weight hit the hood, sliding inevitably toward the earth, leaving a trail behind him. He was reaching into his coat, somehow finding the strength to go for his gun. Jill fired her last shots into his neck. He was still smiling a toothless death's head grin, one eye missing now, as he hit the ground.

"Fucking die already!" Reaper shouted, stepping on the Fat Man's arm, pinning the gun, extending the stubby 12 gauge toward that nebulous smile. *BOOM BOOM!* Point-blank range. It wasn't pretty. Reaper stepped back and wiped his arm across his blood-splattered face. "You ain't coming back now!"

I shoved a fresh magazine into my STI. "Get Bob on the radio."

"He says he's okay," Reaper answered. "And—"

"Down!" Valentine shouted. He was closest to Jill and shoved her aside. I hit the deck as another sedan tore past us, muzzle flashes strobing out the open window, bullets whizzing past. Eddie's maniacally grinning face was illuminated for a brief instant. He must have gotten into the car while we were distracted by the Fat Man. Hawk fired his .44 one-handed at the speeding car as it bounced down the road. The concussions were deafening, but then the car was around the hillside and out of sight.

"Everybody okay?"

"I think so," Jill answered from the ground.

"Reaper?" *No answer.* I scrambled over to my friend. He was on his back next to the headless body of the Fat Man. "Reaper? Reaper!"

A bullet had smashed his chest plate. He was bleeding badly from the side of his head. I shook him. He opened his eyes, looked around in confusion, then grimaced. "Ow, shit, that hurts." He rolled over and put his hands on his skull. "He shot me, and I hit my head on the car. So quit yelling at me! Oh, man, he shot me in the arm too." Sure enough, there was a wound on his bicep. Jill knelt by his side and put pressure on it. "I hate getting shot!"

"You'll live," Jill said.

I could be relieved later. I pulled Reaper's radio off his vest. "Bob. Can you hear me?"

"Yeah, bro. I'm good. That was close."

Somehow we had all survived. "If you see another car moving down the road, kill the driver."

"He's already around the hill. I can't acquire."

I swore as I keyed the radio again. "Get down to the road as fast as you can. We'll pick you up in a minute."

"*I'm on my way,*" he answered.

I stuffed the radio in my pocket. Valentine had picked up the big MG3 and taken up a defensive position. I started for the closest sedan. The door was unlocked. No keys of course. I whipped out my multitool and cracked open the cover beneath the steering wheel. It took all of thirty seconds to get the car hot-wired, and that was between bouts of violent coughing and blood trickling down my arms and making my hands slippery. The engine turned over as I struck the wires together.

The others were already cramming into the sedan. Valentine had to maneuver the German machine gun to make it fit. The entire prison camp was burning bright now, and we needed to get out of here before the authorities showed up. I slammed the car into gear and floored it as soon as everyone was inside.

The car was dying. Something must have been hit as we were unloading on the Fat Man. All the warning lights were on. The engine was coughing almost as badly as I was. Jill was squished against me, with Bob and his body armor taking up most of the front seat. All of us were filthy, sweating, and half of us were bleeding. Bob's shocked reaction to seeing me under the car's interior lights when we had picked him up told me about how horrible I looked.

"We're almost where we left the vehicles," Bob stated calmly. He was covered in desert dust. His rifle was between his knees. The fire from the work camp was just a visible glow over the hill behind us.

"Status back there?" I asked. "Hawk? Reaper?"

"It's a shallow cut." Hawk had his shirt open and had shoved a pressure bandage on his side. "Nothing bad."

"The kid's going to be okay. Bullet grazed his bicep, missed the brachial artery. I've got the bleeding under control," Valentine said from the backseat.

"I suck at this stuff," Reaper whined. "I keep getting shot."

"You'll be fine," Valentine said flatly.

"Bob, I need you to get these guys out of here before the cops show up. They need medical attention. Think you can handle it?"

"No problem," my brother answered. I knew that he'd been some sort of medic in the National Guard, an 18 Delta he'd called it. "But I think you need a hospital."

"It's better than it looks," I lied. There were deep lacerations on my face, scalp, and down my arms. My hands were a blood soaked mess. I had first degree burns on much of my body, and from the throbbing nerves down my back and legs I knew that there were some spots that were much worse. I couldn't stop coughing.

But there was no way in hell Eddie was going to get away.

"*Holy shit!*" Reaper suddenly freaked out. "Look at this! Look at this!"

"Crap. What?"

"I think it's Eddie's tablet!" he exclaimed.

"So?"

"He's *logged* in!" Reaper cackled in glee. I was too out of it to see the significance. Gunshot wound forgotten,

Reaper madly started fiddling with the little gizmo. "Oh, now this, I am good at!"

The car died as we rolled into the rest stop. I jumped out and started toward the stolen Explorer. "Where do you think you're going?" Jill asked.

"After Eddie." I opened the door. "He told Gordon that he'd flown into a nearby airport."

Valentine spoke up. "There's only one around here. It's not far."

"You're injured! You need medical attention!" Jill insisted. She was right, of course. I was running on nothing but adrenaline and anger now.

"I'll be fine," I said. "I'll hook up with you later." I didn't want them with me. Gordon had probably notified the authorities, and surely word would reach the cops in Quagmire about the massacre at the old work camp. I grabbed the wheel. My vision was blurred and my head was swimming. Bob was helping Reaper into the back of the G-ride Suburban.

Valentine tossed the keys to his Mustang to Jill. "Follow Bob," he told her. "And take good care of my car."

"Lorenzo . . ." Jill trailed off. She was filthy, stupid pink outfit splattered with blood, her hair tangled with dirt, hanging like a dark shadow over half her face, a stolen handgun dangling from one hand.

She was beautiful.

"I know," I rasped.

Valentine opened the passenger-side door and slid in, maneuvering the big German machine gun to fit between us.

"What the hell are you doing?"

"Just *drive*." He slammed the door.

I pushed the Ford up to a hundred and five. It wouldn't go any faster. The highway was virtually deserted, and I had the gas pedal floored. I wasn't worried about being pulled over. God help the stray Highway Patrolman that got between me and Eddie.

Valentine held onto the *oh, shit!* handle as we barreled down the road. I passed a slow-moving semi truck like it was standing still, pulling back into the right-hand lane just in time to avoid hitting another car head on. The Explorer was vibrating like hell.

"We're almost there," Valentine said. "This airport has been closed for years. Your guy must've had his boys come pick him up. There's nothing there but a few run-down buildings."

In the back of my mind, I wondered why Valentine came with me. I doubted he'd tell me if I asked. Just then, my cell phone vibrated, disrupting my thoughts. I pulled it out of my pocket and hit the talk button.

It was Eddie, sounding as shrill and oily as ever. "Ah, Lorenzo. Just checking. I thought that was you I saw standing on the side of the road back there. Did I kill any more of your friends with my little drive-by? It was so invigorating! Like one of your American rap-music videos!" The psychopath giggled.

"No, Eddie, you're a lousy fucking shot." The sound of his voice made me push the gas pedal that much harder.

"You certainly are hard to kill."

"You won't be," I promised. "What do you want?"

He laughed, somehow managing to sound girly and sadistic at the same time. "To taunt you, of course. My plane is taking off as we speak. I imagine that you're trying to catch up with me, but you will be too late. As soon as I hang up, I'm going to ring one of my associates, and then the fun will begin. I'm not just going to have your loved ones killed, I'm going to have them tortured first. I'm going to take your little nieces and nephews, and I'm going to have them raped in front of their parents. I'm going to make them *watch*. I will—"

I ignored Eddie's ranting. "Where do we turn?"

"Right here, right here!" Valentine said, pointing.

"Hang on!" I'd nearly missed the turnoff. Hitting the brake, I cranked the Explorer to the right, nearly putting it up on two wheels.

"Ow! Damn it!" Valentine snarled as the heavy machine gun slid over and struck him. We sped down a narrow deserted road. The airport wasn't far. After a minute or two we shot through an open gate on a rusted chain-link fence and careened onto a wide-open paved area. I smashed the brake, making a tight turn as we crossed a parking area, passed the dilapidated remains of a hanger, and sped onto the tarmac. The airport obviously hadn't been used in years. The runway and taxiways were cracked and faded, with weeds springing through splits in the pavement. Eddie's car, now empty, was parked off to the side.

"There!" Valentine shouted, pointing down the runway. At the far end was a speeding Gulfstream jet. Its engines screamed as it built up speed.

Eddie was still going on, screeching like a lunatic. "— you hear me? Nobody crosses Big Eddie! *Nobody*! I've got to make an example out of you, Lorenzo. Everyone needs to know the consequences of my displeasure!"

The Explorer skidded to a stop, leaving a trail of rubber. Valentine leapt out, pulling the machine gun with him as the jet jumped into the air. He set the barrel over the junction of the door and frame, crouched down, and squeezed the trigger.

The MG3 roared, sending a stream of tracers down the runway after the climbing jet. He hosed the rest of the belt, at least fifty rounds, at the target. Bullets streamed into the air, but fell short. The jet was just too far away. The MG3's bolt flew forward on an empty chamber. That was it.

"That's the best you've got, Lorenzo?" Eddie cackled. "Not a scratch on me!" I stuck the phone in the front of my armor.

"Shit!" Valentine shouted. "I'm out! He's gonna get away!"

"No," I stated calmly. While he was shooting, I had limped around to the back door. I opened it, ripped the concealing blanket aside, and pulled out the portable surface to air missile that I had stolen from the Chechen border jumpers. "He's not."

"What the . . ." Valentine said, observing my weapon in awe.

I set the heavy tube on my shoulder, took one step around the Explorer and looked through the scope. I had read the instructions earlier, and it seemed relatively straightforward. I found the red and green flashing lights of Eddie's jet, centered them in the circle, and hit the lock button. It took a few seconds for the sensor to read. It made a noise like a microwave oven saying that the hotdogs were done.

I pulled the heavy trigger.

FOOOOOM!

The concussion was horrendous. The initial charge threw the missile straight out. A split second later the rocket engine ignited in a massive gout of flame and soared after the jet with a shrieking noise like some obscene bird of prey. The impact staggered me. I pulled the phone out of my armor with my shaking left hand.

"—should have just given me the scarab. I'll—"

I cut him off. "Hey, Eddie . . ."

"What is it, Lorenzo?"

"See you in *hell*."

"What are you . . . evade! Evade!" I could hear him screaming at the pilot while an alarm went off in the background. Eddie was rich enough to afford a missile detection system for his private jet.

Not that it did him any good. A fireball blossomed in the night sky. The entire jet was illuminated for a brief moment as one of the rear engines was engulfed, sparks drifting toward the ground like a demented fireworks display. A wing broke off just as the sound of the first impact reached us. The plane rolled over, trailing smoke, and crumpled into the desert floor in a ball of fire.

I looked down at the phone.

Call Disconnected

Elapsed Time: 4:33

The wreckage continued to burn. It was over. Big Eddie was dead.

My body began to shake, to tremble. All of the pain

that I had forced aside came rushing back, staggering me, sending me to my knees. A year of doing the impossible, my loved ones held hostage, my friends in danger, some hurt, some killed, all had come down to this.

It was over.

"We better get out of here before the cops show up," Valentine said. "I don't want to try to explain to them where you got a Stinger missile from."

I was leaning against the SUV, shaking. I couldn't believe it. I was in shock.

"How about I drive?" Valentine suggested, "Since you're having, um, a moment?"

I jerkily nodded and climbed into the passenger seat. I closed my eyes. The pillar of fire that had been Eddie's plane burned onto the inside of my eyelids. "It's over," I said.

Valentine put the Explorer in gear. "Sure, whatever." He thought for a moment. "So. Who was that on the plane?"

I let the pain carry me into the dark.

. . . *over* . . .

Chapter 30:
What Happens
in Vegas . . .

VALENTINE
Las Vegas, Nevada
June 29
0300

Somehow I ended up back in Las Vegas. It was like I couldn't escape that place. It had been Bob's idea. Vegas was the nearest big city, and we needed a place to go. We found a crappy motel in a crappy part of town, the kind of place where call girls hang out in the lobby and they don't bother asking for ID, and checked in.

Hawk had gone home. As far as I knew, neither Gordon Willis nor any of his surviving men had identified any of us. At least I hoped not. We made a pretty big mess and shot down a private jet. There was bound to be a shit-storm over it, and we decided it was best if we scattered before anyone figured out what happened. If they traced it back to Hawk, or any of us for that matter . . . I didn't know what would happen, but I knew it would be bad.

Bob insisted that Gordon Willis and his people weren't part of the legitimate government. As much as they'd use every resource to figure out what happened, they'd try just as hard to keep things quiet. That made sense to me. I knew things about Gordon that Bob didn't know. I knew what Gordon did. He was a traitor, not only to his country, but to Majestic, the shadowy organization he served. He was probably running just as far and just as fast as we were.

We all had injuries, but with some rudimentary supplies we were able to sort ourselves out. Bob was a medic, and a good one at that. Between the two of us we had gotten the others patched up. Lorenzo had been put down with a significant amount of painkillers. He probably should have been taken to a burn unit for a few spots on his back and legs, but that would've attracted attention, so he was going to have to make do.

Reaper was so preoccupied with the tablet PC he'd found that he barely noticed as we closed the hole in his arm. Jill only had nicks and bruises, but mostly she had just needed to crash. She'd had a hell of a day. All things considered, the girl was doing okay. She was tougher than she looked.

I'd been so close to killing Gordon I could taste it, yet he got away. I needed to get some air, and on top of it I was starving. I left our motel room to get some food. Bob Lorenzo insisted on going with me, which was both annoying and suspicious. It was annoying because I was contemplating just ditching those guys and taking off on my own. That was going to be a challenge riding with the hulking FBI agent in his G-ride SUV.

The ride was awkward, for me at least. I didn't know

Bob, and even though we'd just gone through some shit together, I sure as hell didn't trust him. It was obvious he wanted to talk to me about something, and I wasn't comfortable with it.

Bob was quiet for a long time as we fought our way through Vegas traffic. "So, who are you really, Mr. Nightcrawler?" he finally asked. He didn't look at me.

"Are you asking me as a cop, or are you asking me as a guy who just helped me kill a bunch of people?"

Bob didn't respond for a long time. "Don't judge what you don't understand."

A sardonic grin split my face. "My name is Michael Valentine, and I understand things a lot better than you think."

"I believe you," the big man said slowly. "You used to work for Gordon Willis, right?"

I was quiet for a few moments before I answered, trying to choose my words carefully. My gut told me I could trust Bob. Recent experience taught me that I couldn't trust anyone. "Yes. Until a month ago, anyway."

"You seem to have some kind of grudge. Were you in Majestic?"

That's who Colonel Hunter had said he answered to. "You could say that. To answer both your questions, I mean. I wasn't really aware of who I was working for until recently. I'm not sure what Majestic is. All I can find on it is a bunch of Internet conspiracy-theory crap."

"It's just a name. It's every secret, every abuse of power, every bad thing you can imagine. They used to exist to protect us, but now they just exist to consolidate their power. I'm guessing you were Dead Six, then."

I raised an eyebrow.

"You fit the profile," Bob said. "Young, probably former military, and you're not wearing a wedding ring so I'm guessing you're single. No family, either, right? Don't get excited. I've been looking into this stuff for a long time. I was waiting for someone involved in that to pop up. It's my lucky day, I guess."

He knew too much. He looked over at me and squinted. Was he doing the math? Trying to decide if he could get to his sidearm before I could get to mine? Bob was a Fed; was he in on this?

My face went blank. "You've got a forty-cal Sig in a strong-side, thumb-break cop holster that's stuck behind your seat-belt buckle. You won't get it out fast enough."

Bob chuckled before turning back to the road, shaking his head slightly. "Well, I'll be. You're quiet. You're used to people underestimating you, aren't you? But you turn it on like a light switch when you feel threatened. That's something else. But listen, I'm no friend of Gordon Willis. Trust me on this one. Let's just say that keeping up on current events is a hobby of mine. You could go so far as to say that I'm a bit of a conspiracy theorist, or at least my bosses seem to think so. Dead Six was one tiny operation out of many, all of them secret, most of them illegal, and half of them pure evil, all run by men like Willis, and if you get in the way of their power, you die."

"What do you know about Project Heartbreaker?"

"Officially? Nothing. Unofficially, an old friend of mine was the assistant ambassador in Zubara. We were on the same ODA. He knew that I was . . . *obsessed*, I think, was the word he used, about things like this. When things started to go bad there, he called me up, wondering if I could do some checking for him. I did, and found the stink of Willis and his people all over it. I've been doing research into him and the others like him for years. So I did some poking, through sources you wouldn't understand and I wouldn't tell you about anyway, and I learned about Dead Six. I told my friend, Jim Fiore, about what I'd found, and he was dead within forty-eight hours. I warned him not to talk, but he wouldn't listen."

"Why are you telling me this?" I asked.

"Because I want your help," Bob answered. "Because I *need* your help. You know things. Come with me. There are plenty of us in the government, the *real* government, who would love to see these people stopped. We can protect you. You can help us put a stake through their heart once and for all. There are still ways to work through the system. If we shine the light of day on these cockroaches, they'll scatter. If you come help me, we can . . ." Bob trailed off as I chuckled at him. "What is it?"

"You think I haven't heard this line of bullshit before? Come sign up with us, serve your country, fight the bad guys, blah blah *blah*. It's the same crap every time. Well, you know what? I'm *done.* I'm done signing up. I'm done joining the cause. I'm tired of being somebody else's damned *pawn*."

"It's not like that."

"Oh, the *hell* it's not," I said bitterly. "It's always the same. I'm just an asset to you. I used to work for a PMC. I know all about being a commodity. At least Vanguard was honest about it and had a good benefits package.

What are you offering me besides a bunch of rhetoric and empty promises?

Bob frowned. "I don't think you understand the gravity of the situation. These people are *destroying* this country. What you've seen is just the tip of the iceberg. If we—"

I cut him off. "No, *you* don't understand," I said harshly. "I *don't care.*"

We were stopped at an intersection, waiting for a light to turn green, which seemed to take an eternity. Bob gave me a hard stare. I could almost see the gears turning behind his eyes. His expression softened a bit. "What the hell happened to you, kid?"

I looked down at my lap and exhaled. "That's a long story."

"More importantly," Bob continued, returning his attention to the road as we started moving again, "what are you going to do now? You can't hide at your friend's place forever. If certain people find out you're alive, they'll kill you and everyone you know. How long do you think you can stay on the run?"

"Who said anything about running?"

Bob shook his head. "The best defense is a good offense, huh?" he asked sardonically. "I've known a lot of guys like you. Most of them were Special Forces."

"I was in the Air Force."

Bob laughed, somewhat defusing the tension in the car. "You know it won't work, right? I mean, you know that, don't you? Majestic is too big to just take out. You can't kill the beast by running in and shooting everybody. You have to be smart about it."

"I'm not interested in killing the beast," I said. "And there's only one person I need to shoot."

"You intend to kill Gordon Willis, don't you?" Bob asked levelly. I didn't answer. That in and of itself was answer enough, I suppose. Bob shook his head again. "It's a suicide mission. Majestic won't let you touch him, and even if you succeed, you're a dead man."

"See, there's where you're wrong," I suggested. "You don't know everything I know. I don't think Majestic's got Gordon's back anymore."

"What are you talking about?"

"Gordon's gone off the reservation. Project Heartbreaker failed because of his dirty dealings."

Bob seemed surprised by this. "What? How do you know this?" I didn't answer him. He looked frustrated at my intransigence. "It doesn't change anything. Killing him won't change anything. Right now you think it'll settle the score, right whatever wrong happened to you. Trust me, even if you succeed, it won't change. You won't get the satisfaction you want. They'll kill you, and it'll have all been for nothing."

In my mind I saw Sarah falling to the mud like a puppet with the strings cut. *Not for nothing*, I thought.

We went through the drive-through of some all-night burger place. Bob ordered. I was distracted. What *would* happen if I killed Gordon? Would I even succeed? I knew where he lived. I knew everything about him. It was all on Hunter's flash drive. But would I be able to find him? What if he went into hiding?

If those thoughts weren't troubling enough, something else crossed my mind. Ling warned me about trying to exact revenge. She asked me if I thought that was what Sarah would have wanted me to do. I still didn't have an answer that I liked.

"I'm asking you one last time. Don't do it, kid. I don't know what happened, what you lost out there, but I can see that pain inside of you. Don't let the pain steer you." Bob set the bags on the seat and started driving. "Don't throw your life away for nothing." I glanced over at him. He seemed sincere enough. Was it possible he was actually being straight with me?

I wasn't used to that. "I'll think on it," I lied.

Bob started to speak again but had to stop to answer his phone. He listened for a minute, speaking occasionally, before hanging up. "Looks like there's been a terrorist *incident* in my area of responsibility. They want me out there ASAP."

I shook my head at the surrealism of it all as we pulled back into the motel parking lot.

Bob put the Suburban in park. "Will you at least think about what I said? Look. You're right. I don't know you. I'm not trying to help you out of pure altruism. But you helped save my brother's life. Are you sure you want to go it alone?"

"No," I replied honestly. "But it's all I can do. Listen, there is something I can do to help you," I said as I reached into my pocket. I retrieved Colonel Hunter's blood-stained flash drive and handed it to Bob.

"What is this?" he asked. The white piece of plastic looked tiny in his huge hands.

"It's everything," I said. "Everything on Project Heartbreaker from start to finish. The planning, the logistics, the personnel and assets involved. Almost everything, anyway. We picked up a nuke in Yemen, too. No idea where that ended up."

Bob's eyes went wide. He looked at the diminutive piece of electronics as if it were a holy relic. "What? Where did you get this?"

"It was compiled by Colonel Curtis Hunter, the field commander of Dead Six. The last thing he did before dying was give this to me. I've gone over it. Hunter suspected Gordon's activities for a long time and dug up as much as he could. There are still big pieces of the story missing. The stuff highlighted in green is my own notes. I filled in the gaps where I could, but there's a lot I don't know and a lot Hunter couldn't find out. But the hit on your friend at the embassy is detailed on there, though I don't think you'll be able to pin it on anyone. A lot of the info has been sanitized."

Bob couldn't take his eyes off the flash drive. "Why are you giving this to me?"

"You can use it more than I can," I said honestly. "It will help you. It has the complete files of all of the people recruited for Dead Six, from the time they were approached to the time they were killed or went missing. All are listed as KIA or MIA. I've edited my own file, changed it to a confirmed KIA."

"Why did you do that?"

"I was thinking about releasing this whole thing to the news. But I don't know if that would do any good. So I'm giving it to you instead. If you do go public with this, make sure they think I'm dead. Okay?"

"I will," Bob answered solemnly.

"We were serving our country," I said quietly. "A lot of my friends died taking the fight to the enemy's doorstep. And they sold us out and left us to die. Somebody needs to tell the world what happened. Most of us didn't have any family at all. But some did. Their families deserve to know how they died."

Bob gave me a look that told me he respected what I said. He'd been a soldier. He understood. I got out of the car, pulling most of the food with me.

"Valentine, wait," Bob said, quickly shoving the thumb drive in his shirt pocket. "What if they don't kill you? What if you're captured? They'll find out everything. Everyone that's helped you, including me, will be put in danger."

I looked at the ground for a moment. I really didn't have a rebuttal to that. Bob didn't want to let me go, but I'd made it clear that he couldn't stop me. Had I really thought this through? Where would I end up if I went down this road?

My expression hardened as I buried my self-doubt. I didn't have a choice. Bob was right. I couldn't run forever. I wasn't going to run off with him, either. He struck me as a sincere man, but also a lone nut who was short on friends. At least if I went my own way, I had a say over where I ended up.

That's what I told myself, anyway. Bob wished me luck. I nodded and turned away, not looking back as he drove off.

LORENZO

Somebody was singing.

I awoke in a strange hotel room. There were bandages on my head, arms, and the back of my legs. My lungs ached and I could still feel the smoke in my sinuses. An IV bag was hanging from the wall light above me. I tracked the tube down and it disappeared under the gauze on my forearm. I hurt everywhere and my eyes grated in my sockets as I scanned the room. Reaper was asleep on the other bed, his arm wrapped in white and strapped across his torso. The kid was snoring.

I could hear the shower running. The singing was Jill. She was off-key and loud, but she sounded happy. It was a good sound.

The scarab. There was a momentary flash of panic. It was gone. I'd sacrificed so much to get it. . . . The last I'd seen, it had been in the basement of a building collapsing in flames. Then I relaxed. It didn't matter now. Eddie was dead. I was free. I'd never even known what it was, except that it cost too many of my friends' lives. Hopefully the fire had destroyed it, and if it hadn't, then it could stay buried in the desert forever.

I had never even known who it was for. Whoever the important man was that Eddie had been getting the scarab for more than likely didn't know anything about me . . . *Probably.*

The hotel door clicked as somebody used a card key to open it. Instinctively I looked around for my gun. It was nowhere to be seen. I relaxed as I realized it was Valentine. He entered the room with a fast-food bag in one hand and one of those cardboard drink trays full of sodas in the other. "Yo."

"Hey," I responded. "Where are we?"

"Vegas. Wanna hit up a strip club?"

"Only if we can't get Siegfried and Roy tickets."

"What? Siegfried and . . . No, man, one of 'em got eaten by the tiger. Long time ago."

"No kidding? Leave the country for a while and everything goes nuts."

"Tell me about it. Everybody is okay. Hawk's back at his place keeping a low profile. We figured that Quagmire might be a little hot, so we came here. There's no place to disappear like Vegas. Since they grabbed Jill they never saw Hawk with either of us, so he should be in the clear as long as I don't contact him." Valentine set the food on the table and pulled up a chair. "Your little buddy's been busy, going hog-wild over that computer he found. He passed out about an hour ago. He takes his Internet very seriously, doesn't he?"

"That's a bit of an understatement. How's Jill?"

Valentine nodded in the direction of the bathroom. "She'll be fine."

I had to smile. "I think she'll be okay. So what's our situation?"

"Jill insisted that I bring you here, and she's hard to say no to. Your brother's a decent medic, and he got you patched up before he had to go. Apparently some terrorist shot down an airplane in Quagmire with a surface-to-air missile. The terror alert is at red level right now."

"What's the world coming to?"

He looked exhausted. "Jill filled me in on Big Eddie. So your boy is dead. That's two Montalbans I've either killed or helped kill. How weird is that?"

"What are you going to do now?" I asked, already knowing the answer.

"I don't know," he stated flatly.

He might not know, but I knew where his road would lead. I had seen this kind of attitude before, depressed, violent, hovering on the fine line between homicidal and suicidal. Valentine had a weight on his shoulders, and I didn't know if removing it would free him or destroy him.

It wasn't in my nature to offer, but I did anyway. I'd been surprising myself a lot lately. "You want help?"

"What? No."

I nodded. "I understand."

"You won't see me again," he said, "but there is one thing. Listen to me. Your two friends here, Jill and Skyler? You get them out of this life. Look at me. Whatever it is you see? That's their future unless you stop now. You know as well as I do that once you get in, you don't get out."

I glanced over at the bathroom door, then back at Valentine. I cringed at the thought of Jill becoming . . . like *him*.

"I gotta go. Your gun is in the drawer. I got you guys some food. I hope you like burgers."

"Only communists and hippies don't like burgers. Thanks."

"No problem."

"No, I meant . . ." I shrugged. I couldn't have done it without his help. "You know."

He gave me a small nod in acknowledgment. "Just remember what I said."

We were no longer enemies, but we certainly weren't friends. "You want to stick around and say good-bye to Jill?"

"I need to go. Besides, all she does it talk about you. I'm kind of sick of it. I honestly don't know what she sees in you."

"Well, I did take a guy's head off with piano wire for her."

Valentine shrugged. "Girls like romantic gestures like that. Look, I gotta split. Take it easy."

"Watch your back," I told him.

"Watch the news." He didn't look back.

Epilogue:
Requiem

VALENTINE
Arlington, Virginia
July 4
2245

Sweat beaded on my face as I cleared the top of a tall
fence and quietly landed in the grass. I crouched down
for a moment, shrouded in darkness, and studied my
surroundings. Directly in front of me was a full-sized
swimming pool. Beyond that was a palatial home, situated
in the more expensive half of a gated community of "rich-
bitch" estates. The air smelled like gunpowder from the
fireworks being set off in the streets.

I was dressed in dark clothes and had black grease
paint smeared onto my face. My S&W .44 Magnum
revolver was concealed under my shirt. I double-checked
my coordinates on the GPS one last time; I had to make
sure I had the right house. Satisfied, I stood up and moved
silently across the darkened backyard toward the house.

Gordon Willis didn't know it, but he had *company* tonight.

The back patio door was glass. I risked a peek inside and saw no movement. The house was mostly darkened but had enough lights left on that navigation wouldn't be difficult. I'd have to be quick. There was probably some kind of an alarm system; as soon as I busted through the door, I'd have only moments to do what I'd come to do.

Taking one last look around, I reached for the door and tried the handle. It was unlocked. Grinning to myself, I silently entered Gordon's house, shocked that a man like him would be so lackadaisical in his home security. I drew my revolver as the door closed behind me. The tritium front sight glowed green in the dim light.

The house was lavishly furnished with tacky postmodern décor. Half the stuff in the large downstairs recroom looked like it came from Ikea. An expensive-looking pool table sat in the middle of the room. I searched the downstairs area in silence. The lower level was deserted, but I could hear sounds of movement coming from somewhere in the house. My grip on my weapon tightened slightly as I made my way up the stairs to the second floor.

I walked down the second-floor hall. The first door on my left led to a bedroom. The bed was covered with pillows and stuffed animals, and posters of several teen pop idols decorated the walls. A pit formed in my stomach, and I felt *the Calm* begin to waiver. It had never occurred to me that Gordon might've had a daughter. *Shit.* I noticed that the drawers on the girl's dresser had been pulled open and emptied. Had Gordon and his family fled? If so, who was in the house?

I steeled myself and quietly returned to the hallway,

padding along on the carpet. At the end of the hall was a door to what looked like a master bedroom. The door was open, but I couldn't see any movement inside. There was a room kitty-corner to it, also with the door open. I froze when I heard someone cough loudly from that room.

My eyes narrowed as I brought my weapon up in both hands. I took one last deep breath and swiftly entered the room. I was surprised by what I saw.

Gordon Willis sat at a desk, facing the doorway, with his face buried in his hands. A large bottle of vodka sat open on his desk, and I could smell booze in the air. Next to the bottle was a Glock pistol. The room was some kind of study.

Gordon looked up when I entered the room, eyes wide. He swore aloud and reached for the pistol. My revolver roared in the confines of the study. The slug shattered the vodka bottle, blasted through Gordon's hand, and smacked into his desk. Gordon screamed in pain, clutching his pulped right hand with his left. The Glock was sent clattering to the floor.

He stared at the blood pouring down his arm for a moment, then looked up at me. "What took you so long?" he asked heavily, convulsing with pain. "What are you waiting for?"

"It was a long drive from Nevada," I said coldly.

Gordon froze and stared at my face intently for a moment. "V . . . Valentine? They sent *you*?" He paused for a moment, grunting in pain. "Jesus, I should've known. Well, just . . . just get it over with." He looked down at his desk.

"Gordon," I said slowly, keeping my weapon trained on him, "who is it that you think sent me?"

"What? You mean you're not . . ." Gordon trailed off for

a moment. He then let out a pained laugh. "You picked a hell of a day to show up."

"What are you talking about?" My patience was running out.

Gordon nodded his head at his computer screen. *The Drudge Report* had a lead article about Project Heartbreaker and the abandonment of American personnel in Zubara. Bob Lorenzo had come through. He'd leaked Hunter's flash drive, or at least part of it, to the public. "They told me there was no reason for my family to suffer," Gordon said slowly, grasping his bleeding hand even tighter. "They let me send my wife away with my little girl. They . . . they told me to wait here. They said they'd come for me."

"Who?" I asked. "Majestic?"

Gordon managed a sardonic, half-in-shock smile, all while tears of pain were leaking involuntarily from his eyes. "You think you got it all figured out because you found out a name?" He scoffed, wincing in pain as he did so. "You have no idea the forces that are at work here, kid. This is *bigger* than us. They know everything now. They know about the deal I made with Eduard Montalban. They even found out I was proceeding on Blue!"

"I'm not working for anybody. You don't know why I'm here, do you?" Gordon looked at me in silence, inebriated from both shock and alcohol. My face hardened. "Her name was *Sarah*."

"What? Oh . . . right . . . McAllister. I was sent a report about you two."

"I know. I read it. She's dead because of you, you son of a bitch!"

"I know," Gordon groaned, squirming from the pain. "What do you want me to say? I was cleaning up loose ends. It was part of the deal. But that's all ruined now. They found out."

I smiled coldly. "Hunter gave me a lot of information before he died. I made sure it got into the right hands."

"*You*? You did this? Do you have any idea the damage you've done? Well you'll find out soon enough. Or not. I don't know. They'll probably just kill you. You should've taken me up on my offer."

"And you should've listened when I told you not to fuck with me." Then I shot him through the heart. The bullet punched through the back of his chair in a splash of blood, and Gordon tumbled to the floor.

I stood there for what seemed like a long time, not moving. I slowly lowered my gun. It was done; Gordon was dead. I'd avenged Sarah.

Yet I felt no satisfaction. Nothing had changed, except I'd ended one more life. Ling had warned me that if I went down this road, I might not like what I found when I reached the end. She was right. I'd reached the end, and I felt *nothing*.

Turning to leave the room, I nearly ran into the barrels of several suppressed weapons. A full squad of men dressed in tac gear was standing in the hall.

"Drop your weapon!" one of the men commanded.

Very slowly, I laid my revolver down on the carpet. I stepped back and placed my hands behind my head. The men in the hall rushed me then. I was turned around and slammed against the wall. My hands were roughly pulled behind my back and cuffed together.

Searing pain shot through me as one of the men shoved a high-powered taser into my back. I gasped for air, my knees buckled, and I fell to the floor. A black bag was pulled over my head, and I was hit with the taser again.

I found myself wondering if they'd come for me, or if they'd come for Gordon. I doubted I'd live long enough to find out.

LORENZO
Somewhere in the Caribbean
August 28

"It has been a month since billionaire philanthropist Eduard Montalban was killed in a tragic plane crash. The FAA has concluded their investigation and have determined that his Gulfstream jet was brought down by a mechanical failure as the pilot attempted an emergency landing at an airport in rural Nevada. According to the National Transportation Safety Board, there is no evidence that the plane was brought down by a surface-to-air missile, as was originally rumored," the anchorwoman said. Like most cable news people, she was easy on the eyes yet hard on the brain.

The screen switched over to a prerecorded press conference. The caption on the bottom of the shot said Special Agent Robert T. Lorenzo, FBI. Bob looked awkward on camera, enormous behind the podium, and the press spotlights caused a reflection from the top of his bald head. "I can assure you that there is no need to panic. There's absolutely no evidence that there are any anti-aircraft missiles in the United States. Air travel is perfectly safe." My brother lied well. It must run in the family. "The reports of a wild west-style gunfight in the Nevada desert beforehand are nothing more than unfounded rumors passed on by conspiracy theorists. Mr. Montalban's death was a tragic accident. He was a great humanitarian and will be missed by all."

They showed a file photo of Big Eddie waving to the crowd at some bigwig charity function, supermodel on one arm, poodle in the other.

Good riddance. *Freak.*

How could such a pathetic shell of a man cause so much suffering? I didn't think I would ever understand what made him tick, what motivated him to threaten me. The wicked trinket that had cost Train and Carl their lives was buried in a pit of ashes in Nevada. It had gone from one hole in the desert to another. It could rot in those ruins forever for all I cared. It seemed fitting.

The picture changed back to the vacuous reporter. "But with the recently revealed secret files concerning Project Heartbreaker, new questions have been raised. According to the files anonymously placed on the Internet, Eduard Montalban's older brother, Rafael, was one of their targets in the Middle East and was assassinated by members of the rogue operation codenamed Dead Six. Now members of Congress are questioning the NTSB's ruling and demanding that the investigation be reopened."

The picture changed to footage of several men in suits leaving a courthouse. A mob of reporters screamed questions at the men while mirrored-sunglass-wearing security rushed them into large black cars.

"In related news, the Project Heartbreaker hearings have continued. The president has vowed that the perpetrators will be found and that no secrets will be kept from the American public. The House Minority Leader has insisted on the appointment of an independent commission to—"

Jill picked up the remote and killed the TV. "That stuff will rot your brain."

She was wearing a simple white dress and had flowers in her hair. Through the window behind her, I could see the pristine beach stretching into the distance, bright green trees rising behind. Brilliant blue waves were washing onto the sand.

"I was hoping to hear something about what happened to Valentine," I explained. "After he got arrested, he just disappeared into the system. Even Reaper can't find any information about where they sent him."

"You don't even know it was him. They did rule Gordon's death a suicide."

"Suicide?" I snorted. "Five bucks says the kid killed him."

"Maybe." She grabbed my hand and pulled me up. "Come on. We're on a tropical island in the middle of nowhere, and you want to watch the news? That's just wrong." She dragged me up the stairs and onto the deck. Our yacht rocked gently against the wooden pier. I wasn't wearing a shirt, and the sun beat down on the mass of scars that was my back.

It had been one of Big Eddie's boats, but it was mine now. In the confusion immediately following his death, we had gone to work embezzling as much of his fortune as was possible. Eddie's computer had been packed with valuable information. He wasn't worried about password security, because only a fool would steal from Big Eddie. But he was dead now, and you'd never find a bigger pair of fools than me and Reaper. With the contacts I had made in all of my years of doing Eddie's dirty work, and with Reaper's mad skills, we had been able to make an absurd amount of his wealth disappear into a maze of foreign banks before news of his demise spread and his accounts had been locked down.

Basically, we were now obscenely wealthy. In fact, this little island had been Eddie's also. Most of it, anyway. It did have a little town on it. The rest was mine now. Apparently the Montalbans hadn't even used the place in years. Reaper had found it in his frenzied searching of Montalban shell-corporation properties. Jill and I had been holed up here together for the last few weeks. With such a huge burden lifted from my shoulders, they had been some of the happiest days of my life.

And what we did together during that time was none of your business.

My family was safe, and as far as all of them except Bob knew, I was still just the flaky world traveler. Reaper had taken his share of the loot and gone his own way. He'd kept in touch and kept asking if I wanted to go back to work. I always turned him down. Valentine's final words still haunted me.

"Want to head into town?" Jill gestured inland. Her arm was darkly tanned. "We haven't gone dancing for a while."

"I need to talk to you about something," I said. "Something serious."

She stopped smiling, folded her arms, and leaned on the railing. "I'm listening."

"With all of the information about Dead Six public, and with Gordon dead, you aren't in danger anymore."

"I know," she said slowly.

"You don't need to stay hidden. You can be yourself again."

Jill turned away, scanning across the beach as the wind whipped her dark hair around her shoulders. We'd spent a lot of time together recently. Being in hiding tends to do that to people. I was older than her, wearied and scarred by the world. She was a beautiful young woman with her whole life ahead of her. I was a criminal, wanted by the law in a dozen countries and wanted dead by hundreds of evil men. We both knew that though my life was calm and happy now, there was no guarantee that my past wouldn't catch up with us eventually. And for men like me, sometimes the past comes back to haunt you, while other times it comes back to cut your head off.

She'd be better off without me. She'd be safe, no longer a target. "Jill, what I'm saying is, you can go home."

Jill continued to watch the surf and the wheeling seagulls. It wasn't like she needed to stick around for the money. She'd helped us loot Eddie's fortune and had gotten an equal share. The only reason she had to stay now was me.

"You know what, Lorenzo? I think I am home." In one smooth move, she pulled her dress over her head, tossed it on the deck, and dove into the perfect blue water.

I grinned stupidly and followed.

My first official act as the island's new owner had been to change the name from Montalban Island to St. Carl.

It had a nice ring to it.

Home.

ABOUT THE AUTHORS

Larry Correia

Larry Correia is the *New York Times* bestselling author of the *Monster Hunter* series and the *Grimnoir Chronicles* for Baen Books. He graduated with a degree in accounting from Utah State University and went to work for a Fortune 500 company as a financial analyst. Eventually, Larry ended up in the gun business, where he was a machinegun dealer, firearms instructor, and freelance writer for various gun magazines. Most recently he has worked in military contracting. Larry lives in the mountains of Utah with his very patient wife and children.

Mike Kupari

An explosive ordnance disposal technician in the US Air Force, Mike Kupari also served six years in the Army National Guard. He grew up in Michigan's Upper Peninsula and enlisted at the age of seventeen. He has worked as a security contractor with several firms, did a tour in Southwest Asia with a private military company, and is an NRA certified firearms instructor. Mike currently resides in Utah with his iguana.